City of Light

Kerstin Ekman

D1439884

Some other books from Norvik Press

Kerstin Ekman: *Witches' Rings* (translated by Linda Schenck)
Kerstin Ekman: *The Spring* (translated by Linda Schenck)
Kerstin Ekman: *Angel House* (translated by Sarah Death)
Silvester Mazzarella (ed. and trans.): *The Poet who Created Herself. Selected Letters of Edith Södergran*
Victoria Benedictsson: *Money* (translated by Sarah Death)
Fredrika Bremer: *The Colonel's Family* (translated by Sarah Death)
Selma Lagerlöf: *The Löwensköld Ring* (translated by Linda Schenck)
P. C. Jersild: *A Living Soul* (translated by Rika Lesser)
Hjalmar Söderberg: *Short Stories* (translated by Carl Lofmark)
Robin Fulton (ed. and trans.): *Five Swedish Poets*
Gunnar Ekelöf: *Modus Vivendi* (edited and translated by Erik Thygesen)
Gunilla Anderman (ed.): *New Swedish Plays*
Christopher Moseley (ed.): *From Baltic Shores*
Jens Bjørneboe: *Moment of Freedom* (translated by Esther Greenleaf Mürer)
Jens Bjørneboe: *Powderhouse* (translated by Esther Greenleaf Mürer)
Jens Bjørneboe: *The Silence* (translated by Esther Greenleaf Mürer)
Suzanne Brøgger: *A Fighting Pig's Too Tough to Eat* (translated by Marina Allemano)
Janet Garton (ed.): *Contemporary Norwegian Women's Writing*
Svend Åge Madsen: *Days with Diam* (translated by W. Glyn Jones)
Kjell Askildsen: *A Sudden Liberating Thought* (translated by Sverre Lyngstad)
Jørgen-Frantz Jacobsen: *Barbara* (translated by George Johnston)
Johan Borgen: *The Scapegoat* (translated by Elizabeth Rokkan)
Jens Bjørneboe: *The Sharks* (translated by Esther Greenleaf Mürer)
Camilla Collett: *The District Governor's Daughters* (translated by Kirsten Seaver)
Annegret Heitmann (ed.): *No Man's Land. An Anthology of Modern Danish Women's Literature*
Aspects of Modern Swedish Literature (revised edition, ed. Irene Scobbie)
A Century of Swedish Narrative (ed. Sarah Death and Helena Forsås-Scott)
Michael Robinson: *Studies in Strindberg*
Anglo-Scandinavian Cross-Currents (ed. Inga-Stina Ewbank, Olav Lausand and Bjørn Tysdahl)
Nordic Letters 1870-1910 (ed. Michael Robinson and Janet Garton)

City of Light

Kerstin Ekman

Translated from the Swedish
by
Linda Schenck

Norvik Press
2003

Originally published in Swedish under the title of *En stad av ljus* (1983)
© Kerstin Ekman.

This translation © Linda Schenck 2003.
Foreword © Maria Schottenius 2003.

A catalogue record for this book is available from the British Library.
ISBN 1 870041 54 2
First published 2003

Norvik Press gratefully acknowledges the financial assistance given by
The Anglo Swedish Literary Foundation and the Swedish Institute toward the translation
and publication of this book.

Norvik Press was established in 1984 with financial support from the University of East
Anglia, the Danish Ministry for Cultural Affairs, the Norwegian Cultural Department and
the Swedish Institute.

Managing Editors: Janet Garton, Michael Robinson and C. Claire Thomson.

Printed in Great Britain by Page Bros. (Norwich) Ltd, Norwich, UK.

Foreword
by Maria Schottenius

Kerstin Ekman is one of Sweden's most important twentieth century authors, and her oeuvre has crossed the millennium date line with unimpeded success.

The *Vargskinnet* (*Wolfskin*) trilogy will be complete in late 2003, with the publication of *Scratchcards*. (This new trilogy remains to be translated.) Kerstin Ekman's work is both an integral part of the Swedish narrative tradition, and outstanding in its pioneering qualities.

Ekman's early novels, published in the 1950s, were thrillers, and when she made the transition from crime fiction to mainstream narrative fiction, she retained elements of the former. Although powerful, energetic mystery-like strands can be found throughout her work, *Blackwater*, published in English in 1995, is the novel in which she relates backmost explicitly to the thriller genre. Ekman's style is refined and philosophical throughout, at the same time as it also contains elements of "the lower" literary genres.

When it was first published in 1983, *City of Light*, the novel you have just opened, had a major impact on the way Ekman's oeuvre was perceived. It is the fourth and final volume in the tetralogy referred to as *Women and the City*, which marked her shift from thrillers in the 1950s and 60s to more realistic narration in the 1970s. The first three volumes assured her a large, committed circle of readers. *City of Light*, with its rich, complex structure, confirmed Ekman's reputation as one of the most exciting and creative Swedish authors of her time.

The first three books portray the birth and development of a medium-sized Swedish city in central Sweden, from the middle of the nineteenth century and onwards. The community began as a stop on the railway line. Then the trackside hamlet began to expand.

The railway ran like an umbilical cord through the landscape, pumping it with nutrients. The city expanded, its waistline becoming more corpulent. Entrepreneurs arrived, doing business in saws and timber, sledgehammers and machinery. They disembarked from the trains, rented lodgings, wrote in their ledgers, counted their money, and began to build.

While the men created that city, a second city was also germinating. This was the city of the women and the children, a different city that began to grow inwards, toward the courtyards between the residential buildings; the courtyards the women and children had to cross in order to run to a neighbor's flat to borrow a little milk or yeast, or to look after each other's children. The women also retained a more traditional way of counting. What they counted was not only hours, minutes and seconds, but also chores remaining to be done.

Kerstin Ekman's stories wander in serpentines throughout the community and through the passing years. *Witches' Rings* opens with Sara Sabina Lans, who only appears on the gravestone of Lans the soldier as "and his wife". Sara Sabina is portrayed in terms reminiscent of the very lowest flora and fauna: "gray as a rat, poor as a louse, pouchy and lean as a vixen in summer", and "hardy as grass, prickly as nettles". The stories continue, depicting the twentieth century from beginning to end, a century of fundamental changes in the conditions governing the lives of the people of Sweden and of Europe. In just a few decades, industrialization imposed a superstructure on traditional agrarian society and eroded the way of life of the landed gentry who had enjoyed both power and privileges.

One Midsummer's Eve, narrated in *Witches Rings* in a chapter highly charged with symbolism, the reader follows a celebratory line dance in which the nobility, the clergy, the bourgeoisie and the farmers end up topsy turvy. Many such battles in the class struggle were fought before the new social order was established. The power shifted into the hands of the bourgeoisie, and the hunger for it to the working classes (symbolized in the novel in a discussion of who has the right to organize a meeting in the waiting room of the railway station). Both the nobility and the farmers were the losers, disarmed and disqualified. The accession to power of the middle classes is personified in the character of Alexander Lindh, the merchant. He is the key figure in the development of the new city, and this Midsummer's Eve he plays for high stakes, and emerges the winner.

In *The Spring* and *The Angel House* the narrative continues, moving on through the general strike and the world wars to reach the second half of the twentieth century, by which time the city has risen and begun to fall. Initially small and manageable, sometimes even very nice looking, eventually it has swollen beyond all reasonable bounds, extending into the fields and the meadows, and the center is unable to hold.

Kerstin Ekman writes of the city, first as a dream and a hope for the future and then, as the tetralogy nears completion, as a shamefully obsolete phenomenon. She describes it as a disease the progress of which is unstoppable: "The city grows. It spreads like eczema", "multiplying like clusters of bacteria on a glass slide." It is a process that continues of its own accord: "a little city that spreads like a blight on the landscape".

The city is illuminated with "bright red and luminous green signs announcing cut prices and great sales. The city is middle-aged and all decked out like an ageing harlot who can no longer count on the kind of men who can pay generously. But pay they must. There's nothing to be had for free here. She wears her colored ribbons and finery not to please but as an emblem, an irrefutable sign of how she makes her living and what you can expect of her."

Kerstin Ekman opens this fourth and final volume of *Women and the City* with a barely perceptible allusion to the whore of Babylon in Revelations (17:5): "...Babylon the great, the mother of harlots and abominations of the earth." In doing so she opens the gates to a magnificent city, the subtextual world of stories, myths and allusions that provide a context for the reader of *City of Light*. Unlike other subtext, Ekman's does not usually relate to the explicit, visible text of the novel. It is less tangible than that. There are a number of layers with which, once they have been revealed, the text is found to correspond. Thus any given part of the text, or image in it, may have several meanings, one for each level of interpretation.

City of Light – one of the greatest Swedish fiction projects of the twentieth century – becomes particularly effective if read as interwoven with a Jungian process of individuation, the myths of the matriarchy, the story of Jesus, gnosticism, the mysticism of Saint John or that of Swedenborg, and with early experiments in quantum physics.

The text of the novel is structured as a mandala. The mandala, a Tibetan symbol of meditation in which a square fits inside a circle, and in which a configuration of geometric shapes approaches the sacred center, the empty space, can also be found to correspond to the *Women and the City* series. Each little part may be conceived as a symbol or a geometric figure, and its place found in the complex pattern of the great mandala: the characters, the events and the symbolism, beginning with the witches' rings trampled in the grass by the mating roe deer in the novel whose title is precisely *Witches' Rings*.

Jung created a mandala figure for modern man. Kerstin Ekman has created a mandala in literary form for modern woman.

City of Light contains the story of Ann-Marie whose upbringing is quite chaotic, and who appears, when the novel opens, as a middle-aged woman in a small Swedish city. When the novel opens, she has returned from Portugal, where she and her husband live, to sell her father's house after his death. She hardly knew her mother and her now deceased father, to whom she was very close, was an alcoholic.

Ann-Marie was raised to a large extent in the foster care of Jenny and Fredrik. Fredrik is the son of Tora Otter, the keynote character of the first three novels in the tetralogy.

The reader encountered Ann-Marie for the first time in *The Angel House,* where she was merely a marginal character, a little girl sometimes looked after by the ageing Tora. Now, upon her return to the house, Ann-Marie intends to work fast, selling it, turning the furniture over to the auctioneers, and returning to Portugal on the plane where she has reserved a seat in a few weeks. The first thing she has to do is get rid of the three eccentric figures who inhabit the other apartments in the building.

All this is more easily said than done. Ann-Marie's teenage daughter runs away, and Ann-Marie finds herself plagued by anxiety, and overcome by passivity in the face of chaos. After some time, she is unable even to get out of her dressing gown each morning. Two of the tenants are men: Michael, known as "the Whitepainter", and Gabriel. The Whitepainter is a slightly mad artist, Gabriel a man with "a galaxy of dandruff" on his shoulders who is the local proponent of the back-to-the-land movement in spite of his grass allergies. They prove to be Ann-Marie's faithful supporters during the difficult period through which she must suffer. It is no coincidence that they bear the names of the archangels.

When Ann-Marie is forced to descend into her own painful past, they are her supporters, the angels at her side. She knew that she had a lot of "house-cleaning" to do, but the project is not quite the one she had anticipated.

The third tenant, Ann-Sophie, is Ann-Marie's less attractive, less sophisticated double, and her presence in the house gradually takes on its own meaning. As does that of Ann-Sophie's lover, the Magician, with whom Ann-Marie had once wished she could run away.

Ann-Marie's husband, Hasse, remains in Portugal, and Ann-Marie ends up spending a long winter in the house, waiting for a sign of life from their daughter, Elisabeth. She has vanished. No one knows where she has gone. Could she be in the underworld? In Sicily or in Swedish Södertälje? Persephone, Greek goddess of fertility, daughter of Demeter, was abducted to the underworld by Hades, and the reader has every reason to bear her image in mind when reading this Swedish winter's tale.

The question posed in each of the four volumes is what a woman is and does in the community, both local and global, and how she is portrayed and how she acts throughout history. A mandala is known to have repercussions in the life of its creator. It is also a symbol of prayer.

The fictional project of *City of Light* is a journey of exploration in which Kerstin Ekman has used myths and stories, religions and philosophies, and scientific systems. She asks each of them the great questions about life, and examines the strengths and weaknesses of their answers. The tetraology is an experiment, an experiment in life and literature, and its core question is this: what does it mean to be a woman?

However, it poses other questions as well: what happened to the dreams we had for our cities, and what expressions do the longing of human beings today for beauty and meaning take? What does an individual do with his or her powerful inner experiences in a little city anywhere, where Christianity is no longer a powerful force, and where spiritual and religious structures in general are either absent or without significance. Should a person believe in strong flashes of mystical presence and take them seriously? People believe, or are encouraged to believe, in society as a project, but how are we to integrate the other, the inexplicable in our lives?

What happens, for example, when a young, motherless girl like Ann-Marie in this novel, who grows up in an atheistic environment, experiences a revelation? She feels both chosen and afflicted, and she knows that the best thing to do is mention it to no-one, but she organizes the experience in her mind with the aid of her father's natural scientific worldview.

There is no model at hand for a contemporary, secular human being to seize in order to grapple with whatever is going on inside him or herself. Perhaps it is in relation to the absence of this model that the reader is meant to perceive the thought patterns, myths and symbols to which Kerstin Ekman covertly gives shape in her characters, her stories and the places she describes.

If the reader approaches these four novels using the models described here, he or she will have an extremely personal reading experience, because Kerstin Ekman's inner texts are also very private. In this way, *City of Light* fits with the traditions of mysticism, where the sacred is often presented in the commonplace or the trivial. Examples from *City of Light* include electric current in fuse cupboards, and electric stoves and light bulbs, which allude to very special powers, as a running toilet alludes to sacred wellsprings.

God's love is displayed in simple caring. The divinely-inspired life is lived not in sanctified chambers but in everyday life which, ultimately, stands out as what is good and real.

If the reader finds the idea of so much subtext intimidating, he or she is advised not to seek it, but to read on, to dip into one of the great Swedish novels of the twentieth century, inspired by great authors including Selma Lagerlöf, Eyvind

Johnson, Thomas Mann and Doris Lessing. Should you then wish to return to it, recall that this text has within it a gigantic underworld theater that comprises most of our Western cultural heritage and some strands of Eastern culture as well, all sharply observed through the eyes of a woman author whose scalpel has a sense of humor, and who paints a portrait of a lady without flattering ostentation.

This is no innocent work of literature. It has a powerful story to tell. And a unique way of telling it.

Translated by
Linda Schenck

The House

I am in the canopy of the linden and it is in bloom, in bloom. It is late summer, the winds are heavy and warm. All I own is in here with me. I have brought it to nourish me.

All I have ever seen is translucent whirling dust and I am building a different city out of it; I am building different rooms, streets, graves, trees up in the scented wind.

My sleep is warm and salty as seawater. Across my chest is a beam of sunlight but I do not see it, nor do I feel the heat that has made my body damp and my nightgown cling to my skin.

A fly trips along my arm and the swallows cry, whistling as they dive. In wave upon wave come the scents of human beings, cars, bedrooms, earth, debris. The feet of the flies signal through my skin and now I am being born into the city around me, down in gravel and iron at the bottom of a pit.

The sound of compressed air through a nozzle. Sour taste, damp pillowcase, and a beam of dust in the sun. I awaken and between palate and brain it reverberates silently: hell, hell, hell.

Slippers. Mouthwash and water. The kalanchoë is in the bathtub because I washed its leaves yesterday. The bathroom is damp and the light from the waning twenty-five watt bulb is indulgent. When I pee the night runs out of me, strong and concentrated. It fills the air around me with its smell, more penetrating than that of the kalanchoë. The day begins in earnest when I flush.

Hot tea. The sun warming my hands. As yet nothing has happened. The telephone hasn't rung. I haven't opened the paper. It's good to eat in the morning and the flies are wandering across the oilcloth and up my arm. Good little things, good little things, their feet say.

I want to be in peace. I have no desire to open the door if anyone knocks. I do not want to show my face like this, dark gray bags under my eyes, brittle as cheap glass. Perhaps I resemble Ann-Sophie now. I may look more like her now than

12

when I was eight. They danced around us in a circle. It just happened spontaneously. Satin bows in their hair, underwear spotted with pee. Galoshes with clasps that clanked and clattered like little castanets to their singing — or their chanting. A black mass was what it was, not a muddy brown one. Spontaneous evil, ritualized.

I stay at the kitchen table. There is no one here but me. It's only me and the paper, the point of the pen, the ink. I am changing. With every word I undergo a shift. An alphabet is creeping up out of me, moving across the paper like little creatures at the bottom of a stream. I creep up out of an alphabet; all of me is in flux, reflexes on a bed of sand, the shifting of the water and the flashes of light are me. The pen point writes me.

I drive the handwriting into the paper. No, the ink drives me like rain, like a brushfire across the pages. It leaves writing in me, tracks in my flesh, scars full of ink. It's only me, only the pen point moving. Writing.

A couple of years ago I went home to sell a house. I sat on the train looking out at the ponderous evergreen forests. I saw the lakes; saw the manor houses reflected in them. It's a lovely landscape but the beauty ends about half an hour outside the city where I grew up. The woods become scrubby, the willows and alders turn to marshy wetlands. When the sandy, pine-covered area opens up, the city appears, the railway running through it like the spine of a splayed herring. A few decades of construction on flat fields. It's like other communities I have watched passing by, and then being pressed back into time and forest.

It begins with warehouses and stacks of arsenic-impregnated boards. Then come the long, low factory buildings and the spotted plaster housing. When the old post office glides by, with its garlands of concrete leaves under the cracked coat of arms, I shut my eyes. Sometimes I wish the city would sink into a tunnel of oblivion, an old mine shaft inside me slowly filling with water.

Once there was nothing here but woods and gray, ramshackle crofts. Between the mossy groundcover and the fir-speckled sandy heath, a field of oats appeared. A gravel ridge, residue of the ice age river, lay like a huge body in the landscape. No road had yet cut through it. I sometimes try to imagine that there are no rails or embankments and never have been, that ploughed fields of oats, and grazing lands in various shades of brown will sprout up when the long illness of winter has been overcome. People rock along in their carts on crooked roads, oh, so serene. Dunghills and open ditches. Barking and church bells heard from afar. Changes, each year so small they are barely perceptible, and everywhere this serenity about which I can know very little. Perhaps it reeked, sharp and biting. Surely there must have been serenity and returning. Right up until the railway line was laid like a band of throbbing, rushing time, slicing the landscape.

Timber transports began. Quarried stone. Iron beams. Bricks. Hand-hewn sleepers. Even rib-backed pine settles and plaster ceiling ornaments. The rails throbbed and sang under the freight cars, as they have ever since. Strange to imagine that not even during the worst snowstorms has the rail line ever been completely silent. There is always some train moving in the flickering snow and the gleaming lights. Slowly it has huffed forward with the huge iron wings of the snowplough spread before it. The first rolling stock that started on this line didn't even reach the last stop before the next was flagged into motion. And so it has continued, on and on. Without one single snowy Christmas night's interruption in time.

Bearing rucksacks and bundles, people made their way to Göteborg to emigrate. Officials disembarked at the first hamlets, in muddy terrain, to transform them into communities. People have left home to work or find a wife and come back home to plead for forgiveness or for money, and to attend funerals. Like I went home to sell the house. After a few years it's forgotten, or at least it's just as difficult to determine the utility and significance of that trip as of most others.

Boys sneaked into the first-class compartments to ride from one station to the next. Was it Fredrik who told me that? When he and Jenny were newly engaged, they took the train a few miles just for the hell of it. She told me that. Just to to be by themselves. They walked back along the tracks, their arms around each other the whole way. Imagine Jenny and Fredrik kissing with frozen lips in the din of the train to Göteborg that lit up the tracks and thundered past, smelling of steel, as they cowered on the embankment.

Tora Otter told me about a fellow from Vallmsta parish who met The Savior one night in December walking home along the tracks. The man was from Guttersboda and had been in town for a church meeting. The Son of God approached him with open arms, completely oblivious, of course, to the distance between the sleepers that lay bright with a thin layer of frost on them in the starlight. Just before they reached one another the figure dissolved. Vanished like an ice bloom on the windowpane if you move too close with your hot, eager breath. Petter from Guttersboda had gone down on bended knee but eventually he had to get back up and carefully readjust each step to the little stretch of oil-spotted asphalt between one sleeper and the next.

This encounter had no major ramifications for anyone other than Petter and his nearest and dearest.

What probably did affect the communities along the tracks was the goods transported on the railway: all the planed lumber and hand-hewn square timber, the quarried granite, the porcelain water closets and Empire beds have contributed to the change. People who would never have met if the rails hadn't been laid out have interbred on settles and camp beds.

The first people to take up near the station house earned their keep from the next-most elementary task: selling food and drink. To begin with there was Embankment Brita, vendor of dinners and aquavit to the men who built the railway. People say she also let them use her body for a price. Even in those days there was mixing. People I know are the product of it. I may be myself. I have no knowledge of my ancestors farther back than my grandparents on either side. But if they had been from any of the farming communities near Vallmsta I would know.

I think they came with the railway. That they got off and looked around. Set down their bundles and packing cases and asked where a person could lodge for the night. Wondered where they might get something to eat. Tottered along the muddy roads and knocked on strange doors. Peered by the light of a wax candle or an oil lamp to see if there were swingles. Fell asleep and slept uneasily. Awoke to find that the drinking water in the bucket had a peculiar taste. Not even the gruel tasted like home. Then they began living here, from hand to mouth. I'll probably never find out what brought them to this particular place.

After the proprietors of the eating-places, beer halls and wheeled food carts, came the railway officials. They strutted about in the mud in their elegant uniforms, owned horses and pianos, built verandas. They hired field laborers as trackmen. A smith who came to shoe the stationmaster's horse proved to be a mechanical wizard and designed a horse-drawn harrow. Another, a money-hungry fellow, arrived on the train and bought standing timber with borrowed money. He transported hewn spars and pit props by rail. He also began selling the harrows for the smith who had now become a factory owner, having set up an engineering workshop. The timber trader built a warehouse where he stockpiled ribbed back chairs, wagon thills and snow shovels, all made at the joinery that had been built by a tall, cantankerous man who was good at counting money in ways that always made it multiply. He now called himself the owner of a wood products factory.

After this, people say, nothing else happened except that everything grew larger and more complex. Unless you count the clothing factory my father-in-law came here from Västergötland to establish. He was prosperous within three decades and went bankrupt in the fourth. The merchant with the storehouse had built an empire that went on expanding and apparently flourishing right on into the fifties, when it suddenly collapsed. The organisation had outlived itself and was overstaffed.

The smith's workshop was swallowed up by a major Swedish exports concern. The workshop buildings are across from my house. How rotten that company is, no one can say. You can't tell from the outside. But they've started laying people off. When they've all been sacked, that will be the end of this city. There will be buildings, neon, tarmac, municipal greens and traffic lights, people who sell one another fuel, just as many bureaucrats and payroll personnel as there once were in the merchant's overstaffed company, people who do one another's hair and feet, people who nurse, clean, sort, operate, lay pipes, psychoanalyze, connect telephone calls and ring items up at supermarkets. But if no one produces anything that can be transported by rail, they say it's all over. And you can't help wondering whether it may not be already, in spite of the shiny paint and rumbling engines.

But is that really all they've built, the people who have lived here for twelve decades? Steel, gravel, wood and oil — is the city no more than that?

The long goods warehouses where the pigeons coo under the eaves were built all that time ago because people needed somewhere to keep the things that were accumulating. But to the pigeons a city seemed to be being built for them, and they have gone on inhabiting it, without anyone contradicting them.

People built themselves the railway because they needed it, and the railway needed the city and the city needed the things that came by rail. Is that how we are to understand the city? Does it begin just as a little irritation in the earth, a little canker where the first locomotive spilt its oil that went on to grow and grow toward destruction? Was that really all they were building while they were making that airy city for the pigeons out of beams and with long, tiled roofs? Is the city really no more than the sum of its buildings?

People in these buildings live on one another. Live off one another. But as I see it they live very little for one another. When they manage to borrow money from goodness knows where, they build. The city grows. It spreads like eczema.

On the Iberean peninsula where I lived for so long, the old cities stay in place, frozen in their forms, like artichokes of stone. They are on the hilltops, with white heat on the stone walls, or at the seaside, with houses and walls enclosing them like the leaves around an artichoke heart. Inside that heart is the church and the *praça*, with its café and its well. The men sit on the squares with the busses, their *bagaço* in front of them on the table.

These cities have their form in the same way a flower has a form, or a butterfly is complete, pressed tightly in a chrysalis before it appears *in imago*. The notion of the city was there before its granite and stone petals began to bloom.

I don't know what the underlying notion of this city is, or if it even has one. Sometimes when I come here and see how much it has grown since my last visit, I'm frightened. Like everybody else nowadays, I'm scared of cancer.

Perhaps when people build a city, they actually have something more in mind

17

than they realize? Perhaps with their collective efforts they are striving for a goal they never explicitly state from the podium on festive occasions, or at their political conventions, or even in the cigar-scented boardrooms. Imagine if, in the great scheme of things, the city fancies itself as superior to its arrangements and institutions? What if the arrangements are nothing but byproducts?

So what is the idea around which people build? And when does a city stop growing? When has its flower bloomed?

All I have to do is walk down its dingy brown streets and inhale the smell of dog piss, hear the circular saw cut through wood and nerves, and the car tires sputter in salt, gravel and snow to hate the people who made this whole monstrosity and to realize they had no other intentions than those we refer to as pragmatic. I understand that the people here are united only by a system of ownership, the manifestations of which line the streets, their thick façades streaked with rain. And yet I cannot quite abandon the idea that, over time, another city has also been built, like the one the pigeons inhabit.

I arrived one November afternoon. It was a gray day, and the train eventually ran into a rainstorm. I watched the lakes going ruffled and choppy, and the wind and the rain combing the treetops. On the filthy windowpane in my train compartment, rivulets of water trembled in the currents of speeding air.

Probably I was sitting thinking about what I'd do when I got there. My thoughts roved before me like the beam of a pocket flashlight. They often do. In a disjointed, superficial way, they illuminate some spot just ahead of the present. When I'm done with the dishes. When Elisabeth has turned twenty. The spot of light is in constant motion.

I was going to arrange everything and make it impossible for her to go on living here. Sell the house. Pack what I wanted and then phone the auctioneers. I think I also planned to see to it that the grave was maintained.

I go to the grave a couple of times a week. Sometimes more often. I clear it of fallen linden leaves and dead flowers. The stone is flat against the ground and often covered with brown leaves and spotted with dirt from the rain. I think the rain carries soot from the foundry with it. Or maybe it's airborne soot from the Ruhr valley. I clean the surface, polishing it with a handkerchief. It's supposed to be shiny black.

I often take the long way home from the cemetery, walking the brown, muddy sidewalks slowly. I look up as I walk, because brown is so drab, but the trees in this city are lovely. They grow freely, and don't have too much competition for the light. They're mostly lindens. God bless the people who planted them. At the market square there are some weeping willows, and between the buildings there are still one or two pear trees and old apple trees with cracking trunks and gnarled branches that have gone unpruned for decades. In wet weather their crowns are black and drink up the humidity from the air as if they were roots. They are the only remains of what once were gardens but are now nothing but turned-up soil or pavement.

19

The city center is little and winding, and some of the old buildings look out of place. Number 13 Chapel Road is dirty brown with age, and although it's a large house it appears small, across from Swedish Engineering and alongside *The Correspondent.*

It's my house. The timber is rotting and the window panes are so thin they rattle when trucks pass by. It was built in an L-shape, and thus shelters what remains of an old courtyard. Inside the door there's an archway leading to a long hall with a stone floor. The door to the right was painted wavy-grained yellow long ago by a skilled craftsman. If you open it you get to a flight of stairs, the gray wood which used to be covered with a limp rag runner held down at the bend of each step with a metal rod. The firewood bin is still on the landing outside the kitchen door, full of odds and ends. The lid won't close properly. There are net curtains on the windows. The door to the apartment has a pane of frosted glass and a doorbell that hasn't worked for years. When I was a child I used to spin it, turning the knob and round to make it ring. But even in those days it was stuck and silent.

I've come here often. Throughout my childhood, in an everyday way. However, all my arrivals are false ones, because I was actually born here. So there is no alternative but to return.

A few of us got off when the long train had slowed to a stop. I'd been sitting so close to the front of the train that when I got off I didn't end up under the roof of the platform. At the far end I saw older women carrying bags and suit-cases too heavy for them. There was a man, too, who looked as if he had on a top hat and a black sleeveless cloak, a cape. He was the only unusual one. The darkening November afternoon seemed able to suck everything else into it: the women and the rolling stock which, after only a couple of moments, rolled on, and the old, brown roofs that grew up out of their wooden columns and the gray cement of the platform. But it couldn't absorb him. His cloak was so black it glistened. He vanished down the passageway between the station-mas-ter's house and the newspaper stand without a glance.

I walked into the station to pick up a timetable for the inter-city trains. In a few days when everything had been arranged I'd be leaving again.

The waiting room was nearly empty, but it was noisy with the racket of tin against the flagstones. Two boys with tassels on their caps were rolling a beer can with ice hockey sticks, chasing it from wall to wall. On a bench near the door, his back to a painted brown radiator, sat an old man with a very pale face, eyes closed. His head was tilted to one side, and there was a little dribble at the corner of his mouth. He was strangely pallid. In one hand he was holding a crumpled slip of paper, fingering it. I sat down next to him, not sure whether he was merely sleeping or if he was ill and in need of help.

I asked him if he was waiting for a train. He reacted to my voice, but didn't open his eyes.

"I'm not going back there," he said.

He was a very old man with a round face and white hair, cut so short his scalp shone through. He was wearing a black overcoat, but neither gloves nor a cap. It looked odd. Old people are usually warmly dressed at that time of year, buttoned right up to the neck, and they always seem to have something on their heads. I asked where he was going.

"If you tell me your address, I'll get you a taxi."

His head wobbled like an infant's on the stem that was his neck. I took his hand. It was cold and his skin was dry and scaly. I got up and went into the ticket office to ask how long he'd been sitting there. But they hadn't even noticed him. There were two people in there, in the aroma of thermos coffee and underarm perspiration, and they walked over to the door, peering out through the pane of glass. They shook their heads again.

He was about to tip forward, the saliva still dribbling out of the corner of his mouth.

"The man is ill," I said. "Call an ambulance."

They seemed uncertain until they, too, saw him starting to slide to the floor. I reached him in the nick of time and propped him up.

"Get on the phone," I repeated, and one of them nodded and actually began to lift a receiver slowly in there. The boys were still banging the beer can, and the noise was driving me crazy.

"Stop that!" I shouted, my voice echoing in the old waiting room.

Of course they had to hit it a few more times, but then they slammed out, taking their sticks with them. The old man's breath was heavy and labored. His head was on my shoulder, and it felt heavy. He smelled of strong soap, and of something else murky and difficult to pinpoint. Perhaps he was dying. He had little bloody scratch marks on his wrists, and it was difficult to imagine that his own nails, so yellow and hard, could have inflicted these sores. They must itch terribly. Maybe he's come home to die, I thought. He's been away his entire adult life. Now he's coming home. A major event, and yet not.

It may be a very mundane thing, dying. A dry cough, a pain in your chest, inter-

21

minable itching. You scratch yourself bloody, you feel nauseous, and then it's all over.

I wished the ambulance would hurry so he wouldn't die like this, propped against me. The people at the ticket counter kept their distance, as if they considered the whole thing my affair. I could see the veins on the top of the old man's hand, bulging and swollen under the skin. So his blood pressure was all right at least, and his circulatory system working. His heart must be beating, too.

Maybe his life is passing before his eyes, I thought. They say it does at the end. Maybe he is hearing heels clattering against a wooden platform and smelling the oil and coal dust. I imagine he's come home to look for something. But it's gone, been replaced. Please let him stay alive, remain a contemporary, until the ambulance arrives. Dying in someone's arms is so intimate. I had the feeling the gnarled old man's body was assaulting me. As if he might soon start groping me and feeling for my breasts or seeking my mouth.

I tried to straighten him up and lean him against the wall and the radiator instead, but he dropped back to my shoulder. At least he was alive. He was still breathing and his fingers were still playing.

People came in through the kick-plated door. They stared at me and the old man. I realized they thought we were together. The wall clock ticked and in the office the ticket vendors glared at me through the glass.

I tried to turn so I could look outside. Paper and litter that would have been blowing about if the weather had been different lay plastered to the tarmac in the rain. A flock of pigeons was pecking near the black trunk of a linden, the leaves of which had all blown off in the storm. Those pigeons are always outside the station. Well, not the same ones, of course, but their descendants. Pigeons' pigeons' pigeons' pigeons. Mating and roosting and hatching and cooing and shitting and pecking for something edible ad infinitum. Well, if not ad infinitum then for ages. Cars, cars, cars and filth, gray-brown. And they were actually renovating the City Hotel.

If the ambulance didn't come soon I'd have to try to lay him down on the bench.

"How're you doing?" I asked loudly. He didn't move. Why had I gone to him? I could have just told the people over at the ticket counter he was in there and needed help. But I knew I'd done it because I'm a woman over forty and accustomed to playing the mother. Inside, I felt like I was thirteen.

Just then the ambulance came across the big bridge above the post office. Red and blue lights shot through the dull brown haze and two young men got quickly out and lifted a wheeled gurney from the back. When they entered the waiting room the air and the noises changed. Their movements were professional, and they easily got the old man onto the gurney. Lying down, he looked very tall and thin. They covered him with a blanket, moving quickly, like a salesgirl wrapping a present. At the moment they lifted him I saw a first blue gleam under his pale eyelids. So although they were red-rimmed and hazy, his eyes were blue.

They carried him away. For a moment, I felt lonely. Gathered my gloves and handbag and walked hesitantly out through the door. The rain had stopped.

I went down the steps to the market square. The outline of the row of buildings on the other side hasn't changed much since my childhood. But in this gray weather all I could see was the bright red and luminous green signs announcing cut prices and great sales. The city is middle-aged and all decked out like an ageing harlot who can no longer count on the kind of men who can pay generously. But pay they must. There's nothing to be had for free here. She wears her colored ribbons and finery not to please but as an emblem, an irrefutable sign of how she makes her living and what you can expect of her.

I remember how the stall awnings used to flap in the rain on this square where cars park today. There were display cases with flowers inside. Or am I recalling something somebody told me about? A picture?

We feel a longing, without knowing what we're longing for. Then that desire, a little body part we can't identify as an intestine, a nerve pathway or an eye, catches sight of a glass flower case. It reacts instantaneously, with a jolt of mixed pain and rapture. It absorbs the flower case, and becomes one with it. There our longing stands like a little candle flame among the hyacinths and the fragile blossoms we call Christmas roses. It flickers brightly behind the glass, while the weather outside is cold and bitter.

Longing can dissolve glass cases and striped suits, whole carts full of hay, cast iron pump systems, and little houses with pan-tiled roofs. Longing generates our childhood memories for itself. Perhaps it generates all memories.

23

When I was little I went running to Jenny one day when she was washing the dishes in the kitchen. I had the teapot in my arms. I think it was a gray afternoon, maybe in late winter. I can also remember a soft woman's voice reading the stock market report.

"I saw it!" I said. "Look, Jenny!"

I set the teapot on the kitchen table and there it was, as ordinary, chipped, and brown as usual. Jenny looked, dishwater dripping from her hands. I didn't know how to explain. Since I could no longer see what I had seen a moment earlier, I knew she wouldn't see anything particular. Our old teapot. It had been left on the smoking table last night. On the glass tabletop there were flakes of tobacco and rings left by drinking glasses. That was where I had seen the teapot, truly seen it, and I tried to explain that to Jenny.

"I saw it through different eyes," I said.

But she didn't really get it. I didn't get it myself.

The second time, when it happened at Chapel Road, I was almost forty. It was in November 1973, five months before the revolution. I'd come back to do something about Henning. I knew he was in a very bad way, but when I arrived he wasn't in. The apartment was locked and dark. Not until I'd found him and got him into the hospital and sat with him half the night did I finally go back to the apartment.

That was when I saw. It seemed to begin when I was standing by the mirror in the hall, although it may actually have started when I was in the entrance hall downstairs, or even when I was outside the door, looking at the flaking brown paint, when I opened the door and noticed the stone floor of the hall, the net curtains in the stairwell, the frosted pane of glass with the vines, and the doorbell with the tarnished brass button.

I'd left Lisbon that morning, traveled by plane, bus and then train, after which I'd gone all over town looking for Henning. Then I'd been in the ambulance with

24

him and in a taxi home. I'd had a little meal on the flight, but nothing since. A nurse's aide had brought me some coffee while I was sitting there holding his hand. I entered the dark hall and switched on the ceiling fixture. Then I stood looking into the sitting room, which was still dim. I saw.

I saw straight through the layers that hold things together so provisionally and arbitrarily, and I saw the golden dust whirl once again. It swirled in streams of energy and light. I'm not saying the table and chairs vanished, but the thin lines they etched in the light were not forceful enough to press the other vision, the real one, aside. Light and shadow were there, resting side by side in a way I wouldn't have noted just a few minutes earlier but that was now as obvious as birds' eggs side by side in a nest. This was reality.

Did it last for hours or was it only a short while? I don't know. The phone rang and rang for ages before I could get myself to do anything about it. When I finally lifted the receiver it ended. I was back. I saw precisely what I had expected to see in this room, and I heard the slurred voice of one of Henning's drinking buddies on the phone. My feelings returned: the disgust, the compassion and the fatigue.

Just a moment earlier I had been staring at the pinecones in the carved wooden backs of the dining room chairs with the same intensity as at the empty bottle that had rolled under the table, at the bed with its filthy gray sheets and at the table in front of it covered with empties and overflowing ashtrays, the picture of the bowl of violets, the white paneled door, the bucket of sick and piss, the owls on the encyclopedia bindings, the ceiling lamp with all those little insects in it. Now all I could sense was the paucity.

When I stepped in through that door again on the late autumn evening when I came back to sell the house, I was not expectant. I don't think the memory of my vision was any louder than an uneasy whisper. I was on guard, my expectations tempered by experience. The apartment might be in the same state as that other time. At worst I would meet a sight equally ignominious, but this time with hypodermic needles, spotted cotton wool balls, and soda pop bottles of water mixed with blood.

The first thing I noticed was that the rag runner on the stairs was gone. Maybe Elisabeth had dumped it in the rubbish bin. It was probably so full of holes you could trip on it. As I opened the door, I noticed someone else going in through one of the other doors that opens onto Chapel Road. Although I had begun to go inside, I could see that the person entering was a tall man in a cloak, a cape lined with strange red satin. Not until I was halfway up the stairs did I realize he was the same man I'd seen at the station. He wasn't following me. I stood on the stairs and listened. He went in through the door across the downstairs hall.

I unlocked our old door and went inside, and the window rattled. As soon as I was in I could tell it wasn't too bad. Just a kind of girlish, perfumed disorder. Of course there was the sticky scent of marijuana. But there's nothing dangerous about marijuana, mamma! It's nowhere near as strong as hash!

I don't know. Maybe it's not. But in any case I felt affectionate as I picked up a belt embroidered with little glass beads, cheap junk from Monsoon, and a pair of striped cotton underpants that looked just as little as the ones she'd worn when she was five or six.

No, it wasn't the odor of marijuana that was the most distressing thing, nor was it the mess, which was an almost cozy kind. It was the stagnation. Nothing had really changed. There were no signs of life. The underwear. The belt. The empty cigarette packs. But nothing that indicated any effort.

The Christmas decorations were still up. A red, wooly elf dangled from the frame of the door into the living room. I'd hung it there myself. It was during Henning's last Christmas, when I'd made awkward attempts to get everything to seem normal with the aid of crêpe paper and pine boughs sprayed with glitter.

Nothing had happened. The Christmas elf was still dangling from its string, the dust had dug its way deeper into curtains and carpets. Everything was starting to go grimy brown; to take on the very color of the past, the nuance of all that was clumped together, indistinguishable and decomposing. Nothing happens here.

Except that now it's all going to be thrown out. Yes, damn it, I thought, and had the silence in the apartment not been so taut with presence I would have said it out loud.

Without even taking off my coat, I phoned the builder's office. But they'd gone for the day. It had taken forever to get that the old man to the hospital.

I was in a hurry. That was why I'd sent Elisabeth to Taormina. I wanted to accelerate the process of destruction. But the house just stood there around me, dark and taut with time.

So I phoned the builder, a former classmate of mine, at home. When a woman answered, I thought it was his wife. I forget that we have adult children now. I asked her, as slowly and distinctly as if I were speaking to an answering machine, to tell him I'd called, that I had come home to arrange for the house on Chapel Road to be sold.

"He'll know exactly what I'm talking about. Say I'm prepared to sell now."

Darkness had fallen outside. I walked around slowly, my hands in my coat pockets. I think I was trying to postpone having to touch anything in here. The street lights shone into the living room, as usual, and into the study, as my mother's parents used to call it. The streetlamps hang suspended from wires that crisscross the street. In windy weather they sway, and if you don't turn the lights on inside, the rooms take on a eerie sensation. It was cold in there and, as the chill penetrated, fatigue crept into me as well. Although I wasn't hungry, I had a queasy feeling I thought would go away if I had something to eat. But I didn't want to go out, didn't want to be part of the closing time jostle at the supermarket.

I rummaged around the larder and found some spaghetti and a tin of ready-made sauce. The larder reeked, and there were crumbs on the shelves. But there was no point tidying up the cupboards or going through the larder now, when everything was going to be thrown out anyway.

It took ages to cook the spaghetti and heat the sauce. The burners on the old electric stove reacted slowly and solemnly, as if to remind me what a complex procedure it is, after all, to extract power from rushing water, transport it and transform it into heat inside of cold steel. Jenny used to have me run on ahead and turn on the burners when we were walking home from the store. That was at the Upco estate, when I lived with the Otters. But Jenny got a new stove long ago, with glowing coils and white enamel drip trays. Here the coffee grinds and brown burnt milk were hidden under a black rim Elisabeth had certainly never bothered to lift.

I turned on the radiators. They ticked silently. So as not to feel so alone, I ate in the living room in front of the old black and white TV with its cozy buzz. While I was sitting there, the phone rang. I thought it would be Hasse calling from Porto to check that I'd arrived safely and my trip had been all right. But it was a far younger voice, a boy asking for Elisabeth. He hung up without leaving his name. I sat there staring at the black telephone, a heavy old one with a frayed, cloth-bound cord that had never been replaced. Then I called Hasse. He was still at the factory and there was so much background noise we didn't talk long. I said I'd had a good trip. Jenny and Elisabeth were on the plane to Taormina, and now I'd get everything organized quickly. I told him I was planning to unplug the phone because I didn't like strangers calling asking for Elisabeth.

But there was no plug. I had to take the phone off the hook, and when I'd done that I didn't feel comfortable with it. I had a feeling someone might shout my name down the wire, or listen to me through the receiver. Aware I was being both irrational and absurd, I covered it with an old woolen cap.

I was starting to feel afraid of the dark, so I turned the TV back on and roamed around putting things away. Tomorrow I'll get some boxes, I thought. But what was I going to keep? Everything in the place was interrelated. What would the *Nordic Family Encyclopedia* look like in our carved black bookcase in Porto? Or Henning's notes, an enormous paper sack, a pile full of thoughts and moments of inspiration, drunken ramblings and dreams. Perhaps there was an invention concealed in them, a dormant fortune. If only I'd had a son, I thought, and felt the rush of shame I always felt when I caught myself thinking that. I leafed through some of the papers, and noticed that the top ones were about the patent application for the Radax link. The universal ball bearing as he'd called it. He must have had that application on file for eons, and how much had he spent on it? But nothing ever came of it. It just seized up.

The Christmas elf swayed on his string each time I passed. Suddenly the TV broadcasting ended for the day. Suddenly — but several hours must have passed. How? I'd been reading various documents, leafing through the encyclopedia. Folding all the clothes Elisabeth had left on chairs and the floor. Opening drawers full of tarnished silver-plated things wrapped in pink flannel. But still — three or four hours? I found the house slightly intimidating. It gobbled time and awareness. It gobbled my will power.

There were two rooms I still hadn't entered. One was Elisabeth's, which was actually mine. It had been my room when I was a child. The master bedroom is far from my room. I didn't go in there. But I had taken a look in my grandparents' old bedroom that Henning had used as a storeroom for his models and his piles of papers, and into his own room opposite the kitchen. There, as everywhere else in the house, a sense of unresisting subjugation prevailed. Time had been layered onto time but didn't cover it. The Nerman reproduction of the mother and the child was still there. Under the bed were bottles and empty paper cartons still redolent of cigarillos.

My room is across the hall and next to the bathroom. In my grandparents' time it might have been the maid's quarters. I suppose Sigrid did have a domestic. She worked in the shop herself until she became ill.

I didn't go in to the empty master bedroom. I never go in there. And there was no reason to do so now, either. But I had to decide where to sleep.

When I opened the door to Elisabeth's room, I was struck by the sweetish aroma and the heat. Something was glowing in the dark. She had gone off to Sicily and left an electric heater on in her little incense-scented bedroom! I switched on the light. The room turned pink and the odor seemed even stronger. She had hung a red paper Chinese lantern with silk tassels from the ceiling fixture, and it dangled, askew. I watched it sway in the draft from the open door. I thought: if I slam the door shut the paper shade will fall onto the heater and in a few hours it will all be done. No packing. No auction. No tearing down of the house. The builder would undoubtedly prefer that solution.

When I turned off the ceiling light and clicked the desk lamp on, I saw that the room had been repapered. I was startled. Clean beige wallpaper with an indeterminate pattern of some kind, looking like grass and straw. Fifties. She must have found it up in the attic.

The bed was covered with a quilted Indian patchwork spread that repulsed me when I picked it up to fold it. Of course it wasn't washable. But Elisabeth wouldn't have thought of that. She just threw it over the bed on the assumption that anything that came from a shop was new and clean. It was stuffed with Indian rags, in other words with filth and contagion. Underneath, the bed was made with my old pink honeycomb blanket, the one under which I had seen the eye of God, and with Sigrid's sheets. The top sheet had a wide lace border and a monogram — SWA — for Sigrid and Abel Westerdahl. The sheets weren't exactly clean. I pulled them off the bed and flung them down next to the patchwork spread.

There were no more clean sheets in grandmother's chest of drawers. I had to lie directly under the pink child's blanket, which was too short. My feet stuck out, so I went and got my coat. Elisabeth is much shorter than I am. She's skinny, too. Her thin little body had surely made itself comfortable in the oval hollow created by the combination of the bed frame and the kapok mattress. I knew I'd wake up early in the morning with an aching back. But I felt safest here. I could lock this bedroom door.

I was born in this house in 1935, in a bed that is up in the attic with all kinds of other stuff. It has a black iron frame, and there used to be brass knobs on the four posts. I may have been the one who removed them. Sometimes I think I can hear, or rather feel, a golden yellow knob rolling across a yellow and green linoleum floor. But I'm not absolutely certain. There are big stains on the mattress, brown-edged spots. It's probably pee, but I have been known to imagine it being the amniotic fluid from my birth.

In a way this house is my mother and father now. It was always just here. I had the key to it even though I was living with the Otters. Nowhere else on earth do I get this feeling of really being present in a room, a secluded, protected and at the same time extremely frightening room. Outside, there is howling wind, pitch-black rushing darkness or such threatening icy-cold dark that you can see every star in the sky. There's a maelstrom of humanity out there, of intrusiveness, evil and occasional gestures of kindness. I suppose I have long believed this house to be a kind of symbol in my consciousness. But that's wrong. It's right here. It exists and is a refuge in the most perfectly concrete sense. The church for a believer. The lair for a little wild animal.

Now I was going to sell it and it would be torn down. Oh, let this night, when reality and unreality change places, pass quickly.

I found an old transistor radio in Henning's room. The casing was cracked but the radio still worked. He must have knocked it to the floor endless times, groping for his glass.

By the time I'd got into bed, the classical music station had already gone off the air, so I turned it off. I don't like the pop music station, but the silence was too much for me so I turned it back on, so softly the music was only distinguishable as background hum and the throb of the bass notes, and eventually I fell asleep to it. I slept very lightly, and every time I turned over in the rickety bed, I would wake up and be aware of the radio. Later, they played softer music. Somebody once said that Swedish radio plays suicide music between three and four in the morning. But isn't it intended to prevent suicide? I tried to get back to sleep, my mouth dry. I'd slipped down into myself, beneath my intentions, and down there I could locate neither indifference nor the will power to do what I was about to do.

I kept thinking I heard running water somewhere, a vague purling sound. As I slid into sleep, I thought it was voices talking.

"No!" I said. "No!"

But I spoke like a woman who is talking to herself and knows it. Then I reached out and turned up the volume on the old radio, which shut the hum and the voices out.

A voice calling mamma awakened me. As I got out of bed I knew instantly that I was alone in the apartment, but I still walked around, checking all the rooms but the master bedroom. They were empty. I went out into the kitchen and found it empty, too. The thought crossed my mind that a child might be in the courtyard. But I couldn't see anyone through the window. It was still quite dark. Not yet five o'clock.

My heart was pounding, and I was anxious and distraught. Getting back into bed only made it worse. The palms of my hands were prickly and I was starting to have trouble breathing. I didn't think I could get through the night on my own, thought I'd have to phone Hasse. What were we to one another if we couldn't phone up at dawn, when the anguish was unbearable? But standing there barefoot in the hall with the receiver in my hand, having dialed the country code, I had a picture of him sleeping in our black double bed under red sheets with a white bird pattern. That was a different world. What could he possibly say to me?

Ever since I was little, I have known very well that there are worlds alongside worlds. It's difficult for me to find that great container feeling.

My heart was bursting, galloping unbearably.

Unbearable.

What a word! It means no more than Elisabeth's "supercool" and "hyper-high-minded". Don't be so hyper-noble-minded, mamma! And actually there are very few things that are unbearable. Hasse wouldn't have said any such thing, but it was enough for me to think he might have said it. He wouldn't even remark that these calls across the entire continent were going to run up a bill. I put the receiver back down. If I made myself a cup of tea it would soon pass. It was already better.

Elisabeth had herbal teas in crumpled bags. But in the end I found a tin of proper tea. The old stove took ages and there was time for me to start feeling drowsy. I sat at the kitchen table waiting and I think I may even have dozed off with my head on my arms. Then the phone in the hall rang. I thought it must be Hasse who had sensed my anxiety and decided to call.

When I answered, all I could hear on the line was a distant crackling and chatter. After some time I realized there was a foreign language. Then Jenny's voice, weeping and disconsolate. She asked me where I had been. I don't know if she heard when I told her I'd taken the phone off the hook earlier. She was calling from Taormina, a tired and muddled elderly woman who had spent hours and hours on an airplane and then not slept all night.

"Elisabeth never got on the plane!"

I said that was impossible. I had seen them go through passport control, the two of them. But Jenny said Elisabeth had gone back out and the plane had taken off without her.

Afterwards I heard the water boiling away and rushed out into the kitchen. I poured hot water over Elisabeth's old tea leaves and threw her moldy white bread in the rubbish bin. She'd run away!

Of course it was easier to turn tail than to say: I don't want to go to Sicily with Jenny! True to form, she had taken the path of least resistance. Three thousand five hundred kronor! Three thousand five hundred kronor for a trip she wasn't going on. Was money a reality to her? Were other people's feelings? Jenny's, for example. An old woman, alone in Taormina. Disappointed and upset.

I stood there trying to wipe her sticky jar of orange marmalade clean, though I would have preferred just to toss it out. But at least marmalade was better than margarine on crispbread. Three weeks in Sicily and the orange marmalade would have been moldy and the margarine rancid. And leaving the electric heater on full blast! She wasn't bothered about the fire hazard, not to mention the electricity consumption. Or had she been planning all the time to come straight back?

I supposed she'd be along later in the day when she had had some sleep. She knew people in Stockholm. They put each other up. Everything seemed so easy for them. This was a different life, completely unknown to me. A container feeling. Incense and wine bottles. Indian rag patchwork quilts. In a couple of days she'd come back, a sorry figure with a cold. But she'd find me sitting here at the kitchen table like a really unpleasant surprise.

Through the window I saw a young man in the courtyard. It was Gabriel. He lived in one of the apartments on the other side of the hall, although he wasn't supposed to. This building has been condemned. The tenants left years ago, or should have. But Elisabeth let new people move in.

He was standing on the steps holding something in his hands. When he looked up he saw me at the kitchen window. He was carrying a bowl, holding it as if it were a sacred chalice.

I fell asleep and woke up again hearing someone call mamma. So I got up and went out into the kitchen. It was empty. Of course I knew I was alone in the apartment. But those cries had sounded so real and so ordinary.

Then I thought she must be in the hall downstairs, so I put a coat on over my nightgown and went down. There was no-one there, but by the hall door there was a bowl of milk. That was what Gabriel went out and filled up each morning. He had a cat. In fact he still has that cat, and in late winter there's the pungent smell of it in the downstairs hall. Now the bowl of milk was there, untouched, and in the lamplight a big, dark spot quivered on the surface. Some blood had dripped into the milk. I lifted the bowl carefully, so the pattern in the blood was hardly disturbed, but then my hands trembled and the spot began to diffuse. At first it looked like a thinly traced letter of some kind, then a butterfly with striated wings, and then finally it grew and became very blurred, until all that was left of the whole metamorphosis was a pinkish brown film on the surface. I set the bowl down, now convinced my eyes hadn't been deceiving me. At that very moment, Gabriel came out through the other hall door. He was staring at the bowl as I put it down, and looking shaken. Of course it was the spot of blood that had frightened him.

"A rat murder," I said, and he stared at me, uncomprehending. I said it was just that the cat had had blood on its whiskers. But Gabriel pulled his door to without a word.

On my way up, I noticed a little spot of blood on the stairs. It had all but soaked into the graying wood. I touched it with the tip of my index finger, but it was dry. I walked slowly up to the attic to check the stairs for more blood. I should have organized a lock for the attic, but it didn't matter any more. For years, anyone at all has been able to walk straight in off the street and go up into the attic. Drunks have slept it off up there, and once somebody lit a small fire in the wood bin right outside our kitchen door. I woke up to the smell of smoke. At the bottom of the box there were old boots and shoes, smoldering under the ashes of burnt newspapers. The wood bin is still there, charred inside.

The iron bedstead with its blood-stained mattress, the bed I was born in, was just inside the attic door. Lisa had clung to the bedposts, screaming for dear life. A grim procedure. Looking at the pale brown spots on the mattress, I have often felt sympathy for her.

November 1977. Blood on Lisa's bed. A big wet patch.

Next to the bed, with her back pressed against one of the storage space doors, stood Ann-Sophie. I reached out a hand and turned the old light switch so the ceiling light came on. She whined, covering her eyes with her forearm. So I turned it off again, of course. There was enough light coming in through the skylight for me to see the patch of blood on the bed and her ashen face. I asked what had happened. She stumbled towards me, sideways like a crab, and fell onto the bed.

"We'd better go down to my place," I said.

When she took the arm I proffered, it was as if her body were threatening to tip over backwards. She hung on all the way down. Once inside, I gave her some sanitary pads from Elisabeth's chest of drawers and she went into the bathroom. I put on some water for coffee and listened while she ran the water in there. When she came out I indicated a chair I had covered with newspaper so she wouldn't stain the seat with her bloody trousers. I asked if she shouldn't go to the hospital, but she just shook her head. For a few minutes I considered forcing her to. Then I made her a cup of instant coffee and let her sit there, smoking silently.

She was nearly fifty years old. She couldn't be healthy, with such heavy bleeding. But I was embarrassed to ask if she still had her periods. When I did ask what she had been doing up in the attic, she told me she didn't know.

"I must have been really out of it," she mumbled.

I could imagine that. I could imagine other things, too: Ann-Sophie is a stupid cow. I hate our looking so much alike. She turned up at school, a new pupil in a class two years ahead of mine. We looked so much alike the big girls surrounded us, pushing us into the center of the ring, shouting: "Look, it's Sofa's little sis!"

She was an estate worker's kid, and people called her Sofa Sager. Everything about her was bigger than on me. I suppose that was because she was older, but also because she was different. I hadn't known I existed before that. But when they pushed us into the center of the ring talking about me looking just like her, I was born an image, a false image.

Sofa Sager was old now. Her face was thick-skinned, her cheeks rolls of subcutaneous fat that continued down to form double chins. Looking at her opposite me at the kitchen table, I had to give my own chin a pinch, only to feel an odd lumpy accumulation of the same kind of fat, which had collected there without my having noticed. But she had always been stouter than me. Her hair was somehow grayer and blonder at once. Even as children, we were different. It was only our short, quite straight, thin-bridged noses that were alike, and our mouths. Well, maybe our eyes, too, the way they were set, or something about the expression in them. Otherwise why did everybody say we looked so much alike, when I have Lisa's deep blue eyes and she has watery blue-gray ones? Ann-Sophie had bad teeth; she'd never bothered much about going to the dentist. Down by the gums they were brown with tartar and nicotine.

After she left school, I didn't see her for three or four years. One winter evening I went with Fredrik and Jenny to an inn on the north side of town. It was the Craftsmen's Association Christmas party, and God only knows what I was doing there; I certainly wasn't having a good time. The meal was an enormous smorgasbord, and virtually every single dish was smothered in mayonnaise. The women were all over fifty and they rolled like steamships across the floor. Their waists were molded into Spirella corsets, they were wearing dresses they'd had made up by a seamstress and they reeked of dry cleaning chemicals and heavy perfumes. Only two or three of them were slender, and one was still happy. During the entertainment, she came in wearing a tracksuit and a red knitted cap, and sang: "It's not little Sigismund's fault he's a knockout!" The entertainment didn't start until the after-dinner coffee was served, though. Before you could sit down at the table with your plate of herring, you had to queue up outside a special door to collect your glass of aquavit. They'd rented one of the rooms to serve drinks from. The queue was bustling and boisterous. Mostly men, of course. But Jenny was in it. She had an ankle-length skirt on and attracted a great deal of attention. She was one of the first women in town to wear the "new look" .

Why did I go into one of the other rooms? Maybe I was looking for the toilet? This room is buried deep in my memory, the details almost inaccessible. No color, just drabness, the scent of tobacco smoke, some kind of chill, and dusty, scratched surfaces, a sense of shabbiness. There, in the dim light, a girl slumped on a sofa. Her bluish fleshy legs I do recall, the shock of those naked, cold, goosebumpy legs. It was Ann-Sophie and she was in her costume. At the table sat the magician with a drink. He was in full evening attire, and his cloak was draped over a chair.

He was a tall, slim man. I used to daydream about him. But really seeing him up close like this embarrassed me and scared me half to death, as if he might undo the fly of his dress trousers and expose his sex to me at any moment. It was foolish to think like that, those weren't the kind of dreams I'd been having. I dreamed or fantasized that he would come and get me or that we'd meet outside the hotel after some performance. He'd take me to places and buildings where I'd never been.

Actually, he didn't have access to the places I dreamt of seeing. But I didn't need the real him, just his appearance and the things that were unusual, not to say incredible, about him, and his tall, slim body, the cape with the purple satin lining that shimmered when he moved.

I knew perfectly well who he was. His parents belonged to the Craftsmen's Association. His old man was a coppersmith. They were decent, hardworking, penny-pinching folk. They just had this one son, who was over thirty but had never held a proper job. I'd heard he was a drinker. But while people were busy gossiping and feeling sorry for his parents, he was traveling around putting on magic shows. He called himself an illusionist. His real name was Egon Holmlund, but he used a stage name that was also my name for him when I invented our meetings and made up long interior monologues.

Although I don't remember having a conversation with Ann-Sophie in there, I'm sure we must have spoken a little. Later, during the entertainment, she came onto the stage dressed in a sequined bathing suit, with a little tulle tail and high-heeled silver sandals. She handed the illusionist his props, rolled out tables and carried boxes of silk scarves and balloons on and off stage. I assume she was also the one who fed the rabbits and cleaned their hutches

She was surprisingly quick and agile. I recalled Ann-Sophie as a graceless girl who only ran very reluctantly at school when the class played rounders in the schoolyard. But there she was moving light as a feather across the creaky wooden floor, opening her arms out and putting one bare leg in front of the other when she curtseyed. I believe I was mortally shocked. I must have been, because otherwise I would have forgotten all about that Christmas party.

That dumb, clumsy Sofa Sager went backstage and vanished. She packed the bags and took off with the magician. Although I realized they were only moving on to the next run-down boarding house and to another dinner in a party room where the lodgers ate on weekdays, and where greasy, nauseating smells hung in the curtains, I was still astonished that Ann-Sophie was getting to do precisely what I'd only dreamt of doing. He had chosen her, although in reality what it meant was cleaning rabbit hutches and carrying heavy suitcases.

I sat staring at her across the kitchen table, thinking I would throw her out. She paid no rent, and therefore she wasn't here. I couldn't turn her out when she was bleeding, but I would as soon as she was all right again.

Sophie's pedicure salon. She'd put up a sign by the door on Chapel Road. She probably had pedicure equipment in there as well.

I'd toss her out, the lush. She was always stumbling in the hall and bruising her legs. She didn't think I knew. But everybody knew, even I who was so seldom here. I ought to have a word with her of course, say: Ann-Sophie, you've been debunked. Say why don't we go over to AA together right now? But did I actually care about Sofa Sager? She'd made a bloody mess of Lisa's bed, imposed herself on me before I was properly awake, and was keeping me from working out where Elisabeth could have gone. She was just begging for a dressing down, and for pity. I wished she'd vanish from my house and my life without my having to make it happen. Pack her case of pedicure equipment and be gone. I didn't mind if she buggered off without paying the rent. Get her bruises and have her DT's elsewhere. She reminded me too much of Henning with his inflated legs. That little morning puke. I'd heard it a few minutes ago and thought Henning must have risen from the dead to make demands on me. Love, love is all we need, if only ever so little. Even the Sofa was making demands, with a wide-open beak, demanding and chirping and whining and fussing, especially in the mornings particularly through the bathroom door with her dry heaves, so familiar.

Towards afternoon she'd probably perk up again. That was her best time of day. She'd be freshly made up then, with nice unladdered stockings and more or less steady legs. Just a tiny little bit tipsy. A face like enamel. Hi, how're you doing? Breath reeking of lozenges, and hands fluttering. For years when I'd been here visiting I'd met up with Ann-Sophie, and every single time I'd told her I wanted her to move.

Now she'd bled like a stuck pig all over Lisa's bed and spoiled the pale brown mementos for ever. Enough was enough.

She drank her coffee in silence and then went down to her place. She didn't even want a hand getting down the stairs. Not until she'd left did I realize I hadn't been to the toilet either. My bladder felt as if it was about to burst and I was groggy, as if I'd had a bad night. Peeing, I put the night behind me. When I flushed the toilet I was wide awake and I walked out of the bathroom with its pale, thin light coming from a single bulb to meet the sunshine that made all the whirling dust in the apartment golden and visible.

I was sitting at the kitchen table looking through the window at the remains of my grandfather Abel's garden, out at the dog pee-spotted lawn and the lilac that has grown into a gnarled, lopsided tree. Rot has caused the old apple tree to crack, and an iron chain keeps the trunk from splitting wide open. It's been there so long it has grown into the crack. The short poles with sagging metal chicken wire between them that fence in the little lawn were painted green once upon a time, and so they still always look pale but unmistakably green to me. I sat staring at the thin soil in the flowerbed and the little piles of withered leaves, the creepers rustling by the doorway and the leaky rainwater barrel. It's an old oil drum, and it's green in the same way the fence posts are green, only to the eye of the initiated beholder.

Ann-Sophie came out while I was sitting there. She was walking with a determined gait, and straight as an arrow. I didn't doubt she was on her way diagonally across the yard, past the offices of *The Correspondent*, and down the street to the bottle store.

I'd just spoken to Hasse again, and told him Elisabeth had never taken the plane for Sicily. He didn't say much. What had I expected him to say, anyway?

His voice had changed the second time I spoke to him. It was very distant. Was that how my father's voice had sounded to Lisa when she phoned home from the sanatorium? Was Chapel Road pale and gray as a house in a dream when she sat by that black box with the Swedish coat of arms embossed on it, receiver in hand, trying to recall life, her other life?

I heard the sound of a key turning in the kitchen door, and somebody entered the little space between the kitchen and the hall where the door to the larder is. Then there were two men standing before me in the kitchen doorway. One was Gabriel and the other, a sinewy slightly stooped man resting one arm on the lintel and with a towel over his shoulder, was the Whitepainter. Göran Gabrielsson, who everybody calls Gabriel, is the much shorter man, and undoubtedly forty years younger. Gabriel is little and bowlegged, with a round face and long, curly hair.

They were dressed almost identically, in jeans and faded T-shirts, which was what made the Whitepainter look so tall and stooped. His hair is extremely short, crew-cut with his scalp showing. He's the same kind of washed-out Swede as Gabriel, with mousy hair and pale blue eyes. But that's because his hair and beard are now gray; once upon a time he was a red-head.

"Where's Lisa?"

I answered so fast I didn't realize who he was really talking about until after. "She's dead."

Disconcerted by their horrified expressions and what I had in fact said, I was quick to take it all back as soon as I realized they meant Elisabeth. But in my confusion, I'd thought they were asking about my mother. Gabriel asked once again where she was, and I said she'd gone to Sicily with Jenny Otter. He said he knew, but when he saw the lights on in the apartment last night, he'd thought she'd come back.

"That was me. I've come to sell the house."

Then I told them what Elisabeth had done. They listened neutrally and I could hear how bitter my own voice sounded. The Whitepainter just said "Oh, Jeez," and then strode across the kitchen, vanishing down the hall. After a minute I heard the water rushing out of the tap in the bathtub. Gabriel said nothing about Elisabeth and nothing about the Whitepainter's behavior. He just walked over to the sink and started arranging tea mugs and putting water on to boil as if it were the most natural thing in the world. He asked me where the tea strainer had gone without turning his head in my direction. Naturally I didn't answer, but he located it anyway. He also found the tin of old tea. It was on the wood-burning range that was now used as a work surface and had been covered with a yellow checked oilcloth. One or two things had changed.

The Whitepainter lived in the building. He was in my bathroom at this moment. Actually, I should be afraid. Perhaps I was, too, since I didn't throw them out.

He was once one of the painters of highest repute in town, a local celebrity. He had shows, sold landscapes and portraits to doctors and lawyers. Now they called him deranged. He's in his sixties, a thin man with a supple body. He seems to live on nothing but carrots and cultured milk, and his body has retained a kind of lean, wiry youthfulness. All year round, he goes about in clogs and summer shirts without freezing. Now and then he puts on a yellowing sleeveless sheepskin jacket. When he was still young and redheaded he had a dirty beard and wore his hair combed down in a fringe over his forehead. At the time, normal men wore their hair with a front wave and a side part, and so short at the neck you could see the skin. In those days the Whitepainter's hair curled down to the nape of his neck. Nobody called him that back then. He still used colors and was considered a good artist. But of course he wasn't like others, and I think it was because of him the new hair style took so long to catch on here in town in the sixties. No one wanted to be the first one to comb their hair down over their foreheads because they didn't want to look like Michael Palmgren.

"Want a cup yourself?" asked Gabriel, coming over to the table with the pot of water.

"Kind of you to ask," I replied, but he ignored the sarcasm. His method of brewing tea was to pour boiling water right over the tea leaves in the little strainer and into the mug. He made three cups that way, and then rummaged in the cupboard for the bread basket. He muttered to himself that he must remember to buy rusks. I asked if he was living with Elisabeth and he glanced up, truly astonished. I asked whether he had any idea where she might have gone, but he didn't.

Now the Whitepainter came out of the bathroom, his beard dripping. He hung his wet towel over the door and, before sitting down at the table, went over to the sink and spat out what I later realized was a wad of snuff.

"No job to go to?" I said, and they sat there saying nothing and looking attentively at me. I could feel them weighing my bitter comment of a few moments ago and this question in the same scale pan. Neither of them answered. The Whitepainter put five sugar cubes in his tea and mixed it with a brown-stained spoon. It sounded like the chiming of a little bell. I told them they couldn't go on living here, that the house was going to be sold. Since it was being sold for demolition they would have to find somewhere else to live. They both just sat there and the Whitepainter went on stirring his tea, which was getting cold. To keep up the conversation I told them I'd met up with Ann-Sophie Sager and informed her she'd have to move, too. Truth was, I'd done that years ago. I didn't want this place turning into a squat.

They both just sat there staring at me, and the silence that descended when the Whitepainter's spoon suddenly stopped chiming against the edge of the mug was an awkward one. I said she was never sober and she brought all kinds of characters around and Gabriel repeated as if he were the village idiot: "Characters?"

The spoon then started ringing again and the Whitepainter said Ann-Sophie was perfectly sober nowadays. I didn't have to worry about her.

"Well, never mind," I said. "You lot simply can't go on living here, because in a few weeks' time this house will be no more."

No answer. Both of them slurped when they drank. As soon as they'd had their tea they got up and left, and Gabriel said "bye now" a little awkwardly as he walked out the kitchen door. I should of course have told them I wanted the key to my apartment back. But it didn't occur to me just then. I thought the door might just have been open. But when I heard the Whitepainter come back the next morning, turn on the taps in the bathtub and use the toilet, I realized that Elisabeth must have given him a key. He lives in the little room off the shop that was once my Grandpa Abel's office. There's no running water down there. Since he was clearly a man who cared about hygiene, I didn't want to make a fuss about it for the last few days he'd be living in the house. So I just pretended not to notice he was using the bathroom. He never came at all on Friday or Saturday and Gabriel didn't come in and make tea. So at least I'd cooled them down I bit, which I was pleased about. It would help get them out of there faster.

But it didn't. On Sunday evening when I was sitting in the dusky study someone knocked on the pane of glass. Still having heard nothing from Elisabeth, I rushed to see who it was. When I got into the hall and opened the door all three of them were standing there: Gabriel, the Whitepainter and Ann-Sophie. They had bags and bottles. Gabriel announced they'd come to pay the rent.

I should, of course, have slammed the door in their faces. But I'd been alone for three days and nights and had had no news of Elisabeth. Maybe that was why I let them in. At any rate I said they weren't to pay any rent because they weren't tenants. They were living there illegally. They were squatters or whatever you called it.

"Oh, no we're not!" the Whitepainter said. "We've been paying rent all along." That was how I found out where Elisabeth got her money, although she didn't have a job. It wasn't much. The money was still there on the dining room table the next morning with the potato chip bags and paper cups.

When Gabriel walked straight into the dining room and put his bottles on the table I thought I must be dreaming. I just stood in the doorway dumbstruck, as if in a dream. The Whitepainter had given the Christmas elf a push, and it was spinning drunkenly before my eyes. I just stood there while they walked past, smiling and with no apologies. I mumbled softly in a language they couldn't understand. They must have taken my dismissal either as indifference or good will. Or else — and that was a frightening thought — they understood perfectly and were playing a game the rules of which were unfamiliar to me.

I really didn't know any of them. You could hardly say I knew Ann-Sophie just because we'd been at school together, or the Whitepainter because everybody in town had always known who he was. Now these strangers were making themselves at home in my living room. They cleared off the tabletop, exposing all the dull white rings from Henning's glasses. I sat down at the table because I didn't know what else to do. Ann-Sophie had pulled out a chair and was patting the seat, motioning me to join them.

Turning my head, I saw us in the hall mirror. The image shone softly in the dim hall light. All the harshness and dirt were gone. The plastic cups had a friendly sheen, their pastel colors dimmed. You couldn't see the dust on the tabletop or the fact that the slim column of smoke that had begun to wind overhead came from a sloppily stubbed out cigarette in the cup at Ann-Sophie's elbow. Gabriel had a golden-blond head of Jesus hair, and we two women could have been sisters he was visiting: I was the attentive one with my face in deep shadow, she the ministering one, waiting on him with long, strong hands, breaking the bread and pouring the wine. The other man stood there, leaning against the table, slightly bowed, as if standing guard over us.

When I took my eyes off the mirror and turned back to the table, my melancholy returned. It was as if a thin film of dirt and garish colors had overlaid the image. But I was well enough acquainted with the old hall mirror to know that the film was actually in its glass, a blue-gray shadow, perhaps nothing but a slow ageing process that was already well underway when I was a child. The only things the mirror image didn't alter were Ann-Sophie's hands. They were truly beautiful, and she did have long, strong fingers. They were well looked-after, too. Her nails weren't cracked at the tops like mine, but had been filed round and tapering. They were polished pink with a mother of pearl sheen, with the polish so thinly applied it looked natural.

I could see that my hands were neglected, and I suppose I could blame the traveling and the rummaging around in boxes and crates. But they were thinner than Ann-Sophie's, too, the skin on the backs was dry, with a whole matrix of little cracks I could only see with my glasses on. If I extended my fingers the knuckle skin went baggy, like children's stockings used to do at the knees. I remembered the knees of Ann-Sophie's tights from our school days. Unwashed stockings got even more easily creased if they were of poor, wartime quality, of course. I was sure Jenny had seen to it that I had good tights in spite of the cost, and she had kept them mended and smooth.

Our hands were mismatched in relation to our bodies and faces. It looked as if we had reached out toward one another in the mirror glass and swapped.

Whatever had made them think I would sit here and drink plonk with them?

And why hadn't I shown them the door? Ann-Sophie said they thought I must be feeling lonely. It was as if they wanted to show me a kindness. I knew this was a ritual, too. At the end of every month they had a little party and paid the rent. Ann-Sophie had even got dressed up. She was wearing a flowered tunic over turquoise trousers. The whole outfit was synthetic, and I would rather have cut a hole in a sack and pulled it over my head than worn those things. She had thick-soled platform shoes.

Ann-Sophie didn't drink the red wine. She rinsed the chicken down with a soft drink called Trocadero, and I asked if she wouldn't have some wine but Gabriel answered for her that she didn't drink. I said it must be tough for her to sit watching us with our wine, but the Whitepainter answered dismissively that did her good. She had to learn to live in the real world, he said. Ann-Sophie is my age, but that didn't stop them from treating her like a child. And she persevered steadfastly with her fizzy drink that certainly can't have tasted worse than the wine.

There were things about them that surprised me. Ann-Sophie had a kind of natural charm to her way of serving salad from a plastic container. Her gestures were both disarming and ironic at once. The Whitepainter talked to Gabriel about things I wouldn't have believed they were aware of. But Ann-Sophie kept interrupting, urging the Whitepainter to have some more chicken. She was worried about his being so thin, afraid his skinniness was what was causing his ulcers. Without my asking, Gabriel volunteered that the Whitepainter had got his ulcer working in the hospital kitchen. He seemed to do occasional hours cooking there, and sometimes he also apparently stood along what they called the tray line.

The Whitepainter is thin and his body supple. When he is seated, he looks as if he's floating or being poured. His hands and feet are pliant, and he keeps them in motion. The minute he sits down he lets his clogs drop to the floor where they stand, stretched out of shape by his high anklebones, looking like a body part that has fallen off. The way he moves his feet around while he's speaking gives the impression he's using them for emphasis.

Gabriel is short and stout. His face is round and so are his eyes. He looks very childlike, and still has long hair though it's hardly the fashion any more. It's curly and shoulder length. I gathered that he too worked, though less regularly. He took temporary jobs on the hospital wards or sorting the laundry in the basement. Sometimes he did window cleaning for some company. I see him working at one of the checkouts at the Co-op now and then, but they seem only to use him if they're desperate, because they don't like long hair. When he works there, he has to pull it into a ponytail with an elastic band.

Everything he touches at work is dirty. That occurred to me once when I saw him taking somebody's money at the checkout. His fingertips must be grimy with the dirt from banknotes and coins. When he comes home from the hospital his hair and clothes smell foul and dank from all the dirt he's handled. Sometimes his hands are cracked and his fingertips so punctured they get swollen and infected. Bits of glass and hypodermics turn up in the pockets of garments soiled with blood and discharges.

He lives in the apartment next to Ann-Sophie's, and a card on the door reads Göran Gabrielsson. His name is written on it in red Magic Marker, and underneath CHILDREN OF THE EARTH in green. The first time I saw that I thought he must be nuts. But Children of the Earth is the name of an organization he belongs to. In fact it's a cooperative association. The members lease and farm a number of disused smallholdings and crofts outside town. They keep goats and sheep and use horses instead of tractors. The Whitepainter refers to them with benevolent sarcasm, saying they are campaigning valiantly for the return of housemaid's knee and consumption.

Gabriel would give his life to be out there tilling the earth with a wooden plough or an even more primitive tool if possible, according to the Whitepainter. But it's literally a matter of life or death to him because of his allergies. He's tried to acclimatize to dogs' hair and straw chaff and horse scurf, but he's only gotten worse. He's been in anaphylactic shock, and had hospital treatment. Now he lives here and seems to be Children of the Earth's self-appointed ideologist and philosopher. His bookshelves, of the brick and board variety, are full of tomes on ecology. He's funny in the sense that he appears very quiet at first. Or rather: most of the time he is very quiet, but once he gets talking he can't seem to stop. I remember the first thing he said that Sunday evening when we sat down at the table. It was perfectly typical of him. It all began when I repeated that the house was going to be demolished and they would have to move out as soon as possible. I made every effort to sound understanding, and not as if I were trying to decontaminate the place.

"I know you want to go on living here," I said. "You've created yourselves a world apart".

Gabriel answered: "Mankind is incapable of creation."

"Oh, I think we've managed one or two things," I countered, but he persisted:

"No human being is a creator. Human beings are the bearers of life, nothing more."

Then he was silent for a long time, and when we had already changed the subject he interjected that well, possibly a garden was the kind of thing a human being could make. But that was it. And that was just in the spirit of creation. Other things, systems or languages or equipment could not be considered creations, since we could not know what we were imitating. We hadn't a clue as to the mysterious goings-on in our brains, what trails were already blazed.

That was the kind of thing Henning might have said. But Gabriel didn't appear to be drunk. He was a very moderate drinker. Whereas the Whitepainter, so ascetic in all other ways, just swilled the red wine down. That couldn't do his stomach lining any good.

I found Gabriel's words outrageous, verging on mad. To conceal my embarrassment I drank some of their red wine. In the end I drank more than I had intended.

I assumed Gabriel was one of those people who picked up, from radio programs and newspaper articles, whatever philosophical *on dit* was in the air. I didn't imagine him really reading the books , assumed his brain just went on processing all the flakes of soot whirling in the air around him. No, Gabriel is neither out of his mind nor slightly retarded as I originally thought. Though he's not really like other people. Now and then he has severe depressions, and at those times he keeps to himself.

I said something I regretted afterwards. It was after Gabriel said his piece about creation. I said I seemed to have ended up in the local philosophers' society, village genius department.

There was total silence. The Whitepainter downed the red wine he had in his paper cup and held it out to Gabriel for a refill. Ann-Sophie offered me a little more, too, and I was tempted to laugh in her face, sitting there like a dinner party hostess trying to compensate for the shortcomings of her guests. I felt nasty and awkward, and at the same time I didn't think I needed to feel that way. So I had another glass of wine. The Whitepainter asked why I was selling the house.

" I need money, for one thing."

There was actually no cause for me to let myself be held accountable to these three about my life and circumstances. I didn't tell them that if Hasse and I got seven hundred and fifty thousand or even a million for this huge piece of centrally located property we would be able to move back to Sweden. Ann-Sophie was worried about what would become of her.

"I finally have a regular clientele," she said, "and there's no guarantee they'd travel to the other side of town to get their feet done." And the Whitepainter was worried about his studio, in what had once been my grandfather's grocer's shop, and Gabriel was afraid he might have to start working every day if he had to pay proper rent anywhere else.

"In which case I'd never get anything done," he said.

I despised them. I think that's close to the truth. The situation had its amusing sides, and I may also have felt some compassion for them. But in my heart of hearts I despised them.

They, however, didn't seem the least bit aware of it. Suddenly they started cross-examining me. Elisabeth apparently hadn't said a word about Hasse and me, which I found odd. Though of course it was good, too. The Whitepainter was the inquisitor. How long was I staying? Didn't I have a job to get back to? What was I actually doing with my life?

I said I kept house and did the bookkeeping for my husband. Stupidly enough, I also said I did some writing. Naturally they asked what, and before I knew it they had drawn 'Sunbeams' out of me. One thing led to another; I had to tell them I hadn't been on the staff of *The Correspondent* for a long time, since the fifties and sixties. But I'd submitted articles and columns that had been published on Saturdays on what people called the rubbish page.

The Whitepainter guffawed.

"So you wrote articles headlined 'Sunbeams from Salazar's Portugal'? That must be the joke of the century!"

Everything had been so different in the fifties, but they didn't see that. People didn't travel so much in those days. Southern climes were exotic. I mostly wrote about everyday life, about the people in the village where the Ferreiras lived, about the fish market and the little old women who made ceramic figurines. It wasn't at all as mendacious as they thought, and it hadn't been my idea to call the columns Sunbeams. But of course you couldn't write about anything political. They'd never have published it. Personally, I would have liked my column to be called 'Letters from Portugal'. I'd read the letters of Mariana Alcoforado, and had a soft spot for the lovesick nun.

"So what about during the revolution?" the Whitepainter asked. "What kind of articles were you writing then?"

That's what it's like to come home. Here anyone and everyone feels free to fire questions at you about your ideological views and your plans for your life. I just said I wasn't in Portugal during the revolution. "I was at home, in this very house."

They thought my husband owned a garment mill down there, but I explained he was just the manager of a Swedish-owned factory, and that he hadn't had a factory of his own for years, not since the sixties when his father's company had gone bottom up.

"Well, things are tough all over," said Ann-Sophie, who had not otherwise contributed to the cross-examination. She chewed her chicken, swilling it down with Trocadero.

I decided it was my turn now, and started asking them things about Elisabeth. But I didn't learn much. They weren't worried about her, and wouldn't tell me what kind of people she went around with.

"Lisa's quite a solitary type," said Ann-Sophie.

I felt funny hearing them call her Lisa. Of course I went on calling her Elisabeth, that's her name. But it didn't help. She was Lisa, a stranger to me. Her rooms smelled different from ours. She had experiences we hadn't had, Hasse and myself. Shooting up for a kick. I didn't even know if I dared ask about such a thing. Anyway, I couldn't bring myself to say it.

I remembered when she was little and cried because she had to have a vaccination. That childish crying went on for a long time after we left Jaime's office. He was the only one she would let give her an injection. And now?

I said I'd come home because I was worried about her. Jenny had told me she wasn't going to school but didn't get herself a job, either. She was supposed to live with Jenny and go to upper secondary school, but she'd moved into this old house instead. Jenny said she smoked hash and might be doing worse things. When I had got that off my chest, Michael said:

"Well I never, I never, I never!"

I lost my temper and said I had eyes of my own, and he asked me what I'd seen. "This place!"

But they couldn't see what the matter was here. Good God. What could I say to that? She had no initiative. The only hopeful thing I'd seen was that she'd put up new wallpaper in her room. But Ann-Sophie informed me it was Michael who'd done the repapering. When I asked him why, he gave me a weird answer.

"Peel it off and you'll understand."

What a thing to say.

Ann-Sophie said I was taking it too hard. There was no need to worry about Lisa. The Whitepainter said he thought I should go back home and stick to my bookkeeping.

"She'll come back as long as she has somewhere to come back to. Damn it, just don't tear the house down."

That would, of course, be to his advantage. It would benefit all three of them. But I told them I planned to stay and wait for Elisabeth. The day she turned up I'd be here. Even if it took a week. I'd be sitting at the kitchen table.

"Lurking about, like a pike waiting for some smaller fry," said the Whitepainter.

At that, Gabriel got up and walked over to the chest of drawers with Elisabeth's record player on top of it. He put on a record, and I was completely taken aback when the sound boomed out across the room from two speakers she'd set up on either side of Henning's old bookcase.

I hate that music. I'll never learn to like it or even put up with it. Last time I was home there was a rock concert on TV my last evening. I was going back to Portugal the next morning, but Elisabeth had left me with Jenny and come over here. She sat here listening, with the sound at top volume, staring at the flickering images. I tried not to show how disappointed I was. She sat turned away from me, absorbed in the music. For a while I don't think she even noticed I'd come in. And it never seemed to end. It blared on for hours, until very late that night. How I hated those stoned, spineless musicians who kept time with their gyrating crotches as they sang about the end of the world and humiliation in crude caustic voices. I glimpsed swastikas on chains around their dirty necks. They wore dark glasses and dirty, flashy clothes. I think they did their very best to look like criminals. Support your local outlaws, ran the slogan across one of their sweaty T-shirt chests.

I sat up half the night, listening to midnight rock. That was the name of the program. Elisabeth was so engrossed in it the thought of turning the TV off and talking to me during my last few hours in Sweden would never have occurred to her. I was beginning to be scared. That must have been when I first became genuinely frightened. I felt I had to protect her from something life-threatening, but I didn't know how. I didn't even know how to say it. All I wanted was for her to have a good life. That was it. But she seemed just as defenseless as when she was a baby. More so, in fact. In those days I was able to keep an eye on her every minute. I knew what she was eating since I was the one who mashed her bananas, grated her carrots, and chopped her chicken so fine she could chew it. But now?

When that disgusting music gushed out into the room, it all came back to me, and I rushed up and grabbed the record player needle. I yanked at it and the speakers screeched, and Michael shouted at me to watch what I was doing.

Then there was silence. I asked them to leave.

They got up and started clearing away the paper plates and the remains of what they call "party food" at the supermarket. But I told them to leave it. Just get out. I wanted to be on my own. So they left without a good-bye, and I lay on the couch and knew I had drunk too much of their red wine because when I looked up at the ceiling everything was jolting and lurching. I was nauseous, too. But when I shut my eyes and pulled the throw over me the nausea passed, and I think I fell asleep almost at once.

When I woke up it was getting light outside. The remains of the meal were still on the paper plates, and a little creamy fruit salad had dried up on one of Sigrid's little fruit plates. Looking at it made me feel sick, so I carefully got up and started clearing things away. I threw what was left of the revolting chicken, with its coating of rancid fat and "gourmet" spices in the garbage pail. Then I went to my bed but as soon as I pulled up the covers Michael's words came back to me:

"Peel off the wallpaper and you'll understand."

There's no shower at number 13 Chapel Road, just a stained yellow bathtub with a big, gurgling tap. You couldn't shower in that tub. It bothered me at first, then I stopped worrying about it.

No newspaper was delivered. No one expected dinner. I didn't have to freshen up because somebody was coming home.

Every morning I heard the Whitepainter running the water in the bathtub. Since I hadn't returned the rent money they'd left on the dining room table, I let him be. When I got up to pee early in the mornings, I turned on the hot water heater.

What was it that made him take a bath every morning? Had Elisabeth? I tried to remember if I had taken baths so regularly during the periods I'd lived there on my own. But I couldn't recall. Looking back, all I could see were glimpses of events, shreds of memory. I couldn't remember such a simple thing as whether I'd had a wash every morning in the mid-50s. I went and stood at the sink, staring deep into my own eyes in the mirror, trying to make those days take shape in my mind. Naturally, that didn't help. Still, one morning there I was sitting at the table telling the Whitepainter that Henning always wanted toast for breakfast, and a large cup of strong coffee. Towards the end, he had had such severe DTs that he had to hold the cup with both hands. Even then he was fussy about his hot toast. He fussed if I piled two slices on a plate, telling me how the English, who had mastered the art of breakfasting, had special toast racks to keep the slices apart. Henning liked his toast to be so hot the butter melted into it.

Why did I remember that? Was it ever true? The Whitepainter, who had come upstairs so late I was already out in the kitchen getting my breakfast, stood in the doorway with his damp towel over one shoulder, listening with no great interest. When he'd gone I had a feeling I'd been lying to him. Or at least equivocating. But I rummaged through the cupboard under the sink and did actually find our old toaster. Was that proof?

Kurt Lundholm came round. I'd phoned his office to say I'd have to put off selling. I blamed it on the house, on the mess, on all there was to sort out.

So he turned up, an improbable sight in a black checked suit, a striped shirt, and a tie with pheasants on it. Of course he's only improbable in this house. Out on the street I suppose he looks normal. Kurt Lundholm has an aura of school toilet about him. That's because I once heard him tell a joke, when he was about eight or nine. This was it: have you heard the one about the woman who inseminates the cows? She got pregnant. Spilled some on herself.

I'm standing by the outbuildings we used to play ball against, hearing the crude punch lines of his idiotic jokes. The poor man, he will always be associated with them in my mind. Though he doesn't know it, of course. Nowadays he has a secretary with a Tartan skirt, a crystal ashtray and a leather-bound planner. But up here he seems merely comical. Maybe that was what made me say one point five million, just because he was denuded of his crystal ashtray, his devoted, kilted assistant and his office intercom.

"A million and a half! You can't be serious, my dear Ann-Marie."

When he talked about money, his voice took on a kind of mournful, loving quality. I feel very secure with Kurt. He's just like he has always been, and at the same time he looks exactly like what he is supposed to be playing at being, the deputy managing director of an expanding construction company. The perfectly planned life. Ingvar Kamprad calls the young lions at IKEA his enthusiasts, and why not? Kurt Lundholm is Wolfgang Altmeyer's enthusiast.

I haven't spoken to Wolfgang Altmeyer for twenty years. The very thought makes my flesh creep. But he's keen to get his hands on this piece of property, and I'm pleased. I'm sure to get seven hundred fifty thousand for it, maybe even a million. Altmeyer is going to enlarge the print shop. The newspaper's losing money, but the printing business is booming. And he may have other cards up his sleeve, too, that dirty old man. How old can he be?

Considering the seven hundred fifty thousand (that could be a million), it was naïve of the Whitepainter and Gabriel to try to talk me out of selling. A million's not a sum to be sneezed at, even today. We could move back to Sweden. Buy a house. Invest in a business or even a little shop.

At any rate, I liked talking to Kurt Lundholm and I gave him a cup of the instant coffee and some of the rusks Gabriel had bought. Kurt is one of the few survivors of a lost world. All the other people I went to school with have left town, and the people on the streets here are strangers to me. I think most of them are from elsewhere. When I visit Jenny I only see old people. That's put me off the idea of coming back here. The last time I was visiting her I went with her to see an old woman who'd been wheelchair-bound for fifteen years. She claims I used to know her, but I didn't remember. There wasn't much point in making conversation, because she had her hearing aid in a glass of solution. It needed cleaning. She asked me to help her put it back on its cord. She kept dropping wads of soiled cotton on the floor, and I would pick them up for her. The bedroom was full: there was a pulley to hoist her out of bed, the TV, the radio, a tape recorder. It looked more like a workshop or a dentist's office. The living room was chock-a-block with furniture. Some of it reminded me very vaguely of one of the big houses on the north side of town. I'd gone to school with her youngest daughter. But we didn't talk about that, because she kept going on about Meals on Wheels. She didn't like her fish boiled. She liked it breaded and fried. She went through the whole list of peas and beans that didn't agree with her, and the little quirks of all the home helpers. She preferred the men. Jenny and she also took stock of the community's strokes and brain tumors. In fact, she was quite alert and her head was perfectly clear, but her soul had atrophied from malnutrition.

I was never coming back here. I'd told myself that time and again. I don't know what other places are like. Hasse and I haven't talked through our plans in any concrete sense; we've never mentioned the possibility of other towns.

When I didn't have to eat and sleep and wash the dishes, and didn't have to read the paper either, time passed more quickly, strangely enough. It seemed to flow over me. I was the unmoving seabed.

Though I did eat sometimes. I had sandwiches and rusks, and I washed myself cursorily. Hasse phoned a couple of times, and I said I was still waiting for Elisabeth. Kurt Lundholm called too, but I couldn't give him an answer. It was just a matter of waiting now. Waiting. Sleeping. Thinking. Sleeping or not sleeping. Not thinking. Putting things away. But I hadn't packed anything yet, since I didn't know what I'd be taking.

When Elisabeth came back I'd pack. I was the unmoving seabed. over which time flowed. I was quick as a fish in the current of time. When Elisabeth comes back. When I get to Porto. When spring comes.

I started rising early, since it was hardest to sleep in the morning, and I'd sit at the kitchen window with my teacup. From there I could see the door to the hall, the worn grass and a corner of the flowerbed. The house throbbed with music for hours on end. It was the Whitepainter's record player; he played the same music over and over again. But it wasn't that awful stuff at least, it was classical. He must have gone to work sometimes, too, because I saw him cross the courtyard. He was stooped, and had thick woolen socks in his clogs.

I eked out my supplies so I wouldn't have to go out. Late in the evenings I'd walk down to the service station that had a convenience store, for bananas and white bread. I had no desire to bump into the others. It didn't seem they were going to move. I watched them through the window, coming and going as usual.

I didn't want to go into town, where I ran the risk of meeting Jenny's friends and acquaintances. One of them might start interrogating me. What are you doing back home? How long are you staying? When did you get here? I didn't like it when they said "home". It had been years since I'd lived here.

What's Elisabeth up to? Perfectly natural questions. Questions anybody might ask.

And what are you doing with yourself nowadays?

I couldn't use the Nórdica bookkeeping as an excuse, because it was unpaid work, which only made it worse. But I had plenty of time on my hands. Even without a *criada* I had plenty of time. I'm well suited to accounting because I'm a thorough person and orderly, but naturally mistakes did creep in. Every time the hell of year-end closing of accounts came around we'd spend night after night hunting for some trivial number of escudos, getting headaches, our cups of coffee going cold, right through until dawn when the dogs would start to bark and the cocks to crow down among the hens that roosted under us, their tile coops wet with dew.

Hasse comes home tired in the evenings and wants to read. He has been constantly overworked for the last ten or fifteen years. He should have had a better assistant than little Santorio, because he can't keep on top of the correspondence, either. It's impossible for him to fit the bookkeeping into his days. He used to bring his piles of paper home, his ledgers and receipts and records. Towards the end of the month he'd even be bringing the payroll work home. So I started doing Nórdica's bookkeeping in the mornings so we could at least have the evenings free. There was no use trying to negotiate with the management in Sweden, because the factory was already hanging by the thinnest possible thread. One more unexpected expense and they'd shut it down. They almost had, the time Hasse had insisted the roof would have to be repaired because it was raining in on the senhoritas.

Negotiations. Silence. We lived with the threat for several weeks, and the rain dripped down onto the shoulders of the senhoritas and onto the sewing machines. In the end Hasse proposed that the new roof could be done one section at a time without having to stop production, and management gave in. We could breathe again. Hasse brought an expensive bottle of wine home, and I ordered four hundred kronor worth of books from Sweden. We'd been reprieved, but of course the next threat was just around the corner. Between times, we'd forget them. Life would return to normal, the threats would recede, grate less on our nerves.

So I kept the books. I did the cooking. But I'm not claiming this was the justification for my existence. It was more like I didn't need one down there. I don't think I was as good a cook as I used to be, in the days when I had Conceição. Maybe the best thing for Hasse would be if he had both her and me.

The little airing window in the study had been open all night. When I went to close it the frame had swollen and no longer fit. Rain was streaming down the little pane. I tugged at the catch, but when I finally got the window closed, the glass cracked in a very peculiar way, as if it were soggy. It split like satin, and the pieces fell soundlessly onto the gravel in the yard.

I put on a heavy sweater against the chill and started pacing the apartment deciding what to get rid of. I had to be quick now; with the cold air streaming in the floor was getting cold. After some time, my feet and calves were stiff. It didn't take me long to realize this wasn't a job I could do in one day, so I took a cushion and stuffed it in the hole where the window pane had been.

The next morning I heard the Whitepainter come all the way into the apartment when he was done in the bathroom. I know I should have jumped straight out of bed and stopped him. I should have asked him who he thought he was, what right he thought he had to march into my apartment. But I just stayed in bed. My dressing gown was on a chair in the kitchen; I didn't want to go out there in my nightgown.

I heard noises out there. It sounded like he was hitting something. When he'd left I went and looked around, and when I got to the study I saw he'd covered the empty window frame with a piece of masonite and removed the bits of glass that had fallen in.

He came again the next day. I lay rigid in my bed, listening to his footsteps treading quietly past my door several times. I thought he was sounding more and more at home. He didn't seem to be in any hurry, and I heard the sound of his filthy sheepskin jacket brushing against my door.

I got up and put on my dressing grown, cinching the belt tightly and pulling up the collar so none of my nightgown showed. But when I finally had my hand on the doorknob I hesitated, unsure what to say. What are you doing here? What is it you actually want?

I couldn't start asking him such formal questions now that we had spent an evening drinking together. Not that I'd had any choice. Now the boundaries between the formal and the informal were blurred beyond recognition. That makes it very difficult to know how to address one another. Informality with a near stranger is so uncomfortable, it almost feels like unwelcome touching. Like in shops. The kind salespeople. Their faces so close to mine. "Don't those hug your behind a little too tight, dearie?"

Things had happened here in my absence and I could no longer imagine how he would take it if I said: what are you doing here? Would I have to curse him for him to realize I didn't want him here?

That morning he put a new pane of glass in the window. He was a surprisingly handy man. He'd pressed putty all around the frame to hold the glass in place. The next morning again he came in and asked me if it was dry; said he could paint it. He had a can of white paint with him, but although the windows had been painted white once upon a time, I knew that bright white paint shining around one single pane of glass would look strange. So I said no thank you to his offer. A few days later, though, I had to change my mind on that one, because the blue tits were pecking away all the putty.

I had heard that years ago the Whitepainter had had a mental breakdown, after which he no longer painted the kind of canvases that had been his bread and butter. The only color he used now was white. He painted things white, any old things. They said he went around begging things off people, or offering to buy absolutely worthless stuff just to paint it white. He became a laughing stock of course, but his madness was of the tranquil variety, and he wasn't a burden to society.

When he brought his white paint upstairs to paint the window putty, I said I supposed he'd be painting the whole house white now that he'd got started. He didn't look up from his work as he answered. No, he wasn't going to paint the whole house white. He wasn't going to seal it up.

"It's meant to be open," he said. "This is a place to go in and out of." His voice was stern, and quite critical.

He did a nice job. The glass fit perfectly, and didn't rattle in the frame. But when he was gone — I gave him a cup of coffee for his pains — I looked at it again and saw how dead the new glass looked compared with the old panes, which were thinner and more wavy. The new glass looked like dirty, petrified air. The old one had simply been a light film resting on the boundary between two worlds. I recalled one Christmas Eve, late at night, when I had stood there looking down into the courtyard. *The Correspondent* offices were all dark, except for one single window on the ground floor. That was the room of the editor-in-chief, and there was a soft light shining in it. Somebody was sitting there with candles lit, in the middle of the night.

Ada was the only person who would do something like that. But Ada had been dead for years. I stood there looking at that unlikely flame, that living flutter of a thin tongue of light and heat down there, knowing at the same time I wasn't really seeing it. And quite rightly, when I took a few steps back into the study the vision vanished. It had been the reflection of one of our own candles in the window. Both a mundane explanation and something of a relief at the same time. I felt empty.

The sober pane of glass the Whitepainter had put in would never be able to fool me by reflecting a candle flame.

I started sorting things again. I'd decided to collect everything that belonged to Elisabeth in one special box. But there was so little that was hers, a thin layer of clothes just covering the bottom and a pair of worn boots, a few bottles and tubes of cheap cosmetics. Nothing she owned seemed to have been particularly affected by having passed through her hands. The worn, frayed garments were threadbare in an impersonal way. When she was little I knew every seam of her clothes and every broken edge of her wooden toys. Now I didn't know her at all. I knew so little about her that I couldn't imagine what she was doing or where she might be. Somewhere with pavement under her feet, I guessed. When I was worried about her not getting enough to eat, Hasse said on the phone: oh, I'm sure she does. They live on hamburgers and cokes. He must have thought she was still ten. I read semi-pornographic reports about drug abuse in the tabloids. That was all I could base my fantasies on. In the end I reported her to the police. Oh, God, the shame of it.

They weren't terribly interested. All right, they were pleasant enough, but I couldn't see any concern or commitment. They asked me if I had any idea how many teenagers ran away every week. I said I had no idea and didn't want to know. I wanted help finding Elisabeth.

"Is there a boy involved?" they asked. I didn't know that, either.

Walking home afterwards, I felt terrible. I didn't like being out in broad daylight, and I was a bit dizzy. To find out something about her, I started talking to her so-called tenants again. I bought a bag of tulip bulbs and stood out in the yard planting them in the flower bed, slowly and with long breaks, in order to be there when Gabriel came from the hospital. Standing there bending over made me feel faint, and when I straightened up I was weak-kneed. He kindly asked whether I was all right. I found reasons to go in and see the Whitepainter in what he referred to as his "studio", such as to tell him that if he wanted any of the things I was getting rid of for his white painting, he was welcome to them.

"That's not exactly what it's all about," he said.

I looked around what used to be the grocer's store. There was nothing left from my grandfather's day, not even the smell. All it smelled like now was a paint shop. Funny how you can usurp a place that way, I was thinking, and for one moment I felt nothing but hate towards the Whitepainter. Then, of course, I came to myself and told him that if he changed his mind there were things like old vases, and some furniture.

Gabriel hadn't told me a thing about Elisabeth, and neither did Michael. I decided to talk to Ann-Sophie instead. When I heard her out in the hall I asked her in for coffee in the kitchen, although I felt funny about it. Still, I reckoned it would be easier to get her to talk than the other two. We were about the same age, and had even gone to the same school.

"Do you know who Elisabeth hangs around with?" I asked.

But all she said was that Lisa was kind of the solitary type. She kept to herself. I asked if Ann-Sophie had seen people coming to visit her, maybe young men. Not that she could recall. But after a while she let the Dutchman out of the bag. Somebody had mentioned him. But she didn't know his name or what he did. I don't know whether she really didn't know or whether Gabriel and Michael had forbidden her to spill the beans. Let's say that was all she knew. What she really wanted to talk about was herself.

If I had been Ann-Sophie, I wouldn't have. Her life had been a shambles ever since the days she started touring with Egon Holmlund. People in this town had chewed it over and spit it out so many times it was amazing there was anything left of her private life. Could she even remember what it had really been like?

What she liked talking about best were the days before she became a real wino. She'd worked in a stocking shop in the Grand Arcade for a few years. I had bought nylons there myself, and left old laddered pairs in for mending. She had been a real lady in those days, her hair in a French twist with a thin hairnet on top. She'd combed her curly bangs down over one eye. And abandoned her dialect for a high-brow way of talking. When I took stockings to be mended, she would ask:

"Are they dahhhmp?"

I didn't understand what she said, and she had to repeat it. The memory of Ann-Sophie with a fancy hairdo and penciled-in eyebrows was a little embarrassing too. And would I really have taken unwashed stockings to be mended?

She told me it was Bertil Franzon who had given her the job.

"You remember Franzon. Who owned the Grand Arcade."

Did I remember him! The whole town was alive with the gossip that Franzon had opened a stocking shop for the mistress he was keeping. The only person everyone assumed knew nothing about it was Gerda Franzon. She went into the shop and was waited on by Ann-Sophie and seemed happy as a lark.

"Franzon wanted it to be an exclusive stocking shop. He said the men in this dump of a town needed to learn to give their wives nylons as presents. So he wanted a good-looking shop assistant. Well, I didn't look half bad in those days," said Ann-Sophie.

He called the shop Cadeaux, but nobody could pronounce it so it wasn't a very good choice.

"But gosh," said Ann-Sophie. "In those days you could sell nylons as if they were really something special! Nowadays there are stacks of them in every department store. And nothing but pantyhose. I would show the stockings, lifting them up and drawing one over my hand. 'This is a lovely nylon,' I'd say, 'really superior quality. Or would you prefer something thinner?' You had to take good care of your hands when you were going to draw nylons over them like that, believe you me. But I've always put a lot of effort into my hands."

She extended them across the kitchen table, showing me her manicured and polished nails, with their mother-of-pearl sheen. Ann-Sophie had strong nails. I couldn't resist asking her if you could do anything about nails that had a tendency to chip and crack.

"Oh, Lord. Let's see. I'll bet you do the dishes without rubber gloves, eh? That's the worst thing for your nails. Dishwashing liquid and laundry powder."

She promised to do mine for me so I could turn over a new leaf with rubber gloves and have long, lovely fingernails.

"But what do I care, anyway?" I objected.

"Don't say that! Once you start letting yourself go, the end is near. You're asking the right person. Before you know it you'll be old and heeled down."

That was ridiculous. What could I say? I decided to pretend I hadn't heard her. She went on about how she'd learned manicuring when she was working in a hair salon.

"That came in useful when I decided to learn the pedicure business."

Listening to her, you could imagine she'd climbed the career ladder from Cadeaux to Sophie's pedicure salon and never looked back. But I couldn't imagine she didn't think I knew. Everybody knew.

She offered to bring me a vitamin B supplement. To strengthen my nails.

"We'll get them all sorted out," she promised.

I regretted having asked her in. Now she'd be dropping by all the time. But at least she'd told me something about Elisabeth.

I went back to the police station to tell them about the Dutch guy, but they weren't particularly interested, I think they thought I was being a nuisance, maybe acting hysterical, because one of them said:

"You can't expect us to put out a national alert for your little girl, ma'am. She hasn't exactly committed a crime."

That was how they saw it. She'd just gone off. Which wasn't a crime. Did I know how many kids ran away every week?

"No!"

All I knew was that things weren't supposed to be like this. Children shouldn't go off without anyone caring. They just sat there staring at me, I slammed the door and then looked back at them through the rippled glass. They were kind and good-hearted and very patient. This wasn't about *their* children.

I was living under a tremendous strain, always fearing the worst, my mind full of images. I can't say I could see them. I could just sense the flicker. They were quite gray but certain words could make them stand out in Technicolor. Then they'd begin to flow, wanting to become stories, seeming to develop their own clarity, because suddenly I could see them. Not behind my eyelids but beyond them. If I stared down into a tabletop the picture would be there, just below the surface. I could see her down there in a zone where no matter seemed to exist, nothing but the power of thought. Sometimes when I woke up in the morning I would see her before I opened my eyes. Her body was naked and stabbed all over. Some sense of decency prevented me from making this into a series of images, a course of events. Slowly I allowed myself to experience a highly censored series of images that provided me some relief.

I might have been too attuned recently to what was happening inside me, or just under the surface of the tabletop. Sometimes I didn't notice that reality was changing.

When Gabriel the Whitepainter and Ann-Sophie brought me the kalanchoë for my birthday, I knew something had happened. But I didn't know how it had happened, or even when. Why would they give me a such an expensive plant, and how could they know it was my birthday? Ann-Sophie did hasten to say that she'd cut a coupon out of *The Correspondent*. If you took it to the shop you got ten kronor off any plant that cost more than forty. But still?

When I was little, I wasn't afraid, not this way.

Children aren't afraid of cruelty in the agonized, averted adult way.

As a child I was wide open to terror, to the stink of corpses, and to the cellar-chill of cruelty. I saw a strong hand strike, and a head swing , trembling like a fruit dangling from a tree in a storm. I stared, not even turning away when blood began to drip from its nose.

On the floor in front of me lay a newspaper with pictures from the concentration camps that had recently been liberated by the allies. It said: SEE OUR EXCLUSIVE PHOTOS OF THE HORRORS OF THE CONCENTRA-TIONCAMPS. The caption to one of the pictures lying on the plank floor was: Piles of Bodies Crawling with Maggots. I was sitting in the shed where Tora Otter kept the sweets she sold at the market. I was reading on the sly.

When I pulled down the wallpaper in Elisabeth's room that had once been mine, I found pictures of corpses. The papering hadn't been done too well. When I picked at one of the seams, it came away and exposed the pictures. I saw the body of a man in jeans and a bloody shirt. His chest was riddled with bullet holes and his trousers were torn away at the front. They were black with blood, with newsprint, with ebony newsprint blood where his sex had been. He was wearing sneakers, those leather and canvas gym shoes you can buy at a department store anywhere in the world. Perhaps they were plastic and imitation leather, a cheap pair of worn-out shoes. They were not going to be used any more, would be disposed of. But if he had lived I imagine he would have worn them a while longer.

Then I realized that they would have been thrown away long ago, were perhaps already decomposing.

I tore down the wallpaper, ripped it to shreds. It had been put up with flour-and-water paste. She'd been in a hurry, hadn't even taken the time to go to the hardware store for proper wallpaper paste.

No, it was the Whitepainter who'd been in a rush.

I pulled away faces and bodies with the shredding wallpaper. But what was left was quite sufficient. I understood that the entire room had been papered with corpses.

Was she out of her mind?

The Whitepainter found me. How much time had passed I did not know. He said I looked sick, and asked how my face had gotten all dirty. Then he went out to the kitchen, maybe to get some water or something to eat, and he passed Elisabeth's room and saw.

"Well I never, I never, I never!" he exclaimed.

I asked him if he could figure out what it meant. Why had she papered her room with photos of the dead and maimed? I walked behind him and we looked into the little wallpaperless room. Most of the pictures were torn in two and white gashes of paper and glue split faces and images.

Why had she done this? It must have taken ages to collect all the pictures. She must have been cutting them out of the papers for months. There were people who had been tortured and executed. There were twisted limbs in mass graves, piles of bodies in extermination camps, terrorists shot down lying in pools of blood on the pavement, burned children's bodies and victims of traffic accidents covered with blankets. There were also some very old newspaper pictures. I recognized them from my childhood. SEE OUR EXCLUSIVE PHOTOS OF THE HORRORS OF THE CONCENTRATION CAMPS. Why had Elisabeth put all that up on the walls? Was she mentally ill?

The Whitepainter said he didn't know, but he didn't think she was crazy. Might have got that way eventually, though.

In fact he knew nothing, not even how long she'd been living with all those pictures on the walls. He hadn't heard anything about it except that she said she had been going to repaper her room. And when she started tearing down the old layers of wallpaper, a layer of newspaper emerged that had pictures from the concentration camps. That had got her started, and she built it up from there, cutting out newspaper photos every day, and sticking them up. She had never explained why. He'd happened to see it all one Sunday morning not very long ago when her door had been ajar. He'd gone straight up to the attic and got those old rolls of wallpaper, mixed up some flour-and-water paste and put up that paper over the whole hellish mess as fast as he could, he said. She hadn't protested. Pale and petite she had sat curled up on her bed that he'd shifted out into the middle of the room, smoking the whole time he worked. I asked whether she smoked hash and he answered he supposed she did sometimes. Was she a drug addict?

"Jesus, what the hell is with you? Have a wash. Eat something. I'll be up to check on you."

He slammed out the door, the pane of glass rattling as he left.

One afternoon when I had been to the cemetery the apartment smelled different when I came in. It wasn't an unpleasant smell. When I passed Elisabeth's room the door was open. There was new wallpaper up and now I recognized the smell of wallpaper paste.

The Whitepainter was at the kitchen table, his tea mug in front of him. I asked if the wallpaer was his doing, and he replied he'd got hold of some rolls cheap.

"I think you should sleep in there again," he said. "Shit, sleeping on that damn living room couch will make a hunchback out of you."

I didn't know what to say.

He'd put up beige paper with little pink flowers. It bubbled a bit on top of the rough walls, but it was clean and pretty. That evening I carried my bedclothes in and put them on the bed. He'd found wallpaper not unlike what had been there when I was a child. That might not have been a coincidence. I imagined he'd seen the old paper when Elisabeth slept there.

I lay there at night, not thinking too much about the photos that had been on the walls. That were still under there. There was something comical about Michael's having to repaper this room over and over again.

One of the first mornings I was back in the bedroom, which still had the lingering almond-like scent of wallpaper paste, something happened to me that hadn't happened in years. I had thought it was all over, it had to be. But it wasn't.

The wind breathes in me, a warm wave rolls through myself and the treetop. It fills the white curtain so it billows, leaves it empty and trembling, fills it again. I can't see the trees. I don't know what trees are, or curtains, or body or house. Someone larger than myself and larger than this room is breathing and filling my lungs, too, with wind.

In this scruffy, shabby room in a house that stands surrounded by small industries in a little city that spreads like a blight on the landscape, I can still on very rare occasions re-experience moments when absolutely nothing is trivial, not even breathing.

In this house I have experienced things that can only be recalled by the movement of a curtain in front of the open window, a curtain that eventually went yellow and stiff with dirt. I took it down to wash it, but it was so old and delicate it crumbled to shreds. I put up a new white curtain. It, too, moves with the draft, billows and swells; I anchored it to the windowsill with a weight. I lie there waiting, but it won't come when I keep watch for it. It stays still. The cautious fish senses the presence of the mink in the shade of the rock. It waits and then takes a different route. When it does come it won't necessarily even be summer or windy.

I have experienced something that can only be called back to life by the wind in a thin piece of fabric, the creaking of a wooden stair, bits of wallpaper under the fingernail, the acrid odor of vomit and day-old urine. Some of it would probably be better forgotten. It might be good for me to forget it. But I don't want to.

One afternoon there was a knock at the door. It frightened me not knowing who was there, although the knock sounded familiar. It wasn't the Whitepainter. If he came up without his key he would pull at the door so the glass rattled, shaking the handle up and down impatiently until I opened. Ann-Sophie and Gabriel both knocked on the pane of glass. This was someone knocking persistently at the wooden frame around the window. It couldn't be Elisabeth, because she had a key. I sat still, curled up in my armchair until the knocking stopped. I heard footsteps disappearing down the stairs, and I knew I had experienced this before. But I couldn't remember when. Deep down inside me those footsteps resounded, those fists pounded. So I walked over to the kitchen window and hid behind the curtain, peeking down at the courtyard.

Naturally, it had been Jenny. I realized three weeks had passed, the length of the package holiday I had arranged for her and Elisabeth. I kept stock still behind the curtain because I didn't want her seeing me now. But I went out into the hall and put the telephone back on the hook, and then I went into the bathroom and turned on the hot water heater.

She phoned just an hour later, very upset she hadn't got hold of me more quickly. When she heard that Elisabeth hadn't come back, she started to cry. I didn't know what to say.

"I'm coming over," was all I could get out. "I'll be right there."

But I didn't actually get out until about seven that evening. By then I'd bathed and washed my hair. Still, the first words she said when she got a look at me were critical:

"What have you done to yourself?" she asked. "Are you ill?"

"I've lost a few kilos." I said. "It's not so dramatic. Haven't you ever heard of crash diets?"

She kept harping on about how unwell I looked. When a person was fasting they were supposed to drink vegetable juices to get their vitamins. Had I?

Jenny has an eminently Swedish conviction that you will be a happy, successful person if your body functions smoothly. That may be right, how should I know? No, actually, I do know that your body can't just function smoothly, it also has to be looked after with dental floss and vitamins, fiber and protein, it needs to be cared for like an expensive, imported dog at a first-rate kennel. It's like a religion. There's no way she'll ever abandon that belief. She said it was terrible to see me looking so run down.

"You used to go through times like this, in the old days. I thought you'd outgrown it." But I said the only kind of growing I had done was around the middle. She'd already started making me a meal.

Jenny lives in the middle of town in a big apartment building with shops on the ground floor. It was where the bottle store had been when I was a child. There was in an old wooden building here in those days. I recall it as dingy brown, but it may have decomposed and taken on the color of long ago. Anyway, the scouts' meeting room had been on the top floor.

I can't say that when I visited Jenny I felt as if I were going home. To me this city was now a world of old women. They lived like Jenny along the busiest streets, they were frightened of burglars and muggers, drunks and flashers. Their apartments were dark and overburdened with memories and the bric-a-brac of long lives.

Jenny felt deserted. Fredrik died of a heart attack a few years ago. Before that she had nursed him for a year and a half after his first infarct. I remember how slowly they would walk through town during the time before he died. I don't think I'd ever seen him out walking before. He had become very thin and gone pale and circumspect. I decided this wasn't really Fredrik but just a blue-gray shadow pretending to be him. His clothes hung baggily from his body.

Afterwards, she led a very dull life. There's no doubt about it, she felt deserted. But I believe she was trying to accept it. She made lampshades and played bridge. Sometimes she'd say she had been thinking about setting up her loom, but the more she thought about it the less point there seemed to be. She admitted how she felt:

"I'd only be doing it to pass the time."

She was isolated. She often said so to me on the phone. "Well, it's a lonely life," she'd say. "I just have to make the best of it. But the holidays are hardest."

Statistically speaking, I'm inclined to think she had a larger social circle than I did in Porto. But that wasn't the kind of isolation she meant, she was talking about the beginning of an even vaster solitude. This often made her speak bitterly to me. "You've got such a full life, you do," she'd say. "You've got so much ahead of you, too."

I didn't recognize that as a description of my life, but it was how she saw it.

She spoke of other elderly people in the bitterest, most hard-hearted way. An old friend of hers kept going from one doctor to another because of a sore on her leg that was infected and full of pus. The friend claimed she'd been a victim of malpractice.

"But she keeps scratching the wound open herself," Jenny told me.

"What would she do that for?"

"She wants punitive damages for pain and suffering."

"Isn't she rolling in money already?"

"Sure, but she needs to prove someone's been in the wrong. She'd do anything to have her case upheld."

I thought every story she told was sadder and even more tragic than the next.

"Ingrid Johansson's killing herself slowly but surely," she said. "She just sits chain smoking at the kitchen table."

Ingrid had pulmonary emphysema and the doctors had forbidden her to smoke. "But she just keeps on. She wants to kill herself," said Jenny. "You should hear how she heaves just coming up a flight of stairs."

She said of another of her old friends that people had started calling her loony. She had four dogs. I didn't exactly consider that convincing evidence, but Jenny pointed out that a dog license now cost a hundred and fifty kronor. And that wasn't all. This friend was also filthy, aggressive, and out of control. She might stand right in the middle of the street shouting at people. But she would only do that if she were provoked. Like when someone complained when she didn't clean up her dogs' messes.

"Are you supposed to?"

"Of course," said Jenny. "The town supplies dog owners with special little bags."

"And if you don't do as you're supposed to you're considered a nutcase…"

"You twist everything a person says," said Jenny.

I didn't really believe that business about the plastic bags, but I've seen them since. They've got a picture of a German shepherd squatting.

She said Ingrid Johansson was dying, but I thought she seemed pretty sprightly the last time we visited her. She did smoke, though.

Sometimes I think Jenny's impossible. Other times I just feel sorry for her.

"Arne Johansson's been sent home from the hospital now. But he's practically an invalid."

I didn't know he'd been unwell.

"And he hasn't. He got mugged. On Walpurgis Eve behind the department store. He was crossing the parking lot when he caught sight of a group of kids pushing one another around in shopping carts people had left out there. They were bashing them into parked cars."

"Were they drunk?"

"You bet your life. They were being ever so rowdy. But Arne's used to working with young people, he's been the bandy coach for years and years. Don't go thinking he hollered at them. All he did was tell them to stop. 'Cut that nonsense out right now,' he said. He knows how to talk to kids. But it didn't help. They kicked out his front teeth and broke several of his ribs. They might have killed him if a car hadn't come and scared them off. He was unconscious."

"Hush," I said. "What did you have to tell me that for?"

"Because it happened. We were devastated over it."

"I'm not surprised Ingrid smokes, after that."

"And Konrad's in the hospital now, too," said Jenny. "Her brother. He's over eighty. Best thing would be if he could just slip away."

It wasn't an uplifting conversation. The city of my childhood was transformed into a paved inferno when Jenny produced the scenario. I suppose the cruelty's always been there. I recognize it in spite of her saying it's new. But I imagine she wants it to be. Lukewarm, ludicrous, and even laughable behavior pop out in her stories as often as cruelty. I let them wash over me. I could stop listening, interrupt her, change the subject. But I rarely do. I let the city wash over me. As it washed through my insides when I was growing up, rounding the sharp edges. Wearing and shaping. These are familiar waves.

Jenny told me about Ingrid Johansson's elderly brother Konrad, that he had made off from the old people's home, quite simply run away. She thought he was senile, and not accountable for his behavior.

"Anyway, somebody found him at the station. He was so bad by then they had to call the ambulance to take him to the hospital. They say Ingrid's constantly at his bedside. That doesn't seem fair to Arne, if you ask me. He's been very poorly himself. But that's how she is about Konrad. It's always been Konrad this and Konrad that. He's just about had it now, though."

I remembered Konrad Eriksson. They called him The Commie. There was one more in town, well, maybe there were others, too, but the only ones everybody knew about were The Commie and the Damn Bolshie, an old foundry man. I was scared of them when I was a child.

Jenny still thinks of Konrad as Evil Personified, as she saw him when he first crossed the courtyard of 13 Chapel Road. I like Jenny when she sticks to her old antipathies. Most of the time I think she's unfaithful to the past.

The morning Hasse phoned and asked me to come back was the Monday or Tuesday after the first Sunday of Advent.

"Come by Christmas," he said. "I don't want to spend Christmas alone."

The previous evening I had sat watching a television drama about the people in a small town in Sweden where the main industry folded. It followed the lives of four different families in which the men had lost their jobs. One took to the bottle. One had to sell his house, after which he developed an ulcer and had a nervous breakdown. The third drove his wife to the verge of insanity with his silence and his depressions. She was committed to a mental hospital and the children were taken into care. In the fourth family, the man was young and was retrained and got a job in another town. He and his wife were able to buy a house.

The morning Hasse called, the rain was beating at the windows. It was dark when I woke up. I went to the downstairs hall to pick up my newspaper, in which I read an article about a middle-aged housewife who was sickly and married to a sadist. She wasn't employed, and couldn't have got a job if she'd wanted one. Their children were grown up. All she had to work on was her own suicide. That's what she said, apparently: "It's the project I'm always working on."

She claimed that the depth of her problem (she said that, the depth, or at least that was how the journalist put it) had to do with the demand today that everything be so efficient, rational and profitable. If you were unable to perform perfectly, society imposed the feeling on you that you had no right to ask for anything. Often it began with physical weakness. You fell ill, or all the pressure sent you to rack and ruin with drink or some other kind of escape.

I read that article slowly and carefully, and then cut it out. After that, I turned on the radio and heard that one of the big industries in Västmanland was threatened with closure. I switched to a different station, and heard a deep male voice saying:

WE MUST NEVER FORGET THAT WE WILL DIE

Then I made tea and waited for a while. When I turned the radio back on, there was organ music. And at that very moment Hasse called from Porto and asked how I was doing.

"Well, I'm not exactly living it up," I replied.

"So what are you doing, then?"

I said I'd just been reading in the paper about a housewife whose husband was a sadist.

He found it odd that I'd already been out to buy the paper at that hour.

"I haven't. I have it delivered."

He didn't say anything for a while. Then he said he wanted me to come home. I didn't know how to answer. I was ashamed. But I had actually only subscribed to the paper for a month. Should I have told him?

"I've got to stay here. At some point Elisabeth is sure to come back."

There was total silence at his end. I started thinking we must have been cut off. But then I heard his voice, soft and gentle as if stripped of its layers of years and experience, his young voice:

"Come back now, Ann-Marie. I don't want to spend Christmas alone."

I said I'd have to think about it.

Later that day I went over to Jenny's and she told me I ought to move over to her place.

"You mustn't sit over there in that old house any longer. Surrounded by those weirdos."

She must have said the same thing to Elisabeth, lots of times.

"I'm not staying much longer," I said. "Hasse wants me to come home for Christmas."

"I see," said Jenny.

I knew exactly what that meant. Oh. So I'll be all by myself then. I just have to make the best of it, then. Holidays are hardest. Everyone has their own life. That's it. Nothing to be done.

"Yes, well of course you must go" she said then. "Elisabeth's probably not going to come back anyway."

"How can you say that?"

She turned her back to me, fussing with her idiotic coffee maker. It's electric and drips and hisses hot water over a filter with coffee grinds.

"You might as well give up on her," she said.

Sometimes she says things like that. Once she said about Henning: "Well, he's a lost cause now."

Lost.

There's no use disagreeing with her, or trying to hold her accountable, or arguing. It rises up out of her own intense bitterness about life; it is irrefutable.

Elisabeth was living with the Otters in 1973 when I came home to look after Henning. She couldn't very well have stayed at 13 Chapel Road, with the state he was in. That fall she had started school in Sweden. She'd been at the French school in Porto before, and none of us realized how difficult it would be for her. All I could think about that autumn was Henning, No other human being was really real to me. And Elisabeth so seldom spoke .

She didn't fit in at Swedish intermediate school. She didn't even own a quilted jacket, or a pair of jeans. It took some time for us to realize how important those things were, and to buy them for her. Jenny thought it was very odd that she went to her first school dance in those blue trousers, and to tell the truth so did I. I didn't even know they called it a disco. She didn't even get herself home from that dance. A teacher phoned Jenny to say someone would have to come and collect her. It was unfortunate Jenny's number was the one they had.

She went off in a taxi late that night to pick Elisabeth up; they'd found her in one of bathrooms. She'd drunk herself into a stupor. Jenny should probably have taken her to the hospital, but she didn't. She tucked her into bed and sat by her until her pale little face began to get some color again and she started throwing up. Jenny changed her sheets and held out a basin. She didn't call me until morning. I could hardly believe what she was saying. It didn't sound like Elisabeth she was describing. I thought I'd never be able to tell Hasse about it, but eventually I did.

Afterwards the whole thing became more comprehensible. Elisabeth had always been a quiet, introverted child, but she explained that she had felt friendless at the party. She was shy and no one had paid any attention to her. Everyone had just been talking and laughing and dancing. Then some girls had offered her a drink. They had probably meant to make a fool of her, but she didn't see that. All she could remember was feeling violently sick and going to the bathroom.

She was so sweet then. Thirteen years old. On the last day of term at the French school in Porto she had worn a white dress with a full skirt. Hasse had had it made by one of the senhoritas, and embroidered with flowers by an old, very good seamstress in Porto. He'd taken her to the photographer. Hasse didn't like her going off to Sweden without us, and if there had been a job for him he would have moved back. We had realized she needed to finish her education in Sweden. We had so much good sense.

She looked so pretty in those photos. Fragile, of course, but she was starting to fill out. She had developed some completely new features, a kind of transparency. When I looked at her I thought becoming a woman was such a beautiful thing. Or rather, when I looked at the pictures Hasse had taken.

Jenny told me she didn't fit in at school and was unhappy. But what was I supposed to do? School was school. I couldn't explain to her why girls were so catty. I realized she was going to have to change, and wondered what Hasse would think. She got platform shoes and went around in a very strange leather jacket with a silver and blue eagle on the back. It was sizes and sizes too big. She said one of the guys had lent it to her. I saw it as providing her some kind of protection. She had a boyfriend. You seemed to have to have one in this world. She had a swastika around her neck, too. I think it, too, was a kind of talisman of redemption. She said her boyfriend had given it to her. She couldn't take it off, it was like an engagement ring.

"But a swastika?" I asked. "Nazism. Hitler. You aren't for all that, are you?"

"Aw," she said. "This has nothing to do with that stuff. It's a thing of its own."

Her black hair was long and parted in the middle and hadn't been trimmed or cut all autumn. She was extremely pale, and starting to look stooped from just sitting around. Intermediate school girls almost all skipped P.E.

At Christmas she brought home bad marks, consistently "poor" and "fail". Perhaps that wasn't so strange considering she'd changed school and language. I think that was what I thought. If I thought anything at all. Or was that what Jenny said? In those days she wasn't as deeply pessimistic as she is today. Yet it was only four years ago. And now she could stand there fussing with her coffee maker and telling me I might as well give up on Elisabeth.

"How in the world can you say such a thing?" I asked. But of course I didn't get an answer.

I have always found it difficult to walk out of Jenny's and slam the door behind me. Even on those occasions when I should have done so. What seems to happen is that I sit there saying nothing and she says nothing too, fiddling with her coffee or her sewing or whatever she has at hand. After a while we talk normally again.

Walking back to Chapel Road I realized how tired I was of just waiting for Elisabeth and how tired I was of doing nothing and of not having anyone to talk to. I started packing my bags as soon as I got upstairs, and planned to call and make a flight reservation. I would do as Hasse had said.

He was right. I had to go back if I was going to be able to cope with all this in the long run. I wouldn't have the energy for Elisabeth if she came back now, wouldn't be able to handle seeing her helpless pleading defiance — since I couldn't control my own bitterness and didn't even dare to talk back to Jenny. Not to mention if she'd caught a cold while she was gone. Nothing made her look so little and pathetic. I wouldn't be able to deal with it — Jenny was the one who coped. She would tell her off in no uncertain terms and make her hot milk and preach at her and sort things out and have forgotten all about having advised me to give up on Elisabeth.

I'm too tired to be a mother, I thought. The griddle has finally gone cold. At last I've been delivered. Though the contractions certainly had to be induced.

I'm too tired and suspicious. You'll have to get yourself a teddy bear pillow or a dog, Elisabeth. Or a fiancé. A religion. Or join up with Gabriel's environmental activists.

But I hadn't been delivered. My bag was packed and was out in the hall. It ended up staying there. Dusk fell, and blue darkness. In the end Hasse called again and I told him I wouldn't be able to make it home for Christmas. I was sure that was when Elisabeth would come back.

This city in the December chill and raw fogs, lusterless mornings, silent and gray. No rosy sky. No song. But toasters, tea makers, Christmas lights, instant coffee, toilet paper, marshmallows coated in shredded coconut, headcheese, lutefisk sauce, Carmen Curlers, toothbrushes, sheepskin rugs and plastic carrier bags. Carrier bags, carrier bags, and more carrier bags. Jenny demanded that I come to stay with her for Christmas.

"If you don't, I'm going to turn out the lights and sit here in the dark."

"Why would you do something like that?"

"So no one will see I'm all alone."

I said I'd come on Christmas Eve, and I did.

We went through all the rituals. Jenny had made enough food to feed an army for the two of us. I sat down to write little couplets to go with my presents. "I rhyme all the time. Jenny slaves and behaves," I wrote on one card. That was the best I could produce. But at least I tried.

We spent two hours giving one another presents and opening them. I don't know how we managed to drag it out, but we did. I got bath salts, talcum powder, a red blouse and a cookbook, and lots of other things. We put Elisabeth's presents away in the walk-in wardrobe. When Hasse called on Christmas morning it wasn't precisely either calm or bright. He told me he'd been to midnight mass, but for us the little Lord Jesus was already out with the bathwater. I couldn't possibly tell him what we'd been doing.

A week before Christmas the first snow had fallen, at least. We began to be able to imagine a white Christmas. The air was full of whirling and swirling, people's collars were snow-covered and their knitted caps grew tall and white. When you walked around town your face would get wet, and snowflakes would fall onto your neck and melt. The tree branches were loaded with precarious little drifts and the light glimmered through their fragile white latticework. I couldn't work out what the city was reminding me of, but there was something. Maybe a small town in an

73

American movie from the forties, where the snow falls gracefully to music and ringing bells. Or was it my own childhood that was sculpting itself in snow and soft, muffled sounds before my eyes? The most amazing thing happened, too — I rediscovered the glassed-in flower stand. A nursery owner from Vallmsta had set it up at the market, complete with glass cases, lighting, and hyacinths. I bought three from him. I gave the pink one to Jenny and set the blue one on the kitchen table at Chapel Road. It reminded me of Tora Otter, who always had a blue hyacinth on the table at Christmas time. The white one, which hadn't opened yet and was covered in pale green buds, I set on Sigrid's chest of drawers, next to the photo of Henning.

On Christmas afternoon when everything had gone dirty brown again and the snow had melted in the gutters, Jenny asked me if I would be offended if she took the pink hyacinth up to the terminal care ward at the hospital. That friend of hers who had been wheelchair bound for so long had been admitted there now. We were going to visit her. I said I didn't want to come. I was afraid she would ask how Elisabeth was. Jenny said she'd deal with that.

"Don't you worry about a thing," she said, plucky yet bitter.

Jenny's friend looked different lying down, a little head atop a huge, swollen body. Although she wasn't ill she was now bedridden and appeared to be nothing but a receptacle for medicines and meals. All she could talk about was her body and what it was taking in. From out in the corridor I heard voices singing Silent Night, and after a while a sermon being preached. I thought: now she's going to change the subject from medications and meals any minute, she's going to ask about Elisabeth. And I beat a hasty retreat.

I walked in the direction of the sermonizing voice down a wide corridor with polished, vinyl linoleum and heavy doors. A nurses' aide was walking ahead of me, her eighteen-year-old bottom swaying under her white polyester uniform. She was wearing white knee socks and clogs. This struck me as a fantastic outfit to see at a hospital, where the hymn singing reminded me of sisters at the clinic where Elisabeth was born.

I reached the common room, with glass partitions separating it from the corridor. There were Christmas decorations taped to the glass: cut-out snowflakes, woolly birds and glazed ginger biscuits dangling from ribbons. A little choir was singing around a harmonium played by a tall man dressed in black. Possibly the same man who had held the sermon a few minutes earlier.

The day room was crowded with people. I went in through a door on the side of the room and sat down. There were healthy middle-aged people dressed in their best, sitting next to wheelchairs with old people who looked very pale. The room was hot and stuffy.

That was when I caught sight of the old man who had been taken ill at the railway station. I saw him through the glass and I suppose I would have recognized him anyway. But Ingrid Johansson was sitting next to him now. It was him, all right. Konrad Eriksson. At the station I hadn't had a clue who he was.

Their hands were intertwined. His bony fingers with tough yellow nails and with spots and thick, sparse hairs on the backs rested in her smaller hands and her fingers, not as pale but thin and ageing, were sticking up from between his. It didn't look as if they were planning to let go for a long time. Was she asleep? I couldn't see her face because she was bending down towards him, her head resting on his sunken chest.

I thought I'd go out into the corridor and say hello to them. But I didn't. They were sitting so still. His mouth was close to her hair, and his head kept wobbling. They were so peaceful and self-contained on the other side of the glass, I didn't want to disturb them.

She didn't come back. And nobody asked about her, either. It had been ages since the telephone had rung and a voice had said: "Elisabeth?"

Not even Hasse asked about her. I still knew he was phoning to find out whether she had come back. But he didn't ask. Maybe it was the same for him as for Jenny. They avoided asking to spare me the pain of having to answer no, I haven't heard anything.

I know there are rituals associated with mourning a death, there are ways of behaving. But for mourning a disappearance, there is nothing. That makes it difficult. Blank. Maybe there was nothing odd about their pretending everything was all right. They can't have known what to say or do. I didn't know myself.

One day I found a photo in Elisabeth's desk drawer. I hadn't expected it, I had been through all the things she'd left behind so many times that my hands and eyes knew those closely-written pages, hair clips, belts and underwear by heart. But the little color photo had been stuck between the lining paper and the bottom of the drawer. My nails hit one of the white corners, and I pulled out a very recent picture of Elisabeth. How thin she was, almost transparent, and she was laughing slightly, as if embarrassed, when the picture was taken.

I didn't like that photo. There was nothing wrong with Elisabeth's thin smile, but the background was dull and drab. It was as if she had been nowhere and asked someone to take this snapshot that arrived here in my hands out of nowhere. I cut away the gray background, leaving her face in profile. Then I stuck it into a vase of dried grass she had put on the windowsill herself. I arranged the thin strands of grass and their shadows over her face until it looked perfectly natural. Then I took a shot of it with Henning's excellent old camera, the one with a full set of interchangeable lenses. A narrow, mocking face was what I saw through the viewfinder, a young woman in a Savannah, in a forest of high grass, a kingdom of reeds. Her face was both in sunshine and in shadow, in this forest that had never been but that now was. It took me a long time, but finally I had a natural, convincing scene in the viewfinder. It was a difficult task. I had to color the cut edges of the profile so they wouldn't show up white when I zoomed in with the telephoto lens. The shadows had to fall just right, so it wouldn't look like I had simply photographed a flat picture. I was very happy to have achieved that picture of a moment that had never been but that I had still managed to capture.

I took the whole roll over to Prontoprint and explained that there was only one exposed shot on the roll, and that I needed it developed fast. They promised me a special arrangement, so I would be able to pick my picture up the very next day. But when I got there they told me they hadn't been able to print it. The negative had just been black. There must be something wrong with the camera.

Well, I didn't know where she was, what she was getting to eat, or what she could see around her. I didn't know where she was sleeping at night or whether she actually had anywhere at all to stay. Nothing. A black hole. No notion at all but those damn images of dead drug addicts on bathroom floors. I told myself it couldn't be that awful. No one had said she was so far gone. Jut a little hash. Marijuana, actually. There's nothing dangerous about marijuana, mamma! It's nowhere near as strong as hash!

I guess she's flipped out, I thought. Was that the expression? Wasted. Shoplifts from department stores. Isn't that what they do around here? Smokes hash. Goes drinking. Nothing worse than I did in Uppsala. Once I threw up in the bathroom at the student union. Philip held a hand on my brow and Veronica stood next to me smoking. She was swaying slightly. I remembered Veronica swaying twenty-five years ago but I couldn't imagine Elisabeth now.

There had been things to do, but they were done long ago. I had convinced the police to put her down as a missing person. I had phoned every single classmate she had had before she dropped out of secondary school and asked if they had any idea where she might have gone. I had spoken with thirty-one reluctant voices. Four of them had moved and were difficult to locate. I got satisfaction out of its being difficult and time-consuming. None of them had a clue. None of them had seen Elisabeth since November.

Now there was nothing left for me to do but to try to imagine, create pictures in my mind, put words to the blankness that was called up when I shut my eyes and said her name.

Elisabeth. Elisabeth.

Elisabeth Maria de Lourdes.

Maybe she's in bed now. Sleeps all day. Gets high and sleeps the days away so she won't have to live.

I'd like to reach her and tell her: it's all a mistake. It's like in a play with costumes. Really you're my sweet little girl. I love you.

I scribbled on pads and thought the answer would suddenly spring out of the words like a pattern. But nothing happened. This sticky mess of worry, disappointment, anxiety. The chill, pure horror — is that love, too?

Her rooms smelled different from ours. I mustn't forget that. She had been through things we knew nothing about, couldn't even imagine. Who was the man with all the bullets in him, under the wallpaper? What did they mean to her, all those bloodied, mutilated figures?

I wished Hasse would come and see what was under the wallpaper in her room. During the days, I lay on the sofa in the dining room listening for footsteps on the stairs. Not just for Elisabeth's light ones, but for Hasse's as well. I wanted him to come and share this torment. But I couldn't ask him to come. That wouldn't have been fair. He couldn't take vacation days or ask for a leave of absence right when they were making the spring collection. I tried to write and tell him how I was feeling, but no letters materialized. All I could produce were tirades on the pages of my spiral notebooks, and I was too ashamed to send them. No answers sprang out of the words, yet I couldn't stop writing.

Thinking about her was like breathing. I was the mother of an infant; I was stuck like a clock that had stopped, out of order. And I knew it. But she could really be in as much peril as the time we were driving back from Portugal via Paris and she couldn't keep anything down, not even liquids.

I remembered that in the old days when I worked at the paper, we published photos of runaway girls. There were whole articles about them. The last traces of them before they vanished not to be seen again were followed and investigated. One had ironed a blouse with her hair in rollers, said good-bye to her mother and left. One of them was called Viola, I sill remembered her. But nowadays the papers seldom published pictures of missing girls. There would have to be something very special about the case, the police had told me.

I suppose there was nothing special about Elisabeth. I'd given them her photo and they had assured me that her name had now been posted all over the country.

But what did that mean? Was anyone really looking for her?

I had made Jenny call every single person who'd been on that charter flight to Sicily. I made her ask them if they'd noticed Elisabeth disappearing from the airport or if they'd heard her say anything about not planning to come along. The travel agency was reluctant to give Jenny the phone numbers of the people on the flight. She found the whole thing upsetting, and it got us nowhere. But it did keep us busy for a while.

I hoped she would eventually phone. She might not call me or Jenny, because she was probably ashamed of herself, but she might phone someone else. A school friend or Gabriel. Or the Whitepainter — he'd been good to her, after all. Why didn't she phone him? If she would only let us know she was alive, everything would be different. But she didn't. It was as if she were getting back at us. But what for?

Maybe she wasn't phoning because she was completely spaced out.

The weeks passed. Sometimes I was afraid, truly and deeply frightened. It was as if a wound had opened up. Suddenly I realized I was bleeding. But mostly it was just a kind of dull presence. I inhaled it. I didn't even know what to call it any more. Grief? Or worry. There was despair and horror. There was anger with her, a helpless, slightly fading anger.

But mostly it was the sense of estrangement, of our slipping apart and of things happening I knew nothing about and never would.

All the bad things, all the difficult things we'd been through together I could recall, but nothing else. Sometimes I had a feeling I was also remembering things that hadn't happened. I saw her face, slack and drugged, saw her glaring scornfully at me. I slapped that face. But that couldn't be true, could it? I had to take out her school-leaving picture and put on my glasses and look long and hard at it, see the white dress Hasse had had made, the embroidered pink flowers and her black hair brushed tightly back, held in place with a white plastic slide, fanning out across her shoulders, black with a red tone. Not black like Conceição's, but with red highlights. Where had those come from?

I didn't know. I knew nothing. Her face was so young in that photo that it was almost not yet a face. It was nothing but smooth skin and dark irises and lips so pale they might soon be eradicated.

Where was she? If only I could have seen her, truly seen. I thought about those people who can, clairvoyants. There was one in Porto, a woman. Maybe I should get Hasse to consult her. But surely this was too far away? Could she possibly see things across a whole continent? God only knew.

I would at least have liked to have someone lay out a star for me, preferably someone old and wise, a fortune-teller who was level-headed and who had experience in addition to the gift. She'd spread her cards for me, shift them around slowly and say:

"You needn't worry. The person you are waiting for will return. It will take some time. But she'll be back."

I stood at the window in the study and watched the people go in and out through the door of the editorial department. They seemed very young, the people who worked at the newspaper nowadays. Did they have any idea they were working in a chapel? Once upon a time that building was built as a meeting-house. There was a Jesus painted on the inside eastern wall. He was depicted as a strong man with curly brown hair. His arms were wide open and he was stepping towards the people he hoped to redeem. He had a blue mantle and pink feet. I suppose that fresco is still there under various layers of paint. Perhaps one day it will be restored, and attract some arty or religious cult.

I wanted to go inside but at the same time I didn't dare. Early one morning I finally crossed the courtyard. I went in through the back entrance, where the composing room had once been. There were people sitting there, typewriters and flickering television screens. They noticed me. I hadn't expected that. In the old days people came and went here all the time. The wooden floor had been pitted with comings and goings. Now there was linoleum everywhere. The floor was flat, footsteps obliterated.

A boy in jeans and clogs came up to me and asked what I wanted. His style and dress were childlike but he had the face of a thirty-five-year old.

"Could I please see the archives for the last month?" I asked, sounding like something straight out of the days of the meeting-hall. Actually I didn't want anything in particular. I just wanted to go inside. Have a look. But I had to say something; you couldn't just come in there for the fun of it. The clog lad looked doubtful. At that very moment Bertil Sundh came out of what had been the copy editing room in my day.

He opened his arms wide, and exclaimed:

"Ann-Marie!"

Then he hugged me with everyone watching. We were never so demonstrative with one another when I worked for *The Correspondent*. We hadn't even got to the stage of using the familiar form of address. But he couldn't possibly behave as if that had been the case now. In those days he had only been a news editor. Today he's editor-in-chief. He's balding and has a paunch and wears very tight trousers. I felt awful when I saw him. He asked, I suppose he was joking, if I was coming back to work there, and that was a pretty foolish thing to say after all that time. But I answered that I just wanted to catch up a little. Would he mind if I had a look through the files?

"Anything for you!" said Bertil, and in a way this new cordiality of his was perfectly in line with his tight-fit shirt and the green trousers with their flared legs. He was wearing neither jacket nor tie and his shirt was patterned with little green squiggles I couldn't identify without my glasses. Probably butterflies, though. His hair was combed forward and then off to the side, probably to conceal a hairline that was migrating upwards. Wise of him. It was eminently clear in here that age was no merit. To me he looked as if he was dressing up as someone else, because I couldn't eradicate the memory of his neat side part and his charcoal gray suit.

He ushered me into his office. The office of the editor-in-chief was unchanged, so unchanged I found it oppressive. It was obscene for Bertil Sundh to be sitting at Ada's desk, with her globe next to him. Ada used to give it a light pat to set it spinning. She had smoked cigars in this tiny little room and her globe had spun more and more slowly and finally stopped. It was a wonderful old globe. Ada had had a whole house full of lovely old things.

Bertil Sundh's gesture was different. He sat in his chair with one hand on that globe. Who did he think he was? Napoleon?

"What are you up to nowadays, anyway? Moved back home?"

When I come here and have to answer questions like that I feel as if I don't belong anywhere. I'm neither fish, flesh nor fowl, want to be all of them and not have to make up my mind. But that's not realistic. People like to pin one another down. They want to stuff you, skin you and nail your hide to the wall. They want to know and be certain about whom they're dealing with. Every time I see Synnöve the question comes up. I'm not saying she fixes her eyes on me and asks it straight out, not like the time we were sitting under the picture of the city at Anker's café and she said: but you must have some idea of what you want out of life!

We were so young then, and Synnöve so direct. She's become more tactful with the passing years. Or perhaps more subtle. But she's still the same old Synnöve who considers it her right to ask. Like Bertil Sundh with his professional efficiency. And the Whitepainter and Gabriel. And Jenny. I'm sure they asked

Elisabeth, too. Like Jenny asked me. And herself.

Yes, Jenny must have asked herself lots of times: what am I doing here? What's my excuse for living, actually? Barren, I wander through all this simmering activity and rub surfaces that need polishing, rub halfheartedly. They could actually be rubbed better.

I had just begun asking myself the same thing when I captured Elisabeth. Seized her.

When I was down in the basement at *The Correspondent*, where they archive the back issues, I had a stupid idea, about something I should never have done. I was sitting reading on a packing case outside the fireproof door to the archives. The basement smell that surrounded me was unchanged. I heard the gurgling of the toilets one flight up, the water running and swishing in the pipes that ran down through the ceiling above me.

At one point I thought I might try to find some of my old 'Sunbeams' in the back files, or even those 'Father and Daughter' columns I wrote when I moved home from Uppsala. But I couldn't be bothered.

As always, *The Correspondent* was full of recycled information. People who had attended a meeting wanted to read that the meeting had really taken place and that they had been there. Preferably there would be a picture of them as proof. But nowadays they were different meetings and different people. A people of strangers. On page three were the cantankerous letters to the editor. I recalled Konrad Eriksson's long harangues about his philosophy of life and world politics, and wondered whether anyone missed them. Nowadays letters to the editor seemed limited to the nuisances of dogs' messes and motorbikes.

When I got home I wrote a letter to the editor. I made myself out to be a man. When I had finished I found Henning's old Remington and typed a clean copy. The carriage return was stiff and the ribbon frayed, but the letters came out: large, beautiful and pale. That evening I crossed the courtyard in the dark and put my manuscript through the letter slot on the door of the editorial offices. Two days later they published it. I had started buying the paper just to check the letters to the editor. The rapidity with which it happened shocked me and frightened me slightly.

I'm sitting waiting for a missing child a to return, it began. I don't know where he is or what he's doing. I can't even imagine. When I open the newspapers I see pictures of dead drug addicts. A couple of weeks ago there was one of a boy who died with his head down the toilet bowl. That picture haunts me. I've got nothing else to put in its place.

Two weeks ago I had to take compassionate leave from my job because I couldn't manage both working and looking for my child. But since then I've hardly gone out at all. When I need something I get it at night when there aren't so many people around, from the kiosk or the convenience store. Before I go in I peer through the window to see whether there's anybody I know inside. I'm afraid someone will ask me where my child is. I don't know what I'd say if they did.

I'm constantly expecting the phone to ring. When it does I'm scared, and don't dare to answer it until after two, three or four rings. By which time the person on the other end has often hung up.

I am most aware of waiting at night. I listen for footsteps on the stairs, and lie tense, waiting for the phone to ring. I have stopped sleeping regular hours or for long stretches. All day I brood over what I did wrong. I remember all the hard, bad things between us over the last few years. I remember slapping him once when he came home drunk from a school dance, I remember when he took money out of my wife's purse and denied it, when he lied to me about where he had been one night we sat up waiting. I cannot remember anything happy or good, although I tell myself there must have been such things too.

Sometimes I realize I shouldn't be shutting myself inside. I should go out into town and ask whether people have seen him and ask other parents whose children are also missing what they are doing to get them back, I would like to know the reasons and what we did wrong. Can we do anything to make our children come home and to give them a better life?

Pappa Ben

It was a silly name. It just came to me. But I didn't think anyone would see Pappa Ben as a silly man.

Two days later, someone answered. A woman wrote in and gave her real name, which made me feel ashamed. She wrote to say that the parents at Rosenholm School had started an anti-drug abuse parents' group and that Pappa Ben was welcome to join. She even put in her phone number.

I never called. I never went to a meeting, either.

A couple of days later Jenny mentioned that Håkan Hernström's father had written a letter to the editor they'd printed in the paper. Håkan had been a classmate of Elisabeth's. She showed me the letter she'd cut out. It was mine. I asked her why she thought it came from Håkan's father.

"That's what everybody's saying," Jenny replied. "He called his son Little Joe

83

when he was a kid. Like in Bonanza."

I'd invented Pappa Ben. I'd made him up. But nothing comes of nothing. They call that creating, and mankind is not a creator, as Gabriel's always pointing out. Pappa Ben was made of scraps and bits of truth, of things that whirl in the air, gossip and talk and half-forgotten memories that eventually sink to the bottom and become the clay we work into figures. I knew the Hernströms had a son who'd been in trouble. I hadn't thought about it until now, though.

Nearly everything in Pappa Ben's letter eventually came true. That was his revenge on me, his maker. I no longer wanted to go out. I went to the convenience store late at night. But I was never able to go and meet the other parents. Maybe he wasn't either.

The snow fell so softly. In Porto I often sat at the window listening to the rain pattering on grass and leaves. But you can't hear falling snow. I felt lonely when school started and the factories opened up again after the long holidays. Now the houses were cleaned, the aquavit bottles emptied, the boredom and despondency put to flight. Now the men were back at Swedish Engineering, at half past six in the mornings there was congestion in front of the gates on Chapel Road. I was envious when I saw them chatting with one another as they disappeared inside. The doors to the editorial offices banged all day long. But what I was feeling was not only loneliness and envy; I was also secretly pleased not to have to go, not to have to face the monotony. All those pallid people in the newsroom. The hissing of the coffee machine. The tobacco smoke. People treading the floor in clogs and moon boots and high, Lapp-style shoes. I often thought how damn fortunate I had been not to have to live with all that.

Bertil Sundh actually called a couple of times when he needed people. But I said no. I told him I was clearing out the house, preparing it for demolition. "So not just now. Maybe later this spring."

Now it was only January and the snow fell heavy and gray. But in this cold, silent winter I still had a strong sense of life. I often stood at the kitchen window looking down at the courtyard, so often that the time I didn't spend there vanishes afterwards, fades so I think I spent the whole winter standing there and that time was unified, as it actually is. I thought it flowed faster and faster like river water rushing when the snow is melting, and I heard it swooshing like the rapids. Though I suppose all I was really hearing was our voices, our quarrels and our small talk, our agitated disputes and the inarticulate endless phrases that are hardly communication, more like sympathetic noises. I could distinguish both friendly repartee and coughing and shouting and nagging — persistent, childlike nagging. I told Michael about it but that was foolish of me because he didn't take it seriously, or perhaps he took it too seriously, how would I know?

"If you're hearing voices you fucking ought to have your head examined," he said.

Jenny harped on at me. She didn't like me going on living in the house. I should move in with her. It wasn't good for me to be alone, it never had been, she said.

It is no one's business how I live. I was tired of all the surveillance and of all the busybodies' interference.

"Let me be. I need some time. A week. A month."

I explained that it was no small task to organize all the junk that had collected here over the years. I had to call the Salvation Army and the auctioneers, try to decide what I wanted to keep, have a dumpster brought round, and pack.

"But you've got nothing done yet," said Jenny.

She offered to help me. But of course I didn't want her here. Nor did I want her rummaging through Henning's papers or putting her hands on Lisa's old, flimsy dresses. I didn't mind how long it took. Lots of people have lived here. My maternal grandfather built this house. It isn't something you can arrange overnight.

"You're burying yourself in all that," said Jenny.

But that wasn't what I was doing. I didn't want to tell her what it was. I was trying to imagine. That was what was occupying me.

I worked hard at it. I no longer had time for anything else. I tried, for example, to imagine that something more mundane, something less dramatic was happening to Elisabeth than those things the newspapers described. But the panic didn't recede; it lay in wait like nausea at the back of my throat, and in a way it was a relief the times it filled my mouth with sourish regurgitation, and I could vomit. The telephone ringing and ambulance sirens frightened me. My genitals and stomach began to throb when I heard them. After a phone call I always felt sick, even if it was only Jenny. If an ambulance passed down Chapel Road on the way up to the hospital I didn't dare stay inside near the telephone. But I didn't dare take it off the hook, either, so I would rush down to the Whitepainter's if he was in and sit listening to the records he was playing. In a way it was a calming thing, hearing the same music over and over. If he wasn't there I'd drop in on Ann-Sophie. She would give me a manicure and nag at me to take care of my nails the way she'd told me to. She could always chatter on and that was sort of reassuring, too. I didn't really have to listen hard because I knew what she was going to say anyway.

I did a lot of walking those days. I drifted up and down the streets all the way to the edge of town and along the gray-black roads until I got so tired of the monotony of them that I had to start walking in the woods. I often penetrated pathless terrain, exhausting myself by striding among logs and trees uprooted by the wind. One day I came to a little lake with reedy banks at the edge of the woods. I could see a blinking light under the blue-black water. The ice had broken and thin sheets of it were afloat. Near the shore there was a semicircle of ice that had sunk to just beneath the surface.

The amber light under the water was blinking and blinking. It was out in the middle of the lake. Thin, black branches blocked my view, and behind me was the dark fir forest. The clouds darted past, quick and soot-gray in the sky. The only thing that had any color was that inexplicable light. Then I noticed a second blinking light, and saw that it was a railway crossing on the other side of the lake. It was the warning light flashing yellow in the cold air being reflected in the middle of the lake. Strangely enough, I was pleased there was such a trivial explanation. I found myself standing there laughing. When the light had been blinking down in the depths I was frightened and tense and felt an odd, ominous sense of foreboding.

I couldn't forget the light under the surface despite the fact that I now knew it had a natural explanation. As long as I believed that the source of the light was really out in the water, under the broken ice floating on the dark surface, I had found it both lovely and frightening. The light had given the grayness of the winter day some depth; I do not believe I have ever seen such a soot-gray, whitening, chilling sky as just then. I had the water in front of me and around me in different manifestations — as razor-sharp sheets of ice, heavy crescents drowned in black water, snow, freezing mist, haze and droplets. But it was difficult to recall that there really was matter, such as stone, wood and iron. The landscape was a tinted picture. Yes, it was easy to believe that it really was a tinted picture and not that it just resembled one. If that light hadn't been blinking and eventually led my thoughts to glass, railway tracks, sleepers, arsenic impregnation, gravel, tar, steel wires, I would have been standing in front of a work of art I could have entered.

No.

The light under the water made the picture both possible and impossible. I felt relieved when I was able to leave it.

If I was going to start anywhere, it would be with Henning's papers. They were all over the apartment, mainly in what had once been Abel and Sigrid's bedroom, but also in the dining room and in his own room. They were piled up on top of bookcases and stuffed into drawers and closets. Naturally, the easiest thing would have been to toss them straight into a dumpster.

I leafed through these heaps of papers time and again, wondering whether they could possibly be of any value to any human being alive today. Still, it was horrible to think of his notes and drawings scattered over a rubbish dump, blowing around in the sickening smoke and then reappearing somewhere, half-burned and soot-edged, where someone might read them. They were all written in Henning's fine, even script with the long, pointed upstrokes and the frills that crossed the f's. and t's. I thought I'd burn it all up in the tile stoves, but couldn't get a single one of them to work properly, without smoking in. They hadn't been swept in decades, and the flues were probably clogged with soot and dead birds.

There was no one I could consult, either. Who could possibly say anything about the value of Henning's papers or tell me whether it was a desecration to incinerate them?

The snow fell thick and even outside the window. There were cold days when the surface froze to a hard crust, and thaw days that packed the snow heavy and wet in layer after layer the sun would later bore through. They weren't far off now, the days with the simple two-tone flute song of the blue tits and the dripping from the drainpipes with their rust holes. The water from the melting snow would run along the cobblestones in front of the door, old birds' nests tumble out of the drainpipes, and dog messes float back up together with pine branches and litter. Over by the corner of the house, I could see now how gray and peeling the paint was, knowing that the light of a March afternoon would expose it as in even greater need of repair. When I sat curled up there with Henning's papers on the kitchen table in front of me, I was sometimes not sure whether the high-pitched cutting sound was coming from a distant circular saw or if the workshop in the old laundry building had sprouted again like a crocus in the depleted soil. Perhaps everything comes back, like the trilling of a blue tit, falling leaves and crocus buds, and maybe even workshops would if someone planted workshop bulbs?

The spring sun sparkled in the old windows where so many of the panes were still the original, convex, hand-blown glass. The paint on the windowsills was cracked and peeling. Sometimes the loose flakes looked like the ethereal apple blossom petals that would be whirling down here in a few months' time.

If only the house and the trees were allowed to remain standing, the old apple tree would lose its leaves once again onto the tufted grass and the leaves would turn brown and be pulled underground by worms or become trembling white webs when only their exposed nerves remained. The snow would lay a new blanket over the courtyard gravel, a frayed net curtain so thin the pattern of the rake in the gravel was visible beneath it.

But no one raked the gravel any longer on Saturday afternoons, no one came out through the doorway in a white shirt and drew the rake through the gravel with long, smooth strokes. Things were still quiet on Saturday evenings. Surely dusk fell and the air went gray on early summer evenings full of the scent of lilacs and of fuel from the road, as gray as a June night can get? Perhaps the gravel crunched underfoot when someone tried to get away quietly. Or did none of that happen any more? Was there never anyone who made love here and then left unseen on summer nights, in thin-soled shoes? Were there little green unripe apples in the grass and an empty aquavit bottle under the lilac? Was there still anyone who tried to get in through the door? Couldn't summer nights sometimes still be so warm you might fall asleep with your bottle beside you under the apple tree? Waking up here in the morning sun must be terribly cruel, waking up when doors began banging at the print shop and when the whistle blew at Swedish Engineering.

Then the frosty nights would come, making the grass stiff and shaggy white. The wind would howl and tear at slanted windows and TV aerials. At night the brown leaves of the apple tree flew in the wind at the window panes, as frightening as bats. They stuck, they wanted in. You could hear them as agitated voices in the gusts of wind, in the noise of the workshops, in the roar of fire — I could still hear it softly on windy days, hear the thundering storm of fire in an old wooden building, hear again the pounding at the door that woke Henning once. In the middle of the night there was still pounding, although the fire was extinguished long ago and the bits of scrap iron cast here and there in the sooty boot-trampled snow were no longer steaming, the pounding remained in the house, alive in it like a heart.

On the gravel there were leaves that had dried up and lost all color. They had shriveled to little cups, and when the wind blew they scattered here and there over the gravel with a dry, hissing sound. Looking at them brought Adam to mind for me, and I scoured my memory for pictures and voices associated with Adam Otter and the dry little leaves. I was a small child standing at the window watching them blow around outside in the wind, the tiny things rushing around like little animals running into the flower bed and settling by the stone foundation. Behind me adult voices were talking, and one of them belonged to Fredrik's brother, the elegant Adam. Gaiters with little buttons he had, and elastic bands under his shoes. Hand stitched suede gloves. Dark, parted hair so drenched with tonic from the blue bottle it looked black. The comb had furrowed it like the raked gravel in a churchyard.

He was leaning forward over the kitchen sink, and Jenny was looking at him from the side. He said to himself or to her in a voice imbued with desperation:

"Why are we alive, actually? What's the point?"

No, that's impossible. Not Adam. And what would he have been doing in our kitchen, anyway? But the image is there and the sound of his voice and the little rat-like rolled leaves blowing across the frozen gravel.

I tried to imagine what had happened, but that frightened me, too. I was afraid to ruin it, to transform the singular compound of auditory illusion and real sounds, of visual memories and scents from the old house, into something as dead and terrible as the tray of Fredrik's old slides Jenny keeps, or as weird as my Grandpa Abel's collections in the attic.

There wasn't much in the apartment worth saving and packing. Everything that could have been converted into cash for spirits had been, of course, long ago. Once I decided what to do with Henning's papers, there might be a few books I had loved as a child. But what sense did it make to keep the *Nordic Family Encyclopedia*? In Lisa's wardrobe, there were thin dresses and blouses of thirties design, and one single pair of shoes. I knew that without opening it. I didn't want to go into that empty bedroom and open the wardrobe door. I was planning to ask the Whitepainter to do it when the time came. It wouldn't be right just to leave the things there. When an old house is torn down, its insides are exposed. I didn't want Lisa's dresses to be lying in a pile of mortar and rotting timber or to be fluttering from a wall that remained upright until the excavator operator returned from lunch.

When I opened the sideboard in the dining room, I found tarnished silver-plated cutlery under pink flannel. It probably wouldn't be saleable at an auction. In the attic there were pieces of broken furniture and clothes rotting to rags. But beyond Henning's blueprints and notes there were no papers in the drawers. This was because my Grandfather Abel had salvaged everything he judged to be of interest and put it away in his boxes.

Abel did not live for his grocer's shop, he lived off it. His main interest was collecting. Eventually, it became his only interest. He collected testimonies to the past. He did so with such zeal and such precision that the present had barely had time to happen before he transformed it to past by adding its testimony to his collection. When he came home from an evening's entertainment at the community park, the first thing he would do was to put the program, including the name of the operetta, the cast and the summary of the plot in a box labeled *Community Park*. When he died, it contained a complete set of programs, from day one. When he had been unable to go himself, he'd asked someone else for their program. He had other boxes, too, labeled *Bandy*, *Obituaries*, *Eccentrics*, *Superstitions*, *School Reports*, and many other things. He cut out all the articles in *The Correspondent* on local history and all the interviews with elderly people about what life had been like in town when they were growing up. Eventually he was also interviewed himself, and asked to exhibit his collections. But he hadn't kept articles relating to his own life in any special box. They were sorted under *Local News*, *Birthdays*, and *Old Team Players*.

When he was in his thirties, he began keeping a diary and saving all the letters he received. He'd been collecting post cards since childhood. When he had sold the shop and moved down into the little apartment where Gabriel lives now, he began arranging and cataloguing his collections in earnest. Every time I came in he would show me something he found of great interest: an old issue of the members' newsletter from the sports club, a bill where you could see how much the milliner had charged for a hat Sigrid ordered in 1922. To me, looking through his old newsletters had been the height of boredom. I'd seen his postcard collection so many times I'd lost interest in what our city had looked like before it was a city. Abel showed me how elegant his home had been when it was first built.

Many of his clippings were about people who had too little to eat and who lived in misery, about frightening murders, disappearances and embezzlement cases. He often spoke about how wretched things were for people during the Great War, and about all the suicides there had been after the general strike. I don't believe he thought things had been better or that people had more fun when he was young. Maybe he just thought life was more real then.

The last ten years of his life he hardly went out at all, and he didn't increase his collections much. To him, time had probably stopped. When he wrote his will, he decreed that all the things he had collected in his long life by way of papers, letters, and photographs should be donated to the municipal archives. But the cartons and boxes were still up in the attic. Maybe the municipality had refused them.

I took a little look through the boxes labeled *The Community pre-1917*. I was most curious about Abel's diaries, and upset about his wanting to give them to the archives, where anyone at all would be able to look at them. But reading them was both a disappointment and a relief. He hadn't been the least bit personal. They didn't even say when Lisa was taken to the sanatorium. What he had noted down was the weather, every day for more than forty years' time. He wrote about things you might have read in the papers: the outbreak of war, a serious railway accident 10 kilometers outside town that he had cycled out to see. When the workshop burned down he wrote about that, and one of his last entries was from the time when he was overweight and crippled and almost blind and he made his way up to the schoolyard on the last day of school to watch the upper secondary graduates stream out, and to hang a bouquet of flowers on a raffia string around my neck.

When I opened drawers and cupboards in the apartment, and when I sifted through chests in the attic, I thought at first it was strange that I couldn't find the things that were missing from Abel's collections. There had to be personal letters. Surely Lisa had written to him from the sanatorium. Every single picture postcard Sigrid had received from her women friends during the time she was at the home for chronic invalids had been saved, they were part of his donation. But Lisa's letters weren't there.

They were gone. He'd had plenty of time to arrange the past, that was for sure.

Naturally, there would have been no pleasure for Abel in documenting his own life and the misfortunes of his family. Unplanned pregnancies and running away from home. Addiction. Bankruptcy threats. And illness, illness, and more illness. That had also been a peculiar dictum of our lives. But incontrovertible.

No, he didn't bother with the personal things. He avoided them for obvious reasons. Time also passed through old football scorecards, through Co-op receipts and time sheets from the workshop. And I think time was what he was after. When the present melted in time and ran off, the personal was not particularly relevant. All this paper rubbish must have been that pouring to him, that gushing sludge which is time, and he collected it in stagnant pools, drawing his own attention to the fact that it was not really passing.

I began to realize that Abel had not been a nostalgic man at all. To him, life was undoubtedly much nicer as the boxed past than when he was running from herring barrel to cash box, or the first time he had to go out and pay Henning's drinking bill so they'd let him go home, or every afternoon when he went to the chronic invalids' home to take Sigrid her newspaper. No, Abel had been a harsh realist, a stern commentator. Look at this: death. And a devoted mystic. Look at that: eternity. What a fine time he must have had. What pleasure he must have derived from his collections of receipts and his piles of photographs on thick paper. More than from any woman or the new leaves unfurling in spring. He was not collecting the history of the city or the grocer's trade in his boxes; he was creating a nest for his soul. Souls need to be nested. And yet most of them flutter like moths in the mist and haze on a cold, penetrating summer's night. Abel feathered his nest with old receipts. I'm cushioning mine with ink penned leaves from keepsake notebooks.

During the time I spent rummaging around closets and cupboards, Kurt Lundholm kept calling, wanting to discuss the sale. When I kept not giving him an answer, he came round to Chapel Road. This time he brought his secretary along, and a young man I assumed worked at the office. I could tell there would be a deed of sale in the briefcase the young man was carrying. I saw them coming before they went into the hall downstairs, because I was standing at the kitchen window. Before they could get up the stairs I had run to the attic.

I felt more secure up there when I heard them knocking at the door of my apartment. I could, of course, have locked it, but it's creepy hiding behind a door someone is banging on. It makes you feel both threatened and deceitful.

I could hear their soft voices downstairs. In the end they left. They went down the stairs more slowly than they had come up. I lay stretched out on Lisa's bed waiting for silence to descend.

I have a former classmate who lives in Södertälje. Her name is Barbro, but we always called her Babba. She was a good, quiet girl and if she hadn't phoned me to say she'd seen Elisabeth, I might never have thought about her again.

One afternoon she was standing ironing blouses in her kitchen, glancing out at the street from time to time. That was how she happened to see Elisabeth walking along with a heavy case. She rang the doorbell of the terraced house across the street, and was let in.

Babba knew very well that Elisabeth was missing. She'd been to visit her mother, who lives in Jenny's building, at Christmas. People will talk. Now she didn't know whether to phone her mother and ask if the girl was still missing, or rush out and try to catch up with her. While she was vacillating, Elisabeth came out of the neighbor's house and saved Babba the decision, by ringing on her doorbell.

Babba opened and said hello, but Elisabeth didn't realize she'd been recognized. She wedged her portfolio into the doorway, explaining she had artwork for sale and would like to show it. The strange thing, said Babba afterwards, was that she spoke in English.

She let her in, or perhaps Elisabeth just barged in. At any rate, before Babba knew it Elisabeth was in the living room opening her case. Then she perched framed paintings on the sofa and the armchairs. She described herself as an art student from Amsterdam, and the paintings as hers. She was traveling around selling them to finance her studies for the following year.

Babba should probably have told her she recognized her, but she couldn't bring herself to. Her own English isn't very good and in her astonishment and confusion, she didn't realize she could have spoken Swedish. The real reason was probably embarrassment, though. Elisabeth talked on, sounding convincing and extremely serious.

"Art is all my life," she repeated several times. Babba was able to remember that afterwards. She had never heard Elisabeth was an art student and she knew

94

very well she had been at school in Sweden. And still she said nothing. As she talked, Elisabeth set up more and more paintings around the living room. They weren't cheap and Babba started to worry about feeling she'd have to buy one. She told her she wasn't going to, but it didn't have any effect. So she pleaded having no money in the house. The girl packed the paintings back into her case and walked out without saying good-bye. She seemed to be under pressure, Babba said. She was thin and very pale. She was wearing jeans and no overcoat, but a thin denim jacket. Babba stood at the kitchen window and watched her go into the next house. Then she phoned her mother and a little while later she had me on the line. Elisabeth must still have been at the neighbor's at that point.

"Run and get her," I said. "Tell her you've changed your mind and you want to buy one."

By the time I got to Södertälje, nearly two hours had passed. And I'd driven fast. But Elisabeth had left. She'd gone off in a big black car that had been waiting for her at the corner of the next street. There was a painting on Barbro's couch and she said she'd paid five hundred sixty kronor for it.

"I'll give you the money," I said. "Why didn't you keep her here?"

"I couldn't."

She had probably become suspicious when Babba tried to spin out her purchase, and offered her coffee after the transaction.

"She doesn't drink coffee," I said. "But as far as I know she doesn't speak English, either, or at least not particularly well. She does speak French. Are you certain it was Elisabeth?"

"Yes, I wouldn't mistake anyone for her. She's so dark and has such a special look."

"Did she look well?"

"She was so slim. Terribly thin."

We went into the living room so I could see the painting. It was leaning up against the back of the couch, and had a white frame with little flecks of gold in it. It was a landscape with snow-capped mountains against a blue sky, white houses, and trees with pink cherry blossoms.

"This is a mass produced piece," I said. "Was her whole portfolio full of this kind of thing?"

"Well, I didn't think it was real art," said Babba. "Even I could see that. But some of them were really pretty. And I don't believe a machine could do that."

"That's not really what I meant. But they're industrially produced. They use stencils, make lots of copies."

"Well, how was I to know?" Babba asked.

There was something absurd about the situation now. It was as if she were trying to defend Elisabeth against me. She described her as extremely convincing, and as having spoken excellent English. I asked again if she was completely certain it had been my daughter she had seen. She was.

Myself, I didn't know what to think. The painting was standing there anyway, pink, white and blue. Babba said she had to start dinner.

I found the smells in Babba's kitchen and living room revolting. They were sharp, pungent odors from synthetic fabrics, as well as a sticky scent from her own body and off her clothes. It was getting worse by the minute.

Her husband and two daughters had come home. They stared at me, and that was when I realized how I must look. I'd just thrown a coat on and rushed down to the newspaper office to borrow a car. My hair and my clothes were very different from Babba's. They weren't really like mine, either, but there was no way for these people to know that.

I sat down at their kitchen table and looked out into the street. It had begun to drizzle and it looked cold out there. But there were children playing out of doors. They were running around the yellowing lawns. I thought about the fact that just an hour ago they'd watched Elisabeth pass with her case. The car I'd borrowed at *The Correspondent* was spattered, and there was a brown film of dirt on the back window. I had driven fast, but not fast enough. I sat there wondering if I should have done things differently. Perhaps I should have started by calling the police. But I didn't want the police picking Elisabeth up.

Babba was frying meat, and the smell made me queasy. Her daughters were quarreling about whose turn it was to use the hair dryer first. Her husband was sitting in the living room leafing through the paper. When I was saying good-bye to Babba, he came in with the picture and asked her how much she had paid for it. I had forgotten to reimburse her for it, and now I had to tell her I didn't have enough cash. So he carried it back into the living room.

"You keep it," I said," and I'll send you the money anyway."

Babba rushed back into the kitchen to pull the frying pan off the burner, and I just stood by myself in the hall for a moment. I looked at the pictures that were hanging in the living room. They weren't much better than the one she'd bought that afternoon. The smells in the house had become so sharp and pungent they were making the inside of my nose prickle. The house felt dry and dusty. I looked around, trying to impress it all on my memory: the over-fertilized potted plants, the synthetic tulle curtains, the shiny tiles with their stylized mandala pattern, the nylon jackets and fake fur hanging in the hall. Elisabeth had been here. They say the dust in the air is primarily composed of flakes of skin. Billions of particles are constantly coming loose, falling and whirling in the air. There were dead fragments of her skin in here. Perhaps on the television screen, on the leaves of the monstera, in the deep pile of the Rya. But none of it was visible. Everything was shiny.

It was a big city. I couldn't recall having been there before. Afterwards it appears to me like a city in a dream, and I have in fact dreamt about it many times since. At first glance there was nothing unreal about it. There were streets, shops, cars and tall apartment buildings, buses, traffic lights and pavement, like everywhere else. Neon signs shone swollen and misty in the rainy haze. On the streets in the city center car engines revved and growled. I had to drive slowly, but I would have anyway, looking for Elisabeth outside the restaurants and hamburger joints. How would a girl with at least five hundred sixty kronor in her pocket spend her Friday night?

Only the young were out. They roamed the streets and gathered in clusters. I was part of a stream of cars, where I could see back seats full of young men and women. It was difficult to get out of the flow. I had to go along with it to the outskirts. I was about to turn back towards the center of town again, when I noticed a large tentlike structure a few hundred meters down the road, a plastic dome with inside walls that appeared to be inflated with air or gas; so it stood there, round and shiny, dark and damp. With its arched, bloated forms, its smoothness and blindness — having no windows — it was nothing like any of the other buildings nearby. It rested on the ground like the egg of some giant bird, looking as if it had just floated down through the nasty, sourish air.

There was an entrance haloed in bluish lamplight, and from inside came the thump and pulse of the kind of music that frightened me even when it issued from Elisabeth's little record player. I approached it slowly, driving along the edge of the pavement, until the car was opposite the entrance. There was a long line of people waiting to go in, they got their hands stamped when they paid. The bouncers didn't let the drunk ones in, but when I'd sat there a while it began to seem to me they were being quite arbitrary about who they kept out. Some who were reeling and holding each other upright got in anyway. I saw some very drunk girls, and had an urge to drive off just to spare myself seeing Elisabeth in that state. But I forced myself to stay in the car, looking at every single girl who went in or out.

When they came out they were often in the company of young men, and most of them didn't go farther than to some car to drink straight from a bottle in the glove compartment or the back seat. Many of them went to have a pee on their way back in. There were some apartment buildings nearby, and people stood on the balconies of the closest ones watching the kids go in and out. The voices and music from the loudspeakers must have been a continuous intrusion on their home life.

The kids who needed to relieve themselves went into the courtyard and found hardhack bushes under the balconies to pee between. Some did it openly on the grass. Girls pulled down their jeans and exposed their bottoms. Up in the windows, older men stood watching them. They didn't shout at them to get out of their courtyard. I wondered whether they didn't dare, or whether they were enjoying having a look. Some kids came out to throw up, too. A tall, thin man in shiny black jeans stood groping the back pocket of a vomiting girl.

I would have left if I hadn't kept seeing girls who looked like Elisabeth from behind. There were plenty of girls even darker than her. Sometimes I thought I must be in a southern European city, until a group with fairer heads and stouter bodies passed by.

More than once, kids stumbled or were pushed against my car. But no one noticed me sitting in it. At first I was frightened. Then I started feeling invisible.

I'd been sitting there in the cold evening air for nearly an hour, staring at the queue and the groups of people coming outside, when I discovered there was another entrance at the other side of the tent cathedral. She might have gone in ages ago without my seeing her. Of course that meant I had to go in and look for her, but I wasn't sure I really dared to get out of the car.

I don't know what I thought would happen, but slipping across the street didn't turn out to be any different from staying in the car; I was invisible. Not even the man who stamped my hand looked me in the face. I followed the slow stream in. The top of the tent was very high, and you couldn't see the entire inside structure from the entrance. The tent was partitioned, and behind taut fabric walls other music came throbbing and pounding out. It was duller than the music blaring from the arena that was sometimes flooded with flashes of white light, sometimes spotlighted with rushes of red and violet. The audience was sitting in a semicircle on a high, tiered stand around the stage where the bodies of the musicians gyrated and pitched. The musicians held their flat guitars low, as if to conceal their genitals, or replace them with their bright instruments.

Loudspeaker voices broke through the noise. One made an announcement about the rotunda of death, where a motorcyclist was going to ride a rotating drum. I followed a slow mass of bodies in rustling quilted jackets in the direction of an opening in the partition, and found myself inside the wooden walls that ringed in the drum. A young man walked out onto the stage. He was dressed in riveted, star-studded leather. The thundering voice announced that he was the man who was going to risk his life on the track. His face was red and pimply. He'd brushed his hair back in two huge waves, and it was full of some greasy cream. It looked like a fifties hairdo.

Another voice was describing a magic show, tantalizingly, urging us not to miss the most shocking performance in the history of magic, although if we didn't have nerves of steel we shouldn't go in.

There was music coming from two directions, with brutal amplification. I walked around slowly, searching from behind for long, dark hair and a thin girl in a jeans jacket. Every time I saw someone who resembled her, I would walked around her to be able to see her face. I started to feel uncertain about what she actually looked like. There were so many skinny girls. I tried to hold on to her image. Thin and pale. Ultra-tight jeans. Red highlights in her dark hair.

Along the walls were a series of little rooms where you could watch films of people copulating. Girls fornicating with serpents or rifle barrels or mules, men fucking sows or other men. I hated the thought Elisabeth might be around. The short, crude previews of intercourse, massacres and catch-as-catch-can that flickered on the video screens by the doors filled me with an intense, groundless sense of shame. I hadn't made those movies. I hadn't asked to come to this place. I just happened to be here, along with this fluttering flicker of constructed situations and faces acting out ecstasy and terror. It was all unreal; there were flashes of light and not a sound to be heard when a jaw was crushed or when a jackass brayed as he rose on his back legs. The music from the arenas blanketed it all. Had I been living in the days of Augustus Caesar, the scenes would at least smell.

There was a silly old-fashioned ghost train that went in through a wooden tunnel and vanished out along one of the long sides of the tent. Above the door were brightly colored painted cardboard bats and skeletons. There was a gorilla with the bloody corpse of a woman in its mouth, her clawed, mutilated breasts protruding from a bathing suit and dripping with dark red blood. There may actually have been something crudely comical about these images. But when I looked into the tunnel where the creaky train vanished, full of people shouting with anticipated pleasure or horror, I was frightened. I wished I'd been as wasted as everybody else.

It was difficult to get a look at the girls' faces in the crowd. Lots of skinny dark-haired girls stood with their backs to the doors of the film booths watching the roving white dots and streaks of lightning on the screens. Many of them were smoking. I looked upwards, but the arched ceiling was so far away. I didn't know whether or not the material of which this place was made was flammable. It might even be explosive. Or perhaps it would just melt down over us if it were exposed to the heat of burning wooden tunnels, partitions and doors. Maybe what had been our clothes and our flesh, our legs and shoes and keys would be transformed to plastic sculptures with insides of crumbly ash.

There were young men standing at game screens with wide-barreled machine guns, turning a wheel or pressing an animated trigger to shoot at little figures who either fell down dead or got away. Some of these games were awfully unsophisticated; there was something absurdly old-fashioned about the whole set-up. Little slanted-eyed beings dressed in green ran across the screens. They were probably supposed to be Vietnamese.

A heavy-set guy reeled out of a fighter aircraft simulator, the stress of which had clearly been too realistic for him. He felt his back pocket for his wallet but it wasn't there. He started shouting at the ride attendant, who refused even to consider that he might have dropped it on the catapult seat. The guy's voice grew louder and louder, outraged, offended, a naive roar of fury into the attendant's shut face. Out of nowhere, two uniformed bouncers appeared and removed him.

I watched the dancers, and saw any number of thin girls' bodies. But not Elisabeth's. Most of them were too lightly dressed to be out on such a chilly evening, They had on short jackets and low-slung jeans, and I could see their cold flesh in the gaps between their garments.

I had only been looking for girls in jeans, but now, outside the room where the loudspeaker was still booming about the most shocking show in the history of magic, I saw a bare-legged girl with a poplin raincoat slung over her shoulders. She crossed the floor nimbly in open-toed silver high heels, and went in through a door. She walked like Elisabeth. Her dark hair was pulled back with an elastic band. I was so close when she disappeared I could have reached out an arm and touched her.

I was sure I had spotted Elisabeth and I rushed forward to try to get in. Of course the guard sent me to the ticket booth, where I had to queue up.

When I did get in, the place was only half full. The loudspeaker voice was still urging people not to miss the show, but performance time was past and the audience was getting impatient. They were whistling and stamping.

I couldn't see how to get into the wings. The stage was high and there were no steps up to it. Suddenly the magician came on, tipping his hat. He bowed to the rowdy audience and the spotlight beamed white on his face. A girl in silver sandals came tripping in, but not the one I'd seen outside. This girl was fair. She was wearing a blue bikini with silver sequins, and she began efficiently handing the magician boxes and wands, and he did his tricks with them in an old-fashioned, quite elaborate fashion. Music started coming from the speakers behind them, obviously out of synch. The audience booed at the whole spectacle. The music was Latin American with heavy, complex rhythms.

I didn't know what to do. Elisabeth might be in the wings. Certainly someone had turned on the tape recorder after the other two had come on stage. But I didn't dare walk up and interrupt the performance to ask about my daughter. I wasn't worried about how the magician might react, but there was the audience.

It consisted mainly of young men. I glanced sidelong at the ones by me. Several had thighs and arms as broad as logs. Shouting and rude gestures couldn't possibly be a sufficient outlet for everything they had inside those powerful, awkward bodies. There must be so much pent up in them. They were impatient and loud, and that scared me. I was appalled by how ugly they were. I had seen so few people recently. I thought: can they really be so unattractive?

The magician was working up a sweat on stage, with them shouting at him all the time to hurry it up, to get down to business. He maintained his old-fashioned demeanor, doing his whole act systematically — no short cuts to climax. But the atmosphere was growing tense. They shouted at the young woman as she bent over the equipment:

"Come on now, ass up. Give us a look, damn you!"

"Show that cunt of yours, too."

I couldn't believe they were allowed to scream such obscenities and not get thrown out, couldn't believe someone didn't just stop the show, but nothing happened at all. The girl just tripped along, turning towards the audience and curtseying first with one foot in front, then the other.

"Fucking fat legs!"

"Get a move on, dammit. Let's see some sawing action."

The magician was ashen. He was doing things really fast now, and sometimes fumbling. That provoked clapping and laughter from the audience. They had managed to hurry him though his program at some speed, after all. He said a few words to his assistant, and she tripped out. There was a rustling sound as she crossed the stage.

She came back in wheeling a box on a stand. It looked like a coffin, and she got a great round of applause for bringing it on stage. They obviously knew what they were here for. Now they roared with approval as the magician waved his magic wand over the box. When he raised his hat you could see a sharp, red mark on his brow, except for which he was pale gray and perspiring in the white light. His big, yellow teeth had more color than his skin. It was a face of bone and leather. But he maintained his smile throughout, with admirable stamina.

I kept thinking he looked familiar. I know that's a symptom I get when I'm tired and stressed, that I think I know people, take them for others. But he did really look like Ann-Sophie's lover Bertil Franzon. Sometimes I was sure he was Bertil Franzon even though I knew it was impossible. He's a wealthy, respectable man; he wouldn't do magic at a cheap sideshow. I felt as if the heat from the spotlights, the shouting and stamping were rocking me. I was wide awake, but dreaming. I put both hands on the back of the bench in front of me and held tightly to the wood.

Now the girl in the bathing suit was getting into the box. She looked very chipper, waving before she put her arms at her sides. Soon her silver slippers were protruding, her feet wriggling gently. The audience reacted roughly:

"Get a fucking move on!"

But she just winked, smiling brightly, her face sticking out the other end.

The magician rolled up his dress coat sleeves and raised the saw. When he started cutting through the box I had to admit that this cheap vaudeville performance was better than others I'd seen. The saw blade didn't just glide down into a precut groove. He sawed right into the wood, the sawdust whirled. He had to work hard. His hat toppled askew. Urged on by the crowd, he worked the saw back and forth.

"Heeeave — ho! Heeeave — ho!"

At last there was some spirit in the room; he had them wrapped around his little finger. Or maybe they had him. Their shouts helped him saw rhythmically. Grimacing, he drew the blade back and forth.

Suddenly the girl began to moan and jolt, as if she were trying to break out of the box. Then she began to cry, babbling incomprehensibly, her screams fusing with the roaring of the crowd. As they shouted with glee, most of them rising to their feet now, I got up and rushed towards the back. I wanted to leave, hardly dared to look but couldn't help doing so with all the screaming. I saw blood dripping from under the saw and him sawing more slowly now and with exaggerated effort. The girl was shouting in pain and terror. Her neck had gone rigid, the whole box wrenched with her violent tossing. Her feet circled stiffly and she was tossing and straining to get free and pleading with him to stop, praying for her life as he sawed.

He stopped cutting for a moment to comfort her, at the same time instructing her to lie still so he could get it over with. When she wouldn't stop jerking, he slapped her face, to tremendous applause. The room was ruttish with male aggression now, and I was so frightened I didn't dare move. The audience was shouting that he was such a fucking loser they could die.

"Get a move on now! One more pull and she'll snap!"

He drew the saw hard, and the blood gushed out. Now he'd sawn through her, the girl gave a jolt. She went stock still, her head thrown back as if her neck were broken, her eyes staring straight up, round and blue. Her feet hung lax, one sandal dangling. The stage looked like a slaughterhouse floor, and I suddenly understood that the rustling sound when she had crossed it was the protective plastic. But I didn't smell blood. Finally, I was released from the tyranny of odors.

The magician rolled the box and its stand into the wings, and the audience had already begun to file out by the time he came back for his bow. In all the commotion, I, too, had been screaming. I had been retching and trembling. Now my whole abdomen felt tender, but I hadn't vomited. I supported myself against the wall, afraid of being crushed in the throng. The magician just stood there bowing, holding a microphone. He was urging the audience not to reveal the high point of the show to their friends and relatives. But to please tell them if they had enjoyed it.

"And if you didn't, tell me," he said, but no one was listening to him by then.

I was jostled along with the crowd and had to follow. Once back in the main tent I made my way to the wall and found a door, banged on it. But no one answered. So I just opened it, and there was the magician, standing by his revolting box having a smoke.

"I saw my daughter go in this way," I said.

"Fine," he answered. "Come on in."

There were two girls in there, the one I'd seen in the box and another who was dark and had her hair pulled back in an elastic band. Both were wearing silver slippers. They were busy with the contents of the box, wiping up the mess. I saw thin balsa wood and torn bloody plastic bags. One black coffin side was waiting to be reassambled. The dark-haired girl didn't look a bit like Elisabeth from the front.

"I was wrong," I said. "That's not her."

The girls barely noticed me. They seemed completely disinterested, and the fair one started pulling a sweatshirt over her head.

"That was awful," I said. "What a horrible show."

"Did you think so?" asked the man in the dress coat. He was delighted. "Won't you sit down? Coffee?"

He gestured in the direction of a thermos.

But I didn't want to be there. There was no point in my staying, I wasn't the least bit interested in him or his assistants.

"Why are you parked here? Is there a problem?" The face was close to mine but on the other side of the rain-streaked car window. His voice sounded muted, as if it were coming from under water. Uniform buttons. The rain streaming off the brim of his cap.

When I started the engine, my hands had stopped trembling, I was no longer feeling sick, and I hadn't thrown up. The car pulled out into the wet street and I was grateful for the seclusion it provided me. I left the outskirts of town, where the tent was, driving slowly to avoid hitting the bodies staggering past in the rays of my headlights. The music receded, I could only hear the thudding of the bass. Then that, too, disappeared, and all I could hear was the engine and the way the tires whined on the pavement. When it began to rain even harder, I turned on the wipers, and their rubber edging whispered against the windshield in a steady rhythm.

I headed home although I could have gone on looking for Elisabeth or to the police station. If I had wanted to, I could have driven in the direction of Stockholm instead. I could have stepped on the accelerator and driven straight into one of the steep rockfaces along the road. But I did none of those things; I just went back home instead. I was aware that I wasn't actually making this choice, it was just happening. The key had been turned in the ignition, I had shifted gears and was steering in what I believed to be the right direction.

I could see everything clearly now, and knew that my worries of the last few weeks had been unnecessary. It wasn't a matter of loving. There were no causes and no effects of actions, at least none that could be distinguished.

Ana Maria Conceição would have prayed to Maria de Lourdes if she had known that her child was in this town, that at this very moment she was folding the bloody plastic sheeting and rinsing it clean for the next performance. But some other daughter than Conceição's was folding that plastic, some other mother was weeping or indifferent. Elisabeth was not there.

She was gone because that was what she wanted to be. She was not dead, not even unconscious. She was walking the streets with a heavy case, telling lies in broken English and tricking people into buying pictures.

I wasn't quite sure that everything I had experienced had really happened.

Looking back, all I could see were fragments, broken bits that were not easy to piece together into memories. I would have to narrate it for myself, and how could I ever be sure of what had actually happened? I understood that there is nothing else, everything is what we see. Nothing more.

The causes would not make themselves known if I stayed six months or a year at Chapel Road. Maria de Lourdes would not step down from her niche and comfort Conceição no matter how hard she prayed and wept.

Maybe Elisabeth would come back on her own. I would be happy or angry when she arrived. But I'd never know how long it would be and whether it should be called love or hate.

I had a husband and a daughter and a foster mother. A few weeks ago I would have said that I loved them, and I would even have been able to rank my love for them. Now I did not know whether I ever wanted to see any of them again. The key had been turned in the ignition; I was traveling in the settled direction.

I had a husband, and just as much a right as anybody else to use the words love and lovemaking when I spoke of him. But it had come to feel easy to be away from him, easier and easier by the week. I wasn't longing for his embraces. That was it and no one could say why.

My daughter would be eighteen that summer, but I had been looking forward to her turning twenty-one for several years. In the old days you became an adult when you turned twenty-one. Perhaps I imagined my worries and my responsibility would come to an end on the twenty-third of June 1981.

Now I knew I might just as well wish I would never have to see her again. Longing for her to grow up was just a kind of hypocrisy. Why do we give everything such fancy names?

I couldn't take it any more. I didn't know what you did then. Maybe you drove into a rockface. Maybe you just lay down and let time pass. I didn't have to make up my mind. It would be made up somehow. Keys were turned in ignitions. Gears were shifted.

Outside it had begun to rain cold and hard and the trees were flying by like rags in the glow of the headlights. Now and then approaching vehicles momentarily blinded me, but when they had swept by I was alone again. All I could hear was the even beat of the wipers on the windshield and the singing of the tires on the tarmac. There was nothing else.

Ishnol stood before me in all her glory. I did not know if she had stepped out of the dimension into the world, or if I had been shifted instead. She smiled as if she had heard my question without my having enunciated it and I felt that ancient comprehension; I relaxed into it.

She was wearing her veil of pearls, and each sparkling drop reflected all the others.

"Lambda!"

I had forgotten the greeting of Choryn and couldn't fool Ishnol; she knew I was just imitating her with my "Lambda!", but she was obliging. She smiled as if at a child. I began awkwardly testing the complex patterns of meeting and greeting in Choryn, my hands recalled clumsily and Ishnol regarded me with patience, and with the light swirling around her clothing.

"Little Snailshell," she said. "You are among friends. Do not fear failure. Of course you remember! You're doing very well."

I concluded the greeting.

"Fly," said Ishnol. "Fly, little Shard."

"I cannot!"

She was silent and I felt myself being lifted by the warm swell. I was no longer in bed, not with my legs twisted in damp, sweaty sheets. I was in the swell of leaves, in the high treetops — I was rising and falling. The warm, acidic wind ran through me and the world, through the lung of leaves that was breathing me and filling my veins with light. The tips of lung, the tongues of sun were licking me as I rose and fell in the leaves' embrace, and their membranes opened to my body and opened my body so that I streamed out toward the tips, the tongues, into the light that was pulsating me. Then I streamed gradually back into the arteries of the leaves and sank. Slowly Ishnol lowered me with her gaze. I sank back.

"Oh yes you could," she said. "Was it nice?"

My gratitude choked my voice. I couldn't speak. This marvelous heat that was spreading up the insides of my thighs, a hot, licking fire that did not burn, did not even warm, just tickled and caressed.

"Thank you, highness," I whispered. "Goddess!"

"You are fortunate, little Baby Snail. You are resting on leaves and wind. You are among friends and your time in Choryn will be constant marvel and enlightenment."

She used charain, the word for both light like a torch that burns in humid darkness and for inspiration.

"Only *one* crime has been committed and shall be punished."

"No crime!" I screamed.

"One."

I thought she would invoke the High Choryn but she just gestured with her hand and passed judgment herself:

"You conveyed one word from Choryn out into the world."

"No!"

"Ben."

I began to explain, stammering, I found earth in my mouth and bits of snail shell. Pappa Ben, that's different, really, I had never said any of my names out in the world! She chortled.

"You have no names, little Shred. You have tiny designations."

Then she raised her hand:

"Punish!"

Her voice of ice, and the taste of iron. I expected to see the two Executors appear but they did not come and suddenly I understood that I was supposed to perform the punishment myself. I began to strike. I slapped both my cheeks, slowly, rhythmically, then faster and faster, and I felt the skin grow hot under my hands. Ishnol watched.

"Little Ben," she said, you punish lightly."

I struck harder and faster. The slaps whirled against my cheeks and the whirlwind drew me downward and inward — I lost my foothold and the thin silver air of the dimension was replaced by thick vapors. I smelled urine. I lay curled up, immobile, not wanting to admit that Ishnol had let me fall. But it was true. I inhaled the old, putrid stink of Karun. Along my right cheek was the curved porcelain toilet pipe. And yet I was not unhappy as I began to move my stiff limbs and slowly tried to get up. I looked in the mirror when I was on my feet, thinking with pride that now Ishnol wouldn't say I was punishing lightly. No, I was not unhappy. I knew she would call me back. I had been justly punished and I had stood the test.

"What do you require of me now, High Ishnol?" I whispered inwardly, sound-lessly, since she had withdrawn the dimension. The answer that came to me voice-lessly was irrefutable and simple. I was to go on being Robor until she called me. I was to go through all the motions of Robor thoroughly, allowing none of the sounds or signs of Choryn to slip out into Karun.

Now I had to think hard about what Robor's motions were in this present. I knew I was supposed to wash my face with cold water, Robor's face, and comb her hair. She stared back at me from the mirror and I nearly greeted her: "Lambda!"

But none of the words of Choryn are for poor, ungainly, well-meaning Robor, who has no idea.

"Do," I said to her, and she did everything I told her and I controlled her in the mirror.

The time that followed was the most marvelous time I had spent in Choryn. I got more charain than I had ever had before. I was older now, of course, more grown up. It seemed as if she wanted to initiate me into all the secrets I could possibly comprehend. When I remembered all the childishness she had had to tolerate ear-lier, to teach and initiate me, I was ashamed. The multiplication table in base eight! How I failed at it time and again … I couldn't believe Ishnol hadn't given up on me. She just kept revealing herself, breaking through time after time!

I have never dared to ask why. But sometimes I look at her face when she has the one called damein, the face that can be seen without burning, and I can tell she has chosen me for a secret reason that is clear to her but may never be revealed to me.

I know that when Ishnol shows herself to me in the pearl veil, she does so to give me an image, a gestalt I can comprehend. She has other guises beyond the one I call the Queen, of which the Butterfly may be the most enthralling. When she teaches me about the laws and occurrences in the dimension, she also has them take shapes my brain can comprehend.

I know she wants me to achieve harmony with the dimensions. They embrace all. She demands of me that I shall attempt to understand her images and reflec-tions and abandon the pictures I had before, the distorted, clumsily shaped images. I am no longer allowed to think as I have been taught, but the thought habits of Karun are deeply etched on the slate of my soul, they cannot be easily erased. The stylus has scratched so hard and screeched so loudly that the letters have become indelibly impressed on the lower layer. Sometimes I fear that Ishnol will turn away from these tainted tablets and go looking for a clean one.

I was now subjected to a long learning period. To some extent it was repetition and consolidation of previous experience. But it was also new, and now I went more deeply than I had ever been before in the study of Choryn. Ishnol was completely focused on helping me, I gained full control of Robor and that poor, clumsy assisting creature performed every move she was commanded to make and developed a whole set of abilities to say the right words on the appropriate occasion. She answered questions without my help regarding what she was up to and how long she'd be at home and it all sounded natural to the Karunites. In truth, though, they aren't particularly attentive. They are like Robor in their fumbling and their rigid movements. Their speech is slurred and they seldom make eye contact. Their awareness is irregular and shallow and they are always thinking just a little bit ahead of the present, worrying and planning. Full presence is a state they seldom possess.

Robor was also able to tolerate it for the quite extended periods when I had to leave her body. She grew thin and liquids ran out of her orifices but Ishnol, who knew how important Robor is as a safeguard and a guise, let her lie secure as a chimney swift under a roof tile while the rain passes and the parents are far away in different, milder climes.

The world is whole and all, says the sacred song of Choryn, which is Chosma. The diamond in Ishnol's tiara reflects all, and when she leans forward it occupies the entire reflection in the mirror and is all.

Ishnol sparkles, her tongue is compressed fire, white fire that is the final fire, in which everything collapses into everything. She is made of heavy crystals, her waist is calcite and indestructible, it divides and the split is perfect; a new rhombohedral Ishnol sparkles, hard as glass.

When I was little and she used to play with me, she would float down over my drawing paper, which was a cake box opened out flat. Imagine Ishnol, The Highness, revealing herself playful and good, over that messy cardboard, sticky and covered with pastry crumbs. She would lower herself until she covered a greasy spot I had filled in black with my dull pencil, and I would see to my astonishment that there were now two spots. Then, as she twisted and turned above the cardboard, there would be only one again. The second one would have slid into the form of Ishnol and be rotating with it.

After that she would leave me and my cardboard, abruptly, as if she had dissolved in hot acid and her crystals turned to whirling granules, separating from one another until they resembled Karunish filth and heavy dust, that always falls downward. I would just sit there, still, still, tormented and upset as always in the borderland, staring at the streaks of dirt on my forearms and thinking they might be grains of Ishnol. But I could not be certain, because now she had abandoned me, leaving me in Karun with Choryn's vision, which was the worst of all possible states. The Karunites, in their sacs of skin, full of intestinal wind and smeary excrement, hardly notice their own horrible smells. But for someone who has just been in Choryn, these smells are painful, even tortuous. They do not see their own hairy orifices as they are. They extend their pointed tips, they pat and scratch and bump their runny holes together moaning and groaning good-naturedly all the while because they seem to be content with the materialization of Karun; they live in the best of all possible worlds and work on its decay with their wily brains. They love the decomposition, the runny mass, the sticky, bubbly mush.

Ishnol's advances were always ceremonial, but she did not always leave me alone when she withdrew. She would send Wonda, and Wonda's approaches were completely different. She was always playful. She might appear any place and in almost any form at all and if I did not recognize her right away but took her for patches of sun and leaves on a path in the woods, she would eventually give herself away by her laugh. Wonda might dart like the pattern of a school of small fry on the bottom of a purling stream, golden brown and capricious between the stones. I would sit staring at her without knowing she was there; my brain said nothing but fish and stone and sand. Then she would laugh her laugh under the rippling of stone and water and I knew! There was nothing ceremonious about Wonda, no complex rituals of greeting and no words that had to be pronounced correctly. There was just that chattering fieldfare laugh, coins tumbling in a tin, the jingling of stone and sand, that was Wonda's laugh and there she stood in the leaves and shadowy patches, with her fair neck and the gleam of her black eyes. Impossible she was to reach, but never impossible about playing and pretending. Just when I would extend a hand to hang on to her fringes and flaps, she would vanish down under the stones into a spring I had heard humming under the ground, and the only sign that she had been there a moment ago was a broken flower stalk, a fragile little blink I hardly dared to touch.

I thought she'd disappeared again so I lay down on my back. Above my face a light-green crosier began to open, with green plumes and little light-brown bracts covering them. Then there was one more and one more and they stood there, lovely, surrounding an empty space that should have forewarned me. But I just lay there staring at the tiny saw-toothed branches with their scaly little brown ring of bracts. At that very moment Wonda laughed and stepped out from among the leaves like a blossom bursting from its bud. She had her arms over her head and the wind was slipping slowly in and out between her thin fingers. When I had admired her for long enough — as I assume she thought — she made a face and burst out with a laugh, sharp as when a snakeskin blows away across the dry stones. Then she turned a cartwheel and stood on her hands, her fingers, thin and pale yellow, began to dig in the ground, disappearing into a pile of leaves and moist earth and thread-like roots where timid animals scattered, respectful and faceless.

"Wonda, Wonda," I laughed, exhausted from following her transformations. But at the same time I didn't ever want her to stop changing before my very eyes. Although Wonda was unceremonious and easy to be with, I had to pay the price with a certain degree of uncertainty, even fear. She might suddenly bite or sting, and she did so with the same good humor she displayed when performing her transformation acts.

"Wizardwonda!!! Cruelwonda ... sting-snout, sharp fang!"

Oh, how often you did sting me and how you laughed when I bled and wept. You pulled me forth like a snail is drawn from its shell, and you sank your fangs into my moistness that bled black and ran slimy.

"Take that and that!" you'd say as you stung and I stumbled along your spots of sun as they moved down the path and followed your powdery wings until they rose in the light and were turned into golden powder of spores and dust and me, I just lay there, heavy and unwinged.

"Bleed," you would say. "Bleed until I arrive. And keep the wound open."

The wound not only had to be kept open, it also had to be kept secret. It had to be scraped and renewed several times a day and covered with a sweater sleeve or a stocking. It became infected in the fumes of Karun and ran, pus-filled but secret. Sometimes it resembled a butterfly and then it was the sign for pleasure — like the pattern of the blood in the milk.

Choryn only gives materialization in images. Chosma says: the alphabet is a human matter. My assignment was always to make the alphabet of Choryn. The images were banned. But they were such pathetic images anyway, messy, blurry and uneven on the sticky cardboard, nothing but an insult to Choryn and the teachings of Chosma.

Working on all the alphabets of Choryn was a major task, demanding much rumination and reflection. All other thought was prohibited. Of course it wasn't up to me to work Choryn out or to think out what it might be like. It was conveyed. It came as charain out of the damp darkness, the sparks from torch flames, shadows crossing the stone wall.

The only permitted connection between Choryn and Karun was the alphabet, or alphabets if you like. They were not just permitted, they were desirable. Chosma said: *Everything* has an alphabet. Or: *Everything* should have one.

In the world of Choryn there is no difference between becoming and being. Ishnol once demonstrated this to me by taking hold of one of my legs and holding me like an owl holds a lemming in its clawed foot and lets it squirm.

"I can't see what is the beginning and the end of you, Little Skin," she said, "nor what is up and down, worse or better. You say you start at one end and are supposed to end at the other — but which do you mean? You stubbornly insist that things will be better later — but what is LATER? Is it this end or that?"

And she tossed me in the air for a while before seizing me again with her stalactite claw, saying:

"All I can see is a Little Skin with intestines and chipped teeth, and this little skin is divided into four in the dimension and out of its beak come little time chirps and the ticking of the millimeter counter and we High Materializations sometimes entertain ourselves by turning you upside down and then dropping you again as you tick and chirp and fart …" That was Ishnol in her best mood, playfully teaching me like a lemming.

Choryn's alphabet has no letters but images that become signs and I am the one who has made them all up. There are many alphabets, one is Mathematical and in it the signs have stomachs, huge rumens where the quantities ferment. One is Musical and resembles swallows or flocks of starlings and, like them, is able to move between the trees and give rise to infinite numbers of combinations. There is a Mechanical alphabet and a Manichean. The alphabets are my pride — but one must be cautious about pride or one risks being punished, so I have let the credit go the Karunites. I don't mind.

Using the Mealian alphabet, I let food stream into the world in an orderly, controlled manner. Otherwise it would have been just like the Karunites to let it gush forth like a huge polluted river, a mush of mass and residue. I made their meals and regulations and the significant rituals around the breaking of bread. Now they comply with my alphabetical stipulations both at major banquets and at counters where people eat standing; they have names for everything they consume and special ways of preparing every named kind of food.

Food is of utmost importance to them. They speak of it almost constantly, they write books about it and they long for it when, for the occasional brief moment, they cease stuffing it into or evacuating it from their orifices.

Seeing Ishnol in her crystalline forms breaking through the greasy dirt of Karun is sometimes such a great strain on me that I am afraid I will burst. I am brought up from the depths at far too great speed. I dare not beg for relief, but Ishnol is still often benevolent towards me, sending Wonda who can go in and out of Karun playfully and at will. With Wonda I have evenings when the whole world is perfumed, when she is kind and Ishnol has withdrawn. She lets the little bumblebees find their furry hives and she pulls the swallows on strings right across the pale sky. She allows the water in the stream to talk for no other reason than my amusement, and the foxes she allows to find field-mice, and the little satin shades of the bluebells she allows to remain untorn by the night wind.

Then I wish I could plead to be spared charain. I want to say: this is enough.

The lilacs spread their perfume at dusk, the stream babbles. The feeling of feet is already there on the empty path, in its pale, trampled gravel.

This is enough of time and world.

"Yes," Wonda whispers, "there is a time for everything. The time of chickweed and cow parsley is different from the time of the birch catkins. But male flowers and female flowers share the same time, fortunately and wisely enough. And clouds and sand quarries that get overgrown and pit coal and surging forests and lizards and human beings; to each of them there is a season. Your time is now, little Chip, when the ray of sun is creeping up the stone wall, and it is past when the wall is in shadow."

When Wonda says that I feel the taste of expired time in my mouth and when she has gone into the dappled shade of the alders and vanished I feel dreadfully abandoned. I have been left to the dirt of Karun, to the stink of carrion from the sewers, the clouds of excrement from the cars and the oil-scented band of death that runs through the world, and where the foxes lie in black blood.

But when Wonda has withdrawn I am permitted to invoke her. If she wishes to be called she will allow herself to appear, and the words for Wonda are these:

> sticks and stones
> shards and bones
> stubs and straw
> press them close
> press them close
> broken glass
> bones in bits
> wooden twigs

shards of stone
little pile in the grass
wet tracks
snailshells
moldy smells

mana
mana
mana

in this rain
in this rustling
I shall find thee
I shall find thee

mana
mana
mana

with my hard nails
with Henning's worn pen
with my bony fingers
with head and kidneys
with blood and spit
with shards and bones
sticks and stones
smell of mould
wet tracks
snail slime
shells and rays
dusks and haze
rustle of leaves

mana one
mana two
mana three

mana sticks in stones
mana shards in bones
follow tracks of snails
down the wettest trails
darkness and mull
bones with no fill
oblivion and death

shut your eyes
close your mouth

but there!
in the leaves
gleaming eyes
and a blade of grass swaying
there
there

This time I was transported to Choryn at great speed, I was taken from the band of death and slung into the dimension with no consideration for my long absence and the bursting membranes of lung and brain.

The lessons began at once and continued uninterrupted in materializations but also in long periods of gray haze before my eyes during which only voices from Choryn informed me of what I ought to know. I just recognized a very small number of them and was astonished over how many voices Choryn possessed, realizing that up to this point I had only been permitted to experience a mere pinch of salt from the seas and worlds of Choryn, and that these granules still singed the tongue.

One evening I was lifted above the gray haze and transported to an amphitheater. The stage was far below, with the performance about to begin, and the Bewilderer had stepped forth in his fluttering silk suit and had begun to set up the props. The light sliced wide white bands across the stage, and where the bands of light crossed, on his face and his long, lithe hands, it was intense and blinding. I waited for the performance to begin, perhaps with a wave of the Bewilderer's hand and a swish of silk in flashes from purple violet to sulfur yellow. But suddenly I became aware that it was beginning beside me, it was beginning just next to the seat I was in. A crack opened in the floor just there. It widened, displaying shifting images in black, white and red, no other colors. These images did not represent anything known to me, they did not resemble, did not depict anything. When the Bewilderer performed with his wand and his sweeping cloak, I had anticipated being shown silk scarves and doves and hearing words. But nothing of the kind took place; I was chilled by the beauty of the performance but unable to comprehend the images succeeding one another, and no one uttered a single word to aid me.

When the crack in the floor was at its widest it became rectangular and its color a perfect, deep black. Then a little object was handed to me from the side to play with in the expanded opening. It was artfully fashioned and the size of a small apple or a plum. At the time it called forth no associations, but in retrospect it reminds me of a little skull or of a dried bean inside a whistle. I tried to play with it but I didn't know what I was supposed to do. In the end I threw it down the black opening. I wanted so badly to do it right! But I knew it would never hit bottom. When I listened for the sound of it finally landing somewhere against something and bouncing back resounding or being swallowed up in a torrent all I could hear was a soundless NEVER, like a tone out of the black depths.

I was extremely frightened, far beyond the fear in Choryn, frightened in that sticky, tormented way you can be in Karun, and I began praying to God. I prayed anxiously and intently for light. I suppose I knew this was the wrong place and the wrong god to pray to, but I was praying for my life and my sanity. After a while it got lighter but not like when the lights are turned on by God, or anyone else in Karun. Instead a dawn-like light forced its way through the cracks and interstices between the rows and I thought of the hymn: "Like springtime sun in morning sheen our Lord appeared where dark had been." Choryn responded to this insipid saccharine effusion by making the light blanch and go gray. It was now full daylight around me and I could see that the entire amphitheater was full of spectators I hadn't noticed earlier. The Bewilderer was now dressed in his black suit and was noisily gathering up his paraphernalia. Shortly thereafter it all faded away in grayness and I was left alone with a dry, metallic taste in my mouth.

If I go into a room ticking with Karunish reality, that room appears empty to me between the accumulations of matter. Manifestations of Karun tend to clog together, piling up along the walls, hanging down from the ceiling, and lying thrashed out in slices on the floor.

But Choryn only needs to brighten up this reeking reality for me to see the dancing of the amps in the air. It isn't empty! There is no vacuum in Karun, everything is thick with amps. Nor are the accumulations of matter as solid as they first appear. In them, too, the amps dance in their whirling patterns filled with chor, and this dust resembles fire-bearing flies. I lay my forehead on the table and the fire-flies make it hover with their regular, ceaseless dance, they keep the surfaces apart with their little twirling bounces, and their movements are so quick that the skin on my brow never has a chance to comprehend the vacuum between the sparks. My hand is also swirls of Choryn's charged golden dust which becomes weight and fumes in Karun, my skin is dry fireflies and my nails emit their sparks.

Choryn has enabled me to see this, counterpoising Always Whirling Glittering Burning Never Ceasing Pattern of Firefly Dance against Solid and Immobile and Heavy.

But when I am being punished I can lie for ages and see nothing but particles of skin and fingernails whirling in the air, mutely they fall like snow, always down, and little grains of hair and rugs mix with bits of clothes and books and bread. It wants nothing but to fall, and one thing is mixed with another to a dirty brown, dull grim agglomeration, to slush and grime, to falling time. Yes, all this falls in Karun time like snowflakes float home to their god. And Karun falls and falls steadily, trailing a veil of filth, a train of vapors and particles.

Wonda comes to me in my grief. She transports me out of the zones of clogged up dirt and of rubbish that has begun to lose its stench, like the wilted petals of a rose finally go dry and odorless. The white spot on her throat signals to me from far ahead in a tunnel of green and she whispers:

"To every thing there is a time, Little Shard, to every thing a time. The time of stones is heavier than yours and the time of trees is also stronger and heavier than yours, and yet lighter than the stones. The stones speak, they whisper and mumble but you cannot hear them in your time, and only very seldom can they speak with the trees."

When I stand facing the bright stone, head bowed, and when the soot slowly falls to my forehead and to the shiny surface of the stone, I suddenly see Wonda dancing between the trees. On a stone that has been laid flat, she takes a leap, cruel and lovely and playful, but also gentle and comforting. I think: down there is the subsoil and your solace can't reach that far down; nothing can grow there. It is not even any good as nutrition for a corpse, and no trees can grow out of the subsoil. Their roots are higher up, I know that now.

Wonda dances on the stone in the patch of sunlight like a little leopard. She says:

"Just stand there and go on grieving. It's good for you! But you won't be able to stand there as long as the tree. And when all the trees are dead, a long, long time from now, what is condensed at the very core of the stone will awaken: it will make a movement."

I stand and follow the roots of the tree under the earth and feel their ends seeking between the stones and the mull, searching with thin, blind fingers until they find salts and water. Then trembling little follicles rise all over the finger-threads that have been drawn through the earth and they open wide, transparent to the granules of earth that have fastened onto them and they drink and suck and swell. The salts rise in the water and all the heavy, bright granules of the decomposed stone rise to the light.

But below that is the subsoil where the corpses lie. However they may try, they can never nourish a tree. They are too deep. They are enclosed in iron urns, they are burned and unable to extend their decomposed fingers to search for salt and water. But Wonda dances on the stone in patches of sun and leaves.

"Just stand there and go on grieving," she says. "Just imagine, Shard, when all the trees are dead what is deep in the stone will awaken — and then …"

And then? When the stone begins to give birth. Little dancing cruel Wonda is close to me and slithers out of and into Karun like the snake slithers into and out of new skin. She can comfort me and her lessons are playful. But the lessons to be learned from Choryn also come in the form of pure charain, dense and explosive. I get too much charain and want to beg to be spared. But Ishnol does not cease to enlighten me. Time and again she walks sparkling through the haze of vapors around me and stands out octahedral, distinct. I cannot pull back from Ishnol because she follows me in other formations or comes formlessly, as moss-like masses; white Ishnol may suddenly blacken my fingers, settling on everything I touch.

I had withdrawn into Robor, lain down tired in her old skin and tried to be nowhere, reached by no one, when Ishnol broke through the wall again and again. For a while I believed I had been released and left to my fate like an old hide on a floor. But then I heard the familiar rattling of the Paraphernalia and knew that Ishnol had sent the Bewilderer to me.

He entered the room in his old black cape, lugging his case in the Karunish way. It made me sick to see him screwing together the pieces of the stand, where flakes of nickel had left tired yellow wounds on the metal, and to see him laying out the bits of rubber, slack now, that would be balloons. He stretched them between his fingers as if checking that they were whole and could bear the strain, as he gave me a look that was meant to be mischievous but was nothing but false and repugnant. He folded the sleazy pieces of silk and packed them into varnished boxes, and without minding that I was watching the whole business he set up false bottoms and invisible hinges. Then he took a step forward, opened his cloak so the purple lining flashed, quickly so as not to reveal grease stains and straining seams. He put one foot behind the other, bending his body in a bow that was ingratiating and shameless at once — and the performance began.

The wand! I didn't want to see his old wand. Grinning, he held it straight out so it was pointing at me. Would I be so kind as to measure it? I took the measuring tape from the table in front of him and did as he told me since I knew there was no point in refusing. Then he swished his wand and it gleamed in the air. Finally, he held it still right in front of me. It was now resting, horizontal, the ends left-to-right. Once again I had to measure it and pretend to be amazed at the result.

"You are surprised," he said. "You are astonished because the length of the wand has changed — and just because it is pointing in an unusual direction."

No, I was no longer surprised. I was nothing but tired. I knew his wand was merely a swarm of amps charged with chor and migma. They rushed about shoving for space and always keeping their distance from one another but none of them could be held down long enough to get a clear idea of how far that distance was because then you would cause that fragile structure of swarming, dancing amps to come crashing down. There was no measurable distance between them, they simply had a tendency to keep a certain space and they swarmed and whirled around that point, around their own tendency to stay together and shove for space, it was a trend, if you like, and that trend began to expand in my room; it's always your tired old wand before my tired old eyes, oh Bewilderer who can no longer bewilder anyone.

"Oh, no?"

No, I know your tricks all together too well now. I know that when you set that wand moving its chor changes, becoming an-chor and out of an-chor something else is born, another kind of force the name of which is migma. You wave your wand, Bewilderer, and all its amps call forth migma that does combat with chor and the distance of the amps to one another changes, their swirling, twirling patterns become different and when I measure your wand it is shorter now and it would no longer surprise me if you could also make it droop. No, nothing would surprise me any longer and I wish you would leave me in peace.

But he does not leave me, and from a high point gleaming like white ice Ishnol is observing the lamentable performance, though I don't know it yet. The room where I am lying now rushes at two hundred sixty thousand kilometers per second right up towards her vantage point and the Bewilderer extends an arm with its threadbare tail-coat fabric and raises it from vertical to horizontal as if he were saluting a passing troop. I see his arm being compressed to half its length and, queasy, I turn my head.

"You don't believe me?"

"Oh yes, I believe you, sir."

"Measure."

I have to measure his goddamn arm both vertically and horizontally, and the measuring tape reads seventy-five centimeters in either direction, no more, no less.

"But you saw my arm being shortened with your own eyes. Don't your trust the tape measure? Or your eyes?"

And yet I know the answer: every centimeter on his tape measure shrinks to half when I hold the tape vertically.

But now he repeats his movement and his arm no longer appears to shrink. Relieved, I sink back onto the bed. That makes him laugh.

"You do not seem to have taken account of the fact that a moment ago, when you stood up, your retina contracted to half its original diameter! And now I ask you this: are you exaggerating or reducing all the vertical distances to twice the length of the horizontal ones?"

Although I know there is no use having words with him, I say:

"I intend to go on lying here. I will not bother to get up again. I intend to lie on my couch and watch in the mirror on the wall as you raise and lower your arms and wands. Thus there will be no contraction of my retina and you will no longer be able to deceive me."

"Ha!" shouts the charlatan, spinning an absurd pirouette in his cracked patent leather shoes. "Mirror! Mirror! What do you think a mirror renders? The mirror moves at two hundred sixty thousand kilometers per second and the light bounces back at an entirely different angle than the one at which it shot into the mirror."

The shed wall in the schoolyard. I remember tiredly how I was playing ball against the wall of that shed when suddenly the whole little shed with the dustbins and gardening equipment rushed diagonally upwards in space and my ball shot like a projectile from a canon out of the wall and vanished at an angle behind me.

"Etcetera, etcetera and so forth," the Bewilderer chattered. "Propose any changes you please as we go on! Any speed! Hone yourself down to the zero position and lie flat on your bed — you think you're ground down — ha! ha! — but I'm tricking you, I'm duping you all the time. Nothing stands still. The floor moves, the bed shifts, the mirrors come crashing down! Your retina moves in

121

waves, your old tape measure with its cracked digits slithers like a tortured serpent. My arm, my wand, your eyes are on fire! Ha!"

A paltry spectacle. My eyes are so tired. Oh, Ishnol, why do you torment me so? Is this the only form of charain of which I am worthy, the tricks of a conjurer performed in the light of lamps that have seen better days and in the smell of sweat and make-up?

And Ishnol does not respond.

She does not respond.

I do not dare to invoke Ishnol, butterfly with gold dust on her trembling wings. I am the blind larva, I creep yellow and fat in the filth she has left behind.

Ishnol has held me in her stalactite claw, saying:

"I have seen you once more, little Flake. There may be hope for you after all. There may be something to what you were saying about BECOMING. I do not see a pointer in your bottom, it's not that clear. But I do see a hint, a tendency."

For the sake of that hint, Ishnol has given me a task: I am to eat her waste. What happens is this: for every metamorphosis Ishnol goes through she burns the space around her, and fragments of what burns fall and settle like a kind of soot, a sludge that collects, and it is not difficult to see how these filthy materializations would end up if they were allowed to proliferate at will: new Karuns, endless new Karuns, a Karun in a Karun in a Karun: until the mass of Karun was so condensed it collapsed into itself and burned up. Ishnol has given me the task of consuming this sludge. Fat and yellow I creep behind her, my body feeding on her refuse. I am to eat Karun and liberate it. It is to go through my body and when it has come out of me I am to eat it again and again until the small amount remaining is so miniscule it can neither be weighed nor measured, is nothing but a dry odorless dust that whirls in the winds from the beating of Ishnol's wings. This is my great task alongside the Alphabetization and the preservation of The Codeform.

I live in a core. Ishnol has allowed me to say this.

Deep down in the most secret room of the house I safeguard The Codeform. Its force may cause the film covering the world to burst, but I have been set to protect it and prevent the explosion. This is re-sponse-ability. From out of the re-sponse-ability a force I did not previously possess is being generated.

I want to follow Ishnol when, blinding as white fire, she goes through dimension after dimension, but I cannot. I cannot keep up with the eating, cleaning up after her transformations, and Ishnol has to leave me in zones that are dreary and derelict, that reek of desolation, that are godforsaken holes or even worse: the Slab.

On the Slab I am subjected to all the inconstancy and all the derision that can occur in the borderland between Choryn and Karun. There I am approached by the Garbles, with their salacious sneers. They always stick together, extending appendages for each other to hang on to, to hook into, to intertwine in. They wriggle around, tittering their proposal: now let's Play Games.

I know their games, there's never anything new to them, they rock and sway to the same tired old melodies. I have to trot around their circle, and they raise and lower their arms to their rhythmic song, claiming that chance will decide who is caught in the end, but I know it will always be me. They let me choose between Stone and Sky, between Time and Space and between Sun and Earth, but whatever choice I make they laugh and say it was wrong or I can't choose that one. I don't understand how they can have power over me when they are more obtuse than I am. If only I had some time, if only I could drown out that droning chant and attract their attention I would prove to them that there is a difference between Sun and Earth and between Space and Time. I would tell them I can shut my eyes and still feel that I endure; I feel the marrow of time in my bones. But I do not feel the space. I can never feel my extension when I shut my eyes. So therefore, I would like to tell them, my extension is far more mystical than my survival, despite the fact that you say it's the other way around, and my body is more incomprehensible than my soul, Garbles. Listen to me!

But they laugh their muddied laugh, that chits and chats in the air around the Slab. Then they take hold of my body and beg me to tell them if I am Fish or Fowl, Fly or Butterfly. When I say Fly! they pull off first one of my wings and then the other shouting: Fly now, then! And I have to trip out onto the Slab in my pain, they force me forward, I cannot take off and I must not fall. Then they tear off my legs shouting: run then, carrion! and I creep on my stomach and they laugh at this monstrosity that is neither Fly nor Fish but only pain and weight.

"She is a Book!" they shout, and bend me back and start turning my pages. They turn past the first few pages, exposing my stinging membranes and I scream out in fear because I know they can hurt me.

"Now we're going to read you," they yell, quite distracted with glee, laughing, "now we'll read all your secrets!"

They turn more and more pages but find nothing, and they drive their earth-covered fingers into me saying: "Nothing! There's nothing here. Nothing but emptiness!"

Then they tire of the Book-Game and let me go. One of them, whose name is Wagtail, gives me a kick while I'm still spread-eagled and some liquid from the vessel she's holding sloshes over me and penetrates me, rank and fetid.

"Now you can decide what you want to give birth to," she says. "A bull calf or a hairy baby ape? You give it some thought. There's time."

The worst part is, Great Ishnol, that when I have been in these zones of disease and depravity for so long, I become accustomed to it. In the end I sometimes have a shameful sense of being at home. I resign myself, like a wounded fox in a trap. Because I no longer know there is anything else. I do not sense worlds beyond the urine-stained cement and filthy bars of the pit. When they cease to plague me, I sometimes retreat with a feeling of having returned home. With an exhausted, almost satisfied sigh I make myself comfortable in the rotting straw.

Ishnol allowed me to see the Magician again. He did many tricks before my eyes but my attention was not focused on what he was trying to show me. I was looking at a swelling on his forehead just below the sharp line of his black hat. I saw it getting redder and the skin pulling taut over it. While the old Bewilderer worked with his wands and his double-bottomed trunks, the carbuncle on his brow began to shine and look as if it were going to burst, and I waited for the moment it would crack and the mixture of blood and pus would well out. But the red was so bright it was as if there were a great heat concealed beneath the skin. I began to imagine there was a fire burning in there. Now his forehead was covered in sweat and the skin was contracting in convulsions and under the thin tissue that now shone and was about to explode the carbuncle shone brighter and clearer for every moment. It came into my mind that a precious jewel was about to be born, a ruby or a diamond to be forced out through that heat.

In great excitement I waited for the birth of the gem, never taking my eyes from the brow of the Bewilderer in spite of the way his hands were moving in front of me like old bald birds with creaking wings, and his wand was flashing and the silk scarves fluttering on their strings.

Then the boil burst. In a stream of blood-colored water and pus, a little fetus was rinsed out. It moved feebly, was a sickly yellow color and its tiny extremities lay curled into the body as if it had cramps. It was an odious child, nothing but hair and teeth and flesh. I could see that it was unfit for life, that it was bringing nothing but contagion with it into the world and I wondered if I would be given the task of killing it. I sensed, in spite of the frailty of the little body, that it would not be easy. There was a diseased and dogged force in the compacted limbs of this child, and under its tightly shut eyelids.

At that moment, Ishnol crossed the dimension forcefully and her voice called out, as if from within a bell of incandescent ice:

"You, who have seen yourself born, now rest!"

I retreated to my cage, trying to make the straw cover the cold, filthy cement. I was grateful to Ishnol for having spared me from the killing and the shame. I was to have even greater solace: through the bars I saw Wonda dance, her furry back bright and shiny. She sang to me wordlessly and her song penetrated the sores and cracks in my skin.

"Look at me," she enticed me. "Learn to keep your fur clean. Do not soil it with breeding. Karun is teeming with breeding and births. The newborns swarm on the grassy fields they roam and graze, they teem in the lung tissue and they cluster around the reeds. Karun is stained and besmirched with birthing, there is nothing pure there. It decays in the sun and new hordes are hatched that will live off the rotting remains of their predecessors."

"Come to me," Wonda entices, "learn to live in purity with shiny fur. Learn to live like a beast of prey with clean teeth. Little Shard-of-chip-of-bone, you need polishing in the sun and honing in the wind to make you hard and sharp and pure so no rotting remains can adhere to you."

Wonda dances in the sun among the swaying blades of grass and their rootholds, with rays of sun and of thin blades of grass on her face. She slips with her shiny beak between the thin petals of the pale pink blossoms, and gleams among the anthers, in their golden pollen. Now she glides like the shadow of small fry over a light, sandy bottom. I cannot touch her and soon I can no longer see her. I can only see the rapid shifts of light, the ripples of sand, stirred up by nothing but the light.

Thin ripples borne by soft winds. Wonda wanders in the ripples, touching only the very surface of the water with her dancing feet. The sudden depths are immobile and black and feel no wind.

Ishnol abandoned me. She left me in the borderland. Here I can hear the distant voices of Choryn, but they are distorted by the cutting, pounding, slamming sounds from Karun and I cannot distinguish the words. They are distorted, chattering like apes out of the radiators and off the walls. I cannot see anything. I rest in gray mist, blanketed, surrounded by wet, damp skin, and the taste and smell of rancid fat. In the far corners of the room feet are shuffling, and I sense the groans and sighs of some huge being. I know nothing about how large she is or what she looks like. I can guess at her characteristics from the sighs she occasionally emits, which sound like the belches of an aching stomach. She doesn't bother putting on airs with me, she holds back neither her burps nor her farts. I have been abandoned in the borderland with this witch who imposes her presence upon me, makes herself intimate with me through her gusts of intestinal wind and this constant, discontented shuffling of her feet.

I do not know her name or what she is but I have begun to call her the Shuffle. It's a cheap name, no more than an invention, but I can think of no other. I am paralyzed with the tedium and despondency. When I have fallen asleep she sometimes pokes at my face with her fingers, and in the instant I awaken I can feel her groping and smell her unwashed skin, and I sense her having felt me in my sleep and grown familiar with every nook and cranny of my body.

As soon as I am awake and alert she withdraws to the most distant corner of the room, where she goes on sighing. I could say I detest her if it were not for this awful intimacy I am unable to deny. I know I know the Shuffle, I feel her all over my flesh. Sometimes I sense her wanting to enter me or force herself upon me, and I have to be on my guard unremittingly.

But I cannot always do it. The gray haze and the chatter from the radiators and walls fatigues me. Sometimes I fall asleep and then I am defenseless against her fiddling fingers. Sometimes I hear one of those long, trembling sighs and feel as if they are driving right through me.

I lie in this room with the impenetrable gray haze and I lie in the body of Robor, unable to move it or to raise myself out of it. It is as if the presence of the Shuffle in this room imposed upon me the thought that I truly am Robor. I have no other domicile than her old, tired and abused body. I know all its sores and lumps, I feel the nails scratching the wounds open and I have sucked at her bony knees. Time after time I try to rise up out of her but I have no strength at all.

I think sorrowfully that perhaps I am Robor, and that my fear may be nothing more than a contraction of her tired pelvis and my love no more than her violently aching heart muscle and the fine perspiration of her groin, a plague of presence, an allergic reaction. The nausea, the gushing saliva and the stinging behind the eyelids — that's me. I am imprisoned in this slack sac. I want to turn inward, backwards into the fetal hiding place of my soul. I have to find it somewhere. It has to be there with its fine, moist, membranes, its water, its primal salt and its plasma. I have to search stealthily without awakening the big witch over there in the corner; seek with my eyes closed and charged by the little electric shocks of neuron colliding with neuron. And there — carambolage! My stomach contracts. My mouth goes dry. I am frightened. I have invoked a god from the stone. I am here — internal to myself. Alien. I reach for the stranger and embrace a room and I do it as

126

silently and as furtively as I can so the Shuffle will not notice. But at the same moment the chattering around me expands, and I can make out that they are mocking me and spitting out pejoratives about me, saying that all I found was words, that it was nothing but words I embraced and words I ate and spat up half-chewed and words I gave space to and words I gave arms and necks and kneecaps and intestinal coils to, words.

I try to drown the chatter from the hot radiators and from the crumbling walls. I talk and talk so as not to hear them, but their voices penetrate and speak from inside me instead of through the cracks in the wallpaper and the parched clay air humidifiers hanging on the radiators. They force me to make their voices my own and they say:

"You talk, your tongue flutters and air puffs out of your little holes, you talk all those words and turn away from us but we can give you words, too, if it's words you want, poisoned one. Words of lust, words of air we can give you from Chosma, words with tails, blood words, iron words, words rustling down like sand between stones, water words, fog words, words of steam, of hot, spraying water, ice words, insulting words, knife words, harm words, clamping vice words, weighted words, arrow words, rot words rushing and rushing — enamel words and words of scented wood, words of singing wood and running water, bird words, ape words, dog words and words for serpents, the crooked words of scorpions' tails, words that flutter, and dirt, and the words of fragile petals of sweet peas, all such words, crumpled, preserved through the winter, for thousands of winters under ash, pickle words in ink, fresh and sour like little berries, dead tomorrow as dust and cut-off nails, dead words and life words, blood words, lust words, words of air if you like, Shard, whatever you like …"

And I beg them to stop and go back into their radiators but they do not yet leave me, not for a long time and when they finally withdraw from me and can once again only be heard as a noise from the walls, I am alone with the Shuffle. I listen to her heavy breathing in the corner and feel her grope at me the moment I doze off.

I have to stay awake. I must not let the Shuffle heave down on top of me or sneak her way into me. But I do not know how to keep guard or to whom I should pray. My fatigue is so deep, it comes up out of Robor's spent kidneys and out of her nearly exhausted heart muscle.

Is there no death? Is there no end?

For a very long time I was Robor. I thought her thoughts and did not notice her smell.

She is one long skin, a casing of flesh held up by bones as tightly set as the stays in a corset. She encloses a tube into which nourishment goes down and comes out again; she is that tube. I was Robor and felt the sluggish mass pass through me with heavy, jarring movements. Day after day I was given over to this process; I was nothing but a container for it.

Inert, indolent Robor, whose sores I no longer had the energy to keep open shuffled on and had penetrated right into me. We moved like body and shadow on the wall. I had become Robor and the only thing that reminded me of the existence of Choryn was the voices. But they were now so distant I was unable to distinguish their words. They were mocking me but what they were saying was impossible for me to understand. Even Choryn's words had taken on that heavy, sludge-like consistency in Robor's inner world. They clogged and could no longer be separated.

I went in Robor's body to the toilet and I went to the kitchen. This was her regular stamping ground. There was nothing else to her. The voices were unable to pull her anywhere. Then one morning when I turned around I saw that my bowel movement resembled loose earth and that there were maggots in it. One had a black belly and fine legs, thin as hairs. Its back was shiny and reddish brown with slippery skin. One of them was grayish white and extremely soft with a whole slew of arms or legs. I shook it out and the soft, convoluted skein fell into a regular pattern.

I took this to be a message from Ishnol that my life was once again imbued with purpose and pattern. I was filled with the joy and fear that are anticipation. And suddenly Ishnol broke through! She came straight towards me in an enormous shaft of light that transported her through layer upon layer of the gray, heavy stuff in bolt upon bolt of compact white fire. Between us there was no longer anything other than a thin, trembling film. It never burst but was dissolved after Ishnol's sixth or seventh flash in the light, like polycrystalline gold leaf, and a dust of tiny granules of gold settled on my skin and my outstretched arms.

She kept on coming, but shapeless throughout. Each time, she dazzled the threads of fiber in my tissue and they expanded so I could receive her whole. She came in waves from a sea of rocking multicolored light, in violet and purple waves and arches that met my grayness and kindled it. I was able to follow her from the white spears of fire to the yellow licking mat of flame that sank down into me in redder and redder waves until it ran off in a hot molten stream from my sides. She was vaporized out of her own crater in plumes of yellow and phosphorescent green smoke and sank back again in silent explosions only to pulsate anew into me as long as I was able to open up to her and receive the huge bolts of light. I was a wide-open eye prepared to absorb deeper blindings with every jolt forward and I went on receiving until I noticed that her light was growing thicker and its edges sooty. Then I sank back and heard her voice saying:

"Now, shit-eater, you have your work cut out for you."

Through me runs the way from Choryn into Karun, through me streams Chosma. It may not find its way out, I must store it up and become a vessel for it. If it were to leak out into Karun, the membranes would bleed and burst. It would be a mixture of forms and that blend would be impure. Karun might take over and transform it to mire and mush. I can hold Chosma on the head of a pin or in an infected sore that will not heal. That is my task and I do it through the Alphabets, through the preservation of The Codeform and through eating the slag produced by the breakthroughs of Ishnol. I get more and more charain, although I often have to wait for it, lying in Robor's body for long periods of time. Ishnol comes, bringing Chosma in waves, but I cannot affect their amplitude.

Sometimes she gives me charain gently and allows me to wander through grand habitations and halls to obtain it. That is a blessed existence. I am well suited to it. She has arranged it to enable me to bear it and be in it like a frog in its wet warm pond. I sometimes think she looks down at me with a smile when I am in it, mischievous and attentive.

I want to tell about the time I arrived at one of Ishnol's palaces and saw a huddled figure sitting on the drawbridge. He upset me because it seemed to me he belonged in Karun with his shabbiness and his shrewd, ingratiating grin. I wanted to hurry on past him but he stopped me. I was forced to look at him and remember his ragged garments. On top, he was wearing a sleeveless jacket of matted hide. I tore myself from his sight and vanished into the halls of Ishnol but he kept reappearing at the edge of my field of vision. He was a sty.

He tormented me with his returnings and in the end he had sunk me so low by constantly forcing me to combat his presence that I was lying in Robor's body once again. Her sharp vertebrae were poking my body when I tried to find a restful position. Then I noticed that I was so close to him I was looking straight into the yellow, matted hide. Although a moment ago it had filled me with repugnance just to see it from a distance, my gaze was now drawn into it and I wished my eyes had been able to smell it.

He sat on the edge of my bed so close I was unable to take in his entire body at once and he took my hand and raised it to his chest.

"Feel," he said.

And I felt under the skin of my fingers the soft matted covering on his chest and he helped me sit up with one arm behind my back. Once I was sitting my face fell towards him and I buried it in the shaggy creamy sheepskin that smelled of food and tobacco. I rubbed my face into it and wept.

The Stories

My father's name was Henning. He was beautiful. I remember that his hair was soft and that it curled, despite his efforts to tame it with hair tonic and a side part. It was the color of fine-grained sand, and some strands sparkled the way white crystals of quartz on the beach glitter to the keen eyes of a child. Other strands were dark or red. He was neither tall nor ungainly, but a very fine-boned man of medium height. He was also a genius.

I don't know when people began to realize it because he never talked about his childhood. He grew up in rooms over the courthouse where his father was caretaker, and where they also rented out lodgings to the law clerks who came to town when the court was in session. His mother cleaned the rooms, made the beds and cooked the meals. She wore a hat when she went out shopping and was probably of what people called "a cut above."

Henning lost his father when he was fourteen and I don't know what happened when he left school. The war was on then. Things can't have been easy for him. He was out of work for several years in the early twenties, when he took evening classes at the Technical School. He studied mathematics, chemistry, physics and German, and learned the basics of draftsmanship. But he was also away from town for a few years. His mother had married again, a man with a smallholding in Åsen, a few miles out of town. People have told me that she didn't want anything to do with him in her new life. I once asked him if it was true, but he laughed a little and said it was an exaggeration.

I don't know much about his life before he met Lisa, but I do know that at the time he was working at Swedish Engineering, in the drafting office. I suppose he walked through to the yard behind her father's house and looked around, glanced up the walls, walked over and tried the door of the laundry building. He'd heard there was a something for rent. I imagine him as elegant even though he had very little money. Maybe he had an overcoat belted in back and a soft hat of brushed felt with a black satin band around the crown.

It was my maternal grandfather's idea to put up a laundry behind his grocer's shop. There was an upstairs room, intended for mangling. But it had proved to be too much for people to drag their heavy laundry baskets up the stairs, so no one had rented his mangle.

The mangling room wasn't in use and Lisa wasn't spoken for. In the long, narrow room above the washhouse Henning set up a drafting table and a workbench with vices. Did he occasionally see Lisa in her kitchen window? Was there just as much ivy outside the window then?

He didn't have many tools and it never got cluttered or dirty up there. There were protractors and gauges, of course, tongs and clamps, screwdrivers with pear-shaped handles and hammers that looked like small plump horses' heads with their ears back. He used fierce little wire cutters and steel scissors with lizards' jaws. I liked watching him work with them, but he thought I should learn their real names too. What I remember best are the beautiful French precision files called fluteroni and barrettes.

If he needed something turned or drilled he had to take it to a machine shop, and of course he couldn't do any forging up there either.

My father didn't have a workshop yet for the simple reason that he didn't produce anything. He was an inventor.

I've sometimes wondered where he and Lisa went when they wanted to be alone. There was no bed in the room above the laundry. I'm sure he couldn't take her back to his room in the boarding house. Did they make love in the attic? Or did they borrow someone's room? Maybe other people in the building were privy to their secret.

When I was born in the winter of 1935 they had been married for four months. They lived with Abel and Sigrid. Of course they were supposed to move to a place of their own as soon as they could afford it. They never did. Sigrid's arthritis got worse and finally she had to be put into a home for the chronically ill. Lisa, who had already been running the household for several years, couldn't abandon Abel.

I think Abel and Sigrid were kind people. But what I remember most clearly about them are frightening details: Abel's cataract-blinded eye, and Sigrid's hands, twisted with pain, on a blanket, a paintbrush handle protruding between thumb and forefinger. She painted bouquets of flowers and some still lifes of vases and fruits. She was determined not to succumb to the pain that was crippling her hands. I still have one of her paintings of a bowl of flowers on a lace doily. They're violets, with small, evil monkey-faces staring out. It's as if, in the end, the crippling pain left its mark on everything she tried to do. Her late snowdrops no longer wept, but just

133

hung heavy, yellow and inflamed.

My first memory of Henning is in the kitchen. He's watching Lisa work, then stops her from turning the handle of the food mill and, his hand on hers, rotates it so slowly the applesauce just barely seeps through.

He couldn't see an ordinary kitchen gadget, be it an onion slicer, a nut grinder, an egg chopper or any other device, whatever its degree of complexity, without wanting to improve on it. True reverence he felt only for the simplest of things, the whisk and the corkscrew. He studied Lisa beating egg whites and his gaze followed the movements of her hand and the symmetrically arranged wires working air into the viscous substance, willing its metamorphosis. He swept a flyswatter through the air in slower and slower circles. Eventually I too thought I could see the air flowing silently through the tiny holes that perforated it and I understood why the flies failed to notice it before it was too late.

There are people who, when they enter a room, have the habit of stopping and facing whoever is there; they reveal themselves full-figure. Henning does that in my memory. From my early years there is also something that tenses in him when he looks at me. His curls are just about to spring loose from his slicked back forelock. His chin is raised as if he is just about to be photographed.

My mother doesn't do that; she doesn't reveal herself. She slips away, a face of recesses and shadows. I see hands, of course, moving and whisking, flowered apron damp from dishwater and a foot in a brown shoe on the sewing machine treadle. But was that really her? Afterwards I call that Lisa, but it may have been the women who helped us when she had gone away. My memory of Lisa is fragmented into bits of blouse fabric, strands of hair, the smell of food and little coughing sounds.

I only have one complete image of her. She'd already begun going away. She went to a sanatorium. Sometimes she came home and then she went off again. The only time I remember her completely intact was when I was playing in the empty, unheated bedroom. There were marks on the linoleum where my parents' beds had stood side by side.

I knew she had gone away. They said she was far away and that meant she was dead. When people with that look in their eyes told a little girl that her mother had gone far, far away she was just as dead as the lifeless fish I'd found on the stones at the beach. There was something about it all that made me queasy, something about coldness, swelling and stiffness. People didn't talk about it, nor did I want to expose Henning's lie. She'd gone away; that's what they said, and I played on the floor in their unheated bedroom.

I stepped into the wardrobe. Some dresses and blouses were still hanging there. When I pulled them they fell to the floor and I could dress up in them. I put on a silk blouse with multicolored flowers. It had a long row of little buttons, but I didn't have the patience to fasten them. I slid my feet into a pair of Lisa's high-heeled shoes. They were beige suede and brown leather and had knotted tassels. They were so big on me I tottered, parading in front of the mirror.

The mirror was all that was left. The furniture had all been carried out of the bedroom. There were marks on the walls from picture hooks, and all that remained of the pictures were rectangular shadows on the wallpaper. There was a pair of lovely hangers in the closet. They were tightly wound with silk yarn in all the colors of the rainbow, and under the hook they had flowers crocheted in the same yarn. I wanted to take one down but I couldn't reach it. So I grabbed a couple of dresses and shook them. Finally I managed it - several hangers came clattering down, and the clothes with them. This exposed the back wall of the wardrobe, and I saw that it wasn't really a wall at all. It was a door. Not a wallpapered door like the one to the wardrobe, but a heavy paneled door, painted white, exactly like the ones between the rooms in the apartment. I opened it and stepped into another cold, unfurnished room. There was a chair in the middle of the floor and in it sat Lisa. She was dressed in a white nightgown with a gray sweater on top, and her hands were on the armrests of the chair.

She reveals herself clearly to me when I open the door. Her face is young and round with a sharp little chin. She has circles under her eyes, her skin is brownish there and looks delicate. Her mouth is barely visible. It's small and her lips are pale. Her hands keep gripping the armrest of the chair. As her knuckles move they turn white.

That's all. I don't remember any more.

I know I don't have anything to complain about. Every family has its problems, after all. Sorrows and aggravations, major and minor misfortunes, it's always on those terms. But I can't reconcile myself to the fact that it's all gone now. I feel as if I am walking where a forest has been felled, unable to recreate the space around me. It was the trunks and crowns of the trees that once bounded the space, but now they are gone, and so is the moss-covered ground with its boulders and roots. The trees have been cleared and hauled away and the ground is torn up, the roots dislodged. The boulders have been overturned, exposing the vulnerable undersides that no one had seen before. You trip when you step over piles of underbrush and splintered wood that are moldering and rotting. It's death and devastation and little empty mouse holes in the ground, it's dry and charred and hacked to bits.

We had our entryways and holes, our dens and cozy mouse nests under the roots. But we can't find them now. The entries are dead ends now. We provided one another with hiding places; perhaps we were fooling ourselves being pleased and proud of things that would later flutter away and collapse or disintegrate into dry little piles of cinders. It does no good to say that after all, I have my hiding places now too, but under different roots and stones. Those others were mine as well. How can what's mine simply vanish?

We lived at 13 Chapel Road and a hallway ran down the middle of the house, splitting the world in two. On our side there were rotting wooden stairs and worn rag rugs in pale colors. The pane of glass in the door rattled when you opened it and inside the apartment stood Abel and Sigrid's dark furniture in its timeless order. There were pinecones carved in the backs of chairs and owls in gold leaf in the binding of the *Nordic Family Encyclopedia*. There were dead insects in the lamp fixtures; you could see them when the lights were on. Most of it is still there in the material sense just as there is still underbrush and scrap in the cleared areas. But the owls have lost their power, the gold is dull, the pinecones have no fragrance, the specks in the alabaster globe of the lamp are dry and unidentifiable.

Early in the morning in the region between sleep and waking I sometimes find myself in the room with the white curtain. But when I awaken I'm in a strange room and everything that was mine is gone. Nothing happens any more in this desolate place. Henning reveals himself with the wave in his hair, stiff and smiling. Lisa flutters past, a snippet of blouse fabric, a damp spot on a sheet. Deep inside the house is death, tucked away like a heart. The floor is cold but it is real in there. You find this eternal standstill is unbearable. You have to piece stories together.

Henning and I were out for a walk. He was holding my hand and I could feel the thin gray suede of his glove against my bare skin. I was a little worried that my fingers were dirty. We had walked across the footbridge over the railway tracks. There was a Sunday stillness in the air, a heavy foreboding silence that had as little effect on us as the dust and cooking smells have on the polished objects under a dome of glass.

The street was straight and long. Actually, beyond the last house it became a gravel road. We came to a pine-covered hill separating two large homes. There are apartment houses there now, but you can still recognize the spot by the flat rocks between the buildings, although of course they look smaller and more worn. Moss and ferns no longer grow in the cracks. In those days the ground below the rocks was covered with pine needles and the thick roots of fir trees. A woman was squatting there.

She had spread the hide of a newly skinned animal on the ground. The inside shone white, spotted with pink bloodstains. Her manner was deliberate as she sat heaping pieces of meat and large bones on the outspread hide. When she had finished she gathered the corners where the legs had been and tied the whole thing into a bundle. When she left she carried the entire load in her arms.

"That's beautiful," Pappa finally said. I felt solemn. I want to say that we walked on, but I don't remember any more.

Another Sunday:

My grandfather Abel had taken me with him to visit an old man who lived in a little house. The veranda glistened white and the evening sun gleamed brightly on the blue, red and green panes of glass. We had stopped just inside the gate and the old man came toward us. He probed his way along the gravel with his cane, keeping between the large white seashells that bordered the path. Sometimes his cane struck one of the shells, and they sounded as if they were made of china.

When he'd reached us Abel instructed me to give the gentleman my hand. I did as I was told, but then after we'd said hello the man didn't release my hand. He grasped my other one, too, dropping his cane in the gravel. Abel picked it up and stood holding it while the man's hands wandered up my arms and took hold of my shoulders. Then he put the palms of his hands against my chest and groped down to my stomach. I stood stiffly. His hands wandered upwards again, finding my neck, and then he used his fingertips on my face. They were rough and coarse. I shut my eyes. He felt my hair and ears. When his hand wandered back down toward my stomach, I tore myself away and took a step back. But Abel held a firm grip on me and said:

"The blind see with their hands."

Grandfather sat me on his lap and drew a house. Then he divided it in two because the couple who lived there didn't get along. He gave them separate doors with pine branches on the front steps, and separate windows to look out of. The old man saw the old woman leave home with her bucket, and he thought she must be going to the well. She went but she never came back because she fell into a hole. First she got out but she fell back in and then she got out again and fell in again and finally she hurt herself so badly she couldn't get up at all.

So the old man went out to help her. He walked round and round and in the end he fell down where the old woman had fallen and where we all end up sooner or later. And there they both lay.

Right!

But then I looked down at the drawing and it was no longer a house. The whole thing had turned into a cat.

I once saw a hairless ape-like man dressed in a striped suit, his large body rocking back and forth. And yet I know that no matter how clearly I can see him he was not in any of the houses we visited.

Henning had often said that there were two kinds of inventors. One took advantage of nature. He forced her to yield economy, comfort, even pleasure. As child I saw everything in concrete images.

Henning said: he thinks he's creating something out of nothing, but without his paraphernalia, his nuts and bolts, pistons and valves, he's not even capable of seeing the world. It's empty and meaningless to him. But he sees himself as a God stepping down into the paraphernalia to make it rattle and smoke.

Now I know that the man in the striped suit was the Demiurge, a blob of brain tissue on legs. He creates nothing.

Henning didn't talk about the other kind of inventor. But I knew him. He was my father. He was a playful boy and a bold, tender lover. He was surrounded by dormant powers, easily awakened and awesome. He was clever and cunning; he played with the powers and entered into pacts with them. However old the world became and however much it rattled and shook he would always find something to play with.

My father was a shaman although he was born when the world was old and full of gadgets. He always looked closely at whatever was in front of him. That was why he thought it was beautiful to see a woman spread out her apron in the grass and fill it with pinecones for lighting the fire. She wrapped her apron around the load to pull it together and make it easy to carry. He liked to imagine how people had come up with things like that. He saw them standing by the flayed, newly skinned hide of a wild animal. Then he described how they piled bones and pieces of meat onto it, wrapped up the hide and carried the bundle just as the animal had recently so magnificently carried the weight of its body. He liked these simple analogies. He claimed they were man's contribution to the creation.

He showed me a cross-sectional drawing of the spongy parts of the human femur. Alongside it he had placed a sketch of the tensile stresses and strains in the girder of a crane. The principle was identical, except that the girder was a more primitive, less complex construction. It makes me sad to think how clumsy and derivative all our undertakings are. But it never made Henning sad. The only thing that depressed him was that people didn't think about it.

He was a draftsman at Swedish Engineering, but he couldn't support me and Lisa on that. So he had to learn how to make more gadgets.

I don't really think his little invention business was absolutely pristine even before I came along. Henning lived in this world. He wanted nice suits and expensive hair tonic, to go to the barber, have fresh rolls for breakfast, subscribe to a daily paper. And he wanted fame. Yet I don't think he had started palming off widgets and gadgets on others just because he fathered me. He wanted to come to grips with the world; he wanted to find the metaphors that made it resonate.

There's nothing I can substantiate before I was seven and started school, which took place on a given day, in a given year, namely the year Hitler's army was surrounded at Stalingrad and Jenny leaned her forehead against the cabinet above the kitchen sink and cried about the German boys. What had come before hadn't happened. It just was. Lisa hadn't died. She'd gone away.

139

Henning applied for patents on his inventions and then tried to find buyers for his mechanical devices. When he wasn't home I stayed with Jenny and Fredrik Otter. He was a foreman at Swedish Engineering. She told stories about what had happened and, in a way, made them happen.

The same year I started school (and the German boys were locked in at Stalingrad) I began selling sweets at the stall on the square run by Fredrik's mother, whose name was Tora Otter. The next year we learned to add two-digit numbers in school, but I already knew how from handing back the right change at the stand. When I became thin and wan Jenny thought the milk and sandwiches we had in school weren't substantial enough for me. I started going to Tora's for lunch because she lived nearest. It happened because it could be fixed in time; it was the same time the Hungarian refugee who had been staying with Fredrik and Jenny moved away. It was before the bird feeder blew over and before Fredrik got the pipe rack for his fortieth birthday. Jenny had an inexhaustible supply of stories about what was happening and what had happened and I understood that I was living among other people. Before that I had only known about Lisa and Henning and the law of leverage and other great things that were contemporaneous and not mutually exclusive.

Now Jenny made something happen called: Henning has started living it up. It was talked about in low voices and wasn't intended for my ears. At first I didn't really know what she meant but then I worked out it was the brandy. But this hadn't happened. Jenny was wrong. Henning smelled like that; he had brandy on his breath. That was him. You couldn't say he had started living it up. I was supposed to stay with them more and more often because Henning had started living it up or Henning had gone away, "gone away" with a little quaver in the voice, not to be confused with "gone away" with a big quaver. Jenny manipulated events for her own purposes. She wanted me. She had no children of her own so she tied ribbons in my hair and washed out my white anklets. She told me to use toilet paper even when I wee-weed, so my undies would stay clean longer. In short, she was playing mother.

I could see right through her with the side of me that had no history, that was uncivilized and lived in the house at 13 Chapel Road. I also discovered that sometimes she'd tried to fool me. Henning wasn't always gone when she said he was; he was in bed or at the living room table. There were glasses and bottles on it. His head was heavy, resting on the tabletop. But he was there. I got into the habit of checking the house. By then I was living with Jenny and Fredrik, but every time my father was home I was supposed to visit him. The part about every time I had made up myself. I was learning how to write history: every time my father comes home I go visit him.

The living room was stuffy and smoky. There had been men there. He was asleep in his clothes and had forgotten to turn off the light. I pulled the cord, and the room grew dimmer. The streetlight shone through the window, illuminating his face. The tremor in his eyelids was less distressing now. Someone had to be at home and turn off the light and put a blanket over him. I called Jenny and said:

"Pappa's home now. I'm staying with him."

He woke up Sunday afternoon and came out to where I sat drawing in the kitchen. He was glad to see me and asked if I had been there long and if I'd had anything to eat. The first hour was a little bleak. He spent a long time in the bathroom. I heard the bottle of aspirin clatter against the bottom of the bathtub when he dropped it.

When he came out I was making cocoa. He turned away. He couldn't stand the sight of the skin on top. He didn't have any milk so I had to make it with water. I went across to Fru Westman's and borrowed a little cream to dissolve the cocoa in. Pappa didn't want any sandwiches either but he took out a beer.

Everything got warmer and more ordinary toward evening when we could turn on the lights. Pappa cleared the living room table, wiped it, and put on the crocheted silk tablecloth after shaking the ash out of the window. He wanted things neat and tidy. Jenny called him pedantic. That was another of her meaningless assertions. He wasn't pedantic. What there was was an orderly room, a certain pattern that had been disturbed and that the two of us had to restore before everything could become completely real again.

He went to North's Boarding House and brought back roast veal with cucumber salad, boiled potatoes and cream sauce in a cake box with a handle. We warmed up the meat and potatoes and ate at the kitchen table. Afterwards we washed the dishes, not the Jenny-way, but the way dishes were done here at 13 Chapel Road, with detergent and various hot and cold rinses under running water and in the basin. When we finished we sorted the silverware, making piles of knives, forks and spoons. We wiped the oilcloth and gave the kitchen table, worktop and stove a final inspection before going into the study and sitting down.

Pappa sat on a leather armchair next to the wooden Negro servant dressed in a red uniform with a white cravat holding a beaten copper ashtray in his gloved hands. I sat on the floor at their feet. Pappa read the newspaper and I waited, waited silently, with my knees drawn up and all my energy taut like a metal spring inside me. Then he looked over the edge of the newspaper and whispered almost inaudibly:

"Anaximander."

I flew to the bookcase, jumped up onto a dining room chair and took down the heavy volume, the owl resting against my palm, and before I was even off the chair the pages were fluttering and turning. I found Anaximander, read the entry, tested my memory, and finally dared put the book back, return to the study and say:

"He was a philosopher of the Ionian School who held that all things originated in an eternal and immutable primal substance that was, moreover, animate and in perpetual motion. All things derive from this primal substance, to which they also return in order that a new creation may begin and so on and so forth *ad infinitum.*"

He nodded. He looked interested. And he grabbed one of Anaximander's coattails as he flew by, he grabbed the Ionian School, and said the words over the edge of the newspaper and I was flying again, and on it went with rustling pages, with gold leaf and dust from the Ionians and Heron's steam-powered projectile and the Voltaic pile to Papin's pressure cooker through dead space to Huygen's pendulum theory. This game was governed by rules I can't account for now because they developed as we played, grew like a coral reef and spread like the feathers in a peacock's tail from inside Henning's head and from inside mine. He asked about things he didn't know and about things he knew perfectly well. He asked some real quiz show questions - What did it take to build Cheop's pyramid? - and got answers other than those he expected: a hundred thousand men and twenty years instead of two point three million blocks of limestone. Then he raised his head and pursed his lips in a thin, almost imperceptible whistle, and I knew that together we had accomplished something unexpected: a living flower had bloomed in the coral reef pattern of motionless branches, golden owls were flying between us and the air glittered when the sunlight struck particles of golden dust. It was simply fun and good and thoroughly useful. The world was a huge cheese and I crept through the tunnels for him, a hunting hound, a mite, a bookworm. But when I emerged I had the wings of a butterfly. Everything was either useful or beautiful or both, everything was pervaded with meaning in the same way as the cheese, punctured a thousand million times, is still whole and connected.

By late evening when the hunting hound was panting and the butterfly wings were threatening to droop the next time they opened, the telephone rang. In those days it sounded like a bell. Reverberations enveloped the sound of the telephone like crystals of hoarfrost layered on a tree.

We looked into each other's eyes for the entire duration of the silence between the first and the second rings. When the second one spread through the room I walked out into the dark hall and lifted the receiver. I knew exactly what was happening: otherwise I wouldn't have dared answer. When I answered I was talking into an artificial ear. Together, just as Reis had done when he built the prototype, we had drilled a hole in a wooden cylinder, stretched a thin membrane over the hole and glued a tiny blade of metal onto it. There was a metal spring on the blade connecting it with our energy source, a flashing battery. Then we had wound wire to form a coil around a metal spindle. When the sound waves made the spindle reverberate, the membrane and its metal blade were set in motion. So I knew what was taking place, and just as I had suspected, it was Jenny's voice producing the sound waves. It took ages for my brain to decipher them; in fact, it couldn't be done without transformation. Like a trembling little sausage casing connected to a knitting needle I buzzed her words, and Henning reproduced them.

"Of course," he said. "Naturally. Let's go. You have to get up early. Sewing lesson. Yes, of course you'll sleep at their place."

Jenny said "natchully." Henning said "naturally." The world was like that. It was made up of different worlds lying side by side, as one snowflake lies beside another on a branch, silently, as a matter of course.

We walked across town. He had stood by the mirror in the hall watching me tie my cap under my chin. One of the clasps on my galoshes was broken and it clanked and clatttered as I walked.

Now we left the rosy lamplit world where the wings of the golden owls shone, and entered the white street-lit one with black puddles. After passing through five worlds we reached a two-story single-family home where I lived with the Otters. Jenny untied my cap and gave my galoshes to Fredrik to see if he could fix the clasp. I had milk and toast before brushing my teeth and then I lay in bed listening to Henning talk to Fredrik and Jenny. His voice was low and intense. I couldn't hear his words, but I could hear them laughing, frequently, appreciatively, in surprise. All was well. All was really very well.

When I was little, I went to Stockholm with my pappa to visit the Technical Museum. He showed me the lovely old machines from the previous century and demonstrated a model of the solar system. But the most important thing we saw, the true object of our visit, was Christopher Polhem's Mechanical Alphabet.

In those days it hadn't yet been put on display in cases upstairs. Pappa had to request permission to see it and we got to follow a curator and an attendant down into underground rooms. They unpacked the alphabet from cartons and released it from paper and wood shavings. Then they set it up on two shelves. And there stood the little models of darkened wood, no larger than toys and each equipped with the necessary cogs and wheels, dowels, articulated rods and swivel shafts to depict the transfer of power or motion each individual model described. We weren't allowed to touch them. We weren't permitted to use a lever to move the articulated cog-bar up, or to spin the eccentric disc to see how the movement shifted back and forth, back and forth. No, the pendulum hung still now, but if it had begun to swing the cogwheel would have rotated and when the plated shaft began to turn, the upper arm would be jolted into motion.

The attendant in his gray coat stayed with us the whole time with his hands clasped behind his back. He was there to make sure we didn't fiddle with models. He swayed back and forth on his feet in flat black shoes, and never left. We had to imagine it all. That was, of course, very easy, because the little cogs and wheels were so meticulously made that it was all perfectly clear. Pappa often said that our language conserved all the truths and secrets of all inventions, although most people appeared to have lost them long ago. They honestly believed that it was possible to make something new, that there were things they could add to creation. But he said it was complete. Everything had been there from the outset. All the forces existed in the world long before human beings came into it. And what people did was just to find them, pure and simple. They found them in their hiding places. They found them and found things out. And wrote them down. This was Polhem's way

144

of presenting a set of notes, in beveled carving wood, with glue and with pegs. And today we had the opportunity of reading his findings.

I asked Pappa who had activated all the forces in the world. The question, of course, was superfluous. I knew that in school the answer would have been God. But Pappa wasn't interested in him. I don't understand hallucinations, he said. But I liked asking the superfluous question to have him confirm that most of what we learned in school was preposterous and applied nowhere but within those four walls.

Pappa said that the world was full of forces at work. To him, that was the only important thing.

When we stood there in the long underground corridor I felt a cold gust of wind around my legs and when I turned around I saw something that resembled a little gray animal come scurrying along so fast it looked as if it was rolling along the floor. When it got closer it no longer looked like a body but was translucent. The next draft from an open door farther down the cellar moved the round thing in under the cold lamplight and showed that its fur consisted of sparse, loose knit dust with nothing inside. It was swished in under a shelf and vanished. The attendant started rattling his keys in his pocket and we realized we would have to get going.

Understanding the forces at work when the pulley ran through the block or when the cogs interlocked was much easier once you had seen Christopher Polhem's Mechanical Alphabet. But it wasn't a creaking wooden wheel that drove the earth around the sun, and to understand those forces you had to know mathematics.

The principles of mathematics are the alphabet with the aid of which God wrote the world, according to Galileo. At school mathematics was called arithmetic and I found it difficult to master arithmetic reliably. If you had done a problem correctly, the result would be the same whether you did it once or ten thousand times. I failed at that. I would try twenty-seven times, sometimes twenty-eight.

To aid us in our arithmetical operations we were given the multiplication tables on pinkish gray cardboard, and we had to learn them by heart. The cardboard got stained and dog-eared, but I only very slowly succeeded at learning the right answers. Pappa saw how difficult and dull it was and he sat down with me in the study and examined the multiplication table in the light of the lamp with its pink silk shade, which made the tired meaty-gray cardboard of the table nearly colorless. He asked me how much six times six was and I answered thirty-six.

"Are you sure?"

I was, nearly. All the formulas that were rhythmic and where the numbers repeated, I found easy to learn. Seven sevens were forty-seven. Eight eights fifty-eight. He was silent, and just stared at the figures on the paper.

"This would have been easier if our numerical system had been in base five," he said. And then he demonstrated it to me. We moved over to the living room table.

"You have to learn to understand everything from the inside," he said.

Then he showed me how to write five in a base five numerical system: 10.

"In our ordinary numerical system, 10 means one times ten. Here, it means one times five. Six is 11, Seven is 12. What's eleven?

At first I couldn't tell him, but he showed me how it was 21. After a while I had understood the base five numerical system. I could write its numbers and I understood that its multiplication table was different looking. I could add 3 plus four so they made 12. That was impeccably correct, said Pappa. 13 plus 14 was 32.

"There's no saying that ten is the best base for a numerical system," he said. "Twelve might have been better. It has been considered. And is still in use in England. And the Babylonians used sixty. We even use it ourselves when we tell time and measure angles. And no one's the least bit bothered."

After that I understood the multiplication table from inside. When the teacher asked me to repeat the seven times, which was generally considered difficult, I didn't manage it. But I said out loud so the whole class could hear that the base ten numerical system wasn't at all the best one. The teacher looked taken aback, and then he burst out laughing. He carried the class with him in gales of hilarity. I could tell they didn't really know what was so funny by the way they were laughing. Then the teacher brought down his heavy pointer hard on my desktop. It landed just a fraction of an inch from my fingers. He roared at me to recite the seven times. He had made a dent in the yellow varnish on my desktop. After a little while when the class had calmed down and a monotonous girl's voice was intoning the sevens from the back row of the room, I poked about in the yellow powder lying in the injury to the wood. After that slam I was unable to recite any answers by heart at school. Verses of hymns did take shape in my head when he asked me to recite them, but in a form my instinct for self-preservation told me not to let out. While the class waited for my answer in tense silence, I sat there mute, the words resounding in my head:

Oh Lord our aged help in past
Our hope for ears to come
Arithmetic impossible
Just smile and head for home.

146

Or in some other equally unutterable form.

Henning had talked about Forces and Laws on the train home from the Technical Museum in Stockholm. The rain had been coursing down the window panes as the train thundered us closer and closer to our neck of the universe where neither laws nor forces applied, but where everything grew unpredictably and seemed to have taken shape any which way. He talked about Education and Humanity and Schools. But he must have meant the Ionian School or something, because I was now in the third year at school and it just stunk. The teachers must have hated it. They couldn't have seen a single Ionian or human thing in it because they were shut up for life in that foul stench of piss and chalk dust. You could tell they knew they were in there for good from their boredom, their wrath and their cantankerousness. They were doomed to go around in there where everything had just been pulled together quite randomly and undependably. It kept changing. Yes, the ground was always just a little aquiver. If you were attentive you could feel that it was shifting slightly more than imperceptibly. We were supposed to learn the meanings, like when the blind grope over bodies and surfaces without knowing what holes or crevices their fingertips will find.

In front of the schoolhouse there was a big graveled yard. Nothing could grow there. We would have pulled it to pieces if it had. We plucked at things like monkeys. Below the school was a triangular park between the two streets that forked at the Country Road. There was a thick tangle of rose hip bushes, and we picked the berries. We pulled off the petals, crumbled the anthers on the stamen. At the center of the tangle some rose hips somehow survived to ripen anyway, but we scouted them out. The hedge, which stank of dog urine, scratched our cheeks when we stuck our heads into it. We dismantled the rose hips and picked out the seeds. They were hairy as could be, and when we stuffed them down someone's back they became itch powder.

On the ground floor of the school were the toilets, where we learned how children came into the world. I had once come scampering into my life like a squirrel can come climbing down into the fireplace. For a long time I had no need for any other notions, but they were forced upon me in the school toilets where the stench of ammonia was so strong that only the torment of desperately having to pee could make me enter. This was where you learned about the things that are deepest down and farthest out, about willies and cracks and how they met and were united and what they gave rise to, and it was all indescribably revolting.

There were bigger girls who nonchalantly inhaled the stifling air of the school lavatory, and they spent a lot of time there talking about all the bottomy things they could think of. There was a clique whose specialty was pricks and holes; one of them had a knitted angora cap and a trench coat. Others just listened, with hot cheeks and short breath. Of the many levels of the school, this was the lowest of the low.

Another was by the wall of the outbuilding, where the balls slammed against the yellow boards. A third was in the middle of the desolate schoolyard where we were meant to play. The children made up a big body, a horde of maggots full of separate, creepy-crawly lives but all moving sluggishly in the same direction. The army of maggots was a body with a back and a belly, and the games determined who belonged to the upper and who to the lower strata.

Those lowest down were dragged out onto the schoolyard for general entertainment. Individual larvae were extracted from the horde, and their antics displayed. For nearly two years I was the doll-baby with whom the angora cap and her entourage entertained themselves. Then Ann-Sophie Sager appeared. All the bad things that had been attached to me until then, all the ridicule and the stench of fear, shifted over to her. It was like taking off an old coat. At first they mocked us collectively, but very soon I slid imperceptibly out into the circle and the Sofa was all alone in the middle, weighted down with dumbness and inadequacy.

Every day between eight and three we were closed up with our teacher. He was a giant, with a red face and short gray hair that stood on end and had once been blond, and he had light blue eyes. He was fat, or rather massive, a pillar of flesh. He loved music. When he put his giant hands on the keyboard of the pump organ, his fingers moved as if they were independent of those clod hands. Music issued forth from the harmonium, and we sat silent, straight as ramrods in the chalk dust, waiting for his preludes to shift into the melody of the morning hymn. But there were days when he never got to the hymn. It would turn into a Danish song about the ripening of the grain instead, or "The Last Earthly Journey of the Fiddler". Everything he played was diffused with a tender melancholy.

Suddenly he might cut himself off and begin a lesson, without our having sung the hymn. His world-weariness and his power were boundless.

He liked the girls well enough, at least ones who were bright and well-behaved. He was ruthlessly sarcastic toward the less intelligent ones, who were doing their very best. This reached us mainly, I suppose, as a vague but constantly heightened sense of discomfort, since none of us understood sarcasm.

Several times a week, and during difficult phases several times a day, he lost his temper and lashed out. He only visited corporal punishment on three of the boys. The first was Palle, poor and idiotic, gaping and with green snot trailing from his nostrils, always in the same brown and gray checked pullover with a hole in the front. The second was the Shag, wily, thin, quick and anti-social. He was just as penniless as Palle, but he had a father. The third one was the boy we called the Rat, who was the son of a widow. He was short and skinny and he always had a cold. The insides of his desk were in chaos. His rat's nest, our teacher called it.

These three were so poor, so stupid and so frightened that they could never put their cases to anyone and be listened to. Nor would anyone pay any attention to what their mothers, or the Rat's father, might have to say, because these parents' health, morals, finance and intelligence were not up to snuff. He knew it. On the surface it just seemed he hated them because they were so poor and so stupid, hated the Shag's scornful face and Palle and the Rat's submissive looks, because he was trapped with us and thus with the three of them, closed into the smell of piss and chalk dust for life.

I think when he looked up from the organ and met our gazes, he saw dogs begging for sugar, dogs that know how to avoid being kicked. But he couldn't beat any of the rest of us. I don't think he whipped a single girl in his career because if he had he would also have lashed out at Palle's sister Sylvia, who had terrible earaches and was always having to stay after school.

When he meted out corporal punishment, it always began with a slap across the face, quick as a flash, hard and apparently unpremeditated. Then he would strike again and once again. The boy's head would flop back and forth between his hands — he used them alternately — and he would also grab the boy's hair, pulling and tugging. After that he would slam the head of the delinquent down onto the desktop, pounding it time and again against the scratched wood. Some of us would look away. The Rat would weep. He weighed twenty-five kilos and our teacher ninety-five. It looked absurd. He was so little our teacher could have lifted him up into the air with one hand while boxing his ears with the other. Sometimes he would just bend him down over the desktop, holding him tightly by the neck and pressing his nose to the ink-stained wood, all the time detailing for him what kind of a boy he was.

He hit the Shag hardest. There was something of love in his mockery. He gave him a nickname: Snot-Nose. That happened when he caught him picking his nose. He took every opportunity to call him Snot-Nose after that, and it didn't take long for the whole school to be calling him Snot-Nose instead of the Shag, which was a wild, dangerous name.

We scorned the three of them. I liked the Rat but at the same time I disdained him. He was cute. No, his face wasn't cute but his littleness was. I liked him and scorned him.

Watching this abuse made us neither upset nor indignant. I think it made us scared and toughened. We learned to be able to watch and to stand it. It wasn't all that difficult. To begin with you felt sick and were frightened, but you got used to it. In the end we understood that there are people in the world who are abused and that it was all right for us to hold them in contempt.

We never talked about these things, because there was nothing to say. As we knew in advance who was going to be beaten, we had no need to speculate. I don't know whether Palle, the Rat and the Shag discussed it with one another, but I doubt it.

However, sometimes at least, after a lesson when there was ear boxing and pounding against the desktop, I would run all the way down to the kiosk at the end of the Country Road and buy sweets with my money if I happened to have any. There was a risk I would be late coming back, because the kiosk was more than halfway to the bridge. Sometimes, though, I couldn't possibly wait until noon when we had our lunch hour.

Because Jenny's mother-in-law sold sweets at the market, I had been living around sweets for several years. I knew the aroma of sweets by the box load, which was completely different, a far more massive, heavier sweetness than what emanates from a little paper bag containing a few chocolate creams. But not until now did I begin to ask her for some for myself. Tora was surprised. I had never asked before because, to me, sweets were things to be sold and to take responsibility for. She let me help her weigh them, I folded paper into cones and took payment. To me it had been a matter of dignity not to ask for anything for myself, not to be like all the other kids, the ones who didn't have access to infinite quantities of sweets.

Now I was letting her down, but I couldn't help myself. Every time the teacher gave someone a beating, I craved sweets. Tora gave me some the first couple of times, but after that she refused me outright.

I had known for years that she kept her sweets in the long, narrow, gray wooden shed in the courtyard of the building where she lived. I hadn't given it a thought except on Wednesdays and Saturdays when she opened the shed to load boxes and crates onto a horse-drawn cart to go to market. Now my thoughts began to circle around that narrow building where there was also a woodpile behind which the dustbins stood. I started hanging around there when Tora wasn't at home and I could smell the mixture of sweetness and rubbish. Once I went and got the key to Tora's apartment from under the doormat, opened the door and took down the key to the shed from its hook beside the stove. I knew she wouldn't be back for a couple of hours, and he had given each of the three a beating that morning.

That was the first time I had been in there alone, and I stuffed myself indiscriminately. I pried off tops and stuck my hand into boxes. I dug for the soft raspberry wine gums and I crushed the chocolate mints to get at them. I didn't dare stay as long as I might have, and afterwards I tried not to think at all about what I'd done. I was sure it would never happen again.

But it happened time after time, and always for the same reason. Sometimes I was such a bad girl I took the key down even when Tora was at home and crept in. I became much more selective. Of everything in those boxes, I chose the expensive marzipan sweets and the fresh marshmallow snowballs. I took arrack-filled chocolate miniatures as well, and always saw to it that I crumpled their tinfoil wrappers and stuffed them in my coat pocket. I liked the thin chocolate of the bottles, the sticky arrack inside, that was both strong with alcohol and sweet as well, but almost best of all was the sugar coating. I ate them while leafing through old newspapers so damp with age that the yellowing paper often crumbled to the touch. There were articles about the concentration camps in those papers. I suppose Tora had hidden them so I wouldn't read about it. But I wanted to. I had to. It brought me relief.

It didn't last long, though. Tora went off for a stomach operation and never came back. Now I was so big no one insisted on telling me she had gone away.

"She's dead," Jenny said.

We often played in the churchyard. We chased each other up and down the rows, and I often hid behind the largest gravestone, the one that said Alexander Lindh Wholesale Merchant. From just behind his grave came the slamming of the foundry.

It wasn't actually a churchyard though that was what it was called. It was just a cemetery with a gray concrete crematorium and a chapel that would have looked like a country gazebo if it hadn't been for the gilded crucifix over the door.

We played here, in the city of the dead; it had streets and blocks just like the city of the living. But the proportions of this one were better for us. When, as an adult, I visited a playland park in Denmark, I immediately recognized all the proportions from our cemetery. There was everything here: splendor and squalor, iron-link fencing and completely unenclosed graves. There was gold leaf on the stones and dry, crumbly moss around them, there were bouquets of flowers in vases, miniature rakes, white marble doves and little lamps. The tiny gravel beds that were the gardens of the underground homes were neatly raked.

The houses of the dead were not to be entered. You could only set flowers at the doorway and depart without a word. Here, ultimate seclusion prevailed. They had gone underground with their lives. No one knew what the dead were doing.

I believed that people who had died lived in ordinary houses like us but never had visitors. Now and then you could catch a glimpse of their silhouettes, beating a hasty retreat when we alien visitors arrived. So I'd heard.

My mamma didn't have a grave here. She was one of the retreating figures I would glimpse, but not here. She was elsewhere.

As the inhabitants of these houses were never again to be seen, their name plates were more important than on other houses in town. The grown-ups wouldn't have been able to locate their dead kin without them. Once, I'd had to show Tora where her husband's grave was. She had never learned to tell from the treetops where he was and when the names were buried deep in the snow she was as frightened as if the dead had vanished.

Once, while we were playing hide and seek in the cemetery, I found myself hiding way at the back of the crematorium. I heard the footsteps of my pursuer in the gravel, and crept in through an open cellar door. My attention was focused out into the bright sunshine and the slamming from the foundry as I pressed up against the wall. I was listening for the steps of the seeker when I heard someone behind me. I turned around. I was at the start of a long, dimly lit cellar corridor. A man was coming toward me, dressed in a dark gray work shirt and tattered trousers. He had fine ashes or soot on his face, and his hands were dirty, too.

"Ann-Marie!" he exclaimed.

It was Ruben Sjurman. I knew he was in charge of the crematorium, but I had never really thought about what that meant. I had pictured him wearing clerical garb at work.

I ran away without a word. The dirt and the soot and his threadbare work overalls had upset me. His hands, unclean, and his heavy work boots somehow distressed and pained me. But it made sense in relation to other things I'd seen. The graves ended over by the railway. On the slope down to the tracks there were bits of silk blowing in the wind, from the rubbish pit where the wreaths and ribbons lay rotting. Nothing was deader than the brown carnations with their heads held up by green wire mesh, and nothing spoke more clearly of decay and decomposition than the soiled silk ribbons with their semi-effaced words. Their letters had not been printed, but painted carefully in gold. After a few days the rain dissolved them. Once I tried to recover one of those soaked silk ribbons to play with, but the finishing was all washed away and it was frayed and loose.

There were things you weren't supposed to know about death but that the grown-ups didn't always bother to conceal. There was something seedy and slovenly about it. Now and then the thought crossed my mind that the dead weren't at all keeping themselves to themselves in their underground houses, but had started mixing with one another and with rats and birds. I had long known death was shameful, because nobody said outright that my mamma was dead. I also saw that the graves might not really allow for lasting seclusion.

When Tora Otter died I was in the crafts room, sitting there with two enormous pieces of material I was supposed to join together to make a pink nightgown without using the sewing machine. Our class teacher came in to tell me I was to leave school and go straight home to Fredrik and Jenny's. I put away the pieces of cloth with the dirty thread creeping up and down in hard little knots and stitches. In spite of realizing something awful must have happened, I was pleased.

Out in the hall, the teacher told me Tora Otter had died in the hospital. I was to hurry straight home. I did as he said, not bothering to pull my coat on properly, working my arms into the sleeves as I went out to the street. I ran just as fast as we did when we ran races, but after some time I got tired and had a pain in my side. So in the end I found myself walking along just about as usual. I looked up at the sky covered over with ruffled clouds, a pale red sun glimmering through. Up there, I imagined, was Tora Otter, an old woman riddled with tumors, on her way to heaven. Her soul was flying up there. Might have been there all afternoon.

Her soul was making its heavy way through the clumps of cloud cover. It looked like a paper kite but instead of a wooden frame it was held taut by of something that looked like human rib-bones. Between the crosspieces there were thin membranes. These were made of such delicate material they could easily have become stained during a person's lifetime.

It was a great undertaking for Tora's soul to make its way through to heaven, and I couldn't follow it very far. I knew this was all my imagination, and when I tired of these fantasies I began to feel anxious. I didn't want to think about her body. I had been to the hospital to visit her and I hadn't liked the smell of ether. Her foot had been yellow and dry looking when they lifted the cover to straighten her sheets. She had still been alive then but had been dying from below; her heel looked like white horn.

When I got home, Fredrik was sitting at the kitchen table, inarticulate. Jenny was occupied, I don't recall with what. But I do remember her stern fretfulness. She kept looking at Fredrik as if he were ill, and he just sat there, not moving, bent forward, not saying anything.

The funeral, and even the whole unusual week prior to it, was filled with rituals that served many functions in their lives. Now I learned to mourn their way, and I learned that just as I had learned everything else — to walk, to read, to sew — solemnly. I could imagine Tora in two ways: either with curiosity or with anger, as if she were still alive.

I was angry with her for having slapped my face. I hadn't thought about that for ages, but now my anger resurfaced. She had been trying to keep me from reading things I wasn't supposed to read. In the newspapers there were pictures from the concentration camps. In the thick smoke from those crematoria, no souls rose up to God. There were different kinds of death. Some deaths were like being tossed out into a pit past which the hooting, thundering trains rushed at night. Other deaths were hymn-singing and the scent of carnations, and black coats. This was the kind the soul survived. You had to learn that.

I got a black coat. Jenny made it out of an old velveteen garment that had belonged to Tora. She put a little gray Persian collar on it. I wore my rabbit fur cap and my brown galoshes. Right when we were going to go out to the taxicab, that had already been waiting for quite a while, I noticed that one of my galosh clasps was giving me trouble again. The two halves wouldn't close properly. At the very last minute I pulled the galoshes off and stuffed them to the very back of the boot shelf. But Jenny noticed as soon as we sat down in the cab. She started fussing at me. Was I planning to ruin my dress shoes? Fredrik leaned back against the seat in the car and turned his pained face to the window. I wouldn't tell her what I had done with my galoshes, but she went in and looked till she found them.

When we walked out into the churchyard after the ceremony at the crematorium, it was exactly as I had feared. We walked in a long procession, and ahead of Jenny, Fredrik and myself there were the pallbearers with the brown coffin. Tora wasn't going to be cremated, they had said. I didn't know what the word meant. Now the gravel rattled softly under the soles of our shoes and that was the only sound you could hear except for that fateful clicking of the two halves of my galosh clasp, forever knocking against each other, unable to join.

When Tora died, it began with her being removed from our ordinary way of life. She went into hospital. Everything about her became more and more secretive as the weeks passed. She was in a private room, Jenny said. Those were the last few days. Now, at the end, she was carried under strictly regulated conditions to her total seclusion. And the sorrow her death brought with it was like that, too, severe and silent. Fredrik bore it behind his unflinching face. People drew apart, shutting their eyes to keep the tears from leaking out. Gestures were few and rigid, voices low. In this silence, the clanking of the clasps of my galoshes was as unbearable as the fact that the chrysanthemums in the pit by the cemetery went brown and rotted without anyone bothering to cover them up.

This was the churchyard. The most private of private places. I myself had also begun to have secrets. When I went into Tora's shed and ate sweets after our teacher had given somebody a beating, and when I read newspapers I wasn't meant to read, all this was forbidden and detached. No one knew about it but me. Perhaps I had some idea of what was coming from now on: separation, successive separations, until the anxiety-ridden and painful separation that will be my solitary death.

Now I had to learn all this and I had to learn to grieve so beautifully and so silently that the soul of the person who had died would fly up to God. But the people who taught me performed the rituals in a slipshod way themselves. They forced me into galoshes with a broken clasp. Their faces grew liquefied and red behind

155

their mourning veils. They were unpleasantly reminiscent of rotting flowers. They didn't last. There was something ambiguous about the whole event. They tossed their bouquets onto the top of the coffin down in the pit and it wasn't difficult to imagine what was going to happen to those chrysanthemums and roses. Everyone was peculiarly dressed in borrowed or old, altered black clothes. They didn't seem to think it mattered. The tail-coats the men were wearing were made of coarse, machine-woven fabric and were obviously hired for the occasion. Neither Adam nor Fredrik would ever have put on such a poor suit, normally. It disturbed me that they had forced me to be part of the ambiguity, the sleaziness, by wearing a broken galosh.

I hesitated so long when it was my turn to throw my flowers down onto the coffin that Jenny grabbed my wrist and shook it so the bouquet fell in. At that moment footsteps resounded behind us. Everyone turned around. It was my Pappa who had arrived. He had not been there before. Now he was walking the long path down from the road.

He looked different from everyone else. No one had such a fine overcoat. He was bareheaded! Naturally, he wasn't wearing galoshes, but was striding toward us in newly polished, burgundy dress shoes with perforated caps. When he reached the grave he stood upright, civilian upright. He was not the least bit awkward or hesitant. He bowed his head and stood there for a while in that pose, looking down. Then he straightened back up and stood there, just as erect as before, and then, without a glance at any of us, he turned and walked away.

My Pappa! Afterwards, at the Urder Lodge used for coffee after funerals, people whispered that he had been given leave. They shook their heads and dunked their Danish pastries in their coffee.

No one but my Pappa could have done what he did. He hadn't given me so much as a look. And for that very reason I was certain: we two are the only ones who know. We know how things are supposed to be done. Here they are, snuffling and dragging their galosh-covered feet through the gravel, here they are, dipping their Danishes and wiping their mouths with their crumpled hankies. I will never be theirs.

Pappa used to have parties when I was little. They were nothing like the Otters' dinner parties, planned weeks in advance. At his parties, there were neither soufflés with creamy chanterelle sauce nor meatballs, no glass bowls of herring nor tightly-corseted ladies with silk stretching across enormous bottoms and breasts. Only other men used to come, there were glasses and bottles on the table, and blue clouds of smoke hovering up toward the ceiling. Chess clocks rang harshly, and the plucking of a guitar could be heard from the corner of the drawing room. By late at night the little nigger servant's copper tray was full to overflowing, and sometimes I couldn't resist giving a little blow to the compacted, pale gray ash just to see it whirl in the light of the lamp with the silk shade. A swarm of particles held in a sensitive equilibrium thanks to electromagnetic forces and taking up space by displacing all else that might try to enter — that was a body, said my Pappa. My body, too, was nothing but a cloud of whirling particles, no heavier than ash by lamplight. Those evenings I had nothing to eat, but ever so much soda pop to drink, its bubbles rising in my Grandma Sigrid's seltzer glass.

When the men sat around our dining room table, I was lifted from lap to lap and rolled against their hard thighs and their slippery suit fabric. Their cheeks smelled of after shave, and their shirt collars were so starched they shone. They had friendly, rumbling voices and just about everything made them laugh. I used to take my little finger and fish up bits of wood chip from their grogs. There were almost always some little bits stuck to the bottom of the blocks of ice pappa hammered into pieces and then rinsed in the colander under the tap. My eyes were so sharp I could catch sight of tiny granules of wood floating on the golden liquid. The men praised me when I captured one and held it up to the light of the ceiling fixture on my pink fingertip.

Now I was no longer little. I was too big to sit on men's laps. My legs were long and I had bony knees I used to sit and suck on. The guitar and the chess clock had fallen silent and nowadays there were seldom more than three or four men

157

round the table. They just teased me.

Nor did they listen to Henning the way they used to when he talked about infinitesimal calculation. I don't think they had always understood what he was talking about, but they would laugh heartily and freely in those days, and lift their drinks to him in a toast. Perhaps it had made them feel implicated in the febrile excitement that had seized a small group of people a couple of hundred years ago when they believed they could apply the principles of mathematics to touch the very core of the cosmos. Once Henning had extended his arm through the airing window, tumbler in hand, reciting:

Oh, lumpen Folk enclosed in prison-like Minds
Who are not moved by spirit to Define
Nor Postulate to Urge or to Reflect
Nor Axiom to assert the Truth Correct!

The others had raised their glasses, too, and encouraged him to continue, and he did so, mocking all those who were out there with their chopped herring hors d'oeuvres and their dull passivity. He spouted verses I'm still astonished he was able to invent.

Nowadays they would pull him back when he started shouting out the windows, and react to his harangues with "all right, all right", as if to a nagging child. Which was all the more bitter, as it was now he really had something important to inform them of:

"The world is falling apart," he would say. "You've got to hear this."

But he had become too heavy and depressing for them. He, who had always spoken to them of Forces and Laws, now said they no longer existed, or at least that they only had an extremely limited range. He showed them books which, if they were read and understood by all, would make life meaningless and the world a broken-down engine. But they couldn't follow him that far. They collected their coats and hats and emptied their glasses and shamefacedly put Henning's hat on his head and told him he could use some fresh air. But he didn't move. He just stayed at the table with his gray felt hat askew, staring straight out into the smoky air, and his eyes seemed to me to be clear as glass.

I was terrified about what those eyes could see that others knew nothing about. Now he only had me to talk to and I had to make a huge effort to not only comprehend what he meant, but also to understand what he was saying. His lips seemed a little stiff, as if he'd been out in very cold weather, and his speech was slurred.

" I understand them," he said. "It doesn't surprise me that they don't want to hear any more. I wish I'd never read this myself. It's so preposterous. It makes reality so completely absurd."

I didn't know what absurd was, but I imagined that reality had to keep on being "sirred", like we said "sir" to our teacher.

"I feel as if my own body is dissolving," he said. Then he raised his head and looked me right in the eye.

"The atom no longer exists," he said.

"What does exist, then?"

He couldn't tell me. He held out his hand and examined it. The room was completely silent and from the little window we had opened to air out the smoke, the voices of the men walking noisily across the courtyard abated.

"There's something called quantum theory," he said. "It dissolves everything. Matter …"

He went quiet and for a few minutes it looked as if he had fallen asleep or left his body. I was scared. When I pulled him gently by the arm his eyelids fluttered and a I caught a glimpse of his blue eyes.

"Heisenberg," he said. "His matrix mechanics. He calculates and calculates. But he is unable to tell us how things really are. Do you see? No one can know. He no longer talks about what will happen or when it will happen, only about probabilities. Quantum theory makes everything unreal in that it makes elementary particles unreal. See?"

"No, not really … this is a body, isn't it?" I asked, pressing my hand hard to the tabletop. "Particles at equilibrium. The forces. I can see it right here. I can feel it, too, I mean my hand can feel it."

"It's nothing but words," said Pappa. "Thoughts. You think you can feel it. Those elementary particles … are nothing but thoughts people have worked out. No one knows anything about them. They don't exist. In his matrix mechanics, Heisenberg calculated the motion of electrons and the way atoms emit light. But those things both happen and do not happen. It is probable that they happen. But it is just as probable that they don't. There may be two worlds. One where they happen. And another where they don't. "

He was silent for a long while and I thought he'd fallen asleep with his head on the tabletop, until he said:

"Maybe the world divides every time something happens. Splits into one world where it happens and one world where it doesn't. Every time…"

I had brushed the ashes on the dining room tabletop into stripes of dead gray powder with one hand, and now I was thinking about whether there might be one world where the ashes were brushed together and the tabletop was matte, and another where they were still spread all over and the dark wood glistened between the granules.

"On the border between possibility and reality," said Henning. "The possible is just as real. World upon world upon world…"

His sorrow was as tangible as the chill in the room that was now creeping along the linoleum. In the end he fell asleep with one cheek on the tabletop. Behind him on Sigrid's chest of drawers were the books he had taken out to show his guests. He said that those books had broken his world down and I knew it was true. To him, the world could fall apart inside his head.

I didn't know what to do. We ought to go to bed but he no longer reacted when I tugged at his arm. I had ashes on my fingers and they were leaving spots on his best summer suit. That scared me. In the drawing room there was such strange light coming from the floor lamp. It kept getting weaker and weaker. Then I noticed that there was light coming from outside, a gray, tired light coming from the wrong direction. I had never been up so early.

I didn't dare go to bed while he was lying like that. I may have dozed off on my chair. When Pappa woke up he was embarrassed and spoke softly.

"We'd better get to bed now," he said. "Lucky it's Sunday."

Out on the street there was sunshine now, and I saw people passing by carrying cakes from the cake shop. When I looked at them I was scared. The sun went up and down and we couldn't do a thing about it. People came out with their boxes of cakes when it was Sunday, with their bicycles and lunchboxes when Monday came round again. They were unstoppable. There was nothing we could change.

Jenny was annoyed when I got there on Sunday afternoon. She didn't like my staying at Pappa's for so long, but she didn't say much about it.

"Ooh, you reek of cigar smoke," she just said. "And your eyes are all red."

Fredrik and she were at dinner, having pork chops. He even ate the thick edges of burnt fat and chewed on the bones. Fredrik liked things people usually left on their plates. Tough pork rind and the skin of stewing chicken, the cartilage of joints and the pungent edges of cheese. From fish heads he poked out the white eyeballs and ate them first of all. Then he would suck on the bones in the fish head and pry out the tender meat from the jowls. Jenny made trotters for him, and even ate them herself, though she was the one who had brushed out the dirt from between the toes.

When I had had too little sleep, nausea sometimes came over me. I couldn't eat a single bite and I lowered my eyes when they pressed their soiled napkins to their lips. I was so painfully aware of all the smells in the stuffy washroom and the bodily odors when one of them had just been to the bathroom. I felt I would never be able to fall asleep under the satin coverlet that smelled just as strong and oily as a human presence. So I went off to Chapel Road again that evening. I didn't bother telling Jenny, because she wouldn't have let me go. I thought Henning could phone later and explain.

But he wasn't there. The apartment was empty and had already begun to feel cold. There were no other smells than dust and cigar ash. Dry, factual smells.

I went there every evening to check. But it just stayed empty. Jenny and Fredrik didn't tell me anything. Business trips often took him away for a day or two. But I knew he hadn't had any plans to travel now. There was something wrong about his absence, and it was best not to ask any questions. Twice I heard them on the phone, talking in low, worried voices, and I knew it was about Henning. But they didn't say where the calls had come from. Every time I saw that old wooden wall phone the Otters still had, a police officer came to mind. The box under the receiver had a big coat of arms on it.

I went back and forth between Upco and Chapel Road every evening. It was a long way from Otters to us. The darkness under the trees in people's gardens and the darkness between the piles of planks opposite the freight yard was harmless. There were only two different kinds of darkness, two kinds of matter. It was worse in the center of town. There, the other kind of darkness came creeping, darkness with human breath. When I was younger I had vanquished it with breathless storytelling. I would tell myself I was walking there by myself as I walked there. I was a girl in a blue trench coat walking through a forest of stone and there were trolls in their lairs all over the place in there. Now, all that seemed ever so childish, but it was still sometimes tempting to try it out, like when you find a box of old paper dolls and can't resist dressing them in the hand-colored outfits. Those trolls weren't sitting on treasures but on secrets and they were sitting there to keep an eye on me and to hold me accountable for whirling around in their stone forest. When I was little two or three years ago I had been afraid of the lady at the sausage stall. She had bright red dyed hair, and stared at me out from under her pitch-black eyebrows. I had a name for her I could no longer recall. The hunchback at the newspaper stand would lean out to see who was passing. I pretended he had strong thick glue on his index finger, and that you had to hurry past so he wouldn't get you with it. Babyish, babyish games. Tufts of gray steel wool were growing out of the ears of the man behind the counter at the bottle store. He had to stay behind the counter, but he could send out his dog, whose mouth lapped fire water. That dog was an alcoholic, and had survived a mouthful of broken glass. At the lending library there was the thick-snouted toad lady, who croaked when she tortured her victims.

Gaping snouts, crooked fingers, ears flapping in the dark. Trudge on, trudge on. My Pappa was out of town and I pretended he was at a huge castle battling serpents and dragons, as well as the constant threat of rats and insects. He had left the princess behind and she had to live with a witch whose heart was kept in a big stone crock full of cold, sour, lingonberry preserves.

I went to school and learned to read about flowers and kings and wars, and at story hour we got to read about trolls. That they tripped up human beings with their long, crooked toes resembling the roots of pine trees, and that their way of having fun was to bang one another over the head with boulders, which everybody knew anyway. But that they heated up their ovens until the doors glowed and murdered children, piled them up and tossed them into their bread ovens after removing their boots and caps. That kind of thing we had to find out by ourselves.

I had. I had shut myself in with newspapers and read about it, an escapade that had earned me a slap on the face that made my head buzz.

Trudge on, trudge on. Soon I would know everything there was to know. I had walked this adventure path so many times now I was quite familiar with it. I sometimes had to take my Pappa by the hand and lead him past the most dangerous dragon lairs. One day there was an old woman I knew who wanted to be taken by the hand and led to a place where people had crawled down under stones and stopped moving. She wanted to find one specific stone but it had been snowing all night. Not one single bump was visible in all the whiteness. But I still recognized the place. It was where two tree branches met in a very particular way. I didn't mention that. I just took the grateful, astonished old lady to the right spot. Yes, strange things happened sometimes. People you thought had crawled down under the stones for good began to move again. You mustn't trust anything, especially not the natural sciences.

Cunning and shrewd, that was what you had to be to keep the trolls from getting you. Walk cautiously and whistle a tune. The fog is clingy and drippy and if you take a pair of scissors to the woods, they will hear you. There are sharp teeth everywhere, and cocked ears. Your foot might get stuck in deep holes, and you would have to pull it up again, with great effort, only to find your stocking caked with black mud. Now you can't see your hand in front of your face even, and you are at constant risk of having it chopped off. Slippery and slimy, horrid and dark. Just then the moon appears, a glowing melon. Trudge on, trudge on.

Now you can hear a plopping in front of you and a persistent grunting and moaning. You go closer to be able to see in the dim light, and become aware that this must be the marshy den of the snout-faced toad, where the sulfurous calla lilies grow. Here, gas bubbles rise from the water and you have to watch out for the burning mire. Every time you hear one of those fat animal ploppings, you smell the stench of cracked, unhealed wounds. You'd better try a song to give yourself courage. But you can't. These are the only words that come out:

> here are eyes like glass
> lead jaws
> hands of wood
> here I enter into blood
> in a shoe of iron

Words like that frightened me. Where did they come from? I hadn't invented them. When they rose up in me and I got to places like that, like the swamp with the sulfurous lilies, I found myself facing something alien that made me experience sheer terror. I decided not to play like that any more.

At times like that, I really enjoyed sitting at Jenny's kitchen table cutting out dresses for old paper dolls and listening to her endless stories about this city and its people.

World lay alongside world, I had long known that. When I got to Jenny's, to her little house down at the Upco estate, I was released from the school's smells of pee and chalk. I didn't talk about it, because there was nothing to be said about it in Jenny's world. I wouldn't even have known what to say if I'd tried. Should I say: "Our teacher beats Palle till his nose bleeds and once the big girls dragged me into the toilet and poked around where I wee from and I've kicked Sofa Sager in the shins lots of times and once she fell down and tore a hole in her tights"? There were no such words. Jenny knew that schools smelt of lilies of the valley and the children sang Rock a Bye Baby and our teacher was musical because he was the director of the Glee Club, in which Fredrik and Henning sang.

I didn't know where Henning was, but once before when he'd been away a long time he'd told me he'd been at a big castle. He'd been quite pale when he got home and had described huge rooms and a mysterious park. I made the mistake of telling Jenny one day when she was standing there ironing. She snorted, grunting loudly through her nose, and told me I was too big to believe in stories.

"Henning's there to dry out."

I'd made a serious blunder and was very upset about it.

I knew perfectly well there were different worlds and that each had its own names for things. But worlds were not alongside other worlds any more like they had been just a couple of years ago. It seemed as if they sometimes overlapped. There was also something unmatched and ill-fitting about them.

I should never have told her what Henning had said. I realized now it might be my own fault when worlds wobbled and didn't stay separate. It was my blabbering, it was the loose, untrustworthy sides of me that made them unable to fit together. I had this fault, of not being loyal. Other people had qualities. They were clear and stable inside their trench coats and sweaters. But I was slippery slidy. I nothing and everything at once. That was bad.

I knew Henning's castle really existed. It was on the map. It was even described in my history book. By chance I found out you could get there if you changed buses in Vagnhärad. I decided to go there. It was a major undertaking, but I wasn't a child any more, was I, at least not a little child. I ran errands to make some money, and I think the Otters were surprised because I had become both so docile and so greedy. I saved up those coins but they didn't amount to much until I got a whole five kronor coin completely unexpectedly from a watchmaker named was Krantz who had known Tora Otter.

The next Sunday I went down to the bus station at the market square. I had told Jenny and Fredrik I was invited to Synnöve's for Sunday dinner.

It took a lot longer to get there than I had anticipated, and I didn't really have enough money for the ticket. But the driver of the bus from Vagnhärad let me on anyway. He dropped me on the main road, and I couldn't see any castle anywhere. All I could see were meadows, and along the edge of the country road ran ditches full of hawkweed and thick, dusty leaves of the wood dock we children called coffee.

I found a tree-lined lane and was soon walking down it. I still couldn't see any castle. The trees planted to ornament and shade this lane were birches. But they must have been planted a very long time ago, because the ones that were still alive were cracked, their thick trunks spotted with black. Some had been struck by lightning and killed, but not removed. They were still reaching out to catch passing shreds of cloud. So far, the arrangements and setting were very fairy-tale like and appropriate, and the best was yet to come. The lane ended at a little wooden bridge, and finally the castle was in sight. It was on a little tongue of land, floating in still, green-reflecting water. There was a strong smell of decaying leaves in the park, from the beeches, oaks and sycamores. Here and there little wooden bridges dotted the scene, connecting the land between inlets of the green lake. There is still no scent that fills me with such a strong sense of anticipation as that of slowly decomposing leaves.

For the moment, I was keeping away from the castle. Having made it this far, I suddenly realized how ridiculous it was to imagine they would let me in, when I was only eleven years old. Half hidden behind the smooth gray trunk of a beech tree, I stood peering at the portal at the top of the long flight of stairs. Then I heard a distant sound, and turned around. I caught sight of a troop of people crossing one of the bridges. Some of them vanished behind a hazel hedge, and then reappeared. They were in a long line, I counted eleven of them. They were walking slowly. One was shuffling his feet.

At the head of the line was a person dressed in blue and white, with a sweater around his shoulders, and further down the line there was another blue-and-white one. The walkers were not looking around. None of them saw me. Neither did they see the trees or the squirrels, the gleam of the lake water or the moss-capped stones. Somewhere around the middle of the troop was Henning. The first thing I noticed was how thin his hair was. It couldn't have happened that fast, but still a very upsetting notion came into my head. I can still see that image: his beautiful hair fallen off, lying in a dandruffy, brownish-gray pile on his pillow. He was wearing the strangest clothes, made of cotton. There was something saggy and droopy about both the trousers and the jacket, they didn't become him at all. I couldn't conceive of him being persuaded to put on a pair of trousers like that, not to mention the shoes, which were more like bedroom slippers.

Then the blue-and-white leader caught sight of me and there was a bit of a stir. But Henning wasn't as surprised as I had imagined he would be. They let me come inside the castle. It didn't look the least bit as I had imagined. There reigned boredom, law and order, a frenzy of cleanliness, a blasting radio, Mother-in-law's tongues on the windowsills, and an unmistakable odor of urine. I remember the beds lined up in rows and I remember the helplessness. Henning could barely raise his own coffee cup. When we were sitting in the huge common room, an old man came in; he was playing with his fly. He started to pee on the seat of a chair, and actually did get a few drops out before they removed him. My Pappa never even noticed.

One of the blue-and-whites was playing Parcheesi with a man who didn't want to play at all. Another was watering the potted plants. The light brown coffee in Henning's cup was slopping about dreadfully. Someone came in and said I shouldn't be there but that my Pappa and I could take a little walk in the park.

It was a very pretty castle and full of history. Counts had resided here, and their dreams had been plans for new, even larger, even more beautiful castles. The era I was living in had begun to fill such buildings with the helpless and the intoxicated, and sometimes the muddled and the deformed.

Now Henning and I were having a walk on the leaf-strewn paths and across the little wooden bridges. A blue-and-white was following us at a distance. Between Henning and me things would soon be as usual. But he wasn't quite as usual, of course. His gait was slow and I noticed his eyes kept brimming over for no reason at all. One of the first things he mumbled was that he wished he could give me some money, some sweets money, but he didn't have any. For a few minutes I considered the fact that I didn't have any money to get home with. I decided not to think about that any more.

"Well, I take my daily walks here," he said with a sweeping gesture, and suddenly I saw the moss growing, the leaves rotting and the cold snails slowly inching their way along the paths and the wall with the ironwork portal. But when I commented on the yucky snails he got excited. He told me they were called vineyard snails, and that they were edible. They had been set out here by the lords of the castle, who had eaten them au gratin and bubbling with butter. As always, he had soon persuaded me. I no longer found them the least bit repugnant. We started to collect them, agreeing that I would keep them captive until he came home. Then we would prepare them as a culinary delight. He claimed to know that what they needed was to live on a diet of lettuce leaves and milk for three weeks, which was precisely the amount of time he would be here, if everything went smoothly.

We had nothing but my cap to put the snails in, and we had to pick them up one by one and extremely furtively, so the blue-and-white-lady-warden wouldn't intervene and spoil our plans. We assumed, quite correctly, that everything was prohibited here. In the end my cap was full and we counted twenty-seven snails. We tied them in with the string from his slipper-like canvas shoe.

"I'll tell them I lost it," he said, and now he was just about like usual, much less tired and with no tears in his eyes.

I hid the stuffed cap by the stone gatepost and went back in with him. I still hadn't mentioned not having the money for the bus home. There wasn't anything he could do about it, anyway. The Matron had obtained information about where I could catch the bus back from Vagnhärad, and they told me I'd have to hurry. They also told me I must never come back. It was prohibited.

Pappa and I didn't touch one another in the presence of the others. He just stood looking at me, perfectly erect. When I saw he was able to stand up straight if he wanted to, I could imagine that in three weeks he would be putting on his own suit, the one with the pressed trouser creases.

The trip home didn't work out very well. The driver was annoyed, but he took me to Vagnhärad anyway. He noted down Fredrik Otter's name and address, which was what I gave him when he asked who my parents were. Because I knew Henning didn't have any money, of course.

They made me phone Jenny from Vagnhärad. Not only was she furious, she even wept. After the receiver had exchanged hands any number of times in the office where they had the timetables, it was clear that the last bus had gone. I had to wait on a bench for a very long time for a taxi they sent from home.

As for my edible snails, I could tell from the very outset that Jenny detested them and had no intention of having them in her house. I realized they would be gone when I got home from school, so I took them with me, hiding them in my desk. There, they led their slow, searching lives, and through the desktop I could hear the little snails colliding, with muted thuds.

I had the key to our house on Chapel Road in my possession. I had realized early on what a precious item this was, and never told Jenny about it. Pappa knew, of course. He was the one who'd given it to me. Now I went over to Chapel Road after school and put my snails in an enamel hand basin, on the bottom of which I had spread some moist sand. I set a saucer of milk in the middle. There wasn't any lettuce, though, this late in the autumn, so I put in a handful of leaves instead, some of them frostbitten and spotted brown.

The next afternoon I went over to give them fresh leaves and a sip of milk I'd saved in my lunch bottle. But there wasn't a single snail left in the basin. I felt like an idiot. It hadn't occurred to me they would be able to climb the slippery sides.

I was soon able to locate most of them, and I covered the hand basin with a pillowcase before I left. The next day, however, they'd escaped again. This time I didn't find as many of them, although I scoured the whole apartment. One snail was sitting on Sigrid's painting, the one of violets, as if it had thought they were edible. And I found some under the radiators, and others on the bathroom floor. I started feeling anxious.

By the time Henning got back there weren't enough of them left to be worth preparing. We let them out in the yard instead, and he said they could be the beginning of a huge snail farm, just like in the castle park. Both of us knew that there weren't many trees in our courtyard. They would seek out other spots, where there were decaying leaves. I still sometimes find empty shells in the apartment, from the snails that starved to death and dried out in here.

Henning soon went away again unannounced. When he had been gone a long time, I went to Little Heavenside one afternoon after school. I went there because it was a castle, too. I wanted to see it because I had never thought about what it looked like. The path was difficult to walk on, gray and brown with deep wheel ruts. It resembled poorly-healed scars on the pitted skin that had been soft and dusty in early summer. The wood dock had gone to seed, and all the thistles and grass along the roadside had long since finished blooming. It was overgrown, and covered with a film of caked mud.

I didn't dare go all the way up to the castle, because people were living there, so I stopped in the meadow behind the stable. There wasn't much to see there, though. Nothing but hawkweed and yellowing grass. Then I heard the murmuring of voices, eager and enticing. I went into the shade of a grove of alders, and fell to my knees alongside a stone foundation that was protruding from the damp grass.

In amongst the alders, there was a running spring, and the water spoke eagerly as it purled over the stones and the gleaming sand. I knew instantly that this was a sacred place, and when I pushed the grass aside, I found bones. There were lumps, glowing white, and bits of brittle shiny bone with gray, porous surfaces where they had fractured. I gathered the bones and stones and snail shells I found to form a little heap; anything that might be a remarkable relic, I gathered before me. I imagined I was the first person in centuries to find this place. Perhaps there had been a convent here, or another, older castle, and perhaps treasures and remains of people who had lived long ago were buried here.

I poked eagerly around in the soil with a stick. It was moist and loose and full of rotting leaves. Secretive animals escaped stealthily into hollows and crevices, fleeing from my hands and from the sunlight falling in among the alder leaves, making a patchy pattern that shifted over the ground when the wind moved the boughs. Suddenly I hit a hard little shard. At that very moment, I heard a voice speak. I cannot repeat its words because my memory was unable to retain those syllables, which had no meaning to me at the time. But the same words were repeated three times, and the echo surrounding the voice rose louder each time. It sounded as if the voice were coming out of a huge iron bell.

I was on my knees, and now I fell forward, leaning my brow to the damp earth, I was agitated and frightened, and I lay there perfectly still for a long time, waiting for the voice to return, or for someone to seize me. But it was quiet now, and the spring continued to purl.

What I had heard was a voice from another world than that of the spring. In the end I dared to move, and my hand explored the topsoil where the stick I had been digging with had come to rest. That was when I felt the little shard against my fingertips, and raised it to the light.

For a few days after finding the shard, I was liberated from all smells. And all sounds were very distant as well. I hardly dared think about what I had experienced, and the few times I did let my mind touch on it, my throat constricted as if I were about to weep. It was a lovely feeling.

Sadly, I wore it out by recalling it too often. I also noticed that all those stale, horrid smells began to come back. When I stood too close to anyone, I became aware of the scent that surrounded them. Not too long afterwards I was back in my same old den of hopelessness and misery, and the memory of the time I found the shard had begun to blur. In the end it seemed sort of pathetic. I went around with the shard in my coat pocket, feeling it now and then among the waxed paper wrappers and bits of string. I didn't want to take it out and look at it. I was afraid I would find some chipped fragment of an old china dinner plate.

But one afternoon we happened to stay on after school with a few other girls, to write notes to boys. There were four or five of us. I didn't really join in from the beginning, and they got annoyed with me and made me write

DEAR JAN-OLOF,

LOVE ANN-MARIE

on a page of the pad. This was the accepted formula for love letters, and I didn't dare not write one. One of the girls was going to deliver the note to Jan-Olof's house. They were cousins. Suddenly an elderly teacher from the primary school confronted us. She must have known we were doing something we weren't supposed to be doing, and immediately asked what we were so busy writing. The others looked at me and said they had no idea what I had been writing.

"Let me see that note," she said.

Then she made me empty my pockets and show her what was in them. I took everything out of my right-hand pocket and gave it to her. There were mainly candy wrappers, but also some torn bookmarks. She couldn't find a note anywhere and ordered me impatiently to turn out my other pocket as well.

"I know you big girls pass notes with dirty words around in class," she said. "Turn your pocket out."

I felt the sharp edge of the shard against my fingers, and at that very moment a voice coming from an electricity transformer on a post behind us said:

"Hide it."

I was terribly frightened the others might have heard the voice, too. Then I realized the only way to obey it was to run away. I turned tail and ran as fast as I could. I got a pain in my side but I still didn't stop until I was high up on the ridge and sure no one was pursuing me. Then I made my way to 13 Chapel Road.

I do not remember the punishment I must have been subjected to for running away from that teacher. But everything that had happened at Little Heavenside became real again. The voice was there. I was liberated from scents and nagging noises and the hopeless drudgery of my arithmetic book and sewing class. I may have done quite a few of the things I was told to do. But I could do those things without being present. My mind was constantly preoccupied with the voice, and the world it had let me glimpse.

I could think about those things while riding my bike, and even when I was sitting at the Otters' kitchen table eating prune compote. But I did my best thinking when I was able to go off where no one would disturb me. I could lie on my bed, curled up under the pink blanket, and not even notice the passing of the hours. If I couldn't find any other place to be in peace, I would go up to Chapel Road and lie in my own bed. It was cold up there when pappa wasn't at home, but I would lie under a pile of blankets, quite still.

The voice did not speak to me again, but I noticed I was still being given knowledge. It came to me from inside where there were lots of voices talking and purling and always had been, without my having noticed or been attentive to their chatter. It was like listening to the treetops, to the aspens and the fir trees, and suddenly understanding what they were saying.

In that way, I was given knowledge of the shard, learned that it was so sacred and so powerful it had to be kept concealed, and that I was its guardian.

Everything that was said inside the constant murmur had to be listened to very closely. Words that were clumped together and indistinguishable gradually made sense, after patient listening. The name of the shard was The Codeform.

At first I called the world behind the voices The Dimension, but I probably just made that up. Later I learned its name was Choryn. It also appeared as images, and

I now realized that the images, too, had been there all along. But I hadn't been paying attention.

I had hidden the shard deep in the cellar of the house on Chapel Road. That was a place I didn't usually dare to go. The cellar wall was made of huge, embedded stones, and there was a strong smell of earth down there. I was deep down below the roots of the trees, deep down below the layers of soil people's feet tramp. Water dripped out between the stones, cold, ferrous water. In one corner was the old furnace with its rusty grating. Along the wall there was a huge coal box, with a plate-metal chute running into it.

The inner room of the cellar had no windows. You turned an old, black light switch and, with a solemn click, a bare ceiling bulb lit up. The room wasn't perfectly square, because the stones had determined the shape. Drops fell from their cold surfaces. I would never ever have dared to go in here just a couple of weeks earlier. But now I was no longer alone. This was where I was to bury the shard.

It was white and slightly rounded, and on the gently cupped inside it had the sign of Choryn, which is The Codeform and which looks, to ordinary people, like a little blue flower. The very first time my fingers brushed against it, I was prepared to obey the voice. Even then, I realized, if only in a dim, unenlightened way, how great was the risk associated with the shard.

Using a rusty knife I found on a shelf, I delved around until I found a little crevice and removed the earth between two stones to make a spot for the shard. After pressing it in there, I gathered up moist gravel from the floor and covered the hole. It wasn't actually gravel. It was as fine-grained as soil, but reddish-brown and dry, not at all like the clods of rich topsoil in vegetable gardens. I pressed with my fingers until it was smoothed over and no one would be able to tell where I had inserted the knife.

In bed that night, I summoned Choryn. I could do so silently, so no one in the house could hear me. I called straight into Choryn, with which I was not familiar at the time, asking whether I had acted correctly. I thought I was shouting into darkness where there was nothing but a voice. Choryn answered me as so often later, when things were well between us. It took a while before the answer arrived, though, and when it did, it was with a sign. So that night I had to lie alone and confused under the honeycomb cover, unsure if I had acted correctly and whether or not the voice was pleased with me.

"You can't just lie here like this!"

Jenny was standing over me. She had pulled down the bedspread and the covers, exposing me to the damp chill of the room. It was like lying out of doors. Behind her face a second face had emerged, rigid with desperation.

We went back to Upco. I walked behind her, staring at her back, and at the seam running down her brown coat. All around me the sickening sounds began to arise out of the still air of a Monday afternoon. There was scraping and hissing. In the window of the cake shop, the marzipan had changed a little since I walked to Chapel Road. We passed the fire station and the florist's. Now the smells were beginning to return. The leaves were decomposing and the apples rotting under the trees, brown with white specks of mould on the skin. When we got to the Otters' house I knew I couldn't go on this way. I had to get back under a cover and lie down. I planned to invent a stomach ache.

A neighbor was planting bulbs, her huge rump turned toward us. Jenny and she exchanged a few words, but I didn't hear what they said. When we got inside I could smell the wallpaper glue and hear the hissing of the heating pipes.

"What's got into you?" Jenny asked. She sounded upset and near tears. What was I supposed to answer? I saw the teapot still standing out on the table, and for one moment I thought I'd try to explain. Once I had seen it with new eyes. But now I couldn't.

As to the other worlds, the ones that wouldn't open up any more, I neither wanted to talk about them nor was I permitted to. They had abandoned me. There was only silence from there.

Jenny gave me some drawing paper. She'd bought a roll from the shop, white paper smooth on one side and rough on the other. It had been purchased expressly for me to draw on. But now I didn't want to draw. I was sick and tired of those crooked pencil lines. They never managed to look like the things I could see in my mind. And besides, I wasn't allowed to draw anything from Choryn.

"My stomach hurts," I said. "I want to go to bed."

"Come along," said Jenny, pulling me toward the sitting room. On the glass top of the smoking table, there was a bowl of sweets.

"Sit down," she said," We'll play cards."

I don't know how many days or weeks passed like that, abandoned.

One night I woke up. A bright light was beating at my eyelids. When I opened my eyes I saw it was coming from a point on the wall diagonally behind me, to the left. I turned my head and saw the face. It was coming out of the wall, blindingly bright. It was gold and shone with an expression I had never seen on a human face. I was so terrified I thought my heart had failed. I didn't dare turn away, the face just kept beaming down, blinding me. In the end, it sank back into the wall and everything went dark. I hadn't died. Now I could hear Fredrik snoring again, and feel how hard it was to breathe the heavy air in the confined bedroom.

It took me days to understand what I had seen. It was Ishnol. Now I could lie under the covers or out at Heavenside beach in the old canoe shed and the revelations swept over me. They came as light behind my eyelids. They came as names and words from the murmuring I could always hear. That was a good time. Even Jenny seemed pleased again, although she had no idea what had happened. All she knew was that I was no longer biting my nails down to the quick, or pulling the flowers off her potted plants or picking the sugar pearls off her sticky buns. When Ishnol was with me I was able to behave precisely like Fredrik and Jenny wanted me to behave. Not even school was much trouble. You're a bit absent-minded, was all they said. But absent was exactly what my mind wasn't. It was exceptionally present.

One day on my way to school, I saw Wonda. I didn't know her name yet, though. It was the first time I saw her. I was walking through Spring Park, in the shadows under those big alders. It was late autumn, but the alder leaves were still green. Even the ones that were falling to the ground at my feet were dark green and brown. Up on the slope, the secret water was purling under the stones. I had always been aware of it as I passed, but without knowing what the sound was.

In the patches of sunlight on the path in front of me, among the still-soft curls of brown leaves, Wonda appeared, dancing. I stood there for as long as she was visible. Then I had to run to school, but I got there late anyway. When the teacher asked why I was late, I told him the first thing that came to mind:

"There was this big dog in Spring Park!"

He laughed and the whole class joined in. I didn't know what was so funny, but I had long ago stopped bothering about them. That afternoon I walked home through Spring Park as well, but Wonda did not appear. Where she had been dancing I just saw a little mouse on the path. It was dead. One of its eyes was bulging, and there was blood on its face. It frightened me that Wonda had left me this sign, and I ran away. But on the slope up to the chapel I stumbled in the gravel and scraped my knee so hard my stocking ripped. I had cut my knee and it was bleeding. I realized at once that the cut was sacred and had to be kept from healing. Every time a scab developed, I picked it off with my fingernails. It didn't hurt. Light red blood dripped out, and the cut looked alive and well again. But at night after I had slept, the scab was brown and too thick for my nails to break. So I took the nib of a pen from my pencil case and cracked open the thick, brown cake. I did this for several days, but one morning I forgot and in the end it healed. Then I was miserable and abandoned again, and all the voices were silenced. I had betrayed Wonda. There was nothing but grayness around me. I remember standing in the milk shop, where Jenny had sent me on an errand, and searching for signs. I thought there ought to be some there. But there was nothing but gray cement and rusty handles, and the dull sound of the milk cans when the ladle hit the sides.

Now, once again, I was a rejected, abandoned person. Not until now did I truly understand that I couldn't go into and out of the worlds as I chose. I remembered the very first time, when I had been so happy. But that time I had produced so much of what happened in my imagination. And I could no longer do that. I realized my fantasies were just as insipid as my blurry line drawings.

The next time Ishnol showed herself, I was not in bed. This time it happened in the schoolyard, against the wall where we played ball. There was no way to postpone this encounter or to avert my face from hers. I reeled right back against the wall, as Ishnol's bright face appeared time after time. The others were shooting the ball at it. They were chattering and shouting just as they had been before; she did not appear to them.

Afterwards, my mouth was dry, and my heart pounding and throbbing. I sat on the damp grass catching my breath. But when my heart had settled down and I was breathing nearly normally again, I started wondering why she had especially chosen me.

One of the children playing ball against the wall was Synnöve. Her hair was blond and ringlets fell from under the edge of her cap, which was a really pretty one, with a knitted pattern and a square inset at the back. Those caps had come to Sweden during the war, with the Estonian refugees, and Synnöve's mother had knitted her one, in pale gray, white and pink. Synnöve's ringlets danced on her back. She was so pretty and she was always at the head of the class. Why hadn't

Ishnol chosen her?

Now I had to stay with Ishnol for a long time, and she was relentless. She wanted me to learn all about Choryn and there were many things I didn't understand. In the end she left me in a great void and I longed for a sign from her or from Wonda.

Every morning that autumn I had inspected the hedgehog's milk bowl for a message. Once there had been blood in it. But the saucer was licked clean until one day when it was untouched. The hedgehog had gone into hibernation down underneath the steps in the leaves and the sticks for the winter. So Jenny stopped putting out the milk and the saucer. I had to look for messages in the thin ice on the puddles, and among the cones that had fallen from the pines. But there was nothing else.

Pappa had come back from his drying out and he didn't even ask about the snails this time.

I felt longing and fear but my visions had expired. My experience gradually paled. It was like an old photograph that is fading. The light breaks in from the edges. The image disappears into light. I could recall nothing more about Ishnol than that she was the light.

One morning I went down to the sitting room before Jenny and Fredrik. It was a Sunday and they had had a dinner party the evening before. The playing cards were still on the table. There was also a fruit bowl with nothing in it but the stalks from bunches of grapes, and on the plates there were just dry seeds people had spit out. Everything looked so forlorn. Above the sofa there was a big framed needlepoint tapestry of an elk, a sunset and some pine trees, all in shades of gray wool. The room was so bright you could see the moth holes in the picture.

Imagine if they never came back into this room. If no one were ever to touch those playing cards again.

What happens to abandoned things in a room no one enters? That was how I had felt since Ishnol left me: like an abandoned room.

Pappa and me on our way to Marstrand in July 1948. I am carrying a little suitcase and wearing a braided straw hat with an upturned brim. Pappa has on a light gray suit. He looks kind, sober and decisive. Behind us the steel side of a train carriage with a big, dirty white number three on it. Jenny must have made my blouse. It's white, with a checkered yoke and cuffs. The skirt is of the same checked material and is ruffled, with a wide elastic waistband. A sinewy girl with straight, fair hair. She is mamma to me, not I to her.

We spent two weeks on the island of Marstrand where the air, according to Henning, smelled of sodium chloride and iodine. A big blue sky stretched above our activities. The rocks were warm, some sparkling gray, others rosy pink. There were crevices where we found sea asters and sea rocket. We didn't have a flower press with us, but we had brought reams of gray pressing paper. We filled a couple of drawers with stones and pressed the plants under them. On every leaf we put a label, where Pappa wrote the Latin name, the date and the location of our find in his small, pointed handwriting. For that, not having written the labels myself, I would later be reprimanded at school. At the start of term, I brought one hundred and four flowers to class with me. That number I shall never forget, just as I shall never forget Tora Otter's telephone number.

We were actually staying at a boarding house on the nearby little Cow Island, a drafty, white wooden house. Everything there was bright and clean and it was less expensive there than on Marstrand island itself. You got there on a little tram-like ferry boat.

Sometimes there was sand on the wooden floor when I went to bed. We brought it in on our shoes. Little bits of dried seaweed would fall out of my beach robe when I unrolled it. Pappa hung our damp swimsuits on the balcony. He covered me with an extra blanket at night because the air got a little damp inside from the drafty, ill-fitting windows.

We ate in the boarding house dining room, and both of us had milk with our meals. On our table there was a little holder for salt and pepper, vinegar and mustard. We had envelopes for our napkins, too, on which we were supposed to write our names. Pappa wrote "Filon of Constantinople", and no one was offended.

When we had had dinner we took the ferry back to Marstrand and walked over to the Society Ballroom, where we heard a brass band play and watched them lower the flag at sunset. Afterwards we walked the narrow, winding streets down toward the harbor to look at the sailboats. Tanned, well-dressed people swarmed in and out of the hotels. Pappa held my hand, and on the ferry back I would fall asleep. The very air smelled strong. It must have been laced with medications from the spa.

While I was falling asleep in the evenings, Pappa would lie on his bed, slowly turning the pages of a book. When I peeped out I could see the shiny gold edging. Even deep in sleep, I could hear the waves.

The only people we talked to were each other. Of course he would occasionally say a few words, usually in jest, to the people at the tables near ours in the dining room. There was one woman who was on her own. She was extremely large, considerably bigger than Pappa, I think. She was good-looking. Her hair was ash blonde, and was styled in a wave across her forehead. There were diagonal waves across the top of her head as well, and curls at the bottom. Her profile was forceful and flawless, and her lips were painted red. People tended to stare at her as she passed through the dining room in her flowered sundress and a bolero. At dinner she wore a tighter frock, pulled smooth over her stout behind. At first I hadn't paid much attention to her, but suddenly I started thinking about her often, without knowing why. She reminded me of a she-lion.

One evening Pappa asked if I would mind missing the sunset music. Of course I didn't mind a bit.

"What're we doing instead?" I asked.

But his plan was that I should go to bed early. He had bought me a ladies' magazine, a Children's' Digest, and a bag of sweets. Himself, he was going to accompany the woman who looked like a lioness to a bridge tournament at one of the Marstrand hotels. His voice was soft. It turned out there had been bridge down in the boarding house dining room after my bedtime. And he had been playing.

My chest felt like an ice box. I was a little dizzy, too. At half past seven I found myself in bed, with my sweets and my magazines. It was ridiculous for me to try to fall asleep that early, Henning agreed upon due consideration. He wasn't very happy either by the time he left.

I sat there perfectly still thinking about the she-lion. Now I remembered some of the things she had said, although I hadn't paid them much heed at the time. She had said that she preferred dark meat to light, and that her feet were always nice and warm. And she had told one of the other lady guests, very softly, that this boarding house was so old-fashioned it was difficult to keep yourself decent. I thought about that one for a long time. I didn't know what she meant. But I had understood from her soft, secretive voice that it was one of those important things people didn't talk about. I remembered *The Physician's Handbook* in Jenny and Fredrik's bookcase.

I couldn't stop thinking about her. She grew more lively, larger and warmer than before. I thought about her feet.

I hadn't yet opened the magazines or touched the sweets. I got up and went to her room when I was sure the ferry had left. I looked out of the window and could see that it had almost reached the other side. The lock on her door was just the standard one, and it opened readily with our key. When I had closed the door behind me I could feel her presence as strongly as you could sense the scent of a lion in its concrete pit at the zoo.

She had a very tidy room, even tidier than ours, in fact, and we were pedantic. Henning might set a book down on his bedside table, and my rubber beach shoes were full of shells and perching on the commode shelf. But the lion lady had left nothing out. Which was why I had to open her closet. She had at least fifteen dresses with her. On the floor were several pairs of her big shoes, with broad, high heels.

I went to the chest of drawers. In the top drawer she had beaded necklaces, handkerchiefs and a container of pink powder. When I took off the lid to sniff, my hands trembled and I was afraid it would spill. There was also a lipstick, as dark as clotted blood. Next to the lipstick was a little box with a tube in it. On the label it said this was a cream for the removal of unwanted hair. She also had a bottle of perfume to cover her smell.

In the other drawer were her underthings. At the top was a big, shiny Spirella corset. It was black. I had only seen Jenny's pink corsets. This one made me think of death, and the thought crossed my mind that she might be in mourning. The rest of her underwear was more summery: big pairs of flesh-colored knickers with no elastic at the bottoms, and loose, flappy legs. There were also three charmeuse nighties, neatly folded, one on top of the other.

The deeper into the she-lion's room I got, the more frightened I felt. I had originally had an urge to do something to her things, or take something, but now I didn't dare. I did use the lipstick, painting my mouth bright red in front of the mirror. It felt greasy and sticky, made me look different. Then I left the room, locking the door carefully.

178

My heart kept pounding for quite a while. Now it seemed a dull occupation to lie down and read the magazines Pappa had bought. I wanted someone to see me. At home, of course, I couldn't have gone out with my red mouth. People would either have laughed or been indignant. But here they wouldn't see *me*, they'd see a semi-adult girl, a stranger. I walked with my head held high and with an eager, wild, sorrowful expression. I looked like someone in a film.

When I got to the ferry it had been there for a while. There were a few people on the seats, but I didn't look at them. I had my wild, sorrowful expression on, and my dark red mouth; they looked at me.

Then I caught sight of pappa and his bridge partner, as if in a flash photograph. They were sitting opposite me. I don't know what they'd been doing. Perhaps they'd stopped to talk to someone, or taken a walk. However it happened, they hadn't taken the earlier ferry.

Pappa crossed the aisle right away and sat down by me. He pulled out a big, white handkerchief and handed it to me. Naturally, I knew this meant I was supposed to wipe my mouth clean. Then we quickly disembarked from the ferry. I don't know where the woman went. He said something to her, softly. But then it was just him and me, walking toward the boarding house.

The last few days the weather was more unstable. At night you could feel humid gusts of wind coming through the windows. The sun was less bright during the days too, and the walls of the houses, where the little flies crawled, were less white. I often woke up at night and checked to see whether Henning was still in his bed. The light from the lamp fell on his cheek, and on his sand-colored hair, that was no longer so thick and high that it stood up all by itself. His wave fell gently toward his brow, and now and then he would push it aside with his hand just before he turned the page. If I called him, he would come. No matter how soft my voice. He would always hear it.

Sometimes I heard the jingle of a glass, and caught sight of a bottle he took out of the commode. That didn't at all bother me. I didn't want to change anything about him, not even the smell from his mouth.

The remaining days had no scent of wild animals and were very peaceful.

We lived on an island of tranquility but all around our yard was the clatter of an active world. Printing presses rolled and roared, cross-cut saws sang murderous melodies, and early in the mornings compressed air hissed out through a hose. That was usually the first sound I heard when I woke up at Chapel Road. From the foundry came the dull banging of tool against die, and the persistent sounds of hammers knocking away excess metal. On warm summer days when the windows of the editorial offices were open, you could hear the patter of the typewriter keys against hard rollers, and swearing when the keys got stuck. From the ground floor there was the peculiar, soft clanging of the setting machines and the banging as the rows of composed words settled into their cases. Clogs clattered on uneven floors, bundles of newspapers were loaded into trucks, and their tired engines started, coughing and barking like old dogs. Late in the afternoon the whistle at Swedish Engineering blew, and shortly afterwards there was the rattling of bikes. On rainy days their tires hissed against the pavement when whole hordes of workers rode past on the street.

As a child I must always have heard these sounds. But I wasn't aware of them until they became torture.

I had woken up one morning at the Otters' and found a blood stain in my bed. Looking down, I could see that my nightgown, too, had a stain as large as the palm of my hand, and the shape of an insect. I'd never seen anything like it. It was as frightening as finding a monster in my bed, this cut I didn't know where I'd got. Jenny gave me pads, hard, hand-crocheted ones, and an elastic belt and safety pins and, at the eleventh hour, explanations: rueful, comforting explanations.

I went home to Chapel Road instead of going to school, and I lay in my bed. The dragging, insistent pains in my abdomen radiated throughout my body. My back and my thighs seemed to get drawn into the pain the way porous paper attracts and absorbs water colors, spreading and blurring the paint. I fell asleep but the sounds coming from the foundry and the street kept waking me up. My stockings and my camisole were glued to my skin with sticky cold sweat. The moment I woke up the pains would start again, a suction cup at the small of my back. I wept over this misery that had made its home in me. Jenny had said it would be back, once a month, year after year. It will get easier when you have children, she consoled me.

I disliked the dark blood. It came from a wound that had long kept itself secret and I didn't need the tone of Jenny's soft voice to know this was something shameful that had afflicted me. The smell was quite enough.

The menstruation and the melancholy brought in their wake this hypersensitivity to sounds, making me suddenly aware of how we had been living for all these years. I felt what a violation the heavy rolling of the printing presses was when I lay curled up in bed trying to read, with the sensation that a saw blade was splitting my eardrum. I began to feel an extreme aversion to the intrusive sounds of everyday life, toward the cacophony around me, and I must have put it into words, crying or cursing, because I recall Henning's hand on my shoulder and his voice, jesting yet intense as always when he had something important to say:

"My dear girl, haven't you noticed them building a community all around you?"

That image has stayed with me. When I think the word community, I see myriads of men hanging onto a huge, shaky scaffolding, hammering, soldering, bending reinforcing irons, filling foundry dies, clattering, nailing, starting pneumatic drills and compressors. Everything is shaking and rocking. But what are they building? And what am I doing here, actually? I feel strange, like a red fox in sharp sunlight.

In the evenings, when it was quieter, I went out. There was never total silence. Even when the city was asleep, a train might come clanking in with hissing valves and the stink of oil and greasy metal. I would stand on the bridge and watch stained, decomposing bits of paper flutter along the track. The train yard was a place of rubbish and paper as well. In one of the flowerbeds there, I once found a bottle containing a little mouse that had crept into it and died. When I inspected it I felt more than just repugnance. Another feeling rose in me as well, but it refused to come into focus; it was a memory, tantalizing. But it sank back down and left me in the ugliness.

I wanted to tell Pappa about all this, but I couldn't seem to: your community is ugly. It's a crime to leave so much ugliness lying around. Every time I saw the rotting waste and paper blowing back and forth in the wind I realized that some day this entire shameful world would be lying here, abandoned by its inhabitants. But I couldn't tell him.

181

Sometimes I would also go out in the mornings before school. I would roam through Spring Park, listening to the murmuring of the water, and walking among the sparse trees at the edges. Sometimes I would see things in the patches of sunlight on the path, things I couldn't identify. I would feel a sense of anticipation and fear, but I could never capture those dancing patches, they would vanish and I would be standing there, poking my foot around in dry, rustling leaves. One morning I crushed a snail under my shoe and stood there for a moment, quite still, staked to the spot with horror. After some time it passed, as inexplicably as it had come. But it had been just the same when I found that dead mouse in the bottle. That time, too, I had felt more than just revulsion and pain, something else to which I had been unable to give a name. And as I walked it seemed to me there was a swarm of voices following me. For a while they were so clear they reminded me of seagulls in the distance. Yet for all these years I knew nothing about them, even though I was sometimes so close to them.

The workshop moved into our courtyard, with soot and oil. The sledgehammer pounded against a hot white slab and rang out against the cold anvil. Reality had forced itself quite a lot closer. It had begun with a machine for making marshmallow snowballs. Often, when Henning designed things in sheer playfulness, he succeeded. He produced efficient, you might even say serious, gadgets. This one began on the outside of a flattened-out cake box. I was sitting there eating a marshmallow snowball, and as I was eating it I was drawing a machine that made new ones, a perpetuum mobile spitting out snowballs. Clouds of beaten egg whites migrated down from the heavens into its insides, and a flurry of desiccated coconut I dotted in with my pencil was pulled down into a funnel. I was quite little when I drew it and Henning was sitting next to me, listening to my explanations. Suddenly he was interested. He started drawing himself, first on the cake box and then on transparent design paper he tacked to a board.

A blacksmith made the real machine. It was an unwieldy monstrosity. Henning asked Tora Otter, who sold sweets at the market, to try it out. Fredrik was nothing but contemptuous at first, they say. But the machine really did produce snowballs, white inside and dense as little heads of cabbage. Now and then it would have a clamorous breakdown, an intimation of overheating and intertwined cogs from deep down in the steel-plated heart of civilization, after which it would turn the snowballs into pancakes, and mix lubricating oil into the white mass of meringue. Then they'd send for Henning, who would come with his ashen face and his toolbox full of monkey wrenches and soldering irons. He might lie there underneath it for half the night, on the floor of the cold hallway with Fredrik, until the heavy, rattling sound took over once more, and the machine began to spit out its puffs, the first ones gray inside and still tasting of oil, then gradually whiter and fluffier.

Fredrik overcame his scorn for the bumbling machine, and for the smell of brandy and the hangovers; he began to admire my Pappa.

Fredrik was professional and strong-willed, responsible, persevering and realistic. He was worthy of a talent like my father's. But Henning was the one endowed with it.

When Fredrik was a little over thirty, he was promoted to foreman at Swedish Engineering, and eventually he became a supervisor. During the Metalworkers' strike after the war he developed gastritis and insomnia. He would wake up very early in the mornings and wander around the house all by himself. Sometimes he would tackle a repair job. I might wake up at four or five in the morning to a dull pounding.

In 1949 Henning designed the Universal Ball Bearing. By that time the puff machine had been standing rusty in the basement of the Angel House for years. It had been down there since rationing, when there were no ingredients to be had. It had been too cantankerous to be worth any more work or a patent application. But the Universal Ball Bearing was different. Fredrik admired its simple, almost self-explanatory design, and told Henning he stood to make his fortune. The Universal Ball Bearing would be marketable and perfect for serial production.

Yes, he even went so far as to say that all the things Henning had invented thus far had been in preparation for this.

Thus this ball bearing seemed to have been waiting, curled up somewhere in the universe just waiting for Henning, the same way the snowball machine had been waiting for me and my newly-sharpened pencil point.

And thus the workshop came into being, and reality came to our courtyard. Number 13 Chapel Road ceased to be an enclave of contemplation and melancholy. All the bottles of drink were gone. The pounding and hammering began to be far outside Henning's head. These were his most sober years, years of optimism and daylight, pounding, milling, the smell of oil, and confidence.

It would begin on a very small scale in the big, disused laundry building my Grandpa Abel had had built to compete with the big municipal laundry. A blacksmith out on the edge of town had died recently, and they purchased all his machinery and tools at auction.

They had no trouble borrowing money. Fredrik was a man with a spotless record, who punctually repaid the mortgage on the house he had built and, when it came right down to it, my Pappa was a genius.

The smith's black old equipment was terribly dilapidated. For weeks, they spent every evening doing repairs and making improvements. They produced their own drill chucks and revolver heads for the old lathe. Fredrik devoted all his vacation time to the project. He didn't dare give his notice at Swedish Engineering until autumn. The first morning he no longer had his supervisor's booth to go to he was standing at the file bench looking extremely pale when Henning came in around seven. He'd had a sleepless night. That was how it began, and how it often was. No one knew what time he got there; he was always first.

Almost too much reality came into our courtyard. I didn't dare tell them how much I hated the high-pitched whining of the polishers. I couldn't tell Henning, and I certainly couldn't tell Fredrik. But dreams had also come into our yard, a new kind of dreams. I was drawn into them, too, and started imagining things.

It was all gray around me. No one was starving, but it stunk of rats. The only beautiful thing I had seen was the sunset out beyond the foundry, yellow, deepening into red like the cooling castings. And the treetops.

The lindens were tall between the houses. Their branches drew in the light from the sky, no matter how grim and sooty it was, and their huge root systems sucked the moisture and salt out of the ground beneath the cobblestones. They grew taller and taller in constant starvation; their longing for the forest was the only nutrition they had.

Everyone was fed up with all the rationing, I saw that their faces were gray when I began to notice them outside the house. The heavy ones looked like they were suffering from stomachs full of gas and bad food, the thin ones were stacks of bones, grimacing.

There was nothing to draw, except snowball machines. I tried to draw love, flowers, princesses, frilly clothes, but nothing came out right.

I got to know a wealthy girl. Later I would call her Kaa. Her real name was Ingela Iversen-Lindh. She lived in a big house full of objects that gleamed mysteriously as we passed them, in unheated rooms. There was something wrong with their wealth. It was diseased. But I didn't know in what way, nor that the illness was incurable.

Their riches still existed, and it made the cocoa taste different. I told Kaa. It's Van Houtens, she answered pragmatically. She lived in her wealth like the lampreys in their rushing river, wouldn't notice until it dried up.

There is money in every nook and cranny in the world. Mattresses and pillowcases are stuffed with it. There's money in tea caddies and wall safes, in bra cups and briefcases, between rounds of crispbread in the bottom oven, in the fist of a dead man, in hymnals, in stockings and in bouquets of roses. Until I got to know Jenny I believed that money was distributed arbitrarily, like a cloud of golden sperm; money pollinated whoever it encountered.

She taught me that money comes to those who deserve it, and that the dealer is the incorruptible world order. Poverty is a sign of moral laxity. You didn't get up early enough in the morning, you didn't change your underwear. The reasons can always be traced, although you sometimes have to look back a couple of links in the chain.

Today, Jenny is nothing but a tired old woman who takes the bus and has trouble getting on and off it, wears a woolen coat although she could use a fur, and buys soup bones when they're on special offer. Healthy young men go by car, furs walk around with tax dodgers inside and barbecue chickens fly into the mouths of those who turn up their noses at a mess of porridge. But that hasn't kept Jenny from believing in the world order. What she believes is that, after having forced mankind to fast for forty days, it is now shepherding us up onto a high mountain. She, however, is resisting. In those days, before the world order had begun offering mankind temptations, the principle of fair distribution applied up to our sort, and even a little higher. Then logic and justice were suspended. The very rich were simply participants in a huge, mad lottery. A wheel of fortune spun, spraying gold onto the crowd.

I sometimes saw Patrik Iversen-Lindh, Kaa's pappa, hurrying by. He was friendly, rushed, and burdened with worries about his rotting wholesale empire. I don't think he ever derived the slightest pleasure from all the money that passed through his accounts and ledgers. God only knows if he had ever even seen a pristine banknote. The Iversen-Lindhs were living with the after-effects of their wealth, and I can now imagine that that was like waking up one March afternoon after a long fever. But the paintings were still hung, the silver was tarnished but still in its cases.

It was patently obvious that if my Pappa and I were ever going to have any money to throw around, it was not going to be acquired by the sweat of our brows or by prudence. The Universal Ball Bearing had not come into being because Henning had been an early riser. I knew precisely what happened when he had a brainstorm, how he walked around daydreaming. Most of his ideas came to naught. Frivolous or serious? You couldn't always say. But there was happiness, always happiness.

We would go by car, we would have a Bokhara rug with an elephant foot pattern against the deep red, satiny background, we would holiday at the seaside, with a room at the Lysekil Beach Hotel, we would sleep in pink cretonne sheets, no question about that.

But more importantly: the grayness would fade and dissolve. The voices would be gentler, the stones kinder, the rain softer, the faces livelier. I had become an adult, biologically speaking. My body could be impregnated. But I never gave that a moment's thought. Instead, I had been reinitiated into melancholy. The dreams had crept up on us. They were like a film of oil in the air. Even Fredrik dreamed, wide awake and sleepless, and Jenny dreamed over her sewing machine while she was altering clothes. But I think I was the only one who dreamed outright of wealth; puberty can be crude and honest. Both Henning and Fredrik saw money as basically indecent. To Fredrik, Labor was sacred, to Henning Ideas were. But I dreamed, perfectly trivially, that the Universal Ball Bearing would give us piles of money, old silver, Van Houtens cocoa powder, leather-bound books, the glow from the fire inside the windowpanes and the rain on the outside.

I suppose Henning was born too late, into a world where the important technical inventions had already been made. I believe he actually dreamed of Watts' and Boultons' little workshop in Soho where the primitive prototypes of steam engines clattered and hissed in an environment that was still peaceful as the countryside, a heather-covered hilltop with a running river that made the belts and the wheels go around. From there (and from our laundry building) change would be wrought upon the world!

Fredrik dreamed about having one of those little, all-round workshops with skilful craftspeople, a place where just about anything could be made to order from a design, where the welding work was impeccable and the forging well and efficiently done.

They could only afford to hire two lads who'd just finished their seven years of comprehensive school. They were called Ove and Morgan. But after a year and a half the firm had four partners. There was Arne Johansson, a former bandy coach who had once been a prominent player. During his years of greatness in the thirties, Swedish Engineering had given him an easy job in the stockroom as a way of sponsoring his bandy career. After the war he had resigned and moved to a little foundry town where the bandy team, on its way into the national league, needed a coach. He'd done well for three years, but the year the team was relegated Johansson became the scapegoat and returned to town, out of a job.

The other one was a herring dealer. Way back before the war he'd stormed out of a mechanical engineering workshop when he and the owner had clashed. He was a skilful smith (even when he was a herring dealer people still called him Blacksmith Rundgren), and Fredrik admired him both for his professionalism and the pride and courage he had displayed toward his former employer.

But he was no longer as proud as Fredrik believed. He'd been worn down by pounding the pavement between the station and the market square with his herring cart, by the newspaper he wrapped it in, that covered his hands in newsprint, by the fish scales that stuck to his clothes and the smell, that eternal stench of fish. I think he had his regrets. He was deaf from the noise of the workshops, which also made him touchy and suspicious.

The old laundry building where they worked was a long, narrow room. At one end, where the hearth and the chimney were, they had built in a brick forge, with a hood over the deep pit where the coal glowed. I would sometimes stand watching Blacksmith Rundgren lift a piece of work that just a few minutes earlier had been a cold iron rod, out of the forge. It was heavy and white when he set it on the anvil and raised the sledgehammer over it. First the rod grew yellower, then redder. When the iron began to cool, Pappa explained:

"That's how the stars cool down. The hottest ones are white, the ones that will soon be extinguished are swollen and red."

"Are the stars made of iron?"

"Yes," he said. "Probably they often are."

In the courtyard under a corrugated metal roof far from the stars, there were flat bits and I and U bits.

I didn't understand much of what was going on in there. I didn't know what die stocks were. Morgan and Ove looked stupid, but they didn't hesitate when Fredrik told them to go get one.

When Pappa bought a set of German-made tools, I was told to sit down and try to translate the instructions, because I was doing German at school. I sat with the thin, transparent paper one whole evening, but my book learning was useless in reality. Fredrik got impatient, cursed, and figured the whole thing out by staring at springs, nuts, and blades. The instructions are still folded into my German dictionary: *Eine Feder drückt einen der Schenkel gegen den kurzen Hilfsschenkel, ge stattet aber, das Werkzeug ohne Verstellung des abgenommenen Masses über Hindernisse, Eindrehungen usw. hinweg zu heben.*

I had pink fingernails in a world where everybody else's fingers were black, firmly blackened with oil and soot. I knew nothing. Oh, how hard they worked!

They had to take in repair work. There were problems about the patent and the name of the Universal Ball Bearing. There was already a bearing known as the

Universal Link. Henning probably shouldn't have given in, but he did, renaming his design the Radax Link because it was a combination of radial and axial bearings; it transferred both radial pressure and pressure working lengthwise on the axis. At any rate it was meant to. But there were problems with overheating and cracked castings.

The problems gathered like house sparrows in our courtyard.

One day Jenny was standing in Pappa's and my kitchen looking down at the courtyard.

"That wretched man," she said, softly and bitterly. "I wish he'd never walked in here."

I went over and looked. Her gaze was following a tall, thin man who was just walking across the gravel over to the laundry, where the doors were open. There were the sounds of the shaper and the miller from inside.

The figure crossing our yard was a familiar one. Everybody in town knew who he was. He was Konrad Eriksson, better known as The Communist. He had worked at a bakery, but been fired. Now he made his living as a jack of all trades, and as a cinema projectionist in the evenings. He was always writing letters to the editor of the paper. He wrote well and often critically about the local social democrats, so our non-socialist paper was happy to publish them.

The Communist was Arne Johansson's brother-in-law, which was how he got involved with the workshop. He found the company extremely interesting, not seeing it as a firm with four managers and two workers, but as a cooperative worker-owned enterprise. None of them had seen it like that.

Konrad Eriksson was tall and stooped. If you saw him in just his shirtsleeves, his backbone stood out sharply. According to Jenny, all he ever did was blabber and breed babies. His head was round, his ears large, and he was so thin his shoulder blades protruded from his back like incipient wings.

He would turn up toward the end of the work day and talk with his brother-in-law and the two lads. From the beginning, Blacksmith Rundgren didn't take part, and Fredrik just turned his back. Pappa sometimes enjoyed a discussion with him, but he never took their talks seriously.

After some time it became clear that The Communist had a plan. He was urging Ove and Morgan to demand to be made partners in this worker-owned enterprise. And, true to form, one Friday afternoon when Fredrik was giving them their pay packets, they stood there spouting what Konrad Eriksson had taught them. There they stood in their clogs and oily work shirts, with their big hands sticking out of their too-short sleeves. They were afraid of Fredrik, who laughed good-naturedly and asked whether Morgan was planning to be chairman of the board and Ove vice. They left, embarrassed. The next week they were at it again, though, saying they'd joined the union. When Fredrik heard that he was dumbstruck at first, and then went white.

He replied: "I s'pose the thing for me to do now is join the Confederation of Swedish Employers."

His voice was grim and jeering. But he meant the sarcasm as much about himself and the derelict laundry as he did about the Cheeky Sods, as he called them. All he said to Henning was that they couldn't possibly know that what the partners shared evenly were mortgage and interest payments on the loans, but no profits to speak of.

"I have to tender lower and lower to get any commission work at all, and they have the gall to come and demand wages in line with the collectively bargained agreement. They have their nerve!"

I think Pappa and the others had noticed how he'd started saying I instead of we. I can't order semi-oval irons for that one little repair. I did the figures on it. I put in a tender. It just won't pay.

Fredrik wasn't very old but he was still a supervisor of the old school, skilled at all the kinds of work he monitored. Piece work rates, time studies and shift work had forced him out into the no man's land between laborer and purchaser of labor. Until the Metalworkers' strike he had had a tough life; during the strike I believe it became intolerable. His insomnia and stomach troubles multiplied. If anyone had known what it was to be depressed, I am sure people would have said he was.

His dream had been of a workplace sheltered from the tough labor movement struggle, an exceptional little place where all that counted was being good at what you did. When the Universal Ball Bearing/Radax Link didn't work out, he demanded that they work on contract for one of the larger local workshops, supplying them with some kind of relatively simple piece work they could do large numbers of relatively fast. Soon Morgan and Ove, too, were spending their days polishing the surfaces of flatirons. When there was no other work, even Arne Johansson had to do some polishing. Blacksmith Rundgren was getting uneasy. For the moment there was plenty of forging work for him, they had lots of repairs. Fredrik cursed farmers who had used their equipment so hard it broke, but he should actually have been grateful to them. He who was used to the kind of manufacturing and the resources available to a large workshop, though, didn't like having to fix rubbish. They had no choice now, however. If they didn't, they wouldn't be able to meet the payments on their loans. Henning ran back and forth to the bank with pieces of paper reading: ".... Please pay to myself or order, against this sole bill of exchange...", oblong pieces of paper Jenny found just as disagreeable as condoms. Now Fredrik started demanding that Henning, too, do some of the contract work. Of course, that was insane. He withered like a flower in the dust from the grinder.

Altogether too much reality in our courtyard: the nerve-wracking whistle of the polishers, the men behind the sooty windowpanes in their yellow protective goggles, box after box of semi-finished flatirons coming in through the archway. And Henning seldom at the drawing board, not even in the evenings any longer.

He called the area upstairs of the laundry his design workshop. He'd set up there in Abel's day, and I'm sure that was where he took Lisa. Fredrik called it the office, and the others ate their dinners up there. They'd started sitting around after Fredrik had gone home in the evenings, too. They sat there having endless discussions with Konrad Eriksson the Communist. Tense, ashen and sleepless, Fredrik dragged through a spring and a summer. In the autumn there was a huge row up there. He threatened to throw them out. Nothing happened except that a cup of coffee got spilt out onto the oilcloth, the rest was verbal warfare. But Konrad Eriksson now had a foothold upstairs in the laundry building and the others refused to see him tossed out. Probably this was less out of loyalty to Eriksson than because they resented Fredrik putting on managerial airs.

At home Fredrik called it ridiculous, said it would have been laughable if it hadn't been a matter of life and death. When he said life and death, he meant loan payments, pay packets, reputations and the future. They sat up there, Blacksmith Rundgren who was so deaf he couldn't hear what the Communist was saying, and Arne Johansson who never uttered a word if he didn't have to and had nothing but bandy in his head, and the Cheeky Sods, not to mention Henning, who was an intelligent man. They all just sat there like sleepy, hypnotized frogs in front of a snake. They started asking others up, or else the others just dropped by uninvited. The electric heater glowed all evening long and they made bitter coffee and let it stand on the stove as long as there was any heat at all. Henning got sick of it. He had never been interested in politics, and the discussions were growing more and more political.

I don't know what happened up there after Henning stopped going. I don't know if Jenny was right when she said: if only that wretched man had never walked in here.

No demands were ever made after the meetings upstairs in the laundry. They just talked and talked, but Fredrik thought that was bad enough. Now, Damn it, there was work to be done and mouths to be shut. So he shut his mouth and went straight home after work. He started spending his evenings in other ways than sitting bent over tender bids. Jenny got him back. Sleepless and bitter, he turned his back on their dithering and their plans.

The seats of the chairs in the office, as he called it, were black with oil and polishing dust. On the wall there was a calendar with a well-endowed girl posing in the middle of a tractor wheel. Her breasts rose like creampuffs from a sequined bathing suit. Henning's drawing board stood in a dark corner; they'd moved his light. On the desk were the yellow time sheets with Fredrik's dirty fingerprints. They put coffee cups down on them. I think that caused him more pain than anything they might think of to say. They may not have said anything important at all. I saw the lamplight over the desk and, if I stood at a certain angle in our kitchen, I could see the glow of the electric fire.

One night they forgot to turn it off. A couple of time sheets probably fluttered down, hitting the hot coil.

I was spending the night at Jenny and Fredrik's, and the phone call woke me. But Pappa told me what had woken him was a pounding on the door, so loud he knew instantly something was wrong. When he opened the door, the person who had woken him was already halfway down the stairs again. Henning looked out the vestibule window, and saw the laundry building in flames.

It burned to the ground and the machinery was ruined. They managed to drag the big tool cupboard out, but the heat had already ruined most of the things locked inside. In the morning there was expensive lathing steel on the kitchen table, and they were trying to wipe it clean and sort it out. Fredrik had gone into the burning building several times. He brought out the marbleized ledgers where the accounts were kept. Most of them had scorched edges. He injured his hands, and both his shirt and jacket were sooty. The fire brigade had trouble getting into our courtyard, so their firefighting efforts were delayed.

Blacksmith Rundgren and Arne Johansson were there of course, helping. But no one had told Ove and Morgan. In the morning they walked into the yard as usual. I saw them through the kitchen window. They stood there, side by side, staring at the sooty snow, at the smoking laundry foundation and at the machinery, resembling the charred bodies of animals who had died in their cages.

It was cloudy weather with rain in the air. When I lay in my bed looking out the window, all I could see was a gray square. It could be absolutely any season. The darkness grew slowly up out of the corners of the room. There was some kind of tension in the furniture, as if its weight had increased with the darkness, and it needed to expand. I could have turned on my bedside light and stayed in bed, but in those days there was some restlessness in me that drove me out onto the streets in the rain and the cold. I called it going to the library.

I was a skinny sixteen-year-old in a brown coat, a black beret with a little silver pin and with crêpe rubber soled winter boots on my feet. I was carrying a pile of books.

I walked out into the High Street, passing the silent, black row of buildings on my way toward the square. There were people about down by the bus station. The light from the kiosk shone on their faces, and white vapor rose from the sausage stall and into the cold air. Many shop windows were dark. The sidewalk slanted down toward the street, and the rainwater murmured softly in the gutter.

I continued down the High Street and all along Industry Road to the last building, which was the hospital. The streetlamps were high up on their brown poles, few and far between, and they seemed to be heads, observing my route. I walked home along Maiden Street, because it was less ugly. I liked the gardens of the big houses, with their scents wafting out of the darkness even this late in the autumn: apples and leaves.

I was cautious on the unlit stretches of road between the streetlights, because I knew the pavement was potholed. Along the steep rise leading up to the Highway Bridge, chestnut trees grew. Sometimes I could see the red of the sunset beyond the concrete spans of the bridge. The strange trees, with spiral blossoms on their branches in the spring, the clouds in the sunset and the sounds of the shunting engines under the bridge all excited me. I often stood there for quite a while, pretending I was in a different city. Sometimes it was Dublin, sometimes Leningrad or

192

Milan. I had no idea at all what those cities looked like. I was simply testing their names against the hazy red sky behind the smokestacks of Swedish Engineering.

Behind the chestnuts was a small house with two sun porches. Sometimes I could hear someone playing the piano inside. When the windows were open in the gray wooden house opposite, I could hear Wickström the baker's children and their parakeets, and the radio that was always on.

A bumpy road led down past the railway tracks by the square. There were no streetlights, but I was never particularly frightened walking there. On one side there were long rows of silent freight cars, and on the other was the wall around Wilhelmsson's joinery. There was a smell of newly-sawn lumber from the wood-pile, and then it was suddenly replaced by the clingy, poisonous smell from the yard of the pharmacy, with its big glass demijohns in their wicker baskets, insulated with wood shavings.

When I crossed the trampled gravel of the square, it was so quiet I could hear the footsteps of people on the wooden stairs leading up to the bridge across the tracks. In the summer the fountain splashed, sprinkling the weeping willows. Then there were voices in the evenings, and cars coming and going behind the newspaper stand.

When I got back to the High Street, I had walked a couple of kilometers, still carrying the pile of books. Sometimes I would just go home, others I would really go to the library and exchange them. The first part of Store Street was quite well-lit. Down by the building that housed the wine and spirits monopoly we called the bottle store, it was very dark. A stranger to town would never have found the library on Hovlunda Road without directions. The door was on the courtyard side, and on the street side there was a big, thorny hedge. Children's books were on the ground floor. Although I now had the kind of library card that allowed me to borrow books upstairs, I was still as afraid of the children's librarian as I had always been. You could smell her sulfa cream all the way out in the main hall. Her cheeks were spotty, full of scars from old pimples, and caked with medicinal cream.

I was an upper secondary schoolgirl now, a young woman on her way to adulthood. But the children's librarian still had the right to bully me. Someone had found a book on a bench in the city park, destroyed by the rain, and handed it in to her, probably just because they were too lazy to go upstairs. But it was a book from the adult shelves, by Vicki Baum. I had read almost everything by her, and the children's librarian knew it. She claimed I'd taken it from the library without having it stamped. Endless harassment. Sulfur-scented accusations. Ashen pale denials. To what end?

Probably to no end at all, but not for no reason. Pappa was bullied at the Poly. Bullying was the order of the day.

It could have been worse. It could have started earlier. I remembered The Rat and Snot-Nose. But in those days Henning was still quite composed, good-looking and neat. Although he had begun making those trips to the peculiar castle, he was never hospitalized or arrested.

Now the experiment of the workshop was over. Fredrik had gone back to work for the big company, pale and stiff on the outside, wild with humiliation inside. Pappa had descended a peg or two. He'd begun rinsing his mouth with grog. That's how I remember it.

He had always looked tidy and well-kept, and his habits had been fastidious. The first sign that he was going down was this: he began to swill his mouth with diluted brandy.

He would fill his mouth with the light golden brown liquid, not swallowing it right away but keeping his mouth full. Rolling his cheeks, lips and tongue, he would swish it around. From the beginning, of course, he had only done it when he was alone, probably because he loved the taste of brandy mixed with vichy water, mild yet with a sting. I suppose his taste buds gradually became dulled to that taste, and wanted more. Or was he just trying to make each sip last longer? I realized it had become a habit of which he had lost conscious control. He had no idea he did it in the presence of others, or that this procedure produced a noisy, unsavory slurping sound. I was ashamed when he swilled the drink in his mouth like that. I took over the sense of shame he would have suffered if he had suddenly become aware of what he was doing.

Perhaps he swished his vichy water and brandy mixture around in his mouth because it was his only pleasure?

One day, the joy went out of my father the way a bird's little air sac is emptied. He stopped singing. He never tried to fly again.

I couldn't see any pleasure anywhere in this city that was holding us captive in a mold hard as cement. All I could see was cruelty and caprice. I was at the newly-built upper secondary school with pastel murals on the walls of the auditorium and the dining hall — a nation of young people dressed in blue and marching into the future. But the little painted leaves on the trees were squares and triangles.

When it was summer you could see the real leaves. Then I cycled and smelt the water from the lake and danced on swaying boards and kissed someone occasionally, held the hand of a boy with rough, aftershave-scented cheeks, sniffling the collar of his clean, white shirt.

There was one persistent fellow who was almost always trying to get me. His name was Hasse, and he was the son of Curre Clothes, the big garment factory. That was what people said: his father is Curre Clothes. He was good at kissing, even better at hand-holding, and he taught me to fish with a fly rod. But he was a year younger than I was, and I suspected he was only going with me because he knew what state Henning was in — Hasse Curtman's mamma was an alcoholic, one of the most talked-about people in town. He and his pappa tried to keep her indoors, but sometimes she would wander out into the streets, looking for drink. She still had a distinguished air about her, slightly disheveled, but distinguished. She probably wasn't as far gone as people said. But they just said it and said it and said it until Astrid Curtman took her own life toward the end of the winter of 1952 by drinking a whole bottle of whisky to rinse down a whole jar of sleeping pills.

In the local rumor mill there were endless versions of how she had done it: cheap aquavit, hanging, the jugular, a crack in the ice out by their summer place, rat poison, prussic acid, car fumes. But much later on her son told me what it had been, and it had been Ballantine's whisky and barbiturates.

This may have frightened me. We didn't hold hands for a long time. He must have felt very lonely, but I didn't think about that. I didn't think at all. I didn't feel much, either.

Jenny was the one who had taught me to live in this world, and I assume I owe her a deep debt of gratitude. If I had been alone with Henning I guess I would have had about as much of a chance as a hummingbird in a concrete silo. Jenny knew a great deal about the world she had lived her whole life in. Down there at the bottom were the corpses of Astrid Curtman and other little birds. Jenny taught the art of living through things. She did it by telling stories. You could also say she was a gossip, a talker of crap. She told stories for years on end and it got monotonous. But you learned such a lot. Here are two of her stories, frequently repeated.

The first one is about a man who was a tobacconist and who people called The Goat. One day he was behind his counter, I imagine it was twilight on a winter's day, while the slush and the gravel were spraying up from the tires of the cars on District Road. He was helping a woman who had come in to buy *Women's Weekly* or one of the other things he stocked for irreproachable people to purchase. The Goat carried smutty magazines as well. They were called things like PIN UP, COCK-TAIL and TOP HAT. In those days it wasn't all that easy to get girls to pose in the nude, so The Goat's magazines mostly contained pictures of no-longer-very-young-ladies, and not the prettiest ones at that. In some places they were as hairy as she-apes and probably scared the wits out of the boys who smuggled them to one another. They were relatively fully-clothed, with lacy black garter bands, frills and ruffles around their cracks, and midriff bulges. I never read the texts, but I understand they were lame. It a line of business that hadn't yet come into its own.

Inside the shop a customer had just paid the Goat. He was fussing with his paper bag and his change. I don't know if his wife was crippled or if he had been frightened by a hairy she-ape in his youth. Maybe he was perfectly normal. At any rate, he picked up a magazine, a PIN UP. He did it covertly, which is easy to understand. He was ashamed because he was a school teacher. That's what Jenny said, so of course it's the truth. He was a comprehensive school teacher and a social improver, and the man who had founded the local art appreciation society.

He dropped the magazine into his paper bag, just letting it slide down surreptitiously, blocked from view by the woman with *Women's Weekly*.

But that lady saw him do it. She was an irreproachable citizen and the wife of a hauler from the north side of town. She was shocked, her heart began to pound. It's all very easy to imagine. Here she was, really in the thick of things.

She waited until the teacher had left the shop. Then she said: "He stole a magazine."

"What?" asked the Goat.

Mutely, she pointed to the magazines no decent woman would call by name. Then she walked out.

The Goat must have spent a long time,considering how to handle this delicate matter, because he didn't go to see the schoolteacher until that evening when he was sitting listening to his daughter practice the piano. Undoubtedly with the parish magazine on his lap. The Goat asked if he could have a word in private which, of course, gave rise to a family commotion.

They had their conversation in the dining nook. The family cannot have heard a word, simply seen their profiles against the frosted pane of glass in the door. The Goat waited patiently through the schoolteacher's denials and his pleas, through his offer to pay *at least*, and finally while he went into the bedroom and got the magazine. He brought it out wrapped in *The Correspondent*.

Having seen to it that justice was done, The Goat was now ready to torment the teacher a little. But how? He told him, presumably in an offhand sort of way, about the irreproachable woman who had witnessed the awkward event, the actual theft. This is where my ability to empathize fails me. Jenny, too, dried up and kept it short. But she always told it the same way.

The Goat demanded that the schoolteacher go to see the irreproachable citizen and apologize to her. In fact, that was the one condition upon which The Goat was

196

prepared to keep the matter to himself. Which, of course, he was unable to do any-way. As the schoolteacher surely knew would be the case.

So why did he go, then? We do not know. Undoubtedly he was petrified. After worrying over it for two days, he went. I assume he inventoried all the options: bar-biturates, rat poison, prussic acid from the cake shop, a drinking bout and freezing to death, hanging, going through the ice, a lorry on the Highway Bridge.

Is there a lesson to be learned from this? None. That's the lesson. There is no meaning, no logic, nothing that could have been predicted, The Goat was making up his own rules. He had the game in his hand.

Jenny did not tell this story as an example of anything, or because I was sup-posed to learn anything from it. She told it because it had happened.

Her other story was about a building contractor and his wife. He had inherited the business from his father, and he was pretty flush. His wife had a Persian lamb coat with a muskrat chasing its own tail as a collar. She was little and black-haired, an irascible looking woman. One of their sons was in my class, so I spent some time at their house. In the palace of the contractor she walked around in a flowery housecoat, short-temperedly brandishing a feather duster. He may have grown tired of her, or he may have cared about her in a quiet, middle-aged way, who am I to say? Whichever it was, he fell for another woman. She was an unfortunate creature who spent her days behind the counter of a jewelry shop and was a divor-cée. That was uncommon. It indicated chinks in the armor or character flaws, unless the man was a drunkard and unusually bastardly. But there was no infor-mation on that because she had moved to town alone.

They didn't see one another in town, neither of them dared. They must have been very much in love, because they took the trouble of going to another town nearby, she traveling by train and he by car. There they took separate rooms at the hotel by the station, and spent the night in his. He told his wife he had to go out of town on business. But it didn't take long before she knew all about it. A friend of hers knew the woman who worked the switchboard at the station hotel. And when it came right down to it, the next town along was in the same galaxy, even if it didn't feel that way to the lovers when they came together in that little room with its bright electric heater and its tulle curtains pulled closed.

The contractor's wife asked the switchboard operator to call her the next time he reserved a room at the hotel, and so she did. They had just come in. It was a cold, raw October night. He had ordered a red wine toddy to be brought to his room. So there they were.

His wife hung up and called a taxi. It cost a pretty penny but she didn't mind.

They were sleeping when she caught them. They'd fallen asleep on top of the bed, naked, with the counterpane over their legs. He came home with her. The engine gave him some trouble that cold night.

When they got home and were getting undressed in their own bedroom beside their own double bed, she noticed he didn't have his underwear on. He'd been in such a hurry to get into his trousers when he woke up and found her standing in the room brandishing her sharp sword that he'd forgotten them.

And now the question arises: is the rest of Jenny's story actually true? Did she demand that he drive right back and collect his briefs? And did he really do it?

Well, that was how the story had it, anyway, when it slid out into the city on its slithery stomach. You'll do best to believe it, if you know what's good for you.

One evening I came walking down Cobbler's Row past the silent Carlsborg building where the pay desk and offices of the town finance department were. The thuja bushes were capped with the snow that was falling fast and gray. Around the streetlamps, though, it whirled and swirled like flakes of gold. I had been at the library right up until closing time. I was carrying the pile of books I had borrowed, nervous the snow would soak them and I would have more trouble with the librarian. At that moment I heard a loud thud behind me. The sound came from the intersection I'd just passed, to see what had happened I had to retrace my steps a little way. There were two cars in the middle of the crossing. Not until I was very close did I hear that one of the engines was still running. The snow was muffling all the sounds. The library and the Baptist church were closed up tight, dark and silent. Across the street were the city park, and on my side Carlsborg, empty in the evening. I had been the only witness to a collision.

It wasn't a serious accident. Henrik Sterner, a teacher at the upper secondary school, had driven his Opel into the Ford Eiffel belonging to Torben Holmlund, the pastor of one of the nonconformist congregations. He'd had that Ford since before the war, and it didn't have so much as a scratch on it. I heard that now, through the snowfall. They both got out and were talking, loudly at first and then more and more quietly. In the end they both got into Holmlund's car, and I assume they settled the matter there. I couldn't see what they were doing. Then the pastor drove off. When Sterner was getting back into his own car he caught sight of me. I had him for geography and biology. In fact, he was the one who had taught me how the reproductive organs work, although I wasn't thinking about it at that moment. But I was extremely embarrassed to be caught standing there watching. It was obvious I'd been there for a while, because the snow had accumulated on my shoulders and beret.

I started walking, but Sterner drove up alongside me. He wound down the window, getting snow on his lips and eyelids.

"Ann-Marie, would you like a ride home?" he asked. "What a snowstorm!"

That was completely incredible. I didn't know what to say, so I just walked around to the passenger side and got in.

Mr. Sterner was a tall, thin man with black, bushy eyebrows and upward-combed spiky hair. I think we girls considered him good-looking. He was extremely patronizing, with a touch of sarcasm if he was in a good mood.

Now he was entirely different. I was very attuned to the unreality of the situation. The snow was falling so heavily the car headlights could barely penetrate it. Sterner babbled nervously and was driving me in the entirely wrong direction. I could smell drink on him, there was no question about it.

He kept inserting my name into his sentences. He never called us by name otherwise. He just said "you" and we said "Mr. Sterner". But now, upset and confused, he was completely transformed. The stiff Mr. Hyde turned into a chatty, entreating Jekyll. Was it the drink? Or that he was afraid I would tell someone he'd been driving under the influence? I don't suppose he was all that drunk, but I could smell liquor on his breath.

He'd turned into one of the little streets above the cemetery, stopping the car in front of a brown wooden house.

"You'll come in won't you, Ann-Marie?" he asked.

He never told me what he wanted. Never, although I stayed for a couple of hours. He just went on talking and talking. We were sitting in a cold little room just inside the basement door. I knew it had been a waiting room in the days of the previous owner, who was a vet. I thought I had seen a light on in an upstairs window. I was constantly on edge, afraid his wife might appear.

He spoke about school, and how much he hated this city, but above all he went over and over the accident. He repeated that Holmlund had been at least partly at fault, but that he hadn't wanted to make a fuss. Pay up and shut up, that was his line, he said. It sounded light-hearted but light-hearted was the last thing he looked. He sat opposite me on a wooden chair with no armrests, his knees locked and his hands on the seat of the chair under his scrawny buttocks. My knees were also tightly closed, and my shoulders and hair were damp where the snow had melted. There were puddles around my boots.

A bare light bulb hung from the ceiling and I was feeling no more cheerful than the dogs who had once waited there on their leashes, to be seen by the vet.

He seemed to have been seized by a sudden interest in my personality and my destiny, because he started asking me whether I liked school and why I didn't work harder — I had talent, of course. It truly astonished me to hear him say that, and when I thought about it I didn't believe him. I didn't answer him at all, just bit my already cracked and peeling upper lip, not knowing what to do with my soaking wet mittens that reeked of wet sheep. I didn't even want to answer his question about whether or not I enjoyed school. In the first place I thought it was a stupid question, like asking if you enjoyed being imprisoned at If or Alcatraz. And in the second place I was certain he was trying to get me to say things he planned to use against me, in one of his terrible caustic eruptions in class, or at a staff meeting when marks were being discussed. When he put his hand on my forearm, or rather on my damp brown coat sleeve, I went rigid and panicky. I thought for a few minutes he was going to start groping me, as people said. Maybe he'd had more to drink than I imagined. I kept expecting him to ask me not to tell anyone about the accident. But he never said anything that could be interpreted that way.

He said over and over again that he was sure I understood him. But I was getting confused. I didn't have the slightest idea what I was supposed to be understanding.

"I've got to be going," I said.

It was already much too late. Jenny must be worried. Although I was out almost every evening, I never came home late. I got up and pulled on my wet mittens, but he just kept on talking.

"I've got to go."

"Oh, of course, of course," he said.

He opened the door for me, no longer mentioning driving me home, which was a relief.

It was a longer walk home from here than from where we started on Cobblers' Row where the two cars had collided. But the snowstorm was over. It was a beautiful evening, and all the trees now had fluffy borders and brims of snow. There wasn't a soul about on Store Street. The cinema had finished ages ago. There had even been time for the snow to cover all the film-goers, footsteps. The shop windows were dark. Suit jackets and dresses, china mugs and books were now at rest in a gentle dimness, only lit up from the outside by the weak glow of the street-lamps and their reflections in the snow. Store Street stretched out ahead of me untrammeled, with not so much as a single black exhaust mark coughed out of a car engine. It was coated in soft, clean, new-fallen snow.

I stopped, uncertain for a moment as to whether I dared walk in it.

I'd walked along here so often, wandered up and down the streets, willing something. Something would happen.

What would happen must have to do with the color of the sky behind the foundry at sunset. Sometimes I had been so sure it was going to happen that I had made bets with myself. And lost them. During some periods I had also anticipated events; I had daydreamed as I walked the dim evening streets in to the city, where the light of the occasional street lamp glowed in the brown puddles. I walked between derelict sheds and empty freight cars. Set in dewy yards, the houses gleamed like lanterns. In the darkness between the timber piles I stumbled over a couple of boards and my shoes and socks got soaked but I didn't mind, just stumbled on with my hands in my coat pockets. I was in a waking dream.

Nothing happened and nothing came of it. I actually knew it would be like that. It was just a way of keeping myself going. I felt threatened, but not by external dangers. What I was terrified of was the tedium, that it would crush me or more like squeeze me to death, slowly, like a duck press when someone pensively tightens the vice and the duck is still alive.

I don't know when I stopped. Suddenly it was just all too meaningless. I had started reading at the same time, initially for the same reason I daydreamed. Often the books provided me with the material for my dreams. But I'd stopped dreaming, I don't know when. I learned French irregular verb conjugations by heart, and I still know them. But I've forgotten when I stopped having waking dreams. I only know how it feels when the duck is in the press and the vice is slowly being tightened. No escape is possible, no rescue, no matter how she quacks. The tedium, the compulsion, the repetition are squeezing all the juice out of her. I am I. Nothing helps.

I had compulsive thoughts as well. If a train passed under me as I crossed the Highway Bridge, it would happen. It would happen that very evening if there were pigeons on the roof of the post office.

It was a kind of ultimatum I'd given life. But I had nothing to threaten life with.

Now, however, it had happened. It had happened one evening when the snow was falling harder than usual, and when it finally happened I didn't realize it. I just felt extremely discomfited, almost afraid.

All the ultimatums I'd issued to life had long since expired, and expired again. But now, at last, it happened.

Life was a word I often heard. Human life. We used that word. We said: the meaning of life. Life has to be …

But that evening as I walked home from the Sterners, and it had stopped snowing and Store Street lay silent and clean, I realized there was no life. There was nothing but me and the snow and the houses where all the lights would soon be out. It was night. The stone walls were asleep. The crevices were dark.

Jenny was kind about it when I got home. I said I'd bumped into Mr. Sterner who had been in shock after a car crash and needed someone to talk to. When I said it that way it didn't really sound too peculiar. I heard in my own tone of voice that I sounded grown up and a little ironic.

I'd figured it out! There was nothing. But you had to get yourself something. It had to be something protective. Not to protect you from life but from nothing. Sarcasm. Conviction. Humor. Or fighting spirit. I hadn't figured out how you were supposed to do it, just that it was absolutely essential.

Jenny didn't think there was anything strange about it when I told her about the car accident and what happened afterwards. She just told me I should have a cup of cocoa and put on some warm dry socks after sitting around in my damp coat for so long.

"You could catch cold," she said. Then she started asking me about what the Sterners' house was like inside, and found out, to her disappointment, that I hadn't got past the dogs' waiting room.

In August 1954, I left for Uppsala. Jenny and Ingrid Johansson saw me off on the train. I remember thinking they looked both dowdyish and kind. I must have been extremely overwrought. I may have seemed edgy and not myself at the station. Fortunately, I don't remember. I saw the world I was leaving as small, gray and insignificant.

Of course we got to the station in such good time that our farewells were drawn out and awkward. In the end we ran out of subjects for conversation. Then Hasse Curtman turned up. He was carrying a bouquet of flowers. They were sweet williams: burgundy, purple, violet and white. Ingrid insisted they were graduation flowers and had been bought to celebrate my finishing school: I think she was a bit worked up herself. I was wearing my graduates' cap and I think it really got to her to be standing there with someone who'd managed to complete upper secondary school. Most people like us didn't.

When it was finally time for the train to depart, I kissed Jenny and Ingrid on the cheeks and they hugged me, clearly revived by the fact that the long wait was over. I kissed Hasse on the mouth, to my own surprise. Where we lived it was extremely unusual to do such a thing in broad daylight and in the presence of older ladies. But I did it anyway. Wound up as I was, I had already put the conventions of small town life behind me.

I had'nt organized anywhere to stay when I got to Uppsala, but Jenny'd given me the address of one of her distant relatives. His name was Lager, and to me the name had a ring of distinction and wisdom to it. Carrying my two heavy suitcases I asked my way until I found his address, 2, Main Square.

The main square actually turned out to be a little one, smaller than the market square in my home town. The bus station was there, and it was guarded on all sides but one by large stone mansions. In one of them I learned later, Karl Wilhelm Scheele — whom my Pappa had very much admired — had lived. There was also a cake shop. That was my first stop in Uppsala. I sat in its stuffy air, a mixture of cigarette smoke and coffee smells, staring at the house diagonally opposite. I was quite simply afraid to ring the bell at Johan Lager's.

He and his wife lived in a one room apartment around the back. When I was finally standing there with my two suitcases, they just stared at me, horrified, quite simply. Hardly saying anything, they indicated their cramped quarters. Every nook and cranny reeked of poverty. He worked at a meat packing plant on the edge of town, and he was also the caretaker of the mansion. His wife's job was to keep the enormous, winding stone staircases clean. She cleaned other people's houses as well. Her hands were swollen and covered in a rough rash. I felt so sick and so frightened by their poverty I barely dared to breathe in their kitchen, which smelled of leaking gas pipes.

He ran out to borrow someone's phone, and less than an hour later I was in a taxi, on my way to an address on the other side of the river, in Svartbäcken. It took a long time to get there. The road grew more and more potholed, less and less urban, and the streetlamps farther and farther apart. Finally we stopped in front of a three-story building. The wind had worn down the bushes by the door. In the twilight I could see the sweeping Uppsala plain and a barn-like building I later understood was a brickworks.

I lodged there throughout my time in Uppsala. My landlord and his wife were distant relatives of the Lagers. They were a young couple who'd had a shotgun wedding and, in their panic, had rented a larger apartment than they could afford. So I moved into the biggest room and paid a hundred and ten crowns a year in rent. I didn't dare try to bargain them down. He worked in a shoe factory, and every morning just before six she took the baby to her mother's so she could go to her job in the kitchen at the Rickomberga Home for Crippled Children.

They had hardly any furniture, and most of what they did have they moved into the smaller room where they were going to live. I got a rollaway bed, a chair, a chest of drawers and a sewing machine. The sewing machine was the fold-down kind, so I could use its stand as a desk. I sat studying with my feet on the treadles. From the ceiling hung a white globe with a seventy-five watt bulb in it.

My relations with these two bitter, terrified human beings were such that he and I couldn't stand each other and she and I got on fine. She wept a lot and told me what it was like to have been forced into marriage. I never dared to move out. Once I hinted that I'd like to, but she started crying and saying I was the only person she could confide in That probably wasn't true. But how would they ever find another student to rent their room? It was so far from the university. No, I didn't dare move out because they had taken me for the simple reason that the Lagers had talked them into it. But eventually I found myself spending as little time as I could at their place.

The first few weeks weren't like that, of course. Then I didn't know a soul. I had signed up for Nordic languages because Jenny and Fredrik thought I should be a teacher. Pappa had unrealistic suggestions about subjects none of us had ever heard of. But the higher education advisor who had been to our school had told us that if you took a suitable combination of subjects, introductory and then continuation courses, you could earn a degree. It would take me five years if I kept my nose to the grindstone. Then I could get out of there and start teaching.

I took the bus to my lectures, which were held in a building called Philo-logicum behind the English Garden. Everyone in Nordic studies seemed to know one another already. They talked about things I'd never heard of, about professors who taught I-had-no-idea-what subjects, about words like cum laude, orals and compendia. My situation was a classic one, I'm sure, but I had no idea at the time, so that was no comfort. I didn't know there had been provincial students before me. If anyone had compared me with one, I wouldn't have seen what they meant, either. I wore tight black trousers with a red elasticized belt at the waist, and a black tunic one of the third-year girls I met at the Philolog told me was existentialist. Now I called it the Philolog and I knew what orals and cum laude were, too.

Once a month I went to the Swedish Commercial Bank at The Square and cashed in my student loan. I got seventy-five crowns a month and was in a constant state of starvation which, to begin with, was quite becoming. Instead of food, I bought cheap blouses and elasticized belts, lipsticks and brassieres with hard, pointed cups. When my landlords were at work I made porridge from their oatmeal, terrified he was keeping track of how much was in the bag. He was constantly suspicious, but I never got caught because I wasn't so dumb that I would help myself to sliced pork or sticky buns.

My whole life changed at the party for new students at the student union. I was a little scared to go because I had heard they hazed new students. And they did, but if you were a girl and not too bad looking you got off quite lightly.

I had on my best dress. Jenny had made it and it was thin, light blue wool with a wide skirt, gathered at the waist. Under it I was wearing a starched petticoat with embroidery. The collar was white piqué with lace edging, tied at the neck with two cords of the same blue material. I had a wide patent leather belt around my waist, about which Jenny was none the wiser. I cinched it very tight.

I went to that party frightened, shy, and having persuaded myself that I could always go home if it got too awful. But it was not a bit like I had imagined.

My face was small and pale, with neither distinguishing nor disfiguring features. I assume I looked sort of sweet and fresh, as new students do. My hair was tightly curled with a permanent wave, and was newly washed with the astringent shampoo we used in those days. It hung like a cloud, almost as fair as the glitter on a Christmas tree. And then there was the tight patent leather belt and a bright red mouth to go with it.

I had no idea that the slightly older male students at the party were patrolling us like pikes amongst a floundering school of small fry. In every group of first-year students there were a few girls who were selected as easy prey, the cute ones with the tight belts. Myself, I felt incredibly well looked after, as if these older gentlemen who were all of twenty-five or twenty-six had decided to spoil me. I spent an enchanted evening. I danced, I sipped their mixed drinks. Suddenly I was liberated and carefree and dared to chat them up and retort wittily when they teased me. I wasn't the only one who thought the man who kept asking me to dance was the very best looking man in the whole student union. He was known, as I found out later, as Philip the Handsome. He held me close when we danced, his lips brushed my cheek. The atmosphere was orgiastic, though I was hardly aware of it. I was too carried away with my own success. I simply didn't realize that people were drunk. Perhaps I was too used to it. I still never really saw when my father was plastered.

When people started to leave, Philip took me by the arm with a secure sense of possession.

"My sweet little thing," he whispered in my ear. I heard that. I'd previously only heard those words at the cinema, or rather read them in the subtitles on the screen. All around me he was getting smiles of complicity from the other older fellows.

For what happened then I will never forgive that Sven-Åke Philipsson, who absolutely refused to respond when addressed as Sven-Åke. He asked me if I wanted to come up and see his etchings. I had no idea that this was a turn of phrase so I said yes, and told him how my foster father back home was a member of the art society and that we attended the openings of all the art exhibitions. That damnable Philip the Handsome gave me a perfectly serious look and we went up to his freezing, tobacco-impregnated room in the student housing next to the union building. When we got there he immediately began to kiss me and we forgot there were supposed to be etchings on the walls.

I must have been quite tipsy, because I cannot remember thinking twice or dreading losing my virginity. We undressed, that is he undressed me and then himself much faster, and we got into his slightly gray sheets.

That Sven-Åke Philipsson, known as Philip the Handsome, and whom I did not know, put me in his saggy bed, parted my legs and then went down on his knees on the floor in front of me. He held me by the thighs I was trying to pull closed, and kissed me ever so passionately in the place women called their private parts in those days. In spite of my intoxication I was so horribly embarrassed I would gladly have passed out. I had never even considered the idea that anyone might do what he was doing. I just wanted him to stop and I didn't dare to move because I was afraid of making a fool of myself or seeming inexperienced. What I did realize was that this was not an occasion for playing the virtuous damsel. Things had gone too far. How and when I had crossed the boundary I didn't know. Philip kept whispering (between mouthfuls, was a thought that crossed my mind) lines that could very well have been subtitles on a film screen.

"My dear, sweet thing, you are divine!"

"You're mad," said I.

"Right, about you," he whispered, and this was as new to me as everything else.

As I said, I cannot recall dreading penetration, but I started thinking he was taking an awfully long time. I was ready to get it over with. Maybe I hoped I could just run home afterwards. But nothing happened hurriedly here. He went over to the closet and took out a bottle of eau-de-vie. We had more to drink. I ate a banana. I got ever so giggly; relieved he had abandoned his post between my thighs. I smoked his cigarettes. The world was spinning. He was pale and there were beads of perspiration on his top lip.

"My dear little darling," he said. And then he started adding, over and over: "Forgive me, dear one."

As I said the sheets were dingy, there was an overflowing ashtray on the table, and a bunch of flowers beyond identification. Most of the petals had fallen onto the tabletop around the vase. There were also open books, cufflinks, a lighter with his initials on it. I started to feel more self-assured, and to think this was marvelous. I had never in my life seen a room so filthy and permeated with smoke, never been in a bed so close to an overflowing, stinking ashtray. I thought: this is the life. It was congruous with my black tunic and the red ribbed belt. This, I thought, is existentialism.

"Forgive me, darling" Philip whispered, caressing me more and more intently between the legs. He went on until I finally told him to stop. I had no choice, because I didn't know what I was supposed to do about his methodical rubbing, didn't have the slightest idea where it was supposed to be leading. I felt desire only when he kissed me, and even that desire was beginning to wane because I was so tired. He fell asleep, and went on begging my forgiveness, even in his semi-dormant state.

I slept in the gray room and woke at dawn. The bedside light was still beaming right down on us. I was so thirsty I could hardly stand it, so I lifted up the vase to drink the water. But the stale smell sobered me up. I made my way out to the bathroom and drank water, drank and drank, wetting my dry, swollen tongue. I was hung over for the first time in my life and couldn't imagine why I felt so strange. The gray room had all the modern conveniences. There was a shower in the bathroom and I got in, allowing the tepid water to run down my body, washing my hair with his Palmolive soap, and drying myself on a grimy towel.

He was still asleep, his regular features and soft brown eyelashes very handsome. His skin was a little darker than was normal at our latitude. When I had tottered up I'd pulled the sheet off him, and now I could see what a lovely stomach he had. I stared, too, at his penis, recumbent against his thigh, huddling down by his scrotum. It was the first male sexual organ I had seen, and I thought it was gorgeous.

I reckoned he had refrained from making love to me out of consideration for my youth and our short acquaintance. He had asked me to forgive him and I thought he meant for having been so brutally lustful. I liked being the object of his raw desire. If I crept back down into bed with him we would wake up together for the rest of our lives and by evening I would no longer be a virgin. When he was sober he would realize this was no fly-by-night drunken fling but his great, enduring love. Then, of course, he would have no qualms about taking me.

In spite of my headache, I was happy. I had had all these powerful experiences and survived unscathed. The future was staked out. That handsome man in the bed. Everything dull and blurry and indefinite gone from my life. He was a law student, I knew. I could be the wife of a lawyer or a judge. I remembered the lawyer's daughter who had been two years ahead of me at school. Her tailor-made suits. Her layered hair after she'd been to Stockholm. Her father's car.

But in the end I decided to go back home to Svartbäcken. I didn't dare to stay, because my landlords would notice if I'd been out the entire night. I inspected him more closely as I dressed. The lamplight didn't illuminate much of the room, but it lit up his skin intensively. I could see every single strand of his hair. He was no mangy beast, but his whole body was covered with fine downy hairs. I once knew a midwife who said that some newborn infants are perfect specimens of human hair growth. It begins as a curl at the top of the head, spiraling out from there all over the body. Those were the little hairs the lamplight was now turning gold. On his chest they were thicker and curlier. There was a narrow brown stripe combing down over his abdomen and then spreading, soft and auburn, around his sex, which rested curled between the pebbles of his scrotum. His foreskin was wrinkled, the glans exposed, shiny and so intensely pink you could see that it was really part of his insides.

He had dark hair all along his legs down to his fine ankles. Stepping even closer I could inspect his hands and noticed that the hair on the backs of them continued to the first knuckle of each finger but it was so soft and fine it would have been invisible had he been blond. On his cheeks and chin a dark shadow was developing; under his nose it was already so thick I could imagine how he would look with a mustache.

He lay on his back with his head to one side. His eyelashes looked long against his cheek, and he had a childlike expression on his face. Resting against the grimy sheets, he made even them look beautiful, their folds and shadows. The wallpaper behind him was a backdrop for the brownness of him, nothing else.

When I left, I found I had to walk all the way to outer Svartbäcken, because the busses hadn't started running yet and I couldn't afford a taxi. My newly washed hair became a frozen cap on my head. When I fell into bed, I was still happy. I could see him in the lamplight, and thought about not yet having met him only ten hours ago, and that now my entire life had changed. It was tied to his with invisible filaments. The scent of his skin and his hair, every nuance of his voice and the color of his eyes bound me to him. When he woke up he would shave away the whiskers I'd seen, and the five o'clock shadow which had made my top lip and my cheeks red and tender. I had learned so terribly much about him in this short time. I knew his nails were rounded and that there were nicotine stains between the index and long fingers of his right hand. There was a tiny depression just at the top of his behind, precisely where his buttocks split with a dark indentation. His ears were very, very flat against his head. I fell asleep to this knowledge and intimacy.

I woke up a couple of hours later thinking I must be having a heart attack. I didn't dare move because I knew the slightest shift would be the death of me. I realized it was probably also fatal to breathe, so I tried not to for the longest time, and then only inhaled gently and very cautiously, exhaling again almost indiscernibly when I absolutely had to. It was as if I were trying to deceive someone next to me, make him believe I was already dead, so there was no need for him to murder me. Never for a moment did I imagine anything but that my heart was acting up, and the only thing I feared was death. It was close to me, nosing around.

My consciousness was a black, sucking vortex. Although I was afraid to breathe too deeply and die, I also felt the downward pull of the center of the whirl-wind, down where there was extinction and rest. I was lying most uncomfortably out on the very edge of my rollaway bed, but I didn't dare to change position. My mouth was totally dry, my tongue swollen and rough. But there was no way I could get up for water. I didn't even dare moisten my mouth with saliva. The entire earth was rocking under me and around me, as if it wanted to entice me to take a deep breath and be dragged down into unconsciousness and death. It was a seductive, dangerous rocking motion. I resisted, lying stock still and breathing imperceptibly, like a hare who knows a bird of prey is hovering, poised for the onslaught.

Eventually, the attack passed. I could begin to breathe more normally, and I dared to get up and make my way to the bathroom. I was still afraid there was something wrong with my heart.

I slept almost all that day, and when evening came I got dressed and took the bus into town. Of course I went straight to his place. It never occurred to me he was doing anything but sitting there waiting for me, since we belonged together now. It astonished me when he didn't respond to my knock. I went back down to the street and walked around the building until I could see his window and that it was dark. Then I went in to one of his neighbors, a more conscientious student, and asked if he knew where Sven-Åke could be. He had no idea who I meant until I said Philip.

" Carousing, most likely," he said without interest.

I wasn't prepared to believe that. I walked up the entire flight of steep stairs to the housing above the student union where his best friends lived, and eventually I found somebody who had been so hung over he couldn't go out with the others. He said Phillip had gone to Gillet with a bunch of people. I wasn't about to turn up at the best hotel in Uppsala wearing my black trousers and tunic with the ori-ental collar. They wouldn't let you in to the dining room at Gillet dressed like that. It made me realize how hungry I was, though. I sat on the steps outside his door to wait, certain he'd be back soon.

After the studious fellow came out, perhaps to take his habitual evening air, I was ashamed to be sitting there, so I went and stood in the vestibule of the build-ing. It was large and had a sloping marble floor. I stood with my back to the out-side door, looking out into the leafless yard. The hours passed. Sometimes I sat on the marble floor. They were strange hours — they passed so fast. I didn't even real-ly feel impatient. There was nothing else I could do but to stand here.

In the end he did come home, part of a large, rowdy crowd. I cannot recall there being anything tense or awkward about our reunion. I was simply thrilled.

Philip was not a successful student. He was studying law, in the sense that the crumb-covered books open on his table were on the reading list for the introductory course. He ate breakfast on them and he dined on them. Brandy splashed on the pages, and cigarette ash dropped into the sticky crevice at the binding. Naturally, these books were legendary. He was proud of them and would have been irate had anyone closed them. This arrangement on his table was the emblem of an extravagant, reckless man. Crumbs, filth, grease stains, glasses of liquor from which all the alcohol had long since evaporated — it was all part of the picture, and everyone who came to see him was very careful not to disturb this still life, originally arranged by chance and idleness but now preserved as the kind of work of art that wasn't exhibited in Sweden until the sixties.

Otherwise, this room with its flecked beige wallpaper was no more than a passageway in his life. Not even when he had women there did he really live in this room, I don't think. He lived for the long, gentle evening hours he spent out drinking. In that world, he was loved and known by all. He owned one dark, good, just-frayed-enough suit. The middle class men with the affrontery to enter that world did so in suits with pressed trousers, and silk bow ties under their chins. Phillip's shiny, burgundy tie, his thin black shoes with holes in the soles, the gray-white-yellow cuffs of his nylon shirt were all absolute perfection. His slim brown wallet seldom had anything in it. Sometimes he would borrow money off the maitre d', which didn't seem to alter his virtually regal status at Gillet. They may secretly have held him in contempt although they served him so eagerly. That never occurred to me until much later. They let him drink on credit, of course, because they knew they would be paid. He'd be coming back. Who would he be otherwise?

Now I was his girl, and I learned about evening life in rooms hazy with smoke and the smell of good cooking. Some evenings it was hash, schnapps and beer. Others it was a private smorgasbord with a fruit platter to follow, as exclusive as you could get. Those evenings there were champagne punch, arrack and the Curaçao that made your vomit toxic green. In between there was every possible nuance of evening entertainment, every possible kind of food, red wine, spirits, grog, liqueurs. Including violet Parfait Amour and sticky yellow Crème de Bananes.

I discovered I didn't really dislike drinking when I was taking part in it myself, and I appreciated the muffled sounds, the soft voices and the music. This was Henning's world, too. I had collected him at the City Hotel, and I recognized the prematurely ageing men in the black suits playing up there on the stage, the clergyman-like maitre d', and the timidity of the middle class guests who felt out of

211

place. They were here so seldom they never got over the embarrassment.

When we ordered our food, drinks and utensils according to a solemn, unalterable ritual, I felt myself going through a metamorphosis, or even metamorphoses. My frigidity and anxiety fell away. The depression of outer Svartbäcken and its semi-starvation vanished in the warm haze and I regained my dignity, yes, my human worth. I was a participant in a mystery, sometimes I was one of its high priests — like when I inserted my knife into a Chateaubriand, revealing it as medium rare. I had begun to realize that Uppsala, that the world, was full of such participation, large or small societies where cults performed their rites. Until now I had fluttered like a moth between firmly closed-off worlds. Now I was in.

As opposed to Philip, who was doing his sixth year in Uppsala, I still went to lectures and seminars. But I was distracted. The whole thing was so unreal. We had to learn to conjugate non-existent cases of dead words. The participants in these mysteries wore thick gray sweaters and sensible footwear. I myself was always cold because I still went around in my black outfit with an unlined black jacket over it. I had no money for winter attire. What Jenny and Fredrik sent and my student loan were spent financing the mysteries. But my black clothes were also taking on emblematic status: I was the blonde who wore black, and who washed her hair every second day so it rose like a white cloud around her head. I had also acquired a long, black cigarette holder, which is the only thing in this context I feel embarrassed about afterwards.

This was around the time Philip and his friends had begun to show an interest in reading. They lugged carrier bags of novels, splitting at the spines, with them from hangout to hangout. There were Henry Miller's *Tropic of Cancer, Sexus I* and *II*, and various other things you could only get in English. Of course I read them, too. I went on reading until I happened into a book called *The Carnal Days of Helen Seferis*, in which a group of men got a woman and a mule together to see them copulate. I was overpowered, in spite of my poor mastery of English, by such revulsion that I never touched one of their books again. I kept my reaction to myself because they would have regarded it as neurotic. We were living in an emancipated age in which the fusty, morbid view of sex that had been prevalent for so long was supposed to be replaced with fresh, seething sensuality. I don't think Philip and his crowd were really the champions of this new movement. Their main interest was drink, and it is common knowledge that Bacchus never had any children. However, my course mates, the gray gang from Nordic languages whose flesh was seldom rosied by the soft lamplight of eating and drinking establishments, displayed a fanatical interest, and learned to steer their girlfriends across the floor like wheelbarrows and have anal sex with them.

There was a scientific side to this emancipation movement, and I quickly adopted it. It had no room for hanky-panky and obscenity. At the café in the basement of one of the university buildings, someone introduced me to a man who was doing a PhD on Old English verb endings. He launched the theory that, by natural selection, most women were what he called "back-cunted". All sex, said this man who was balding prematurely, was initially rape. Women protected themselves by turning onto their stomachs. The ones whose vaginas opened farthest back were the ones who were fertilized. We had long discussions about the logic of his theory. I sounded as cool and objective as any modern woman could be expected to sound, and before I knew it I was brandishing the term back-cunted as my own personal banner of liberation.

My own sexuality underwent no change after that first night with Philip. Our physical relationship did, of course, become more and more sophisticated as the pile of books in the carrier bag diminished. I learned to take his penis in my mouth and sometimes a desire for revenge or a longing for true emancipation must have crossed my mind vaguely and rapidly, because I recall thinking it was amazing how blindly he trusted me not to bite it off. But in the technical sense I was still a virgin. Philip would retreat every time when it came down to the final, decisive step. The only difference was that he'd stopped saying: "Forgive me, darling". Instead, he'd say "Dear one, I know how you feel." He must have known intuitively that our relationship would end the pallid moment I whispered that I'm not afraid any more now, so come!

It was just that I had never demonstrated the slightest fear. Now, though, it came, rising from the same source as the tears of an actress or the cries of pleasure of a whore.

Philip wasn't consistently impotent. Had he been, the girls would have brought his lady's man act to a quick, cruel demise. No, he was ill a lot of the time, and he drank too much and partied too much, had various stomach ailments and took charcoal tablets for his diarrhea. I knew this although he refused to discuss it.

My studies weren't going too well, but looking back I believe that until Christmas time I was still keeping up. I had a vacuous, dull holiday season, staying with the Otters. Jenny gave me aprons she made herself. Henning was there too, of course, but I remember thinking of him as shabby and mundane. I smoked and walked the gray streets. The day after Twelfth Night I went back. The situation then changed completely.

At the beginning of the term, a new girl moved into a room at the student union. She was from Stockholm and her name was Veronica. I don't know why she transferred to Uppsala, and I don't remember what she was studying. We never really talked about it.

Veronica attracted attention. She had a triangular face with slanted, gray-blue eyes. Her hair was the color people called platinum blonde in those days. Like mine, it was fluffy and dry from constant washing. She wore no lipstick, but what she did wear was a thick layer of a make-up called Pancake that you applied with a moistened sponge. It made her face pale, smooth, and expressionless. She, too, preferred to dress in black, and I think we had a lot in common. But there were two definite differences between us: my red mouth and her riding boots.

She wore those brown leather boots, well-made and somewhat the worse for wear, every day. There was no one else who had them. We wore wellington boots in the rain and walking shoes with thick India rubber soles otherwise. Veronica's boots and her Mongolian facial features lent her a Russian air.

The first time I saw her she was standing in one of the round turret rooms at the student union surrounded by Philip and his entourage. She was smoking. I saw her more distinctly than you tend to see people. I thought she seemed to be looking at me with her lips, those pale, unpainted lips, the bottom one of which was a little chapped and cracked. Her eyes narrowed. There were stray blonde hairs on her black sweater and skirt. She just stared at me the whole time, as Philip put his arm around me and said:

"Have you met Veronica, sweetheart?"

Then she walked across the stained parquet floor to the ashtray on the grand piano with her loose black skirt swaying and the heels of her riding boots clattering. When you saw the rooms in daylight, everything looked dusty and worn from decades of partying. With Veronica standing by the black excuse for a piano the room looked like a set built up around her by a stage designer. I had a strong foreboding of imminent danger.

Sometimes I think about how immediate my feelings were in those years. They had no names. They were seldom deformed by words and reflection. The danger surfaced in my stomach or groin or windpipe. Words, my own and Philip's, fluttered by like crude clichés in the subtitles on a cinema screen. I never worried over things Philip had said to me. But his arm around my shoulder at one moment and his mouth very close to Veronica's ear the next haunted me night and day.

Our triangle also took shape almost without words. Philip put his arm around me one evening when we were in the turret room, crowded and smoky, and he whispered just beside my ear: "Isn't she gorgeous, sweetheart?"

My ear went hot. I saw Veronica, one boot on the floor, the other angled sole up, toe down, and beads of perspiration broke out in my groin. The next morning after my class in applied Nordic linguistics, I went up to Philip's room. He woke up as I undressed and got into bed with him. He whispered that there was still winter air in my hair. Then there was a knocking or more: someone clawing at the wood of the door, scraping her long nails against the grain.

"Come in, Veronica," said Philip.

She opened the door and stood there framed by it, smiling with her pale, pursed lips.

We were seldom perfectly sober. If nothing else, we were so dead tired we lived in a kind of trancelike semi-lethargy, not unlike inebriation. Most days, the Nordic seminars went on without me.

I had realized the danger inherent in Veronica's riding boots. She had a short, slightly stubby body and a heavy bottom, a narrow waist and extremely small breasts. Her nose was gently aquiline. It was her slanted eyes and her artificially pale lips (I had discovered that she covered them with Pancake), her triangular face and her hair, which was fairer than my own, that gave her such a striking, almost sensational appearance. And yet I sensed that the danger came from her riding boots.

One morning I was outside the Philolog with a girl from my Nordic class. Another girl came riding on horseback down the Stockholm Road, and turned to circle the stone wall around the Botany department. My friend, whose name was Barbro, said hello to her. Afterwards she explained that the girl was the daughter of the professor in whose house she boarded. Just a few days later I found myself having tea at their home, a villa with the name "Tranquility". The daughter came in from her ride, greeted us nonchalantly and put her heel into a boot jack.

Barbro had her Icelandic grammar book on the table and said we should test one another. Her monotonous voice conjugated four cases of Njorðr. She had a love bite on her neck. But she wasn't like me. She didn't use lipstick and she had a steady boyfriend. In the spring she would become engaged to a historian whose children she would bear and whose doctoral thesis she would have to proofread and index. She would organize his footnotes as well, and iron his shirts and buy birthday presents for his mother.

In those days, I hardly had any lucid moments; I simply sensed danger like a roe fawn senses the presence of predators in the tall grass. I fled from potential PhDs in hand knitted pullovers, the incipient junior lecturers who frequented Bruhn's restaurant and the young civil-servants-to-be who still had pimples but who had begun to look around for girls who typed well, had good Fallopian tubes and firm breasts.

Myself, I'd stopped menstruating some time ago. Perhaps it was the semi-starvation and late nights alternating with orgies of sleep and food, and constantly being so overwrought, on my guard against Veronica, scrounging for money, avoiding Jenny's worried questions on the telephone and the outbursts of my landlord when the cheese shrank or the level in the cornflakes package had fallen. I tried to keep track of the date on which the pawnshop ticket on the briefcase Fredrik had given me when I finished school would expire, and I was forever taking short-term loans at the student union to pay off my debts to my friends.

Still, I wouldn't have changed places with Barbro for anything. I fled from the India rubber soled souls, attracted instead to the souls in thin soles, the men who shivered in their dark suits.

I took the boots one Monday morning when Barbro was at a seminar on Swedish fourteenth century lawmakers. I had become familiar with the habits of the professor's family, and went out to "Tranquility" when his wife was shopping. The boots were at home when their daughter was at the Domestic Science Seminary. They never locked the front door.

I had only worn them a few times when someone came knocking on the door at Svartbäcken asking for me and saying I was wanted on the telephone. It was quite late one evening and I had to go downstairs, outside, and up the stairs in the next entrance and into the apartment of a woman I had never met, who indicated her telephone, on a table in the hall. When I heard Barbro's voice I realized for the first time that it's a small world, or rather that the worlds that are there, alongside one another, are not separated by watertight bulkheads as I had believed in childhood.

"You've got to give her boots back," she wept. "They're throwing me out. They're going to report you to the police and call my parents, too, if you don't return the boots."

The shock made me weak-kneed. I just stood there.

The only way to get out to "Tranquility" was on foot. It was so late the buses weren't running. If I had had the cash I would have taken a taxi with the boots in the dark of night.

In the end I did head off on foot, around three in the morning. I had the boots in a big paper bag, and when I got there I left it by the front door. The house was silent and asleep, the curtains unmoving.

After that night I couldn't go back to the classes in Nordic languages. Barbro might burst into tears or run out of the room if she saw me.

It was also lovely weather that spring, the beginning of a hot, sunny summer. We — Philip, Veronica and myself — started spending our days at the student union recreation center, which was on the shore of Lake Mälaren. Now I had seen him put his lips to her pale, tight ones many times. But I couldn't get used to it. It made my heart hammer every time, and my genitals feel heavy, as if my guts were twisting.

After May Day we started sunbathing on a blanket, and Philip complained that our shoulder straps would leave ugly white marks. So we sunbathed without our swimsuits. We had isolated ourselves behind a little alder grove. The ground under the blanket was bumpy. There was a scent of marshy water and rotting reeds. We heard children shouting over at the beach, but their voices sounded very distant, and the clatter of the pebbles being washed up by the waves was soporific. Student mothers sat knitting by the jetty. There were rumors that swimming in this tepid, turgid water might be prohibited. I recall it as green, blooming with drifts of sperm from the trees.

There were the sounds of people behind the alders, and we knew it wasn't just Philip. We heard the rustle of voices and branches snapping. When it was perfectly silent but we knew someone was there, I would get that heavy, lustful feeling again, and press myself hard toward the ground. Veronica squinted through one eye, the other half of her face pressing into the blanket. We were lying on our stomachs with our legs toward the alder grove. The sun ricocheted toward us off the water, the reflections blinding you if you opened your eyes. I knew it though I didn't dare look.

"Oh my God it's hot," she said. "We ought to have a swim."

We knew nothing about one another, didn't want to know. I had entered a world where there were no questions. With eyes as quick as martens' or little foxes', we learned by looking. The drinking, the pawn shop, the smoky party rooms at the union — we learned everywhere. It was not a matter of life and death but of style, a slightly chilly, indolent, shabby elegance Philip may not have invented but that he chiseled out in such fine detail that even its headaches and cold feet were just right, the perfect accents.

I'm sure we were shallow, we didn't see much of the world around us, but it was one of the few times in my life I have had a sense of belonging. I was part of a community of spirit that had nothing to do with one's antecedents. I had practically no idea of what courses Veronica was registered for, didn't know what Philip's father did, and had only the vaguest sense of how old they were. All such

217

knowledge was superfluous to us. What we knew, we knew without it, with the precision of a troupe of dancers.

When the term ended I did not want to go home. I went to see Fredrik and Jenny for a weekend, and told them I had to stay in Uppsala to study for a big exam. When I got back, summer was in full bloom. The weeping willows reflected in the green water of the river. The pond in the park was sludgy with swan droppings, and the jackdaws didn't make themselves known until evening, when they rested in the spire of the cathedral after the day's raids on the plains.

Now most of the university students had left town, and the tourists had arrived. They moved from one cool church to the next, stared at us on the streets and from their café tables at Flustret. Philip wore a gray suit and had his shirt unbuttoned at the neck. His tie stuck out of his pocket. Veronica with no stockings on, in a pair of black high heels that were too big for her but that still looked molded to her feet the way our eyelids are molded to our eyes. When the heat forced her to abandon her riding boots, the magic didn't desert her. Myself, I wouldn't put on any of the summer dresses Jenny had given me, but wore cotton trousers and a man's shirt with the ends tied under my breasts.

We made an outing from Flottsund to Skokloster on one of the little white steam boats. There was a whole gang of us, but Veronica and I were the only girls. The others were medical students Philip knew, and they had hospital alcohol with them. I didn't dare drink it, because my mind filled with images of embalming and of pus-filled, open wounds. But someone must have poured some into the mock champagne I had brought in the picnic basket — white wine mixed with soda pop. I was tipsier than I had been in a very long time. When we had disembarked, I changed into my swimsuit behind an ice cream stand. Then I ran straight out onto the jetty and jumped into the water. I still recall the euphoria of the moment I jumped, the cheering medical students and Veronica's laughing shout. My field of vision included a swan, the silky-blue water of the bay, and swaying leafy branches. I jumped in and came up with a mouthful of water tasting of sewers and diesel fuel. I found myself wading to shore among ice cream wrappers and floating fruit peels, not completely sober but enough so to be terrified I was going to cut my foot on a broken bottle under the water. There was a film of oil on my skin, but I didn't bother to wipe it away, just pulled on my clothes as fast as I could so no one would see how I looked. Then I took several swigs of the wine mixture to rinse my mouth, and went to find a good spot for our picnic.

We sat in a palace where a tree had been felled and chopped. The pile of wood cast deep shadows and down there, under the branches of an oak that had either been struck by lightning or rotted with disease, I saw a snail.

"Look," I said.

"It's a vineyard snail," said one of the medical students.

"I know. Helix pomata."

He stared at me, accustomed, I suppose, to less well-educated girls. I took him by surprise.

"There must be more."

I headed into the park, reacting with annoyance when I heard his footsteps behind me in the gravel, and soon his voice as well, meddlesome and magisterial. Apparently he needed to rectify the misunderstanding about our educational levels.

"In sunny weather like this they will have withdrawn into a shady place, with damp leaves or rotting stumps. If we stay until evening, when they come out again, we might be able to gather a couple of dozen. As you know, they're perfectly edible."

He stopped but I went on. So he kept following. The voices of the others were gone now, and it was cool under the trees. I kicked off my shoes when I reached the grass, crossing it slowly, exploring for snails with my feet. I poked around piles of rotting leaves with my toes. There was that smell that's always there where vineyard snails can be found, a hint of autumn, a scent of death. We found shells, but they were empty when we turned them over. I felt like weeping over each empty, dead one. Dried up traces of them glittered now and then when the sun fell on the leaves. They had left their slimy trails on leaves and grass, but we could not find a single living snail. There were pupae in the piles of leaves, and we scared up big black beetles there. The fieldfares followed us at a distance, jabbering, shrilly and indignantly. Ringworms, three-legged mites, springtails. I thought about all the things we couldn't see, and I told him about them.

"Every time you put your foot down you trample on about twenty thousand lives," I said.

This upset him, not the lives under the soles of his shoes, of course, but the fact that I was teaching him something. Out of me had emerged a girl who knew what she was talking about, a girl with a halo of golden owls. They were whispering all their secrets to her.

He was now searching like a madman for a single snail shell containing a living snail. His long white fingers groped; I don't suppose they'd ever been so dirty before. What a triumph when he turned up a pair — they were stuck together!

"They're mating," he said excitedly. "Look!"

But they had pulled apart. Chaste and still, they were now resting heavily in the two striped shells in the palm of his hand.

"They're hermaphrodites," he said. He crouched down, trying to get the separate snails to conjoin again.

"Stop that," I said.

"When they initiate mating contact, they start by feeling one another up with their fleshy feet. Then one of them shoots a love dart. Look, here it is. Broken off."

He had a sharp little calcified bit on the tip of his index finger.

"One of them drives his long sharp love dart up into the thick muscular mass we call the foot but which is actually just the beginning of the body. It contracts with both pain and desire, after which they crawl out and start touching one another. The penis and the vulva protrude. They seek, and each finds a partner. They have double equipment, you know. Their mating act is a long one. Hours. All day. It takes an incredibly long time for them to deposit a batch of sperm in each other's vulvas. Now, let's see if we can stimulate them back into action. I'll see if I can use this dart."

"Don't!"

I pulled one of the snails out of his hand and slung it far off in the grass. I knew I ought to have kept as calm as I had when the PhD student in Old English verbs had launched his theory of the location of the vaginal opening. But I didn't care if he decided I was a sexual neurotic. I had found forgotten words, rediscovered lost knowledge and I am nearly certain I spoke in the voice of a little girl.

"Hush up," I said. "Let them be, you sickening slob."

When I was a child, I was often alone. Perhaps that was natural. Maybe all children are alone a lot. The intense sense of belonging together we imagine and even see between mothers and children may be no more than physical intimacy, the taking possession of an object one owns or an appendage of one's own body with the lovely smell of soap and talcum powder. When my Mamma had disappeared I was alone in a strictly physical sense, too, of course, in the same way old people who live on their own are; they are hardly ever touched. That may have been what made me almost dizzily enthusiastic about collective projects. That was what it had been like when Pappa sat under the pink lampshade and sent me on missions to the gold owls, and that was what it was like when Tora and I counted up her income from the sweet stand together. When Jenny sewed me dresses and did fittings on me I didn't experience that dizzying feeling at all, only dull aggravation. Her plucking fingers turned me into an object among other objects — bits of thread, dust in a ray of sunlight, leftover pieces of fabric, and pins on the floor. The odor of her skin was insistent. The touch of her fingertips when she fitted the waist, or of the ice-cold scissors on my skin when she adjusted a neckline, they were all the same to me.

But in this sense of belonging with Philip and Veronica I walked around giddy, in a euphoria stronger than any I had known before. Veronica and I may never have been more intimate with Philip than are two dogs with their owner. We may have been nothing but accessories, two well-groomed silver poodle bitches that showed off his lifestyle. I'm still not really prepared to believe that, though. I want to believe we made that lifestyle together, performed it like complex dance steps, and that all three of us were equally important; there was no master and no object. This, like most of the things that interest me, cannot be proven.

Initially all I could see in Uppsala was the others' sense of belonging, the signs and gestures of community, impossible for the uninitiated to interpret. I came from a small town upper secondary school where the only tradition was the Christmas concert, and I had only the vaguest ideas about what a university education was, even in the technical sense.

The students who had Anglo-Saxon oriented parents of the progressive, middle class kind said tiddly-pom when it snowed. I didn't have a clue why. At first I was foolish enough to think all you had to do was pretend to know what they were referring to. Whenever someone mentioned a book — be it Montaigne's essays or the Gilgamesh epic — I therefore answered nonchalantly that I'd read it last spring, but that I'd been so worn out I didn't remember much. I assume if I'd gone on that way I would have been intellectually done for as well. I stole things, I had gonococci in my throat, I told lies about doing exams. But suddenly I had to draw the line. I don't know why. One day I was sitting in the coffee shop in the basement of the main university building saying to a comp lit student that I'd read a book called *A rebours* by J.K. Huysmans.

"In French?" he asked.

I felt like the fox about to step into the trap. Caught the scent of human fingers on the carrion bait and turned tail. I realized it was very possible there was no Swedish translation of that book. I'd been in Uppsala for three months and I was nobody's fool.

"*Naturellement*," I replied. That was supposed to sound like a joke, a way of weaseling out of the problem.

"*Vraiment?*" he asked, and I saw the look on his face. He'd taken me seriously but didn't believe it was true.

A rebours began to plague me. It was the shame, and the memory of his suspicions that plagued me. So I got hold of the book in French. I got someone to borrow it for me from the university library, since I didn't dare go in there myself. I got through a couple of pages with the help of a dictionary. It was difficult but not impossible. Just six months ago I'd had French twice a week. I managed to run into the Huysmans enthusiast again, and to slip allusions to *A rebours* into the conversation. Afterwards I was sick to my stomach. Now my self-loathing truly began to torment me. The embarrassment would come over me, my idiocy, my ingratiation, my childish boasting. The only penance, obviously, was to read *A rebours*. Slowly, I dragged myself through the atonement. The book accompanied me everywhere. It was there in the snow and on the sun-heated jetty planks. We spilled wine on its open pages. Some time after I had passed the two-thirds mark, the French language suddenly opened up to me. It was an indescribable experience of depth and nuance. I had been living for so long in the painful light of self-contempt, obligation and tedium. I stepped into that book, which is about the attempts of a degenerate member of the nobility to reawaken his dulled *joie de vivre*, as if I were entering a forest full of elegant, leafy trees.

I suppose I also borrowed one or two things from it to supplement Philip's lifestyle that we were shaping together. There was no question but that Philip was the protagonist of our triangle. We three were making something gorgeous and idle of our lives, of a few months of our lives. That was what we thought then, and I do not mean to deny it now.

Then Philip left. He was offered a chance to stand in for a museum guide at San Michele. This was in July. Veronica and I were left alone.

We had started going to the nineteenth century bathhouse by the river. It was right by the place I lived, the first and only time my digs were ever close to anywhere. This was the last summer of that old wooden building. It was in utter disrepair, officially not even open. We sometimes put a foot through rotten planks or leaned against balustrades that gave way. On sunny days the disintegrating wood of the benches and the graffiti-covered walls still exuded the smells of perspiration, tanning oil and urine. Under the long verandah that served as a jetty ran the turgid river water, and the building snowed heavy flakes of paint into the water. The little listless, erratic currents that tugged at the slippery grass beneath the surface carried them along.

One afternoon Veronica and I were alone there, undressing in the gloom to the purling of the water. The smells here always frightened me. When Veronica had pulled her dress over her head and removed her panties, I set a towel under her bottom before she could sit down.

"Careful," I said, recalling residue of Jenny's admonitions, "you never know what you might pick up here."

"You mean *here*?" Veronica asked, grabbing her labia and the surrounding hair with her thumb and index finger. She pulled her legs up, leaning back as she did so with a look on her face we used to call smutty on the boys at school. She burst out laughing.

"You're incredible!" she said. "A whole school year of being with Philip and his full-blown gonorrhea, and you're worried about what you might catch at the *bathhouse*!"

She couldn't stop laughing. My throat constricted and I was completely unable to think a sensible thought. But there was one sum I could do:

"What about you, then?" I finally asked.

She went serious for a second, no more.

"It's difficult to cure," she said. "Almost impossible."

Then she threw the leaky door open to the sun. The light flew like sparks of magnesium through her dry, blonde hair. Carefree once more. Carefree once more?

We used to sit and wait for Philip at the Ofvandahl cake shop. I recalled the sign of the outpatient clinic for venereal diseases on the side of the building. Had Philip and I sometimes waited for Veronica there, too? I just didn't know any more. Was she lying? She could lie through her teeth with the ease of a monkey swinging from tree to tree.

Philip didn't come back. He wrote two letters from San Michele. Then I never heard from him again. So I thought he had stayed down there. Several months later someone let on to me that he was spending his days as a bank teller in Söderhamn and his evenings at the City Hotel there. He'd left Uppsala in the only way he could without destroying our fragile structure.

Having learned belonging, I now learned solitude. When I first came to Uppsala I was as lonely as a single little fish separated from its school. The jackdaws dived from the spire of the cathedral with suicidal cries. I could have found support for my predicament in every single volume of poetry that has ever been written in this town.

I had already followed the stone wall of the cemetery, wandering the long path leading from the old hospital for contagious diseases and then down Cemetery Road, I had walked the cobbled streets between the stone buildings.

This city had skin of stone and if you tried to get under it you ran the risk of hurting yourself. Once during that time I stood watching a cobbler at work in his cellar. This was on Cemetery Road, in a dark room where the corners looked almost black. He had one single lamp, focused on his work. But the light fell on his brow as well, and I can still recall how yellow and hard the skin of that stooped man was. This far but no further I thought, when I saw it. This far but no further.

At the end of the summer term Synnöve returned from the United Sates, where she been a college exchange student for a whole year. By the time she arrived my life was extremely complicated — or extremely simple if you like — because it had grown so messy there was nothing to be done about it. I was no longer able to borrow a little money here and there. Philip still hadn't come back. I prowled around the building, looking at the dirty curtain in his window. Someone else had moved in there, one of the studious fellows who did his drinking at given times and his studying at equally given ones. I sometimes saw him come out of the door, a coarse-looking, sturdy type who was sure to succeed. The only likable thing about him was that he hadn't washed that curtain. It hung there with the same creases, the same stagnant dust, as in Philip's day. Down below I stalked, transformed into something like a dog.

Synnöve thought the worst thing was the typewriter I had borrowed from the student union so I could type the final version of a paper I never actually finished. I'd put that typewriter in hock. There was no way I was going to get enough money to redeem it. The student union staff were very cold to me now. A penetrating mist hung over the river, and the bathhouse had been torn down. Veronica was seeing an ethnographer who had been offered a radio job. We waved at a distance. I hadn't been evicted from my room out in the sticks at Svartbäcken, but the only reason was that they knew they didn't have a chance of getting in any rent over the summer if they let me go.

"What are you living on?" Synnöve asked.

I shoplifted things, but I couldn't tell her that. I walked around smoking. Inspected the gravestones of renowned Swedes including Fröding and Pontus Wikner. I read the city library's books. I wasn't exactly miserable, but I had a toothache. Synnöve came back from the States and tried to get me to see that I had to do something about my situation.

"But what?" I asked.

I sat for hours in the basement of the university talking to weirdos. The lights were so weak there, behind their parchment shades, you couldn't see well enough to read. But the woman who ran that café was so nice she didn't even throw us out when we'd sat for three hours over the same cup of coffee. It rained on my face when I went outside. I read books I could forget the next day.

Synnöve started doing things for me. She had enough vitality and will power for two, as always. In one of the novels I read and forgot there was a woman and her "lame ducklings", people she took under her wing. I was Synnöve's. She applied splints to me and fed me and gave notice on my room, she must have spoken to Pappa and Fredrik, too, because money arrived for the summer rent. She arranged for me to live in the same student accommodation she was in, and for Fredrik to sign as guarantor on a loan for me. She went with me and got the typewriter out of hock, squeezed oranges for juice, made me a dental appointment and decreed I wasn't allowed to smoke more than a pack a day. I officially terminated the course in Nordic languages I had unofficially dropped out of long ago, and registered for English like Synnöve. I ate hearty fare at Delmonico's student restaurant with her and her course mates.

But her ugly duckling didn't turn into a swan. At Christmas break we went home, sitting side by side in a railway compartment. For a month and a half she had stood guard over me like you stand guard over an alcoholic. On January the tenth we were supposed to be going back side by side. But we didn't.

"But *why?*" Synnöve asked. "Your whole future's at stake." It would probably be no use to explain to her how little such an expression meant: your whole future. She spoke of my future as if it were a house. Some solid object.

"It makes me absolutely heartsick to hear you talk like that," said Synnöve. "It makes *everything* meaningless."

There we stood. We were on the square and a freezing cold wind was blowing. Sharp little granules flew through the air, stinging our cheeks.

"Well, for one thing I think studying English is boring," I said.

"Boring?" she wailed. "You don't get it do you? You have to make sacrifices if you want to get anywhere."

"But I don't want to," I said. "I don't want to be an English teacher."

Synnöve was, as always, kind and strong-willed and full of empathy. She said we had to discuss my future. Before I knew it she had made it into a problem. She made it sound like another sort of object. We went into Anker's bakery and cake shop to get out of the wind. I liked the smell in there of coffee, tobacco and sweet biscuits. Synnöve was talking at me the entire time.

"You must have some idea of what you want out of life," she said. But she couldn't come up with a single thing I'd be good at, a single job that would suit me.

"I can marry somebody," I said.

She nearly shrieked. I envisaged — without putting it into words — myself married to a dentist or an English teacher. I thought about long, silent afternoons in an apartment, books, snow on the windows. Myself going out to buy daffodils, putting them in a pewter vase his mother had given us. About having a cat.

"You'll be having a baby," Synnöve said as if she had broken right through the barriers of my soul.

She was sitting under a painting in shades of yellow, gray and ochre.

It was a picture of a city.

"How realistic that is," I said, and she cast a glance over her shoulder.

Then she paid no more attention to it. But inside me — or perhaps in the painting — something amazing had just happened. I had gazed at that picture lots of times before. But now, at the highly inappropriate moment when Synnöve was talking about my future, I saw it in a way I'd never seen it before. It gave me a sudden vision, rending my senses, my sensitivities and sensibilities.

When I looked over her shoulder, something extraordinary had happened to the painting. It had always been of a Mediterranean city. Cube-like houses cowering under an empty sky. But now the referent of the city had changed. I could no longer hear what Synnöve was saying. I was just afraid she would move her shoulders in her burgundy wool coat so she blocked the painting and made it change back.

Scraps of sky and sea broke unexpectedly into the stones and the walls. It was no longer possible to tell what the subject of the painting was: was it the reflections of the sky and water, or was it the shapes of the houses? It was no longer possible to say what was roof in sharp shade or ceiling opening to the heavens. The light from the sea had moved into the stone, and the skies split the shapes of the houses. Instead of a city of stone and shadow it had become a city of light.

The moment she shrugged her shoulder and blocked the canvas it was as I had feared: my vision vanished and I was unable to blink it back again.

We got nowhere on my future. She went back to Uppsala without my having told her what a fool I felt among the other students in the English course.

Now I was back in the house at 13 Chapel Road. Jenny made no comment. Henning wasn't home very much at the time. I think he was still making quite a decent living. I survived January curled up in his armchair under the big reading lamp with the silk shade that had once been pink. The snow fell outside the window. No one nagged at me.

The sun bored holes in the snow. Our metal roof started to rust, brown water dripping into buckets and hand basins on the attic floor. The sound woke me from my winter torpor. Not all at once, but it drilled me into wakefulness. Drop and drip. Up and live. Up and be.

The crosscut saw, stock exchange reports on the radio, the car tires in the slush, the whistle from the world order at seven a.m. and five p.m.; I rose from hibernation. My eyes burned and my skin stung.

Now I was really back. Uppsala had been like a state of inebriation or like performing a difficult balancing act. The main thing had been not to think. Now I had so much time and so little company I almost had no choice but to think.

It was as if I had never really seen the familiar people passing in the street until now. The main difference between myself and them seemed to be that they were so very busy. They were constantly on the way to somewhere or had something to do that could not wait. They were occupied. But with what?

I knew, of course, that they had their hands full of perfectly normal things, like boiling the potatoes, writing letters to the editor, turning brake blocks. But I didn't think anything I saw was the least bit significant. I kept asking myself: why? Of course I knew people boiled potatoes for dinner. But every day? Were they really hungry by noon every day? I wasn't.

What made the workers cycle to Swedish Engineering each morning? If I went out onto Chapel Road and asked them, they would answer: you have to make a living, don't you? I had spent nineteen years of my life here, after all, this was not a different planet I'd landed on.

I knew the answers. But they didn't make sense to me. I would have liked to ask someone: is it really necessary to live like this? Who said so? And why do you listen? And that inhuman toil of theirs in the heat of the foundry, for so little recompense — it looked insane when you watched it from the outside, or rather from the window of the living room in our house on Chapel Road. Where did all the toil end up?

I hadn't yet heard of added value. Most of my thoughts were as somniferous as they were abortive. I thought they were new. I had begun to think without having learned how, I did suspect that, and kept finding myself bewildered and forlorn. When it came right down to it, I was as ignorant of religion as of politics. I knew there were people in this city who paid homage to a supernatural being. They congregated and sang songs in its honor. They called themselves wretched and sinful to its face and said in no uncertain terms that nothing they undertook made the least bit of difference. They supplicated the being for food and shelter. And still they toiled by the sweat of their brows and were ever so busy the moment they left the premises; they behaved as if no help would be forthcoming.

In the whole city I only knew of two people who had seriously questioned the prevailing order of things. One was Konrad Eriksson, The Communist. In his view there were two kinds of people, the ones who were always lining their own pockets at others' expense, getting richer and fatter the more the other kind toiled. People said Konrad was a shirker and a nutcase. The second person was a watchmaker at whose home I had often been when I was little. Pappa had said Krantz knew his Spinoza and his Schopenhauer. People thought of him as slightly off his rocker, too, but he ran a successful watchmaking business, so they were prepared to regard his philosophical speculations as more of a hobby, a harmless obsession. He did taxonomy, too.

I recall from my childhood how, in the most trivial situations, watchmaker Krantz would suddenly come out with statements such as that human suffering and human passion were transient phenomena. Intellect and the volition by which mankind was created were what endured, as well as the human capacity for both suffering and love. Watchmaker Krantz was also a person who tended to talk about The Being instead of God. It certainly did sound different.

I wondered to myself if it was possible to read Spinoza and Schopenhauer to get answers to the questions that were working in me like ghostly beasts in the mist. They reminded me of supernatural creatures because no one else seemed to have noticed them. With the possible exception of Konrad Eriksson and Krantz the watchmaker. I had often read Eriksson's letters to the editor in my school days. They were about precisely the kind of thing I had now begun to ponder: why people just accepted their allotted estate.

I would never have dared talk to Eriksson, although I knew his sister Ingrid Johansson quite well. Jenny had scared me off him. She called him a threat to society and said he was ridiculous and crazy to boot. That didn't really make sense, and in a way I knew he couldn't be as Jenny described him. But he still intimidated me. I was afraid he would tease me and be scornful if I talked to him about the things I was thinking about.

As for Krantz the watchmaker, he was dead. But I seriously considered reading Schopenhauer and Spinoza. I didn't dare ask for them at the library, so I scoured the shelves at random. I couldn't find them, though. It's very likely I was looking in the fiction section. After three terms in Uppsala, the only things I really knew how to locate at a library were the novels.

I went on reading those, although they didn't make me feel any more at home in the world around me. Everywhere, according to the novels, people were engaged in matters of life and death, or subject to conditions they had to muster all their strength to overcome. But where I lived they just seemed to muddle along without passions. I was surrounded by people who believed in nothing, but who still struggled and endeavored as if there were something to believe in.

One might have thought that if there really was no particular meaning in all these efforts, people would have lapsed into irresponsibility and taken every opportunity for pleasure and extravagance. But they didn't. On the contrary: if they ever allowed themselves any pleasure or gave way to their passions, they seemed only to do so clandestinely and with guilty consciences or even feeling as if they'd committed a crime.

They kept a close eye on one another, and this surveillance was what seemed to drive them. It was what made them go to their jobs in the morning, no matter how strenuous and tedious the job might be. It was what made them weed endless rows of vegetables, knit gray woolen sweaters, stay with wives whose breath reeked, and make sacrifices for children who treated them badly and whom they had long since ceased to love. They dusted, cut rags for rugs and scrutinized their gravel paths, armed with weed-pullers.

At the square there is a café called Future. There it stood, big and gray and smelling of dirty dishwater. I would have liked to point it out to Synnöve.

I got Hasse Curtman to take me to the City Hotel. That was the best entertainment I could come up with. He hadn't yet finished upper secondary school. He had plenty of money.

Hasse had fallen two years behind me at school. Originally it had only been one; he's a year younger than I am. He went to work for his father at sixteen. When he was eighteen he was already overburdened with the problems of piece work rates and fabric deliveries. He never mentioned them at school, of course. He was a quiet young man, always had a stomach ache, sometimes severe. Strangely, he was dark-complected when he was younger. Dark and sinewy. He quietly lived the life of an adult man in the midst of our world of make-believe where the teachers prowled the halls on the lookout for those of us trying to skip assembly. Naturally, he got reprimands and poor marks. In the end they even forced him to repeat a year. Although he had so little time for his studies, he really needed a school leaving certificate. To him it would be more than an ornament. It was vital, to keep him from being in limbo between social classes. And now he was jeopardizing it by going to the City Hotel.

I took pleasure in the fact that he would do as I asked, and in the possibility that a schoolteacher might very well come into the hotel dining room. Hasse settled on a compromise, cautious as ever. He took me there for dinner, but he didn't have any alcohol.

Since I had been sitting thinking for over a month, I could tell him what was wrong with this city, and I did so over the schnapps I had with the starter.

The first thing was its lack of beauty.

You had to be utterly brainless to build something so ugly, or to live in it.

"I'd never thought about it," said Hasse.

"A place without beauty is like soil without selenium or something. The cattle fall ill. But when the whole herd has the same disease, no one notices. "

I went on to tell him that a brainless herd of cattle suffering from selenium deficiency would never learn to think.

"This town doesn't even provide facilities for that activity," I said.

"Oh?"

"There isn't a single café where people meet to discuss things and to think. Or library."

"Come on now, we do have a library," said Hasse, though I don't think he was quite sure.

"Yes, but with what kind of books? Berit Spong and Louis Bromfield and the Rotary Club's annual reports."

I continued as he ate his herring, saying that in this city no one acknowledged sexuality as the basic human drive it was. It was pursued covertly. It was viewed as nothing more than some kind of hanky-panky people busied themselves with between the sheets. While in reality it governed our lives.

"Is that so?" asked Hasse. "I don't think I've ever heard anyone talk about sexuality like that before," he said, but without even a trace of astonishment. In a way, he hasn't changed much since.

"What's more, people have forgotten God," I said, which really did make him look up. I still think I was right about everything I said that night. But I neglected the fact that, fundamentally, whatever I was I had become in this very city. I made fun of the people passing by in the slush with their Co-op carrier bags and their scruffy briefcases with thermoses and sandwiches inside. But I had failed to recall that they taught me everything I knew. If they had told me when I was a child that spirits dwelt in the trees and we must worship them and carry little bowls with our offerings out to them I would have done so. Bowls of cold rice pudding, prune whip and cultured milk. There would have been nothing absurd or ridiculous about it. I would have made sacrifices to the spirits in the lindens and the apple trees and later when I had gone out into the world and met other people who told me those things were forbidden or unnecessary or mad, I might have stopped. But I would always have known there were spirits in the trees.

I am what they made me.

Although I granted Hasse the privilege of taking me out to dinner and paying the bill with Curre Clothes' money, the moment I had my schnapps he ceased to be any more present than if he had been invisible. His suit of nubbly gray homespun cloth dissolved, and from behind it Philip's black elegance emerged so clearly I imagined I could see his frayed jacket cuffs. What tenderness I felt for that shirt collar with its curled ends, for the dirt under his index finger nail, and for his burgundy tie. It was Philip I was talking to after I drank my aquavit, when I said:

"I can't feel my nose any more!"

"Can't you?" asked Hasse, while Philip would have said:

"Well it's still there, and damn stunning!"

And then he would have raised his glass to me, asking:

"What'll it be for the main course, darling?"

"Medallion of pork."

It existed in the material world, and came in on a silver-plated serving dish. On the stage over by the kitchen door a solo violinist was playing Vilja's song. Vilja wandered among the gentlemen in their dark jackets and around the dusty pillars and tables covered with white cloths like altars. She was laden with the scents of food by the time she got to us. Hasse ordered a red wine called Le Vallon Hanappier. He placed his order in a way that sounded as if he knew exactly what he wanted and always did, and I guessed this was the wine his father drank with Sunday dinner. I wanted him to say something about me, about my appearance. I put my hair playfully up on my head, though it wasn't quite long enough.

"How do you like my hair this way?"

"It's all right."

"All right?"

"Yeah."

I had thin, shoulder length hair that curled in blonde waves around my neck. Some strands were darker; I was as stripy as a tomcat but didn't want to go on using peroxide because it was so hard on my hair. I was wearing a low cut, black sweater and a strand of beans. I liked the contrast between the beans and my neck, which was pale and so thin the veins showed.

I skewered the last mouthful of my pork medallion on my fork between two French fried potatoes, using the tomato butter to hold the whole thing together. I swilled it down with Sunday wine.

"Don't drink that wine when your mouth's full," said Hasse.

He was drinking sparkling water. When the waitresses kicked open the kitchen door you could hear the clatter of dishes and the frantic voices of the kitchen staff. I couldn't feel my chin any more. When I dropped my fork all the sounds had become so rounded and muted I could barely hear them. When I laughed, people turned toward our table and stared. The maitre d' made a sign, a waitress toddled over with a clean fork. She looked at me with forbearance. I suddenly remembered that Pappa was a regular customer here.

I had coffee with Parfait Amour and got my fingers sticky. I suppose I must have dipped them into the glass. The ceiling lights were dimmed, the violinist left the stage. Hasse paid the bill after having scrutinized every item in great detail. Seventy kronor for two. Philip's lines floated around in the air, but didn't find a single mouth that could have uttered them. We were leaving and I was at the absolute zenith of well-being, right where the wave breaks and the dip of queasiness begins. I felt like opening my mouth wide and sticking my tongue out really far to get some air. Slowly and hazardously I navigated my way between the tables.

"What charming drunken dignity you possess, my dear," Philip would have said. But he said nothing. He was rotting away at the City Hotel in Söderhamn. The cloakroom attendant trudged back and forth. "Your coat, madame. May I? Thank you sir, thank you ever so much."

Hasse had learned to tip. We emerged onto the street and my shoes filled up with slush.

"Don't you have any galoshes?"

No, I didn't have any galoshes. I didn't want any galoshes. I didn't really even want to be in a place where you needed them.

The next morning I woke up in my narrow bed. On the desk next to me was a whisky tumbler full of water. I sat up, focused on keeping my tongue as far from my palate as possible and my mouth wide open so I wouldn't get that bad taste. First I drank. Then I realized Hasse must have been the one to put the glass there and it made me think of his mother. He had put it there out of goodness and tenderness, but also out of habit, and perhaps even resignation. I began to feel ashamed, as ashamed as only a twenty-year-old can be. My black raincoat with the missing buttons was on the chair. My necklace had broken during the night, it had only been a strand of beans. Now they looked like black teeth on the sheets and it didn't strike me as the least bit stunning any more. I wondered if my neck had been grimy. My stockings were dirty and had been for three or four days. Hasse had decent habits; he hadn't undressed me, thank God.

It was a time and a community so feverish with activity that you had to be extremely strong if you were going to persist in not working. Now I spent my days at the Lindh manor helping an elderly woman relation of the deceased merchant draw up an estate inventory. Work had come sniffing me out as well.

The house had been sold to the city, the goods and chattels were going to be auctioned. They had been collected, once upon a time, by the merchant, who wanted to own things by the cartful. I got the job because I had been at school with Ingela Iversen-Lindh. She was in the hospital with leukemia, but had told them to ask me if I wanted to do it. Perhaps she hoped I would come visit her, but I never dared.

The name of the relation was, as I had been told "Fröken Lindh". She had a large bottom, a tweed suit and sturdy walking shoes. There was no heat on in the house. Before we stepped on the parquet floors, we wrapped our shoes in rags. I hated wearing those bundles of cloth on my feet, even though no one but Fröken Lindh saw me, and she didn't really. To her I was a device known as Fröken Johannesson, fitted with arms, hands and fingers that could pound her dictation into a tall, black typewriter. I sat in the faux fur Pappa had bought for me; it smelled like piss in wet weather. My wrists, protruding from the fluffy cuffs, were bluish-red and thin. We never said one personal word to each other. I wrote:

> Bohemian crystal chandelier.
> Early nineteenth century. Blue drip-
> rings. Brass chain. Six arms.

Fröken Lindh stared up at the ceiling for a few seconds. Then she added:
"Gift from the then Countess of Västerbotten province to Merchant Lindh."

That was shamelessly presumptuous. A bold-faced lie. Invention. Practically poetic. She was mad. The whole town would laugh in her face when the list of items for auction became public.

She was the daughter of Merchant Lindh's younger brother Adolf, and her profile was very noble. Her broad, aquiline nose, her thin legs and her enormous, rocking body made her look like a sheep, an aging ewe. If a sheep started to surround itself with objects it had collected and then tried to lie down on them all at once, it would be put down as mad. I watched that woman in the tweed suit handling silver vases and paintings of decapitated heads and I saw an aging ewe lying at the very top of a heap with a peculiar accumulation of pine cones, stones and twisted tree limbs under her.

I realized right away that Fröken Lindh was no collector and organizer like my Grandfather Abel. To her, the most important thing was the personal connection. If there was none she made one up. She wanted the mark of ownership on every item.

Her uncle had brought all this matter together. Now it did not suffice that it was to be dispersed, she needed to bind him to it with more and finer filaments. Had she been able to claim that he had given birth to the chairs that belonged to the eighteenth century group by mating with the sofa, she would have. Without so much as blinking, she instructed me to write that the human hair used to embroider some of the finery came from the Lindh family heads. Even I could see it was nothing but junk from some run-of-the-mill itinerant pedlar.

Instructions ran into my brain from hers and out through my fingers to the typewriter keys, and I typed a neat and orderly stack of lies. It sickened me. Was there blood in the dusty bottles of vintage wine in the basement, the blood of the Lindh family? I spent my lunch breaks at the café next to the town hall, where I had big open sandwiches of liver paste on dark bread, or hard-boiled eggs and anchovies, and drank milk. I ate in protest against this foolish, deeply religious woman, who did not seem to require sustenance, who lived off lists of objects. She stayed inside the house counting silver tankards and waiting for me.

The blood, sperm, brain cells and hair of Alexander Lindh the merchant couldn't possibly have forced their way out into these objects and taken possession of them, I knew that. The objects had all been transported here, and now they were to be taken away. I needed those breaks at the café to enable me to cling to that understanding. This whole city was one big transport chain, when it came down to it. Aggregations of matter people had exchanged, purchased, acquired, given as payment in kind, dumped, bartered for credit, lent, bargained, bought under the table, over and underbid, saved, brought to fulfillment, invested. This was called the economy and had given rise to all these items that had been transported here by rail. The Bohemian crystal chandeliers and the silver cutlery from the Lindh mansion. The concrete bridge spans and the iron cemetery gates. The granite fountain on the market square. The more solid the matter, the more economy was in it. All that is not solid rots and melts to waste. The blood of Lindh the merchant would have liked to flow out into a set of silver tankards and solidify in perpetuity.

One day a man appeared and stood watching us from the doorway. Fröken Lindh was in the process of removing one volume after the next from a little eighteenth century book collection, and I was noting down the titles. He stood there with the light behind him, looking into the dark room that gleamed with silver. We could not see his face, but it was Wolfgang Altmeyer.

He was born in Austria, and during the war he came to stay with the Iversen-Lindhs. By my calculations, he was forty-three the summer I worked for him, though I thought of him as an old man. When he walked past me and went over and kissed Fröken Lindh on the cheek, there was an expensive, pleasing scent about him. I hadn't expected him to introduce himself to me, but he did. His stiff head was pressed down between his shoulders, his hair was black and straight, parted in the middle. I had heard a lot about him but would never have imagined him as friendly. He asked us about our work and then he picked up a few pages from the draft list of items and sat down on a sofa to read it. When he finished he replaced the pages very carefully alongside the typewriter and praised my neat work and my typing. He praised Fröken Lindh as well, but differently. He told her she had done a tremendous job on this inventory and that it was really much too much for her. He was afraid she would overtax herself. I realized what he was getting at and I suppose Fröken Lindh did, too, because she assured him it was nothing, nothing at all. She wasn't the least bit tired!

The next day a woman phoned from merchant Patrik Iversen-Lindh's office to inform me that my job at the Lindh mansion was complete. If I came to the office with my references I could count on a position in invoicing.

I never went. The list for the auction was eventually published but the text bore no resemblance to the one Fröken Lindh had dictated to me. It was factual and totally unobjectionable, drawn up by a firm of auctioneers. I found it dull and felt sympathy for the old looney. Which I hadn't when I was shut in with her.

"Have you heard about Altmeyer buying *The Correspondent*?"

This was a standing joke. When the person who was asked said no you're kidding, well who would have thought it, they were told Altmeyer had been to the newsagent down by the square and bought a copy of the paper.

But then Altmeyer really did buy *The Correspondent*.

I had daydreams about being on the staff of the paper. I would submit a column that would turn out to be the wittiest, most eloquent writing they had ever seen. I would slip my manuscript through the slot in the door of the editorial offices. Once the whole town was talking about that fantastic column I would look in and tell the editor:

"I'm the person who writes under the name of ..."

But I couldn't settle on a pseudonym. I considered STAR, PLUCKY, ROSE and THE PEN.

One morning when I was passing the editorial offices I heard an angry voice through the window:

"These archives are a goddamn shambles!"

After which there was the slamming of cupboard doors and then silence. I stood where I was, stock still by the wall of the building. That shout had come at me as if it were a message. I rushed home and washed my hair in the hand basin and dried it over the stove until it was fluffy as a cloud and glistening. Then I went over to the paper.

The editor-in-chief was sitting in a crowded office that was broiling hot from the electric radiator and freezing cold from a draft along the floor. Her name was Ada Wallin. She had a big body and a fine-featured little face. She sat there in her swivel chair, with a globe on the desk next to her. Whenever it slowed down she would give it a little pat to keep it spinning.

I had been sitting in the secretary's office rehearsing how I would put it, but now I forgot what I had been practicing: "I live in the building next door," I said. "My name's Ann-Marie Johannesson and I've heard your archives need reorganizing."

She gaped of course.

"I thought I could do the filing. I need a job."

She still didn't answer, so I said:

"I'm pendant."

The minute I said that I could tell it was inappropriate and I started to blush and could feel the tears rising. Pappa and I had always said *pendant* in jest, and in imitation of Jenny. It had just slipped out.

"Where did you hear our files needed re-organizing?" Ada Wallin asked

"Through the window," I said.

I did get a job but not the filing. She gave me two tickets to *Showboat* at the community park and told me to review it. It didn't take her long to worm it out of me that I wanted to be a journalist and that I had a year and a half of studies at

Uppsala behind me.

I went and saw the show and spent all night working on my review. But I still didn't finish it. By dawn I felt so sick I just had to lie down on the bed for a little while, and I nodded off. When I woke up it was eleven and by the time I had typed the final version of my manuscript on Henning's old typewriter it was nearly noon. Too late, or almost too late.

When I brought my manuscript to the office, Ada had already got someone else to prepare a review from the program notes. I said good-bye and backed out through the door.

I spent a lot of time in bed, some of it crying. I hadn't realized how much it meant to me. Now and then I dozed off, and when I woke up I thought it might have all been a dream.

In the end I actually got taken on. Ada called me in when I was passing outside her window. She told me my review had been far too long, would almost have taken up a whole page of the paper. She also said I was a terrible writer. I should stop trying to be funny. Write like you breathe, she told me. Calmly.

"Still, it was good," she concluded. "Very good."

I didn't understand. Until she went on and told me it was well thought out.

When I left her office I had a job on a trial basis doing general journalism. We hadn't mentioned pay; you just didn't ask about such a thing. I went home and washed my hair again and when I came to my first day at work, it was bristling with static electricity.

Ada had succeeded her father as editor-in-chief. He was the one who would assign a photographer to go get a picture of the people outside the bottle store. When people got their pictures in the paper in that line, they would be too embarrassed to go and buy their rations for some time. Wallin's ambition was to use his power for the good of society. Which ended up being an attempt to teach the people how he thought they should live.

When he died, the newspaper went to his two daughters, Ada and Lisa. Ada suddenly appeared at the office. For the last few years she had been wasting away, living the dull life on a little estate not far from town. This genteel poverty hadn't agreed with her at all. She was a dynamic, outgoing person. When she walked through town the air crackled.

She and her sister became the majority shareholders, and Ada persuaded Lisa that they should share the position of editor-in-chief, too. Their father had designated a crown prince, Magnus Swärd, who had been writing celebratory cantatas for public occasions, obituaries and articles about historical monuments for *The Correspondent* for decades and who had gone gray and bony waiting for Wallin to release his grip on the paper. It's amazing he didn't die of a broken heart when Ada took over and appointed him head news editor. He'd been a news editor all along.

Lisa refused to call herself editor-in-chief. She'd worked at her father's newspaper ever since she finished girls' school in Norrköping. She did the 'Thoughts for the Day', which were devotional, and the family page. But she did not want power. She went on doing her 'Thoughts for the Day', as before.

When I got to know Ada, she was fifty-five. She had a stiff cloud of graying once-red hair, a bush rising from the top of her head. She smoked cigarillos, and people said they had seen her wearing Wellington boots with her walking suit and a hat with birds' wings in the rain. I'm not sure that was true. Ada was one of the personalities of the city; she was sent out to do things no one else dared.

There was an indignant period when she tried to get into Rotary because the editor-in-chief had always been a member before. There was no question of that now.

She had kept her Deutsche Kraftwagen from her days at the manor, and it bumped and rattled forcefully down the muddy roads.

Ada treated me as her protegé. But I think I disappointed her. I was something she just couldn't comprehend — quite lazy.

My first day of work at *The Correspondent* began with Ada walking me to the foot of the stairs to the newsroom and shouting:

"Here comes Fröken Johannesson! She's new!"

Climbing those stairs, I couldn't imagine who would be at the top. My hands were clammy and I had cinched my black patent leather belt very tight.

I got up to the newsroom, a big, empty room with phones ringing. At the far end was a glass cubicle, where I could see Lisa Wallin. She was sitting there cutting things out of the paper. She was little and stooped and several years older than Ada. It took her quite a while to straighten up when she rose. I think she had a lot of pain. When we had shaken hands she asked me what my duties in the newsroom were. I thought I'd burst into tears. Anyway, she showed me to a big book with brown covers, instructing me to cut the death notices from that day's paper and paste them in. She didn't explain why. When she had given me my instructions she returned to her cubicle and went on working. Her baggy, machine-knitted yellow cardigan hung over the back of her chair. I peeked at her now and then and realized how pale she was. She had dry, cracked skin, like a bowl of dough that's been left to rise for too long.

In spite of not knowing the purpose for which I was doing the task she had assigned me, I thought I'd better do it well, so I cut out the notices very carefully and then shaped the edges. I put all my energy into organizing the pages of the book to fit as many notices as possible.

Afterwards I learned that the book was used as a list of funerals to be covered during the coming week. The relevant data was copied from the notices.

The telephones kept ringing but I didn't dare answer. Now and then someone would rush into the room and speak into one or type a few lines. They greeted me as they passed. One introduced himself as Karlman, another didn't identify himself but I heard them calling him Uno. There was a photographer who ran through the newsroom on his way to the archives occasionally. His name was Pippo and he was a familiar figure in town.

When I finished the death notices I didn't know what to do with myself. I brushed dead flies off the windowsills and dumped them into the wastepaper basket, wrapped in tissues.

At noon the building grew noisy. I realized, with a sense of physical relief, that this was the press starting up. Now something would have to happen. But the only thing that happened was that Karlman came back, his hands black with newsprint. He gave me a copy of the paper and told me I could go to lunch.

I didn't dare go home. I had a feeling that if I went back to my own kitchen table I would end up staying there. I knew Karlman had only sent me to lunch to get me out of the way.

I went to a café for a sandwich and a glass of milk. When I returned things improved slightly. Karlman, who was always rushed, showed me around the offices. The teleprinter in its little alcove was just pecking out a message about five British citizens who had been arrested for naval espionage. It had just happened, in London. Karlman liked my being impressed. When we walked out of the cubbyhole it went on chattering on its own, in fits and starts. A long strip of paper slithered out. We didn't need to bother about it, said Karlman. We couldn't print anything else until tomorrow noon, anyway. Not even if the Bomb fell.

He showed me the archives. They weren't, as I'd imagined, the place all the old cuttings were filed, but rather a repository for photographs and printing plates. They were kept in shoeboxes and envelopes. The sharp edges of the plates had split the sides of the envelopes, and all the spookily black faces were getting mixed up with one another, the city council with the American president and the Kramfors bride with Andersson the Swedish naval spy. I asked Karlman if anyone would mind if I came in and did some sorting when I was not otherwise occupied. He looked taken aback, but said it would be all right

There was a manuscript lift that rattled on a chain, lowering manuscripts down to the composing room on the ground floor. Karlman never had the patience to put his work in the lift. He he ran his manuscripts down the stairs instead.

In the afternoon I was given proofreading to do and put in an office in the basement with a man whose name was Victor Bremer. He looked about forty-five and treated me with irony and a large dose of chivalry. He made me deeply insecure.

We became a proofreading team. I would sit with the manuscript and he would read aloud from the proofs, reading about serious things in a mocking voice. He read a bunch of 'Thoughts for the Day' that way. Fröken Wallin wrote several at a time in advance. We spent the afternoon on material that didn't have any news value. It made me realize what a full larder of that kind of thing a newspaper has to have.

No one showed me the composing room. But at some point I was told to take something there. It wasn't really considered our territory.

When I went home at the end of the day I had the feeling that if I didn't go in again the next day no one would ever remember I had been there. Later, though, I learned from Victor that I had been wrong. That was just their way of not showing amazement or appreciation or anything that might seem unsophisticated or naïve. In reality I'd made a hit with my low-cut, washed out cotton top, my patent leather belt, my bitten-down nails and my high-heeled shoes clattering on the stairs to the newsroom. I had also, Victor added, been highly perfumed.

When I was little I always lived with my Pappa. I hadn't suffered when he was away. Jenny and Fredrik took good care of me — though I really lived with my Pappa. All other living was like sitting at a bus station. You don't suffer from waiting. You don't really care what you are doing while you wait.

When did it end? I don't know. I guess it ended when we started being embarrassed in one another's presence.

I came home from Uppsala and he didn't ask any questions. I thought I must have had the wrong idea; he hadn't expected great things of me. It was perfectly logical for me to have failed.

It might have had to do all those things that were awkward for us to talk about. I kept my sanitary pads hidden away. I never spoke of Philip. Having those pads and that bleeding, those risks and feelings and men so close to my skin, that may have been the root of my failure. In which case it was innate to and sprang from my body. It was destiny, it even contained an element of sickly desire. I was born with millions of genetic traits for failure stored deep in my body. Some of them would surely grow and develop. Pappa turned away, embarrassed.

Fredrik couldn't be Pappa when Henning was away. He was just Fredrik. Thumped me on the back and played around with me as if I were a puppy dog. He hadn't noticed that I was almost twenty-one. He gaped with astonishment when I drank the schnapps Jenny poured for me one Saturday at dinner.

But now, every weekday morning, I sat opposite a man in a gray suit, a thin man with a polka-dot bow tie under his chin, and between us was that tension I hadn't felt since Pappa had started to be embarrassed and then left, gone away without me to make his fortune.

I read proofs with Victor. Even when he was reading the description of a football match or an exposition on local taxes he aimed his voice at me, full of tension, of sarcasm. Sometimes I could barely discern his face through the cigarette smoke. I could just hear his voice, rougher and hoarser as the hours passed. Sometimes he would break off and cough long and loud. Then he would light another flat Turkish cigarette from the butt of the previous one and go on. The smell of oriental tobacco made me nauseous at first. Then I got used to it, and soon I couldn't smoke any other kind myself. I have thought about it often. I inhaled his cigarette smoke and listened to his biased and sarcastic rendition of the events and lives of the city.

He was the one who really looked after me when I started working at *The Correspondent*. He taught me proofreading. He was the person who read everything anyone wrote, and who cleaned up the language of the whole paper. On the days he was hung over and pathetic (as he said), he didn't bother, and then the newspaper was a disaster for linguistically sensitized readers. When I started to write he corrected all my efforts before I sent them downstairs in the manuscript lift.

Victor was thin and not very tall but he didn't come over as either small or skinny. He had a large head. I think his hat size was sixty or sixty-one, and it was difficult for him to find headgear that fit. He always wore hound's-tooth suits, he must have had three or four, with different sized checks, to alternate between. He wore gray or blue shirts to work and bow ties of polka-dotted silk. His changing his tie was a big event for me — that's how quiet and regular our routines in the newsroom were.

His face was very sharp-featured. He had large, dark blue eyes under heavy eyelids. Even when there was no question that he was awake and alert, his eyelids drooped over his eyes. The whites were yellowing and a little bloodshot. Now, long afterwards, I realize how extraordinarily keen-sighted I was in those days, and I am often embarrassed when I see young people scrutinizing me. Could Victor have felt that way? Were his sarcasm and joking a defense against my ruthless youth?

He had black-framed goggles, and I suppose I really only remember his eyes from the occasions off work when he removed them.

He only ever referred to his body as the old cadaver.

"The old cadaver's happy today," he would say. "It's had a rest. It's taken a Sunday stroll."

I was, of course, curious about whether he had ever had any love affairs. He was a bachelor, and extremely reticent about his private life. He sneered at total honesty and said the old cadaver had seen better days; he was too old for love.

He claimed to have a materialistic world-view , and not even now can I really understand what he meant. He was outspokenly, almost programmatically, atheistic. But he spoke of Jesus more often than any other person I had ever known. He

245

called him Our Savior, and appeared to identify with him, because one day when he was going to leave early he said:

"You'll have to go to press yourselves. Then will I no longer be among you."

He detested men of the cloth and was relentlessly ironic about the death notices I pasted into the brown ledger.

My first assignments were related to the church and the clergy. I read the proofs of the coming week's parish events, and every Sunday afternoon I had to go to the empty newsroom and phone around to every congregation, ask the ministers what weddings and funerals were upcoming, and record their answers on wax cylinders. Eventually I also got to write up the reports on funerals. I was also in charge of the boxes on the shelf in the proof room containing the excerpts from the parish registers of births. We would go through them every day to see who in town was having a big birthday, and then write articles honoring those who were men and sufficiently well-known. At ninety even women and men of lower social position got mentioned.

When I had been on staff for a few weeks I was allowed to go out into town to interview people who were having important birthdays. I was scared to death that they would feel put upon in spite of their obvious, even laughable willingness to see me. I had also begun to write columns. I wrote about Pappa's and my life at 13 Chapel Road. I didn't write exactly the truth, since, at the time, Pappa wasn't at home. But I wrote what could have been true.

When I had some extra time I sat down in the picture archive sorting printing plates. It was my favorite part of the job. The files contained stacks of pictures of people who had succeeded by pulling themselves up by their own bootstraps. There were three shoeboxes full of Fabian Bärj, chairman of the town finance department. People recognized him wherever he went. And yet he didn't own much. He lived in one of the weatherboarded houses at the Upco estate, where Fredrik and Jenny lived. He didn't have a car. Although he wasn't a wealthy man he had succeeded in making himself more real than most people in town. I stared at big, rectangular printing plates from which his face shone black with silver eyes. But the air he inhaled into his lungs was no more real than mine, and the water didn't taste any stronger when he drank it.

I found Victor Bremer to be an extraordinarily remarkable person. But he hardly existed. No one outside the paper knew he cleaned up all the language in *The Correspondent*.

"Uh oh, Fabian Bärj is about to tip his bucket over us again," he said when one of his speeches to the city council came into the newsroom. But when he read the proofs he put right the worst of the howlers.

I don't think there is a photograph of Victor as an adult. His resistance was faceless, averted, ironic. Every time he removed an erroneous double negative or corrected a pronoun referent, it was as if he had squeezed the pus out of an abscess or operated on a sty on Fabian Bärj's fat, bloated body, and strangely enough he seemed to do this work out of love.

One morning when I got to the paper, Victor wasn't there. Just before nine I went around and took orders for cakes and buns to go with the morning coffee. His swivel chair was still empty. On the desk was a whole stack of proofs waiting to be read.

Uno asked for two cinnamon rolls and a pack of Marvels with his coffee. Karlsson wanted an iced almond pastry. Pippo's standing order was creamy yellow coconut macaroons that left him sucking at what was stuck between his teeth for the rest of the morning. But I just stared at Victor's empty chair, unable to remember what he usually ordered. Ginger biscuits? Plain sweet rolls? Something must be his thing. His absence ate away at me like acid. It was a gaping hole in my memory. I even felt uncertain about how he looked. I wanted to hear his voice, and I asked Karlman whether we ought not phone and see if he was all right.

"His kidneys are acting up," Karlman answered.

Kidney trouble? Was he in pain? Bedridden? I wondered if he wore pajamas.

Victor was gone for three days and during that time the paper was full of misprints. His absence revealed to me how dull life in the newsroom really was. The hours crumbled down to minutes, the manuscript lift rattled and I knew by now what was in it. It thumped when it hit bottom. The teleprinter spat out a couple meters of text. The pigeons scuttled around on the metal roof, and I heard their footsteps in a little pool of silence in the very midst of the noise of work. I didn't even think it was particularly exciting to have to go to the composing room any more. I sometimes went by there when I was feeling reckless and newly-perfumed. But now I realized that I hadn't done it because the comments turned me on, but to tease Victor.

I stood by the brown table, cutting. Lisa Wallin sat in her cubicle, a ruffled bird accustomed to her captivity. All that ownership, the house and the newspaper, huge rolls of paper, even a delivery van, cameras, cases of font styles, composing machines, God only knew what, and to sentence oneself to life in a cage, to voluntary captivity, to writing "and Jesus said". The same baggy, machine-knitted cardigan week out and week in, brown stockings and tie shoes with perforated caps. A little grayer, a little more stooped for every day that passed. The best years of one's youth run through one's fingers. Life, where is thy Victory? It runs out into a pit, settling, going foul.

I left. Went to the proof room to look at Victor's empty chair. The seat must be cold now. My chair was warm, I sat quite still. Like the furniture. Like the filing cabinets, full of rubbish. The sun sent a wide beam of light through the room and in it the dust whirled, dizzying and silent.

The dust particles were always whirling although we couldn't see them when it was cloudy and dark. Whirling and settling, being set in motion and whirling and lying down to rest. They lay on the shelves and the desk and in the curtain folds. First a layer of dust accumulated, then it ate its way in and became grime. In the end it was that grayness that never disappears, no matter how hard you rub and polish. On everything. The pages in the files yellowed. They are yellowing right now, growing slowly but steadily brittle. The sun bleaches the curtains. The furniture creaks and rots. The occasional cracking sound. You only hear it on Sunday afternoons when you're alone in the building. But it is actually clicking and eating away all the time. It is time. It rushes in your ears.

Something clicks in you and your blood stops rushing. Victor had said it wasn't nearly as big a deal as people made it. But it interested him. He often talked about it. No one else did.

I understood time was eating away at me, too, although it was easier to see in the furniture, the curtains and Lisa Wallin. The skin around my nose and on my chin was getting rougher. You think you live on events, Victor had said. But you live on time. Not on five minutes at a go, but on whole, unbroken rushing time.

I wanted him back. I wanted to sit opposite him and whisper this secret:

"Life is boooooor-ing."

And he would whisper back: "You're right, it's dull as dishwater. It is bore, bore like the feet of fat pigeons on a metal roof."

I hung around the newsroom all afternoon. It got quiet and hot. The sun baked down through the windows. In the end I plucked up my courage and lifted the receiver, dialed Victor's number. He sounded gruff when he answered. My anxiety stole away the reason I'd made up for calling. I just said:

"When will you be back?"

He was perfectly silent. Then we switched to our regular newsroom jargon. It was over. But it had happened.

When I walked outside my sharp heels went down through the hot tarmac. We were having a heat wave and the streets reeked of fuel.

Now I realize it was as natural for me to fall in love with Victor as it is for a young she-monkey tossed into a strange cage to choose the burly older male who is the leader of the pack. I had understood that he had power. If there was calculation in my romance it was deeply buried. Falling in love was the behavior that was possible.

I had spurts of being interested in my own psychology. I would list my qualities on a piece of paper, good ones in a column on the left and bad ones on the right. I wrote:

intelligent	lazy
thorough	shy
good speller	easily bored
sense of humor	untruthful

But there wasn't a word about my sexuality, and I think that for a number of years around this time it was my most salient feature. It was my communication and my perception, my way of coping with life in the world and my only instrument of power. But I didn't think about it. I went to work with freshly-sharpened breasts. They were supported by bra cups that were hard and pointed, I swayed with a wiggle when I walked and kept my belt pulled tight, wore shoes that made my feet more pointed than my breasts, had red nail polish and a collarbone that protruded from my low-cut tops, but I attributed none of this the slightest significance on my list. I was a lazy, shy, easily bored girl who spelled well. I wonder if the men in the composing room would have recognized my description of myself. Ada's secretary stared at me as if the Leviathan or Zarah Leander had entered the room when I came in in the mornings. I don't think I ever understood why. When I thought about Victor I was only afraid he would find me stupid.

There's one place where a shy person can very agreeably exercise her sexuality, and that's on the telephone. Every Sunday afternoon I went to the newsroom to phone the local clergy. I recorded their information about weddings and funerals on wax cylinders. The ministers were difficult to get through to, their wives equivocated cheerfully about their not being at home. When they did come to the phone they were annoyed, and talked too fast. But I think I can say that if there was one thing I managed adequately, it was the clergymen.

One hot evening I had kicked my shoes off under the desk where I sat calling around. My feet were dirty and swollen from walking with no stockings in my shoes. My hair was sticky at the temples. But it didn't make any difference, since the clergymen could only hear my voice. When it was time to change the cylinder, my fingers were fumbly and swollen from the heat, and I dropped the used one. Some little bits of brown wax split off when it hit the floor, and when I got it back into the machine and put on the headphones, the only sounds were buzzing and crackling.

I panicked. I certainly couldn't phone the ministers again. They would surely be annoyed and uncooperative. The newsroom manager would hear about it. I started to cry, banging my fists on the typewriter keys so they bounced up, and their metal rods got all tangled. Then I began to howl.

The next time I looked up, Victor was standing there. I had been crying to an audience. He extended a blue-checked handkerchief and I cried for a few more minutes before accepting it. He had not needed to come in to the office on a Sunday. Since he returned after his illness he had been cool and ironic with me. But now he was there.

He put on the headset and listened. He told me I'd only lost the beginning of one funeral, and that I could go look up the name of the deceased in the cuttings ledger.

When I put on the headphones to listen again, he stood behind me with one hand on my neck. While I listened to the minister talking, his hand rested there.

After a while Victor took it away and left the room. When I heard his footsteps on the stairs I assumed he was going down to the proofreading room to get a cigarette lighter or something. But the street door closed and then it was quiet. He's gone to the cake shop, I thought. But he didn't come back.

When I was twenty the city was a stage set for my own dramas. Institutions, companies, political bodies — they were all painted on stretched canvas or presented like set pieces. There was no point walking around looking at them. I didn't believe my eyes but I couldn't imagine there being anything else behind them, either.

Social criticism was like shooting at these painted figures and facades and scoring bull's eyes. Ada did it sometimes, which I thought was funny. But I couldn't imagine that what she wrote was really true. It was brash, unflinching, urbane — but just as unreal as holes in paper targets. It didn't bleed.

At *The Correspondent* it wasn't the news staff who revolted against the management. The editor-in-chief didn't sit censoring articles that might annoy advertisers and subscribers. On the contrary, Victor and Karlman would go into Ada's office for long discussions in which they tried to get her to call off her dogs in the editorials. The paper wasn't selling.

But Ada was brooding on plans, unbeknownst to us, and that autumn she actually made the city bleed and squeal like a stuck pig. She wrote a novel. It was entitled *Safe and Scintillating* and was the story of a small railway town and the problems associated with the building of a big new office complex for the local government. A slimy scoundrel with black hair parted in the middle by the name of Atle Wolfpaw was a member of the working committee and decided what plot the building would go up on. Then he sent out his henchmen to buy up the real estate. He sold it for a high price and the chairman of the town council who weighed a hundred and ten kilos and had chilblains big enough to sculpt, whose name was Laban Boulder didn't blink an eye. After the meetings there was plenty of wining and dining and the whole story was as crude and as simple as only reality can be.

Ada was trying to kill two birds with one stone, so she wasn't content with exposing the lying and robbing that goes on in the upper echelons of society. She also wanted to get in a dig at the rotten sexual mores, so she added an element of violent young love to the drama. There were stiffening nipples and hot lips, and even legs that parted, owing to which Ada was sentencing herself to the loss of the confidence of her fellow citizens. She was valiant as an Amazon about ensuring that when people wrote letters to the editor claiming she ought to be put behind bars or institutionalized, they were published. But it's one thing to show courage on the battlefield. The post-battle scenario was worse. That was the time of ridicule and contempt. Subscribers cancelled, advertisers switched allegiance to the *County News*. Ada was lonely and unusually quiet that autumn. Her sister Lisa went off to Skodsborg spa in Denmark to recuperate, and when she returned her mouth looked as if it had been closed up with stitches.

The balance in the building shifted. Lisa's voice got sharper. Magnus Swärd left his office more often. Ada's door was usually closed and most days of the week the editorials consisted of material submitted by the local Social Democratic party office. I don't think Ada's novel was very good. But it has a scent of unaired sheets and dirty socks about it that hits the nail on the head. Even in those days I knew she had captured the tone accurately, and I could suddenly see how the big, newly-built local government office building was more than a stage setting, that it was a real place with employees who didn't wash their feet all too often.

But it didn't ring quite true that Wolfgang Altmeyer was a lying, cheating rogue. He definitely kept his hands, feet and underwear clean, you could see that from a mile away. He wore Swiss Bally shoes, tailor-made suits and hand-stitched pigskin gloves. All that spoke more clearly than Ada's inept novel.

Altmeyer had acquired *The Correspondent*, beginning with Lisa's shareholding, and we were his employees. At first we didn't notice any difference. The manuscript lift rattled, and at half past nine there was the smell of coffee as always. Ada was still editor-in-chief then, although no one knew what the future would bring in that respect. When the consequences of her first novel began to be evident in black-and-white circulation statistics, in the fact that advertisers and subscribers were switching papers, Altmeyer came to see her several times and they had long conversations. But no one knew what they talked about.

One Sunday she drove up to the offices at two-thirty in the afternoon, her DKW bouncing through the puddles. I was looking at her from our living room window, watching her not bother to keep her feet dry as she crossed the yard.

Around five I went myself to phone the ministers. I knew Ada was in her office right under the room where I was, but I didn't hear any noise from down there, no rattling of the typewriter, no turning of pages. When I had finished and was going home that evening, her office light was still on. I felt uneasy. There was something odd about this behavior. She didn't usually come in on Sunday afternoons, and it was unlike her to be so quiet.

I went back to the newsroom. I hoped I'd bump into her. I wanted to know what she was up to. But I was too timid to go to her office door and knock. I had started on a little piece about a wedding in Vallmsta church when I heard her door creak, and after a few minutes the building door closed and Ada's car started in the yard. I stood at the window and watched her drive off.

Since I was there anyway I went on writing a few bits and pieces, but my back was starting to ache and my throat was raw from smoking. I don't know how much time had passed when the incoming news phone rang.

It was a man calling from a little farming village a few miles out of town. He said Ada Wallin had crashed her car and was dead. I still remember how his voice sounded.

"She'm crashed and died," he said. "The police're here. She'm drove right into the rockface."

I didn't know what to do. I think I said thank you. When I hung up I heard how silent the offices were and I was frightened. Ada's death was a kind of news in itself, I did realize that. Perhaps I ought to call Karlman or Magnus Swärd. But I didn't dare stay in the building.

Ada had left her door open down there. When I passed by I could see through the secretary's cubicle and into Ada's office. There was a lingering smell of cigarillos, and clouds and ribbons of smoke hovering over her desk, slowly sinking and dispersing. At that moment I realized how unreal life is.

Ada's body, with its good-looking slim legs and enormous torso was autopsied, and whenever I thought about that, it made me feel sick. It was hard to sleep when you knew. Every time I passed the office of the editor-in-chief I sniffed the air to see if it still smelled of smoke.

They said the post-mortem indicated death from a heart attack. The car accident had come afterwards. I don't know if I ever believed it. Having seen those bands of smoke over her desk when she was already dead I didn't really believe anything I saw any more.

I hadn't been to a funeral since Tora Otter died. In those days you stood outside, in summer rain or in cold weather, seeing the remains on to the next thing, the thing we don't know anything about. Surely everyone who attends a funeral is keenly aware that all our contraptions and conceptions are no more stable than the wooden planks around the open grave. Behind them and under them is the other thing.

When Ada died, they had begun burying people mechanically. Ada's coffin was in the crematorium, and it was lowered into the basement with music and hydraulics. What happened down there I did not know. But we all had the impression that even the next stage was under control. There was something known as "removal to the chapel" that was part of the ritual. But it was quick and there were very few of us there, as if the knowledge that the other thing existed were shameful.

At the reception afterwards, the real autopsy of Ada began over coffee. It was carried out with spite, sentimentality, and ridicule. She was unable to do anything about it now, couldn't come storming into the room in her Wellingtons and her hat with the bird's wings. Now she was theirs. They could dissect her as they pleased.

After the funeral we went back to the paper in our black garb. Ada's secretary was already sitting there weeping. She looked like a soft little mound in her black sweater set. She had been so fond of Ada and so ashamed when she wrote about nipples. We invited her into the proofreading room with us for another coffee but she said no. I suppose she didn't like our swearing.

I had been too timid to approach Ada and too full of my own dramas to listen to her properly when I sat across from her to proofread the editorials. I had very little to defend her with when the autopsy got going.

I don't think I ever managed to release myself from the city's opinion of her. She appeared both Romanesque and silly, brave and comical and a nervous wreck, hysterical, honest and obsessed with sex. She lay there in little boxes packed by others. Spleen there, brain there. I sensed even in those days that she was a wellspring in the forest I had walked straight past.

What frightened me most was to see how social control was exercised over the dead as well. People didn't even let go of the corpses. No one gets away here, alive or dead he was theirs. They could have chopped the nose off a dead person if his profile was too cocky, and that afternoon I sat in the photo archives weeping with horror and thinking of my Pappa and myself. I hadn't realized how frightened of them I was.

Of course Victor came in and found me. He wormed it all out of me. Strangely enough, though, he gave me no solace. He just said it was a good thing I'd figured it out.

Victor looked both scary and almost absurd with his shiny spectacle frames and his bow tie like a little propeller under his chin. When I heard him say that, I thought life was asking too much of me, at least here. At least everywhere I had been.

There were also days that were chinks in the wall, pierced by rays of sunshine, smelling of fresh, white rolls. Particularly in the mornings, summer mornings. My body was healthy and light, fifty-two healthy, lusty kilos, freshly-washed in the old, dark, bathroom at 13 Chapel Road.

One morning I was walking across the city. It was a time of blessed tranquility for the non-industrious of the earth, when the others were shut in with their work, and the streets were quiet. Ladybugs crawled around in the yellow blossoms of the tufted vetch hedge. It seemed so inviting and so right on a morning like this for the houses to be surrounded by blossoming walls. Right in the middle of the city, between the houses, there hovered a scent of fresh bread and of fuel. A dog was basking in the sun on the steps in front of a house, a woman in a green-flowered housecoat and clearly corsetless was unabashedly having coffee in her garden; there were pockets of peace to hide in. The lilacs cradled baby swallows. They were waiting for their parents to come and feed them. These parent birds were toiling eagerly in front of the bakery, collecting the cake crumbs people were dropping as they ate from grease-spotted paper bags.

I was on my way to the hospital to see if I could get an interview with an eighteen-year-old girl who was the only survivor of a car accident in which four people had been killed. Car crashes still interested people. There were long articles about them, accompanied by Pippo's shots of bloodstained tarmac. They had sent me because I had the best chance of getting into the women's ward. On the way I passed the Curtmans' gray functional-style house. The curtains in Hasse's room were drawn. The school term hadn't quite ended, but I figured his first class started late that day. I saw that his father's car was gone and thought of Hasse lying there in his bed. The sunshine must sparkle through the cracks along the edges of his blue window shade.

The idea came into my mind that I'd take him breakfast in bed. The door wasn't locked, his father must have left it open when he went to Curre Clothes.

The house frightened me once I was inside. It smelled stern, and the furniture was so dark. In the kitchen his father had left a Cona coffee maker half-full of coffee that just needed to be reheated. I didn't have the slightest idea what Hasse had for breakfast but I made toast the way I usually did for Henning and found marmalade in a cupboard. I moved around silently and stealthily.

They had so few knick-knacks around them, Hasse and his father. It was strict, almost Spartan in there. And yet it looked very wealthy. The gilded ornamental timepiece, the books in their calfskin bindings behind glass, the plush easy chairs and the polished tabletop between them made me feel timid when I peeked into the living room as I went past with the breakfast tray. The walls shut out the chirping of the birds. The only sound I could hear was the refrigerator humming.

Hasse's door was shut but I didn't knock. The moment I opened it he woke up. Typical him, I know now. Alert, present. He looked genuinely astonished, of course. But he pulled himself together, put his arm around me, pressed his face to my blouse and nuzzled my breasts when I set down the tray. He took a few swallows of the reheated coffee before he managed any words.

"You're nuts," he said.

When he had had half a slice of toast he went out to pee. I heard him brushing his teeth, too, and my groin began to tingle.

His room was so bare. There was no tennis racket or butterfly collection, no balsa wood model planes, nothing but his physics book on the bedside table next to his smokes. He had a photo of me on his desk. I found that touching. I felt much older than him. He was still a schoolboy, hardly dry behind the ears. His classmates had just finished morning prayers.

When he came back in, I was lying in his bed. He didn't look very surprised and that annoyed me. I felt almost aggressively reckless. Perhaps it was the proximity to his schoolbook on the bedside table. I decided to seduce Hasse C:son Curtman. To a certain point, of course. I was going to show him how it was done. In Uppsala. Out in the world.

So I showed him. My shoes were on the striped rag runner. They looked as if I had jumped straight out of them and up into his narrow bed with its pink plaid cover and its lace-edged sheets. Here we went. He had a smooth, hairless chest and his body was thin and a bit bony. Under his pajamas was an erection. I extricated his penis and did everything Philip had taught me. I expected he'd just about lose his senses and ejaculate the minute I meant him to. But when he came close, he drew back.

"Hang on," he said.

"Don't you want it?"

"Quiet," he retorted simply.

A few minutes later we went on. I still had my clothes on though he had unbuttoned my blouse. More and more of the tricks I'd learned from Philip were coming back to me. Hasse pulled away from me again. He lay still with his eyes shut. The sun shone right in on his face; I had pulled up the shade when I came in.

It was a tense, pale face. He was working too hard. Our playfulness hadn't released the tension there. His eyelids were thin, a little bluish. Now, eyes still shut, he extended a hand and found my hair. He lay running his hand through it.

"You're so chilly."

"Chilly?"

His hand in my hair made me aware I should have washed it.

"But I don't feel at all cold."

What shame I can still feel over that reply! I didn't get what he meant at all. I lay there quite still, quite horrified without really understanding why. Just a moment ago it had all been fun. Now the air was rife with danger. Hasse went on talking softly with his eyes shut and his fingers in my hair.

"Don't you care for me?"

After a long time I managed to say:

"Well of course I care."

He crept right up next to me and lay his lips to my throat. I didn't like his head being lower than mine. But I lay perfectly still. Slowly he began caressing my arms, as if there were something special about arms. But they were nothing but arms, skinny little ones. He must have felt the bones through my skin. I thought: this is how he likes it. He is a different kind of man. I have to wait, be careful about what I do. It was like dancing with someone who didn't do the usual steps: one, two three — together. You couldn't be certain what was coming.

He removed my blouse, turned me over in bed as if I were a big doll, and undid my bra. The cups were a little dirty-looking because I had on a black sweater the day before. But I couldn't start telling him. I slithered out of my skirt and panties myself. I was afraid the panties might not be perfectly clean. Lying there on the floor they just looked pathetic. Washed-out cotton, threadbare and graying. Hasse went on caressing me but not as if he wished to give me pleasure so much as if he were inspecting how I was made. He rolled the skin on my collarbone back and forth.

"You're so thin," he said when he got to my stomach. "But it seems to me you eat enough."

That gave him an idea and he raised his head.

"Maybe there's something wrong with your metabolism!"

He was perfectly serious.

"I think you should see a doctor," he said. "Have some tests."

In those days I didn't yet know that Hasse was — and would remain — a hypochondriac who also had a great interest in others' illnesses.

When his lips touched my thin, light red pubic hair I could feel he had a new erection and thought he must be wanting sex anyway. Like Philip after all. I parted my legs. But Hasse pressed them back together and lay on top of me.

"I don't like it when you're so chilly," he said.

What was I doing wrong? Now I was very near tears and regretted having come to see him. But I couldn't run away, not in the midst of defeat. I lay very still, stretched out. I had heard there were men who preferred passive women, which was the only explanation I could come up with.

But he gave me a little shake.

"What's with you?" he asked.

Then I really began to cry. It was the last thing I wanted to do, but I did it anyway. The tears were running down onto the pillow case, although I wasn't sobbing.

"Come on," said Hasse, with a consoling little shake.

Everything I did after that I did very fearfully. I put my arms around his neck and we kissed on the mouth. He seemed to like that. Then I discovered he didn't have his eyes closed, so I didn't close mine either and we lay gazing into each other's eyes. I thought we must be as close as people could get. Just seeing two eyes. I said so to Hasse, but he corrected me:

"You can only look into one eye at a time."

He was right.

"If you want to lock eyes with someone," he said, "really win their respect, stare at the bridge of his nose. He won't be able to catch your eye then." So we stared for a few minutes at the bridges of each other's noses. Then he started kissing me on the lips again. His right hand was wandering across my body, moving downward, and then he parted my legs. Apparently it was all right if I let him do it himself. Then he sat up. He had a handsome, not particularly large penis with a good-looking erection. That was when I realized he intended to have intercourse with me. I couldn't explain to myself how I had managed to get this far without working that out.

"Wait," I said.

He waited, sitting up with his weight on the palms of his hands. I didn't know what to say.

"What is it?"

"I haven't done this before," I said.

I was more ashamed afterwards than at the moment I said it. He shut his eyes and lay down on top of me without saying another word. But he had no intention of stopping. We were both bony and thin. Our hip bones were sharp against one another, it hurt a little. His body was so fine, a warm, supple boy's body, floundering a little to find a position. Yes, this was very different from anything I had done before. It was neither playful nor artful, it was perfectly serious. Angular and soft at once, warm and rough. And there was shame. I was ashamed of what I had done before. But he didn't seem to give it a thought. He was intently preoccupied with trying to penetrate me. The round glans of his sex kept poking and he was even helping with his fingers, wetting them and trying again. Everything I had read told me that if things were as they should be he was supposed to thrust into my wet vagina. But I didn't seem to have a vagina at all, just a hard, little reluctant mouth with pursed lips.

"Are you scared?" he asked.

I shook my head. What could I say? That the sunshine was so brash, that we were so sober, that I had never thought it would be like this. That I hadn't even thought about not having done it before. But that was so peculiar he wouldn't believe me.

He entered me millimeter by millimeter. It was perfectly undramatic, although at first it felt as if there wasn't room for him. But there was, and he slid gently up and down while kissing my throat. I was wide-awakely aware of exactly what was happening and he didn't seem especially dazed either. When he lay still I thought it was lovely. Our thin bodies pressed into one another. It was a kind of intimacy. I came to think of my mother. I hadn't thought about her in years so it was truly odd that I should do so just now.

Lying skin to skin, hipbone to hipbone. Without feeling embarrassed, without pulling away or doing any tricks. That was how simple it was. Neither more nor less.

Every now and then Hasse would move, but mostly he lay still, I think he had noticed I liked that. He look attentively at my face when he moved. When resting on the ridge of my hips got too uncomfortable he rolled to his side, pulling me with him. The sun moved. It was no longer so harsh and yellow over the bed, having migrated to the rug, my shoes and my white undies on the floor. Hasse's alarm clock ticked loudly and I became aware that time was passing. He wasn't just late for school now, he was playing truant.

Dust whirled in the sunny air. There was a scent of pine soap on the skin of his throat. He pressed even closer to me, pushing as far in as he could. For a moment, I felt a little pain.

I think several minutes must have passed, or more. Then Hasse started moving again and the next time he grew both still and very tense at once, and then he withdrew. I watched him ejaculate. When he looked up he was embarrassed.

"I couldn't hold back any longer," he said. "Even when I tried thinking about Brattström."

He was the religious studies teacher. I'd had him, too. Hasse lay there for a very long time with his face to my breasts. I wondered if he planned to skip the whole school day, and thought about my interview. In the end he mumbled he needed to get a move on.

He splashed a bit in the bathroom, came out and got dressed. He had white underpants and a beige shirt with a pocket that closed with a little brown button. Then he put on gabardine trousers in exactly the same shade with brown trim. No one in the whole school dressed as well as Hasse.

He spent a little while buzzing an electric razor, and then he came and kissed me. His skin was cold and he smelled of toothpaste now and even more strongly of pine-scented soap. Although he was solemn and hurried, I could tell he was happy.

I didn't need to leave when he did. I should just slam the door behind me, he said. It was quiet when he'd gone. From upstairs I couldn't even hear the humming of the refrigerator. Everything felt so dull and trivial at once, almost deserted. I considered whether I should try to get the bottom sheet clean. As soon as I could I should go back to the paper and tell them I didn't get in to see the injured girl. No one would be surprised. It would have been perfectly true to form for me to fail when I was sent out to do a report in the city. The only places I was any good were in the archives and at the proofs table and, in fact, occasionally at the typewriter.

I dozed off. The big functionalist house surrounded me with gray silence. This was where Hasse's mother had sat with her bottle every morning. Vermouth? I thought about sweet, dark vermouth, fell asleep and awoke to the sound of a car engine. Low gear. There was a growling and metallic creaking right under my window. Then a moment of silence before the door opened and shut. I realized Hasse's father had come home.

At first I thought he had just come home to get something, but then it sounded as if someone was on the rampage down there and I couldn't imagine what he was doing until I heard the whine of the vacuum cleaner. It was a good one. It roared. Maybe one of those industrial ones from mill For a few minutes I thought it must be someone other than him. But a cleaning lady would hardly have a car. I got up and looked out the window. It was the Curtmans' black Mercedes. The company director owner had come home to do the vacuuming.

Later I found out they had never had domestic help. They couldn't, of course, when Hasse's mother might go on a binge any time. People would talk. When she no longer bothered to clean, Hasse and his father did it themselves. They kept it up after her death. They didn't want a stranger in the house. Hasse's still like that; he shuts his door. He doesn't want others to know any more than the bare essentials about him.

Now his father was doing the stairs. Had he decided to come home because he had a little free time or because he needed to get away from something? I knew he didn't like negotiating with the local union. Hasse had told me. I lay curled up in the bed, thinking he wouldn't come into Hasse's room. I didn't need to consider one of those silly moves like hiding in the closet. Now he was in the upstairs hall, putting the plug into the socket. In the noise that followed, even louder than before, I was entirely unprepared when he opened the door. We looked at each other.

He was a small, quite fat man, dressed in a pin-striped suit. He hadn't loosened his tie to vacuum. I had pulled the blanket up to my chin and wasn't moving. When we had stared at each other for a few seconds, he shut the door.

It went quiet. "Jesus, what's he going to do now?" I wondered. But he must just have stood there thinking for a while. The vacuum banged the wall along the stairs again; he was on his way down. I heard things falling and bumping in the cleaning cupboard. After a while the front door closed once more and I heard the car start.

Hasse's father and I never acknowledged having seen each other that morning. I didn't tell Hasse. None of us ever mentioned it.

"You're one helluva lousy journalist," Victor informed me. "But you write well."

I was nervous and hated to disturb people or to seem pushy. I was ignorant, unprofessional and dreamy. I had no head for figures and a lousy memory for names. I was better with colors, moods and, well, atmospheres. If they had let me spend all my time in the newsroom I might have managed better. When I found myself out there in the city was when I became forgetful, overwhelmed with impressions and my own misgivings. But the only page that was done from entirely inside the offices was the family page, and it belonged to Lisa Wallin.

Everything had worked out as she had wished. She had divested herself of her earthly possessions. It was rumored that she hadn't got a very good deal when she sold her shareholding in *The Correspondent* to Altmeyer. She donated the money to the Missionary Society. Now she really was an old family page editor in a worn cardigan and there was no doubt as to whether she would slink through the eye of the needle. Her feet were cold in her glass cubicle. The road to heaven was wide open.

Except that she had killed Ada. Wolfgang Altmeyer and Lisa Wallin had done her in just as surely as if they had dragged her down into a cellar and smashed her skull with a sledgehammer. I knew that.

After Ada's death I had rediscovered an ability I had possessed as a child. I could see both lies and truth at once and I knew that there are sometimes no words for the truth. But that didn't make it any less true.

The words ran over reality like polluted water. They circulated in thousands of rivulets, no one could control them. They said that things were thus but at the same time so, and that every cause had a cause, and that what you could see was not all there was; things were complex and could only be described in very difficult and intricate ways.

But under the ground the truth runs clear. Under many things there is a ground water of truth. Inside me, too. I sometimes wondered if there could possibly be words for it. Not that I went around cogitating about it. It just stirred in me, a query.

When you work for a newspaper you have to go in there each day and take over where someone else left off the day before. The language was made of lead and lay waiting in the type cases. You were not allowed to awaken to see the city being born out of the hole in a construction site, a mound of iron and gravel, ready to take shape in a new language. That was not possible. "It's common sense and plain as the nose on your face," bellowed Uno Kampe who was now community affairs editor in addition to everything else.

But I had an inkling of the truth after Ada's death and I knew that I could not keep it to myself. I couldn't possibly speak to Victor about it. It was too intimate. He'd only be sarcastic.

It was summer. Hasse scraped by in school and came out with the qualifications he needed. We went to the community park and danced to Hasse Kahn's and Seymour Österwall's orchestras; pressing our sharp hip bones against each other's and inhaling the smell of soap from each other's necks. We often made love out of doors, on the ground. He would spread out his poplin coat for me to lie on. Sometimes he'd borrow his father's car and we would wedge ourselves into the back seat. Sometimes when there was no one around we would go back to his bed. We kissed with our eyes open and lay still, with him inside me. I never thought very much about our thing, our love affair. I suppose we were actually going together. As they said. But I didn't put a name to it. It was just part of my life; it smelled of soap and clean shirt cloth, and sometimes fresh and pungent from his semen.

Hasse was the more prudent of us. He was the one who was concerned about the fact that what we were doing could have consequences. But now that people knew we were going together he couldn't keep going into the pharmacy for condoms without bringing shame down upon me. It might even get back to Jenny, because the pharmacy owner sang second bass next to Fredrik in the men's Glee Club.

We borrowed Hasse's father's car and went to Norrköping so a doctor could fit me with a Dutch cap. We couldn't do that in our town, where the doctor not only belonged to the same Rotary club as Hasse's father but also prescribed Antabuse for mine.

Hasse sat waiting for me at a cake shop across the street while it happened. I was terrified. On the ring finger of my left hand I wore a ring with a blue aquamarine in it, and I had turned the stone inward, hoping that the narrow gold band would give the impression of an engagement ring. When the doctor instructed me to climb up onto the examining table and spread my legs into the stirrups, I panicked. Had there not been a nurse in the room I would have turned tail and run. The physician was in his fifties and smelled of cigarette smoke. I lay there, bared to his eyes, his instruments, his contempt. I was sure he could tell I wasn't engaged. In Uppsala I had been dangerously close to the outpatient clinic for venereal diseases. Well, all right, all I had done was to have coffee and cakes in the same building, but by now I did realize how close I had actually come. I would definitely have been able to waltz right in there with Veronica, quite cool and unperturbed. But Uppsala was in some other galaxy.

I knew nothing about how I looked inside. When we had that lesson in biology about reproduction, I had either been absent or not listening. Now I learned, at least, that there was a little ridge in there, a bony edge somewhere, behind which the diaphragm was meant to lodge. You try doing it now. No, no, put it in yourself. Oh yes you can. I refuse to give you a prescription until I know you are able to insert it. That's right. Good girl. One more time.

It looked like a little cup, or a yellow rubber shower cap. When I finally got it in place, he felt it with his bony fingers that were covered with a thin film of glove. I was in pain from the tension. The tears ran down my cheeks and the nurse scolded me.

"Honestly, it can't be all that bad," she said, sounding exactly like the physical education teacher when I refused to jump the vaulting horse.

I got down to the cake shop with wet furrows on both cheeks and my genitals aching from straining when the doctor had been groping around my insides. Hasse got terribly upset and had second thoughts about the whole thing. For a while we considered just not going to get the diaphragm prescription filled.

"What if using that shit keeps you from being able to have children later?" Hasse asked.

To my mind, the idea that I might be able to have children was perfectly inconceivable in any case. I had come along to Norrköping for Hasse's sake, to put his fastidious mind at rest.

"You've got to ask him! Go back up!"

"You must be mad," I said.

But he insisted stubbornly. I couldn't imagine why he cared whether or not I would ever be able to have children. My *not* having any was what was of interest to him, and that part I could understand perfectly. That was why I had come along to Norrköping and subjected myself to this painful experience. But that was where

I drew the line. I was not going back up there.

Incredible, incomprehensible Hasse. I see him crossing the street in his poplin coat and his suede shoes with their India rubber soles. Two months earlier he had been an upper secondary school student. Now he went up to the doctor's office to say he was my fiancé and to ask whether there was any risk that I might not be able to have children when I stopped using the diaphragm. I just sat there, bent over my cup of lukewarm cocoa and cold whipped cream, the reward he had offered me as a consolation. He came back after a little while, sat down across from me and had his coffee cup refilled.

"What did he say?" I asked, mostly to find out whether they had laughed at him up there.

"He just said it was all okay."

He stirred hard to make the sugar dissolve in his cooling coffee and then gave me a little grin: "To tell you the truth, what he said was — 'I'm sure you can count on little princes and princesses when the time comes.'"

At the end of October Magnus Swärd called me into his office and talked to me for a long time, but I didn't get the point. I came out with one single word intact: commission. I said it to Victor.

"From now on I'm on commission."

He must have understood, but he didn't say anything. Shortly thereafter, the paper took on a new journalist. He was Bertil Sundh, who wasn't much over twenty at the time. He got the desk opposite Uno Kampe's.

I noticed there was less for me to do. I spent more and more time in the archives. Hours and days. But I didn't even realize I'd been sacked when I got paid for two columns. That was all the money I got that month.

It was November. Rain running down the windows. I sat in the archives replacing torn envelopes in shoe boxes. All the organizing was done. But as people were always tossing their used printing plates every which way, the files always needed straightening. I was sifting through the familiar black faces when the secretary of the editor-in-chief walked in. She was irritated because she had had to waddle up a flight of steps just for my sake.

"Miss Johannesson, you're wanted in the editor-in-chief's office," she said.

I fixed my face in the cramped toilet where I sometimes sat smoking to pass the time when I didn't know how to fill the day and didn't want people seeing I was idle. It smelled like sewage in there. There was probably no clack valve for the drain.

I didn't like going into Ada's old office, but now I had no choice. This was the second time since her death. When I knocked and entered it was not Magnus Swärd sitting in the swivel chair. A compact, familiar silhouette was reflected against the light by the window. Altmeyer!

He was so kind. God, how kind Wolfgang Altmeyer was to me. He offered me a seat, he expressed his appreciation of my columns, he said he could tell I liked being around the paper since I dropped by the newsroom so often. He gave me a letter of reference. Which, of course, I would need when I applied for my next job. What were my plans after this extended summer adventure?

Naturally, it was Swärd who had written the testimonial. I saw that when I got back out into the lobby and ripped open the envelope. But he hadn't had the courage to talk to me a second time. I never went back to the office. I was so ashamed. That afternoon Victor phoned and asked where I was.

"I've been sacked," I said.

He was silent, but didn't seem surprised.

"They still want your columns though," he said.

So he'd known. Everybody had known. And I had walked around the newsroom for nearly three weeks without getting it.

I had a pappa, just like everyone else. Of course I didn't see much of him, but there was nothing odd about that. I was grown up now. Henning and I couldn't go on keeping track of each other's every move as we had when I was a child. I didn't want him to know all about me and I certainly had no desire to know exactly what he did when he was away.

It is true he was something of a drinker, he was known for it. But I didn't take that too seriously. I had seen a lot of boozing in Uppsala. He was still good-looking. When he walked down the street from the station, swept along in his light summer overcoat, his well-polished shoes with his hat always at that perfect, becoming angle, and I walked toward him — my heart would flutter. Oh my Lord, he was of a different race altogether than the sloths who plopped their hats straight down on their heads and walked as though they had orthopedic arch supports.

When he caught sight of me he would tip his light gray hat. And then turn as if to change course, although he simply walked over to a flower and vegetable stall on the square, lifted a bouquet of stocks out of a bucket, wiped the dripping stalks with his handkerchief and proffered me the bouquet at the same time as he extended a five kronor note behind him. Without looking back, without inquiring about the price.

Then we would go home to the dusty but tidy apartment where the stocks would smell of fading summer in my room. On the way we would buy pork chops and a nice piece of cheese, or prawns and a loaf of fresh white bread, or sweetbreads, and a tin of the smallest French peas, *les petits pois*. We prepared our meal thoroughly and methodically. And we ate and talked and sipped the wine he had brought and he did it so cautiously, yes, so discreetly that all the rumors and gossip about his having a drinking problem seemed petty and foolish and nothing but envy, people's eternal desire to find fault with anyone who is different.

Then we washed the dishes, our way. Pappa fixed himself a grog. He gave me one too. I was a big girl now and he offered me the leather easy chair. But I didn't want it. It was quite sad to see how the pink shade on the floor lamp had split and the stretched satin was beyond repair.

When Henning had come home that way he might shut himself in for a long time. I knew what he was doing: he had his hands full of the future. I had known that since I was little. He was more an explorer than an inventor. To him, the future was a place. It was reality, a country that already existed out there, like heaven exists for the deeply religious, on high yet also dwelling in them. The point was not to create it, not even to invent its devices, but to discover it. The future lay inside the inventions, dormant in them. To Henning, people did not have futures in the sense that they would change their attitudes. They would remain egotistical, cruel, rash, prudent, idealistic, narrow-minded and tender-hearted. Among people, everything existed at once.

But progress was another thing entirely. He admired it, he was its servant. He attributed ambition and objectives to it, and literally endowed it with power and feelings as well. Not to mention rights. That may have been accurate, because the very word pro-gress contains the idea of how everything which is to come is actually already there, just waiting to go forward, to de-velop like the puckered wings of a butterfly in its enveloping cocoon. Maybe his belief was that nothing can possibly be any different from what it was intended to be, in which case that restless, creative person who was Henning, my absent-minded inventor of a father, was not a believer in the un-created potential of the world or in what people mean, fundamentally, when they speak of change.

When I returned home from Uppsala, chemical experiments began to make our apartment reek. I saw huge demijohns and pails of solutions in Sigrid and Abel's bedroom. The evenings he was at home, he sat in there with the door shut, and the odor of strong fluids came seeping out. During the day he would send off packages. He would carry lots and lots of identical parcels down to the post office in paper carrier bags.

One day when he was out, I was looking for something in my grandparents' bedroom and noticed a lot of little boxes Henning had set up. I opened one. It contained hair rollers, thin bits of rectangular paper, and two bottles. On the outside there was a label: FIX — the easy, safe home perm. The permanent wave of the future. Instructions enclosed.

Of course I was dismayed. There was a great deal I was prepared to accept, but not that the future was in the home perm. I knew Henning had a partner now, a man called Larvinge, I think he'd changed his name from Larsson. He called himself a businessman and had undertaken to launch Pappa's inventions and see to it that he made money out of them. But ever since they had met, Henning had only had little assignments on the go. Mostly appliances: cutters, choppers, mixers and cream whippers. They hadn't tried to market the Radax link again. Larvinge contracted out the production of Henning's devices and tools to little workshops with one or two men working out of a basement or a bike shed. Then he sold them, by advertisement, for cash on delivery. But I had no idea they had moved on from there to selling things Pappa hadn't even thought up. I assume they had to. But it was strange to think of Henning having sat there pouring the foul-smelling perm fluids through a funnel into little bottles.

At one point Larvinge sold fur coats. Nothing odd about that, he was a businessman. I didn't think Henning had anything to do with the furs. When Larvinge advertised in the paper that he was showing a collection of furs at the City Hotel, Pappa took me along and bought me my faux fur jacket. Larvinge sold lots of black Persian lamb coats up there, and he also took some customers into a nearby room to display his crystal chandeliers. But he sold them for such low prices he asked the customers not to tell anyone where they had come by them. Special deals for his best clients, he said.

The autumn I lost my job at *The Correspondent*, Larvinge and my pappa were charged with handling stolen goods.

Henning had nothing to do with the crystal chandeliers, or with the fur coats. He couldn't have. They were too tawdry.

They convicted him anyway. He got a six-month conditional sentence. Perhaps they were sentencing him for his ignorance. I assume there's a law against being completely ignorant. But the people who bought those fur coats and chandeliers were permitted their infinite ignorance. They ate Sunday roasts with creamy gravy and marinated cucumbers under their crystal chandeliers and read about the trial in *The Correspondent*.

It was in Växjö. When I read about it I thought: Victor must have seen this in the proofs, could he have kept them from publishing it? There were no names in the article. But it was easier to figure out who was on trial than to win *The Correspondent's* Christmas crossword prize. And undoubtedly just as much fun for most readers in their cozy armchairs.

He came home. It was an afternoon in November, at twilight. When I heard the key in the lock I went out into the hallway. The light wasn't on but I could still see his face. He was so pale. The skin around his nose looked pitted.

When he caught sight of me he seemed, at first, to be unable to make out my face in the dim light. He appeared to be unsure of who was standing there. He must have recognized my voice, though. Still, he didn't smile. He looked at me the way an animal does at another one who has occupied the lair it left that morning at dawn.

He said I think I need to be alone for a while and his voice was loving but so thin I hurried into my room and threw a few things into a hold-all. I didn't want to hear it crack. Pappa and I had always brushed one another very, very lightly. He never said an unkind word to me.

He had two briefcases with him when he came home, and I heard a sloshing sound as he passed through the living room. The sound was muffled, reminiscent of heavy oars in water. It frightened me. I had to leave. I said bye, then, in a voice just as thin, and I could hear that I sounded like a child.

When I got to the Otters, Fredrik and Jenny were at the table. They were clearly visible through the window, now that Fredrik had put up a fluorescent light fixture in the kitchen. There was something unimpeachable about that light, nothing could be concealed in its whiteness. They were sitting opposite each other, eating. Jenny had covered the yellow and brown checked oilcloth with a large napkin. It was spotted red from pickled beets, and reminded me of the sheet on Hasse's bed the first time we'd lain there.

Theirs was a kind of love lair as well. I think that around this time their meals began to replace caresses, eating together becoming their main source of shared joy and pleasure. They planned their meals, agreed about what they would have, allowing themselves things that would never have occurred to them before. Most evenings they would have a bit of a sandwich. As now, this might actually be a whole little supper at the kitchen table. There was aged cheese, cold fried herring, trotters in aspic and beets Jenny had pickled herself. Clearly, Jenny had brought out the trotters to take Fredrik's mind, for a few minutes, off all the things he had been reading about the trial. They talked about what good aspic these particular trotters were in, instead of trying to understand why things had gone so badly for Henning. Through me they felt related to him, and his shame caused them pain. Henning had drawn Fredrik out into the only adventure of his life. Now he'd been back at Swedish Engineering for ages. Maybe they were sitting there thinking how he might have become involved in similar dealings himself, been convicted in spite of his protests of innocence, his objections that he'd had no idea what was going on.

Their meals turned my stomach. They loved each other with their digestive tracts, or at least that was where they expressed their love. I didn't belong here.

It struck me that they, too, were failures. They'd sent me off to Uppsala as an experimental balloon. It hadn't worked out, and that probably hadn't caused them much pain, since academic degrees and scholarly discoveries were fundamentally alien to them. It was no different than if they had had a son in this landlocked town and then sent him to sea. Of course they wouldn't have been surprised if he had turned out to suffer from seasickness and had to return home.

But I couldn't tell them I'd had to leave *The Correspondent*. There were two categories of people whom Fredrik truly despised: people who wrote for the local paper and schoolteachers. He was a tireless discoverer of factual errors and incredible statements in *The Correspondent*. So anyone who got themselves fired from there for incompetence just had to be the lowest of the low.

Had I been able to tell them how much it hurt, they might have felt sorry for me. But I couldn't possibly tell people who ate trotters and drank milk.

"Would you like a sandwich?" Jenny asked, kind and tired.

I said no thanks and that I wasn't staying, just happened to be passing and thought I'd drop in.

When I got back to the apartment, Pappa had locked the door. I knocked but there was no answer. So I used my key. I felt strange and intrusive to be going in when he had said he wanted to be alone, but I had no choice. I entered and, without removing my coat, walked straight through the living room and stood in the door-way to the study. He was sitting in the armchair, his back to the window, and I was unable to make eye contact.

"I have to be here," I said. "There's nowhere for me to go."

He didn't ask me what I meant. All that came out of him were a few gentle sounds. His voice was no longer tense. He'd had quite a lot to drink.

Dusk had faded to evening, but he hadn't bothered to light a lamp. The last of the daylight rested in the mirrors, and in his hair. We spoke to each other, slowly, not about what had happened, there was nothing to say about it. Things had gone badly for us. There was nothing amazing about that.

Now, in the dark room, we talked about things we had talked about before. He asked me how the typesetting machine transported the lines it had finished print-ing down to the box where they fell in order. I thought about it. I could recall the sound, I could hear it. But I couldn't remember the mechanism that pushed the rows of lead types down. I was ashamed. It was such a long time since he had been able to demand of me that I understand the things I used. I had been at the paper for several months now, but I still didn't quite know what happened when the lines were composed. I hadn't cared. The typesetters were gnomes whose quick fingers were supposed to run over the rustling keyboards and who were supposed to notice the smell of my perfume. That was how unreal the world had become to me. It had become so gray, it had dried up. It was full of tedium, heavy as boulders. But he, so much older than myself and so incomparably much more badly treated, had retained his curiosity.

He didn't ask anything else about my job or about the people there. He wasn't at all curious about people. So few had accomplished anything he could admire.

We talked with each other like train passengers. His face had vanished into the darkness for me. I could only see a silhouette. There were soft clinking sounds

273

when he moved the glass and bottles around. There was a dreamlike sensation: as if we were on a train and would be disembarking in a few hours. But we didn't tell each other where. We simply conversed for a while to hold the loneliness at bay. Silent stations waited in the darkness, the faces of clocks, tarmac shiny with rain, streetlamps, tracks.

It was so real to me that I had to make a great effort to bear in mind that outside there was nothing but Chapel Road, the newspaper building and the graveled court. All that was across the street was the Swedish Engineering plant, not a steep rockface with headlights at the bottom.

"I think I'll make a cup of tea," I said, speaking louder than before. He didn't answer. It was becoming eminently clear that we were getting off at different stops. When I left the room I heard the sound of drink being poured into a glass and I felt frightened of what I was going to have to be part of.

That night I couldn't sleep, couldn't get myself to wake up and read, either. My narrow bed with the depression in the middle had become a nest. I could not be more secure than I was here. Around one o'clock I got up, half-asleep, to go to the bathroom. A tap was dripping and everything looked untouched. I could still smell my toothpaste. When I had been, I tiptoed over to Pappa's room and peeked in. But he wasn't there. The door was ajar and the spread still on the bed. I walked over to the window and looked down at the courtyard and the newspaper building. A street light was shining right into the window of the office of the editor-in-chief. There was a linden tree partially blocking it; it looked as if the light itself were lying in a loosely-woven basket. It cast stripes and patches of light across Ada's desk, and they shifted uneasily when the wind blew through the treetop. Neither light nor darkness were constant there. There would be a lurching, a movement that rearranged the image of an empty desk with an empty chair and a globe once again. It was hard to maintain my grip on what I knew about what had happened in that room.

I went back into the dark apartment, fumbling my way down the hall toward the entrance and the living room. I didn't dare turn on the lights. Pappa was still in the study. He had been sitting in the leather easy chair, but had slid down in his sleep. He lay with his left arm twisted under him. It should have hurt, but he didn't feel it. When I turned his body over, pulling it upward so his back would be supported in the chair, I saw his arm hanging limp. I didn't want to embarrass him by trying to wake him up and help him into bed. Shifting him into a more comfortable position would have to do. I turned the light on in the room to get a look at his face. It didn't shine too directly on him. His skin was gray, all the blood drained out. But he was breathing, panting unevenly like a dog that had been at the chase.

When I saw him the next afternoon the arm he had twisted so far under him in his sleep was aching. He said his arm really hurt, but he couldn't imagine what he'd done to it. After that I moved him as best I could when I found him lying in an all too unnatural position. It wasn't embarrassing for either him or myself because he wasn't conscious.

I don't know if I realized he needed medical attention. We didn't believe anything good could ever come from outside. My dreadful suspicion that the world was an unsafe place, full of hollows and fissures and shadowy jagged walls in caves and cellars had been confirmed. You were sacked or given a conditional sentence out there. Your skull might get cracked. You had to be a tougher sort of person than we were to act in such brutal scenes. We withdrew voluntarily. We felt sorry for ourselves. Actually, we were pathetic. If anybody else had felt sorry for us we might have been able to go back out there again. In November, frost and damp rotted the plants down in the flowerbeds and the windows rattled in the wind. We just let the telephone ring — oh, the forlornness after that last ring! — and thought of ourselves as all alone. Yes, it was like a railway journey but we didn't disembark as we had intended. Out of consideration for me, I would like to say out of love, Henning didn't drink himself paralytic. He lost consciousness before he reached that point. Out of concern for him, out of love, I didn't leave, didn't go looking for a way out — whatever that might have been. An office job. Marriage. Or gritting my teeth and growing up: back to the university. This was a love that suited us, it meant doing nothing, at rest in the eye of the frenzied whirlwind all around us.

Henning had always spent his periods of humiliation by himself, and so those horror stories had never been told, just barely sighed about by Jenny and sometimes paid for by Fredrik. Sometimes he really had drunk himself paralytic. But now, when we were traveling together, we maintained a delicate balance. The smell of vomit was very discreet. He splashed aftershave around the bathroom before he left it.

I, too, was reticent about my misery. I tapped away at the typewriter when he was conscious so he would be sure to hear it, and I mentioned being paid on a commission basis several times while we were having tea.

Food made him feel sick. I went to the pharmacy for vitamin pills. According to Hasse, that was what I should do. And I went on making slices of toast he couldn't say no to since they were perfect, golden and still warm. I suppose that was better than nothing, at least I managed to get something solid into him.

Though he was a true master of the art of the silent puke.

We thought of ourselves as alone. But there were footsteps on the gray wooden stairs and the downstairs hall doors would slam. We still had a caretaker in those days. He stoked the furnace and shoveled the snow in winter. The last day of every month the people who lived in the building came and paid their rent. I sat at the dining room table and wrote their receipts. They tried to peep into the study, as if they had a feeling Henning was sitting in there. I didn't object to their looking, because we still lived neatly. But it must have reeked of dust and cigarette smoke.

In the living room there was a tall, narrow bookcase. The two top shelves and part of the third held the *Nordic Family Encyclopedia*. Henning had emptied the rest of it to make room for his own books. He had moved into his in-laws' home more than twenty years earlier, but with the exception of the now unheated and unfurnished master bedroom none of the rooms had been changed since Sigrid and Abel's day. He had just lifted down his in-laws' books and stacked them on the floor of one of the big closets. They were still there. It was a random collection of books, the kind you can find in the homes of most families that have books at all. There was the A to Apollo volume of a reference work they'd been giving away for free. A couple of yearbooks from the Swedish Tourist Authority. Religious tracts in rough paper covers. Booklets on regional historical sites. Two novels by Runa. A book of cake and cookie recipes. With the exception of the religious tracts, which were Sigrid's, there wasn't much testimony in that pile of books to the spiritual life of my maternal grandparents. It meant no more than all the other rubbish that was gathering dust in boxes and cupboards: keys that no longer opened any doors, rolls of oilcloth and cotton wadding, pocket watches that no longer told time, balls of twine.

Henning's books and papers were different. He cherished them. Since the workshop burned down, his books were all he owned beyond a few clothes in the closet, his aftershave and his suitcases. I was well aware of the law of the city: you are what you own. Most people's ownership was an elaborate cake plate arranged around them: their bodies were pears, preserved and candied, centerpieces encircled by property. Even the poor sat there like sour wild plums in a Poor Man's Cake.

But Henning's affinity with the papers and books in that bookcase was different. It was so fragile. It only emitted the softest of sounds. You couldn't tackle that easily-obliterated reality with a crosscut saw and a riveting hammer. That was precisely how I saw his relationship to the books — as so much more fragile and gray, as if some kind of blood plasma or lymphatic fluid ran with those pale printed letters into his veins, or as if the flesh of his face were aging like paper.

The bookcase contained a tool catalogue called *Materials*. It was a lovely book, bound in green leather and illustrated with minutely detailed drawings. There was the Karlebo engineering manual in its soft leather binding, black with soot from the workshop and full of tables. He had books of logarithms and thin gray textbooks from night school in the twenties. There were two linen bound volumes called *The History of World Industry*. There was one book called *The Nature of the Physical World* and another that was Theordor Svedberg's *Matter*. A thin booklet less than fifty pages long that had cost under two kronor when he bought it in the early twenties was entitled *Einstein's Theory of Relativity Made Simple* by someone called Pflüger. Henning had subscribed for a set of books summarizing everything from the world-view since the theory of relativity to the structure of matter, the nucleus of the atom, radioactivity and the transformation of chemical elements, not to mention the principles of physics governing rotor ships. I found a list on which he had marked the ones he planned to order and others he might want. I still have it and it reads

> What is the atmosphere?
> What's wrong with my radio?
> What is death?
> What is homeopathy?
> What is Christianity?
> What is life?
> What is meaning?
> What is a capon? A complete description of cockerel
> castration with illustrated instructions.
> What is the truth?

Where I grew up it was unusual for people to bother with thoughts and ideas that had no direct application in the practical world. Everyone knew they were there, of course, like we know dreams are there. But as opposed to dreams, these shiftings of the soul hardly had a name. Thoughts were too general, thoughts described the beginnings of tangible actions. This was nothing but a sort of slag, the refuse of the psyche. Henning was a person who had no natural outlet. The waste products accumulated in him, clogging up his mind. That was how people saw it, I knew, and to me it was a great source of comfort to see that list of some of all the WHATS we ask ourselves about. Except for the matters of caponization and radio repair these were still the kind of questions that could puzzle anybody at all, but that most people were able to rid themselves of the minute they sensed their presence, thanks to their exemplary mental peristalsis.

Henning had neither bought nor read all the booklets on the list. He was particular about keeping his world coherent and he did not allow trivia or adiaphora into it. I have probably done more reading than he has, but it has dissolved into flakes and fragments most of which never sank to the bottom and settled. I have also listened more to the radio than he, I have read the papers and watched TV, and therefore I could never claim that my bookcase is the history of my soul or the bundle of necessities I take with me on my journey. My world is a junk world, a dump. I have received rather than sought. Sometimes I fantasize about waking up with no memory, and I wonder whether in that case I would be at the shore of an ocean with the horizon swept clean. I imagine the precision with which I would select the furniture and fittings of my soul the next time, how I would guard against clutter and overload. But I soon realize that without a memory I would simply awaken with a feeling of missing something and of contextlessness. I wouldn't be selective at all, but in utter panic would wish to have the whole lot back all at once, be born right there in the rag and bone shop, surrounded by all my familiar rubbish.

At the age of twenty-two I stood in front of Henning's bookcase touching the bindings, feeling the stiff blue cloth binding of *The History of World Industry* and smelling the paper of his blueprints. I touched these papers affectionately for the first time. They were already memories. He never opened the books any more. But he still took a pile of papers with him into the study now and then and looked as if he were balancing equations and writing out long tables. I didn't know what he was busy with. Since the home permanents I didn't want to ask. The papers reminded me of Heisenberg's matrices, and filled me with a tenuous respect.

I didn't want anybody going in to the inner room where he was. Sometimes he flopped in the armchair abandoned to himself; he was nothing but clothes covering a frame with a white face mask. The voices from the street didn't reach him, and when the wind blew through the trees at night the shadows from the streetlights wandered over his face but his eyelids didn't flutter.

Some days he sat in the living room, shuffling through his papers. He dropped them on the floor and tried to gather them back up. But his fingers fumbled and he had trouble bending down so I was usually the one who put them back on the dining room table after he went into the study. The lamps were always out in there now, and no light irritated his aching eyes.

I spent my days in the kitchen. When the first sensitive period was over, Jenny took to popping in. She never went farther than the kitchen and she always brought things to eat. Delivery men came as well. I never saw their faces or how much they were paid. We were in dire financial straits, I knew that much. The rent money vanished fast from the soup terrine on the sideboard. So I needed to start writing columns again. I had lived in so few worlds and had to take what was around me and write about it. Since the trial it had become impossible to go on writing the Father-Daughter columns. But I wrote poorly disguised, idealized descriptions of the Upco Estate with Fredrik and Jenny in the main roles. I called them Aunt and Uncle and they didn't object. Reading about their everyday lives in a sheen of gentle jesting amused them. When I caricatured Lisa Walling and Magnus Swärd they were not only flattered, they paid as well.

Christmas time came around and Hasse came home from Sollefteå where he was doing his military service. He realized that we couldn't see very much of each other. Henning couldn't be left alone; that was something he could readily understand.

Still, Pappa was well enough for the two of us to spend a few pallid hours celebrating Christmas with the Otters. We hadn't bought them presents, though, which became embarrassing when we had to open a pile of gifts from them. I stayed seated at the kitchen table while Jenny washed the coffee cups and Fredrik tried to get hold of a taxicab for us. He clicked the receiver into the cradle time after time, but he never got a line.

I saw Jenny looking disappointed and tired and I thought about how she always looked that way nowadays. So I apologized to her for our not having given them any Christmas gifts. Then I started to cry. I hadn't cried once until then. But at Christmastime the air is thick with cigar smoke and the smell of wax candles, you're heavy with marzipan and bottled-up emotion. Jenny surprised me by saying she was really relieved we hadn't bought them anything. Then she told me about a recurring dream she had been having for years.

She dreamed it was Christmas Eve and the shops were about to close. People were rushing home to light the candles in their trees and exchange presents. She hadn't had time to buy any, though. She hurried into a shop. It happened to be a men's clothing shop because that was closest at hand. So that was where she had to buy all her presents, for me, for her mother-in-law Tora, for her own mother Stella who, in the real world, had been dead even longer than Tora, and for Fredrik and Henning too, of course. But there was nothing to buy. There weren't any goods left. All that remained was some rubbish the owner brought up from the basement, toys his children had played with and broken, cheap junk he had really meant to throw away. She had to pay a fortune for it and walked out into the road carrying a load of rubbish.

She told me that this dream had haunted her for years and that she had recognized the anxiety in the air from it when she discovered we hadn't bought any Christmas presents, Henning and I. But suddenly she had felt relieved and pleased, in fact she felt like bursting out laughing, she said.

I couldn't really understand her.

"Good grief, Christmas presents are just a load of nonsense," she said.

I found this distressing, didn't want to agree with her. I really didn't like her laughing when she thanked me for not having bought any Christmas gifts and thus possibly having set her free from her dream. Do we have to learn everything in such a bitter, blunt way?

The feeling in the air throughout that winter and the long, cold lead up to spring is easy to reconstruct. Rabbit's burrow. Fox's den. Reality pounding, ordinariness howling outside the door. We lived off the rent money, the columns, Henning's pitiful income from patents, Jenny's cabbage soup and her rice puddings with their raisin reproaches, almond admonitions and insistent cinnamon curiosity.

Her puddings were often burnt around the edges. Henning couldn't stand sloppily done, quickly whipped up things. He averted his face from Jenny's desserts. His handsome profile grew increasingly translucent. Soon it would be paper-thin.

I saw Hasse when he came home on leave, Victor Bremer now and then at a café farther down the road, and Synnöve on the rare occasions she came back for the weekend. I told her I was working on commission now. I understood from her that a legend was taking shape: I was guarding my father, preventing his suicide since the conviction. I was sacrificing myself to him; it was for his sake I didn't go out to work full time. That was why I was writing on commission. Synnöve, with her easily-touched warm heart was one of my most ardent hagiographers. But the shame regularly reminded me of what things were really like. Perhaps Henning had a secret truth of his own, too? Deep down inside, did he know what he had always known about the origins of the Persian lamb coats and the crystal chandeliers?

When spring came around, Henning and I were taken on a trip to Copenhagen. Fredrik and Jenny treated us, of course. They must have had endless conversations over the beet-stained tablecloth as to what they should do for us. In the end they decided we needed cheering up. They were kind people; they would have been prepared to allocate a percentage of the national product without blinking an eye if it could make people like us be like them.

The men's Glee Club went to Copenhagen, their women in tow. Pappa had been a sporadic second tenor so we were automatically invited. We took the night train, and I fell asleep to barbershop quartets and the clinking of bottles out in the corridor. I took it for granted that he would behave himself and keep his drinking moderate. We had lived for several months in an ambiance of discretion and consideration. In the morning we went aboard the ferry. Soon the spires of Copenhagen could be seen: there was a shimmer to them. The water rose and hissed and fell again at the bow of the ferry, and seagulls cut the air with their knife wings. On the deck, the women traveling with the chorus turned their faces to the sun as they strolled. They were wearing their spring suits and light gloves. On a graying photo where our squinting is the only evidence of how blinding the sunlight was, Jenny and I are standing by a lifeboat grinning childishly, like an entirely different race from the human beings alive today. Jenny has taken her hat off and tied a scarf over her hair. It is fluttering rebelliously — but no rebellion is imminent. Nor were we as naïve as our smiles might have implied. I am clinging to a handbag that looks like a binocular case. I have a hat on, and white gloves with embroidered backs.

All the men were sitting at the bar. They were drinking Elephant beer. You just had to, it was so cheap. The barbershop quartets were already sounding gravelly. When it was time to disembark at Copenhagen, things got chaotic. The ferry was crowded, and people clustered by the gangway. The voices of the Glee Club could still be discerned in the crowd, and the members located one another by waving their white caps.

Jenny and I had managed to find Fredrik and Pappa. The crowd was dense. The bodies of strangers pressed against my back and legs. Henning seemed agitated. He was trying desperately to find a way to get out of the crowd, a hole to sneak through. He was pressing against the flow, and that upset people. We were supposed to be moving forward.

Henning's face had gone absolutely ashen. I thought he was going to be sick.

"I have to go back down," he said, trying to shove his way backwards. But his body was too thin and his movements unsteady. He wasn't getting anywhere. There was a barrier of flesh, clothes and heavy bodies on all sides.

"Easy does it," Fredrik said, annoyed that his friend was embarrassing him.

Henning was bareheaded. He had lost his cap. He didn't like the glee club caps, said scornfully they made them look like would-be academics. His fair ashen hair fluttered in the wind, and I saw how thin it was now. Fredrik and he had shoved their way back a bit, but now they were stymied again, getting nowhere. Pappa's gentle curls blew uneasily among the caps. We lost sight of them when, once the line really started moving, Fredrik used his heavy body to help Henning wedge through the crowd. Now he was pressing forward, but this aggravated people, too.

Nobody had the right to push their way to the front of the disembarking crowd. When we got out onto the pier, I could see Fredrik there, but my view of Pappa was blocked. The Glee Club began to gather where they were standing. I heard peals of laughter.

When we got over to them Henning was standing there leaning against a corrugated metal shed. He hadn't made it. There were dark gray streaks down his trousers, and a huge spot at the crotch. He had wet himself. He seemed to have pissed gallons. I heard the comments between the guffaws.

"That Elephant beer will always do it!"

"Cheers, Henning! Don't take it too hard. Your trousers will dry in no time in this weather."

Somebody had set an oversized glee club cap on his head; beneath it his face was extremely pale. Fredrik propped him up as we walked to the chartered bus, but he still kept stumbling, and at the foot of the bus he dropped to his knees. They lifted him aboard amidst roars of laughter. Fredrik had stepped aside, wan and resentful. They laid Henning across the back row of seats. His face was gray against the brown upholstery, his eyes shut tight. I didn't want to see him so I sat at the very front behind the driver.

We were late. The bus was supposed to take us to the hotel first, but instead we were taken straight to a village some twenty kilometers outside the city, where we were welcomed by a Danish choral society and children waving stiff Danish and Swedish paper flags. The Glee Club stood in formation on the worn village green and sang a Swedish folk song and the Danish melody about the ripening grain. Their voices sounded raw in the strong sea breeze; I noticed they were out of tune. The wives listened, faces to the sun and handbags to their bellies. My Pappa lay in the bus with wet trousers. He was soaked, down to the socks in his shoes.

There was no getting away. Where could I have gone? We were traveling as a group so I couldn't even take my ticket and go back home. I followed passively along. There were long tables with open-faced sandwiches and the incessant popping of beer bottles. Others started looking a bit the worse for wear too, but nobody else wet his trousers. The proprietor of the medical appliance shop took the floor, fumbled with his crumpled notes, began to speak in his deep voice, lost his place and locked eyes with his helpless wife. He managed to remember the words, and concluded his speech successfully. His wife was white as a ghost. She must have been first horrified and then relieved.

The choral societies exchanged little table flags on silver-plated nickel stands. There was coffee with hot almond biscuits so heavy they felt like little animals in one's hand. After we had been served a second cup of coffee I managed to sneak away. I followed my nose toward the sea. The grass became sparser, my heels sank into the sand so I had to take off my shoes and walk in my stocking feet. Behind a thin curtain of fir trees was the water. It seemed to be swelling in the sun, sparkling with confined light.

On the beach were rolls of barbed wire the air and salt had corroded to red rust. There were bottles and shoe soles, scraps of rubber, rags, and rotten fish with empty eye sockets. The sea rolled this conglomeration with every wave it cast up. The smell of coffee was gone as well as the muddle of Swedish-Danish voices and that Danish melody about the grain none of us really understood.

We spent the night in Copenhagen. I walked alone on streets lined with buildings that made me think of grim, beautiful faces. Henning was in bed at the hotel. He had tried to persuade one person after the next to go and buy him a bottle of schnapps. They had refused, puffy as jelly doughnuts with the moral code they called "all things in moderation". I went and bought him the bottle he craved, and when I stood in the doorway with it in my hand we saw one another in a way we'd never done before.

Pappa didn't want to see me, and I suppose that wasn't surprising. With the exception of that one naked, I'd almost say objective look across the room at the Mission or Salvation Army hotel or whatever it was in Copenhagen, he didn't want to see me. He accepted the aquavit because he needed it and his need was so implacable that even his shame had to step aside for a moment. O my God, the morning light and his eyes, so pale, so lusterless. All the color had drained out of him, out of his skin and hair and gaze, and his hands lay idle on the blanket. I thought about his penis, and I truly never thought about it now that I was grown up, but now I realized it must be just as drained, just as slack. His jacket hung over the back of a chair and I supposed his trousers were at the laundry. He couldn't possibly go anywhere.

On the way home he got off at Alvesta or, to put it rightly, no one saw him after Alvesta. We didn't hear from him for three weeks. God knows where he got money from. Then he phoned us from Dagöholm where he had been admitted to dry out on Abstinyl.

I arrived back at home, Chapel Road in the gray morning light and all the usual clatter outside. It was endless. Sometimes I thought this pounding clacking city was a madhouse where the inmates beat their spoons against table top and bed frame, tirelessly, without a pause, with rapt grins on their faces as they imitated zeal and enterprise as only idiots can, nonstop. Of course I somehow knew they would be mutely miserable, like diseased animals, if they stopped even for an instant. That was what happened, sometimes the moon shone right in their faces when their grinning had left them bare and I knew, at moments like that, their souls were calling like foghorns chained to buoys in a cold, nocturnal sea.

One morning I woke up, still alone in the apartment. I paced the cold linoleum barefoot. I thought he might come back when his money ran out but he didn't. We had still not heard from him and no one knew where he was. I slept uneasily at night and listened for footsteps on the stairs, for the scratch and rattle of the glass in the door. But it was perfectly silent all night every night.

A murmuring sound had woken me at daybreak. It was the sound of running water. It frightened me and that fear must have started in my sleep because it had already reached a pounding, prickling, panting pitch, as if the volume of blood in my body had increased beyond what my vessels could contain.

Otherwise the apartment was as quiet and forlorn as always. I noticed it was misty outside. There were no noises, and no bird rose from the tree outside the kitchen window. I just kept hearing that rippling sound of an underground stream, of water babbling, cajoling and, strangely enough, terrifying me. A numbness, a kind of paralysis had crept up on me. I knew I ought to get out of bed, that I absolutely had to. I thought about the things I was going to do. Turn on the burner, run water into the pan. Open a window. But I couldn't.

This purling water gave me the feeling that there were faces, blurred faces pressing against a windowpane, faces wanting to get in.

I woke up at dusk, very thirsty. The sheets smelled and when I got up I saw I had wet the bed. But the spot had dried. It was going brown at the edges. I could still hear that underground water but now that it was getting dark out I was less frightened and was actually able to get myself out of bed and the bedroom. This was just before the streetlamps came on along Chapel Road, and the big Swedish Engineering building looked as if it was rising out of its own darkness to be sucked into blackest pitch. Then suddenly the bright streetlights were lit and I went from room to room turning on the lights. I drank some water in the kitchen and then I dared to look around for the cause of the sound of purling water and I found it, too. It was the old WC running.

I turned the water off with the tap on the long pipe running from the porcelain tank up by the ceiling, and the sound ceased at once. Then I walked all around the apartment and turned off the radiators, too. In those days we still kept the furnace going, and the water circulated with a hissing sound when it was heated up. I didn't bother making tea nor did I eat anything. I wasn't hungry. I drank some water and took a glass in and set it on the desktop near my bed. Then I got back under the covers. I should have changed the sheets but my energy had dissipated for now. I was sucked back down into my torpor the moment my head hit the pillow, which was still damp under my cheek.

I don't know how long I slept, but when I woke up my whole body ached. I could hear the purling water again. In fact, I awoke surrounded by running water. My body was rippling as if thousands of tongues of water were lapping at its crevices. Very slowly I rose to the surface, and found myself lying on my back in my narrow bed, my legs entangled in the sheets. I was sticky with chilly perspiration. Suddenly I realized what I was hearing was rain. I stayed there, lying on my back talking silently to myself: there is nothing other than this rain falling on the metal roof. It is gathering in rivulets and running down the corrugated metal into the gutters, taking with it flakes of black paint and yellow spotted leaves that were stuck to the roof, pigeon droppings and feathers. It's that filthy rainwater that's purling in the gutters and rushing down the drainpipes. There are no voices. Everything is as you see it. That's all.

There's nothing else. Just metal and rusty water.

Then I was able to get up and go to the bathroom. My bladder was tender. I turned the water back on before I peed so the tank would fill up and I could flush. Then I stood watching the water drip down. A little trickle ran slowly down the porcelain, that was brown with rust. I was listening to the murmur of running flush water, that was what I was doing and I knew it.

Then I walked through the apartment opening taps and letting the water flow, ecstatic at having vanquished my fears. The house had gone chilly, so I turned the radiators back on.

Perhaps it was to prove to myself that I wasn't scared that I went back out into the kitchen and turned on the tap over the sink and let a little stream of water run down. Then I went into the living room and lay listening on the sofa. It was true that there was some resemblance to voices. But these voices were saying: don't be afraid. If they were saying anything at all, it was that. Not with words but with something else, possibly ordinary sounds. How silly that I had been scared of them all my life.

In my semi-stupor I now heard that old familiar heartbeat phrase. It was: give in now and you're dead. Your heart will thump one more hefty beat and that will be the end. But now I was able to think that this must also be nothing but my imagination. There's nothing to be afraid of: giving in is just letting out the breath you've inhaled.

And yet I still went giddy as if I had been standing on a very high promontory when I did it. Sheer horror. But it was too late.

The next time I opened my eyes the sun was out. A beam of illuminated dust danced in the sunlight. The whole room was full of it. I was actually inhaling it every time I breathed, although I could only see it out there in the ray of sunlight. I was always doing things I had no idea of. Being filled with the world invisible.

I fell back to sleep in the rippling sound thinking: how foolish of me to imagine I was going to have a heart attack. I'm lying here now unscathed hovering on a cloud of voices.

The next time I woke up I felt rested but thirsty. It was late afternoon. I had some water, got dressed and went out. My thought was that it would be good to get out in the clear, cold air and not be drawing so many particles into my lungs with every breath, not so much of the world.

It was still hazy out there. The air was thick with atomized, solidified, stagnant water. The trees stretched their knotted black shapes up out of the fog only to be dissolved again at a distance. I passed houses with rain-spattered facades. The gravel in front of my feet was full of little streams; the rain had not been a dream. I met people in the fog, but they were nothing but specters of thickened air, accumulations that soon dispersed. I was being pulled away from the streets toward the woods. There was that smell of rotting leaves that always made me tingle with anticipation.

As soon as I got away from the human-stained areas I could feel the significance of what I was seeing very strongly. The meaning of a stone, of its entirely unique form and location. The unfathomable meaning of boughs, of the grass having been bent in a certain direction by the streams of rainwater a few hours or days ago.

Yes, this landscape was full of meanings.

I reached a little lake lying still in the fog. I could hear the soft chatter of ducks I couldn't see. The reeds were bent, thin brown lines. They would decompose and drop into the water. I thought about everything the water had to absorb and transform and wondered how it could manage. Drops were falling from the trees and hitting the surface of the water, and there was a sound I had never heard before and at first didn't understand.

Then a light penetrated the haze. It was not coming from the sky but from below, from the depths of the lake, from inside the water.

The water was illuminated from a hidden source and the lake was expanding. It was like a flow of heavy white metal before it vaporized in the light that was seeping in everywhere and making the trees along the shore glow and grow brighter and brighter until they turned white and stood there as if they were blooming from crown to roots from the heat.

The light also filled me and made my veins glow, coursing all the way into my minutest vessels. My heart fluttered and I stood trembling with light like a tree in a forest fire the instant before it really catches and begins to burn. I know how the filament in a light bulb feels.

Then, very slowly, everything began to grow dark. The white mist sank and yellowed. Everything around me went charred and I felt sick from something clingy in the air. The yellow light had darkened to red and gone as brown as burning butter. I felt something hard at the small of my back. It was a tree. I found myself sitting on the ground leaning against a tree trunk. Yes, a tree trunk.

That was the first word that came back to me. Then I realized this was the same position I had ended up in after Ishnol showed herself against the outsbuilding at school.

I had my memory back.

Choryn is not a country in which I grope my way forward. It is a shifting of light before my aching eyes or inside them. You stare at all the green, and gray-green and green-gray shapes, their bizarre repetitions verging on shapelessness, you stare to find the green hunter who is hiding fully visible with his loden green coat and his loden green trousers and his beard like fir lichen in the chaos and suddenly without warning the light and focus of the image alter and completely different colors and figures emerge from the surface of the picture, in the wink of an eye, in a moment of distraction. If you walk too close to the picture all you can see is the grid, the big dots into which everything eventually dissolves. But if you move even closer, so close that the film of your vision splits, you see a different kind of light than the light that comes from outside, a light coming out of the dots in the grid itself. Yes, it is quite simply a kind of light and between the dots is the picture, the other picture. Choryn is there. But it is difficult to pin Choryn down, it keeps dissolving into gray on gray and roughness, the black grid threatening to take over.

The small of my back aching, I sat warding off the grid. I sat by the little lake, leaning against a tree trunk in the gray-green, and yet I was in Choryn. I had that fizzy drink feeling in my body like when I was a child, a sense of anticipation that made me bubble. I got up and walked home, my steps were light. Not a sound, not a single nasty gust from Karun did I have to pass through. It didn't reach me.

But it was there, on the verge of breaking through, and it had to be warded off, like a whiff of sewage.

Now I had to be left alone. Choyrn needed time in me. Luckily, I was shrewd. I was filled with a cunning that seemed to come from my rapid steps and rise up in my body. I was like a fox nosing about in a pile of refuse, amongst peels and papers with his sharp muzzle and sending a glance up toward the windows now and then, keeping an eye on their darkness.

At home the curtains were half drawn, and lights I had forgotten to turn off were glaring. But I was wily now, and switched them all off. In the chilly rooms slight breezes seemed to come and go. I felt them touch my nose and upper lip. The phone rang. It had rung earlier, too, but not until now did I acknowledge the ringing, crystals on a bough. I had to make my way in from the far end of the branch toward the trunk and down into the roots in order to understand. My shrewdness prompted me to answer. Of course it was Jenny. I told her I was going away and her questions pattered like rain on a tar-paper roof. I said:

"Uppsala."

That was a good word. That was new hope, charged with a future. Maybe she believed me, maybe she didn't. In the midst of her questions, I hung up. The Bakelite receiver fell heavily. Explain. Explain. She had pattered until I put black Bakelite in her voice. Oh, Jenny, how could I ever explain to you the terrible break-through of a sun different from the flat disk that shines while you are cooking the beans for dinner?

Yes, I am dauntless.

I remain undaunted.

Dauntlessly, I balance up there. I could hardly have dared imagine it as I walked home, but it is true: this treasure is mine. I have recovered it. My hands were full of gold and I was afraid it would slip back down into the surging water where I captured it. I was also afraid it would turn out to be glitter or leaves. And so I needed to feel undaunted.

It was gold! I remembered now that I caught the first glimpse of it on my knees at the foundation of the old house next to the stream at Little Heavenside. The shard in my hand. Wet snail tracks. And the purling chatting comforting cajoling voices.

But now they had been silent for a long time. Or: I hadn't been listening. Intrusive and ignorant I had let their murmurs sink down into the thick mat of noise all around me. They had given me tireless guidance and I had rejected it. They had laid leaves at my foot and given me the incentive to read the old books, Henning's

289

piles that smelled sharply of dust and obscurity. When I finally listened it happened as if I had given in to a temptation.

That was when it happened. I stood there with my hands full.

Dusk became, without my noticing, morning in the rooms with the light breezes and the gift was still there, the gold in the stream. It hadn't turned into dry leaves nor to copper ore — brittle fool's gold in my hands.

Everything had its place inside me now. Apparently this country that was not a country had been spreading inside me for a long time. Like a map on stretched parchment it was there on the inside of my skin, where the blood vessels outlined rivers and winding tracks I could follow if I had the time and patience, fragments of paths, never properly trampled, only just begun. Brook-threads, thin, splintered arteries seeking a sea or a lake beyond the map.

In fragments and images, Choryn had made itself known. Sometimes as an intimacy with a few bending blades of grass as signs at my feet, or with the light shooting out of a mirror in an otherwise darkening room.

I lay in bed thinking about all the things I didn't know. That's not really true. You can't think about what you don't know. But I was thinking about the absence of those things, their shadows. The shadow body of everything I didn't know grew clearer and clearer, more and more tangible, beneath me. It was the deep, evasive shadow below me that had filled me with lust. I realized that now.

I wanted to surrender to it but noises from the courtyard kept interfering. Footsteps came and went to *The Correspondent* and I was aware I was lying there thinking. I was thinking about the light between the dots of the grid that had penetrated out to me and I heard the little impulses of light saying: we found an eye!

But I knew that if the pane of glass in the door rattled and Henning walked in I would start talking to him about what I was thinking and it would all be over: the leaves, the glitter, the flakes of pyrite would be washed back down into the stream by the rain. We would discuss light's quality of reality, and Henning might say that matter is what has happened, energy what hasn't yet occurred, and I would try to imagine a light that had not yet found an eye with a retina exposed to change, the cones and rods of which signaled their presence. But the pane of glass never rattled and I don't know whether or not the phone rang. I thought about Jenny now and then, thought of her as a swarm of amps, a thickening and concentration around a name. They tried to stick close to the name and to the behavior, which wasn't allowed to change too much from time to time. But I am thinning out, I thought, like distracted moths around a failing light. I giggled over that image. There were so many amusing things. Lusty's the name, full of lust.

I lay with the lights off, because a person living in Choryn needs neither the light from glowing filaments nor food. I didn't have to be disgusted by food any more. My intestinal system might dry up and be resorbed, peristalsis, secretion of porridge again, that whole sickening routine would be over! Intake and excretion cease! I would be released from spinning in this wheel where you are dropped down into the dung for your intake and swung up into the light for your excretion. A human being must be more than just a meat grinder with a sausage stuffer attached. But people who live in Choryn need water. The nature of water is weakness and strength. The body consists primarily of water. No surprise that it ripples in response when the waters call to it.

"Little Chip, why haven't you been listening to us?"

They never gave me a real name in what I called the dimension when I was a child. That was my freedom there. I was the nameless one but jestingly Ishnol and the others called me Shard, Splinter, Little Chip or Ben, and thousands of other variations, lusty and loving and all of them referring to my task as the guardian of the nameless shard that bore the sign "Codeframe".

"Listen here, little Bone-shard, the water is rising around you, it's time to leave all this thinking, all your little words."

I asked them if Ishnol wanted to crystallize, but they withdrew, annoyed, into the din once more and left me to all my cold thoughts. I imagined what might have happened by the lake, wondering if new mountains had been born from the heat into the light. But if they had then they, too, would be ground down to dirt and dust. All earth is dirt, is ground up dust from extinguished stars. It struck me that the heat had been so great the carbon from the incineration process might have been pressed into diamonds. I ought to go out to the lake and prospect for them. I lay like that with my cold thoughts like plucking, scratching fingers in Choryn and the voices went silent, of course. I wanted to find Ishnol in Karun, so hard she couldn't be ground to dust, an Ishnol who couldn't pass through any intestinal system and be altered. But all I found was my own cold fingertips, my thoughts picking at things.

I think I went out again, at least somehow I was at the lake watching the pond skaters dart. My face was so close to the water that I could see the indentations from the feet of water boatmen on the viscous surface. The leaves lay like little boats out there, sail and hull of a piece, waiting for wind. Above them were cold air and wandering clouds, and under them I saw the lake bed with sand worms swaying in the sludge, wooly brown branches and the shadows of fish. Then a face cut right through the layers of lake bed, surface, cloud and water, eradicating all else. It was a Robor mask, a skin of stretched parchment with holes puncturing the surface. It gaped expressionlessly and wanted to arch and cover me so the only way I would be able to see was through its eye slits. But I pulled away, retching.

The heat that followed the light from the lake must have opened the earth down to the deep strata where the oviducts run through the deepest bedrock and the octahedrons of Ishnol gleam under the vernix. But my fingers only scraped decomposing pine needles and the brown tangles of heather roots. I found cocoons, hard little brown treasure chests in which bodies were stored in anticipation of resurrection and wings. There were eggs in hiding places, lying in wait for life. I heard Wonda laugh. Shards rattled, and I saw her flapping unsteadily, possibly enticing me to follow her and get even more cuts on my fingers. But I knew her back was pitted, that the eggs hung in clusters from all her pores and cracks, and that everything she excreted was twirling, twisting and turning with incipient life, searching and scratching, with antennae and snouts, trying to plaster itself onto one of the pitted spots, seeking a damp crevice.

Ishnol did not appear but she touched me. A swell passed through the leaves and breathed me calm. I lay listening to the rippling of wind and water, but I could not reach it, other sounds got in the way, sighs, sucking sounds from clogged channels where dirty water was seeking to escape, the lowing of underground pipe systems. The body of Robor and the sounds of Robor. I lay listening to the lapping and the clucking from her stomach. That was it. Always this intestinal system making itself known. There is no silence in me. Nerves jolt and blood hums in my fingertips and my underarms.

I was a sludgy riverbed full of little animals that had burrowed down into me and sometimes moved around, trying to dig even deeper. My tongue groped around the backs of my teeth. A little oval fence of damp bone, chipped but still strong. The space between my tongue and my teeth filled with saliva, warm and tasteless. It ran down into my throat. There was clucking and lapping down there as it found its place in the system. It sounded like feet padding around a swamp and then like a series of little cries.

I begged: Ishnol, release me! forgetting that she could not be summoned. Nothing happened of course. The small of my back and the soles of my feet were hot. When I opened my eyes I was looking into the round, uninformed face of the clock. It had been one and it was un-one, the only fathomable thing about it. The factory whistle sounded and un-sounded. The clicking followed me into the darkness, little recurrences I could lie and anticipate. Not recurrences of the same thing, but of roughly similar things that would fill me with desire, fool me into thinking they were Exactly the Same Thing. But they weren't. The clicking sounds followed me now like a little troupe, they would stick with me now, for sure. Eyes closed, I expected the recurrences, but they were being diluted with something inconceivable, and they grew farther and farther apart, more and more irregular, and eventually they were gone. My body had lost its shape the minute I closed my eyes. I had ceased to know distance, and just lived in this sack of flesh with its lapping and sucking and buzzing and heat and the little prickles and jolts. But I didn't know how long it was or how far away anywhere else was, and I didn't want to know. People born blind know nothing of distance. If they regain their sight, they still prefer to grope their way forward with their eyes shut, that's what feels most secure to them. When they open their eyes they are scared of colliding with the mountains over there in a world that is nothing but surface, splotches of color alongside other splotches of color, all on the same plane.

Then finally she allowed me to be released!

And in Karun, Robor dressed me in her rags, skin and hair and chipped teeth. She began her eternal trudging between kitchen and bathroom, between kitchen and bathroom, between kitchen and bathroom — that's all the imagination Robor possesses.

But Ishnol had removed me from time, out into the great landscape where I had to climb over the tree trunk that was my own corpse and spend time on plateaus of life.

I was whole and utterly vulnerable when I stepped forth from this bath of images. I wanted to stay in this wide open tranquility like a person sunbathing in an open spot in a gentle forest. No hooks or knives reached me, no scabs of illness or evil could stick to my warm skin. I begged for that. And I lay out my comfort like clothes on the still-damp grass. But Ishnol's tranquility was not a forest; it was moonlit fields of ice and plains that could have been frozen water or dust. I saw all these One o'Clocks and whatever else they were called; they were sludge thrown up from the riverbed, but I was the one who cast them up on my journey. Ishnol let me travel. There were no movements and no forces beyond my own movement, my journey, my circumventions and clamber-overs, my roundings. I traveled in Ishnol's landscape deep down into the sludge like a lamprey travels with the water flowing above it, ready to enter her stillness when all my sludge had sunk to the bottom and the water above me cleared like a big bell jar of glass.

But it didn't happen.

I was doomed to live in Robor's insides, in her sludgy stinking wastewater. I lay whispering in her chest, which was full of the polluted water, and I asked Ishnol: why couldn't everything rest in you? Everything is already there in your crystal forms, the branches, the grapes, the nursing breasts — but immobile, resting in sparkling light. Why does it have to be dissolved into dirt and sludge? Why does it have to grow and sprout in the dirt? And why do rotting, moving branches reach out to the light?

Ishnol, I know you are light of light and that you breathe by diving into yourself and that every dive of light makes you more intense, that all the hardness and mass are born from your breathing light and the vapor of light from the heat of your mouth is crystallized like branches and frostwork on a pane of glass. But I don't understand the water.

Why didn't you stay as hardness? Why did you let the water erode your stone? You lowered your hardness into water and now you are overgrown. Boughs and arms extend towards their decomposition. I stand upright in you like a cup lichen open to the rain that will rot it.

But all this was mind exertions and words. Ishnol did not reveal herself. I lay lapping in the chest of Robor, in the foul stench of bloody water and saw her hand on the cover, thin and veined, a kind of branch in itself, reaching out eagerly for her death.

There was a glass of water on the desk, and someone behind the glass, someone who filled it and let it stand until it bubbled. There was someone who came back and poured the contents of the glass into me. These hands, less branch-like than Robor's, firmer, had tightened a screw and now there was a continuous clicking sound. The idiot face of the clock changed every time I looked at it. He had tightened the screw and closed me in with a clicking insect. That was how he was controlling me even when he was away. When he came back with a cup of white bread soaked in warm milk, I asked: is that the deathwatch beetle you have shut me in with? But he answered: you know it's the alarm clock.

I felt transparent and ashamed. I knew very well I had been putting on a miserable act. I wanted to throw something in his face the next time it turned up in the doorway but I was too weak. Soaked bread ran down into me only with the greatest difficulty and some ran down over my chin. He poked it patiently in. He looked like a commonsensical mother hare under a pine tree. It wouldn't surprise me if you developed an udder, I said.

Now he wanted me up out of bed. Until now, he had changed the sheets by pushing and pulling underneath me. I said there's one thing, just one thing, I have to ask you first, and it's serious. No games, no puns. I really mean it, it's something I've been pondering for ages. Don't mind my hoarse voice, I need to ask you now. You took the fast track at school, and did more biology than me, so you might know. It's also related to your clothing industry, you diligent squirrel. Moths and body lice and the like, but a little worse.

"Hasse, listen to me. A fellow near here on Chapel Road died last month. Henning knew him slightly. They weren't precisely drinking buddies, but I think they got their booze from the same source. He died and no one knew. They didn't find him for ages. The police were the ones who told us. You know, *The Correspondent* used to call and check for stories. Every morning we'd phone and ask if there was anything new. One morning I walked past the police station and went in to ask. They gave me a cup of coffee and an almond pastry and this story. He was a young officer, I guess he either needed to get it off his chest or to impress somebody. So: they found him and he was riddled with maggots. Now to my question: where do they come from? He was alone in a locked apartment, in a bathroom, even. Where were the eggs? Do we have maggot eggs in our skin? Answer me! Or deeper inside? Answer me!"

He really answered me. He said he didn't know and he couldn't care less. When you were dead you were dead and you no longer minded what happened to your body. When you were alive you were supposed to eat and sleep and try to stay healthy.

He took me to the Otters' house in a taxicab and he had personally packed a tote bag with my underwear and blouses and toilet things.

This was a time when I wandered around at the Otters shredding all sorts of things. In the morning I started by crumbling the piece of toast I was supposed to eat onto the oilcloth. Distractedly I plucked buds and leaves from Jenny's potted plants until she noticed and shouted: what are you doing? My nails, that I'd been letting grow so I could polish them pink like Hasse wanted, I bit down to the quick and thought it felt nothing but good. One evening I sat on my bed thinking or dreaming and twirling my Dutch cap on my index finger. I liked to watch the little rubber disk spin round and to see if it fell off. With my other hand, I caught the thick little rolled edge around its metal spring, and pulled. The index finger of my hand stood straight as an arrow, the yellow rubber going white with the pressure. And then it split.

I stayed with the Otters for quite a while, afraid Pappa would come home, and hate and shame would be let loose like beasts of prey in the apartment. Because I hated him for doing what he did on the ferry. I didn't feel he had let me down by drinking too much Elephant beer, O God no, I wasn't that childish. I wasn't much of a psychologist in those days, either, but I do think I tried to figure out why I felt like there was an animal biting at my stomach, at my intestines, every time I thought about him standing there on the jetty, leaning against that metal shed, with wet stripes running down his trouser legs. My only conclusion was that it would have been better for him to throw himself overboard than to have let that happen. And I think that was exactly what his own conclusion had been, but the crowd prevented it from happening.

In the end I went out to Dagöholm to see how he was getting on. But he asked them to tell me he couldn't see me that day; he had the most terrible headache, otherwise things were fine. I forced my way into the doctor's office and he, too, told me things were fine.

"Johannesson isn't doing too badly," was his pronouncement.

I don't know what his standard for comparison was, but it certainly wasn't himself. However, he had no idea what an expert I was at reading upside down. I had learned it sitting opposite Victor in the proof room. So I could see from the records that Johannesson had a white coating on his tongue and poor eye contact, rectal cramps, vomiting after meals and headaches. He showed indications of anxiety and *depressio mentis*.

There was nothing I could do. Fredrik and Jenny were fed up. Their faces were solemn as gravestones. They asked what I was planning to make of myself. Evidently they had heard or figured out I'd been fired.

Well, I didn't really know what I intended to do with myself. For the moment columns would have to do, pieces about the landscape, since I couldn't think of a single amusing thing to write. The good old trustworthy landscape — I hadn't given it much thought since the days when I started playing truant from school, but it was a fine structure for giving expression to my melancholy. Bursting buds sounded better than cramping rectums.

When I was falling asleep, an alien world would appear, strange voices quite near at hand. But I never managed to capture them, never succeeded in hearing what those voices were saying, and they didn't turn into sleep and ordinary dreams, but an angst that brought me wide awake. I developed sleeping problems. Although I was aware that I'd been ill and having weird dreams, the details kept eluding my grasp.

Things only got worse after I'd been out to Dagöholm. The animal kept biting at me, and it didn't help a bit that I realized it was possible to have several emotions at once. I kept on picking at things and pulling them to pieces, would pull a loose loop on a sweater Hasse had given me so it laddered right across; it was like pulling the little tab on a pack of semi-soft cheese. I could hardly believe such a tiny action, such absent-minded fiddling, could possibly have such conclusive results. Sorrow rose in me like the liquid in a jug. It was out of control now, I could feel it. Pull yourself together, said Jenny. A young girl like you wants to be out and about, you've got your whole life ahead of you. Oh, Lord, I'd give anything to be twenty again! Or she'd phone to say she'd baked fresh Danish pastries and I was invited over for coffee. And by the way, she'd say, she'd bought a remnant and was making me a blouse.

I shredded one of her Danish pastries to little flakes, and let her give me a fitting.

"Your arms are like matchsticks," she complained. "Chin up, now. Straighten up and fly right, why don't you?"

The secret with the garments Jenny made was that they required a certain posture to fit right. Otherwise they'd wrinkle up somewhere or a seam would pull. That posture affected your personality so you stiffened up. At least it that was what happened to her.

I wasn't sleeping a bit well, most nights I wasn't sleeping at all. But Henning had a medicine cupboard full of pills. I guess the doctors wanted him to try something different, they laid out a lavish spread of pharmaceutical delicacies, but he stuck to ethyl alcohol. There were pills to help you sleep, and I took a bottle of them and put it on my bedside table when I moved back to Chapel Road. Then I started crumbling them and nipping at the edges with no more intention than when I plucked the buds off house plants or ate flakes of Jenny's Danish pastries. Though I suppose our intentions are buried deep inside us, below our reason, and they trickle past it just as the ground water finds its way around rusty, leaking pipes.

At any rate, I was cutting my life up as if it were semisoft cheese. Jenny and Fredrik had gone to Oxelösund for the weekend and I slept or was unconscious for three days and nights, I realized afterwards. When I woke up the bed was covered with patches of dried-up pee, and the room must have stunk. I couldn't stand upright, it was as if I were drunk or hung over. Black specks and spots spattered my field of vision. I couldn't even get rid of them by shutting my eyes. Everything ached, my joints and my head. My tongue was stiff. I got out of bed but couldn't stand up, I had to crawl over to get some water. How long it took me to reach the tap on the bathtub I'd be hard pressed to say. Everything I did or tried to do must have taken hours, but the clocks had stopped so I couldn't really tell. I didn't realize what a bad state I was in, though. At first I thought I'd just slept one night and all the next day. It was dusk when I woke up. When I was able to shape words again I called the shop and asked them to leave some milk outside the door, and then the hard part began: keeping Jenny and Hasse away. It was only possible for a day or so, then they came. But by that point I was on the couch in the living room and saying I'd had a stomach bug and just wanted to be on my own. All I felt was shame, bottomless shame.

For several days I had no energy at all, couldn't even manage to wash my hair, and my joints and muscles just ached more and more. But I wanted to survive, just as badly as a fox that's been shot in the leg. I drank milk and threw up but was finally able to keep some down, and phoned for bread. I must have called at the right moment because a big fresh white loaf was delivered, its warmth was alive and it smelled wonderful. Henning had explained to me how the yeast consumed the sugar inside the bread and turned it into alcohol and carbonic acid and how the sugar in the crust became dextrin when it was baked. That created most of the aroma, he said. Who the hell cared? It smelt of life! When I broke it there was the smell of a nipple, of sun and clean cotton cloth, of the dry coat of a healthy animal, of leaves in the wind, of clean sheets and apples and nuts — it smelt of life!

I ate bread and egg yolks to keep myself alive. I only needed to see my sunken face and dirty hair in the mirror to know that death is a terrible disgrace. I thought about all the childish ceremonies I had attended, about there having been a soprano soloist accompanied by a cello at Ada's funeral, and about people having moved along slowly with rigid faces and medals on their chests. But death is only shame and stains, as I now knew. It must be resisted even after all its legs have been shot away. It must not happen. It is humiliation in mud and gravel and rotting shrouds. It sneaks up on us as soon as it has the chance, with the odor of ammonia from leaking urine and spots on our hands and bags under our eyes. But there is nothing natural about it, it is not the bread you eat and that shines your teeth, it is muck and filth.

I was back in bed, having managed to pull off the sheets and turn the mattress. The window was open onto the little garden where the lilac was in bloom. With every second breath I gagged, the phlegm pushed up into my throat and I was sure I was going to have to bring up the little I'd eaten. The alternate breaths filled me with oxygen and health. There was a breeze coming in from outside, too, billowing the curtain, the sweetness of the lilac alternating with its sickly cloying scent. Both were so intimately intertwined that I knew there was no choice but to wait, but to breathe.

Victor was the only person to whom I ever confessed what I had nearly done. When I could walk a straight line again without having to hold onto the wall for support I tied a scarf over my dirty hair and went to meet him at a café. He told me it was one of those things some of us had to go through, a kind of virginity that had to be lost, and now I had done it. I replied there must be one helluva lot of virgins walking around in this world and he agreed that it was so.

While I was still seeing spots Hasse came up to see me, and he touched my sensitive body. He was very gentle and I had bathed and washed my hair now and put on clean clothes, because I wanted his closeness. My Dutch cap was cracked, of course. Hasse was fastidious; he checked with his index finger for the rounded little edge with the spring in it. So I used it for his peace of mind. I couldn't get pregnant in my present state. But I did.

When I realized, I spent some time feeling the same disgust with life that I felt with death, disgust with the breeding and hatching in every conceivable crevice and hollow, even the ones that were diseased and fractured, because it never gives up trying, and groping like the digger-wasp with its oviduct to find the weakest point, even if it turns out to be a pus-filled sore.

I didn't go around with that feeling for long, though. It passed when I told Hasse. He was very excited and started talking about "the baby" right away, and I was ashamed of not having thought about it as a child but more like an abscess or a jellied lump with eyes, that was full of vicious life.

He thought it would be just as well we got married as quickly as possible. People would only talk more and more as my stomach began to show. "Little mamma" he called me, the phrase millions of animated young men must have used before him, patting my inconceivably flat tummy. In fact, the whole thing was actually quite inconceivable. It was like chemistry, a reaction that had been triggered but that hadn't yet become cloudy. But he called it "the baby", and that was ever so sweet of him. Hasse's never been much of a talker, never had a way with words, although he's been quite good at finding the right ones on occasion, the words with life in them.

My breasts changed. They became beautiful, taut. I really wish I could remember it, recall every minute of that brief period, but I can't. I tried to imagine a little person in there, sprouting inside me. But I don't remember. The body has no memory for anything but pain. It is as empty as a gutted fish.

We got married when I'd only missed one period. Hasse wanted it that way. Pappa didn't say much. I had seen him treating Hasse like an adult for years now. I don't think he ever found out I was pregnant. Two sisters of Hasse's father came in from out of town, and there were separate engagement parties, one at the Otters' and the other at the Curtmans'. Not until later did I realize Hasse's father could never have invited his fellow rotary club members to the Upco Estate.

Jenny made me a pink cotton dress with a bolero top that I wore to their party. For the other one Hasse bought me a light blue satin dress and a marcasite brooch. The house smelled of coffee, perfume, cigarette smoke, dry cleaning chemicals and sweet pastries. Because I was in the early, sensitive weeks of pregnancy and also still weak after my overdose of sleeping pills, I felt sick throughout. Middle-aged women screeched like gulls and hovered around the table where the presents were laid out. We were given blankets and toasters and towels, a rolling pin, a Foley food mill, vases, an onion chopper, a glass-covered cheese dish, and napkin cases. An assortment of household gadgets rolled into my life with demands about capability, knowledge, interest and, yes, get-up-and-go. There were towels to hem and monogram in cross-stitch, pastry dough to roll out thin and fold with cold butter between the layers, dinner guests to invite so they could wipe their mouths on the napkins.

A whole lifetime grew up around me with its paraphernalia, and I didn't know how it had happened. Was all this really initiated by my breaking the skin of my Dutch cap with the nail of my index finger? Or had it been triggered earlier?

Whatever we didn't get as presents we had to acquire, and Jenny took it upon herself to make lists I had to run dizzily all over town to deal with: dust cloths, Lustra floor wax, a measuring cup, a potato scrubber, a feather duster, a fingernail brush, a dishwashing brush, a clothes brush, sponges, canning seals, a thermometer. A big funnel. Extension cords. A bread box. She suggested I take some things from home, from Chapel Road. The kind of stuff Henning never used. For instance, she told me, we had an excellent larding needle. Needless to say, I couldn't possibly remove anything from there. If Jenny didn't realize that 13 Chapel Road was a universe in which every component was equally important as every other, I couldn't explain it to her. Now I was supposed to build a world of my own out of this chaos of extension cords, skirting board brushes and bread boxes. I had no idea whatsoever of how to do it. I would have to find the proper actions as well as the proper order of doing them in.

When I looked at Jenny I understood that it wasn't about being orderly, either. She did all those things, I knew, she was the person she was supposed to be, although she wasn't at all orderly. Something else was required, a kind of identification. Maybe she had enough of that for both of us, at least at first. With determined enthusiasm she sat down to make me a bridal gown, grim because of the pins between her lips. Five meters of virgin white panama silk was spread out on the dining room table. Hasse would have been happy to have a seamstress make me a gown, and his aunts would undoubtedly be dissatisfied with Jenny's handiwork. But I didn't mind. She had made my confirmation dress, my white suit when I graduated from upper secondary school, and the light blue party dress I had worn to that new students party in Uppsala, the one where Philip had discovered me. It was integral to every ceremonial moment in my life to look a little home-sewn. I tried on the dress, which had long sleeves and a high neck with no more than a tiny lace-edged slit in which the most exciting thing to be seen was my gold confirmation crucifix necklace. I would have preferred to get married in the barbarian glory of a folk costume from Dalacarlia or Morocco, but Jenny wanted me to look first-rate. She was so busy dressing me up as the quintessential bride, I didn't have the heart to tell her I was pregnant. I told myself I had ages to go and things would work out, maybe I'd go past my due date and no one would ever know. But when she did the final fitting she commented that it was odd how tight across the bust the gown looked, she'd have to unpick the darts and let it out a little. Funny, she said. My breasts were swelling like August plums. All I could do was hope I'd still be able to get into the dress at all on our wedding day.

Jenny was concerned and slightly uncertain. Perhaps she was beginning to realize the results were not going to be an adequate reflection of the love and pride she felt. The dress pinched and creased and, worst of all, it "drew", as she said, across the bust. I just can't figure it, she said, and that was one of the few times in her life I've thought Jenny was being rather naïve.

It looked like the product of a crafts project. Even a dress bought off the rack would have been better. Her fingertips, sore from pinpricks, pulled and pinched, postponing the inevitable. But there were still six days until the wedding. She took the whole armload of panama silk, thread end dragging and pins falling out, and carried it down into the living room, where she had her sewing machine set up.

I stood there in front of her bedroom mirror looking at my thin body with its red-veined breasts swelling up over the edge of my padded bra cups. I was wearing a white half-slip with embroidered edging, just an everyday slip. When I twirled before the looking glass I saw reddish-brown spots at the back. Oh Lord on Thy heavenly throne, what had I done? I twisted the slip from back to front and stared. The engagement party and all those presents! And Hasse. What was I going to do? In the distance I heard a barking dog and loud voices and footsteps coming upstairs, but I rushed into the bathroom and ran cold water over the stains. Not until they failed to disappear did I realize they were rust spots from Jenny's old hand-turned wringer, and I rubbed the streaks and wetted them with spit and more water to be absolutely certain. In the end I pulled down my panties, too, but there was nothing there: I was pregnant and no one could accuse me of deception.

So I was standing there, skinny and pale with two little brown streaks on my slip and a big wet spot, when the crooked bedroom door opened, and masked figures scurried in. They held me tight and blindfolded me with a rag. I'd registered noise when they were coming up the stairs, but now they were quiet as mice.

I felt soft hands bundling me into some kind of cloth, how good they smelled. They were suppressing their giggles and setting something tall and rickety on my head. Around my waist they were hanging noisemakers, and then they were shoving me out into the hall, and beginning to maneuver me down the stairs. I could hear Jenny laughing and the news on the radio, so it must have been half past six. Buster barked loudly throughout from behind a closed door; he had good instincts.

They put me in a cart attached to a bicycle — I figured that out because someone warned me to keep my fingers out of the spokes. Then Jenny brought out one of the kitchen chairs. I was raised out of danger and we rolled unsteadily off. They were perfectly silent, probably so I wouldn't recognize their voices, but we seemed to be going a long way, and I couldn't keep that grin on my face forever. I started feeling melancholy as the cart bumped along and I smelled the peonies and the horse manure in the little gardens of the Upco estate.

Long, long, was our route through town, and the silent figures surrounding me who knew how everything was supposed to be done were apparently taking me through the market square because I recognized the smell from the yard behind the pharmacy and heard the freight cars rattling along the tracks. The fountain splashed and one or two of the people we passed laughed softly. I sat trying to smile while inside me some kind of sorrow and wonder were growing: is this my city? This gentle splashing, these soft voices, this dialect that sounded so special to me now after I had lived in Uppsala, the musty smell of dog pee, the scent of flowers and the sickly smell of the pharmacy. I was sitting less erect now, because I was cold. I pulled my legs up under me on the bouncing chair and stared into my eyelids at images of what was passing me by. I noticed they were pulling me up towards the churchyard, and began anticipating the heavy smell of leaves and decomposing wreaths and wet gravel from there. But I no longer felt anything. It struck me that everything out there could perfectly well have been replaced, that I might have been imagining the scents and the sounds. Perhaps I would find myself in another city when they removed the blindfold.

But first we had to go up some stairs and then they put a cold glass to my lips. I had to swallow some liquid with little chunks in it and I thought: this could be anything, blood, impurities. But it was wine, of course, wine without much of a kick, and afterwards they told me it was wine punch with soda pop and fruit cocktail.

They tore off the blindfold and shouted a toast to my health, and we were at Synnöve's parents' and she was standing there right in front of me herself, looking elegant in a men's dinner jacket. Babba was there too, in a frock coat and sweatpants, and Ing-Gun from the post office, wearing a night-shirt and a red knitted ski cap. Karin Tervard, who was so shy, was standing there in plus fours that pulled across her big bum and with a charcoaled moustache below her nose. Ulla Karrén was there, too. She was a couple of years older than the rest of us, and already married to a curate. She had a battered hat on her head with artificial tulips sticking up out of it. Ingela Iversen-Lindh hadn't come. She was too ill.

We had more of the punch and they took me over to a big mirror so I could see what I had been wearing when they dragged me through town. On my head I had an upside down lampshade. It resembled a huge crown, out of which a not-very-clean lace curtain flowed like a train. On top of the lamp-crown they'd set a raggedy old soft toy, a plush squirrel. I suppose it was an allusion to the squirrel on the Curre Clothing label, and I could see Synnöve's embarrassment when I took the crown off to examine it. Well, it may have been a little tactless of them to dress me up with a squirrel, but they were excited and had got carried away. And of course they were right: the most noteworthy thing about this wedding was that I was marrying the Curre Clothing Company Ltd., and everybody in town was talking about it. The girls had wrapped me in sheets and tied a rope around my waist, from which there was a jangling bunch of kitchen gadgets that were meant as presents. Synnöve, who had come straight from Paris where she was taking a course at the Sorbonne, had brought a garlic press and a potato cutter from the Prix-Unique.

The excitement was wearing off. We drank more punch but it was too weak to get us back in the mood. Synnöve had written a funny and touching verse, and she was handsome in her tuxedo with her hat at a rakish angle. It was as if she were trying to make up to me for the squirrel on the lampshade, because when she had finished reading, she came and sat down next to me and explained that I had been missing Hasse when I was in Uppsala. That was why I had never been happy there.

"You just wanted to come home and be with Hasse the whole time," she said, pronouncing her verdict on my time in Uppsala. She may have been a little tired, though she didn't look it. It wasn't exactly a cushy life acquiring that demanding, expensive French education, and God knows she may also have been in a lull between flings just then and been a little envious of me that evening. The others had their ideas, too, and the room was full of romance, along with the pop and the sweet white wine, and I could see that Synnöve, who put such high demands on me, was pleased for once — a person could make a career of love as well. But I felt sick at heart because I knew that it had to be true love in that case, so I felt I was faking — I wasn't so deeply in love. I wasn't really living up to their standards. Ing-Gun at the post office had been engaged to a classmate since the day we graduated from upper secondary school, a fellow from the Bible Society; she had adopted his faith. He'd proposed right there on the school steps when we were all rushing around in our graduation caps, and she'd been waiting for him ever since, for him to get his degree from the Stockholm School of Economics. Of course she had never touched another man, in fact she might not have touched him much either. Karin Tervard had been in love once with a young man in the vocational program who had betrayed her, and she had nearly grieved her heart out. When it happened, she had wailed and raged and downed a whole bottle of furniture polish. And good old reliable Babba was also pure-hearted because she was in love with a young man who worked in the foundry at Swedish Motors. That was peculiar since she had gone on with her own education, and her father owned a big paint shop. But her young man was going to night school now and Babba, who had gone to teacher training seminary and was a qualified handicrafts teacher, knitted and waited. Any one of them would have been more worthy of Hasse and of Curre's Clothes than I was; Synnöve who was so talented and beautiful or Babba who was so strong and independent or Karin Tervard who was so passionate — or Ing-Gun at the post office who was surely a more virtuous virgin than I had been when I got together with Hasse.

But somehow it was me, and they congratulated me and then we talked about the engagement parties, about cheese slicers and tea sets. Hasse and I were going to live in quite a large, centrally located apartment, and have checkered bedspreads. Was I making them with a valance or just plain?

It was odd being with them again. They were like little blue tits around a birdfeeder, gray and fluffy. Synnöve was the only one who chattered a bit more loudly, boldly. And I was probably the most tit-like of all, thin and beige, with whisks and ladles and can-openers strung around my waist. But at least I had been rescued from utter destitution and invoice-writing. I was quite clear over the fact that it wasn't precisely going to be all fun and games from here on. Fredrik and Jenny had given us a vacuum cleaner for our engagement present. I would vacuum up bag after bag of dust and while I did so Hasse would be taking over the business and we would buy a house and our children would have good educations and when I had vacuumed up a mountain of dust, so much that a whole city could be covered with a gray layer like the ashes from a huge bomb, then we would at have a fiftieth birthday party catered for Hasse in the party suite at Rosenholm, and that was about as far as I could think because after that it was all false teeth and beet stains on the tablecloth and possibly the sound of soft violin music from the crematorium.

I wished I'd been like Synnöve, that I had been successful when I was able to get out of here after we left school. But I just couldn't figure out where the key to success lay. I knew I'd been lazy in Uppsala and that Synnöve had been full of go. But that wasn't what it was all about, it was something else. I knew I could have been as quick as a slithery little mink if there had been any point. But I never had. And why not?

There was no way I could ask Synnöve. She thought things were working out for me now. And in a way I agreed. It wouldn't have been any better to have become an English and Swedish teacher. Have to get up for an eight o'clock start every morning, get eczema from the chalk dust, mark tests all weekend, take long walks with the biology teacher.

I was starting to feel glum, but Babba had made coffee and Ing-Gun from the post office opened the box with the cake in it. Once it was on the cake stand we all agreed it looked weird — a green marzipan cream cake with pink marzipan decorations. Instead of the usual rose in the middle, there was a pink thing that looked like a log or little candle stump or maybe a sausage. All around the edge there were more decorations, the same sausage shapes but even smaller. They were all in a line, and we poked at them, Kari Tervad saying they reminded her of baby field-mice. Then Ulla Karrén lifted the centerpiece log, which had sunk down a little, and commented that it was the strangest thing she'd ever seen. Suddenly we all knew we were looking at pink marzipan penises. It was a joke on the part of the pastry-cook, he'd heard that the cake was ordered for a hen party. It was horrifically embarrassing, what with Ing-Gun being so religious and Ulla Karrén married to a clergyman. In fact Karin was the one who got most upset; she cried.

As always, Synnöve had a solution. She lifted off the decorations with a table knife, sweeping them back down into the box. But nobody seemed overly keen to eat the cake anyway. Karin wouldn't even taste it.

After that, the party broke up quite fast. Everyone hugged me, and things got a bit more cheerful again as people were putting their coats on. Synnöve and I were left alone. She brought out a bottle of port and we finished what was left of the cake. In the end we gobbled up the pink field mice too, without thinking much about it. I drank most of the port because she had to get up early. I felt like asking if I disgusted her. I was thinking about her orderly life, studying for exams and learning stenography on the side. In addition to which she expected herself always to have nice-looking hair. And be happy. Of course I knew it was important to have ambitions. That was much better than floating around like me, just as it was better to have long fingernails than to bite them, there were no two ways about it.

But when I said to Synnöve she seemed overworked, she retorted that you had to steward your pound. People tended to quote the Bible more in those days. Nowadays people talk about self-fulfillment, as if the self were inside you like a pancreas or an appendix, invisible but indubitable. In those days, however, it was stewarding your pound, and I said:

"Come on, call a spade a spade! You're working your way up in the world, heading for the good life, the icing on the cake. Being one of the crème de la crème, the people with time to read books and take walks, the place there are the most interesting jobs for the people who have itchy feet and want full planners. Up at the top is where the fame and the rewards are, we know that. Synnöve, you can't argue it. When we finished the years of schooling the law required, you and I could have left school and taken jobs stitching shoulder pads if we had come from that kind of family. But we had a choice. I don't think about the people who spend their days down in the basement of Curre's Clothes as seamstresses very often, the women doing the stitching in the shoulder pad department. I don't think about their pounds or their souls. I've never even been down there. But I do happen to know someone who works at Curre's, and she's no fool. I think she's quite a lot like you but she's never had the opportunity to rise to the creamy top, and as far as I can see it isn't bothering her particularly. There are different lives, thank God. Maybe things aren't so bad down where the masses are, or inside, in the guts. No, I don't really believe in all that pound-stewarding crap. What it's all about is staying up in the creamy bit because we think things are best there. What kind of obligations are we supposed to have in relation to any pound? I mean, I like you and admire you but you are, forgive me Synnöve, of normal intelligence, *forgive me!*"

But she just laughed, she was a good egg.

"Well, isn't that the way it is?" I asked. "Lots of people are of normal intelligence but you have your determination and you are also absolutely sure deep down in your bones of what it's all about. Not slipping down to the bottom. Isn't that the truth, Synnöve? Answer me!"

She was nibbling little field mice and watching me, and her mascara was starting to run and I don't think she gave me much of an answer, there just wasn't much more to be said about it. We unstuck the centerpiece from the bottom of the box and had half each.

"It's really only marzipan," said Synnöve. Apparently she had taken in something of what I meant when I exhorted her to call a spade a spade, after all.

The money the girls had pooled for the hen party covered a taxi ride home for me, so Synnöve called me a cab and lent me a raincoat of her mother's. We kissed on the cheek and said good night, and I was off in the direction of the cemetery. But being in the taxi immediately made me retch; somebody had been smoking there. I had been unable to stand the smell of smoke since very early in my pregnancy, and I haven't smoked since. I simply lost the taste for it.

I paid the taxi driver and got out. This was on a long street that runs down the ridge and is called Geijer Street. Nowadays there's a street in the town named after every single famous person in Swedish history. In the old days the streets were named after Merchant Lindh's wife and children, and even his wife's lapdogs got a little cul-de-sac each. Victor lived on Geijer Street, and I found myself walking straight up to his house. I was tipsy and wound up and needed to talk. Synnöve was sweet but she couldn't let me give vent to my confusion: she just superimposed her usual grid on it and thought everything would be fine if we were just industrious and loyal and if the Bomb didn't fall. But I could talk to Victor, he was able to latch onto some aspect of the confusion, show me what I meant.

Still, I can't remember what Victor and I talked about that night.

We went for a walk; his apartment stank of tobacco smoke so I couldn't be in there. We'd taken these walks before and a couple of times we had walked all the way out to Little Heavenside and borrowed a rowboat. He lay on his back with his head up on the hard edge of the hull, eyes shut and perfectly calm. His large, bulging eyelids were motionless and I sat there with the oars in the air, water dripping down into the fresh, lily pad-covered lake, letting us drift with the current, and I stared down at his face as if it had been a forbidden landscape.

I suppose Victor had been quite lonely while I had been running around buying lampshades and skirting-board brushes. I think he was nervous now. We hadn't yet mentioned my approaching marriage. Perhaps he had been hurt by having to find out in the paper about the banns being published, what did I know? But I hadn't had the guts to tell him, hadn't been able to find the right level of sarcasm.

By the time we reached the beach at Rosenholm he was tired. His old nicotine heart was aching he said, and the cadaver wanted to be horizontal. We couldn't find a single rowboat that wasn't locked up, and as we walked around among the reeds at the lakeshore it began to rain. We took shelter under the gable of the old canoe shed. The rain swished on the water and leaves that summer evening, the tiny drops bounced against the surface of the water and then burst into pearls and splashes. The cobwebs in the juniper bushes shimmered like gossamer. We forgot to talk because there was so much to look at. There was a strong, sickly scent from a tall, pinkish green bush Victor said was called Valerian, and all kinds of scents were gradually being released from leaves and grasses and water. Little Heavenside manor shone white through the veil of rain, looking like it was floating on the surface of the water because the mist was shrouding the old, gray patio stones between the house and the shore.

My back hurt from leaning against the canoe rack, and Victor offered to put his arm in between. But then he noticed how cold I was and I explained that under the raincoat I was wearing nothing but a bra and a half-slip. He immediately removed his coat and sweater, offering me the sweater. But it stank of tobacco and I said I couldn't put it on because of the smell. He insisted I wouldn't notice it under the raincoat. So I unbuttoned Synnöve's mother's raincoat buttons and Victor forgot for a moment who he was and stared at my breasts. I found myself just sitting there, the cold air on my breasts, taking his hand and setting it on the taut, vein-mapped skin protruding from the cup.

"What did you do that for?" he asked, and I didn't answer. Then I gave in to my weight and leaned back onto his arm and for a moment I thought he was actually going to take it away, because he stiffened. But then he kissed me of course.

When you make love with someone, when you go to bed with them or whatever you call it, you presumably do approximately the same things you have done with someone else if you have been there before, and I cannot explain where the difference lies. I don't know why Victor was more delightful to me than anyone else, why everything that was him: his skin, his hair, his scent, was the most heavenly thing I have ever known. Perhaps it's not worth trying to explain, since I have no idea why I was so pleased with him the minute I touched his skin and felt his hair, at first pleased as a child with sweets, and then forgetting absolutely everything, I felt such happiness, such sincere happiness, and I took him to me and deep inside me I knew all along that he was the one, the one and only. Because no one else had that scent, that scratchy chin, that tongue, no one else breathed like he did, no one had those hands. I knew who he was so definitely, as if I had never known who anyone else was or is. He took me to him in the same way, I know, I didn't doubt it for an instant even then. We lay down on the ground, he put his raincoat underneath and it rained the entire time and I noticed that too. There was water running off his hair down into my face while he was inside me, and the root of a tree was hurting the small of my back. But I didn't want him to stop, I wanted him to stay inside me and keep looking at me. That night with the terrible, ice-cold rain I was *seen*, that's the only way I can explain it; he saw me.

It was awful when we got up afterwards. I began to shiver with the cold, my teeth were chattering beyond my control. Victor began thumping me on the back, and he forced me into his sweater that reeked of tobacco. Then he took me by the hand and we ran through the scraggly birch grove up the slope toward the dressing rooms. At the entrance to the Ladies there was a roof I could shelter under while he went across to the caretaker's office and tried all his keys in the lock. He couldn't get the door to open and suddenly I heard a crash and the sound of a great deal of glass breaking on the pavement. He'd smashed the ticket window to reach the telephone. I heard him call a taxi. When the taxi arrived, its headlights blurred and enlarged, we were standing there, soaking wet and muddy.

There had been an accident, Victor explained quietly, pulling me into the back seat and giving the driver his address. I whispered that I had to get home. But he whispered back that I must go home with him, we were meant to be.

But I didn't. Nor can I explain it. I went to Chapel Road and was nearly hysterical when I couldn't get in. I didn't have the keys with me, of course. I sat on the firewood bin out in the vestibule and wept, trembling from head to foot. After some time the lamp in the hall went on, the pane of glass rattled as the old door opened, and there stood Pappa, pale and newly-discharged.

He asked me no questions, of course. Who would he have thought he was to start asking me why I looked as if I had been rolling around in a ditch? He carried extra blankets and a big glass of hot milk into my room. Then he phoned Jenny and told her I was at Chapel Road so she wouldn't worry.

Less than a week later Hasse and I were married at Vallmsta Church. There was a heat wave. Everything had happened so fast. I had become pregnant when the first sign of red on a bud of the peony had made itself known, and on the morning of my wedding day when I went out barefoot to get the newspaper from the Otters' mailbox, I waded through drifts of soft petals. It was the heat that had made them bloom and wither so fast. I raised handfuls to my nose, taking in the sweet aroma, and wishing my bridal bouquet could have been these peonies, if they hadn't already been past their prime. But dreams of such barbarian, shocking pomp were not the kind of thing I could communicate. All around me there was expertise about how things were supposed to be done. Jenny had even persuaded me to have my hair cut and permed, so now I had little curlicues all over my head.

The morning of the wedding, the bridal bouquet Hasse had ordered was delivered. It was a nursery arrangement of pink and red tea roses, white freesia and one or two other things. It reminded me of beet-and-herring salad. We went to the church together, the Otters, Henning and me, irritable with the heat and the tension, and we nearly had a row about who would sit where in the car. I ended up in the front with Fredrik, my train folded in my lap. Jenny and Pappa sat in back.

Fredrik had an old Ford Anglia he had bought second hand from somebody who had kept it on blocks during the war. He parked outside the church, so white in the sun it made your eyes sting to look at it. The last of the guests were just flapping and fluttering in through the door, all organza shawls and black coat tails. We tumbled out. Fredrik's dress suit was already damp with the heat, he was steaming and his collar pinched. When Henning got out into the merciless sunshine his dinner jacket had dog hair on it. Not just a few strands, not a little bit you can swish off with your hand. He had a fuzzy coat of Buster's graying fur right down his back and even his trouser legs. Jenny had been spared, thanks to her dress of sleek duchesse satin. The Anglia had mottled gray upholstery, so they hadn't noticed a thing when they got in.

Henning was furious.

"This is just typical," he raged, and they knew very well he was referring to their general untidiness and way of keeping house. Fredrik turned on his heel and stormed off. He waited in the shade of a big ash tree over by the wall. You could see he had a headache and was beside himself. Jenny brushed with her hand, and was angry as well. Of course there was no proper brush in the car. Jenny and I took turns slapping at the tuxedo and pulling off one hair at a time, but it didn't seem to be doing any good. Hasse peered out from inside the church, because we were late by this time, and when he saw me crying he ran out and helped us brush.

"That's the best we can do," said Jenny. "No one will notice once you're in your seat, anyway."

I'd given up and withdrawn into the shade alongside Fredrik. I wanted to scream, I wanted to run way. My heart was pounding heavily from heat and exertion. My Pappa in a tuxedo in church, his back furry as a dog, ridiculed, a good story for years to come. Just like Copenhagen. But sober this time, pale as a corpse, and the shame none of his own making. He had been released from Dagöholm less than a week earlier.

Suddenly he shoved away Hasse and Jenny, who were still madly brushing his back with their hands, and crossed the lawn to me.

"Ann-Marie," he said softly. "I'm not going in."

I nodded, unable to answer. My heart was pounding so hard I could hardly breathe. As he walked toward the line of waiting taxis Jenny shouted shrilly: "You can't do this Henning! You can't do this to your daughter!" Such an idiot, that Jenny. She couldn't see that he was doing it for my sake. This time there was no crowd to prevent him from getting to the railing.

Yes, Victor was a peculiar person, I could see that sometimes. A middle-aged proofreader with a passion for spelling and grammar, a fundamentally very lonely person who sat in cake shops and cafés with a girl twenty-five years younger than himself, gaped at by the proprietresses and waitresses, recognized by customers who went home, carrying paper bags of cakes to go with their evening coffee, and to whom it would never have occurred to spend any time at a café table. A whole evening. Sit there talking and smoking. The owners didn't like it. His visits were far too protracted. One had to keep an eye on such dubious clients through the window in the door to the kitchen. Pass by and wipe a nearby table with the dishrag, trying to eavesdrop on the conversation taking place over there under the dusty cissus. Those two were talking softly, much too softly. And they hadn't been drinking, either. In the end you had to go up to them and say: "We're closing in a few minutes."

Your voice might belie your words, since there was over an hour till closing time. But they'd leave, quietly. He paid. They would just move on to the next café, take another table, pour their own coffee since nobody did it for them, crumble their iced almond pastries, no more than poking at them on the cake plates. But they were perfectly good iced pastries! It was as if they didn't notice what they were eating and drinking. They just gazed into each other's eyes and talked and talked. And her supposedly a newlywed. Had to be thirty years his junior. Nails bitten down to the quick. Headscarf over her hair and high-heeled shoes whatever the weather. At least he looked properly dressed, with that bow tie under his chin.

That's how I imagine they saw us. That's what we looked like at Ankers, where there were mirrors. But we had stopped going there. Our pact about avoiding the places right in the middle of town was a tacit one. Naturally we knew people were talking about us, but we never said a word to each other about that, either.

We talked and we talked. We'd had sex now. We'd had part of a night of love. We didn't talk about that. But it had created a fissure. Opened a crack through which fresh water could seep. Anxiously, we now strained to remain open, intimate and serious. Still it slowed and stagnated surprisingly fast. We would have had to be together, be close to each other, but I didn't dare.

He was so different from Hasse. That was practically all I could think about when his face approached mine. His lips were dryer, his bottom lip larger. His tongue had felt older when he kissed me; well, he was older of course, had a rough, old tongue, dryer skin, a different scent, a completely different smell from Hasse, who had an aroma of pine needles and fresh skin. He looked straight into my eyes and I could see his were bloodshot and that the whites were going yellow. It was all so damnably distinct.

Our jargon started to return. What was initially desire and sadness when we looked at each other across the crumb-covered café tables soon turned to poses. We were being watched, of course, and that affected us though we tried not to show it. Soon we sat there like parodies, talking softly and smoking. A Humphrey Bogart who had already begun to cough and his young love, bad and beautiful. But not really as bad as she believed, and not so beautiful, either. And Bogie looked like a small town accountant or, quite simply, like a proofreader at a provincial paper, a man with a guilty conscience.

We were distorted by being observed. Not even chimpanzees can stay lively and natural in such a situation. Nor did we have anywhere to take refuge. Or at least we couldn't figure out where we could go, what we were going to do, although Victor was always asking:

"What's to become of the two of us, then?"

One evening Hasse came home from Curre's Clothes and told me we were moving to Portugal. He was going to be a trainee with a major clothing manufacturer. He didn't ask whether I wanted to come along or not, or whether I thought we should go, or anything. From which I understood that he had heard I was sitting around cafés with Victor Bremer.

We left not only Victor, but the skirting-board brushes and the breadbox and the extension cords: we left it all behind. In a suburb of Porto we rented the ground floor of a villa, which was actually no more than a studio apartment, one big room with a flagstone floor and a tiny, newly done up bathroom. The walls were white plaster. There was a big bed with a black and red woolen blanket for a bedspread. Just inside the glass wall that was both a sliding door to the garden and the entrance to our studio, there was an old oval table of polished wood. There was a high-backed armchair with a black leather seat and back, and an enormous candleholder with drops of yellow wax on the wood where the gilt had flaked off. There were

314

also dining chairs with hard, stuffed, red velvet seats. On the floor on Hasse's side of the bed was a tall wardrobe of brown oak with twisting black columns.

That was all. We bought a set of bedside tables and a radio, and rented a heater fuelled with *gas butano*.

In the mornings there were some kind of little animals on the floor, rolled into tight little coils. I called them rusk worms because they crunched under foot, and I avoided walking around barefoot inside.

I made a habit of having a vase of white callas and bougainvillea in on the table. We had to share the kitchen with our landlords, who lived upstairs. They were French, a couple who had come to Portugal after living in North Africa; he speculated in real estate. The woman's name was Chantal, and she was only a few years older than me. She was extremely thin and had bleach-blonde hair, so stiff it looked like stalks of dried grass. I often sat on a stool in their little kitchen while she was cooking. She was a chain smoker, but I could tolerate the smoke again now. Or perhaps I learned to put up with it because I needed her company.

The kitchen was on the north side of the house. It always had a scent of damp stone, as well as of hare blood and butchered meat, gas, garlic, and moldering summer from her tins of Herbes de Provence.

Her husband bought her beautiful dresses. He despised cardigans, trousers and flat shoes. Chantal wore the more faded of her party dresses for everyday. I remember one that was pink wool, a tight, dainty little frock. The darts at the bosom showed dirt.

She prepared hare, chicken or fillet of beef, cut potatoes into chunks and deep fried them in olive oil. They had a salad with their meal, and cheese after, always two or three kinds of cheese on a china tray. Sometimes I thought her life was as dull as the world of those cheeses, her only future shrank a little bit with every passing day. She was maturing, as one said of cheeses that were going pungent. But hers was also, as I quickly came to see, a well-defined life in which there was tranquility.

Their son, Jean-Loup, was already old enough to go to school. He was the spitting image of his father. His feet, his ears, his body language — he already shuffled around like a little *propriétaire*, with a mouth like the moist petal of a flower, and a reluctant, appraising look in his eye.

Chantal taught me to cook. She splashed olive oil out of a tin can, clicked the gas burners. Meat sizzled and browned. She turned it quickly, before it could begin to exude pink sweat. Fish was not eaten in her household. Roger said he wasn't working his butt off for fish or ground meat. That was the kind of thing we told

315

each other. About our husbands. Chantal once said: *les hommes*! swishing the spatula, rolling her eyes. Then she asked me how to say that in Swedish. *Männena*, I said. Even thinking about it afterwards, I thought that was the best expression. Chantal beat time with her spatula, repeating it with sharp e's: *ménnená*!

We fantasized about making a Swedish dinner for Roger, and I told her how you made meatballs, boiled brown beans to a pulp the shade of nylons and seasoned them with cinnamon, spirit vinegar and sugar. Chantal laughed so hard she got black-and-blue mascara rings under her eyes.

I needed her company, could spend hours on that stool, watching her perform her rites with a spatula and flannel potholders. But I was quite happy on my own, too. I often think back to that big room with the flagstone floor, the old wooden table, the callas and the whitewashed walls. I think of it as a room for the soul, that's the only way I can put it into words.

Something happened to me again, just as something had happened when I returned from Uppsala. I thought I might have a soul after all, or be developing one. And I mean something complete, not just a flutter of thoughts and impulses barely held together by a way of being.

I know I should have constantly been listening inward for the fetus growing inside me. But I was longing for another thing altogether. I wanted to recognize myself, have a feeling of familiarity when I turned inward. Feel — feel — feel. I did not know what all that really was, and most of the time I didn't believe in it. It seemed as improbable as my having become pregnant. Of course one could create a space around oneself as Chantal had done, rather than inside oneself. One could restrict, cut oneself off, in order to have a sense of tranquility and familiarity. If I looked inward all I saw was contradictions, anyway. In there was the denial of everything I said, the mirror image of everything I believed in — inverted. Every evening I could repeat the exercise, like a kind of yoga, if I chose: now I shall turn toward my nocturnal sun. At the very bottom of the lake is a sky. In me, too, my opposite rests as in a deep bowl.

But the sense of peace I experienced when I did this was not what I was looking for. It frightened me. I wanted to have a soul. I wanted to have a soul more than I wanted to have a baby.

I was often anxious at night. Hasse was a light sleeper and I didn't want to disturb him by turning on the light to read. He was so tired after work. He sneezed fabric dust, and he had a crease across his brow I hadn't noticed before. It looked kind of old-mannish. He was starting to look like his father, just as Jean-Loup looked like his. Perhaps I was carrying a little Curt Carlsson Curtman the second in my belly, a worried fetus with knotted fists, willing himself to sleep so he would have the energy for the ambitious life awaiting him when he opened his tightly-shut eyes.

I would put on my dressing gown and slippers in the darkness and shuffle across the stone floor. Every now and then I would crush a rusk worm under foot, and I might bump into the edge of the table before I reached the glass doors and slid them open. Outside the cicadas were still chirping and the darkness smelled of strange leaves. To get up to the kitchen I had to climb a narrow set of rough stone stairs at the back of the house. Sometimes a cat would try to slip in with me, but in the darkness it frightened and disgusted me. I went upstairs to heat some milk on the gas stove and sit on the stool reading in the light of the lamp over the sink. The hissing of the gas and the whispering of the milk as it began to simmer felt like company. And sometimes noises also seeped out of the bedroom, although it was at the other end of a hall with a cold stone floor.

They quarreled. Chantal's voice could sound like a shower of bullets striking sheet metal. It would soften as time passed. She screamed when she wept, a peculiar, birdlike scream. In the end he sometimes struck her. She may have been hysterical, and the blow for purposes of mental hygiene. But in point of fact I don't think he was much of a psychologist.

Naturally, I would never have dared to go knock. During the day I never even hinted that I knew. Some days her face was a little swollen, but it was impossible to tell whether that was from crying or from being hit. There was seldom more than a single blow. Then she would start to cry like a baby, as if being struck loosened a stopper inside. Occasionally the thought crossed my mind that somehow being hit like that was good for her. She would start to cry normally. He would comfort her. Then silence.

Jean-Loup? I don't know how deeply he slept. I would set my mug in the enamel sink and turn out the light. Silently, I would sneak off, taking one tiptoe step at a time so as not to graze snails, rusk worms, cats.

One day I went to get some ice cubes for our Camparis from the freezer compartment. I found a bird there. It had been cleaned, was half-frozen, a tiny little bird with a gray and brown striped coat of feathers and a red spot under its chin. The thought that they ate songbirds sickened me. But I'd never seen Chantal prepare them.

A few more times I found birds in that freezer compartment, desperate for a defrosting. Once the whole fridge smelled so awful I got suspicious and tore open a little cling film-wrapped packet I found among the drifts of frost. It contained a little semi-decomposed bird, the kind we call a shrike at home.

Chantal was embarrassed. No, they didn't eat them. She sent the birds to the Natural History Museum of Norway, in Stavanger. But I mustn't tell Roger.

Eventually I got the story out of her. It had happened when Roger was selling property in Capri. He had rented a villa in Anacapri, and she was often on her own. Jean-Loup was a baby. It was toward the end of April. Every day thousands of migratory birds would land on the island, and up at the bird sanctuary above San Michele the ornithologists set up their fine-mesh nets in the bushes to catch them. They didn't kill them like the boisterous Sunday hunters, who came by boat from Sorrento, or sometimes all the way from Naples just to pellet little birds with buckshot. They identified them, ring-marked a spindly leg and registered them in a ledger. Then they let them go.

Chantal got to know a Norwegian ornithologist. He taught her the name of every kind of bird they captured. She had never given birds more than a passing thought before. She had probably seen most kinds in Africa, but she didn't know any names. She hadn't given much thought to the men who shot them, either. Big, black-haired heavies. Sometimes she would come upon them in the *macchia*. Paths ran through it like tunnels in the thorny undergrowth. Of course she didn't dare walk there all alone, so the ornithologist went with her. She carried Jean-Loup in a pack on her back; he was just a baby and couldn't tell his father.

Stein was a bashful, sensitive lover.

"Ann-Marie," she said, "forgive me for asking. But does Hans make love to you that way?"

She used the French expression, *faire l'amour*. I confirmed that Hasse did it like that, that Nordic men made love that way, sometimes.

She hadn't heard from him since he left Capri. But she stressed that she was the one who had insisted he mustn't write to her. Roger had the key to their postal box.

When she found dead birds she would save them because she knew Stein wanted them for his museum. Sometimes little boys killed them with their slingshots. She would store them in the freezer compartment until she heard about someone who was flying to Northern Europe and would be able to put them in a postbox at the Copenhagen or Frankfurt airport. Otherwise they would rot on the way, Chantal said gravely. She also told me once that she would love to visit the city of Stavanger in Norway and see her birds at the Natural History Museum. She had sent him all kinds, including the southern European nightingale, the golden Oriole and the bee-eater. But it might not be a good idea to see Stein again. I thought she was right.

There was a country restaurant we would go to, a kind of inn owned by a man named Arturo. We would order *frango* from Arturo's wife and sit at rough-hewn tables overlooking the yard, where Arturo's son Gomes chased the wing-clipped cockerels. When he caught one he would cut off its head on the chopping block, and then stand there holding the body for as long as the wings went on flapping and the blood spurting from the neck. Then he would wipe the hatchet clean and toss the *frango* on to the kitchen steps. Sometimes he would be in so much of a hurry that the blood would go on running from the neck of the rooster down the kitchen steps and a pool of dark red blood would collect underneath. Meanwhile the guests had been served a jug of the fresh green wine, and had lit their cigarettes. It was a very popular place with whatever tourists found out about it. People would even rent cars just to drive out to Arturo's for his *frango*.

After a while a tall, slim girl came out and sat down to pluck the cockerel. She plucked at the feathers with determination, tearing them from the limp body that had had all the life pumped out of it. The sun was scorching, she sat there on the top step trying to get a little shade from the door frame over her head. Her face was bright with perspiration.

This was Ana Maria Conceição. That was how I saw her the first time. She gathered up the feathers in the lap of her burlap apron, and not until the very end, when she had to be very thorough, did she look at what her hands were doing. The minute a man crossed the yard she tossed out a comment to him. I suppose they were indifferent words, everyday chatter. But it sounded more significant if you didn't understand it. Conceição had a high, yelping voice. It could sound different when she was worried. But that was later, much later. Then it got hoarse and deep.

When the body was more or less plucked clean and lay there on the burlap, pitiful as an aborted fetus, she reached into the kitchen for a knife and an enamel bowl. She slit open the belly of the fowl and released from its muddle of dull yellow intestines the shiny purple stomach and the dark purple heart that was still throbbing. She tore out the lungs with her fingernails from where they were attached at the back, and the rough skin of her fingertips were covered with blood and gall. It took me some time to realize that her surly indifference was feigned. It was part of the show. Conceição knew very well that she was being watched and admired for her part in the mystery being performed in the hot yard. As soon as she had slit the craw and cleaned it of stones and grit she put it and the heart and the gizzard into the bowl and carried the body, dangling by one wing, into the sanctum sanctorum, the hot, cluttered kitchen. Sometimes the tourists would go stand in the kitchen doorway to watch Arturo fry the frango in amber olive oil. They would remember this, yes they would. The heat, the dog lying waiting for the scraps, his whole neck scratched raw with eczema. The braids of garlic, the baskets of peppers and onions, the half-eaten loaves. The swollen calves of the senhora, and her club-like feet in black felt slippers. Sometimes they tried to take pictures of the dim kitchen and of Arturo who, feeling he had nothing to hide, grinned at the shutter. People who had looked into the kitchen tended to order strong spirits before the meal, a *bagaço* or two. Arturo served the bird on a stainless steel platter that was his pride and joy, surrounded with big chunks of deep-fried potato. Conceição hadn't singed the cockerel, and bits of down and feather were still on it, particularly around the anus. The tourists ate this real frango and drank the indubitably real, rough wine and smacked their lips and shouted in a way they would never have done at home. I behaved that way myself the first time. I was under the influence of the *bagaço* and the wine in the sunshine, and I think I had also come with a strong desire for reality. But when we had lived there for some time I started shielding myself from it. I stopped drinking the tap water and started buying *agua mineral*, I pulled down the blinds when the sun got too hot. On Thursdays the local Swedes took turns serving pea soup dinners, and Hasse and I began to attend them. We would drink hot Cederlund arrack; the first time we brought a bottle of Skåne aquavit as a gift.

Conceição came to us because Arturo, who was her uncle, asked if she could start to work at the garment mill. But Hasse didn't have a job for her.

"Couldn't she start out helping around the house?" I asked.

What was Hasse supposed to say? There were a lot of us around the table, Arturo was leaning over us anticipating an answer. And so I got myself a *criada*.

Of course I had no need of a domestic. But everyone I knew here had one, and having a girl in the house was no expense at all. I wanted Conceição around me. I liked her. She exuded reality. Around me things were stagnant, like images, and exceptionally pretty. The Bougainvillea and the sea. The heavy Kosta goblets Hasse's father had given us, and the Spanish Fundador cognac shining in it. The stiff, lawn, cut short. We rented the whole house now, because Chantal and Roger had gone to France and wouldn't be back for a year.

I wanted to get at Conceição's reality. Sometimes I went with her to the outskirts of town, where she lived. But when I got it under my skin, the smell of fish and piss, the dusty road, the body of the cat hanging from the tree, the shouting voices, the smell of hooch, the faces of the children covered with scratch marks, the oily old felt hats on the men's heads, the drops of blood on the cement, then I warded it off and wanted to go back home. I returned, had a Fundador and a shower. Then I sat staring at the television. I powdered myself with talcum powder. I used mouthwash. I played records. I read the precious Swedish novels that arrived having crossed the sea or all of Europe.

At any rate, I liked to listen when the *criada* told stories. They were mainly about the complex hostilities and the many attempts at revenge between the Ferreira and Valvente families. I never really worked out if they were truly afraid of each other, or saw the whole thing as a kind of game. The Ferreira children grew up on hatred of the Valventes. It was like the smell of sun dried fish and piss. They never thought about it; it was part of their lives.

A stone broke the window when they were having dinner. Fragments of glass showered onto their meal. Of course when they rushed out into the darkness there was no one there. The stone was on the cement kitchen floor and they gathered around it. I never heard how they retaliated for that one.

I saw the cat myself. It was hanging by its back legs from an olive tree. According to Conceição, it had been there for a week. They had no intention of taking it down. It was just as well people saw what the Valventes were like, and what they had done with the Ferreiras' cat.

"But did you care about it?" I asked. "Wasn't it just one of those cats that prowled around your house?"

Its body was long and had become even longer and all stiff from hanging there, with dark yellow patches on its coat, that was all matted, and dirty white paws. Eventually the blood must have drained to its head, and it stopped struggling. Its brain may have burst, which somebody thought was a good joke.

"The Valventes," said Conceição. "The Valventes hanged our darling cat. Maria Graça and little João cry about it every day."

The old olive tree was probably planted before the war of independence from Spain. It had dusty leaves and a gnarled, cracked trunk. The cruelty was even older. It turned my stomach. I sniffed my hand that still bore a trace of the scent of soap, and stared at my shoes on the dry, brick-red road. I tried to fight down the nausea,

322

and the saliva that filled my mouth. I didn't believe Conceição's talk about the cat having been held so dear by her little brother and sister, because none of them cared a bit about animals. It had been nothing but a cat that hung around the piles of rubbish outside the Ferreiras' house. Conceição gave me a sentimental version, adapted to my Nordic nature, my softness and my innocence.

Perhaps hanging a cat by its back legs outside someone's house was an ancient insult, how was I to know? I recalled gestures I had seen, exposed body parts. There were words I didn't understand and didn't want to ask Conceição about. She also wanted me to retain my innocence. She was sixteen and I was twenty-two when we met, but she treated me maternally. Sometimes I didn't want it like that. Then I would give her orders in a high-pitched mechanical, upper class voice. I had good teachers. There were plenty of women in our neighborhood to learn that from. But my change of register bothered Conceição no more than an afternoon shower. She stood there ironing my white blouses. The iron thudded against the felt-covered board and there was the smell of clean, hot, cotton cloth. She sang as she ironed and my bad mood evaporated.

"A senhora quer café?"

"Sim, uma chávena."

And we had our coffee with *pastéis de nata*. That was when I started gaining weight.

Sometimes when I'm ironing and I smell the clean cotton and the hot iron I find myself missing Conceição. Of course I am perfectly able to wash my floors and iron my own blouses, but I smell the strong scent of reality that surrounded her. Most of all, I suppose I miss her taking care of me. She was old for her age and maternal. I think she was born to mothering. That was what Elisabeth would have had. All that. The stink of piss. The disgusting *bacalhau*. Conceição's thin, tanned hands smoothing and stroking. Her chattering and tidying. The Valventes' hate. Maria Rosario's shrill voice and hard hands and the love, the love that was always there, above and beneath every sound and smell, like the playing of the cicadas in the dark of night, like the smell of the sea, like the taste of salt on one's lips.

That is her rightful legacy, just as Maria de Lourdes is her name and Ana Maria is Conceição's. But I took it from her.

I got my baby in haste. There are no other words. I talked Hasse into it. The whole thing happened so fast. It had to be fast, fast. Why? Would he have refused otherwise? Of course I cannot know, but he was definitely reluctant. I imagine he would have liked to think it over, take his time. But what was there to think over, I asked? Genes. Absurd. Genes were just ridiculous. We would outsmart every gene with our competence, our vitality, our potential for happiness! It was my will, my accursed will, that was the way. I suddenly knew what life was supposed to be like. I was meant to have a child, there was no doubt about it. I imagine I thought I was made for it, a real genius in the mothering department. Yes, we were quite simply suited to happiness, Hasse and myself. Everything was going to be fine. I was in control of reality, wasn't I? Finally in control.

Of course that wasn't what I had in my mind then. But when I saw Conceição skinny and weepy, and heard that low, hoarse voice she had that winter when she was trying everything, even doing it with a parsley root, and when she ran away from the man in Miragaia, the one with the dirty hands, just got up off his oilcloth-covered table and ran, it never so much as crossed my mind that anything like that could have happened to me. Or when I heard Maria Rosario's loud voice, raw from so much shouting, saw her leave João at that indescribable crèche outside the factory gates, a storage shed with a concrete floor where two woman looked after the children in the sense that they kept them from crawling out from between the partitions where they were encaged like calves or dirty laying hens — that was most definitely not my world, it was nothing but cruelty. I don't think I ever thought about what kept me apart from that world. It was money, and money alone — and not even all that much money, either, when it came right down to it. I honestly think I imagined that I was in greater control, had more will power, and more of a right to happiness.

We were married in a breathless rush and scurried off abroad. Every morning Hasse went off in a little black Anglia and I sat trying to learn Portuguese from a textbook written in French, and I spelled my way through the newspapers as well as I could and made our meals. I was frightened all the time. And only grew more frightened with every passing day. The feeling didn't go away as Hasse had said it would, it intensified.

I started looking in the phone book, at first randomly I think, but I was looking under the heading *Médicos*. What I was looking for I am not really sure. But I wanted, although I didn't dare to go back to that hale and hearty type who prescribed my vitamins and checked my urine for protein, to tell someone I was afraid.

That was how I found Jaime Oliveria-Cruz listed under the subheading *Doenças de senhoras, Ginecologia*. Strange to think about my having found Jaime by letting my fingers do the walking through the yellow pages of a phone book.

He was a dark-skinned, handsome man, not at all overweight in those days, and he spoke excellent French. On his desk he had a lovely little lacquered model of a uterus with the Fallopian tubes and ovaries, and he used it to show me how the egg had been fertilized and how the normal course of events would run. He was extremely patient and took plenty of time. But it didn't help. I was full of terror and thought I was going to die. What little I knew about childbirth I had read in the *Nordic Family Encyclopedia*, volume III, from Ca to Dr. If this fetus, now only the size of a thumb according to Jaime Oliveria-Cruz, was allowed to go on growing, it would inflict a bleeding wound on me, and when it forced its way out it would kill me. He did not find it strange at all that a woman could be frightened of giving birth.

I was in bed the afternoon the bleeding started. Jaime sent a nurse. I saw her arrive on her bicycle, her wimple flapping above her derriere. She helped me to get to the hospital, and late that night the fetus I never saw was expelled.

Jaime was the one who phoned Hasse and told him I had been taken to hospital and was miscarrying, and when he came to see me the next morning it was already over.

He cried. Yes, he wept. He sat next to me leaning forward, laying his head on the pillow of my hospital bed, crying because there wasn't going to be a baby. I am still almost unable to understand it. He was so young then. Nothing would have been easier to comprehend than if he had been reluctant to be married and have a family. And here he was, unhappy because it came to naught. He also said he felt terribly sorry for me. I brooded over that a lot.

It was a miserable winter. The house turned out to be a cold dwelling, and we had to get several electric heaters. The camellias clung to the tree. They never wilted, just rotted. The callas in the flowerbed reminded me of Swedish funerals, of wax flowers and wreaths for All Saints' Day. The boxwood hedge reeked of cat pee, and the butterfly-like petals of the bougainvillea dried up like paper. I read my books and wrote my columns for *The Correspondent* — thank God for those 'Sunbeams'. The early columns were quite touristy I expect, because learning Portuguese turned out to be harder than I had anticipated. The strange thing was that Hasse was quickly speaking fluently in spite of the fact that he had never held a grammar book in his hands. He learned by talking with the senhoritas at the factory, whereas I would stammer the minute I had to say anything beyond the set phrases. It was my accursed shyness! It made me lonely. I sat at home in the villa, staring at the rotten camellias and not daring to complain. After all, I only had myself to blame, didn't I?

I didn't have to do very much. Not much was expected of a middle class woman here. Synnöve was a thousand kilometers away! It was basically quite sufficient that my hair looked nice and that I had elegant shoes and perfect nylons. It helped if my nails were well-manicured and dinner was tasty. But I was a bit bored. At home I had always walked in the woods; when school was too dull I had skipped classes and walked the forest paths. But here the countryside consisted mainly of rubbish dumps and the occasional *boa vista*. There were the mountains, of course, but nobody went walking in them. People went on outings by car and walked on sandy paths in parks. It was so much simpler. Why make things difficult?

I cannot claim that I was suffering, but I was stultified. One day I counted my shoes, and discovered I had thirty-two pairs. That horrified me. I weeded out a whole pile, and gave them to the *criada*. Although we both knew that Conceição wore size 36 and mine were 38s, we never mentioned it. She would sell them of course, but there was no need for me to know that or think about it.

Everything was much better now that I had Conceição. I woke up every morning to quite a pleasant routine. I heard dogs barking and cocks crowing. I knew what kind of a day I had ahead of me. All I really needed to do was to make a nice evening meal. Conceição did the topping and tailing, the peeling, the chopping, and the scrubbing. We made real deep-fried potatoes, frying wedges in deep olive oil until they were golden, fresh chicken and little *codornizes*, soup of strained vegetables, and lovely *pudim flã* made with real egg yolks and a vanilla pod boiled up with the cream. That was the kind of thing I served when Hasse invited the company's Portuguese owner to dinner, and for the Swedes we made a roast with creamy sauce and marinated cucumber. Afterwards we usually had fruit or cheese, a rich *queijo da serra* I can still crave. This gastronomy, not mastered by Conceição — nor by me, either, from the outset — was the justification for my existence. Well, that, and its offshoots: flower arranging and finding pretty pastel colored candles to match the table linen. Washing the expensive embroidered cloth from Madeira. No one could do those things but me. Hasse actually had no idea of what Conceição did, and I was careful not to exaggerate her skills. Nor did I tell him she was the one who brought reality to the house where I was as shut in as the cicada who got stuck behind the sliding door of the closet. It chirped for three weeks and was driving us insane, until it starved to death.

I was in Jaime Oliveira-Cruz' office again, sitting in the patient's chair with the pretty lacquered model in front of me, a shiny, little pear-shaped container holding the Fallopian tubes graciously in front of it, with their swaying cilia to catch the egg. Jaime sat leaning back, his white coat unbuttoned so his cream colored shirt and elegant gabardine trousers could be seen. The way he was sitting I could see the swell of his sexual organ beneath this trouser cloth. I was fascinated, and thought it was because in those days it was still unusual for a man to wear such tight-cut trousers. I felt no desire for this man yet, or at least I didn't know it.

I had made an appointment and was sitting there to ask him if he would consider performing an abortion. Instead I said something completely different. He was politely conversing with me in French because my Portuguese was still fairly weak; I spoke it like a child. Jaime said:

"Now tell me, Madame, what I can do for you. You cannot be in poor health — you look far too well and beautiful for that."

When he spoke French, he sounded pleasantly ironic. Our conversations were always slightly imprudent, or perhaps I should call them lighthearted. That may have been why I dared to say things I would otherwise never have dreamed of saying. This time I held a whole little diatribe, and to my vast surprise I thought it sounded both considered and well-prepared. I did not ask him about the abortion, but instead about whether he thought it would be possible for me to adopt a Portuguese newborn whose unwed mother was unable to care for it. She was a girl who had run away from the abortionist's at the very last moment because he had frightened her. I told him she was my very own *criada*, Ana Maria Conceição Ferreira. She had had the misfortune of having given in to the eighteen-year-old she was in love with, and was now pregnant. That would not have been a disaster, of course, if he had married her. Her own mother had been having babies since she was seventeen and was still having them at forty-six. But José Antonio Dimas, that was his name, had enlisted and was now in Moçambique. He hadn't been in touch. There was no question but that he intended to abandon her, and all she had before her was the prospect of shame and an impossible life.

"My husband has only been here as a trainee," I said. "Now he is going home to join his father's business. We have already bought a home, in fact. Everything's arranged."

"Excellent," said Jaime. "So you will return to Northern Europe. And you want to take your *criada's* little baby with you."

"What does your husband have to say about it?" he went on to ask.

What could I say? I certainly couldn't tell him Hasse had no idea about my plan, that I hadn't known of it myself until I was sitting here in his patient's chair.

"Otherwise the girl will have to leave the baby at one of those horrid crèches," I said. "If she ever manages to get another job, at a factory or as a *criada*. And the shame. No one will marry her."

I felt sorry for Conceição, and I had gone to his office to ask if he could perform an abortion for her. But how would she have paid for it? Conceição wept constantly and was thin and hysterical. She saw no way out. She had developed that worried, hoarse voice I had never heard before. On Christmas Eve she suddenly collapsed onto the couch when we were taking the Christmas decorations out of their box. I had asked her to pull our tree out of its cardboard roll and she removed it so roughly I got annoyed. It opened like an umbrella and the branches, fully equipped with plastic needles, were pulled tight with a little mechanism you had to be gentle with. She pulled so hard most of the decorations, little glass ornaments and glittering hearts, went flying to the floor.

"What do you think you're doing?" I asked.

She wasn't herself, and I said so. I held an instructive little sermon to the best of my ability, because I felt she was losing interest in her work and was always in a foul mood. I may have been a bit too hard on her, because she lay down on the sofa, sobbing. Then it all came out of her, José Antonio and the parsley root and the abortionist, and how when she found herself there she got cold feet. I was upset. I had no idea at the time of how common her story was. She told me her cousin, who was married, had had six or seven abortions and nearly died from the last one. She was quite sure her mother had given herself abortions with a crocheting needle. She had been in the hospital for some time a couple of years ago with a fever. But Conceição had been too frightened. Scared to death. She sobbed until her whole body trembled, her thin shape torn this way and that by the hurricane of tears. I had no idea what to do or say.

"It costs so much money, senhora," she said. "Sixty escudos is what a dirty swine like that man in Miragia takes. And it's so painful, that's what my cousin told me, you aren't allowed to cry out because then people in the building would know what he was up to. You can end up in prison yourself and he threatens you if you cry. Sixty escudos that swine costs, I wish there were someone else. But a midwife who does it on the sly costs even more and a doctor, well that's the best way to do it, but a doctor costs two thousand, senhora! And you have to have an address, and that kind of address isn't easy to come by. Oh, what am I to do? José is never coming back, that's one thing I know. Not back to me, anyway. He despises me, senhora."

She was speaking from the depths of her experience of that scoundrel José Antonio, whom she had loved desperately just a couple of months ago and whom she must have trusted. I told her that I had been pregnant myself when I had got married, but that nothing came of it. I imagine she knew, although we hadn't told her about it. Then the little nut wept again, saying poor, poor senhora Ana Maria, you lost your little child. She sobbed so hard she soaked through the plush cushions on the sofa and I told her to sit up and blow her nose and calm down. Now we were going to fix ourselves some coffee and drink it and then go on getting things ready for the Christmas Eve dinner. We were making a rabbit stew with red wine, and we had the potatoes to peel and the olive oil to heat, and we were just going to think about the practicalities that had to be accomplished so the house wouldn't plummet into chaos and senhor Curtman lose his temper and be upset when he came home from the mill. And then I would figure something out.

The best thing I could come up with was to go and see Jaime Oliveira-Cruz. But I never asked him to perform the abortion. The plan about adopting Conceição's baby must have been there, complete inside me, lying in its cardboard roll, and when I sat there in the patient's chair staring at his gabardine trousers, it popped out.

I asked Jaime to talk to Conceição and propose the adoption to her. She came from his office the day after *Véspera de Reis* with a crumpled, soaking wet hand-kerchief in her hand, to tell me he didn't perform abortions and that he didn't know anyone who did, that it was a terrible thing, and a violation of the laws of both God and man. A doctor who did such things ran the risk of being convicted to two years' hard labor he had said, and been very stern (of course he had been speaking Portuguese) and instead of thinking of that kind of way out, she should be thinking of having the baby and giving it up for adoption, he had said. If he could only find a kind, well-to-do couple for parents, the baby would have a good life, that was his conviction. The only thing he could help her with now was a prescription for vitamins and a promise to ask around for a childless couple who would be willing to take care of her baby.

He did that, and Conceição was extremely astonished and enormously grateful. Her mother was told that she was pregnant and that we were going to adopt the baby once it was born. Maria Rosario gave her daughter three hard slaps on the face, one on her right cheek, one on her left cheek, and another on her right. She shouted and screamed for an entire evening. But her husband, who was at a football match, never heard anything about it. Jaime arranged things so that Conceição got to go off to a private clinic up in Tras ó Montes. At home they said doctor Oliveria-Cruz had arranged a position for her in a good family, and when she came back to Porto there would be a job at the garment mill, Hasse had organized that. His contract would be coming to an end soon, and I went home before him and started making curtains for the house.

I made curtains and selected furniture upholstery and waited for my baby. It was growing in another woman's body, that was true, but just then that meant very little.

Elisabeth was born on São João's day, 23 June 1959. Jaime went up to see Hasse himself that evening to tell him. They went out to dinner together after Hasse phoned me.

That evening I felt lonely. I sat there in the semi-furnished house not knowing whether I should bike over to Jenny's or open a bottle of wine all by myself. I had been very surprised when the baby was a girl. I had believed all along it would be a boy, and I had been afraid, at least a little bit afraid, that he would look like José Antonio Dimas, who was certainly not the man I would have chosen to father my child. Now, to my astonishment, I was pleased it was a girl, and all my fears that this child would bear any external or internal similarities to José Antonio were gone with the wind. However, I wouldn't be able to name the baby Henning, as I had intended.

I took my bike and went over to the Otters to tell them the news. They didn't display as much pleasure as I had expected. In fact they had been quite reserved about the adoption throughout.

I felt extremely odd. In Porto people were celebrating the feast of São João, but here we were sitting outside behind a house in the Upco estate, chatting. Not until later, when we drove out to Vanstorp for the midsummer fest did I realize what I wanted the little girl to be named: Elisabeth, naturally!

It was a windless, warm midsummer, and Fredrik's little car was very stuffy.

330

This was the first time he'd bought a car that wasn't second hand. It was a green Volvo sedan, and he was so proud of it he couldn't just get himself to drive straight to Vanstorp, he had to take a long detour, so we were on the road forever. He talked on and on about the car, and his voice was loving. I sat in the back seat feeling car-sick. When we finally got out to Vanstorp it was very late. They had already put up the maypole and now people were just milling quietly around in the field. It was that kind of thin, blue twilight I had missed so when I lived in Porto, where the cicadas chirped in the darkness. But now I couldn't take pleasure in it. The smell of birch leaves and coffee just made me feel lonely. I wanted to be happy, but I couldn't. I was getting more and more irritated with Jenny for her indifference and her nega-tive attitude, and with Fredrik for being so foolishly enamored with a car, with the festivities going on around me, and the fiddlers fiddling away, so enthusiastically and so out of tune. When we got back to the Otters' I sat out on the patio in the cool summer night thinking about the baby. In the morning I had a fever.

Jenny said I'd been too lightly dressed. "This isn't Portugal my girl," she said, and God only knew she was right about that. I couldn't think about anything but the baby girl and I think it was my happiness and my concern about her that gave me the fever. I wondered if they would let Conceição have the baby with her or if she would never see her daughter. If they let her hold her and nurse her, perhaps she wouldn't want to give her up. How would the baby be fed? Jaime had said we couldn't have the child until she was two months old, because before that there was no way of being sure there weren't any hereditary deformities or diseases.

I had to find out if Conceição had returned to Porto or if she was with her baby. I had to ask Jaime to arrange to get her away, but I was ashamed. It felt niggardly to begrudge her holding the child in her arms or to her breast. I think it was that evening in the Otters' crowded sitting room with the curtains pulled and the blue flicker of the television screen, with the smoke from Fredrik's pipe and the mid-summer sun stubbornly trying to get in through the cracks between the curtains that I felt, for the first time, some uncertainty about what we had got ourselves into. I had an anxious inkling of the fact that feelings cannot be governed by will power, and I wished I had someone to talk to. But Hasse was far away, and Jenny thought I had already been talking about the baby too much. She would be pleased when it was a reality, she said. She emphasized the word reality. But the child was already a reality.

That made me realize that they'd probably christen her at the clinic. The nuns would, of course, be eager to make a Catholic of her. I didn't mind that, but the bad part was they would surely give her a name that wouldn't work in Sweden, particularly not in a Swedish school.

Early the next morning I phoned to instruct them to christen the baby Elisabeth. I was told she had already been baptized, and that at the request of her mother she had been named Maria de Lourdes.

"But that's not what we want!" I said. "We don't want her to be called Conceição or de Lourdes or anything to do with miracles. She must be called Elisabeth!"

"That's also a name linked to miracles," said the clinic director dryly, bringing the conversation to a close.

I decided I would have her name entered into the parish register as Elisabeth Maria de Lourdes here in Sweden, when we applied to adopt her.

It was a long wait. Those two months passed slowly. Finally, in early September, I went down with a little suitcase full of baby clothes. I flew to Lisbon and went on to Porto by train. Hasse met me there, and Jaime Oliveira-Cruz drove us to Tras ò Montes to the clinic.

The nuns would come toward me down a long corridor, and one of them would be carrying the little girl — that was my mental image. But Jaime said she had developed an infection and hadn't quite recovered yet. I was frightened, but he laughed at my worry.

"Even little babies get colds," he said. "That's all it is."

Instead, they took us down a long corridor to a room with one single crib in it. It looked like a little enameled box. I saw through a window set in the wall that there was a baby in the box. A dark head of hair against the white pillowcase.

"Goodness, why is she all alone in there?"

The director answered that she might be contagious. The room was cool and smelled of laundry bluing and lavender. On the white wall above the enamel box was a black crucifix. The director bent over, her wimple blocking my view of the little face. I was afraid she would wake her too roughly, so I grasped at her arm.

"Don't pick her up," I said. "She might start to cry."

The others went and stood by the window, waiting for me as I bent over the child, who was sleeping deeply. I touched her cheek lightly with my index finger, but she didn't wake.

"I don't want to wake her," I said. "She might be frightened. If I could please have a chair, I'd like to sit here until she wakes up."

"Faça como quiera," said the director, waddling off in her starched habit.

Jaime got me a chair from the hallway, and he and Hasse went down to the garden and sat on a bench under a frangipani tree that had finished blooming months ago. They sat there smoking and talking, and every now and then I walked over to the window and waved to them. I sat waiting in that room for a long time for the little girl to open her eyes and look at me.

I have so often wondered what it is like to give birth, to actually bear down until a hard head, a slithery body, and a cry slip out between your thighs. I have wondered what one feels for the child one has carried.

There is a kind of astonishment in some female animals when they give birth for the first time. They sniff at the newborn with their muzzles or noses, as if it were the most alien thing in the world. A few moments ago it did not exist. Immediately, they use their tongues, and taste the film of mucus enclosing the body. The instinct to nurture, to lick clean and dry, to release from suffocating membranes, and anything that might prevent breathing, is triggered in a trivial and ingenious way by the fact that it tastes good to them.

It has been a long, long time since we did any licking. We deliver, equipped with the expectations and knowledge with which we are imprinted. Queens and prima donnas hold their babies, as we are to hold ours. They look happy. You can also see how to do it if you go to the beach on a summer's day and watch pappas and mammas hold their children, skin to skin.

When children get beatings you seldom see it. We whip and torment in secret because we are a hypocritical species. A female animal routinely and quite openly kicks away the kid who has suckled long enough. A gentle but firm kick.

We take love and torment to extremes. Sickening tangles of caresses and corporal punishment. Insidious love. Hate with embroidered edging.

Are we fundamentally alien to that which issues forth from our bodies? Had we not been taught otherwise, we might have poked at it as if it were some anomaly we had produced: a pimple, a discharge, a little spot on a gall apple that houses a black worm and may contain death.

I do not know if there is one single primal, unambiguous feeling innate to a woman who has just given birth. Possibly exhaustion. Even the pride of having brought forth a being who did not previously exist is conditioned by circumstance. The woman who gave birth in solitude and tightened her hand around the neck of her bastard child, born in secrecy, has also given birth to her shame. Poor women bear anxiety, headaches and worries. Bear toil.

The feelings we call primal spring up most readily in newly-built homes with garages and bathrooms and guest toilets.

What did Conceição feel? Pain? Shame? Relief? I suppose I will never know.

The first thing I saw of Elisabeth was a head of dark fluffy hair, the contour of a cheek and a wrinkled red hand in a tight fist on a pillow. All my hale-and-hearty newly-built-home-primal instinct fell away like a singed layer of outer skin. I was frightened. And a day or two later I felt certain I was frightened for good reasons.

She had an ear infection. They wanted to keep her at the clinic a while, for observation and treatment. But Jaime Oliveira-Cruz, who was there with Hasse and me, settled it. He wrote a prescription for penicillin and we took Elisabeth off with us in a white bassinette. First to Porto to pack the last of the things in the villa, where we had broken our lease. Then north by car, heading for the newly-decorated house in Sweden. Our lives were charged with the prerequisites for happiness, like buns filled with raisins.

At the border between Spain and France, the little girl developed diarrhea. We gave her more penicillin and hurried on through France. A stream of yellow excrement the color of gall ran ceaselessly out of her tired, tormented body. Her little legs and arms trembled, her face a tight grimace of pain. I watched helplessly as the insides of her thighs and her little rump grew red and blistered with the chafing diarrhea. When we got to Paris she had begun to show signs of dehydration, and I sat in a hotel room trying to feed her sugar water by the teaspoonful. She was limp and had stopped crying. Her eyelids were shut tight and creased.

Hasse drove around Paris in the hellish traffic to find a doctor. Paris is a rough city where people are polite. At the hotel reception desk there was a corpulent middle-aged woman with a head of gorgeous red hair piled up in a cloud and stiff with hairspray. Her eyelids looked like black swallows' wings, at the top which green eye shadow shimmered. Around her neck she wore a double strand of pearls the size of cherries. They were artificial, of course, but still beautiful. I recall her as if she had been a graven image, a shining, elegant, reproduction of power and perhaps charity. She was all I saw of Paris, and I talked to her about Elisabeth, about my anxiety that had crescendoed to terror, and about the suffering and limpness of the baby that seemed to be transporting her closer and closer to death by the hour.

"Toujours des malheurs, madame," the goddess image pronounced solemnly but mechanically. "Toujours des malheurs."

A pathetic blonde mother seeks a mother of her own while a little child is dying in Paris. Le grand malheur! I wonder what it would have taken to shake that goddess up. Hardly the Bomb or the plague. But the loss of six hundred new francs for an unpaid hotel bill, it transpired before our sojourn was over. When I came down to the lobby one morning, a guest had run out on the bill, and she was in a fearful uproar.

By that time the little wrinkled creature upstairs had begun to straighten out, her limbs no longer trembled. Her bottom was dry again. An aged Jewish physician who looked like an anti-Semitic caricature and extracted payment before he would even unwrap the child, had explained that she was allergic to penicillin. I trembled with gratitude.

"But her ear infection?"

He shrugged his shoulders demonstratively.

"Il faut choisir, madame."

We were back on the road to Sweden ten days later. I had been frightened, so deeply frightened that I could only see one solution: get me home. Because the awful thing was not actually that there could be a painful ear infection in the world and a concomitant allergic reaction to penicillin. The awful thing was that people shrugged their shoulders demonstratively and admitted it outright. At home where I came from, chaos and blind cruelty were not acknowledged. Order, justice and social democracy prevailed. The main thing is not what you have but what there is a consensus about your having.

We got home and things settled down. I sat with the thin little body of the girl in a house I had furnished but that was alien to me. The little body was alien to me, too. One of the worst nights in Paris I had fallen asleep toward morning and dreamed a dream about brutal, atrocious death for the child. It was my hand that tightened, my beak that pecked. In the dream I entered a room where Hasse was sitting waiting for me, and I said: "It's over now." I felt liberated, as if I had been able to vomit, or some pus-filled abscess had burst.

Afterwards, the dream filled me with horror and shame. That was one of the reasons I wanted to get home as fast as possible. Now I was home. There was the smell of wallpaper paste, wood, and new fabrics. I had never really partaken of the security that was said to prevail around me. I had hovered above it, wandered between worlds. I had believed that acquiring this baby would be a sure ticket into a world where order and consensus reigned. I never thought about realities. What kind of a mother Lisa had been, what Henning had been like as a father, and that I would probably not be one bit better or worse than they were. Now I sat waiting for security and maternal love, for them to come sneaking they way sleep creeps up on a person who has taken a sleeping pill. What came instead were the after-shocks of the trauma. Perhaps they never really went away. Elisabeth has the scar of her burst eardrum; she is quite hard of hearing in her left ear. A bitter disability for a teenager who never wants to run the risk of being exposed.

I have my own little scar. It is on my emotions. I doubt my ability to love. I have seen it burst, and cruelty and indifference pour out of it.

One afternoon I had gone out into the woods behind the housing estate. I was alone. Hasse was watching the baby and reading the Sunday paper. The house was filled with the aroma of a lightly browned veal roast simmering in a brand new enameled cast iron roasting pan. The radiators were humming.

One hundred, two hundred steps away was the woods. It was autumn now. The leaves had fallen and begun to decompose. It was so quiet I could hear an assembly of little birds busying themselves around a juniper bush. I sat down on a stump and watched them. What were they doing? Flying fussily to and fro, pecking at branches with their beaks. There was a soft chirping sound. Were they communicating with one another, or did these sounds just issue from them for no particular reason? I didn't even know what they were called. They looked like faded blue tits. The stillness was boundless and horrifying and in the midst of it these birds who weighed no more than a letter, officiously preoccupied one late autumn day without passions to puff them up and swell their little bodies. Was everything of equal import?

I thought I glimpsed the bronze goddess with the copper hair and the shimmering green eyelids.

"Toujours des malheurs. Toujours des malheurs."

Her colors belonged to this quiet wood.

It's been cleared now, incidentally. Handsome houses were built there.

Vimmeln is a long, narrow lake. It opens a gash in the landscape, a bloodless wound. At dawn the water is sometimes like thin, gray milk. I saw it through the glassed-in veranda, so poorly puttied that humid drafts of air and bird song pushed through to me.

I have never been there since that late summer morning. But before that I spent a lot of time there. When Hasse went traveling with the company collection and I was left alone at home with Elisabeth, I often went out to the cottage with the Otters. I slept on the veranda, but Elisabeth always slept in the bedroom with Jenny and Fredrik. It could get too cold for her out there. I think, too, Jenny wanted to have her there, be the first one to touch her warm, soft skin in the morning.

The sound of little waves beating against the rocks on the shore and the chirping of the unidentified birds were the first things I heard when I awoke. That morning it was cold, but the early hours of that day merge with other mornings when the milky cold water mixed with the air and the mists. I couldn't see the surface of the water until I sat up. Lying down, I could see the sky and the bizarre collection of trinkets Jenny had on the windowsills. Sand on the floor and mildewed beach robes hanging in the corner. I often said to Jenny that it smelled like the thirties, but she would just chuckle softly as if I had no idea what I was talking about. Perhaps to her the thirties smelled fresh and good, or extremely repugnant, of blood and refuse. Her laugh was uninterpretable.

I stepped down onto the sandy floor and started pulling on the clothes I had folded on the rattan chair. The deck of cards was still on the table, and there were a few sweets, bridge mix, left in the bowl. We had taken it out after Elisabeth fell asleep.

"Well, here we sit, just you and us," Jenny had said, collecting up the cards after the last round. Then she had been embarrassed and risen quickly, mumbling about making a cup of something. The pile of playing cards was exactly where she had left it, under the lamp. Now a matte reflection of daylight shone from the faces of the cards. There we had sat, them and me. To me there was nothing odd about it.

When Hasse was out of town I usually spent time with the Otters. We had no social life, because Hasse wasn't at all accustomed to having people around. There had always just been himself, his father, and the company. In their gray house there had been his mother and bottles. In Porto we spent a lot of time alone, and we didn't mind. Each of us separately and a family was a world. The city was neither as built up nor as built in as now. That was extremely clear amongst *os estrangeiros*.

But Jenny seemed to think I should be a young homemaker tripping through a meadow of social pleasantries and obligations. I had married into the Rotary circle, hadn't I? I could have all the clothes I wanted and I could have venison roasts. She was probably glad I came with them out to their cottage, but she would have been even more pleased if I had been a bit more sociable now and then. She and Fredrik would still have played cards with Ingrid and Arne Johansson, but she could have told them all about me. She would have dealt me into the conversation with a little slap of a card on the table every time Arne started his tiresome boasting about their son Ulf who was the great bandy star of the town and everybody's idol. Ingrid always sat silently when Arne was bragging. She arranged her hand and smoked. She had once said about Ulf — and her tone of voice had been sharp — "I gave birth to him and raised him until he was five. The rest was Arne's doing."

Occasionally I had the feeling she was the only person in town who disliked Ulf. I considered Elisabeth; skin as thin as bougainvillea leaves, soft, black wisps of hair and strong fingers that grasped mine. The whites of her eyes still perfectly white, her short, eager breathing against my neck. Was it possible that one's own flesh and blood could be so totally severed from oneself that one could choose to dislike it? I had seen and could possibly comprehend the dark emotional undercurrents of love-hate and disappointment between parents and children. But the caustic Ingrid Johansson had liberated herself from her son and left her maternal feelings behind like a lump of afterbirth. The rest was Arne's doing, she said, sucking on those eternal cigarettes of hers.

Now and then Ulf and his wife would come too. She was a creature called Marie-Louise who always sat on the edge of her chair.

"We'd better be thinking about getting on home, Ulf," she would say, squinting at her watch that was white gold with a face smaller than a penny. She had a helmet of teased hair and eyeliner wings at the corners of her eyes. I knew their life was planned in detail. When Ulf was no longer able to play active bandy he would become a sales director. That Beowulf who had borne the whole town to victory in the national league would be able to sell anything to anybody. They would have a house of their own with a clematis on the south wall. Children who got good educations. Golf instead of bandy.

His father had been a failure in his day. He had gone on to coach the bandy team of a small industrial town where the business community had decided to sponsor local sports. They had moved there for a while. Ingrid had been unable to get a job, so she knitted display items for a handicrafts shop window. When I brought Elisabeth home she was the only person who hadn't knitted me a baby present; she claimed she never intended to touch a pair of knitting needles again. She had spent three years knitting, and had founded the local chapter of the Social Democratic Women's Association. When they came back to town she went back to Curre Clothes as a seamstress. Jenny found it embarrassing. Arne had been part of the unsuccessful workshop experiment, of course, but later he was taken on in the stockroom of a hardware store. Now he actually managed the stockroom, and Ingrid didn't really need to work.

Marie-Louise, Ulf's babydoll wife, didn't want to spend a minute longer than courtesy required in the smell of the Otters' cottage. She was an upwardly mobile climber on the town social ladder. Jenny glanced at me worriedly.

"Some people are just drawn downward," she said ominously. "Henning always has been, as we know."

I found the thought that I was being drawn downward by playing cards with them in their summer cottage touching. When Marie-Louise departed with Ulf in tow, leaving behind a contempt as tangible as the smell of Hermès from her clothing, Jenny made an unsolicited comment in my direction:

"Well, you're a funny one, you are."

That meant she liked me. I was accustomed to Jenny's double entry bookkeeping. It had nothing to do with falseness. She just wanted to seem wise.

I considered myself fortunate. I was thriving in the welfare state with its confidence in the citizen. There's nothing like the feeling of a pile of hundred-kronor notes folded in your purse. At the time, I kept my housekeeping money in a tea tin. Hasse filled it up. I still have that tin, black with red flowers, and I find it pleasurable to look at. And all those clothes — well-tailored, neat, flattering. We were in the business, you know. They cost us very little. There was no question of expensive clothes, no gaudy crocodile handbags, no light gray hornbuck ones, long, rough and vulgar. No big, ostentatiously silent cars, either, nothing that might trigger some nemesis. For capitalists ("Capitalism rakes home the kitty," said Ingrid Johansson every time I won a hand of cards), Hasse and I were as unassuming as sparrows. We just pecked. Maybe my going along with the Otters to their cabin, my sticking with the cottage folk, was a kind of magic spell I was casting around my good fortune.

But this was the last day dawning milky white, misty gray, and before evening I would be poor again. The lake reflected nothing yet, its surface clouded, awash with mist. The birds were calling in the clouds of haze and the islet where Ingrid and Arne's cottage was hidden from sight. I would have liked to go in and collect Elisabeth and bring her into bed with me, feel her sleepy warmth, the smell of soap and night and pee on her skin. There were children who were night wanderers, who always came into their parents' bed, I knew. But not her. She did not long for my flesh as I did for hers. Washing, combing, and touching were the greatest pleasures of mothering to me, the feelings I wish my empty hands could recall. When I was just looking at her, she was an alien essence. The channels of her blood were not mine. Were no longer mine, I would have said if I had given birth to her. But it probably didn't much matter where she had developed in utero. Possibly a birth mother could have fooled herself for a little longer than I did. But sooner or later she must have known: we are uncorded, severed.

In the mornings she would play on the floor in a big patch of sunlight. The pale parquet floor shone under her. She was constantly moving things around — a yellow and red wooden sausage dog on oversized green wheels with a metal spring tail that bounced to the touch, a rubber doll that squeaked when you stepped on its tummy, my key ring, a coffee tin with a plastic lid. It wasn't nice to see her surrounded by hard objects, grasping at them with her hands. I lowered myself to the floor so she would touch me instead, but she just went on indefatigably making the dachshund's tail wag, giving me no more than a glance out of the corner of her eye. I withdrew, thinking perhaps it was she and I, after all, who were alien to each other. She had not been tossed right from eternity into the world, or from nothingness. We grow into our lives, of course, and it is a slow process. We feel bumps and rhythms, hear distant noise and voices close at hand. A heart pounds, a stomach growls and rumbles. She had been rocked back and forth across a huge flagstone floor, bounced around in Conceição's body in the evenings when her feet and legs were heavy and tired. Perhaps Elisabeth missed that rhythm, perhaps she also missed the sound of crockery and stainless steel bowls clanging against each other in a hospital kitchen. Conceição's hands resting on the tight skin of her belly at night and her voice, that rough Conceiçãoian chatter. Recognition. Intimacy. Perhaps those are the things we want and the things we can give. In the very worst case we have to make do with reminiscences. Bitterly, I compared myself to a wire frame covered with nubbly cloth, an artificial female monkey.

I had sat there in the bare room at the clinic waiting for her to wake up. This would be her second birth. That was how I had arranged it. But she stayed asleep for so long that in the end I had to wake her. I violated her sleep with my alien voice and my unhabituated hands, committed violence against her and dragged her out into the light, to the smell of a foreign person. I should, of course, have given myself more time, stayed there in the intimacy and worked my way in, become one with it. But everything was such a rush. I arranged an efficient second birth for her. The car was waiting. The clock was ticking.

Sometimes it occurred to me that everything was wrong for her in Sweden. The shiny parquet floor, the smell of wood and the slow voices. What, in fact, do we know about the familiar, how deeply rooted it is? I left her every morning in the hands of a young woman with a daughter of her own. She called herself a child minder and charged twelve kronor and fifty öre to look after Elisabeth between eight and three: mashed banana cookies and juice included. I supplied jars of chopped baby chicken with rice or the like. Shiny, new parquet floors, stock market reports, the smell of laundry detergent, and white enamel on an electric stove. Alien voices and footsteps that had to be learned. The alien must become familiar. But what if it didn't?

I heard Fredrik snoring inside. Now she was familiarizing herself with the smell of him at night, and with Jenny's lighter breathing. For every day, every year that passed she would grow more deeply rooted in the world, and it was always us making her choices for her. Most of the time it was me. I, who was barely able to decide what to wear every morning.

I had thought I would go down to the lakeshore, maybe row out and check the fish traps, run a trolling bait for pike behind the boat. I was often unable to sleep after dawn out here. If it wasn't the train that woke me, it was the birds. Land had been so cheap here because the train from Göteborg thundered by just above the property line. You had to cross the tracks to reach the cottage. Paper and waste blew down the embankment and landed in Fredrik's rock garden.

Now I heard it at a distance through the fog. It whistled as it approached the crossing, soon the ground would begin to tremble. When it passed I was standing trying to look out through the mist over the water, and I didn't even turn around. It was piercing the landscape and my consciousness; it would soon be distant, be dull, and then vanish like a shout in a bottle.

Then there was a screech of iron and of welded joints cracking and of steel pressing down on innards of glass, sheet metal and flesh. There was a long humming, the singing of a held note. After which, silence. I couldn't see anything. It took me a long time to dare to turn around. But finally I started running up the embankment and then I could see the locomotive. In the mist it lay there like a predator over its prey. The stink of hot iron and oil. I was not yet able to take in what I was seeing. The first thing I noticed was a little green midsummer wreath on the ground. It was made of fresh, green birch leaves, and had probably been crushed by the iron wheels, I could smell the fresh leaves. Then I saw a face way down on the ground. I still couldn't hear anything but the air hissing out of the valves and the groaning of iron. I fell to my knees alongside the face. There was glass between myself and the eyes that were looking at me. It was part of a window pane, half whole, half broken into long, knifelike shards in the gravel between the sleepers.

It was a man. He was still young. He couldn't move. Blood was seeping out of the corner of his mouth, a little ribbon of blood mixed with saliva. When I moved, his pupils followed. They were black specks in the morning light.

I extended my hand but couldn't reach him. On the side where the glass was shattered hung hot, broken iron. Now there was pink foam at the corner of his mouth. His face grew ashen. A damp shadow crossed it. I slithered down and managed to put my fingertips to the pane of glass. I never realized I might be frightening him. I thought he wanted help and that he saw me clearly. But now I am no longer sure. All he may have seen was a huge, black shadow, fingers reaching, a blurred, swaying illusion. At the time all I could think was that he wanted help. His lips parted as if he were trying to groan or to speak. He had blood on his teeth and looked like dogs look when they are hot and panting but appear to be smiling. There was no longer anything human about him. It didn't cross my mind that the same might have been true about me. All I am certain of is that those eyes saw me. I thought they wanted to lock with mine; I felt my gaze flounder.

I sat crouched there for a long time, as his face grew grayer and grayer. His lungs must have been empty, and he was unable to draw breath. A tremor passed along his face, from brow to chin beneath his damp skin. It may have continued down the rest of his body, which I couldn't see. Then he ceased to see me. His eyes had become bodies of glass or jelly. He had died as we looked at one another, and I quickly covered the pane of glass with the palm of my hand. I heard voices around me now. People were running along the slope, and a woman's voice was screaming:

"Help them, for God's sake! Help them!"

When I turned around I could see that Jenny had come out of the cottage. She was standing silently, arms dangling at her sides, in her pink nightie. A man rushed up to her shouting for a telephone. She shook her head, stepped backwards into the haze and vanished.

The locomotive had crushed a car, and the man behind the oddly unbroken pane of glass had been sitting in the back seat, I could see that now. There were other bodies, body parts, and upholstery and blood. Fredrik came running barefoot up the slope. I thought: here comes Fredrik. Now there will be help for everyone. I rose up on my nearly numb legs and walked toward him. I intended to ask him what I should do, and then to do precisely whatever he told me. But when I got up to him, he vomited. I jumped aside so as not to get it on my shoes. Then I heard a baby crying and started running down toward the cottage. I didn't want Elisabeth looking out of the window.

Jenny was sitting on the bed with the baby on her lap. The room was still dusky, she hadn't pulled up the window shades. Elisabeth's face was tense and pale and she was attentive to the voices penetrating through the thin cottage walls. I held her to me, and the warmth of her rigid body stilled my own trembling. Jenny went outside. She looked terrified.

I tried to talk to Elisabeth, tried to interest her in doing a wooden puzzle with yellow chicks on the table. But she just kept listening. Strangers opened the veranda door asking if we had a phone. They wanted blankets and told me to boil up water for tea and hot sugar water for the people who were in shock. I passed them everything they needed through the door: the camping stove, the water bucket, and even the old bathrobe I was wearing. I didn't want them in the cottage, because Elisabeth had begun to tremble with fear. Now the sirens were wailing, and the noise of motors mixed with the voices. People were saying that there had been four people in the car and that they were all dead. They said they had been on their way home from a dance. It was actually only two in the morning. When Elisabeth heard the noise of the blowtorch she began to cry. I heated some milk, but she was wailing, and threw up the few spoonfuls I got into her. Voices were penetrating the leaky cottage walls. I felt hateful of all of them, of everyone chattering outside and of the people who had died, and who had lived a different kind of life and had dragged us down into its black vortex. Elisabeth was freezing cold now, hiccoughing incessantly.

I took the only covering we still had inside, the tablecloth of slithery linen mix, and wrapped her in it. I pulled it over her head so she couldn't see anything, and I carried her little body, racked with hiccoughs and cramps from all the crying, down to the lakeshore. I put her on the aft bench in the boat and pushed off from shore, rowing away, at first fast and roughly, then with increasing calm and steadiness. I passed another boat in the fog. It was Ingrid and Arne who were on the way over from the little island where their cottage was. They didn't see me. They were star-

344

ing hard at the land, and we glided past. Elisabeth was sitting upright on the bench, hiccoughing. She was holding the old tablecloth around her. I was following the shore, fearful of ending up in deep water in the fog, and I realized I have come to the farm below the cottages when the bow of the boat hit a long, rickety wooden jetty. The house towered like a church gable in the wild gray air, stagnant with moisture.

My arrival didn't awaken the people there, the sirens had already woken them. They wanted to hear all about the accident before they called me a taxi, but I didn't want to talk about it. Elisabeth was sitting on a chair at their big table, staring at the fly paper and hiccoughing, with the regularity of the ticking of the wall clock, though at longer intervals now.

It took nearly an hour for the taxi to get there. When we arrived in town she had been hiccoughing for so long she was in pain, moaning that she wanted it to stop. It hurt. I took her right to the hospital but they had their hands full with people from the accident who were in far worse states of shock, and people waiting to find out if there had been any survivors in the car. A doctor did examine Elisabeth, and said she would be fine when she had some sleep. He pinched her belly and said he thought her hiccoughs were over now. They weren't. She was just sitting there with her mouth shut tight and her body tense. When we got out and into a taxi they started again.

I didn't go home because I didn't dare to be alone. I thought Hasse's father might have a sedative to give her, a sleeping pill or a muscle relaxant, since the doctor hadn't been willing to provide anything. Oddly enough he opened the door almost right away, and was fully dressed. I carried Elisabeth into the living room and went to find a shawl or a blanket to wrap her in. Hasse tumbled up from the couch. He was dressed, too.

I couldn't imagine what he was doing at his father's house. I felt deceived. I ran a hot bath for Elisabeth and managed to get her to take a quarter of a sleeping pill dissolved in a lot of very sweet fruit syrup. I was frightened, not knowing what to expect. Perhaps we would have a dreadful row later; I thought there must be another woman. My mind was in no state to formulate anything but clichés.

When Elisabeth was finally asleep Hasse came up, bringing me a tray of tea. We were in his childhood bedroom. I lay next to her on top of the cover, slowly extricating my arm from behind her neck. I indicated to him that we should leave the room. We tiptoed out and carried the tray down into the living room. Hasse's father was on his way to bed. His face was like gray paper.

Once we were alone, Hasse told me he had come back to town that night after

345

a phone call from his father. They had been talking for hours. They were going to have to declare the factory bankrupt.

At the moment I did not think it sounded real, or very important either.

Then the morning arrived when there was only one single hundred kronor note in the tea tin. I needed several. The phone bill, warm winter boots for Elisabeth, butter, shampoo, compact powder, new upholstery for an armchair. I sat in a beam of sunlight, counting up major and minor expenses. Hasse was asleep. He slept late in the mornings, as the depressed often do. When he was up and about and had had his tea he would look for work. His ball point pen ran down the employment opportunity columns every morning. But it wasn't easy. He had become very specialized, and he had no training in business administration.

In the end he started helping people with their tax returns. Just ordinary folks, who could perfectly well have read the instructions and filled in the forms themselves, but who were afraid they would get it wrong. It only lasted until the fifteenth of February, the deadline. After that he showed the spring collection as a traveling salesman for a big off-the-rack company. He knew the business, but was quiet and terribly honest. They had him on trial for six months, then gave him the boot. He sold sewing machines for a while, but only far from home. We never said a word to Jenny and Fredrik about it. Then he traveled with dresses again, but for a smaller company. He had toughened up a bit, and did better that time.

We had sold the house and moved into a two-bedroom apartment. I still had my nice clothes and the gorgeous handbags; they were still in fashion. But I think Hasse felt he had let me down.

He came home, his clothes smelling of small-town hotels. I wouldn't have been caught dead in the dresses he was selling. Flashy patterns printed on heavy, glossy fabric. Some nights he would call me from a pay phone outside a hotel dining room. I could hear the music.

"There's a big night at the hotel in Vilhelmina tomorrow," he said. "All the traveling salesmen organize their routes so they can meet there on Thursdays. Don't you think I should go, too?"

Irony was new to him. I liked him more this way, poor as a church mouse, sarcastic and nervous.

Until then I had mostly worked for the fun of it, and never more than a couple of hours a day. I wrote columns and sometimes obituaries and birthday notices. I begged to be allowed to do book reviews even though Bertil Sundh was convinced nobody was interested in arts articles. I covered art exhibitions and plays as well, all on a commission basis. The editorial offices had changed. Victor had left town, I didn't know where he had moved and didn't have the guts ask. Lisa Wallin was soon to retire. I would never have dared to ask Bertil to take me on full time. Although there had been staff turnover, I was sure the very air reeked with my failure, suspended particles.

One of my many commissions was to write my father-in-law's obituary. He had handled his bankruptcy flawlessly; they said he had even surrendered his gray, functionalist 1930s home to the administrators and moved back to the countryside where he came from, gone to stay with his sisters. But he didn't live long as an involuntary pensioner. His heart muscle was exhausted.

After his death, I asked one of his Rotary brothers, a retired physician, to write about him. Perhaps because he was used to dictating medical records, the text he produced was dry and lifeless. Trying to think of something that might perk it up, I recalled his sisters once telling me that when he was six he had made a little cap and lined sleeveless jacket for his teddy bear. His father had begun as a tailor and hatter. My father-in-law had not started out empty-handed, but he had worked hard ever since he was a schoolboy. His ambition had been to sell quality clothing. He cared, above all, about being fair with his staff. Wage negotiations were a terrible strain on him, and political innuendo offended him as if it had been an indecency. The thought that he was profiting from the seamstresses' labor was as alien to him as it would have been to slink around the factory trying to slip his hand under their skirts. To him, there was nothing but work, and actually nothing but ready-made clothing. I don't think he pondered over it much, but I could be wrong. He was a quiet man.

Sometimes we looked after the Otters' dog. My father-in-law was surprisingly kind to him. When the dog came his way he would stare as if he had never heard of or imagined such a thing. The dog, who was old but friendly, would trot up to him, get his trousers all hairy, and pant his rotten-toothed, dogfoody breath into his face.

"Poor mutt," my father-in-law would say at those times. He would raise a hand as if he meant to pat Buster, but then had second thoughts. "Poor mutt," he would repeat, with such conviction you would have to look at Buster and think about what his life was actually like. But it was just a dog's life, with a bowl full of food every day and a filthy blanket in a corner of the hall, which he gladly relinquished in favor of couches and beds. He was otherwise timid and self-trained. No one had ever said an unkind word to him. It was a strange idea to feel sorry for him, but perhaps my father-in-law was thinking of his animal nature, his shallow mind and the simple pleasures of his world, telegraph poles stinking of pee and bones dug up in the flowerbeds. He might have pitied anyone who lived a life that was alien and incomprehensible to him. Would he have said: "Poor Irma!" or "Poor Margit!" if he had seen his own seamstresses lumbering over to the Co-op or pulling up their satin-covered acrylic quilts at night?

I asked Hasse if I could add the episode of the cap and jacket to his father's life record and if it would be all right to write that he had been a great animal lover. But Hasse was horrified and told me not to change a thing. The very thought that people might find out anything personal about himself or his father upset him.

I was the one who suggested to Hasse that maybe we should move back to Portugal. I encouraged him to apply for a position at Confecções Nórdica, where he had been a trainee.

We left Henning at home, of course. I had to part from him. He'd have his dinners at the Co-op department store cafeteria as before, and keep busy trying to find takers for his trivial, and now rather old, inventions. He would go to the Otters for Christmas and Easter. It was all a perfectly reasonable arrangement, but Henning was left. Left like an odd sock. We parted. He was in bed that morning, those little inflations in his legs were worse. I hated the way he didn't call them inflammations, he had stopped enunciating clearly. The whites of his eyes were bloodshot and his breath had a nasty smell. I had come to say good-bye at a bad moment. His thin hand rested in mine and his eyelids drooped and twitched every time a car passed by out in Chapel Road. He looked like he had that time Fredrik had tried to get him to spend his days polishing bottom pieces for irons in his workshop.

"Well, we're off," I said. "I'm sure we'll be home for the summer. Let Jenny look after you, please. I'll write. I'll send pictures of Elisabeth."

His hand shifted slightly in mine.

"Take care," I said.

I didn't even mention Lisa. But I think she was the real reason I was leaving. I couldn't live sixty kilometers from the kingdom of the dead.

Year after year, Lisa's name was on every document having to do with the house at 13 Chapel Road. I knew it was possible to keep an estate intact for the surviving relatives, but was it possible to keep it that way forever? I asked Henning once, but he just told me not to worry about it.

The bankruptcy had made me very practical, even somewhat interfering. I wasn't sure of the year of Lisa's death, but the editor of the family page of the local paper could easily find out a thing like that. There were obviously things, many things, about which one didn't talk to Henning, and one of them was Lisa's death.

We no longer had boxes of copies of the information from the parish registers at the newspaper. I had to go to the parish office and ask them to look it up. I found the whole thing more than a little embarrassing. It seemed so foolish not to know what year your mother died.

"She must have passed away in Norrköping," said the minister. "All I can see here is that she moved to Norrköping on 30 October 1939."

I had always thought Lisa died at the sanatorium up north. The idea that she moved to Norrköping and lived out her life there seemed incredible and, above all, uncalled for. I was surprised she had been alive as late as October 1939. That meant she had known about the German invasion of Poland, known there was a World War. If she hadn't been so sick that it had completely passed her by. The thought entered my mind that there was a high altitude sanatorium in Kolmården. Lisa could have died there, closer to Henning. Although I wasn't sure if Kolmården might be a parish of its own, I took a chance and addressed a letter of inquiry to the Norrköping parish office.

I received a polite if brief reply stating that the person I was inquiring about was alive, and lived at a given address. Feeling sick and with my pulse racing, I phoned for more information. I kept telling myself that, as usual, this was one of those times I was getting all wound up about nothing. Something was taking on the shape of an illusion, a grotesque parody of reality. I wasn't sure what. Probably nothing but a mistake, a misreading. At the parish office I was informed that such mistakes were not made. Lisa Johannesson was alive and lived at the address I had been given.

The strange thing was that I had known it all along. I had thought she lived in a city next to ours but that she was dead. When I was little I thought that was where all dead people lived. Nowadays I only thought it about Lisa. It was an image. I hadn't paid much attention to it, because I thought about her so seldom, I just visualized her, living in a crowded little apartment. It was a gray place and not far away. Now I could sense that it smelled of gas, and I could hear the tram on the street outside.

But soon I realized, I don't think it took more than a few hours, that we had a to draw a line between living and dead. A person is either alive or dead. There is nothing in between. You have to make up your mind. That was what I was doing now, all by myself. I didn't want to ask Henning, and not only because I was ashamed to be preoccupied with Lisa, dead or not, like rummaging through old, unwashed clothes a dead or not dead person had helplessly left behind.

She wasn't in the phone book, so I called the parish office again and asked whether she had been registered at the same address since October 1939. When they told me she had I was absolutely certain there had been a mistake after all. No one ever lived at the same address for so long any more. It was an old address, a building that might have been demolished, and a woman who was what the minister referred to as deceased.

That was a relief. Still, I wrote a letter to that deceased mother of mine at a nonexistent address. I felt affected and fake when I wrote, as if this were a set piece I was reciting alongside a coffin, addressing myself to someone who could no longer hear me. While I waited for the letter to be returned to sender, I decided to go and see Henning and ask him where my mother's grave was. It would be awkward for me and perhaps painful for him, but I had crossed a line now, I was going to do it. He was in Småland at one of his manufacturers. Before he got back, though, my letter was answered.

Lisa wrote that she thought I had known something of her circumstances. There were lots of expressions like that in her letter. Known something of. At least a bit. You must find this very odd. The Lisa Johannesson who claimed to be alive did so in an ambiguous, peculiar fashion as if she were constantly in the process of retracting everything she said. I got the letter one morning. The mail comes in the morning when it is light and sober, when there are everyday noises from outside, and the road looks real. My heart was pounding and my knees quaking. Though her words may have been vague, perhaps even intended to be easy for me to erase from my mind, the paper and the handwriting were very real. I could barely conceive of Lisa writing with a ball point pen. The ball point pen should not have been invented when she was writing letters. There was no point in scouring the apartment for a document with her signature on it for comparison. Lisa had been effaced from the memory of the house. Abel had done it. Henning might have contributed, too.

She didn't write a word about staying in touch, or give a phone number. When I wrote to her again asking if I could see her, and for her phone number if she had one, I was feeling something resembling hate toward her, for her reticence and circumspection. But I tore that letter to pieces. When I read hers again, I could see how elusive her words were. She was probably the kind of person who was able to leave an unpleasant letter lying around for months, until it eventually was too late to do anything about it, too late or too awkward.

I hadn't yet begun to think about what her life had been like, or what reasons she might have for shying away. I was brimming with emotions, they tumbled and plummeted out. They had a mamma to rush to, at least a mamma of a few indefinite words and diffuse phrases. The absurd thing was that the ink in her ballpoint pen was also running out as she wrote. It looked intentional, but couldn't possibly have been. Still, I understood she was the type of person whose mind it would never enter to get up and go find another pen when the one she was using was faltering. She would go on writing until she could no longer see the letters. I thought it was a very poor excuse for a letter she'd sent me, and I suspected that I had a very poor excuse for a mother.

When I had thought things over for a couple of days I did write her another letter, and a very straightforward one at that. I told her that at two o'clock on Saturday I would be at a cake shop, the name of which I had located in the phone book. It was on Queen's Street in Norrköping.

It was a clandestine journey. I didn't even tell Hasse where I was going. I was extremely uncertain about what I should wear. I wanted to look good, at the same time as I had a feeling that if I was too well dressed it would be either provocative or embarrassing. I imagined Lisa as poor. That was because of the ballpoint pen and the old address. On the train I went into the WC and washed all my make-up off. I had thought my face looked too painted, but now I was horrified at its nudity and paleness, so I put it all on again. I was pushing thirty, there was no hiding it.

I was at the cake shop in good time, though not at all certain that Lisa would show up. If she didn't come I at least wanted to be sure I hadn't missed her. The waitress asked for my order, but I said I was meeting someone and that we would be ordering together. When I had been sitting there for nearly an hour leafing through crumbling magazines at grinning glossy faces, she came back to say there were other people waiting for tables. So I quickly ordered a coffee and a pastry. But I couldn't touch them. I felt sick.

The shops had closed. The street was growing quieter and emptier and not all the tables were occupied any longer. It was an old-fashioned cake shop, musty and with worn seats, but it had been a fancy place. Over by the entrance there were bronze muses or goddesses holding torches with light bulbs in them.

Opposite me was an elderly couple who kept looking toward the door. They were clearly distressed. I hadn't given them much thought, never expecting Lisa to be anything but alone.

She was short, much smaller than myself. Suddenly we looked right into each other's eyes, and it was like finding an old photograph that had been retouched. Perhaps that was how she felt as well. Each of us saw a face we could just barely recall, something familiar but grotesquely changed. I must have been the one who had aged most dramatically. The last time she saw me, my cheeks were like Elisabeth's, my lips thin-skinned and moist. Perhaps she thought I looked awful now, a made-up likeness, a little child who had developed a disorder of the glands regulating the passage of time in the body. I don't know what she saw, all I know is that I was ashamed.

She was so small and thin. Her hair had no color at all. I suppose it had gone gray, but it was difficult to tell, because she had once been blonde. In addition to which most of it was pushed up under her beret. She was plainly and modestly dressed in a light brown coat. Under the table I could see her legs, thin sticks in shoes, and with socks running up her calves, neatly turned down. It looked peculiar, somewhat childlike. Next to her was a tall man, who treated her like a little girl. He held his hand on hers, and patted it as if to calm her. Now both of them were staring at me. He was wearing an old-fashioned trench coat and a hard little hat of navy blue felt.

I got up. She blinked hard, and her eyelids fluttered as I approached. She seemed to be afraid of me.

"Lisa Johannesson?" I asked.

The man flew up at that. He knocked the table.

"Yes," he said. "That's right. This is her."

I thought she would extend her hand, but she didn't. She appeared confused. The man talked on, but I couldn't take in his words.

"How are you?" I asked her. I meant it literally, because she didn't look very well at that moment. I was afraid she might faint or that it might all be too much for her heart, and that it would be my fault. But the question clearly shifted her into a realm where she felt more secure, because she put her hand gently to her chest and replied.

"Better, thank you. Yes, I am. The years pass, you know. But it's not easy."

"She only has one lung," the man said.

I held out my hand to him and said my name. Afterwards I was embarrassed for having been so aggressive. He was too taken aback to speak, so Lisa said:

"This is Birger. He is my companion."

It came out so fast I could tell she had been thinking a lot about how to introduce him, and had settled on that particular word. Her companion seemed to hearken to the description.

"Well, I had no idea," I said. "Henning never told me."

I couldn't very well say he had said she was dead, because when I came to think of it he had never specifically said so. Abel and Henning and the Otters had rubbed Lisa out, they had tried to erase her face from our history. They had undoubtedly had their reasons. Shame and pain. Some kind of desire to protect me. The easy way out. Perhaps a need for vengeance.

"I wanted to live with Birger for the little time I had left," she said. "We met at the sanatorium."

Her voice faded, and I waited for her to go on. But there was no need to say it. She was still alive. She had gone on living.

"I was contagious, too."

Her eyes sought mine, she was anxious. This was an explanation she was giving, a sort of apology for not having come back to me.

What had it been like to go on living for years after that feverish decision? Was it possible to live for nearly three decades using the love of your life as an excuse? Or did boredom and doubt intercede? There was one person who had no doubt, and that was Birger. I could tell.

Lisa had begun to sweat profusely. There were little drops along her upper lip and along the edge of her beret on her brow. Birger helped her to remove her coat and cardigan. It was only natural for her to be sweaty with all those clothes on. The right side of her chest was concave, and I realized that her voice sounded so flat because she was always short of breath with only one lung. Now she was talking about it. Her other lung had also been infected, but the site had cleared up. It was miraculous. No one had believed it. I had to understand: she had had more than a spot on her lung, it was seriously infected. Her lung had been deteriorating. She hadn't been expected to survive.

I wasn't familiar with tuberculosis terminology. That kind of talk disgusted me. But she took my disgust for incomprehension, and became even more explicit, describing the cavernous holes and the rotting pulmonary tissue. Right in the middle of her description I had to go over to the counter and choose some pastries so the waitress would leave us alone. It was good to get away for a moment. I had a feeling now that the love of her life had not been enough of an excuse for Lisa. She had needed her decaying lung.

They consulted while I was out of earshot, their heads close together. They reminded me of a pair of criminals trying to confer while the judge was otherwise occupied.

Lisa disappointed me. Her proportions were all wrong. She was so tiny and real, and her voice was weak and insecure. I was thinking she had had a pathetic life, I could almost swear to it. The two of them had been shut up together in the same apartment for twenty-five years. When I got back to the table I had made up my mind to ask what their life was like now. But she just kept talking about the past, about her decision.

"I don't want you to think I disliked Henning," she said. "That wasn't it. But this was just so much … greater."

At that, Birger lowered his eyes to the Formica tabletop. I saw that her words made him happy. Maybe I had guessed wrong, they might still be feverishly attached. I asked what Birger did for a living but I should have asked her if there is such a thing as great love that lasts a lifetime; she must be one of the few people who could have given me an answer to that question.

"He's at the gasworks," she said. Their anxious reciprocal concern kept expressing itself through their answering for one another.

"And you?" she asked shyly.

What was I supposed to say? Up against the wall like that, more or less literally up against the gray cake shop wall with my life, I didn't really know what it contained.

"I have a child," I answered. "A little girl who's almost five. Her name is Elisabeth."

That reduced Lisa to tears. Birger glowered at me and put his arm around her. She was, of course, crying because I had named Elisabeth after her, although I didn't realize it until I had said it. Perhaps she was thinking I had gone around pining for her my whole life, that I had a huge cavern inside me.

"I'm married to Hasse C:son Curtman, Curt Carlsson's son, formerly of Curre's Clothes. Hasse's a traveling salesman now."

She should actually have known all about that, but she obviously didn't. If there had been the least bit of what Jenny called *go* in her, she would at least have kept up with the outer contours of our destinies. But she hadn't wanted to know at all, and when I realized that I went silent. It's only sixty kilometers to Norrköping. It was amazing the way she had managed to make herself invisible, blind and deaf.

"What about Henning?" she asked.

"Well, he's all right," I said. Because what good would it do her to know what had happened to Henning? And besides, just then he was pretty much all right.

We were on the wrong track with our earnest but general questions. We were scaring each other. Perhaps we should have spoken of more ordinary things, talked about common acquaintances and the house on Chapel Road. I supposed the reason she had never divorced Henning was that she wanted him to be able to keep the house. Or had she been thinking of me? I understood that Lisa and Henning must have come to some kind of agreement, and that Jenny had certainly known about it. I started looking at Birger. He was the real cause of all this, at least that was what Lisa claimed. He looked quite ordinary. He might have been better looking in his younger days. He was balding and had dark hair. I guessed he was still under sixty. Lisa was fifty-seven, that was one thing I knew. But she looked older, she looked both older and more childlike. As I sat there stirring my coffee and considering a different approach to them, she said they'd have to be going.

"Birger's only off until four o'clock."

I thought that was odd, but maybe they had some kind of shift system at the gas works. She shook her head when I asked if she couldn't stay on. Birger started helping her on with her coat. He took her hand and guided it down into the sleeve.

Then Lisa was standing all by herself in the middle of the floor pulling on her gloves. That was actually the only point at which I saw her on her own. Birger had gone over to the counter to pay. I took a close look at her, a close, almost greedy look, because I was not certain I would ever see her again. I noticed her feet. When she was sitting at the table her feet had looked helpless, as if she had set them aside with those stick-like legs in them. Now I took them in with a driving, urgent sense of intimacy. I could also see that they were the feet of a strong individual.

She had put on her gloves and scarf, and tied the belt of her coat. I could tell she was worried about the cold weather outside. She wanted to live for a long time.

Birger returned and took her by the arm. He had paid the waitress for the coffees he and Lisa had had while they waited, and the pastries I had ordered at their table, but not what I had ordered before I saw them. Before they left, each of them shook my hand. Hers was as thin as I had imagined, and she only pressed lightly. Birger was nearly twice as tall as she was when they were standing.

"We must get together again," said Lisa. But she didn't say when.

I really did see her one more time and Birger was with her then, too, of course. It was over a year later when we were back in Sweden for a visit. I borrowed Fredrik's car and took Elisabeth with me to Norrköping. We never went up to their apartment. The option was never broached. At my suggestion, we went on an outing to Arkösund. Elisabeth held center stage and it was neither as awkward nor as dramatic as the first time we met. Nor did we talk about anything important.

We had a meal at the outdoor restaurant and then I took them home. Elisabeth got to see the windmills, and ate an ice cream in the car on the way home. She dripped on her embroidered dress and we discussed whether the stains would come out. Lisa thought hot water would do the trick, if I soaked it right away. But she didn't offer to have us come upstairs and do it, so we parted outside the big block of flats. I still didn't know Birger's surname, but I no longer cared. I found the whole day kind of dull.

So Lisa vanished from my life again. Or rather, she returned to her place. Now I knew she lived in an apartment in a city quite near ours. And had the whole time. She was a short, physically frail person who had once had the strength to decide to die with Birger. However, she had outlived her decision. After that day she wrote to me every year at Christmas, and sent Elisabeth a present. It would arrive around *Véspera de Reis*. She never bothered to find out how long it took a parcel to reach Porto. We each got a card on our birthdays as well; that went on for a few years. When the cards stopped coming I didn't think much about it.

Jenny didn't find it surprising that we never got together after that. She said that was often how it was, though I don't know where she got her expertise on the subject.

"You see each other two or three times and then it dies out," she said.

She seemed to know what she was talking about.

On the twelfth of June every year, I think: "Henning died to day." One year ago to day. Two years ago today. To day.

The old apple tree in the yard was in bloom. Thin, furled petals were opening in the sun, smoothing out, suffused with something that shimmered like blood under thin skin. The fragile blossoms looked very odd against the trunk, so gnarled and scarred, and the crooked, black boughs.

I wrote about the apple blossoms and about his death in the newspaper. Jenny said it was a lovely poem, that lots of people had said how much they had liked it when they read the death notice. Personally, though, I was ashamed of this invented, comforting death. Untruthful was what it was, devoutly untruthful was about the kindest thing you could say about it. But then you could only use the word devout in the sense of well-meaning.

He was fighting for every breath. When he inhaled, a grating, wheezing sound rose up from his throat. The mild, still air around the bed, the very air he was trying to wring oxygen from, seemed rough and hostile. It sounded as if it was injuring his throat and lungs. I asked a doctor what made his breathing sound like that, but his answers were just vague and evasive. I wasn't sure whether he didn't know or didn't want to tell me. When he had left I tried to figure it out by breathing like that myself. I pressed my tongue to the back of my throat as you do when you gargle, and then forced some air through the little crack that was left. It sounded quite like Henning fighting for breath, but of course I knew the cause was different. Wheezing that way made me tired and dizzy. When I tried to adapt my breathing to the slow rhythm of his, I noticed how irregular it had become. It made me nauseous and exhausted just trying to follow along for a little while. But the hours passed and he had to keep on breathing like that. For him there was no rest and no getting away from it.

I only followed his breathing when we were alone in the room. At night they carried in a bed for me, a roll-away I pushed next to his bed when they had left. I lay down on it and fell asleep, but only slept in fits and starts, and I don't think I've ever had worse dreams.

Several times I considered walking out on the whole business. It dragged on for such a horribly long time. Nothing happened. He lay there breathing just the same as before; I could no longer keep track of the days. Early one morning they came to change him, and they pulled down the cotton blanket, exposing his thin body. I saw purplish bruises on his feet. Of course I panicked and begged them to help him, to do something. But they said there was nothing more they could do.

He was bound tightly to life and to hospital routines by two matte white plastic tubes. One had oxygen and was inserted into his nose to help him breathe, the other ended in a needle puncturing his thick, bruised skin and was taped to his forearm. They were putting fluids into his body so he wouldn't suffer from thirst. His thighs were so thin the rubber pants around the diaper got too big, but no more excrement ran out onto the sheet. He wasn't taking anything in any more, so nothing was coming out, either. I was afraid that in spite of their good will and their competence, the hospital staff actually had no idea of what he was going through. It upset me that his breathing appeared to become more and more painful but that they didn't do anything about it. He was struggling for every breath. It was as if there wasn't enough air in the room. When his battle to take in the hot air with its strong scent of sick body, clean sheets and wilting flowers entered into the third day, I couldn't imagine how he would be able to go on. But he had to get through it. I saw how difficult it was and asked the nurse to please do something. But she said he didn't feel anything. He was unconscious. Then he said very clearly:

"Help me."

His voice was weak but it was his. He was there and had been there all along.

He was Henning until he no longer existed. Now he is one of the dead. He is not in the cemetery under the lindens that are just getting their leaves, and not in the room with the easy chair and the old lamp with the silk shade. Not inside or behind his photograph on the bureau, not with me or in the poem I wrote.

At first I didn't realize. I couldn't see any difference. The nurse stood up and bent over him. He had been quiet for a while but his eyelids had been flicking uneasily. Now she blocked my view of him and when she stood up and turned toward me again she had a different look on her face. She had put it on as you put on a strange, stiff piece of clothing. It had no meaning to me; it looked affected. She had to explain to me what had happened, and afterwards I couldn't remember whether she had said "it's finished" or "it's over now". But she didn't say that he was dead. My impulse was to slap her face, but of course I knew she was a

359

skilled nurse and possibly a kind person. She never hurt Henning, at least not intentionally.

Now she started touching him, but I wanted her to leave him alone. To prevent myself from shouting at her, I turned away from the bed in that hot little room and stood looking out of the window. After a short time, I heard other people come in. She must have called them by pushing the buzzer that was pinned to the cotton blanket. I recognized the voice of the young physician, and there was also a nurse's aide who pulled off the bedding and shifted the drip stand around noisily. Outside the window there was a huge oak tree Henning and I used to look at. In the treetop I glimpsed two squirrels chasing each other. They appeared to be playing.

The doctor approached me. He was an awkward young man with a stethoscope around his neck. From the smell of his breath I knew he had just had coffee. He didn't say anything about Henning being dead, either. I had an impulse to ask him why he wasn't doing anything, or why Henning was lying there like that. "What's wrong with him?" I would have asked.

They had laid him out perfectly straight in the bed with his hands under the blanket. His eyes were closed. He didn't look a bit different than he had a little while ago, but now he was silent. The nurse's aide hade cleared the bedpan and my coffee cup off the bedside table, but there was still some wadding on it. I didn't know what I was supposed to do next, and the others gave me no clues. They just looked at me as if expecting me to say or do something particular.

I went out into the corridor with them. They spoke to me but I didn't really hear what they were saying, and when we got to the big glass doors at the end of the ward I walked away. I didn't know what to do with myself. Jenny and Fredrik were on vacation. They were on a bus tour of Austria. Elisabeth's school term was over and she had already taken the plane to Lisbon where Hasse had collected her.

I left the hospital and walked all the way into town, following the whole of the long Industrial Road, walking on the dark gray tarmac with its stains and its potholes and its tire marks. There was the usual stench of exhaust fumes and filth. Lately I had had a terrible time with smells. I went into the Co-op department store. It was odd to be out among people again after days and nights in the quiet, isolated room. The faces looked harsh and ugly to me. There were the smells of perspiration and food and unwashed clothes and highly perfumed cleaning fluids in there. When I had bought some flowers and candles I walked back. I had planned to take a taxi up to the hospital, but I couldn't find one.

The ward nurse was surprised to see me back. I hadn't meant to come either, but there I stood with my candles and flowers, feeing uncertain. She took them.

"We could have arranged for some flowers," she said. "And there are candles here."

So why hadn't she said so at the time?

They had locked the door. I had to wait for her to come back with the five pink roses in a vase. She unlocked the room and let me in. Everything they had been using for the last few days had been removed. All that was there was the furniture, and Henning, lying with his hands folded on top of the blanket now. His left hand was on top of the right, in a pose that was completely foreign to him. But they couldn't have known.

When the nurse lit the two candles, there was the smell of sulfur in the room from the match. I would have liked to open the window and air it out, but I didn't dare. I didn't know if that was all right. Insects might come in.

"Shall we sit with Pappa for a while?" she asked.

That was exactly what she said. I would have liked to ask why she was calling Henning Pappa, but I didn't. When she asked if I would like to be alone, I nodded. She went out, shutting the door much more quietly behind herself than they had ever done in the last few days.

As soon as she left it was clear to me that sitting there was meaningless. Henning lay under the pale green fabric like a block of wood. From outside, there was the sound of cars and the distant voices of children. There was some banging out in the hall as well. Everything was just the same as before, except that he wasn't breathing.

I had nothing but unpleasant, macabre thoughts. It was only a little after four. I didn't think I could even stick it out until half past. I couldn't touch Henning, and there was hardly any point in looking at him, either. I stood at the window staring at the branches of the big oak tree. I didn't see the squirrels. I went on standing there until the small of my back began to ache.

As I left the room I looked at him, but it was like looking at a piece of wood. There was no point. I was given his belongings to take home in a plastic bag, and when I got back I put the clothes on a cupboard shelf. I set his watch and his signet ring in front of me on the kitchen table.

I slept very little. Now and then I sifted through some of Henning's papers. I meant to phone the funeral parlor but I didn't think there was any rush. In the end the ward nurse called from the hospital and asked if I needed help with what she called "the practical arrangements." She offered to call the funeral parlor. I thanked her but refused, of course, and phoned myself the same afternoon. They wanted to put a death notice in the paper but I couldn't see what good that would do. It would

361

just serve to remind people of how he died and what the last years of his life had been like. I didn't want a funeral, either. I never even tried to reach the Otters so they could come back early from Austria. What should they rush back for, why should they dress in black and stand by a coffin? It wouldn't change anything. There had to be some kind of funeral. In the end it was a ceremony at the crematorium, but I didn't attend. The director told me there would be something called the stone unveiling as well, but that I could arrange a date later. I paid the bill and thought now it was finally over and done with and I would head for Porto. But I couldn't get myself to go. I spent most of each day in bed. I had started to cry, and I wept until I felt ill, and bruised inside. The Otters wouldn't be home for another eleven days.

When they got back, Jenny was dreadfully upset and said I should have let them know so they could come back. She said we had to put a notice in the paper, there was no question about it. We sat down opposite one another at the kitchen table to write it. I found it very difficult and suggested we wait another couple of days. What difference did it make at this point? That evening I wrote the poem Jenny was so pleased with. Underneath we wrote that there had been a small funeral.

Now, said Jenny, we were going to go through Henning's things. Get the whole house in order. His clothing and papers and all the possessions he hadn't sold for drink.

"I suppose you'll be putting the house on the market?" she asked.

I didn't answer. Jenny called the funeral parlor to say we wanted to have the stone unveiled. That time — just over a week after she and Fredrik came home — everything was done according to the book. We three had agreed to meet outside the cemetery a little before one o'clock. A minister had been arranged. I had bought flowers and was dressed as Jenny had told me to dress, in a black suit with a white blouse. At twenty to one she called and said they had ordered a taxi to pick me up at Chapel Road.

She knew how things were supposed to be done, and there was no reason for me to be so desperate or so torn up with grief as I was after the funeral I didn't attend.

The sun was shining weakly when we placed Henning's urn in the ground. We sang hymns Jenny and I had selected. The minister said a few words, well-intended, kind-sounding words that could have described just about anyone. Afterwards we had lunch at the Otters' house in the Upco estate. Jenny had prepared some cold, poached salmon, a meal that could be made in advance. Fredrik praised her sour cream sauce, and I thought it was good, too. She had scraped little new potatoes, and had them ready to boil. They didn't take long to cook, just long enough for us to have a sherry in the sitting room.

We talked a little about Henning as we ate. We hadn't done that in a long time, there hadn't been much to say. The sunlight filtered in through the window and shone on the table, the white tablecloth and their best china and cutlery. Fredrik seemed pensive, and the explanation arrived as we were eating our stewed apples with ice cream. He'd been mulling over a little speech.

It can't have been easy. He said I had lost my father, which was a great bereavement. He held up his port glass throughout, and kept his eyes lowered, looking at his plate. He said he hoped Jenny and he had been some kind of compensation for me, that they had certainly done their best, and that they cared about me.

"We want you to know that you are our beloved little girl," he said.

Naturally, I burst into tears, partly from my guilty conscience, because I hadn't been very attentive to them the last few years. Jenny was crying softly herself and she patted my hand and said the weather was so nice we'd have our coffee on the patio.

I've counted backwards and determined that on that day Fredrik, who looked perfectly healthy, had one year, seven months and twelve days left to live. But that afternoon Jenny was the one who looked unwell, not him. Her black clothes made her look pale, and she was probably tired after their trip. Yet the minute she had poured the coffee she said we were going to start clearing the house out the very next day. It sounded odd: clearing the house out. I asked what she meant. She said it was perfectly obvious what that expression meant, and required no explanation.

"It's high time we dealt with all that old rubbish and got it out of the way," she said.

"It." What was that? Henning, I suppose.

"I'm going to Porto," I said.

Both she and Fredrik started objecting. They were perfectly prepared to wait a few days to empty the apartment and sell the house if I was too tired. But there was certainly no point in postponing the whole matter.

"It," I repeated. "The whole matter."

"No need to be so literal," said Jenny.

Fredrik tried to mediate, but the conversation petered out. We sat there in the sun, stirring our coffee, stirring and stirring the sugar that had dissolved long ago.

Jenny knew exactly how things were supposed to be done. I was grateful, I really was. Henning's funeral had probably been a more pathetic affair than the burial of the Otters' dog a few years ago. Now Jenny had made all the arrangements for the unveiling, and that felt right. But her efficiency was going too far. She was going to obliterate Henning forever. I could see that as she sat there, black as pitch and pale as death, stirring her coffee as it grew cold. I didn't let her.

I went back to Porto the next day, taking with me the keys to 13 Chapel Road.

Many people claim that what made my father dependent on drink was the fuel carburetor for an internal combustion engine. Swedish Engineering had sponsored a number of designers over the course of the years, enabling them to develop their ideas; giving them permanent jobs and the resources of a large workshop. What they didn't get was a share of the profits. If they were lucky they got a lump sum, and a nickname in town, "Chuck-Peter" or "Generator-Lasse". In the public consciousness this was no more honorable than being the owner of a bicycle workshop and nicknamed "Rat-trap-Nisse".

Pappa began experimenting with a carburetor for total combustion when he was working as a draftsman at Swedish Engineering. But he was not keen to take the risk of being a draftsman nicknamed "Carburetor-Henning" for the rest of his working life. He quit, taking his drawings with him to the room above the laundry. Of course he invented other mechanisms as well, and even succeeded in having some of them put into production, but in comparison with the carburetor they were trivial. He never had much hope for any of them, not even the Radax link. Fredrik was the one who thought they could be profitable. But the carburetor, well, the carburetor was the thing Pappa believed was going to make him a very wealthy man.

We never became anything remotely resembling wealthy. Henning found himself in a patent dispute with Swedish Engineering. They claimed that the carburetor had been developed as an assignment from them, and designed by their engineers. They never denied that Henning had contributed a fair number of good ideas, they said. It was all boldfaced lies, and they must have known it. These dignified gentlemen with the straight-as-an-arrow parts in their hair and their pinstriped trousers and suit jackets had snatched my father's carburetor out of his hands the way a jackal snatches a strip of meat from a fox.

But untruths gradually become truths. Henning lost his grip on the patent, and when it eventually turned out to be worthless because there was no market for a total combustion carburetor he was already a returning patient at the detox clinic.

However, although he might have, he never blamed his misfortune on the perjurers at Swedish Engineering. The cause of his problem with the bottle, as he called it himself, was an event that had taken place in late May 1919. He was a young man and out of work. He had rigged up a spritsail on a rowboat and taken it out with a friend. So the event had to do with water, with the gentle lake water in which the boys who were out of work swam on the long, uneventful days at the beach at Rosenholm. It was the kind of water that might release the scent of flowers when it was broken by the blade of an oar or a paddle. It was covered with lily pads and made playful waves when it broke on boathouses and docks. When the sun poured down on it, it looked golden brown, and in May its shallow coves were already warm enough to swim in.

They were above the waterfall at Rosenholm, where the lake was long and narrow, sailing aimlessly and coming about, trying to catch the wind in a heavy cotton sail dotted with mildew. When they had they had been becalmed for ages and downed a few pilsners his friend stood up to have a pee. Henning couldn't really recall afterwards exactly what had happened, whether there had been a gust of wind or the other fellow had made too quick a move. At any rate, the rowboat capsized and they both ended up in the water.

When Henning surfaced he grabbed the rough bottom of the boat and looked around. He saw his friend's head in the distance and shouted to him, then watched him go under again. Henning took one of the oars that was floating nearby and swam to the spot where his friend had disappeared. The water was dark now, and furrowed by a cold, strong wind coming from the wooded side of the long, narrow lake. He swam around searching, abandoning his oar more than once to dive under the surface and try to locate his friend in the golden brown water. Suddenly he felt something around his legs, and when he tried to use them he realized they were locked. Someone stronger than himself had seized his legs and latched tightly onto them. Henning tried to swim using only his arms, and managed to get a little closer to the boat. But when the grip on his legs loosened he felt arms clambering up his body. In panic, he kicked his legs, and the arms locked around his waist. He was pulled under, the stronger one dragging him down, drowning him.

Henning felt strength come to him, though he knew not from where, and he writhed and pulled, forward and backward, again and again, until he finally felt the arms release his waist, only to grope for his legs once more. He managed one forceful downward kick, and felt something happen, felt something both hard and soft vanish down by his feet, and then he was released and managed to swim away from the rowboat and the oars and the brown beer bottles. He came to shore at a muddy, reedy spot and pulled himself up, exhausted. A long while later he was able to lift his head and look out across the water. By then, however, it was nearly dark. He could just barely distinguish the overturned rowboat out there. He knew his friend must have drowned long ago. He said he had never felt so alone in all his life.

This was the event to which Henning attributed his dependence on drink. It may be true, I don't know. We all drag a cloud of causes behind us.

Perhaps one day Elisabeth will have me buried as quickly as possible and with extreme repugnance. And regret it later? But, of course, she's not me.

It was she, not Fredrik or Jenny, who was upset enough about Henning's condition to phone Porto. I recall her soft, girlish voice, so tense with distance and anxiety. She said I'd better come.

I left early the next morning and expected, when I arrived that evening, to find him in the apartment. But it was dark. In the hall downstairs I bumped into Ann-Sophie, who smelled of breath fresheners and was having a hard time staying upright. She said he hadn't been home for days.

I had no access to the underworld where he was. I didn't even know where the entry shafts were. Without Ann-Sophie I would never have found him. I went from place to place by taxi, following her instructions. It was a cold, windy November night, and most people seemed to have gone to bed. There was a little snow. It had thawed during the day and then frozen to a crust that crackled when I crossed strange courtyards and looked up to windows to see if there were any lights on.

Henning was lying in an apartment on Foundry Street, just a couple of blocks from home. But I didn't find him until around two in the morning. I was frozen stiff by the time a tenant arriving home late let me in. The light in the hall went out while I stood there ringing short little bursts on the doorbell of a brown door. I could hear noise inside.

The man who eventually came and opened the door was in his fifties and had a bashed face. Across one of his eyes, the bridge of his nose and one cheek there was a welt. He looked as if he had fallen against something sharp. There was a foul dusty odor in the hallway, and the stench of fresh vomit from the bathroom, where the light was on. Henning was lying, passed out on a couch in the living room. I had never seen him so pale, and I was very frightened.

"Can't you see he's unconscious?" I asked the man, who had followed me on unsteady legs. "Why haven't you got him some help?"

He told me not to start getting on my high horses with him, and asked who the hell I was anyway. Here I came playing Florence Nightingale wanting to do good deeds, he said, and he knew what upper class hookers like me were like. I said I doubted it. The phone had been cut off and I had to wake people up in the apartment next door to call an ambulance. Henning just lay there on the couch perfectly still, his face pale, the whole time, and I didn't dare feel for his pulse. I thought he was dead.

On the table there were bottles and overflowing ashtrays, and he had vomited blood-colored phlegm on a newspaper someone, it must have been the drunkard circling around me, had put on the floor by the couch. It didn't look all that bad in there, actually. The table was the worst part. But they hadn't smashed things, and there were curtains and knick-knacks and even a TV with a nude china figurine on top.

The minute we got to the emergency ward a doctor came up to the gurney and took Henning's wrist. Then he raised one eyelid and shone a bright little flashlight into his pupil. He shook his head. I didn't dare ask any questions, and sat down on a bench to wait. I was very cold in my light poplin coat, and a nurse's aide who noticed brought me a cup of coffee and a blanket. I sat thinking about the poor sod we had left in the apartment. By now he might be lying there as helpless as Henning on the couch. But I couldn't muster the strength to do anything about him. There was no more booze and he would probably just fall asleep.

After an hour they let me go in and see Henning. He was alone in a small room, and there was a tube up his nose. His eyes fluttered but he didn't say anything. I don't think he was quite conscious.

They thought I should go home to bed. They assured me he was no longer in any imminent danger. I didn't know if I dared to believe it. But around four I took a taxi home to Chapel Road.

The world is full of forces at work. Henning was the one who said that. But the world is also full of chatter and murmuring, of restless patches of light and slithering shadows. He must have noticed. There is scraping and tiptoeing, there is cheeping and calling. We are always busy interpreting it. But I don't suppose we invent it, do we? Does the whispering begin deep down in the stones because we have such good ears, because we are so attentive?

Once Jenny stared at the teapot I showed her, and she wanted with all her will power to understand. But it didn't help, because it was over. Whatever it had been. It was no longer there to see. It was nothing but our old brown teapot standing on the table.

"Sometimes when I am washing the dishes I get a glimpse of something like that," she said. "You don't think about those spots, otherwise. Not when you see them every single day."

There were spots in the glaze, she was quite right about that. But they weren't what it was about. At the very instant I lifted the teapot from the table it had vanished. The pot had been on the glass tabletop among bits of tobacco and rings from glasses. At the front, right under the spout, there had been a bulge, and a spot where it looked like there were something inside, right there. Not tea leaves. Not hot water. It had been bulging and dense, almost black, with meaning.

Was it just the light? Had a shadow made the belly of the teapot heavy and dark as if a blood vessel had burst under the skin of the glaze and dissolved the strict contour between the teapot and the rest of the world?

It wasn't what Jenny thought, that I had seen our old teapot as if it were perfectly new and had just been unwrapped out of the paper from Herman Ericsson's Housewares. It was as if I was seeing for the first time, as if I had never before seen anything at all.

I felt a strange sense of loss when it was over. I felt an unbearable absence. But unbearable is a silly word. Most of the time one bears things unless the body bursts or the soul breaks, which is nothing one can predict. Absence turns to missing and missing turns to longing and longing turns to wishing and in the end one just feels a few sentimental jolts when one sees something that reminds one of whatever it is one misses. That holds true for places and men and even children. But it does not apply to my vision, not to the vision I had when I returned to 13 Chapel Road that night I got back from the hospital where I had left Henning.

I had been too long in it. In the past I had had several glimpses after that brief vision of the teapot which was the first one. But they had all dispersed. It didn't help when I tried to reconstruct them. That was just words.

Now, however, I had been able to stay in it for a long time. I thought I would never be the same again.

But I suppose I am walking around looking like I usually look. I am seeing as I usually see, too. Perhaps there is no other way to see, no other lasting way. I don't think it will happen again. I wish it would, but my vision has been extinguished. Of course I cannot walk in through the cracked, brown door without awakening my wishing. This is where I experienced the only real thing in my life.

Just before waking, I had a dream. But now I realize it wasn't a dream, it was a recollection. I am walking on cobblestones and my feet hurt. I must be wearing very thin-soled shoes. At the same time, I like the feeling of the cobblestones under my feet. I am holding a hand or rather: a hand way up high is holding my hand in its, and the grip is tight. It is a fine hand in a fine suede glove. At any moment it may let go because the palm of my dirty hand is sullying the leather. But it does not let go. Instead, another hand grasps my other hand. I release the cobblestones underfoot. I am suspended between those two hands and they lift me up. I am flying, my feet held close together in their shiny strapped shoes, a little way above the cobblestones.

Nothing else. Why is this so crystal clear?

I thought nothing new could happen to me that I had not previously experienced. Then this rises to the surface. Or is it the water clearing so I can see the bottom?

This is a memory I didn't know I had. I seem to be loaded with images like the tray of watchmaker Krantz's laterna magica. Who turns on the light?

I had to clean the apartment, but when I stood there in the doorway to the living room, I hesitated. Was I really meant to alter what was in there? I was cold and I stared at bottles and stained, opened-out newspapers, in which all I could see were the traces of humiliation and hopelessness. And yet I knew I had not dreamed or imagined what had happened. Still, there was no getting it back. There was nothing for it but to clean up.

This was the room to which Henning had retreated like an old badger under a house, sick and alone. He had not expected anyone to come to his aid, and I don't believe he wanted to go out, either. He couldn't be wanting company any more; but it was the need of a bottle that had forced him into the foray that had ended at the apartment on Foundry Street.

I didn't know how he would react to my being at the hospital when he regained consciousness. I might have to force myself on him. But did I want to?

When it came to Henning, I never knew what I wanted. My feelings spanned the spectrum, tacking wildly to and fro. I felt contempt and devotion. I felt the kind of gentle love that went out to a sick child. And desperation, I wished he would die so I wouldn't have to live with this guilty conscience, and at the same time I hoped beyond hope for him to recover so I could get on with my life again elsewhere. For many years I had thought it was all right for him just to have his wine or his brandy or whatever it was he was into at the time. Now and then I felt hate, detesting the curse, the transparent, burning sharp invisible terror. The smell of drink was the smell of horror. But I usually pretended it wasn't there. What good would it have done? I could even have a drink myself without it upsetting my stomach.

When I went up to see him the next afternoon he was lying there with a drip stand next to the bed, just as he had been the night before, but to keep the tube in place they had put some kind of molding around his nose, and now it look like the beak of a bird. He was conscious and able to speak. One minute he would talk about getting up. The only thing stopping him, he said, was the inflations in his legs. Then he would say he was done for. Suddenly and clearly he said, with the old irony in his voice:

"Well, this attempt seems to have come to an end."

"What attempt?"

"Playing the role of a person."

"Come on," I said. Because what can a person say? He sounded so dramatic, so ridiculous. I even preferred his rambling.

They kept him in the hospital almost right up until Christmas, and I stayed on at Chapel Road for the duration. Jenny didn't want me to, but it felt too cramped for me in the Otters' little house. We were always on top of each other. From my old bedroom that was Elisabeth's now there was the constant thumping of music from a record player they had bought her to keep her from playing her music in the living room. When she did, they were unable to converse, or to hear the voices on the TV. But they were actually extremely tolerant of that music. The whole house quaked from it, but all Fredrik said was:

"Heavens, I can't understand that rucus at all. But it seems to be what people are listening to nowadays."

Maybe his hearing was going. Whatever the reason, both he and Jenny coped better with it than I. I couldn't nag at her constantly to turn the volume down or close her door or, preferably, turn the record player off for a while, so I started leaving early instead. Initially, I had gone over there every evening after the hospital and stayed until Jenny switched the TV off and declared it bedtime. Now I went home earlier and earlier, and some evenings I didn't go over at all. There was no guaranteeing Elisabeth would stay in just because I came, either. She might suddenly pull her quilted jacket on and say bye. Without an explanation. And we couldn't constantly be checking on her. It wasn't like Porto here. She wouldn't accept it. Still, it felt ridiculous that Fredrik and Jenny were capable of being tolerant and open-minded, while I was just worried and ill-tempered and demanding explanations.

One evening when the door had shut behind her, I had a strong sense of time having jumped backwards twenty-five years. The same banging of the door. I was sitting on the far side of the living room, where nothing ever changed, with the bookcase and the sofa with its in blue and beige striped upholstery, and the dresser with the photographs. Jenny had a little memorial grove there. Fredrik and I each had a lovely frame, and there was a wedding picture of me alone; Hasse had been sent out to the photographer's waiting room for a few minutes. There were pictures of Elisabeth in embroidered dresses of different vintages, and there were a few objects from Jenny's childhood home, candlesticks, and on the sofa a couple of throw pillows her mother had embroidered. The bookcase contained the old, familiar books, and I pulled out *The Family Physician*. The TV was rattling away at the other end of the room, casting a blue light up into Fredrik's face. I glanced over to see if he had noticed my taking down the book — the guilty conscience was still there after over thirty years. I sat there with it on my lap, turning the pages until I found those familiar illustrations of cancroids and scarlet fever — flaming patches and spots on gray bodies. I noticed how the uterus and fetus were still missing from the see-through pages where you could examine the female body, and the thought, cruel and hasty, ran through my mind that I would comb through Jenny's belongings once she was dead and find that page. She must have hidden it somewhere. Or had she burned it, to be on the safe side?

I actually felt hatred toward her. It was absurd but it broke out in that hot room like a feverish flash of blood coursing through my body.

I have never had a proper argument with Jenny, and I don't expect I ever will.

Henning was going to be allowed out for Christmas, and she thought we should spend the holidays together.

"You never know, it might be our last chance," she said, alluding not to the possibility of Henning's death but to the Arabs having raised the price of oil by sixty percent.

I wasn't too upset about what might happen, since I owned neither a car nor any Volvo shares. But I had made up my mind that Henning and I were going to spend Christmas at home in Chapel Road. He wanted to go home. The doctors at the hospital had very little faith in the prescriptions for Dipsan and vitamins they had written. They thought he was dying. But they didn't say so. Once a nurse had mentioned the words terminal care. That was when he was in a hepatic coma.

Henning's illness had spread to his liver, muscles, nerves and brain. He had absolutely no desire to be sent to a convalescent home after the holidays, which the Otters were insistent about. They meant a detox clinic. We never argued about it, but Jenny once asked me if I felt guilty because Henning had gone right down now that he was on his own. She said I needn't.

"Why not?" I asked.

That was the only time we ever talked about it, but her conviction filtered through, as insidiously as a dripping tap: I belonged wherever my husband was. If all was to be right with the world.

I thought that if all was to be right with the world, Hasse would be able to manage fine without me for a while. I had no way of knowing it would take nearly six months.

Henning came home on the twenty-third, and he sat up for a couple of hours that afternoon watching me hang that Christmas elf in the living room doorway and arrange brown stoneware jugs of pine branches in the study and the living room. Jenny and Fredrik and Elisabeth came over for a lutefisk lunch on Christmas Eve; well actually Elisabeth, who liked lutefisk no better than *bacalhau*, had frankfurters. Henning had no appetite, of course, but he sat at the table with us. That evening he asked why I didn't go over to the Otters for a while. He said he was just going to sleep, anyway. He even claimed to have taken his sleeping pill.

In retrospect I think he started to deceive me that very evening. But I can't be certain. That he was drinking again wasn't clear to me until after the New Year. He must have been extremely surreptitious, and I never saw anybody bring him the booze. But I couldn't be in the flat at all times, of course. His gait was unsteady, but it always was nowadays, whether or not he was sober, he minced or balanced on his heels, stumbling and falling down frequently. He blamed his inflations.

It wasn't him, it really wasn't. I tried to remember his walk, but it was difficult. There were other things he did that were extremely unlike him and that embarrassed us both. It was awful the way his stomach kept acting up, but we pretended there was nothing wrong. Still, I knew he had diarrhea, and he often passed wind. Sometimes I wondered if it had been right of me to stay with him. If I hadn't been there, he wouldn't have had to be ashamed.

He was nervous and despondent, of course, and thought the whole thing was meaningless although he tried not to show it. But by mid-January I think I was the more depressed of the two of us. I had forgotten how early it got dark in the evenings here, how dull and black the mornings were, and the skin on my finger-tips cracked in the cold. I also found it difficult to decide whether I ought to go back to Porto or stay a while longer. If so, how long? Henning was better but he would certainly wind up in a coma again if I left him alone. Now I realized he was drinking again, but that he kept it within limits precisely to keep it secret from me.

To pass the time I took little assignments from Bertil Sundh who, at the time, was a page editor on *The Correspondent*. Just things like reviewing a play by a visiting repertory company, and a couple of exhibitions. He couldn't put me onto anything else. I had lost touch with the community around us and didn't understand the state of affairs that a deadpan TV reporter whose face looked like a cardboard box insisted on calling "the engerny crisis" on the evening news.

But the days rolled on and I barely noticed. This may have been because everything took Henning so absurdly long. I wanted him to eat, and I tried to get him to swallow the vitamins the doctor had prescribed. But some days he had enormous difficulty just grasping the cup with the milky coffee mixture. It looked as if he had to begin by working out which objects on the table he didn't have to try to get hold of. He had to select the cup, distinguish it from the other things by virtue of its shape or temperature or whatever his trembling fingers were investigating. Sometimes, naturally, I lost my temper.

"Drink up now," I would say. "Come on, it's getting really cold."

Then he tried to explain the problem to me and he found it just as difficult to get hold of words as of the cup.

During this period he may not have gotten worse, but he wasn't getting better, either, and when a month had passed I started thinking about what I was actually doing. Did I want him to get better? In that case I should stop pretending I didn't know he was downing some drink every day. He had grown increasingly confident that I wasn't noticing. A couple of times I ran into a man in the downstairs hall. I had every reason to believe this was his procurer. But I couldn't figure out where Henning was getting the money. Every now and then I had the feeling one or two hundred kronor notes were missing from my purse, but I couldn't prove it. I didn't want to. So I never counted my money.

One evening Henning was sitting at the kitchen table struggling over a cup of hot milk. I wanted him to drink it before taking his sleeping pill and going to bed. Out of nowhere, I found myself telling him I thought he should ask me to go to the bottle store for him if he needed booze.

I hadn't thought it through. He was probably astonished, but I didn't see his face because I was standing with my back to him washing the dishes. I did register that he was perfectly silent. Some time passed. He didn't seem to intend to answer at all. So I said it again.

"You can ask me. I won't buy any huge amounts, you know. But I'd rather do it myself than watch that character come and go with his briefcase. And it will cost less, too."

We didn't discuss it further, and he never asked me to go and buy drink for him. Soon it became obbvious he had decided to go cold turkey instead. He was depressed and spent almost all day in bed with his back to the room. He said he felt sick and refused to eat.

"That's crazy," I said. "You've got to."

But he couldn't. On the third day he had some kind of episode and I couldn't figure out what it was. His whole body trembled and he screamed, behaving as if he'd gone mad. I couldn't reach him, and he wouldn't let me touch him. He was clearly seeing things, but I couldn't tell what. Of course I called the hospital. But when I finally got the ward doctor on the line, the one who wrote his prescriptions, the fit had passed. He said it was delirium tremens. I had to go to the pharmacy and get him more medicine. Once Henning was sound asleep I began to tremble myself. I was freezing cold and frightened and felt like I couldn't cope with one single day more locked up with him in the apartment.

I felt like I was shut up with a stranger, and when I was falling asleep I saw his face. It was twisted and distorted, the face of a dwarf, evil and deceitful. That woke me up and I didn't dare try to sleep again. I'm going mad myself, I thought. But I didn't.

In the morning everything was much as usual. Henning was pale and reminded me of a sick little child. I called the doctor and asked if I could give my father a certain amount of wine or some other drink we agreed to every day. He didn't give me a straight answer, and I didn't know what to do but realized I was going to have to make my own decision, and that afternoon I went and bought a bottle of sherry. I thought that seemed about the right strength. It made him incredibly sick. It had been foolish of him even to take a swallow of it, he said afterwards, because he knew what effect it would have. The only form of alcohol his body tolerated now was clear, strong liquor. I trudged back to the bottle store the next morning, and bought a bottle of Smirnoff.

For a long time I told myself I would be able to deal with the situation by pouring him four little portions a day, a shot glass each. Naturally, I failed. However, I had persuaded myself I had the situation under control, and possibly that was what I needed. Meanwhile I was deceiving myself in the same way he had done initially, and I think that deep down, in my own very depths, I knew that, and despised him for it.

But even when he was at his most repugnant, smelled sickening and behaved falsely and even calculatingly, I was able to see the child in him. And when he was most dependent, I might glimpse the adult, the attractive man. There seemed to be layer upon layer of Henning. I was unable to say which one was the real Henning, if there was such a thing. But he was Henning. He was Henning until he no longer existed.

Toward the end we didn't talk to each other much. He found it difficult to find the words, and if he was drunk enough all he did was ramble. He didn't think his own ideas were worth expressing. He recalled how once upon a time he had told me nothing in our brains was our own. I think he actually still clung to that idea, although now it was more tangible. He believed others were manipulating his brain, and putting thoughts into it. Sometimes he saw me as one of those operators. That was upsetting.

Sometimes he also felt his brain was empty, an echo chamber where one single thought was dangling from a nerve end threatening to break. Such images were difficult to counteract. I would be silent and genuinely distressed. It was as if he wanted to frighten me at the same time as he expected me to feel sorry for him.

"I'm trying to hold onto the image," he said. "It's my last one."

When he was sober he spoke of his thoughts and dreams, and about his horrifying, transient fantasies, such as the gray rats.

"They scoot off into the corners," he said. "You can't get a hold on them."

I recognized those gray rats, but they had turned into more than just an image for him. I wondered if they were what he had seen when he was hallucinating. But when I asked he just shook his head.

He didn't have another attack until April. That time he did say something about it afterwards.

"The floor was crawling with them. The whole floor."

That was all he could tell me. It would have been a relief if he had been able to forget the things he had seen, but he clearly couldn't. Nor did his tranquilizers help. He was terrified of having another episode. After a couple of days he left, and was gone for six days and nights during which time I was unable to locate him.

When he turned up again he was so sick he had to go back to the hospital. I thought I would take the opportunity to return to Porto, but there wasn't time. After just three days they discharged him.

He was in bed most of the time after that, and I was tired of things going round in circles. I hoped he would take off and hit the bottle so hard his liver or spleen or heart would give out once and for all. But now he was pale and weak and didn't even want to touch the drink.

"Now I'm done for," he said. "Can't get a single drop down."

He hadn't been able to for ages, actually. To me this was nothing new, but the point was that it was news to him. In fact, he didn't seem to have made the connection between drinking and throwing up until now. Although as usual this was fifty percent lies or drama. He would take a swallow of aquavit and rinse it down fast with fizzy water. That was the only way he could get it down, he said.

In the mean time, the revolution had broken out in Portugal. I was extremely bitter when he didn't really see how important it was, and was unable to muster any interest in what was going on down there. But I'm not actually sure how much I cared myself. For the first few days I was worried about what would happen to Hasse and Nórdica, of course. But the workers never occupied the garment mill. After some time he phoned and said it was all just talk, talk. No work was being done. But they hadn't locked him into his office or taken over the mill itself, as had happened elsewhere. I found it extremely difficult to imagine that our senhoritas would be that militant, and I turned out to be right about that.

My intention was to go back to Porto that summer if Henning would just get well enough so I could leave him. At least he had to be well enough for me to get us both believing it would be all right for me to leave. We got through another month, one day at a time. Hasse didn't think I ought to come down yet. Things were apparently a little messier than he wanted to say.

At the end of May Henning took off again, and all I remember is the relief I felt one afternoon when I came home to find the apartment empty. At first I didn't bother going out to look for him. I sat down at the kitchen table with the window onto the courtyard open, and let the warm wind stroke my cheek. I was so sick and tired of the whole thing, and I hoped the next time I saw him he would be dead.

He wasn't, nor did I want him to be. I knew that the minute I saw his face. He had been unconscious, but they had brought him round. I didn't think he seemed too bad.

But this time he just continued to deteriorate. The change was quite undramatic, it happened as he lay in his hospital bed being looked after, getting injections and intravenous medication and everything they had to offer.

"I'm done for," he said, and that was probably the case.

It would soon be Whitsun; the days were light and the hospital park a beautiful place. He could see out the window from his hospital bed, and I had the feeling there was nothing he wished for, not even aquavit. The first time I came his head was clear, but an hour later he was delirious again. He was isolated, in a room with extra oxygen and lots of other tubes and knobs with things I couldn't identify the purpose of. I found out soon enough. The props of death were what that little room was fitted out with, and they must have thought a person who was sick enough to be put in there would no longer notice what was around him, because they hadn't made the slightest effort to disguise the equipment.

But the things around Henning preoccupied him enormously. He noticed every single detail. His huge eyes seemed to be loose in his head, he could cast his gaze anywhere, in the most unnatural way.

The veneer on the door had a remarkable grain, we noticed. His eyes followed the lines and saw the patterns, he said there was a face in it. Buttons, switches and controls were transformed into eyes and faces. He described them. They were evil, twisted with sneers. Everywhere, these faces mocked him. He was furious with the nurses, who denied the faces. Were they trying to say he was out of his mind? He asked me if there were faces, and I said yes. If he saw them, they were there. He preferred this answer, but was still suspicious. I felt his hatred and his anxiety. They focused on those faces, visible at a distance that made him unable to reach them. He wanted to destroy them he said, but what he wanted was irrelevant. His will had been murdered.

He spoke fast and coherently and it would be wrong to claim that his poisoned brain was done for, because it was working more rapidly and intensively than it had for ages, although not in compliance with any rules. He lived with raw anxiety. But at least he now had the ability of speaking in lots of words once again, in quick, almost elegant turns of phrase. He claimed complex intrigues were being perpetrated all around him. Men got into the room in disguise. They were agents, sometimes dressed as doctors, having put a great deal of ingenuity into their costumes. But a little spot on their skin or a faulty stripe on their ties might reveal them to him as agents. He was constantly striving to expose them, at the same time as he knew he would never be entirely successful. All he could do was keep them away from his life one at a time, and for every success he had on one front there was another where the agents drew closer. They had mathematics and technological inventions at their disposal. Their web was cast all across Europe, and he went cold and feverish when it hit him that they were spreading their intrigue to America as well.

I nodded off now and then, just as he did, and would wake up to find him groping for my hand with his. He wanted me to look out of the window. In the treetops, where the leaves were blowing in a strong wind, there was something happening I just had to see. There were trapezes up there, with little dogs doing pirouettes, flying from one trapeze to the next. The rustling of the leaves could be heard through the little airing pane in the window, patches of sun migrated across his sheets and his face. A nurse brought something in, a bowl or a basin, but we didn't look at her. He held my hand and the doggies just went on performing in the tree, jumping and leaping, elegant and joyous.

His lips were dry and I could see his tongue. It was rough and going gray. When I looked at him the next time, his eyelids had sunk down over the huge globes that were his eyes. He appeared to be breathing not only through his nose and mouth, but through the whole of his skin, through the enlarged pores around his gray whiskers. Time after time he would fall asleep, awaken, and fall back to sleep. I was tired myself.

He held my hand. It was still easy to touch him fondly. I was quite amazed I still wanted to touch him, because his body had become so repugnant, his skin so yellow and mottled. There was a harsh smell about him.

The hours passed and I was tired. I stretched out next to him in the big bed. The sheets were clean, but hospital laundry smelled different to me. We slept and sort of dozed.

Outside the window was a bit of the red brick wall to the right, and to the left, behind the oak tree,were all the other trees, full of leaves. A harsh wind ripped through the treetops, making the oak rustle. Between the park and the brick wall was a patch of sky, bright and empty.

The Cat

Every morning since I came home from Portugal I have had breakfast at a corner of the kitchen table where I have a view down over the courtyard. I have sat staring so hard I called forth figures who moved around the gravel and the barren lawn.

The past does not exist, of course. The girl in the brown coat, well I made her because I needed her. I was using her to fill a hole. But she is thin as paper, and virtually transparent.

The buildings exist, and the streets under my feet. The buildings that are still here are unquestionably as large now as they were then. They have been replastered, repainted, redecorated with new signs, but the core of their walls is still there: brick, mortar, darkening timber. This house is mine and mine alone nowadays, and in Jenny's opinion I should sell it. In fact, she thinks I should have sold it long ago. But I find it difficult.

"You're going down," she says. She has a whole stock of synonyms for that, and she can't see any good reason at all to live as I am living. I can see a few good reasons for living as she does, but not many.

"This isn't like you," she says. But it really is. What it isn't like, in fact, is her dreams and desires. She wants me to participate in them, but I have some of my own.

Last night I dreamed about a woman who lived on her own. I admired the lovely rooms in her apartment, and a collection of glass objects she had in the window. The only thing that made me feel sorry for her was her big pot of garden cress that had gone dry. It couldn't be watered as long as she was living under those conditions. The whole thing was laughably obvious — but it was upsetting as well. I was distressed when I saw the dense little forest of seed leaf in the cress turning into a dried-out brown crust, and I felt unhappy about it even after awakening. But her face was very different from mine. In my dreams I am blurred images awash on glass, streaming down and away, as if snow or rain had eradicated them. In my memories I am roughly hewn travesties, gaudily painted.

The minute Hasse caught sight of my face, he let out an oath. He's not the swearing type, generally. I recall him cursing once, years ago, when one of the senhoritas had been injured in the cutting room. But not until he got her into the ambulance. Now he sat there just the same way, leaning over the table swearing in a voice that sounded almost childlike.

"Merda, merda."

I covered my face with my hands. I felt like I had lost it, or it was fading.

"What have you done to yourself, Ann-Marie?"

I just stood there in the doorway to the hall, in the smell of fried meat that was filling the apartment. My fingers had slid down and caught the skin between my chin and my throat where it sagged. Hasse stared, examining me from top to toe. I had on a fleecy cotton T-shirt and a pair of jeans, clothes that were Elisabeth's but that fit me now. The only thing that was my own was my poplin coat, made at Nórdica.

I heard a sound from the kitchen and looked in that direction. There was a back, and I knew it at once although it was broader now, somewhat sturdier. She was at the stove. The frying pan was sizzling. I think she had dropped something, possibly the spatula, but now she was just standing there, stock still.

"Conceição?" I asked.

As she turned around she also bent over with an ungainly movement to pick up the spatula she had dropped. Were her knees giving her trouble? I hadn't seen her for more than seventeen years, not since the day she left for the clinic in Tras ò Montes. Going through the clumsy motion of fishing up the spatula from the linoleum, she never took her eyes off me.

"Senhora!" she gasped.

"Boa tarde, minha senhorita," I said.

"Senhora Dimas nowadays," Hasse informed me.

"Pode charar-me Conceição," mumbled the woman who both was and was not Conceição. The parting down the middle of her scalp shone bluish white, like a scar. Her hair was gathered at the back. I couldn't see whether she had it in a French roll or a big, round bun. Her breasts were heavier, her bottom wider. No more boniness, no long, loose-limbed legs.

"Como está?"

"Bon, obrigada. Tudo me corre às mil maravilhas."

"Deixa-me muito feliz," I replied. My voice sounded choked, as if it were coming from inside a little box. Hasse cleared his throat and said Conceição had been helping him out while I was away. Cooking, washing the dishes. Cleaning the apartment.

"Excelente!" I said, and then in rapid-fire Swedish: "You never mentioned this."

Not until then did Hasse stand up, and he rose so awkwardly that he swept the *Correio de Manhã* down off the table. When he walked over to me and pressed his cheek to mine, the roughness and the scent were so overwhelmingly intimate that I drew back a pace. I parried his lips, so his kiss landed on my throat. It was surprisingly wet, and Conceição stood there in the doorway to the kitchen, her eyes fixed on us. Hasse's hands felt their way down my body. He explored my ribcage and cupped my behind, where there was hardly a handful to hold.

"What have you done to yourself?" he mumbled.

The smell of fried meat had grown rank now, almost burned.

"Olha que a carne está a queimar na frigidiera!"

"Desculpe, minha senhora!"

She rushed back to the stove, pulling the skillet off the heat. Hasse pressed close into me, at the same time pushing me back out into the hall, where she wouldn't be able to see us. Over his shoulder, I caught a glimpse of our bedroom. There was a hollow from his head in the thick white spread, and a long, thin crater from his body. On the bedside table was a glass with nothing but a melting ice cube in it. Senhor had been resting upon his return from Nórdica. He had had a bit to drink, as his breath also revealed. I asked him to get me a glass of something, too, at which he rushed off, as relieved as Conceição obviously was to have the frying pan to busy herself with. She made plenty of noise when she ran water into it, the hissing drowned out the sound of the TV, where someone had been demonstrating a kitchen blender with endless professional enthusiasm. Was I going to regret not having put my finger on the buzzer which said *4 esquerda*, rather than letting myself in the with the key?

As I removed my coat, I took a closer look at the bedroom. It was very neat and tidy, and everything looked as it always had except that the photo of Elisabeth was gone from the bedside table. My jar of Visible Difference was in place, along with the grayish stone from the beach at Peniche, on the shelf over the clock radio. The red figures in the digital display shone 17:18. I remember because that's the year of King Carl XII's death, and the thought crossed my mind that those particular digits would mean nothing to Conceição.

She had been browning a piece of meat, and was now transferring it to a cast-iron roasting pan. I went over and sniffed at it, saying with the housewife's tone of voice I thought I'd forgotten years ago, that there was quite enough for all three of us.

"Obrigada, minha senhora, mas tenho que me ir para casa."

That seemed quite hypocritical, because there had been two plates out when I arrived, so I just asked her to put out a third setting. Hasse didn't express an opinion, he made himself scarce. But he gave me a whisky before going over and tipping his own glass bottom up.

"I'll go down for a nicer bottle of wine," he said.

When I said I was going to have a shower before dinner, Conceição rushed ahead of me into the bathroom.

"I'll get things ready for you, senhora! Shall I run you a bath?"

"No thank you, I'll just have a quick shower."

Her getting things ready was a clattering business. I went out into the kitchen and discovered that what she had been browning was a fillet of veal. On the shelf over the stove there was a little china Madonna. She had a halo of red and blue electric bulbs. I went out and stood in front of the television watching them julienne carrots on the screen. The situation was absurd. I managed to tell myself that in spite of the state of extreme tension I was now in.

It felt good to close the bathroom door behind me. I took as hot a shower as I could stand. Then I weighed myself on the bathroom scale and put my dressing gown right on without looking in the mirror. When I came back out, Conceição had taken out the ironing board, and laid a dark blue linen wrap-around skirt on it along with a thin batiste blouse. She had also unpacked my bag and put my things away in the bedroom. I wondered if her nightgown had found its way into the plastic carrier bag she had now put out in the hall. The electric Madonna was gone.

She had selected the only conceivable clothes in my wardrobe, my wraparound skirt and thin, gathered blouse. I had lost fourteen kilos, and now weighed fortyeight. I found it a little touching that Conceição wanted me to look attractive.

She sprayed the creased garments with water from a plastic bottle, testing the heat of the iron with her damp finger, although the iron had a thermostat. I curled up on the couch without bothering to turn the television off. A vocalist in gold lamé was singing about her heart, what it was aching for, its qualms and all the trouble it caused her. The whisky, which I had gulped down, was taking firm hold. Conceição must have noticed.

"A senhora quer café?"

I said there was no need to make a new pot before dinner, but she assured me there was a little bit left she could heat up.

"Sim, uma chavéna."

As so often happened nowadays, the past shot out to cover the present like a thin, colored plastic film across the glass of a spotlight. The lighting changed. I had a strong sense of the here and now that seemed to emanate from the smell of scorched cloth on the ironing board when it was dampened and heated. Nothing could have been more real. Or more unreal.

Conceição stands there ironing and the ironing board is reality, the hot cloth, her feet on the floor, *meu coração, meu coração*, on the radio, the coffee cooling in my cup while I ruminated. Everything is reality.

Ruminations are not reality. What was it Henning called them? Gray rats scurrying into the corners. Ruminations ruin reality, they crumble it to bits and make the coffee go cold. If Conceição stood there ruminating the iron would burn a big, brownish-black reeking hole in my best batiste blouse. That would be reality.

"Why do some people think so much?"

"Their stomachs must ache, senhora."

She laughs. It's an old joke, and not much of a joke, at that. She just wants to see if it still works. The stomach, in Conceição's considered opinion, is the source of all evil. If you read books you start to think about things and the result is that you get stomach aches. And vice versa. If your stomach hurts you start thinking, and then you begin reading and thinking even more and your stomach hurts more than ever.

"Don't you ever read?"

"Certainly not, why should I? I have no time to read," she says virtuously. "And all it would do would make my stomach ache."

I knew that answer.

"When you're young, you read," says Conceição. "I read a book called *A enganada* when I was fourteen. It was terribly sad. It was about a girl who fell in love with such a fine gentleman. He treated her very lovingly, very kindly and courteously. He gave her presents and everything. But then, of course, things went wrong. He abandoned her when she was going to have her baby. For her there was no alternative but — swish — Father's razor. Just imagine, senhora! With a razor!"

What is she trying to convey to me?

"Don't burn my blouse now, Conceição."

"I cried my eyes out, wept like a baby the second time I read it as well. It was almost worse that time. I would have done anything to keep it from ending that way. I knew, of course, the minute she went in and opened the cupboard where

386

he kept his shaving things. There was no stopping her. I was so upset I was almost out of my mind."

She irons one of the front panels, where a crease has appeared, one last time, then she turns it over.

"That's the awful thing about books, senhora. They make your stomach ache because what is going to happen is already written in them. It's like destiny."

"Do you think it's possible to change things that have happened by writing that they happened differently?"

"Naturalmente que não! What is done is done; there are untruthful books, I know that. Not to mention the newspapers!"

She sets the hot iron down on the back panel of my blouse with sensual pleasure, as if she had got hold of the most awful *Salazarismo* editor. "But if you aren't sure exactly what has happened. Couldn't you write a book to find out, to let it happen, then?"

"What good would *that* do?"

"You'd be able to stop thinking about it."

"Senhora, a thinker is a thinker. It comes from the stomach. There's not a book in the world that can change it."

We had slipped back down together. This woman was now thirty-six years old, if I was figuring right. I should have asked her what she was doing in my home, because seventeen years ago she had promised never to come seeking us out again. Conceição asked me what tablecloth she should put on the table and I said it didn't matter, we might as well eat on the one that was already there. Then I went into the bedroom and sat down at the dressing table, trying to recreate my own face, which I suddenly desperately wanted back. I was paler than I usually looked down here. When I came out, Hasse was back, and he told me my new thinness was becoming, which was very kind of him but untrue. I must have looked incredulous, because then he added that anyway he still wouldn't mind seeing a little more meat on my bones. That made me feel like a pig that hadn't turned out like it was supposed to, or a heifer. Conceição was rapturous over my metamorphosis when I came out of the bedroom, and my husband — who had had several too many by that time — raised his glass to me again. He was drinking much more than usual.

Conceição had laid the table with one of my best linen cloths, which annoyed me a little. But, strangely enough, she was just trying to show that she was pleased. Hasse had bought two bottles of nice, red wine, a chunk of *Serra da Estrela*, and several slices of *presunto*. He had set a box with a lemon tart on the sink, and Conceição was putting roses in water. He must have bought them, too.

Exhaustion was setting in, from the journey and from the tension. Now I regretted having insisted she stay. But when we sat down to dinner I turned my beautiful pastel-painted slip of a face to her, and heard myself say:

"Senhora Dimas? So you're married now?"

"Yes, senhora. To José Antonio. We got married in sixty-four, before he went back to Moçambique. And we have a son. He's nearly thirteen."

Then she asked softly:

"And Maria de Lourdes?"

"Maria de Lourdes is called Elisabeth now."

"She has both names," Hasse explained. "But we call her Elisabeth."

All three of us poked around with our knives and forks in the mess of rice grains and bits of asparagus and pieces of meat drowning in gravy. Finally, Conceição asked in a voice that was completely unlike her chattering and shouting from the past:

"Does she do well at school?"

"No," I said. "I wouldn't really say so."

Hasse told her Elisabeth wasn't untalented in any way, but that she didn't enjoy school. I noticed he kept calling Conceição Ana Maria so I asked if that was the name she went by nowadays.

"Senhora, everyone has always called me Ana Maria. You were the only one who said Conceição. That was because our names were so similar, yours and mine," she added pedantically.

I could hardly believe that. Had I objected to the *criada* having the same name as me? Had I changed her name as one changes the name of a bitch or an ass? More than twenty years later, my face was aflame.

I took it for granted that she was still working at Confecções Truz where Hasse had arranged a job for her seventeen years earlier. I didn't really believe in José Antonio Dimas as a breadwinner. Hasse didn't help me to break the silence, just concentrated unsuccessfully on scraping up gravy from the plate with his fork. In the end, I managed to ask:

"What's it been like for you at Truz since the twenty-fifth of April?"

"Don't talk to me about April twenty-fifth," she said. "That day put me out of work. The factory shut down. They wouldn't pay minimum wages. Then the new owners came in, but they only hired fifty senhoritas. There were more than a hundred of us seamstresses before."

"So what did you do?"

"I stayed on as a cleaner at Truz."

"Isto é o cúmulo," said Hasse. "You are a trained seamstress, skilled and conscientious. And there you are, cleaning at the factory."

"They have so many to choose among, senhor."

"It's a tough job," he said. "What time do you have to be there in the mornings?"

"At four."

"A couple hours of cleaning work," I said. "Can you make ends meet on that?"

She told me she also helped Senhora Antunes, the Colonel's wife and our downstairs neighbor. Oh, no you don't, I thought to myself. Odilia Antunes is just an alibi. But all I said was:

"Doesn't she use Maria Susete any more?"

"She's got a job at the radio factory, assembling transistors. They want young girls with good eyes and strong backs. So I took on the Colonel's wife. What's a person to do? You know –"

She lowered her voice, speaking in intimate tones as if she didn't want Hasse to hear. Nor did he. He was drinking his wine and staring straight ahead, right out into the vase of roses.

"You shouldn't send senhor Curtman's shirts out to be laundered. They bleach them, I can smell it. They're getting ruined. I'll wash them properly for you."

"You couldn't possibly have the time," I said.

I didn't want to promise her his shirts to wash. We ought to go our separate ways. We went on poking at the gravy on our plates, and she started making snide remarks about Colonel Antues' wife. The conversation perked up. Hasse had stopped listening. He wasn't eating, either, just taking the occasional swallow from his wine glass and staring either down at the tablecloth or over at the refrigerator door. All three of us had had more to drink than we were accustomed to. When I got up from the table Hasse went over to the television and turned on the news, then collapsed onto the couch, but I don't believe he was seeing the pictures on the screen. His eyelids were heavy and his face puffy. I asked for coffee and began to clear the table. Conceição prattled on, the flow of her words steady and soporific. I was extremely tired, and only wished she would leave. She was saying that Manuelo did well at school, and that José Antonio hadn't been able to go back to his old job when he returned from Moçambique. He might go to Frankfurt to work.

All the blood in my body seemed to have rushed to my stomach, which was bloated and working very hard on the heavy meat and fatty cheese. I had not only had more to drink than I could hold, but too much to eat as well. And still I wanted, felt almost tantalized by, the lemon tart Conceição had set out. I took a piece while I was cutting it, with my back to her so she wouldn't see. Then I shifted all the slices around so it looked almost whole again. Just as she was about to lift the heavily loaded tray and carry the coffee into the other room, she whispered:

"Is she sick?"

I knew who she was talking about and quickly retorted that she was fine. Conceição just stood there with her hands on the tray, her eyes glued to mine. I couldn't even see her blinking. To tell the truth, I was only watching one of her eyes. It was strangely like her eyes had been when she was young, brown verging on black with ripples as on a river bed, fool's gold, flakes, muck. The same eye but heavier. With what? I assumed that if I put my glasses on I would be able to observe little ruptures in the white, a fine mesh of minute burst blood vessels that had not been there before. She had a scar on her throat. It didn't look as if it had been stitched. Strange spot to hurt yourself. The nodular stripe of tightly pulled skin was redder than the rest of her brown neck, and seeing it made me feel sick.

She was still looking at me in anticipation, and now I thought of her as older than myself. Her stomach under the apron, wet from washing the dishes, was protruding.

"She's gone."

"Gone? I don't know what you mean, senhora."

"Neither do I. But I wanted you to know at least."

Truth be told, I didn't know what I wanted. It just came out when I was faced with her old, dark brown eyes.

"She ran away four months ago."

"Why? How could it happen? Was someone cruel to her? That old … your foster mother?"

"No, no, and she's certainly no old hag. She's very kind. It's just the kind of thing that happens, Conceição. Lots of young people run away from home."

"What for?"

"I don't really know."

"But didn't she have everything a child could want — a room of her own? A bicycle?"

I assured her she had.

"And no one was cruel to her?"

"No, I swear it. Not that I know of."

I started crying and turned my back on her. I tried to just stand still and hold back my tears, but they ran down onto the tart.

"There must be a man involved! You must make the police find her! Senhora, please speak with the police."

I told her I had, and that we knew she was alive and well.

"She's traveling around selling paintings, the kind they sell at markets."

"Then it can't be impossible to find her," Conceição said. "You must search for her, senhora. You will have to go to all the markets and look. Then I think it would be better if you brought her back here."

She put her arm around my shoulder and led me through the living room.

"Come along and lie down for a little while. You mustn't cry. You will find her if you just keep hunting long enough. Lie down now, you are as white as a ghost. What have you done to yourself? You mustn't punish yourself, senhora. That will just make you ill and unable to go looking for her."

She had turned down the bedspread and got me under the covers. I glimpsed Hasse in the doorway, his puffy face almost blank. He was undoubtedly terribly embarrassed, but Conceição took no notice. She brought me my coffee and a slice of tart on a pie plate, and after a while Hasse passed her in a snifter of cognac and she set it on the bedside table. She stirred my coffee and puffed my pillows.

"Take that away. It's making me nauseous."

"You're true to form," she said.

But I tossed back the cognac, for no particular reason. I ate the whole piece of tart, too, feeling like there was a huge abyss inside me I needed to fill, as if I had neither eaten nor drunk in months. Then Conceição was back with a mug of hot milk. She said it would calm my nerves. There was skin on the milk and I turned my head. She fished it up with a crochet hook from the bedside table. I have never in my entire life used a crochet hook.

"Conceição," I asked, "are you sleeping with him?"

That's right, I took the bull by the veritable horns. I said: "Dorme com ele?"

She held out the milk in front of me as if I were a child, and although I didn't want it, I drank.

"Let me tell you, senhora. You know José Antonio, what he was like?"

"I don't want to hear about him."

"He came back from Moçambique — how shall I put it? Hurt. Yes, — some of them had arm or leg injuries, they shot off all kinds of things. But José Antonio still had everything, he looked whole."

"So wasn't he?"

She tapped her temple with her index finger.

"Answer me," I said. "Don't evade the issue."

I was whispering because I didn't want Hasse to hear me out in the living

391

room. Conceição had lowered her voice, too.

"Estou a responder."

She took a tissue and wiped up some milk that had run down my neck.

"He was so lonely when I came here to help him."

"Deus me acuda! How do you think I've been feeling?"

"And I was lonely, too. I was unhappy and didn't know what to do. José Antonio is gone — I don't know where he is. Sometimes he turns up. Now he says he's going to Frankfurt. I don't know if I'll ever see him again. It was a relief to come here, senhora, but I was ashamed of my thoughts. Don't you believe me? So I went to church, to confession, for the first time since my communion, I could hardly remember the words. I said I had sinned and the Father asked me if it had been with a man. 'Well, what do you think it was with?' I thought. 'A mule?' "

"Maybe he thought you'd done it with yourself."

"Sure, I don't doubt he was an expert at that himself. I should never have gone back there after so many years. But I was at my wits' end. I wanted to be rid of those thoughts. I told him I had sinned with a man in my mind, a married man, and that I was married myself."

"What was your penance?"

"I forget," she replied, ignoring my sarcasm. "I went home after he said, 'My daughter, I absolve you'. It was such a foolish, ridiculously foolish thing to do."

I certainly agreed. Que idiotice!

"Then I sat out there in the church," she whispered. "You know what it's like. That awful smell. Dripping wax candles and mildewed fabric and incense. I thought, 'this is the smell you get, instead of the scent of a man's body'. I was very bitter, senhora. 'You will grow stooped with all the washing and cleaning and you'll come here and sit huddled up in your black shawl, your teeth rotting because you'll never be able to afford to get them fixed. And you'll be full of hatred and cruelty, Ana Maria, because that's what happens to people who have no love in sight' ".

My nausea was now constant and painful, and I knew I was going to throw up. I tried to fight it down, but after a while I had to run to the bathroom, where I vomited up my whole meal, pinkish-brown with wine, and poorly masticated. Conceição cleaned up after me and then brought a glass of water and a box of tissues into the bedroom. I felt empty and quickly fell asleep. She stayed sitting on the edge of the bed, cupping my hand in her brown, rather bony one.

When I woke up I felt soberer. I heard the sound of the television from the living room. Conceição and Hasse were talking quietly, and I had the childish feeling of being awake at a time of night that belonged to the grownups. She came in a few minutes later and when she saw I was awake she said she was going home. Senhor Curtman had told her he would get her a taxi because it was so late.

"I'm not coming back here to clean any more," she said.

She went out and put on her coat and picked up the carrier bag with her Madonna and whatever other secrets she had in it. Then she came in and extended her hand.

"Adéus, minha senhora." she said.

Adéus, she said. Not até amanã and not até logo.

"Adéus," said I. "I have to return to Sweden."

"I know."

"I have to be there if she comes back."

After that we didn't know what else to say. On her way out she suddenly turned around and walked back over to me. She sat down on the edge of the bed.

"Do you know that I saw her once? I wasn't supposed to see her at all, really. It was an awful place, that. No, I'm not being critical, you couldn't pay more for such a long time, it cost a lot of money. I worked in the kitchen, and I don't know if I could have managed just to sit there all day doing nothing, anyway. There was no way you could have known how evil those sisters were. There was a girl named Madalena. She was the one who brought in the baby bottles. The night before I left she took me into the nursery and showed me my little girl. There was a lamp on but the light was very low so I couldn't see much. And Madalena just kept nagging at me, with her "Hurry up, hurry up". She was afraid of the nuns, and of losing her job if we got caught. All I could see was a cheek and a little dark hair. But I'll never forget it. Afterwards I couldn't help wondering if it really was my own child I saw."

"Why do you think it might not have been?"

"It's just that there's no way of knowing if Madalena showed me the right baby. Everything had to be so quick, maybe she just pointed to the cot nearest the door so it wouldn't take too long."

"I imagine it really was her," I said.

Conceição gave a harsh little laugh. Then she pressed my hand twice in rapid succession and stood up and left the room. She waved before shutting the door behind her.

Hasse came into the bedroom when she had left, and I thought he looked relieved. He had put on his old woolen cardigan. Hasse is normally very particular about his clothes and shoes. He orders all his suits from a tailor. His belly protruded a bit now that he wasn't wearing his suit jacket, and I could see that his shoul-

393

ders had sunk. As he walked over to the bed I noticed he had a cold sore, a little red spot at one corner of his mouth. His eyes were red with eyestrain from reading the paper, and he was squinting slightly. He had aged. I felt like I must have been away a very long time. They were of course signs I didn't notice when we saw each other on a daily basis. Now I was seeing him as he really was, a worn, wise, independent human being. A lackluster man with great dignity. How was I going to be able to justify having left and having stayed away so long? How could I even justify it to myself? He touched me very delicately, as though I might vanish if he squeezed, or at least grow weaker. I had changed radically, and there was no way he could find me beautiful, or even pleasing to the touch. But still he touched me. I turned out the light by the bed so he wouldn't see me, and he undressed in the dark. His sinewy thighs and hairless kneecaps were intimately familiar.

But I was hurt and frightened; I couldn't let him get away with not giving me any explanation, so I averted my face and lay rigid, not only cold-hearted but also cold, frozen through and through in the thin nightgown Conceição had set out for me. He could tell right away, of course, because his body knows mine, its movements and scents. He just lay there, stretched out full length, breathing heavily.

"I was alone," he whispered.

"Cona da mãe," I whispered back. We are all alone.

I couldn't see his face, but those words had brought to mind ice floes on a dark sea, and I thought sometimes they collide with each other, apparently. Sometimes we collide.

"But why her, of all people?"

"It just happened. I bumped into her at the café nearby. She was queuing up for *pastéis de nata*, she always loved them."

"She still does, you can see that from her bottom."

"She needed a job. And I needed help, didn't I? There was nothing intentional about it, it just happened."

"Did she move in here?"

"Are you mad?"

"Her crochet hook, and that damn Madonna."

"That was mine," Hasse said. "I won it in a *loteria* the senhoritas were holding. I gave it to her."

Not many hours ago, he had sat in the warmth of her hearth. I wept. He stroked his thin, nervous fingers over my cheeks, trying to catch my tears. I thought about Conceição the moment before I had put the key into the lock, humming over the fillet of veal, and under the apron, damp from washing dishes, deep inside her belly

Elisabeth's unwoken half-siblings, halves of them, as soft as the unfertilized eggs in the entrails of a chicken but many more, like the hard little unripe fruits on a grapevine before they have begun to swell, like green flies clustering around a stalk.

"She's got everything I lack. How could you?"

"She won't be coming back," Hasse said firmly, and I wondered to what *mancebia* I had thereby relegated him. I didn't dare reject him any further, and in fact I was so cold I desired him. But inside I was drier and more fragile than ever, I felt, when he thrust cautiously into me, as if my membranes were made of old, crumbling silk; I came to think of a cracked lampshade, the pale pink one back home in the study, with its smell of dust and its burns from too strong light bulbs. Neither of us really wanted liked having to use lubricant. I imagine he was as turned off as I was of the unpleasant routine we now always had to go through, the gooey gel, the cautious probing, and the long wait until the stinging and tension started to pass and I dared to open up. The cream was cold and I shivered; I was jumpy, shaky, nothing but nerves and nausea and distress, nothing but longing for warmth and calm. We had our rituals, our habits of decades. Hasse had known what he needed to know about my body, it was a labyrinth the twists and turns of which he could follow blind and in the dark, but now there were unfamiliar stones and roots on the path. He cursed mildly again, unlike him.

"Merda, what have you done to yourself? You've got to come back home. What have you been doing, Ann-Marie?"

I had been careless with one of his dearest possessions, abused it into unsightliness. He was having trouble forgiving me, and I felt a bit put off by his grief for the fourteen kilos of fat tissue I had burned, and I thought: "I'll pile books onto the bathroom scale, see just how much fourteen kilos is, see what I've been carrying around, what he has loved " Conceição was heavy and smooth. When I felt his calves, icy cold with perspiration, I imagined how she would have been able to keep him warm, how the two of them would not have collided kneecap to kneecap, no messy lotion, no rubbing membranes. She was undoubtedly creamy as an avocado, but with an *emagrecimento* like this, the truth will out, the truth that so seldom reveals itself.

I woke up early. The sky was pale. It looked for a few moments as if it were going to go white, and the feeling that it was losing color all the time brought soup bones to mind. But then it broke into gold and juicy orange. The cocks down in the yard began to crow louder and more harshly, the dogs to bark monotonously, with neither anger nor the hope of change. Hasse was asleep alongside me, his face a little ashen with old, long-suppressed fatigue. I went out into the living room where there was a sourish scent coming from the now open roses with their ruffled brown leaves. Conceição had dried the dishes and tidied the kitchen before leaving. Not a trace remained of the previous evening or of herself, with the exception of a space between the tea tin and the kitchen timer, where the haloed Madonna had stood, plugged into the toaster socket.

The trees in Santos Castanieras garden began to rustle in the wind, and when I opened the balcony door I smelled wet leaves and heavy earth although we were in the middle of town. I felt sad knowing I had to leave again, but there was nothing else for it. Hasse must have realized it, too, because he had not repeated that he wanted me to stay. He was quiet, holding back; sometimes he reminded me of an old, subdued tom-cat, who never moved unnecessarily, made no more noise than he had to. He was biding his time.

When he had pulled away last night, abandoned himself to his vigilant, always too short sleep and the dreamless state he always claimed he slept in, I had gone out and had a wash in the bidet. I felt I had been treated lovingly, as always afterwards, when I sat there with my soapy hand cupped over *a cona* and his seminal fluid running out into the water, down the drain. At that moment I thought I'll kill myself if she gets pregnant. But of course I wouldn't; I would never be told. In addition to which there was no more prudent man on earth than Hasse, at least no one I have ever met. I thought, how odd, nothing has actually happened, no one has deprived me of anything. Still, I feel as if some quack who called himself a surgeon had cut something out from inside me. I was in pain and something was running right through me and I wept, dry, whining tears for myself alone. *Il faut choisir madame!* But, as always, I had made the wrong choice. I'm hopeless at choices. I don't know if that's a defect in me or a kind of immaturity I might grow out of some day.

I went back to bed, and when my leg hit the corner in the dark I allowed myself a few permissible tears and the taking of some comfort, I sucked it out of his prickly cheeks and his lips dry with sleep, like a bumblebee hungering in winter sucks sugar solution. After that I fell asleep and dreamed I was back in this apartment for good. I was housewifely, cleaning and folding and arranging. I had heaps of cloth and garments to organize. It had to be put into suitcases and drawers. Sleep never releases me from my Martha-duties, it never allows me to pick out the good bits, but rushes me more than waking life, telling me I will never learn to cope with *practicalities*. I am chained to thousands of circumstances and my dreams tell me, cruelly: this is where your excesses get you! All you can do in your earthly existence is to move matter around. Anxiety and intrusiveness steer you. You do and do again and do again and you never get things organized so what you need is packed or unpacked and what belongs in the drawers is there — you're hopeless at choices.

But now it was morning, and the spring sunshine warmed me as I stood slicing bread. Hasse came out blinking, scratching the front of his pajamas, and after a cup of hot coffee he spoke, though not much. Of Conceição we said nothing until he was on his way out.

"Can you get her a job at Nórdica?" I asked.

Making him hire Conceição might have been like hanging a slaughtered chicken around the neck of a dog that couldn't rein in his urge to chase chickens.

"It's not all that easy," he said.

He griped a bit about the state of things since April twenty-fifth. Hasse doesn't think very highly of their revolution. He sees it as nothing but talk and red tape. The cleverest, best seamstresses steer clear of trade union undertakings, he says, so he has to negotiate with the loud-mouthed, ignorant ones. You couldn't just sack somebody, *pôr na rua*, and right now there wasn't a vacant sewing machine. Just about every day there were senhoritas lining up outside the gates asking about work.

"What about in the pressing department, then? Or the cutting room?"

"We'll see," he said, and left.

Before I departed at the end of the week, I went out there with him one morning to see the improvements he had organized. He had had new floors laid in the bathrooms, and the canteen walls were painted a pale yellow. There was a machine now where the senhoritas could buy *café com leite* for three escudos. He had ordered cassettes of Eurovision song contest hits and planned to set up at little outdoor break area for them if he could get the money. He was proud of his arrangements, and almost jolly when he treated me to a coffee from the machine. He said he intended to make Nórdica the finest *fábrica de confeccõeas* in Porto.

There was Conceição already on the shop floor, setting up cloth for pleated skirts on folded cardboard patterns and popping them into a hot steam press. It wasn't precisely the position of choice for a schooled seamstress, but Hasse intended to give her a machine the minute there was a place free. Her grave, brown eyes and the hint of a nod she gave me as I passed told me not only that she was under piecework pressure but also that life seeks its way to the trivial just as water finds its way down into dry crevices; sooner or later everything becomes mundane.

Before I left Porto I had organized a cleaner for Hasse. I should have done that the first time.

I landed one afternoon, finding March spring weather at home. Sickly piles of snow stood here and there in the meadows, and the windshield wipers swept off brown slush the shade of excrement mixed with bits of tarmac the studded winter tires had ground away. I sat watching the roadside ditches swelling with foamy yellowed water and stiff lines of last year's grass coated with a film of dried mud. From the train window I had been surprised, as always when I returned, by the space between the houses. The desolation struck me, along with the light, out of the huge, cold, pale sky.

That evening when I went to bed I thought:Now I'm home. Or am I? I'm back at least. Tomorrow I shall wake up and think the same thoughts, do the same chores as before, and see the same people who will say roughly the same things. I will walk down the same street again, and carry my TetraPak of milk back in a bag.

I woke up at half past five with a blinding headache. The wind tore at the house. Between gusts there were the birds, mostly one male blue tit. The smell of apples that had been lying in a bowl going dry or rotten wafted toward me. It was both sweet and at the same time a little off, a little sickening.

Was I tired of the fragile existence I had arranged for myself here while I waited, an attempt at a life, dull and somnambulant, or was I depressed by the weather or downcast because of Hasse's escapade, or was my sense of desolation attributable to the constipation I always suffered from when I traveled between Sweden and Portugal?

Tedium is a strong propellant, I have always known that. But my own sense of boredom had seldom led me anywhere; I have always wallowed in it. Perhaps I am patient by nature. But on this particular morning, with the wind tearing at the house and the melting snow and dirty slush rushing by outside and the stab of the knife in my stomach every time I thought about Hasse's white back clamped in the vice of Conceição's yellow thighs I thought I just had to do something, that anything at all would be preferable to sitting staring down at the patches of lawn that had appeared under the thawing ice and filthy mounds of snow. *The Correspondent* had arrived in Gabriel's mailbox in the downstairs hallway, and I borrowed it and read it thoroughly. I tried to imagine what it would be like to walk into Bertil Sundh's office and ask if I could start freelancing again on a commission basis. By about eight when Gabriel came up, I had been through the paper twice.

Gabriel spoke in his slow, slurred voice. He was wearing a fleece pullover with a galaxy of dandruff on the shoulders. He looked a bit peculiar to me, but that was because I had just arrived from Portugal. Sitting there stirring his tea, he asked if I had seen it. His eyes wandered to the curtain. I hadn't noticed the letter pinned to the cloth. I had to get up to read the words:

Mamma!

It's lighter out now!
Now, early in the morning, I can see it
and feel it.
It's lighter out now,
longing never ends.

She hadn't signed the note – or the poem if you wish. But she had surrounded the text with flowers and birds with their wings spread wide. One of them looked like a duck.

"When was she here?"

Gabriel didn't know. Some time while I had been away. She was probably picking some things up, he thought. She had, in fact, taken some clothing, as I could see when I went in to look. Then I walked slowly around the apartment, looking for other signs. But there were none. The kalanchoë was well-watered, but I supposed that was Ann-Sophie's doing. There was dust on the dresser in the study, a fine, even layer that was perfectly clear in the gray morning light. There were fingerprints in the dust on the photo of Henning. I felt a sharp, contorted desire to weep, but found myself shivering instead. The electric heating had been off, and the apartment was still chilly.

When I went back out into the kitchen Ann-Sophie and the Whitepainter were there, too. No one said a word, I suppose they were uncomfortable with seeing me so sad. The blue tits chirped jubilantly and aggressively outside the window, and the radiators clicked. Ann-Sophie eventually commented that things were tough all over nowadays.

"God," she said, "she might have a little consideration for you and your feelings, that girl of yours."

I was still shivering, so the Whitepainter lent me his sleeveless sheepskin jacket and Ann-Sophie poured me a cup of deep-brown tea. I leafed through *The Correspondent*, contemplating what it would be like to go back to work there.

"Somebody's discovered a body down by the tracks," I said. "The body of a man. Unidentified! It was buried in the snow until the thaw."

"Let's have a look," said Gabriel, reaching for the newspaper.

What it said was that the body had been lying there since the first snowstorm, and that the time and cause of death had not been established. He had been carrying no documents that enabled the police to identify him. All he had was a train ticket, a one-way ticket from Stockholm, date of issue 26 November.

"That was the day I arrived!"

"Must have been a drunk," said Gabriel.

"Was he wearing tails?"

I was thinking of the illusionist who was on the same train as myself, Ann-Sophie's former drinking partner, lover and employer. She must have realized what I meant, I could see it upset her, in fact more than upset her. She stood up quickly, her face gray. She suddenly looked as if she had stomach cramps. I hadn't realized she was so soft-hearted, and regretted having blurted that out. She walked out without a word, her steps on the stairs slow and hesitant. I hoped she wouldn't throw up in the hall downstairs.

"Tails? Why would he?"

"I was just thinking about that Egon Holmlund," I said. "His mother lives in the house over by the school, on the other side of the tracks. He might have been going to see her."

"There's nothing about what he had on," said Gabriel. He soon lost interest in the dead man and turned the page of the paper. The Whitepainter returned from the bathroom, shaking out a damp towel.

"A society that does not satisfy its obligations," he grumbled solemnly, and I knew this was his formulaic phrase when the water ran brown out of the taps, and there was rusty sediment in the toilet bowl.

Through the window I saw Ann-Sophie cross the courtyard. She was walking fast and unsteadily, and didn't look up at us. I thought, now she'll make a beeline for the bottle store.

"A bungled human creature awash in the general current of life."

"What the hell do you mean by that?" the Whitepainter asked.

I hadn't meant to say it out loud. It was something I had read. I didn't know where. Things I read often surface in my mind. And drown again just as fast. It's like all the rubbish floating in the seaweed along the beaches, broken bottles, driftwood grayed to silver in the sun, gym shoes, bloated oranges. I explained to them that those weren't my own words.

"Well, it was a shitty thing to say, anyway," said the Whitepainter.

Gabriel and he stared at me, their faces blank as those of animals. They reminded me of the stone angels on the house Tora Otter lived in when I was a child.

When they left I felt abandoned. Gabriel soon crossed the courtyard. Off to work someplace, I imagined. The Whitepainter seemed to be staying in, and I decided to go down and see him. I didn't bother getting dressed, just pulled on my poplin coat over my dressing gown. He said nothing when I came in, hardly looked up from the can he was stirring. There was paint in it, of course. Although people said all he did since he lost his mind was to paint junk white, bottles and cartons, discarded purses, mailboxes and old clocks, I could see it wasn't true. Most of the works were things he had made. Oblong boxes reminiscent of coffins but not large enough to hold more than a forearm. He still makes those boxes, always sealing them with white string. No one knows what they contain. Some of them slosh a bit, or rattle like sand or whisper as if balled-up paper were rolling around in them. But some are silent, and they will all be silent one day, anyway, when whatever is in them has shriveled up and been disintegrated.

He has told me he feels confident when he is making them; he feels true. And I think they are true, if there is any such thing as truth. No matter whether they contain preconceptions or hypocrisy or castles in the air, they will eventually shrivel up and be disintegrated. The mummies or chrysalises in the oblong boxes are idols that cannot be invoked. There is no way to know what is in them; the germ of life or a trivial joke. Fragments of words from newspapers. Or just a stain. The seed of physical or mental illness. Or nothing. The whole secret: nothing.

The Whitepainter's work has been exhibited in Stockholm, but people here in town just laugh at the whole idea. Here they know he is nothing but a harmless fool because he no longer runs classes at the WEA. Perhaps he ought to leave town, but I don't think he can. He doesn't like this city and people here aren't very kind to him.

Now his studio is what was once my Grandfather's grocery. His oblong boxes stand there lined up, on end, looking like bones going white, relics. They are frightening and at the same time very beautiful. It is a cruel, sad world we live in and even if we scrape the bones white we will not make it clean. Every time he finishes a box and seals it, tedium is lurking. It's there, in the very dust on the floor, curled up lying in wait in the corners. When the ceremony is over, when the object has been glued, painted and tied up with his white-painted string, he stands there like a tired, downhearted lover. All is as before. When it comes right down to it, I find it strange that he manages to do anything at all. I once asked him about it and he took my question seriously. I sat there watching him, noticing how much he had changed during the time I had been at home. Everything about him was becoming elongated. His nose, his chin, and even his arms were being drawn out. There was something about his gaze as well that I hadn't seen in his eyes before. A kind of watchfulness or chill in them, a gray, dead spot.

"You have to make up your mind," he said. "You have to start somewhere. No matter how smooth the wall may be there is always some chink you can start working on. You have to start there. Otherwise – "

"Otherwise? But Michael, as long as the wall is smooth all the possibilities are still there."

"That is a temptation that must be overcome," he replied. "You have to make up your mind. Start somewhere."

I'd like to tell the Whitepainter I feel like a child.

I am a child. I own nothing. In my coat pockets are candy wrappers and string and a strange shaped shard. I wish for nothing because I actually know very little about the world. For the moment I am dressed up in the blouses, dresses and shoes of an adult woman. In a few years everything I own will have been replaced, or will have disintegrated or spread to the winds.

I have nothing, not even hair and teeth. I am hair, teeth, blood. I do not have a soul. I am possessed, pervaded, illumined. Through me courses water I am unable to retain. I am not a vessel. I move through the world; the world moves through me.

I thought I owned a house and could do with it as I pleased. There was something calculating about me when I traveled home to dispose of it. I was a child, but there was a germ of intention in me. My breakdown was contrived, as when an author composes the culmination or peripetia of a novel.

Our childhoods we mostly use as scrap heaps. We dig and claw to find something useful, something to explain how we grew so gnarled or twisted, or less happy than we would like to be. We seek inequities. This house smells sort of embarrassing, in fact more than a little if you come right in from out of doors. But it is reality. My childhood was the tin of photographs.

I would like to tell the Whitepainter that something happened to me here I have never experienced anywhere else. But I don't have the courage. Perhaps he knows anyway? I rehearse what I would say if I ever told him: I lie here and I see other worlds, and as I do so I am losing weight and developing inexplicable sores on my body. I am sick and freezing cold when I wake up and I have no idea at all of how long it has been going on. For the first few days I spend a lot of time thinking about it, trying to recall what I experienced. But I am unable to salvage very much from the ruins. I try to reconstruct it in words but it just grows more and more blurred. It slips away like a shifting island and in the end I can no longer distinguish it. I

403

only have vague memories of these dreams, or whatever they are, and I feel abandoned and believe I may never get to experience it again. In the end I try to forget it, I believe that would be the best thing for me. Most people do have to live without this — don't they? So I suppose I'll have to, too.

But it seems to me that a vacuum has developed inside me that is constantly longing to be filled. Now there is just a little rubble in there, scraps of memory, fragments — like in your sculptures (though that must be the last thing I would ever dare to say?) and it can be heard for a while, rustling and ticking. Then it ceases.

But the things I have experienced in that way are much more powerful than anything else I have ever known and the vacuum they have created seems to be eating away at my life. Nothing else seems truly real and no projects seem to be worth the trouble in the light of those visions I cannot account for without destroying them.

What is all that?

I don't actually think I want to ask Michael, and there is no one else I can think of. I couldn't possibly talk to Synnöve. She would tell me I am trying to establish my identity. That's what she's always busy doing. "Who am I?" she asks herself gravely, and she is prepared to pay a great deal of money to find out, yes, even to lie down on a gym floor and allow total strangers to caress a personality out of her. She is so robust. I sometimes think about how susceptible she has been in her life, all the things she's been subjected to. Myself, I've always been good at curling up and hiding.

That same spring I sat with my elbows on the kitchen table looking down into the courtyard and waiting for Elisabeth to turn up, Synnöve's mother had a stroke. She was hospitalized, and Synnöve started coming to town to see her several times a week.

Her mother could neither speak nor move. When asked whether she was in pain, she could respond by squeezing your hand twice. They had told her that meant no. If anyone had asked her whether she was suffering, I imagine she would have squeezed gently once for yes. But no one asked that question. The nurse's aides asked if she was thirsty, if she wanted to be turned over, and if she was looking forward to Synnöve's visit. Her weak but insistent squeezes merged and became a number of no's, when she was probably trying to say yes. She couldn't answer questions by squeezing a certain number of times for certain letters; she had lost the ability to count and was unable to put words together. She was most receptive to singing. So Synnöve sat by her bed holding her limp little hand and singing all the songs she could think of. Jenny found it all very upsetting, and didn't want to go and see her in spite of their having known each other quite well. They had been Women's Defense Volunteers together.

"What's the good of their keeping her alive?" she asked.

From the very outset, Synnöve had been the kind of child who pleased her parents. She had walked early, talked early and plenty, and in kindergarten she had made the loveliest coltsfoots out of shiny paper. We finished school the same year, with her at the top of our class and valedictorian. Synnöve's mamma has a photo on her bookcase of her daughter at the ceremony in her white suit, a student cap and net gloves, rows of teachers and students listening attentively to her addressing them.

The year after we left school was her college year in the US, after which she returned to study languages at Uppsala. She starred in student theater productions and later in the Uppsala drama society's annual variety show. That was how she found her way into television. Sometimes when I see her as moderator of a debate on death or young people's drinking habits I remember the student revue that was her first, how she kicked her way into the media world on her long, thin legs in black net stockings, with a high hat on her head and coat-tails waving above her black panties.

She took an advanced secretarial course (she uses her pinky finger when she types), worked as a script girl, took a course in producing, and had a brief term of employment on the civic community editorial staff of the main national daily. By the time she got into the television newsroom she had gone deadly serious. No one associated her performances with leg-kicking any more. Perhaps for her fiftieth birthday some envious, well-intentioned colleagues will find archive footage of that variety show. It was broadcast on the single black-and-white TV channel we had then. But by that time it won't matter.

Now she has her own evening program. She looks straight into the camera and her firm gaze contains a promise of something we all wish, deep down, were true: that every problem has a solution.

Here in her former home town, she is admired. She is often in the headlines of *The Correspondent*, and in the columns, where she is lovingly and familiarly criticized. The readers know everything about her divorces, and thinks she'd make a good Prime Minister. Synnöve is rational, energetic and vigorous. She is those things even when she is in one of what she calls her "crises", for instance when her mother was on her deathbed, or the time she got ominous-sounding results from a cervical smear. Or when she was heading for divorce, as she was again now. At the very same time, she could sit there singing her mother out of life, and keeping both herself and the nurses cheerful. After a while, she asked for a leave of absence and moved into her mother's apartment. Every evening when she got home from the hospital, she would phone me. We never talked about her mother, since there wasn't really very much to say any more except that she was dying and that it was taking some time. Nor did we talk about Elisabeth, because I didn't want to any more. No, we talked about Synnöve's second husband, who was in the process of becoming her second ex; we inventoried his shortcomings.

There was nothing she said I could disagree with. He had certainly proved to be a fairly serious asshole. He had had too many drinks at parties and fooled around with other women right there before Synnöve's eyes. Undoubtedly, that was his way of compensating. He had very simply been unable to handle her success. Once he even gave her a black eye, so she had to take sick leave (that was when she was a news anchor). He had always wanted her to be feminine in a motherly way, and when she chaired discussions it made him impotent. He had never really had much to do with the children, particularly the two from her first marriage.

The decision to divorce him had been made long ago, although Allan hadn't really realized it. He clung on to Synnöve as a symbol of motherhood, and this expressed itself in various ways. For instance he would regularly turn up at their home to discuss what furniture he was going to take and what pieces Synnöve would need. And he didn't limit himself to the large items such as the piano and their pine dining table, he would delve into the books, the vases, the typewriter, their red extra phone and things like that. One might have thought Allan had turned into a cheapskate and Synnöve into a stickler for detail, but that wasn't what it was about. She explained to me how he kept coming over out of a need to prolong their connection. He was quite simply dragging out their marriage; to him it was a victory if they could quarrel about their possessions, a sign of her involvement. It was all emotional, and meant that he wasn't ready to release her. In addition to which it was characteristic of their whole relationship. Allan was a parasite by nature, he had been taking advantage of Synnöve's femininity and motherliness but had been unable to give anything in return. She told me he had been a delayed ejaculator. For most of their marriage he had difficulty climaxing. Sometimes he would have to go at it for hours to be able to present her with a few pitiful drops. This, said Synnöve, was symptomatic, an expression of his emotional parsimony, his dread of losing anything!

But that must be a recent development, I said, because when you were first married you used to complain that he came too fast. She retorted how that had only been for a really short time; this wasn't the first time she was irritated by the arbitrary nature of my memory, either. She was firmly convinced it all had to with how they related to existential being and ownership: Allan was a person whose life was based on *having*, Synnöve's on *being*. This was why she had become the object (that black eye!) of his fixation with the mother. He was a ravenous child trying to find a substitute for his mother's breast, so now he was moaning about bookcases and extra phones in order to replace this surrogate that was being torn away from him in the midst of his midlife crisis. He didn't know what to do with his life. If I understood her account of his own summary correctly, he was going downhill fast, looking in the rear-view mirror and asking himself: was that all?

He had once been a socialist, but now he felt let down, as does Synnöve, although she grits her teeth and says the fight must go on in the environmental and peace movements. She was once an active feminist, but now she thinks things have gone too far. Just look at poor Allan –a victim if ever there was one!

Yes, Allan had also fallen prey to the patriarchy, and there he stood at the top of the hill, with thinning hair and a potency problem – which must be what was driving him to appear extra virile at parties, according to Synnöve. She had recommended rebirthing to him after having been through it herself, but that's a kill-or-cure remedy and I wondered whether poor Allan, on his way downhill, with his delayed ejaculation and his drinking problem, had the stamina for it. You have to lie on the floor with all kinds of other people for an hour and a half to two hours, breathing, with the guru or facilitator walking around checking that you're doing it right, which means inhaling and exhaling so hard and long that your consciousness finally levitates or something. Synnöve calls it a kick, says you're hurled back into your past and if you're lucky and your endurance is good you may get all the way back to your birth and re-experience it. That's supposed to be great. I see it as a way of starting over again, and who wouldn't want to start over?

Synnöve, energetic and ambitious as she is, breathed for two if not three hours, of course, and was duly rewarded. She thinks I should try it, but I don't think it's right for me. I get headaches so easily, in addition to which I couldn't afford it. Rebirthing costs two thousand five hundred kronor. But I don't mention not having the money, because I don't want her poking her nose into my finances. If she ever found out Hasse was sending me money, she'd have a conniption fit. She still thinks I need to make something of my life.

This whole business of everybody having something to contribute and of everybody being creative in some way if they are just given the opportunity has

407

always been a hobby horse of Synnöve's. I think she just cannot accept that some people can't make a glossy coltsfoot no matter how hard they try. She's gifted, extremely talented, and she possesses energy and vitality and a high level of ambition not to mention an iron will. I think she imagines, in her heart of hearts, that my equipment is just the same as hers.

In any case, it is perfectly self-evident to her that I will support myself, and I think it is too, actually. I just can't figure out, right now, precisely how it will happen. If I went to the employment exchange I suppose they'd recommend cleaning, or the supermarket checkout, both of which are horrendous thoughts to me. Sometimes I watch the girls at the register when I am shopping, and am grateful that Hasse can still send me some money. And I have the rent income as well, Gabriel and the Whitepainter insist on paying, and there's no way I can sell the house until I know how things are going to work out.

In my long evening phone conversations with Synnöve, I managed to steer clear of my financial situation, which truly was a scandal for the whole of the female sex. She was extremely preoccupied with her own divorce, and probably didn't think much about me. Now she had put Allan's furniture out in the driveway, anyway. She said she'd done it the last time she was in Stockholm. She phoned him after the fact.

And then came here. Of course she had done it to force him to let go of her. It might sound cruel, but it had to be.

"What if it rains? His furniture will be ruined!" I exclaimed.

"That's his problem," said Synnöve. "He has to learn to take responsibility for his life. He expects me always to be there for him."

I have been living for so long in a country where divorce was unthinkable, that I don't have much experience of all this; I don't know what to say to her. But I don't think what I say matters much, anyway. She just needs someone to listen. I'm terrified she's going to start in on my life, because now that she's put Allan's furniture out in the driveway they're finished with each other, in a way. Synnöve's moving on now. She's come through her crisis — well, there is the business with her mother but her condition seems to have stabilized, so Synnöve's stopped coming to town so often. I can tell she's started thinking more about my situation, because she asks about Hasse. I suppose our friendship wouldn't be worthy of the name if my lips were sealed about everything relating to myself while she so generously pours out her story. In fact she's said as much a couple of times. I didn't like hearing it, but there was more than a grain of truth to it. Synnöve says she has a dream of total openness. People should be transparent to one another. The subjective around us should be as obvious as the objective; there's nothing to be evasive about.

I need my secrets, but I don't feel like saying so to her, it sounds so selfish. She lives for and from making her life, her views and her solutions to problems public. She fillets life like a fish, holding up the bones and saying look, it's as simple as this; you don't have to mystify it. She holds up the bones of solidarity, and the bones of exploitation, and having, and being, and the like. She makes everything perfectly clear and I honestly think she does a lot of good. She's had programs about young people's drug abuse, for instance, and I think it was good for many people to hear that they didn't have the children they deserved — career ladder climbers and materialists and unfeeling egotists like themselves — but that in this area too, a market has developed, there are people who have a profit motive in getting our kids hooked on smoking hash and then moving on to harder, more expensive drugs. She started making those programs when her own son Peter had taken up with a crowd of hash smokers at Bromma Upper Secondary. She founded a parents' group and went out with a film team to drug dens, and worked more or less day and night for three months. She never sat there troubling over what had gone wrong, because she knew. She had dissected the issue long ago, filleted the fish and lifted up the bones for all to see. She had even dug out her own feelings of guilt, although they were as well concealed as that deceptive little extra row of bones on a pike. She rolled up her sleeves and made a series of programs, ending with a panel discussion. She was deeply determined to do good, and she undoubtedly did good, too. In the course of events she was threatened by anonymous callers, and received letters accusing her of being on the side of the drug addicts and the parasites of society. There were editorials where she was rebuked as being tough on crime, and reviewers who called her a liberal fart — and she coped throughout. I never could have.

I am quite sure she will be making a program about terminal care when her mother finally dies, and there will certainly be one about splitting up as well, after this business with Allan, so people can get the help they need with death and divorce. It is important for people to know they're not alone with their problems, that they aren't useless, or social outcasts. I assume she sees our problems as what we have in common. In which case we might as well be transparent to one another.

She holds a conviction: that everyone has something to give, something unique, and that at the same time we all have a great deal in common. Deep down we all have the same desires and the same problems and the same guilty consciences or whatever we have inside. There is something slightly contradictory about it, but it may still be right. She says she has a democratic view of humanity. So she denies that there are any real differences between us. All human beings are of equal value, and I suppose she is right about that. If she says so, she is probably right. Value is something we attribute. It isn't there from the start.

"Good grief, what a nihilist you are!" cries Synnöve at the other end of the receiver. I like it when our conversations don't get too serious, because I know that otherwise I tend to say things I later regret. After all, Synnöve and I have known each other since we were seven, and there isn't actually all that much we haven't already said. But we tend to be able to vary what we have to say in quite pleasant ways.

Allan, however, was a theme we had now varied exhaustively, and with his furniture in the driveway he was relegated to the annals of history. It was completely clear to both of us that it was the only thing to do to divorce this fifty-something swine who wanted not her but a mother figure and a sex symbol.

Still, when Synnöve has been talking for a long time I get tired.

Then I say things I don't mean, or at least don't mean to say. In fact I'm so tired I don't actually know what I mean any more.

We often find it difficult to bring our conversations to an end, despite the heat of the receiver and having to change sides because my ear is hurting. She must feel the same way although she is more robust than myself in all respects.

"But won't you be terribly lonely now?" I ask.

"How can you ask? You can't really think I should sell myself for a little security that isn't really even security?"

"Well, I don't know. Won't it be lonely for both of you this way?"

"I can't believe you're saying that. You know very well that a person is lonelier in a relationship gone sour than out of it," says Synnöve.

"Oh no I don't."

"You must!"

But when I'm that tired all I know is that I am afraid of the dark and lonely and I don't believe in a better solution or a more conflict-free relationship. We talk and we talk and are unable to bring the conversation to closure because we are both afraid of the night. Or maybe she's not?

I am. When the storm tears at the house and exhaustion keeps me from reading, I wander around the apartment. It pleases me if I see a light on when I look out the window. But it's very unusual for anyone to have a light on at night here.

I don't think you could call me an insomniac. I just often wake up and when I wake up I get up and pee and then roam around for a while. I don't think it's personal problems or national disasters that frighten a person at night. If we do dwell upon them, it's to protect ourselves from the deeper terror. At night a few trivial worries suffice to hold one enormous worry at bay. That I will die, that every one of us is alone, is the enormous worry that follows me into my dreams and makes me prefer rambling around to going back to sleep.

The storm tears at the treetops on Chapel Road and at the iron carpet-beating rack in the courtyard. It shakes the house, roaring:

"You will die. You are all alone. You are powerless. You will suffer. Everyone must suffer — do you hear? Don't sleep too deeply. Remember you're no longer a child. You will die, before which you will suffer. You will lose your loved one or you'll leave him alone. You're so powerless you can't even help your own child. She must also suffer, there's no getting around it. You have been careless, and rushed through your life. You committed your greatest errors in your haste and confusion, as in a dream. Your confidence was all show. You actually never believed you could control your life — and you were right! Listen to me howl at the corners! I could tear this house down and leave you all out in the cold. But I won't, not this time. I'll just rip at the roof and the iron of the carpet-beating rack, and if I get really carried away I'll snap one of the boughs off the old apple tree you consider a talisman. Then you'll come out in the morning and think: 'Good God, if the storm takes the apple tree — we'll be done for!' "

As the snow melted, I would sit at the kitchen table and watch the light shift through the window, listening to the sounds of the old house. When Synnöve came she tried to get me to wish I had company but I didn't really, in spite of the fact that I often felt lonely and miserable. Everything did look different, though, when she had been there. All the matter, from the pigeon droppings on the windowsills to the junk piled in the wood bin outside the door. Synnöve hadn't said a thing, had barely let her gaze rest on the piles of paper in the living room. But when she had left I noticed that I had worn holes in the heels of my socks, and the padding was coming out from behind the lining of my red cotton Chinese slippers. I could see that the windowpanes were streaked with dirt and the kitchen floor needed washing. There were dried tea leaves and crumbs in the cutlery drawer, the refrigerator smelled, and the soap in the bathroom was cracked and gray.

There was no point in cleaning a house that was soon to be demolished. I felt like getting away, at least for a few hours every day, and once again I began to consider what it would be like to work at *The Correspondent*. They'd knocked out part of the wall and had big new windows put in, so I could see straight into their white fluorescent world. They were under a lot of pressure down there and never took the kind of coffee breaks we used to in the old days. They would just get plastic cups of coffee from the machine on the wall and drink it while talking on the phone. Every Monday Bertil Sundh gathered them all in the big editorial room. I think he made some kind of speech. I could see them picking their noses while he spoke, although they picked discreetly, mostly at the very edges of their nostrils. They also screwed and unscrewed their ballpoint pens, sitting there on the edges of the desks, feet dangling. Sometimes somebody's clog would fall to the floor. But I couldn't hear it from where I was watching, no more than I could hear the ringing of the phones that sometimes caused two or three people to jump up at the same time.

I tried to imagine working in there, but it was difficult. Would I be able to drag myself out of bed in the mornings? Wouldn't I get dreadfully sleepy from the sounds and the smells once I got inside?

The place has expanded, the building has a new L-shaped wing, and what is now called the main editorial room actually used to be the old composing department. Today people sit in front of flickering screens where there used to be the soft patter of the linotype machines.

To me, that building is inhabited by something other than the present. I can hear footsteps and voices the others cannot hear. Even the smell of the old toilet that used to be in a little closet at the top of the stairs remains as a presence just below what is there now. Ada's harsh voice, her hand being drawn through that reddish-gray hair that usually stood on end — these aren't precisely memories, but more the presence and extension of what there is now. I do not really recall; I am present, and the bands of time we have laid out for ourselves sometimes mean no more than an old belt in a corner that no longer goes with a dress. Sometimes that which is present is the thinnest, the palest stuff of all.

My frequent recognition of things, the past still being there under a wafer-thin film of present reality, disqualifies me for a job in there under the fluorescent lighting. But I thought it might be possible on a commission basis.

Recently the Whitepainter had been behaving like a man truly unhinged. Mumbling, talking to himself even out on the street where he walked with his flapping sandals and his sleeveless sheepskin jacket over his yellowing polyester shirt. The nutcase came up to me now, saying:

"Go and see Ann-Sophie."

Why couldn't he behave normally? Ann-Sophie was in the hospital for surgery. She had been there for a couple of weeks now. It would be nothing but awkward for both of us if I went to see her.

"You have to tell her to come back. She's going to die otherwise."

He was very firm about it. But Michael, people die for medical or, whatchamacallit, physiological reasons. Not because you tell them one thing or another. I thought you were sensible enough not to go for all that mushy, togetherness crap. Maybe you wanted me to hug her, too? Make her feel how much we all love her, that we can't do without her? Ann-Sophie is an old cadaver. She probably already stinks. But I didn't say that. I just thought it while Michael slurped a soft boiled egg into himself and talked to Gabriel about how Ann-Sophie had been vomiting blood.

"You two are really incredible," I said.

But in the end I did go to the hospital. I thought I might ask about the old man, too, the one who had been in the railway station the evening I arrived. After all, he had been Konrad Eriksson who knew my father, and who was Ingrid Johansson's brother. Jenny had said he was pretty much done for.

I went to the old hospital building that is at the heart of the wildly expanding complex of new low buildings filled with bluish white lamplight. That was where Henning had died, and without thinking about it I suppose I believed everyone was taken to the old building when they were dying. But that wasn't the case. It was now the administration building. So I went back to the ward where I had seen Konrad Eriksson on Christmas day. The Christmas decorations had been replaced with plas-

414

tic yellow Easter chicks. Konrad wasn't there. He'd been released.

"So is he better?" I asked.

But the nurse's aide didn't answer. She squinted disgustedly, rubbing her bottom against the wall. She told me to see a nurse, but the nurse questioned me as to my relation to the old man. So I asked about Ann-Sophie Sager, which made everything so complicated she sent for Brother Sigurd.

I still don't know who he was: the Good Samaritan, a volunteer, the hospital clergyman or a just an ordinary person with some bizarre interest. Everyone else on the hospital staff wore short white coats of some synthetic fabric, and you could identify the nurses by the pins on their breast pockets and the doctors by their upturned collars. But Brother Sigurd went around in a burgundy turtleneck and a gray-checked blazer, and his black trousers were shiny and worn all the way down the thighs.

He took me to a room behind the day room with the Easter chicks, indicating a seat in a low armchair. There was coffee in a thermos, but I said no thank you. I told him I was the person who had found Konrad Eriksson and that I knew his sister.

"I just wondered how he was. I thought he might not even …"

Brother Sigurd smiled very gently and looked me in the eyes for a long time without blinking.

"We mustn't be so frightened of that word," he said.

"Well, how is he then?"

"He is a very old man. And very ill. I sat with him as much as I could."

Then, strangely enough, he was quiet for a long time before saying:

"Konrad Eriksson is a person who is unwilling to accept."

O Lord! I could just see it. Sigurd the Samaritan at my bedside, talking me into the inevitable. No, Brother, I would not accept it either! Once I tried to die, and it was disgusting. It was far from a passing vanity. It was the odor of frusty clothing, it was shame and humiliation, and piss stains on the mattress. After that I wanted to live, wanted to live as badly as the fox that has escaped from the trap with one of his legs torn off.

"Aha, so he hasn't got long," I said. "Isn't it odd, in that case, that they sent him home?"

"We wanted to keep him here," said Brother Sigurd. "But home can also be a perfectly adequate environment for death."

He took my breath away. I wasn't quick enough to retort that Konrad Eriksson didn't actually have a home of his own any more. Environment for death. I thought: lint-collecting armchairs, coffee in big pump-top thermoses. Brother Sigurd telling me I am an indispensable member of the community.

"We must respect the wishes of the sick," he went on. "There is such a thing as integrity."

He wasn't the right man to persuade me about that, this man whose very breath felt as if he was pawing at me.

"In terminal care we have to tread cautiously," he said. "And at the same time learn to be honest. We mustn't be frightened of the word: dying."

I could have informed him that there are hundreds of words with which to replace it in the simplest thesaurus and that most of them are old as the hills and not an invention of his hypocritical contemporaries, that there has been a need, for thousands of years, to compare death with sleep or a journey, or to mock it. But I wanted to exchange as little exhaled breath as possible with Brother Sigurd the deathbed specialist, so I asked him about Ann-Sophie Sager.

"Have they told her she could go home yet?"

His eyes grew dark and I was pleased to see that his gentleness, which was surely boundless, could at least be stretched thin. He walked in front of me on silent rubber soles until we were at the foot of Sager the Sofa's bed, where she lay, huge and elevated in a contraption that resembled a machine with which she could shift and turn her way into the kingdom of death all on her own if Brother Sigurd needed a night off.

Upon closer inspection it was not Ann-Sophie who was huge, but the arrangement of the bed, covers, bedspread, drip stand, prop for her arm, pinned-on calling bell, and pillows. Deep down in all of this I saw Sofa's old gray face and her gray-blonde hair and her hand with fingers fatter than mine working the edge of the sheet in that unpleasant way Brother Sigurd must have seen millions of times in the course of his career.

She was asleep and he slipped with habitual ease into the bedside chair, grasping her unfettered hand. I stood at the window. When he pressed her hand, she woke of up course.

"Hello, Ann-Sophie," he said. "Been napping?"

Her eyes were blurry and gray. Her gaze roved, terrified, when she woke up. After a few minutes she adjusted to the situation. Old Sofa was extremely conventional. She looked grateful and silly when she gazed at him. After a while she caught sight of me and was frightened. He didn't notice.

"I'll leave you with your girlfriend," he said.

Ann-Sophie's lips were parched, and she tried to moisten them with her stiff and swollen tongue. I should have gone over and put the glass of water with the bent

416

straw in it to her lips. But I didn't dare leave the window.

"Was it him?" she asked.

I didn't know who she meant. Sigurd? Or was she talking about someone she had just been dreaming about?

"Who?"

"The one who died," she said. "Who they found."

"Down by the tracks? I don't know."

There might have been something more about it in the paper, but I had forgotten to check.

"Was it Egon?" she asked.

"I don't know."

She sought my eyes with her wide open but blurry gaze.

"I cut him," she said. "You saw it. All that blood. He may have gone outside. And it was snowing."

That was when I realized that it had been me, and my thoughtless words about how that man who had been found dead down by the railway and who had been lying there all winter could have been Egon Holmlund, that had sent Ann-Sophie back to the bottle and eventually landed her here with bleeding ulcers.

"I don't know who it was," I said. "But I'll try to find out."

She shut her eyes after that, and I was relieved. I dared to go a little closer. I saw that she had had sweets on the bedside table, chocolate liqueur miniatures. The colorful foil wrappers were still there. I guessed Gabriel was the one who brought her sweets. The Whitepainter had leaned one of his white oblong boxes against the oxygen machine that was not yet in use. Not a cheerful arrangement to the eye. I hadn't had the good sense to bring anything. I didn't even have money on me to go to the hospital kiosk and buy her some chocolate liqueurs if that was what she wanted. My coat pockets were empty.

"Wasn't it you who bled all over the bed in the attic, then?" I asked. "Are you saying it was him?"

She nodded without opening her eyes.

"What did you do to him?"

"I cut it off," she said in a slurred voice.

I had to give her some water now. Her tongue and lips when they sought the drinking straw reminded me of eager, newly-awakened animals . She's delirious, I thought. But I'm going to find out who it was anyway. She thinks he bled to death.

"I'm leaving now, Ann-Sophie," I said. "I'll come back and tell you who he was."

When Ann-Sophie Sager died, it was like when the soil softens up after the spring equinox. It took nearly five weeks, and the last three I was there every day. I sat until twilight fell, a blue, lingering dusk that grew tremulous and unreliable if it was windy out, with rapid clouds shooting across the sky. Then the night shift came on and turned on the lights and gave Ann-Sophie her medicines, the ones to dull her pain and the ones to induce sleep. She was no longer in acute pain, they had stopped the bleeding, but they couldn't halt the course of events. She dissolved before my eyes, and I really didn't want to see it any more than I had wanted to watch Henning die. But I had to. I went there to keep Brother Sigurd away.

I sometimes saw him in the main corridor. He would look at me with those brown eyes of his, inviting collusion. Perhaps he believed we had something in common, a skill or a secret pleasure.

What also evolved out of Ann-Sophie's dissolution was the story of the only act she ever committed of her own free will, or the desire for it. Maybe it was a pathetic story about a pathetic act, what do I know? She was tired when she told it, and sometimes she would fall asleep in the middle, or change the subject. But she always started over again. Her gray, clouded eyes tried to catch mine.

"I did it that same evening you came home," she said. "Up in the attic. He came back the same night you did. I had been sober. Gabriel and Michael helped me, they believed in me. But then he turned up. The swine."

She spoke as she had done in the days before Cadeaux, before the beginning of her fine lady period. I heard the way she rolled her "l's" from the back of her throat, and her long, open "a's", thinking that was how I talked when I was little and when I was growing up; that was the voice in which I whispered to Victor outside the canoe shed: my love, my love.

"At first I said no. But suddenly there I sat, having downed a bottle. With him of course. I hardly noticed. Not until I found myself sitting there with the room spinning. Then he wanted to go up to the attic. Wanted to spend the night in his old room. 'Bring the basin and stuff,' he said. 'My feet need a going over.' It was all just like the old times. 'You shithead,' I thought. But I was scared of him. He'd hurt me so bad."

She looked past me out the window. It was as if the story she had to tell was being enacted out there, in the bare treetops or in the gray air.

"How had he hurt you?"

She grimaced as she answered.

"He called it helping me. He was the one who took me to that quack in Norrköping. I was sixteen. It was down in Salt Marsh. You had to cross the court-yard and go up a set of rickety stairs. I remember the stairs, the stench. He stood next to me, watching. The next time he did it himself. Borrowed a probe. 'Don't be scared, he said, I have skillful fingers, wizard fingers, it's going to be just fine, have a swig now and lie still.' Six hours I lay with it in, I remember the window I looked out. It was in Motala. Every time I hear the name Motala I think of that day — remember how they always used to say "Stockholm-Motala" on the radio weather?"

When she looked me in the eye, when her soon-to-be-effaced gaze captured mine and managed to hold on to it, she could tell I was upset.

"Is this getting you down?" she asked. "Maybe it's shocking."

"I don't know," I said, "my life's just been so different."

"Well, don't think it was always like that. We had good times, too. I mean, there are certain things that stick with you. 'I taught you everything you know,' he used to say. And I guess that was true. He did teach me all of it, every trick in the book. He had no secrets from me."

She grew quiet. Perhaps she slept a while. Or was she lying there thinking about the enormous difference between being the magician's assistant and his apprentice? Both run across the creaky stage floor, bringing him the lacquered chests with double bottoms, the wands and balloon and cases of fluttering doves and compressed rabbits. They have to clean the terrified animals' droppings from the bottoms and they have to refold the silk scarves and see to it that they are nei-ther burned nor torn. But an apprentice will one day be a magician herself. An assistant learns it all; the tricks and the sleights of hand and the equipment, perhaps even the dexterity and the quickness. Just as often as the apprentice, she rescues the magician from an awkward situation. But in spite of her sequins and silver slip-pers she will never be more than an assistant. I have no idea if Ann-Sophie thought about that, if she was bitter. Her memory was groping around the life she had lived, and sometimes she actually smiled. But in the end she always returned to that evening when I had come home and when Egon Holmlund had been on the same train.

"He wanted to go up to his old room, the one he'd rented in the attic. He was a bit unsteady. I went up a while later, quite a while, 'cause he told me to bring the stuff. He said his feet needed a going over. He liked that. Liked sitting with his feet in hot water, getting nice and soft and then having me give him a treatment, drying and creaming them. It was a kind of coming home, that."

She was feverish and rambling. Sometimes her cheeks would go rosy, but most of the time her face was gray with a yellowish tinge in the thin, slack bags under her eyes. I had long ago realized she wouldn't recover. One of the ways you could tell was the nurses, how they went in and out with their kidney basins and drip bottles. Ann-Sophie needed so little. She hardly drank any water at all when I extended the glass. I would insert the straw between her dry, gray lips, and most of the time she made a slight but impatient gesture, shaking her head as if I shouldn't bother her. There was a thin plastic tube running from a bottle and adding fluids and sometimes blood into her body. Her arm was full of prick marks and plasters, and sometimes she pulled at it as if trying to release it from the tube that attached her to life. But mostly she wanted to talk. She would start the minute she caught sight of me as I walked into the room. She didn't always have the strength, and often her sentences were interspersed with long pauses. But when the words came they were like eruptions, and that was when her cheeks might go rosy again, perhaps from the fever, and spittle would run down her chin. Yes, she would spit from excitement in spite of being so weak.

In many ways she reminded me of Henning, and I spent a lot of time those weeks thinking about what it had been like when he died. I remembered when he came home and I decided to give him drink myself rather than taking the risk of his running away again. I recalled how our relationship had changed when the dishonesty in it was taken away. But he was not one and the same man the whole time, hardly even at the end in the hospital. When he was most dependent on me, a child who wet himself and sometimes woke up having messed himself, too, there was a glimpse of the adult man, the man with dignity and *style* — my pappa! One picture overlayered the next, and I could no longer recall how he had died, if he had been like a child or a sick animal. Or if the man in him had glimmered at that moment. I just couldn't recall it; the pictures were indistinguishable. Ann-Sophie's face also flickered with films of already lived life. Of course I couldn't know which one she was of all the ones she wished to call forth, yes, conjure up with her pleading words, the fitful, curtailed stories. They all began that evening she followed him up the stairs carrying the hand basin of hot water, the scissors and the knife and all the things she needed to accomplish her mission.

Her pleading made me tired and sick, because I knew I couldn't do for her what she wished. I did not even really know what she was asking of me. She revealed herself to me. It was shameful and not unnecessary, but it was to no avail.

I would also like to bare myself once, not only undress, removing one garment after another until I was down to my freezing skin, my burning skin, my flayed skin. I would like to take off the house and the city and the corset of habits and the hypocrisy I hold over my genitals, waving it flirtatiously, as if it were a fan, that's the kind of striptease I would like to perform, too. I guess I did understand her, after all, in my disgust. It wouldn't have anything to do with teasing, no it would be an extremely matter-of-fact action, more or less like undressing behind a hospital curtain before going in for an X-ray. But in front of whom, of whom?

"So I'd got everything ready," she said, "everything I needed and the basin of hot water, too. I had to make two trips — remember, I got everything I needed. I mean I'm not saying I just happened to reach for it; it was there on the table downstairs and I took it up with me."

I don't think she had any delusions about coming back home. She never said anything about it, but I'm sure she knew what the outcome would be. Or maybe she didn't even have the energy to think about it. I sat there instead of Brother Sigurd and at least that was as it should be. She said she had tried to talk to him but it had been no good because he didn't believe her or didn't seem to understand what she had done.

"Do you think we have evil inside us?" she asked. "Ordinary people, people like you and me, do we?"

"I'm not sure," I said.

How could I know? But something odd happened to me once. I had forgotten all about it, but when Ann-Sophie and the others gave me the kalanchoë, I remembered. The plant I recalled, though, wasn't a kalanchoë, it was a wax plant. It was in the bay window at Tora Otter's, in her unheated sitting room, and as I recall that plant, it never budged. Never grew. I never dared touch it out of fear that its name would turn out to be true: that it really was a plant made of wax, that could neither wilt nor emit a scent. Nothing ever happened to it in there in the chilly gloom. I thought it was an evil plant. I knew there was such a thing as evil, and I thought that plant possessed it.

One evening I sat in there and watched a nearby building burn down. The fire had started late that afternoon. We had been working at the market, Tora and I. So it must have been a Saturday or a Wednesday. In the first clouds of smoke I saw billow out of a half-open window there were flakes of snow whirling. I think it was early winter, before Christmas.

" Look, over here," Tora shouted. She had become aware of the fire while I was sitting counting the coppers in the cash box we brought home after the market closed. It was an important job, but I abandoned it to run to the oriel and watch the smoke pour out. It was black and heavy and at first it didn't rise, just dropped down toward the street. Someone had opened a window and was screaming. That open window made the fire pick up. After some time we saw huge flames inside. A white net curtain was poised for a moment like a brown lattice inside the window. Then it blazed up and vanished.

The building was opposite Tora's, and down there on the street people were rushing toward the building, staring up at the windows where the fire was roaring. I could even hear it from in the apartment. Window panes were cracking, and glass falling to the street, then a tongue of flame would shoot out of the hole where the window had been. Tora wrapped me in a blanket so I wouldn't freeze in the chilly room, and then she ran out. She must have thought she could be helpful. I was left alone. I sat there all by myself watching the house be completely blasted out by the fire. Hours passed. The firemen had arrived and were dousing the fire with water from their thick hoses. Everything went black and silent in there as they hosed the building down.

Even now I have no idea whether anyone was hurt or killed in that fire. I wasn't very old, six or seven maybe, and I didn't dare ask. But I saw faces and distorted forms in the burning house. Two of them were revealed in the cascades of water from the fire brigade hoses, as something other than what I had thought: they were a dentist's drill in its stand hanging over the dentist's chair. I don't know about the others, nobody ever told me.

I sat in my blanket watching until everything was black and silent. Next to me was that big plant that had caused the fire.

The day I told Ann-Sophie about that, I don't know if she was able to listen to the whole story. She was tired, and when she had fallen asleep she breathed in bubbling, rustling snores I found very upsetting. I shook her gently, trying to get her to change position, and when that didn't work I spoke to her, trying to wake her up. I told her there were lots of people asking about her and looking forward to her coming home. But she didn't seem to care.

It was true that throughout the time Ann-Sophie was in the hospital old men would come knocking at her door. They couldn't believe she was out or away, but would shuffle around to the courtyard to peer in through her kitchen window. Sometimes when I passed I heard the telephone ringing in there: desolate, distant signals.

By now she realized when I was getting ready to leave in the evenings, and she would take my hand and keep me there. I found myself getting away later and later. Sometimes I would sleep in the chair, and when I woke up my neck ached and my legs and back were really cold.

Once I walked out of the hospital at dawn and felt the memory of Fredrik's death rush over me. It was a Sunday morning, he collapsed over the kitchen table when he and Jenny were sitting down to breakfast. The minute the ambulance got him to the hospital Jenny called me in Porto. I was home by the very next day, and we sat by his bedside for several days and nights, taking turns, never sitting together for more than a few minutes in that narrow, off-white room with its shiny nozzles. There was a big oxygen machine that would have looked more at home in a workshop than in a hospital room.

One morning Jenny and I were walking toward each other in the culvert that runs between the hospital buildings. It wasn't even six o'clock yet, I was freezing. The car hadn't got warm in the short distance I'd driven.

I saw her from far away. Her face was literally gray. I was almost scared of her. Perhaps that was what made me start jabbering. I said how cold it was, that Fredrik's car which I had borrowed had been so icy I had hardly been able to see through the windshield.

"You can go back home to bed now," she said. "He's dead."

I didn't know what to say or do. Jenny's face was stiff. She wasn't looking at me.

I drove her home. It was still dark and car engines were starting on the streets, huge clouds of exhaust coming out the back. It was too early to do any of the practical things. Neither the minister nor the funeral parlor director would be awake. She sat down in an armchair in the living room, not bothering to turn on any lights. It had begun to be light outside, so I could see her from the kitchen where I was getting the coffee machine going, her face was the same color it had been in the culvert, and completely expressionless. If a stranger had walked in, he wouldn't have been able to decide whether he was looking at a person who was bored or who had had a fright. While we were having our coffee, she finally started to speak.

"All right, so now he's dead," she said. "He worked himself to death. But I suppose that was how he would have wanted to go."

She didn't look at me as she spoke. There was coffee dripping down onto her lap from the bottom of the cup. I said I was going to get her a napkin.

"He never got a son," she said. "But he never complained about it, of course. Not once."

She didn't seem to notice when I laid a paper napkin between the cup and saucer. I set a second one on her lap for if she started to cry.

"But he did have you," she said. "Though not much came of it."

I didn't know what she meant.

"It was all right for me, I could play at mothering. But you never needed to bother about him. Because you still had Henning."

She sounded openly scornful.

"All you ever cared about was Henning this and Henning that," she said.

I mumbled there was nothing strange about that.

"Oh no?"

She looked me right in the eye for a moment.

"Let's lie down for a while," I suggested. "You're tired."

"No, there was nothing else for you at all. But he was just a big shit. You never realized that, though. He had made his imprint on you, he had. Charming Henning."

"Shush now," I said.

"In fact he never really cared about you. Went off for weeks at a time. The drink. Women, too. And then he would come home and catch sight of you. You were like a puppy. Then he would turn on his best behavior and all his charm for a few days. You never noticed what was going on. He might be more or less legless and talking tripe, you took every single thing he said as if it were the Word of God. The worst part is that Fredrik fell for it himself, too. The two of you. He would fool you time after time. Say he was coming and then not even call. Lying dead drunk in some other boozer's foul lodgings. The number of times Fredrik had to pay his bill. And I had to make up a story for you about it."

"So why did you? Why didn't you tell me the truth?"

"I dunno," she said. "I suppose it was because Fredrik was on his side, too. There was something so amazing about Henning. His ravings. And his mannerisms. He was the pedantic type, you know. And still I have never seen anyone so surrounded by filth. His pens were all lined up on his desk, but his rugs were so thick with dust they were gray. Completely gray. Filthy it was. Filthy dirty."

I had stood up. Now, I thought, she's finally going to cry. But there were no tears. Her face still looked the same. Everything was gray, the dawn coming in through the window, her face, her words. She wanted to bring down my whole life, everything that was mine, out of bitterness she seemed to want to destroy it.

"Fredrik's the one who's dead," I said. "Don't you want to talk about him?"

"What's there to say?" she asked. "To you, anyway. That he worked himself to death. He hardly existed."

Then we sat there silently for a long time. There were never any tears, she just sank further and further down into herself. Finally she got up, blinking rapidly. She made a face, sort of grimaced. She seemed to be trying to bring her rigid face back to life.

"I think I'll lie down for a while," she said. "I'm tired. I might as well try to get a little sleep."

She vanished up the stairs. I think she slept for two hours. Then everything was normal. She cried and twisted white handkerchiefs. Throughout the funeral she held my hand. She had asked me to choose the hymns.

"He was so fond of you," she said. "You pick the hymns."

There were flower scents and tears, just as there should be. I don't even think she remembered the things she had said that morning, right after Fredrik died.

In the big bed on locked wheels, lay Ann-Sophie, drifting, sleeping or unconscious, but if I disappeared too far into sleep or my thoughts, she would fumble for me; I would wake with a start, having heard her sheets rustle, and I saw her blurry eyes trying to find my face.

"I had everything with me," she said.

She was on her way up the attic stairs at 13 Chapel Road again. Her thoughts circled around the big bed up there and what had happened in it. He was sitting on it, on Lisa's bed. Looking foolish. Because in his room there was nothing. It was empty, perfectly empty.

"He didn't think that would happen. Michael and Gabriel had thrown all his things out. They weren't going to let him come back. 'We believe in you,' they said. I remembered that then. He was sitting on the bed, drunk, really drunk. And vicious. He was mad they had tossed his stuff out. He sat rocking back and forth, and then he said: see to it you get my feet looking good now. He sat there on the bed and I pushed over the basin and then I took off his shoes and his sock and he lifted first one foot and then the other and put them in the hot water. 'Is it hot enough?' I asked, and he grunted. Yes, I see what you think Ann-Marie, it shows, but this was what happened, everything was just exactly as it had to be. That was

425

how it was. I remembered my old man. Him I couldn't do anything about. 'Everybody does it,' he said. 'What's with you?' he asked. 'I'll tell mum on you.' 'You'll do no such thing,' he said. And I knew I wouldn't because she'd just be mad at me. 'You're that way,' said my old man. 'It's written all over you. I can't help myself. Been that way since you were little.' I felt like being sick. Egon was having a grand old time. Sat there enjoying himself. It was cold in the attic. Must've been, but we were pretty plastered. 'Don't cut me now,' he said. He actually said that, but I wasn't thinking about it. I wasn't thinking at all. I just cut away. He'd been gone a long time. His corns had grown. High as an elephant's eye, but I just cut. Do you know even Bertil Franzon had corns, high and mighty man that he was? 'You don't have to do this,' he said. But he liked it anyway. 'You're so gentle,' he said. I thought he was so gorgeous I could have saved every bit of skin I cut away. I was so daft in those days — everything was so gorgeous. I wore my hair up you know. You saw me then, didn't you? All clean and lovely. Did my hair up in the morning and it stayed up all day. He never touched a hair of my head, I was just the same when we got up as when we lay down. I did his feet. His wife would never have. 'You don't have to do this,' he said. But he liked it. 'Do like this,' said my old man. 'Just a little. Like that. Such a good girl. Watch him get big. You're Pappa's very special girl, aren't you?' It was 'pappa's very special girl' in those days. I was very special if I did what he wanted. 'You and me, we have a great time, don't we?' I'm so hot I think I'm gonna burn up. No, don't pull the cover up, I can't stand having it over me. I did everything he wanted. Have you ever been drunk? So completely sloshed you were heavy and swollen inside and everything blurred together? There are no spaces inside when you're drunk. You're just drunk. Egon said: 'Dry my feet.' And I dried them. 'Rub the cream in.' And I did. Then he lay back on the bed and opened his trousers. 'Get 'im up,' he said. When I got him right up straight, he just lay there with his eyes shut. 'Not like that,' he said, 'slow down. Hang on, damn it.' Those were the only times Bertil ever touched my hair. He could grab it hard, drive his fingers all the way down to my scalp. 'Slow down', he said. 'Slow, slow.' I knew my stuff. Even then. You might not have thought so 'cause I was so drunk. 'You know every trick in the book,' he said."

She was lying because she wanted to scare me and repulse me. It couldn't be that awful. Awful, but not that awful. Those were fantasies she'd had, or that she knew I'd had, there was some kind of devilment about this that I didn't understand. She was exhausted, feverish, but sometimes her dim eyes had a crafty gleam in them. She seemed to be observing me and my prolonged nausea, my attempts to ward her off. Did she know what had happened, or was she making it up?

Once Ingrid Johansson told me she had felt sorry for me when I was working at the newspaper and living at home with Henning. 'He brought all kinds of weirdos around,' she said, 'and they almost wrecked the place right before your eyes.' She said Jenny had asked her to keep her company to Chapel Road one Sunday morning when she was worried about me but afraid of Henning's drinking buddies. When they arrived they found me alone in the apartment and everything a dreadful mess, with overturned furniture and broken glasses and bottles. Ingrid said they'd even pulled the books out of the bookcase. I'd been lying in my room with a whole lot of Henning's medicines on the bedside table, and Ingrid said she and Jenny had stayed with me all that evening to make sure I wouldn't do myself any harm, as she put it.

I had no memory at all of such an event; I don't think it ever happened. Henning was never inconsiderate of me and he never became violent from drink and never, never did he let anyone else into the apartment when he was on a binge, that's just not true. But Ingrid remembered it and told it to me as if I ought to recall it, and I can't figure out how it all fits together. Maybe there are two worlds, the one in which the apartment got wrecked and the furniture turned upside down, and the other where that didn't happen, and the worlds split apart afterwards and went on that way for ever and ever and always have; I don't know. Ingrid must have been wrong. And yet she's so certain. I don't want to ask Jenny because I don't want to know. Perhaps we don't share a common past. The thought has crossed my mind that a great many of the things we remember so clearly and so well may never have happened. I don't know what that means about Sofa's long story about Egon Holmlund and how she filed and cut with her knife until she finally happened to cut so deep and so effectively. No, not happened to do it, just did it.

"I chopped it off," she said. "It's so hot in here. I'm burning. I need something to drink. If Sister comes she'll make you leave. I know. I'm not allowed to talk for so long. Then I ran away. I hurt myself on the stairs. But I washed the knife, I washed it and put it in the drawer and I thought, I'm not going to die. I'm going to cut away lots of hard bits with this. I don't know how long I sat down there on my bed. It got light, anyway. Then I went up to take a look at him. I wasn't so frightened any longer. But he wasn't there. I sat down on the bed. Right in the blood. When you came up you thought I was the one who was bleeding. I wonder how far he got, I thought. Where he fell. But I never found out until just recently this spring. They found him by the railway and I thought they'd come round asking me questions. It didn't do me the least little bit of good that I cut him. You see that now, don't you? It did me no good at all. I'm so hot. But don't get them to come."

I offered her water but it was tepid. So I went to the sink and let it run a long time. She drank thirstily of the cold water.

"I don't want you thinking too much about it," I said. "He was probably all right. You were both so drunk. You couldn't help all that. Things like that happen."

I didn't know how I could help Ann-Sophie out of her anxiety. Nothing they gave her at the hospital had any effect on it. I had bought fortified wine at the monopoly but I realized she might not be able to take it. So I'd gone back for a bottle of Smirnoff. I still had the bottles in my shopping bag, and I asked her if she wanted any. But I seemed to have misunderstood those chocolate liqueurs. Maybe Gabriel had eaten them himself. In any case, Ann-Sophie had no desire for drink. She was stuffed full of medications, woozy and weak, but the sharp anxiety kept her awake. She believed Egon Holmlund had wandered off in the middle of the night and had fallen down in a ditch over by the tracks and been unable to get up, had bled to death in that ditch, drunk and cold, in the stench of steel and oil when the trains rushed by. She had tried to speak to the chaplain and Brother Sigurd about what she had told me. But it hadn't helped. They forgave her everything.

"Could that be right? Could it?"

"I don't know," I said. "But the way he treated you, I'm not surprised you cut at him. The way he treated you your whole life."

"But when a person sits down in confidence, Ann-Marie. Don't you see? He puts himself in your hands. There you sit with your basin of hot water and he puts his feet in, he trusts you, trusts you to take care of him. And then — it's not forgivable."

"I don't know."

What is a person to say? I just didn't know. I hadn't even managed to find out if the man they'd found had really been Holmlund. No one knew.

"Forget all that now," I said. "He was probably all right. And it isn't like you planned it or anything."

I heard my own kind voice and my polished pronunciation. I didn't want to go on looking at her, I looked at the shiny nozzles and the light green hospital blanket and the thick cardboard kidney basin. I had smashed her world to smithereens with my kind voice, my sober words. I thought I would get up and go because there was nothing more to be done. All I had to do was say: 'Stop thinking about it. He's probably alive. You just get well now.' And I had pull on my gloves and pat her hand and go off and possibly never see her again because she was moribund, I didn't need a ward sister to tell me that.

I had put on my gloves and was standing by the bed. Ann-Sophie was lying there, her head turned to the side, her eyes closed. I removed my gloves again and sat back down beside her. I thought I ought at least to try. But I couldn't find any other words to use than the ones I had already said, and I didn't know what else to do. She's going to die like Henning did. She's going to vanish out of my life right after telling me what she did. And I told her that it was meaningless, and that it never happened anyway. It was nothing but a sordid argument, the kind of things they write about in the papers. Domestic quarrel. The couple had been drinking. She was raving when she told me, and she had been so solemn.

"Ann-Sophie," I said. "Can you hear me?"

Her eyelids didn't flicker. Nothing moved.

"It was a good thing you cut him. That was good."

When I had said it I thought, 'I must be out of my mind'. Ann-Sophie had opened her eyes again.

"You mustn't think I don't know what you're talking about," I said. "Hold my hand. I've been pretty far down myself. You weren't around to see me then, you have never seen me any way but this way. I wish there were such a thing as love without humiliation. But if you shy away from it altogether, you end up like me."

Could I talk to her about my lovelessness? She was listening, at any rate, although she said nothing. She held out her hand, her left toward my extended right, put her palm in mine, and our fingertips touched, hers were no rougher and no longer than mine. I came to think about the old superstition that you should never compare hands with anyone, that it brings on arguments, so I cupped her hand in mine instead.

"I've been such a cautious person," I said. "That's why nothing special has ever happened to me. Whereas you are a person no one has ever watched out for."

Her lips were dry again, I gave her some water but she found it difficult to swallow.

"Do you think some people are lost?" I asked her.

"I don't know," she said.

I thought: she's done for. She has a temperature. She can no longer think, cannot possibly know anything. But she is actually the only person I can ask. I didn't expect an answer. It was forgone. But she moved her chapped lips, whispering:

"I don't think so. There's nothing to lose, is there?"

She lay there holding my hand again, and after a little while she was soaked in perspiration and I had to call for the nurse's aide because she was getting chilled from the sweat and starting to shiver.

429

They came in and took care of her and the room was filled with them and their actions and the rustling of white trousers and coats. She couldn't see me any longer. A nurse came in and took her pulse and then a nurse's aide brought over the oxygen machine. They moved my chair, and when they surrounded the bed they blocked my view of her. I realized I ought to leave.

I went out onto the linoleum floor of the corridor, taking in the smell of disinfectant and sick bodies, passing through doors that were ajar. I smelled the aroma of coffee and the scent of flowers, and heard the sounds of dishes clattering and of squeaky bars on beds being raised and lowered. It was actually midday.

Egon probably pulled through, I thought. He probably bled like a stuck pig, but I don't think there was actually any great danger. That was unreal. She's dying, though. That's reality. She has now done all the deeds she will ever do with her hands and her mouth and her genitals, with her file and her pumice stone and her brush, with her scissors and her knife.

On my way out I saw Brother Sigurd in the hospital lobby, and so Konrad Eriksson came into my mind. Was he still alive? Jenny hadn't informed me to the contrary, anyway. She claimed Ingrid Johansson had left her husband and was living in a little apartment on Hovlunda Road where she was looking after her brother Konrad.

I couldn't imagine what would drive a human being to divorce or separate from her spouse when she was nearly seventy years old. I had always considered Arne boring, but hadn't Ingrid discovered that fifty years ago? Jenny thought it was more than peculiar. She thought it was deranged, insane, and scandalous to boot. She said it was for the sake of that brother of hers, who was now lying there in her apartment waiting out what was left of his life, that Ingrid had moved out. She'd given Arne an ultimatum: Konrad had to be taken out of the terminal care ward and come to live with them. Otherwise Ingrid was going to move out and live where he could be with her. Arne had not, of course, taken her seriously. He refused. And she walked out.

Jenny may have been right about it being insane. Organizing a one-bedroom apartment in Hovlunda Road, moving out half the furniture from what had been the Johansson home, furniture that had been in place there for so long the wood must have screamed when the pieces were separated, nailing up paintings, putting books in the bookcases and china elephants on them, hanging up curtains, Venetian blinds, hooks in the bathroom, lifting and carrying. She would soon be seventy, and had pulmonary emphysema. All that, the stairs, the carrying, and then the vast loneliness awaiting her when Konrad died. Was he already gone?

I wanted to know, and rang her doorbell. It said *I. Johansson* on the door, so Arne wasn't in the picture any more, everything Jenny had said was true. Ingrid showed me the apartment and all the arrangements with great pride, and she showed me Konrad through the door, a sleeping white head on a plumped-up pillow.

While I sat at her kitchen table she told me about how Konrad's time at the hospital had ended. He liked listening to the hymns on Sundays, in spite of being an atheist. We did away with God at a Communist Youth meeting in 1908, he used to say. But when the hospital chaplain heard that he wanted the door ajar so he could hear the hymns during the services, he thought Konrad must be a believer. Konrad was very poorly just then; he slept a lot and dozed and nodded to most questions, and in the end the chaplain gave him communion. Konrad perked up from the wine and got the idea in his head that the last rites had been administered and he was done for. That gave him a fright, said Ingrid, because Konrad has always wanted to live. He asked for his clothes and they gave him them. No one thought he would be able to put them on. They supposed he wanted something from the pockets, something that had been there when he was admitted. They never denied him anything; they idolized Konrad on the ward, all the nurse's aides did little extra favors for him. But they didn't give him his shoes.

It was Sunday afternoon and they were understaffed, so he was able to get into his clothes without anyone noticing, and somehow he managed to get himself dressed and out the door. He was barefoot and didn't make it more than part way down Industrial Road before someone stopped him.

"I don't want to go back there," he said.

The person, who knew who he was, phoned Ingrid. She had been going to collect him in a couple of days anyway, because the apartment was all furnished and nearly ready. So she took a taxi and picked him up at Brelin's tea room where they had deposited him in a chair.

He was exhausted when they got home and she got him into bed but he wasn't able to sleep. He was worried about something. She phoned the hospital and told them where he was, but that didn't settle Konrad down. Not until he had had a cup of hot milk did things clear up. He stuck his long, stiff index finger in his mouth and poked around. Then he pulled out the communion wafer that was stuck to the roof of his mouth. It fastened on his hard fingernail and Ingrid wrapped it in a tissue and threw it away. Then he finally went to sleep, and since then things had been quite unchanged. The days passed, perhaps in a kind of daze for him, it was difficult to say. But he wasn't exactly ill, and he ate a bit. He slept a lot and Ingrid sat there every evening in the cosy light of red and green lampshades, and the blue-white TV screen.

"They think I'm mad," she said. "But I wanted to be on my own, too." I thought about Arne Johansson who had been kicked around and knocked over the head and who had dizzy spells and was depressed and not his old self, and the thought crossed my mind that Ingrid Johansson was being a little hard on him, that she might be a hard person, too.

She had not a crumb to offer me, she said, nothing to have with the coffee because the home help hadn't come, she was off sick. So Ingrid hadn't been able to leave Konrad, didn't even dare to leave him for long enough to go to the store.

"You're pretty tied down," I said.

The kitchen clock ticked. It was yellow with a red frame, red digits and hands. I remembered it very well from Arne and Ingrid's kitchen, and I wondered how they had divided up their home, if they had stood there holding the kitchen clock saying, you take it, it's a kitchen clock and you spend more time in the kitchen than I do. Or had they torn at it like foxes tear at carrion, or just dully packed it into a box, not giving a damn who took it? There's no way of knowing. I don't think I could get divorced. How would we behave?

Then Ingrid said:

"Would you sit here for a few minutes while I go down and get some cinnamon buns? Then I could give you a cup of coffee before you left."

She was very relieved and grateful when I said she could take however long she needed and do all her shopping because I didn't have any particular plans. And off she went with her shopping bag (since Ingrid Johansson isn't the kind to pay fifty öre for a carrier bag when she doesn't need to).

But when she had left I was frightened. Here I was alone with the old man, and the door to the bedroom where he was lying was open. He appeared to be sleeping. His white head rested high on the pillow, he had a perfectly round head and the skin was pulled tight over his skull and it was white, or more correctly it was perfectly free from color. I wouldn't have dared to go in there. Just think if he woke up or died while Ingrid was out. And I thought about that hour or half-hour down at the station — that I had dared back then. I had been a different person. I had had the right girl scout spirit then, somehow. But now — what was wrong with me? Why did I put myself in these positions? I had gone up to Ingrid's mainly to have someone to talk to, to drive from my mind the thoughts of what had been happening to Ann-Sophie up there, and what might be happening right now. And now here I sat with the old man lying stock-still just a few meters from me. I could see him through the door. The living room was silent with the exception of the ticking of the radiators, but traffic, humming, roaring, whining could be heard from outside. They lived in this, it filled their ears all the time, and their brains. Chapel Road was actually pretty quiet comparatively, it was off the beaten track in those days. Whereas here the city rumbled through their heads.

Was he moving around in there? No, he just lay there like a lump, an object. That was the creepy thing. But it would have been even creepier if he had moved, and if he had called out. Though he couldn't, could he? Did he still have a voice? If he did, I'd have to go in, I might have to touch his sheets. He could grab hold of me. The grocer's, the bakery and the national health office were Ingrid's errands. That could take an hour, maybe more. Whatever possessed me to tell her not to hurry, that I'd be fine? I'd better find something to read.

She had a lot of books, old dog-eared ones. Classics and politics and astronomy, a little of everything. It took me some time to realize that most of them were Konrad's. The tops of them were black with dust, they smelled mildewed and musty if you opened them. She must have stored them in an attic. They had, of course, been stored somewhere when he was in geriatric care. And they were probably never very well taken care of. Konrad had lived in cold, damp housing all his life. Krapotkin. Gogol. What a village genius he had been, once upon a time! I remembered his letters to the editor. He had had all these thoughts in his head. And now?

Esperanto! Did he still know Esperanto?

I glimpsed that white skull in there against the pillow, and thought about all the things in the human brain. If he stopped breathing now it would be gone, his brain no more than a soft, dissolving lump, a *cervelle de veau mayonnaise*. No Esperanto, no memories, nothing.

At the bottom of the bookcase there were rows of black minutes ledgers. He had glued white labels on the bindings, with dates and years. No, that was Ingrid's neat handwriting on the labels, inside it was Konrad's. It had to be, because the earliest ones were from before she was born, and they weren't the minutes of meetings, as I could see when I removed one. They were diaries. The nut had recorded his whole life, every single day of it. How had he done it? Where had he got the time from? How had he had time enough to live and work besides? Well, according to Jenny he hadn't actually worked all that much. A lot of politics, a lot of meetings. I leafed through, wishing I could find that meeting where they had done away with God. Had Konrad had any objections?

Local politics, children's illnesses, yearnings, and harangues that might have been philosophical. Children's illnesses and more children's illnesses. The price of pork! I couldn't help thinking of my grandfather Abel and the contents of his shoeboxes. What was it that drove them? The swift passage of time.

But I could already have told Abel and Konrad the secret when I was only seven: life was long, generally far too long and repetitive. Why hadn't he seen it after a few years of diary writing?

This must be the most petty of vices. Running alongside time with a little notebook in hand, running alongside one's own life and not daring to jump down onto the racetrack!

In 1973 he stopped. Toward the end he hadn't written much. I could see that the last four years fit into two books. During the most intensive periods a black oil-skin notebook didn't seem to have got him through more than three months. In 1940 he had filled one in two months!

I read his final entries. They were a bit embarrassing because they were mainly about his stomach. It wasn't behaving, he wrote. And: 'Sunday 2 December 1973. Bowels moved. 1st time in 11 days. Not much.' He wrote that Ingrid and Arne had been issued with their rationing cards, and at that point I thought he'd gone completely gaga. Then I remembered that in December 1973 everything had been doom and gloom and the *Untergang des Abendlandes* was nigh. The Arabs were going to raise the price of oil by six dollars a barrel or something equally horrendous. So what he wrote was undoubtedly correct. They had been issued with fuel ration cards that had never been put to use. That was his last real diary entry. A couple of times after that he had written dates but no more. Had he been too poorly? Or was his mind just empty? At the very end he had written one single sentence in a forceful if unsteady hand. He had pressed his fountain pen hard into the paper and written:

THE SPRINGS THAT HAVE BEEN BLOCKED
WILL BURST FORTH WITH GREAT FORCE

Under this he had drawn two lines that hadn't come out quite straight. He had very clearly balanced his books.

I would have liked to ask Ingrid what she intended to do with the notebooks, but I suppose I didn't dare. It was embarrassing to admit I had been looking at them. Like reading other people's letters or — well — their diaries. That was it. Except that he was nearly no longer alive. An old head, an old body, immobile. There wasn't even any rustling of the sheets in there.

She was all cheery upon her return, as she lined up her purchases on the larder shelves. Then she made some light brown coffee for us and put some cookies from Anker's on a plate. She had a smoke with her second cup, and immediately burst out coughing.

When I finally got away I went up to Jenny's and rang the bell but she wasn't in. After that I didn't know what to do with myself. I didn't want to go home, was afraid to. But my shopping bag was heavy, I had to drag the two unopened bottles

I'd brought back from the hospital around the streets with me, and in the end I went home because I just couldn't think of any other place to be. But I was frightened. The springs that have been blocked will burst forth with great force. They were ringing like a pop tune in my ears, those words. The springs. That have been. Blocked. Over and over again. Will burst forth. Will burst forth. With great force. The springs.

Standing there in front of my door with its pane of frosted glass I felt a strong sense of anticipation. I thought. Now it's going to happen. Now everything will be transformed.

I stepped in and felt how silent the whole place was. As if silence were matter, dense, heavy and pale gray. I set down my bag of bottles on the table. The springs. That have been blocked. Could I actually have heard those words before? Read them?

I felt ill, yes, ill. It was in my chest. Then I thought of the word — oddly enough in Portuguese. *Angustia.*

My ears were ringing. No longer the words, but a ringing sound, soft, distant signals. They say lots of people have to live with that kind of thing. For years. And I felt as if it might make me lose my mind in just a few minutes.

Ringing. Murmuring.

I'd rather hear it outright, whatever it was.

Springs.

Then I did something peculiar. Irrational you might call it. I had intended to put on some water to make myself a cup of tea, but instead I went straight out into the bathroom and opened the little tap on the side of the toilet tank. It started to run, it ran and ran because the tank never got full. I don't understand how that works. You had to shut the tap to get the damn thing to quiet down, and so we always kept it turned off except when we needed to flush the toilet. The Whitepainter knew that was how we did it, so did Gabriel. But now I opened it, put my brow to the cold tiles, and listened.

What I heard was stagnant water that had long been still in rusty pipes. It was running. The tank never filled up. The water shifted but never seemed to get anywhere. It was shut inside its own rusting system.

Then everything really did change. As when the light falls in a different way on a wall, and an opening appears. But light and shadow changed places. I actually stepped out through the portal — not into it as I had believed or imagined.

There was neither an enchanted world nor any wondrous reflection. No spots of light danced in the leaves and there was no series of enormous vaulted rooms.

I stepped out there and it was flat and expansive. I remembered it all. Ishnol, Wonda. But they didn't exist.

Is it really possible for a human being to live in expectation and longing for things she doesn't even remember?

Now I remembered and it was like gazing out over a plain with piles of rubble that were no longer smoking, waste and refuse with no smell.

Yes, a human being can live off this longing.

I realized that I had to get away from here at once. I had been living in this house waiting for nothing.

I had to get out of here. But how was I to do it? I thought about all the junk in the attic, in the closets, cartons, crates and chests, in nooks and crannies, this whole accursed collection of foul-smelling moldy matter that had been pulled together over the course of decades with enthusiasm or at least with energy and concentration and that now had to be disposed of. The thought exhausted me. I alone had to clear out what Abel and Sigrid and Henning and Lisa and at the end Elisabeth, too, had gathered and collected. Not to mention the tenants and squatters and people who had just crashed there in secret, the drunks, the free lodgers. All their shit. I couldn't let Lundholm's excavators go at the whole pathetic lot of it. It mustn't be spread to the wind and made visible to all and sundry.

But I alone? How was I to do it? Had I really seriously considered that when I arrived in November with all my gumption?

And this desperation, this endless, desperate horror.

"At least turn the damned toilet tap off," I said to myself, but nothing happened. I had sat down at the kitchen table and I was frightened and empty. More frightened than I have ever been, I think, because I was afraid of nothing.

So I opened one of the bottles, the sweet fortified wine I had intended for Ann-Sophie. I poured some into Gabriel's old tea mug and drank.

I'll do it, I thought, but I need strength from this mug first. I'll rake up as much as I can of what was left after Lisa and Henning, all the piles of junk and the bundles. And Abel. I can do it, of course. I'm nearly forty-five years old, grown up and competent. It will be all right.

And it is all right to live with nothing. It's probably the way most other people live, nothing remarkable about it.

Most people are waiting for nothing.

"Where shall I start?" I asked myself. The attic. It's always been my intention to start in the attic, sweeping the pigeon droppings off the chests and trunks before opening them. Work my way down through the house. Although I had never given it any particular consideration, I had always imagined cleaning the entire house, from the edges in towards the middle, until I came to the empty bedroom. There was nothing there.

The wardrobe in that room must be empty too. Maybe a couple of blouses, a few flimsy dresses of Lisa's. It was summer when she left the house.

Oh, how I suddenly longed to be able to spend time out of doors, even to live my life at one with nature, under a bare, open sky. Without these walls, without the harsh smell of old dust. How different people who spent most of their time outdoors must be.

I drank while I pondered. The chill crept up my legs, because I had turned the radiators off. I didn't want to hear their ticking, marking time. It frightened me. Because it wasn't really anything but mechanical noise. There wasn't an iota of a message to me in it. The telephone wasn't going to ring, either, because I had bumped into it a few minutes ago and the receiver had toppled off the hook. It had lain there beeping for a long while, but then it stopped.

And the fucking toilet tap just went on runningpurlingmurmuring.

I drank deep, long drafts of the sweet wine that was warming me up. I sat at the kitchen table for a long time. The warmth and the sweetness of the wine did not drive out the fear but it raised me above it so I could stare down into it as one gazes down into the concrete den built for a wild animal. You inhale the stench and wonder what it would be like if you fell down into the jaws and the roaring and the horrid breath. That was the kind of thing I was sitting fantasizing about in the sweetness. Then someone pounded on the door, hard. Perhaps there had been a long period of knocking more politely first, I didn't know. I swigged the last of the bottle before getting up, and out in the hall I hit my hip on the hall table. It hurt like hell. I even cried out, maybe mostly in surprise because I hadn't expected pain to be able to reach in to my insides, surrounded as they were by sweet wadding. Then I put my brow to the cold, polished glass of the door for a few minutes before opening, and there was a wild, no a power-hungry hammering out there, and now I knew who it was. Jenny wanting to get in. Jenny wanting to arrange things.

The door nearly banged her in the head, when I finally opened it. I thought about poor Gabriel, realizing it could happen just that easily. She was standing out there as if she had actually given up hope and was just making a racket because it was her civic duty.

"What do you want?" I asked.

That opened the floodgates, released the flow. If only she could have come up with something new at least. But it was her same old tune, whining and groaning

438

like a hurdy-gurdy, and when that didn't work she raised her voice. It was Henning and spoiling your life and you reek of drink and running yourself down and her whole pathetic repertoire. There she stood in the doorway in her coat with the fur collar and I felt like saying: what good has all your decent behavior done you then, all that doing as one should you have always preached to me about? You don't even have a fur coat, Jenny, and not a particularly clear conscience, either. You got nothing but shit and you are a stranger. You wander aimlessly through your life, you are at home nowhere. But I didn't actually say it.

"Just let me be, damn it. I have things to work out."

"What do you mean, work out?"

So typically Swedish to ask. How I hate those words. What do you mean, work out? What do you mean, love? What do you mean, scared?

"Pack. Clean up."

"I'll help you."

"No, you will not help me. You will not touch one single thing in here, in fact. You will not touch the thin fabric of Lisa's blouses. Can you understand there are things you are not allowed to get your claws into?"

"Well at least don't drink," said Jenny, at which I shut the door in her face, her little turd-gray slip of a face, the one with which she has sucked up so much shit it will never get any color back. I shut the door and the pane of glass rattled and I knew I would start in there with Lisa's blouses, straight down into the den. But first I needed some more to drink, because I was scared.

Now the only drink that was left was the clear spirits, and you have to tread cautiously with that stuff. I took the bottle and the glass with me. I wanted them next to me and I was going to do it. I would be able to do it if I kept an even little flow running, a steady state intoxication.

That door, that French door leading to Henning and Lisa's bedroom, was not locked but it was stuck so hard it seemed to be locked and I pulled at it and half of it opened right into my face, just the same as with Jenny a while ago, except that she managed to step back. But it slammed into me, right above the eyebrow, and the pain vibrated for a long, long time. Yes, it remained with me.

What a strange smell issuing forth from a room that had been shut up for so long. Not a nasty smell, exactly, but a strong one, almost acrid with emptiness. The linoleum was green squares, which I remembered, and the marks from the double bed were still perfectly visible. Everything was as I remembered it. It had been. It had happened and been. No one could say otherwise. I mean, someone might come along in the end and claim that nothing exists, nothing but figments of the imagination.

Things no one remembers have never happened.

The light through the window, the last light of this day. It enchanted me with its softness and the way in which it fell in through the bedroom window. Here this room had stood, empty and shut away, and the light had fallen, it had fallen and risen in this room like milk in a dish, seen by no one.

So: not a single stick of furniture, not so much as a hook on the wall. The easiest space in the house to deal with. In fact, it was already done. Except for the closet and there were just a few pieces of clothing, if there was anything at all after all this time.

Then I tore at the closet door, which had been wallpapered over. Quite rightly, there were clothes inside, thin and flimsy. Nothing a person would have wanted to try on. There should have been a mirror, but there wasn't. So I did have some false memories. I looked for the marks from the hooks. But there didn't seem to ever have been a mirror. It didn't matter, although I wouldn't have minded having a look at the mark I got over my eyebrow and on my forehead. It was swelling up fast and it still hurt. I took the sleeve of a thin dressing gown and dipped a corner of the cloth in my glass, and then I bathed the bruise in eau de vic. I downed the glass and poured another. I had to check whether it was another false memory that there was a door behind the clothes, an ordinary paneled door painted white that led into another room in a closed-off part of the apartment. I sat on the floor sipping from my glass and my bottom was very cold but I had to wait a little while. I think I waited for quite some time and the chill spread along my thighs and up into the small of my back.

The mild, gray daylight had died around me, the light now fell like ash. The alcohol was running down with no smell or taste as if into an abandoned container and because of the chill, my arms and legs were going numb but my head was swelling up; it was heavy in spite of its cloudlike state. I had to transport it gently though this cold room, moving cautiously between puddles of spilt time. In there behind the polished surface of a heavy paneled door there was the poison, or the iron teeth of the trap, the hook into my bleeding gums or the scissors that cut the artery deep down in my thigh.

All I had to do was thud down. All I had to do was tumble in now that everything was numbness and cloud, now that I was resting on a compost heap that was no longer fermenting, snowed under, bowled over. Grope with my hands that are not there or that are there far away on my body between cloudy blouses, between doorway draperies with sweet little tubercular patterns and find the door in. It's

440

impossible to believe that I did it, but I did it. Without courage, I did it. I opened the old paneled door at the back of the wardrobe and came out into an empty room.

Naturally, there was nothing there and there isn't anything to say about it really. I'm sure no one had been in there since they fumigated it after Lisa. The door was locked from the inside and I turned the key and stepped out onto the landing and then went down the other stairs, the ones you get to if you go left along the hall. Which brought me to Ann-Sophie's apartment, precisely as they had to.

On Ann-Sophie's couch I fell asleep or passed out. In the smells of coffee, perfume, and sponge cake, or the memory of those odors. Because my senses were beyond sensitivity, even when I woke up and was sick. I managed not to throw up on her shag rug, I didn't vomit on her rug but, in fact, right into a basin that just happened to be at hand. I vomited over and over again, until there was nothing but bile. And then I vomited bile. My stomach felt as if it had been ripped to shreds, and the roof of my mouth felt flayed from dehydration and pain. Bile in little pools on the linoleum, too, and in the bile little bits, little floes. It looked as if my stomach lining had come up. But at least I spared the shag rug, or my guardian angel did.

Slept.

Then it was dusk, late afternoon, a whole day and night must have slunk past. The light must have once again risen slowly in the empty room and now begun to fall. Here, it fell through Ann-Sophie's synthetic curtains, pale green. And on all the little objects; sea shells, postcards, a white plush dog. Ann-Sophie must love fluff, must never get enough of it. And this toxic headache and parched palate. But I got up on my floppy limbs, managed to stand, drank water straight from the tap, it ran down my neck. Maybe Jenny had rounded up all the social workers on duty now. But she couldn't know where I was, I had certainly locked the door up there. My legs were so light, I had to sit down for a while.

Fell back to sleep, woke up and drank, repeated the exercise several times. It was no longer night, it was morning or broad daylight. There must be something around here for a headache, Ann-Sophie would have something. In the bathroom there was a tube of something called Treo, would that do? They didn't have that kind in Portugal, in Portugal I knew the names of the headache remedies. Dissolved three in water, perhaps that was why they had that name. No longer sick but dull, and with a clear memory of what I had done. There was nothing at all in that room, nothing at all. She had coffee, instant. I turned on the burner and boiled some water, because I had to get something into me before I navigated the stairs. Stale biscuits. Now they won't be in her estate inventory. Nor will this cup of coffee I knocked to the floor. I was on my knees wiping up coffee and bile when the doorbell rang. I raised my head enough to see someone walking in. It hadn't even been locked! An old man, an ordinary old man. Pile-lined three-quarter length coat, boots with zippers, OAP brown.

"Hello at last," the man said in a roguish tone, "I've come the last three weeks at my regular time. But you've been living it up, you have."

Then he looked more horrified than bantering and I realized that his words had been thought out in advance. But what he saw wasn't what he had expected.

"How thin you've got," he said. "How did you do that?"

I was going to answer, try to be amusing, but my voice wouldn't behave. I had to cough up hoarseness and phlegm first. And then I had to go to the looking glass and pull Ann-Sophie's comb through my hair, and there I caught sight of the black-and-blue mark, a swollen welt across my forehead and one of my eyebrows. The old man settled into the couch when he had hung up his coat and put his little brown hat on the kitchen worktop. The he began to remove his boots, which was a quick job thanks to the zippers. But he had trouble bending over, because he was an old man with a stiff back. His hands were large but clean and not hard-worn. He had probably been a pensioner for a long time. Now he pulled off his socks; they were blue with burgundy stripes.

"There's a cold draft off your floor," he said. "My footsies are getting chilly. You'd better fill your basin up. I can sit and soften up for a bit."

He wasn't a dirty old man, nor was he thin-skinned with disease and dying. His cheeks were rosy from the air outside, and he seemed newly-shaved because he had a little cut under one ear. His toes were very white, perhaps from the cold. I rinsed the basin I had been using during the night and refilled the pan on the stove. Then we sat waiting for it to boil and the old man chatted on. I cooled it with tap water and he put his gnarled, paling feet in, sighing with well-being. He liked this. Still, he grumbled a little. Said I usually put some powder in the water. I mustn't forget it, and this water was really almost too hot.

I found the foot salts in the cupboard. All the paraphernalia was there, the files, the pumice stones, the brushes, and there was the knife. It was perfectly clean. The powder made the water bubble up, and he wiggled his toes and blinked his red-rimmed eyelids gratefully. How tough the winter must be for an old man like him with his poor circulation. So easily he blanched.

His feet were extremely clean. He must have washed them well before coming, and last week and the week before as well. What a disappointment when the apartment was empty and no one was going to touch him for another long late-winter week.

I didn't really know what I was supposed to do with his feet, what routines the treatment comprised. But I gave them a long scrub, and he sat there with his eyes shut. Then I lay the whole arsenal of equipment on a terrycloth towel. Knife, scissors and pumice, cuticle sticks, cotton, cream, emery boards and corn plasters. But this old man didn't have corns, no one could say he did. His feet were just twisted and gnarled, they had been well used and were worn out. They had borne the weight of his body and the weight of its burdens and been squeezed into unconceding shoes when he was a boy and grown bony and crooked in every possible way. He had tender chilblains, of course, I suppose everyone in his generation had them. Jenny used to moan and groan when the chill crept down and got to her swollen heels, a reminder sixty years later of what a bad time she had had once in a Stockholm street, queuing for potatoes.

He didn't complain about my amateurish fiddling around with his feet, and he showed no surprise. Maybe I was doing quite a good job of it. In the end I lifted them out of the water that was starting to cool, wrapped and patted them dry in a towel, and then opened the wrapping a little to rub them with cream. But I closed it up quickly again because I could see he liked that best. And while I patted to dry them and keep them warm he leaned back, his mouth agape and his eyes closed like a child's.

But never trust any old geezer at all, no matter how innocent he looks. When I got up he peeked out and I could see the lecher in his eye; he fumbled for me, his hands groping for my waist and my hips, finding the sharp protrusions.

"Lord how thin you are," he grumbled, a little spittle running out of the corner of his mouth.

"I'll put on some coffee," I said.

But he held me fast, his free hand working at his trousers, pulling down the zipper and pulling out his little packet: two stones and a stick was what it should have been. But the whole thing was soft as a babe, he couldn't make anything happen even by shoving my hand down there, and I didn't have the heart to show aversion; in fact I didn't feel any. I felt empty and sorry for him and also kind of like bursting out laughing.

"I can't get me a boner," he whinged and I thought: 'What do you expect of yourself? Haven't you had enough after three-quarters of a century?' But I told him consolingly it was probably because I'd got so thin. He agreed eagerly and then we talked about all the skinny girls nowadays, semi-starved they looked, bony and odd. I put on some water for coffee and when I set the cup in front of him he had pulled up his zipper.

Before he left he wanted to sign something or maybe he wanted me to. But I told him to forget it, it was on the house. Because the national health usually paid for his little adventure, of course, but that required a signature. I told him I was going away and wouldn't be coming back for a long time. There was no use his coming next week or the week after.

"I think you'd better get in touch with somebody else," I said, and he got all upset.

When I was alone again, the fear descended. I thought about what I had done, what I had exposed myself to. But fear was only half of it, the other half was a kind of pity. And actually I felt like bursting out laughing, too. I couldn't pull myself together, and I really didn't mind. I thought: 'If this is as frightened as I get, I'm going to be all right.' Still, my hands were trembling a little. Of course there might be other reasons for that: cold, hunger and my hangover. I couldn't survive on headache pills and biscuits if I intended to go on living.

I had to get out of there but I still didn't have the energy, so I turned up the radiator a little and lay down on the bed. There was no bed in the other room, what should have been the living room of this apartment. There was just a lot of junk. Suitcases, cartons, piles of newspapers. I had imagined this as her inner sanctum, the private area she didn't let her clients see. Maybe with candles in candlesticks, photos, fragile mementos. But there was nothing of the kind. She slept on this daybed in the same room where she heated water for footbaths, a room that was actually a kitchen. But she had covered the wood-burning stove in flowery contact paper, and on the kitchen worktop there was a little electric oven. That was where she baked the sponge cakes that filled the stairwell and the whole hallway with that sweet smell.

She had a chest of drawers with an enormous mirror, with postcards stuck all around the frame. Most of them seemed to be from Egon Holmlund. He had written faithfully when he was on tour. A doll was in the armchair next to the bed, a big baby doll, wide-eyed, in a frilly blue dress. Although I had never been in here before, I had heard about the doll; Ann-Sophie claimed she had been given it when she was a little girl. But I had been at the Sager's place, in one of the buildings where the estate workers from Little Heavenside lived, and there were no dolls there when we were little. So I suppose she had bought it herself. Perhaps to fabricate a better childhood for her visitors, or because she had wished for children, what do I know?

Personally, I've never had a weakness for dolls. They stare at you, wide-eyed, and are rigid to the touch. In one corner of the attic is my broken plastic doll Margareta, named after the princess who is about my own age. She had brown china eyes, and they stare right into the wall. She never came to life. A dead squirrel I found over by the dustbins had more life than that doll. I wheeled him around in my doll carriage. I had already seen other things, heard the rustling and whispers. Dolls didn't come to life on command on a birthday morning. Through the steam from my cup of cocoa her brown eyes stared like buttons and I pretended to be overjoyed, though I was riddled with anxiety.

How much of Wonda is true? Surely something. The glitter. The sheen. The dancing spots. Someone — something. A presentiment that made dolls be dead.

That morning in Ann-Sophie's apartment, I felt absolutely pure; I should have flown to heaven like a white dove. I never wanted to soil my wings again, and perhaps I thought I never would. But I should have looked at the pigeons in the courtyard and considered them. Maybe I did, I don't know. The fat ones, the noisy ones, the thin ones and the one with the bare neck. The dirty pigeons and the one-legged ones who are jumping along as eagerly and wildly in their search for edibles as the others. The ones who huddle up together under the roofing in the gables, the dense, dark cluster of pigeons seeking warmth and intimacy in the dusk. Their droppings, their feathers coming out and dropping down. Their smell. The everlasting cooing through the long late winter evenings.

I pulled Ann-Sophie's fluffy bedspread up over me again, to wait for the forces there must be in me. When I had been lying there for a while, the telephone rang. I didn't know where it was and it took me a long time to locate it in spite of the fact that it rang a second, third and fourth time. It was on the window sill behind a stiff cloud of pale green synthetic tulle. I lifted the receiver and said hello, noticing that my voice was still hoarse.

"Hi there," he said, and it was the man whose toe she had cut off. He didn't have to talk long for me to realize that.

In a bad way, badly battered, possibly ill. And rocking with hangover. That was how he usually returned, I supposed, after a few months, half a year. It wasn't difficult to look back over their lives.

"What's wrong with you?" he asked. "Are you sick?"

He wanted to come back. Everything was going to be all right again, so he thought.

"I don't bear grudges," he said.

Then he told about a performance he had put on at the Långviksmons Community Center and that it had been sold out. He was lying, but so indifferently he couldn't even have imagined he might be believed.

"Tonight I'm in clover," he said. "At the hotel in Bredbyn. But I've just come from two nights at the Tourist Inn in Träske. You know who was there?"

"No."

"The Curtmans' daughter. That dark girl."

"Elisabeth?"

"What's wrong with you? Got a hoarse voice?"

But he didn't wait for an answer. He said he was coming home.

"Was it Elisabeth Curtman?" I asked.

"Yeah, that dark girl."

I didn't take in much of what he said after that. He seemed to be trying to persuade her it would be best for both of them if he came home. He'd never say a word about it, he promised.

When I had rung off I got up and tidied Ann-Sophie's kitchen. I turned off the radiators before I left.

My daughter really was staying at the Träske Tourist Inn; I found her there, not when I asked about Elisabeth Curtman, but by description.

"Oh, Maria Delord," said the owner. He was out in front, messing about under the hood of a tractor. The yard was full of old cars, wrecks half-sunk in the snow that hadn't yet melted up here. It was the inland north, thirty or forty kilometers from Örnsköldsvik. He was a kind man in a snowsuit with Goodyear on it, and a red cap with a high crown and a brim. When I said I was her mother he was pleased.

"And a very good thing you've arrived, Mamma," he said in his northern dialect, after which he wiped his hands on a rag and showed me in to what might be or might have been a hotel, a big, run down wooden building full of the smell of meals past and threadbare furniture, photos, reindeer horns, paintings, wall hangings, funny handwritten signs and less funny ones (on the door to the bathroom). On the counter from which he sold day-old tabloids, cigarettes, chewing gum and sweets, there was a book where my daughter had registered under the name Maria de Lourdes. Something which is all ours, or which we believe to be ours we apparently always want to hang on to. She had been staying there for nearly three months.

"But how does she pay?" I asked. "I don't suppose she has any money?"

"No, she hasn't got any money," he answered. "Not really. But I let her stay on while she waits for her boyfriend."

"The Dutchman?"

"No, Hardy isn't Dutch, I don't think," he said.

Then we went up the stairs, past the TV and the easy chairs at the top of the stairs with their springs close to rock bottom, and over to a door with a number on it. He opened without knocking and we stood looking at her for a little while before he went slowly back downstairs. I heard the stairs creak under his weight and his muddy boots.

She was sleeping in spite of its being afternoon and the room suffused with a sober, almost cold light from the spring sky and the snow. She looked small and

447

skinny and her face was very pale against the flowered pillowcase. Her black hair was longer than ever, but it looked very thin now. It might just have been unwashed and lank. I saw she had a rash on her cheeks when I went closer, and she had drooled a big damp patch onto the pillow, just like when she was little. The hand that was on her shoulder — she looked like she was trying to hug herself — was a thin paw with bitten down nails and dirty cuticles. I didn't recognize it, but it was hers.

I didn't want to wake her. I didn't like the thought that she would wake up and see me standing over her like that either, so after a while I went out and shut the door quietly.

The owner offered me a cup of coffee in a peculiar dining room with plastic over the tablecloths, and I only looked at his face or down into my cup because the paintings and photos and reindeer horns and silly objects hanging everywhere confused me. But he told me that in the summers when the market was on in Kornsjö he would let all his rooms to the hawkers, who were the ones who had given him all the souvenirs. While we drank the light brown, slightly acrid coffee and ate buns sprinkled with cinnamon and pearl sugar, I asked him how much I owed him for the time Elisabeth had been staying there. He answered that it depended entirely on whether or not she left the paintings and I said that she was not, of course, going to take them with her. But I felt uncertain afterwards, sitting there waiting for her to wake up. What right did I have to say she was going to leave those horrid paintings? Perhaps she wouldn't even want to go back home with me.

But she did.

Elisabeth was taciturn and pimply and thin and she looked like a starving child with her swollen stomach.

"Why didn't you come home?" I asked.

She shrugged her shoulders like a southern European and didn't answer. But once when my voice, which had gone shrill with accusations and guilt, almost cracked, she said:

"Because I thought you'd make me get rid of it."

She put her hand to her belly. That was how I found out she was pregnant. It was one morning at the kitchen table. She drank her *café com leite* in big gulps but had hardly touched her sandwiches.

Hasse refused to believe me when I phoned to tell him. But I said there's nothing particularly unbelievable about it, it's the classic story. Then there were lots of arrangements to be made; an appointment at the maternity clinic, vitamins and iron supplements. Jenny took it all quite reasonably, although I wouldn't say she seemed pleased. She bought some appliance that pressed the juice out of vegetables and fruits and gave it to us so Elisabeth would get more vitamins.

Presumably she wasn't a drug addict as I had thought in my darkest hour. But she was uneasy and sometimes anxiety-ridden, and at those times she took pills from the cabinet, old medicine that had been prescribed for Henning. When I hid it she drank from the wine bottles in the larder. If there was nothing at all she stole money from me. I don't know what she bought with it. Once she had a go at my cough medicine. But things went in cycles, a few days of wild eyes and upset, after which she would sink back into waiting.

She awaited the child and, above all, Hardy. She was going to stay here and wait for him and had no intention at all of going back to Portugal.

"You must be crazy," she said. "How could I turn up there with a kid? Even you must see that's just not on."

"But it's all right to have a kid here?"

"Sure," she said. "And besides, we're getting married as soon as Hardy comes back."

That was all she would tell me. But she did talk to Gabriel and Michael, with them she would be elated, drink wine at the dining room table and sing and laugh in that thin voice. Well, to be accurate, there was only once she laughed and sang that spring, which was after Ann-Sophie's funeral. Gabriel and the Whitepainter had organized a meal afterwards, spit-roasted chicken from the supermarket of course, and I don't know if she had too much wine or if there was some other explanation for her being in such high spirits, if it was all just too much for her in some odd way. It didn't upset me anyway, I withdrew. It sounds insane, but I missed Ann-Sophie, and felt sad she had died.

I sat in the study and it was dark in there. Elisabeth was just talking away, and she must have thought I'd gone to bed, because she was being very frank. She told them about the remarkable Hardy whom she missed so much, the seller of paintings, the seller of God only knew what that he often went to Amsterdam to collect. That was how he got the nickname the Flying Dutchman, the Whitepainter had worked out. But he wasn't in Holland now, she gave herself away:

"We're getting married as soon as he gets out."

Or did Michael and Gabriel already know? Maybe she kept less from them? A few hours ago we had buried Ann-Sophie, the four of us and a clergyman. We had sung "God of the living, in Whose eyes Unveil'd", and Elisabeth had joined in, in spite of being uncertain of the words, singing with her thin and fragile but well-pitched and penetrating voice, and I remembered hearing it on the last day of school in Porto, over all the others. She had been cold in just her thin denim jacket in the crematorium, and had stood there, lips tightly clenched, staring down at the stone floor when the coffin vanished. But now this strange elation had come over her. She wasn't drunk, you couldn't say that, but in high spirits. I sat cuddled up on Henning's leather armchair under the lamp with the cracked silk shade, and because I hadn't turned it on she must have thought I was out of the way, which was undoubtedly a great relief to her. With me she never cracked a smile, never said a word more than was necessary about what had happened to her, bad or good. But with Michael and Gabriel she could talk, and that day, at the dining table, she finally told them what it had been like when Hardy got caught for the thing he had been accused and convicted of. She called it a false, groundless accusation, and she had said so in court, too, but they hadn't believed her.

They traveled around selling paintings, she did most of the selling because they did the best business that way. They hadn't had much luck in the villages or at the isolated farms, but things went a little better in the towns. They had been in Sundsvall and Härnösand and Kramfors, and that morning they had arrived in Sollefteå. She spent some time walking around the co-operative department store there, because Hardy had lots of business to do, he always had so many irons in the fire. They were supposed to meet at a parking lot a couple of hours later, but he didn't show up. She had hardly had time to start worrying when a police car stopped in front of her and two big officers got out and told her to come along. They had found hash in the car and arrested Hardy. That was no big deal, she said. But they said it was quite a lot of hash, and she had had no idea what they were talking about. Then they were questioned. Hardy had just been transporting that package for another guy and he had no idea what was in it, and he said so. But they didn't believe him. They had pressed her for answers, too, and she had said that they sold paintings and that was all, the rest was just invention. But they wanted to put *someone* behind bars. So there was a trial and he was convicted. No one had believed her there, either.

"You had a bit of luck if you ask me," said Michael.

Elisabeth blew up at that.

"But what about the package, then?" asked Gabriel. "Or was there more than one?"

She didn't know and she didn't want to talk about it any more now. I think she was crying, that girl who just half an hour earlier had been gleeful enough to sing. I sat perfectly still in the other room and when they started to clear the table I crept through Abel and Sigrid's bedroom into Henning's room where I was sleeping now.

I didn't want her to see me and realize I'd been listening. She didn't want me to know, begrudged me her story.

Late in the autumn of 1977 my daughter vanished down into the underworld I haven't seen and I am told nothing about except what she chooses to tell me. And to me she tells nothing, I've found out everything I know by eavesdropping. She settled in to wait for him at the boarding-house in Träske rather than to come back here, back home, she didn't trust me.

For me, three-quarters of a year had passed since I came home to sell my house, and the time had disappeared. The baby was reality and I believed all the time it would be mine. And this time I wouldn't fail. Sometimes I disliked it, I admit. Maybe not the baby, but that it had happened to her. It seemed to me at times to be more like a diseased growth inside her body than anything else. It was too early, it was battling her for a life that was not yet big enough for them both. I also thought she was being careless with it. She jeopardized its life and health with her pills and her smoking. And I didn't know what she did when she suddenly went away, she never said. Michael told me not to worry my head about it if she went away for a couple of days. Most of the time she was out with those people who comprised Gabriel's sense of belonging in the world in spite of the fact that he couldn't be where they were because of his asthma: Children of the Earth.

He told me he had every reason to hope he might interest her in their way of life. While she was waiting he put his whole ecology library in her hands. The books floated around our apartment; there were Schumacher and Grönholm and Naess and Hartvig Saetra, Callenbach and André Gorz, and Kvaløy and all the big names. But I don't think she read them. She isn't a reader and she was quite convinced that the whole world was going to the dogs anyway, Hardy had said so.

Still she started spending more and more time out there, maybe just so as not to have to be in the apartment with me. When she was at home she sat heavy with the fetus and perhaps heavy with fear of giving birth to it, and we didn't talk to each other much. We might have been pretending we had said all there was to say; we didn't want to show any more.

Those earth nutters had got her to believe hospitals were dangerous places, and in early June when the baby had descended and she had to trudge heavily to get up the stairs, her thin legs far apart and having to have a rest halfway, she suddenly packed a couple of bags and disappeared out to them. She left a note behind saying she was going to have her baby with friends.

I was sure I knew which friends they were and I was out there that same afternoon. The bus didn't go all the way. You had to walk a couple of kilometers from the main road. Behind fields of whooshing green wheat the first thing you came to was an old croft with a veranda that had a corrugated green plastic roof. With frilled curtains and plastic plants in the window boxes, it now had a new lease on life as a summer cottage.

But the croft known as Äppelrik in the district of Skebo, Vallmsta parish, had escaped that worse fate by dying. A mound of grass over the foundation of what had once been the homestead, a cloud of green foliage and heavy bunches of lilacs against what was left of the chimney and hearth, a tangle of pale columbines and strong-smelling herbaceous grass — that was all that remained. It had sunk and was no more. Field mushrooms might still grow in the meadow sloping down to the well. Tora Otter had shown me the spot; she had grown up there.

Then there was the croft that had once been known as Wolf Bog cottage and that was now the Children of the Earth Cooperative. It looked poor but lived in, and in the kitchen at the table of very roughly hewn boards there now sat an entire congregation of deadly serious elders, men and women, holding a group meeting to decide whether or not they would allow my daughter to go back with me.

The children, the real earthly children who had been born out here and nourished on goat's milk and nettle bread, ran around outside while I sat on the steps up to the house waiting for judgment to be pronounced. Nativity was high among the Children of the Earth. They wanted these enlightened parents of their movment to produce offspring, as many as possible.

A few minutes earlier they had explained to me, in the kitchen, that if the only people to have children were the ignorant ones, there would never be any progress. The world would go under.

I sat looking at the kids playing on the hillside by the old barn, with its high grass, the children of the race of pure reason. The idea seemed to be that my grandson or granddaughter would be one of them. I didn't want to contradict them; I knew too little about these things. And yet I felt quite hopeful. I was fairly sure they would let me take Elisabeth along home. She had fled in panic, scared of giving birth and under the influence of her back-to-the-land friends. But I couldn't believe she would really want to deliver the baby out here in this crofter's cottage with the hot water pot on the sooty stove, the big, rough shears, towels made of scrubbing cloth, and the smell of goats. My daughter is slightly fastidious, and in many ways something of a ninny. Not to mention the fact that she wasn't yet of age. If they took things to the extreme, I could send the police out to collect her.

Like all sensible people, they took their time. Elisabeth sat with them in there at the kitchen table, biting her cuticles.

The kids out on the slope were playing with the baby lambs, carrying around those little woolly lambies that can't have been more than a couple of weeks old. I took a walk around the buildings, and stumbled upon more lambs. But these were dead. They were lying there in plastic bags, four of them, behind the barn. A fox or some other animal had ripped holes in the plastic and pulled the rigid little bodies out. Perhaps he had run off with one.

If nothing else helped, I could show Elisabeth the lambs.

But she did come home with me, and ten days later she gave birth to the baby, a boy exactly as she had thought. Just a few days before her eighteenth birthday. I wasn't allowed to come to the hospital. She didn't want me there. I couldn't understand that. She didn't have anybody else with her. I sat at the kitchen table waiting for the phone to ring, but the night passed, and nothing happened. I thought about her tormented, thin body, thinking she was too young and too thin and too small for what was now happening to her. Why didn't she want me to sit through the long vigil of pain and waiting with her?

She named him João Henry. I thought that was mad. Juan Enrique or Jean-Henri or Johan Henrik — but João Henry? Who would be able to pronounce it? I warned her. At school they would surely pronounce it Jo-ao as if it were Swedish.

"I don't think we'll be staying in Sweden," she said then.

We — that was Hardy and her and the child. That was that.

Naturally, I didn't believe her. When she came home with the baby she was tired and fretful. I didn't for one moment think she could manage to take care of him. And quite right, for the first two weeks I was his primary career, undoing the thin plastic tie-pants and removing the diaper, holding his wriggly little legs in one hand and cleaning his bottom with the other. He didn't look a bit like Elisabeth. I had imagined I would be getting her back. But he was different, already larger as a newborn than she had been at the age of two months when I saw her for the first time. He had fair hair, light blue almost gray eyes and a big nose. He didn't cry as much as Elisabeth had. But his cries were fiercer, they exhausted her. He would calm down the minute I carried him to her and put him to one of her taut, blue-veined breasts, which I almost found myself unable to look at the first time she exposed them. I couldn't believe they were hers. In fact I think both of us found it awkward.

When a couple of weeks had passed, she started carting him around. I disapproved. He should lie in his bassinette, he was too little to be taken all over the place. She had a little carrier the Children of the Earth had given her, and soon he went everywhere with her. She exposed him to all kinds of contagion, pour little soul. But there was no point in talking to her. We didn't even quarrel. She avoided me. And she took him with her no matter what I said, carried him into town. Maybe into shops. Maybe to the homes of people I neither knew nor knew anything about. Sometimes she was away overnight.

She'd started swiping pills and some wine again. She stole money from me and went off without saying where. She told outright lies. If only she had at least felt guilty or ashamed when I caught her at it. But she just went on nonchalantly lying and not minding when I found her out.

How had she become so blunted? For a while I thought: she's depressed. She's deeply depressed from this far too early pregnancy, from the delivery, from being tied down to a child when she is barely more than a child herself.

But what's depression? Is it chemistry? Is it a demon? Or was she just longing for Hardy to be released? Or if he was actually already out — to come and get her.

What made her like this? Am I the one who has broken her down? Did I starve her out, like the shade of a larger tree always makes the smaller one fail to grow properly? Or had I suffocated her with caring? Had my angst brought on her illness?

Is she rejected, unwelcome, someone I left in Jenny's care as often as I could; and in the hands of the brilliant Swedish school system? Is she the kind of child who has always seen a closed door?

Or is the very germ of life inside her wounded from loneliness and malnutrition when she was tiny and Conceição was working in the convent kitchen while she was lying there in the white bed staring up into a white ceiling?

I will never have the answers, and I knew it. Still, I tried to extract them from her, as if she had known. And I asked her not to keep going away with João Henry, not to drag him around among strangers.

There were, in fact, lots of times when he was where I wanted to have him, in his little bassinette in Elisabeth's room, sometimes looking out the window. Yes, he was able to focus now. Out there a huge treetop had once swayed. It had blown and billowed and its leaves had turned their shiny sides toward the light, their little tongues into the wind. But it was not there any more.

One night they came and got her. We had finally had a falling out, our only one. Just after it she made one of her quiet, clandestine phone calls, and then she went into her room. I sat there in Henning's armchair, trying to think away my nausea, my shame and the hate I felt for her, to put it bluntly. But I couldn't settle my mind. I thought she was both right and not right, that she was so very young and so very merciless. In the end I went to bed, too.

That evening, the last one:

We had been drinking wine with the Whitepainter and Gabriel. They finally left. I was tired. Elisabeth was standing by the dining room table pouring herself more wine from a bottle that was still almost full. I told her, quite sharply, that she really ought to leave it.

"It keeps fine if you put the cork back."

She didn't answer, just downed her glass and took another without looking at me, took that glass with her into her room and shut the door. I followed her and opened it. She was sitting on her bed smoking and the stale, stifling smell struck me.

"You mustn't smoke in here," I said. "It's not good for João." She didn't answer, just inhaled deeply, blowing the smoke at me, and I had an impulsive urge to slap her, to slap that scornful, lax, intoxicated face of hers. But I checked it, grasping her by her upper arm instead and pulling her up off the bed. I tried to take the wine glass away from her, but the contents just sloshed out.

"Leave me alone, damn you!" she said.

I pried the glass out of her hand and it fell to the floor and broke. I shoved her out of the room very roughly. João had woken up and was crying hard. It took me quite a while to settle him down again and to pick up the pieces of broken glass and deposit them in the wastebasket. I was on my way to collect a broom to brush up all the little slivers of glass that might dig into her feet and injure her. But first I went back into the dining room and what do you know — she was sitting at the table with another glass of wine and another cigarette.

"We can't go on like this," I said. "We've got to get out of here."

"I am getting out of here," she said.

"No, I mean home. We're going to Porto. We have to start fresh. We'll see to it that João has a good life."

"Oh right," she said. "So he's going to have a good life in Porto, you think?

With you?"

"I think so. If we pull together."

She gave me a cynical glare.

"What is it?" I asked, in such a nasty tone of voice I could hear how harsh it sounded myself. "What's with you? If you think I've done things wrong, the least you can do is to tell me so outright. I don't know what I've done!"

"Oh no you've done no wrong," she said. "You're perfect, aren't you? I think you'll be a brilliant mother to João Henry — because that's what you want, isn't it?"

"Well, I do want to help you with him, yes."

"Sure. Go back to Porto and everything will be normal again. I'll wear little frocks again and go back to school, right?"

"Elisabeth…"

I held her, but not hard this time. She lashed out roughly, taking me by surprise.

"Leave me alone, damn you! You go back to Porto! Just go. I'm not coming along. You go back to Pappa and Jaime Oliveria-Cruz!"

A long compact silence ensued. I didn't know what to say. I was dreadfully ashamed. She sat there smoking, staring down at the table top. Finally I said:

"You're talking about things you know absolutely nothing about."

"I know very well."

That, I thought, couldn't possibly be true. But she did know something.

"What is it you know? Out with it."

"That you and Jaime were having it off."

"Nonsense."

"I know it's true, I know it. Remember that time you and I went to Lisbon? After I finished school? We were supposed to have a really good time, go shopping and see the sights. And then we bumped into Jaime on Rua Garett when we were coming out of a shoe shop. My goodness, what a surprise! Jaime in Lisbon — fancy that."

"You're wrong," I said.

"And you proposed we go out to the beach at Estoril, the three of us, and he said he'd treat us to lunch and all. When we passed those big houses along the road I said maybe my father lives there. I said so because I had started thinking quite a lot about him, and I knew Jaime knew who he was. You had told me he was wealthy and his family wouldn't allow him to marry my mother. But I couldn't get an answer out of Jaime, he kept changing the subject. Once we were on the beach at Estoril you developed a sudden migraine, or so you claimed. A really bad one!

Poor, poor you! Jaime would have done anything to help you."

"Cut it out now, Elisabeth," I said. "There's no point in this. You really don't know what was going on."

"Oh yes I do, because I went in! He said he'd arrange a room at the casino hotel for you to rest in the dark and recover from your migraine. And the two of you went off. But I came looking for you, as you may recall. Do you remember? I walked into that room after an hour, told the people at the desk that I was the daughter of the senhora who was ill. She's upstairs with her doctor, they said. And so you were. I remember how it smelled in there when you finally opened the door. When Jaime had finally got his clothes on! You were disgusting. Shit, you were so damn disgusting!"

She drank more wine, but I didn't say anything.

"So why did you come up?"

"To see how you were! And because I wanted to talk to Jaime about my pappa! I imagined him living in one of those villas, because of what you had told me. But it was a lie!"

"How do you know that?"

"I asked Jaime when we were leaving. We walked through that whole long park down toward the beach and he didn't say a word. So I asked him. And he said my Pappa didn't live there. That he wasn't even from Lisbon."

"That's right," I said. "He wasn't."

"So why did you say he was?"

"I don't know. It's difficult to remember after all these years. I don't even remember what I did say."

"You told me he was from a fine old Lisbon family and that he had fallen in love with my mother at university. But when she got pregnant they hadn't been able to get married."

"Well, that wasn't the truth."

"So what is true then? Who was he?"

"It's true that I was having an affair with Jaime Oliveria-Cruz," I said. "It had been going on for fifteen years. But it's not true that we had arranged to meet on Rua Garett. That was sheer coincidence. I didn't know he was in Lisbon. I'm sorry we got you involved."

I could still recall the hot sand, Jaime's wrist with his watch. His voice.

"It was foolish of us," I said.

"My pappa?" she asked.

"Your pappa's name is José Antonio Dimas. He worked in the abattoir in those days, in Porto. Your mother's name is Ana Maria Conceição, her maiden name was Ferreira. She's married to him now and you have a brother who is twelve and whose name is Manuelo." That was it but it was as if she still didn't really believe me.

"It was truly coincidental that we met Jaime in Lisbon," I said. "We hadn't arranged it."

She killed her cigarette in the ashtray with a movement I found awful, and then she said:

"You make me sick."

Then she got up and went out in the hall and used the phone. I couldn't hear what she said because I had gone into the study and was sitting in the armchair. I heard her go into her room and thought she was going to bed.

I went to bed as well. Sleep was beyond me. I lay there thinking about how I could explain to her, realizing that it was impossible. There was no explanation. There is none. I don't know why I wanted a relationship with a man like Jaime. I don't even know if I care about him much, I certainly don't trust him. Yet after all those years it would be madness to claim I never trusted him — so I don't know. I really don't know. Was it sickening? Well, maybe so. But the lust had been stronger. Or had it been so strong because there was disgust attached? Should I have told Jaime: go away. You're humiliating me. Let us go our separate ways because each of us is humiliating the other. But it wasn't easy. That story I made up about her father, I was ashamed about that. I felt ridiculous. How could I possibly explain it to her when I couldn't even remember why I said it any more?

In the middle of the night I heard noises outside the apartment. Soft voices. João whining, doors being opened and closed softly. I put on my dressing gown and went out into the hall. There were people at the dining room table, strangers. At first there seemed to be a lot of them, but in fact there were only five. Two women, or girls really, and three men. One was holding João. Elisabeth came out, carrying two big canvas bags with their things.

"I'm leaving now," she said.

"For where?"

"I'll stay with friends for the time being. It'll work out."

"But where are you going? Who are they?"

She didn't answer. I went up to those people but it was dark in the dining room, just the light coming in from the streetlamps, so I couldn't make out their faces. I went over and switched on the ceiling light. The man holding João in his lap might be Hardy. I had to have a look at him. He had dirty blond hair, a little curly, a handsome aquiline nose, and large round blue eyes. His was an appearance that would attract attention anywhere. But I didn't know if he was Hardy. He had to be a lot older than Elisabeth, twenty-six or twenty-seven, I guessed. I supposed it had to be him. He was holding the baby and stroking him. He even rubbed his nose to João's forehead.

I thought the girls looked slatternly. They had long, unkempt hair, were wearing full-length skirts and jeans jackets. One of them had a thin cotton scarf twisted around her head like an Indian woman's. I saw Elisabeth fixing her lilac scarf in the same way. Then she went to get the carry cot, and the man at the table got up and lay João in it.

"We're going now, Mamma," said Elisabeth. "I'll be in touch."

I shouted at her that she couldn't just go off like this. But she said she could. "I'm of age."

"You're insane! How can kids call themselves of age in this country nowadays? You're a child, Elisabeth! What will you live on?"

I don't think any of them were listening. They walked out with her various carrier and canvas bags. The man with the curly hair had the carry cot with João in it. Elisabeth was the last one out of the door, and she turned around and patted my cheek.

"I'll be in touch," she said. "Not to worry."

None of the others spoke to me at all. I heard them chatting as they went down the stairs. Then I heard a car start on the street. The sound echoed against the stone walls of Swedish Engineering, and then decreased. The person at the wheel was waiting for something. The car was idling, a soft murmur.

If I were to rush down now? If I were to run after you, Elisabeth? If I told you he made me conceive? Then you wouldn't believe me. But it's true.

He was a real magician and a sophist and he did what I asked him without me even really needing to ask. All I needed to do was to tell him how frightened I was. And he explained it to me many times afterwards, making it rational and clear and absolutely necessary. I didn't want to bear children. I was terrified, imagined the baby would rip me up inside when it was born, imagined some kind of awful hereditary disorder. I wanted to be freed of the sick growth inside me, of the thing enlarging inside where my soul should have been developing instead. Hasse had opened me a bank account so I wouldn't have to ask for housekeeping money. I could afford to pay for the conception Jaime Oliveria-Cruz gave me. Three thousand it cost, the price of a soul you might call it, but I didn't really get it in the way I had thought. I had intended to go back afterwards and find Victor.

But that wasn't what happened.

I was delivered, Elisabeth. But what I expected didn't happen, that Hasse and I would be finished afterwards. He was so unhappy. He grieved for that baby who, when it happened, wasn't much bigger than a thumb. And he felt so terribly sorry for me. Because Hasse never found out what I really did.

From that day I was split into two halves, the half where it had happened and the half where it hadn't. But there is truth, Elisabeth. Jaime had made me conceive. He did it with saline solution.

And I stuck with him, one half of me, the half in which it had happened stuck with Jaime not because he was the pleasure and the sweetness and the desire, not only because of that. But because he was also the truth.

That was how, for many years, I stuck to the truth. But I also stuck to untruths, and I did so because I wanted to. I was so fond of Hasse, you see. I still am. But when we come together I am not present bodily. Only my willingness is there. And where it is, there is also my unwillingness. They cohabit.

Now the engine was running harder. The car shifted into gear. The noise echoed loudly between the walls of the building as the car drove away, and I could hear it for a long time on the silent nocturnal streets as I stood at the window, brow to the glass.

There's a swell through the leaves, a swell of warm, pungent wind. I know nothing about the house any longer; it is no longer body around me. I am in the huge lung of leaves that breathes me and the world.

Stacks and haycocks of leaves. They shift and breathe their scent at me. They are mass and motion at once, have the volume of stack and cloud, but still like loose scraps, with little green tongues; I breathe with tongues and lap up air. They eat something we don't want out of the air and return something to us we have to have. When I was little I thought it was the scents and the perfumes. But then I was told it was oxygen. Henning said that when the trees ate it was called photosynthesis.

I can no longer recall what kind of trees they were. Now there is just a twisted lilac left, and that cracked old apple tree. No others are visible from the window. But they may have been lindens. Yes, they must have been lindens, with their heart-shaped leaves. They sometimes live to be a thousand. Here they only lived for fifty years, after which they were taken down because a garage was going up. Oaks? I have a memory of green oak leaves, of holding them between thumb and index finger when they were new, feeling their silky membranes.

I was in the treetops not very long ago, and the city was no more than bits of iron and gravel at the bottom of a pit. I have long possessed the ability to go in and out of worlds. I can do it in various ways and one of them is this: simply semi-somnistically allow myself to be carried along when the warm wind that makes the curtain billow also makes it fall slack, sucking out the depleted air from the room.

For every world I erect another one arises too, equally possible or impossible. Every time I built the house it divided, like in the old children's game. And when I made the city of iron and gravel and waste, another city also arose — of light.

It's still summer but last autumn lies rolled up in this summer, as memory and premonition. Out in the yard, the withered leaves are rolling, pushed hither and yon by puffs of wind. They make me think of Adam Otter, that elegant fellow in gaiters and suede gloves, and of his incredible question to Jenny. Naturally, she couldn't answer him. I wouldn't be able to, either. The point? I don't suppose there is any particular point. Not in my life anyway. If I were to die now I would leave nothing behind but a sizeable pile of rubbish. I have always thought it was, if not presumptuous at least romanticized to assume life had some special meaning.

Adam Otter, the only person I ever heard ask that question outright, has been dead for years. He left a little wooden house on the north side of town with a large but not particularly neat garden. He never had much time for garden stocks and mignonettes, and he died when his heart muscle ruptured. The notice of his death asked:

WHY?

and that was a very good question indeed.

Thinking doesn't take very long when you're not in the habit, I'd say it tends to go much too fast. I try to think slowly, try to hang on to the rolling brown dry leaves with my gaze when they are swept away by the whirlwinds down in the courtyard. Who told me there was no point in life, and that it isn't really proper to wonder whether that is true?

There goes Gabriel, crossing the courtyard, the wind in his face, and putting his hand to his forehead as if trying to keep a cap on. But he is bareheaded. Maybe he's just shielding his head from the wind.

I have been living in this house for months now without, I think, ever seeing who the others are and what's happening to them. Gabriel was assaulted in a building near the foundry, but I didn't notice how much he'd changed until the Whitepainter pointed it out to me. He cried a lot, poor Gabriel, and was depressed. But when it came over him he tried to stay out of people's way. He may not be over it yet.

He can't remember what happened. He had rung a doorbell. He was going from door to door with a petition demanding a popular referendum on the nuclear power issue. They found him on a landing with four apartments, but no one who lived there admitted knowing anything about what had happened. The police said he might have fallen down drunk or stoned and cracked his head on the stone landing. Ann-Sophie believed some pro-nuclear type had assaulted him when he asked them to sign. The Whitepainter said it was true a lot of people were upset after the latest elections, but he still didn't believe they would bang someone over the head without a prior argument. His theory was that Gabriel had been standing there dreaming about a better society and had found himself in the way of a door that was thrown open.

If so, though, why hadn't the person who had opened it seen to him? The Whitepainter said he must have been terrified of getting into trouble. Best to close the door again and pretend it had nothing to do with him. Jenny said, when she eventually heard about Gabriel's accident, some wild drug addict must have done it. Myself, I didn't know what to think. I can't say I really have any definite idea of what happened on that landing. I have too little familiarity with the community I live in; I have become an *estrangeira*.

I don't know much about how Elisabeth is living. I don't think about her that often.

Sometimes the hull surrounding my consciousness is torpedoed. A sharp piece of shrapnel penetrates, rips through. The unthinkable trickles in. Then I'm not happy with myself or with my life. Or with my stomach or the rest of my gastrointestinal tract. I want to eat more and I want to throw it up, too. I see no point in reading or writing. The wind sounds desolate, the metal roofing rumbles, grates and tears. To sleep or play solitaire, to work or not to work, it's all the same.

I wish someone would care for me, correct me and tell me what I should do. But those things don't happen to a grown up person. Something is expected of a grownup: a book, a pot of stew.

I feel desolate and cold inside. It's the inconceivable that has oozed in. It fills me like salt water fills a hull that's been shot to pieces. No, then I'm not happy with my life.

Victor said no one but housemaids were happy. He lives in Eskilstuna now, and has for many years. Bertil Sundh told me. The other day, the other night to be exact, I thought I'd phone Victor. I lay there thinking about him. I thought: he is sixty-nine years old, he has gray hair on his chest, maybe white since it was already salt-and-pepper that time so long ago. His arms are small, thin. He may have no bottom at all, because old men's bottoms disappear. Probably he is bald-headed and has soft ash-gray or white hair only at the temples and around his ears and his neck. But he has the same neck. The same hands, though they may be dappled, speckled with brown like old paper gets when it has been lying around for a long time. He must have the same smell, under all that tobacco stench his skin must smell like it did then. He is Victor, he must be. He is Victor until he no longer exists and he cannot have forgotten me, that's not possible.

But the worst thing is that this longing consumes. It consumes his face, his voice and his smell. They attenuate and fade so in the end you have no idea what you are longing for. Nothing but longing. Nothing but grayness. I lay in bed and I was in my longing, at home in it, full of aching and desire. But far off there was actually Victor, fifty or sixty kilometers of tarred roads, woods, streams, curves, little communities, lakes shining in the dark of night, treetops, rickety houses and barns, far far away in unreality, in the glowing, rosy gray city darkness, in a stone house or in a wooden house, in a bed or at a table in the lamplight, asleep or awake, in darkness or in light, in one world or another.

When morning comes, I thought, I'll go down to *The Correspondent* and look him up in the Eskilstuna phone book. Then it occurred to me that it's perfectly possible to phone directory inquiries at night. I wanted to phone Victor now. I wanted to reach him now, asleep or awake. I knew I would never do it if I put it off till morning came with its gray, sober daylight.

So I got up and dialed the number to those faceless women who say: "Information. Can I help you?" And I said "Victor Bremer, Eskilstuna." It took a little while, and then the faceless voice returned:

"Would that be Bremer, Victor, editor and Ingegerd, domestic science teacher?"

"Yes, certainly," I said, and she gave me the number. But of course I never called.

The grass is bright. At any time of the day or night at this light time of year I wander and I do not have to ask permission because there is no one to ask. I do not have to say that I am on the way to the library or to buy Matanzas for Pappa. It's easy to walk, and it is the same streets, just a few layers of tarmac between myself and the past. But I have to walk much farther now before I get to the woods or the fields. I don't really know where the city ends, there is no boundary like there used to be. It ran by the sawmill and the packaging factory, the railway track down below the graveyard, behind the Swedish Engineering buildings and below the Upco estate. The Otters' house was in the very last row. Below it the fields used to start, and the land belonged to Little Heavenside. But now there are big detached houses there. Houses and streets have crept up on the fields. The city is multiplying like clusters of bacteria on a glass slide. But what do they live on?

I go to the Upco Estate and see the Otters' house that belongs to someone else now, there among the tall trees. I count in my head. Twenty-five, nearly thirty years ago. There's the shady morello cherry that was in bloom the day I was confirmed. Jenny had set the table on the veranda, as we called the slabs of stone set out behind the house. She had made my white dress and put blossoming branches and narcissi on the table. But the morello was definitely the main character that day. Henning instructed me to stand beside it, and took my photograph. Jenny still has that picture on her bookcase. I look embarrassed, slightly stooped, and somewhat larger than the blossoming tree that now shades the house.

Below the Otters was a sparse wood of rowans and birch saplings. A whole new area of houses went up there later, and Hasse's father bought one of them for us. Sometimes I go back there. This time the owners appeared to be on vacation, so I walk boldly right into the garden. I sit on the steps of their little shed, looking at the brown and white house with the blue clematis on the south wall. The wood I am sitting on has grown gray and taken on that soft sheen I thought it took generations for wood to achieve.

I cannot honestly claim to be a stranger to this country, I am just as Swedish as the portly bureaucrat with rat-brown hair and knobbly feet who came out into the garden of the house next to the one we used to live in and lay down on his garden glider. It rocked for a while with its squeaky chain, and the *Daily News* rustled — he gave it an average of thirty seconds a page. Then he was asleep. The newspaper was on the grass. He had started to snore, and his lips were no longer pursed.

Yes, I am just as at home here as Ante Salvehult, local councilor. But where does my feeling of distaste come from?

"You're slipping down," says Jenny.

She sounds muffled and dramatic, doesn't look me in the eye.

"Henning was the same, he was dragged down. Think about that before it's too late."

She is afraid my moorings to Hasse are slipping.

"That house," she says in her radio drama voice.

She hates to see me wearing Lisa's green dressing gown, and she doesn't approve of my having my morning tea with Gabriel and the Whitepainter.

"Get dressed," she says. "And throw that old rag out, why don't you? It must have been around for almost forty years by now." But it's a very pretty dressing gown of dark green cravat-quality silk, with little *fleur de lis* woven into it. One of the pockets was torn, but I've mended it.

Salvehult must have a mortgage of nearly a million on the house, thatblocks the view of Little Heavenside. The amount of his income corresponding to the interest on the loan is tax deductible. I get dizzy trying to work out where all that money *is* — where has the value of the house gone? Does the bank own it? In that case, is Salvehult a tenant? Who the hell owns that huge complex with its shiny windows? How can Salvehult sit there, so secure, napping in his glider? Who owns the houses in the next street? Certainly not the men and women who cut the lawns and run about the streets and along the paths through the woods around here in their colorful Banlon jogging suits.

Salvehult runs too, every morning. I read it in *The Correspondent*. Recently they published his diary for a week. So every morning he subjects himself to suffering, solitude, stress and strain: you would never think it to look at him. He runs on the paved walking paths where the dogs have laid their sausages, and then he runs all the way up to the Heavenside gates and on to the gravel quarry and then he runs the length of the ridge until it intersects the road, and then home on the street. That's no short stretch. Just a few years ago when we lived here people said this country was turning into a land of indolence, where people were devoted to nothing but their own pleasure. And certainly the middle classes did suck satisfaction out of cigarettes, sweets, fellatio, beer and semi-soft cheeses, I can attest to that. But now they have started eating whole wheat and muesli. It won't be long until they can be talked into a war.

But who owns the houses? Does Salvehult even own the glider he's lying on? Sometimes I can see that those scampering, bouncing Banlon people's welfare is an illusion. But it's extremely effective.

And yet I cannot understand, cannot really believe, that the community in which I grew up can have changed so radically in a decade or two that its inhabitants would now be prepared to accept the illusion of ownership. Ruthlessly, unyieldingly, they urge their nearest and dearest: never give anything up. Gather and keep. Lose nothing, forget nothing. Read all the papers you subscribe to. Anticipate everything. Regret nothing. Never let go of your children. Teach your dog to be still when you say "Stay!" Cultivate immortelles. Rustproof your car. Maintain your oral hygiene. Only bathe in water in which you can leave a lasting impression. Write Christmas cards. Do not die.

Maybe I have become an *estrangeira* who actually knows very little about this city. But I can still formulate its first commandment. It was and is:

YOU ARE WHAT YOU HAVE

I despise this city. I wish I could contribute to its annihilation. But like most people in times of tedium and stagnation, I leave the labor of destruction to others. I want to watch.

There is a special ambiance here. A sort of aroma. I can sense it as clearly as if it were a cooking odor or a staleness in the very air. But I cannot reproduce it, even though Victor used to say I was so good at atmospheres. Ada would have been able to. I was only twenty but I recognized that directly in her tawdry little novel. She was able to capture it, whatever it is.

How did Ada do it, gain access to this little Paris of ours with its frusty bedrooms and reeking laundry rooms, its dankest rat-smelling corners? I sat in the auditorium of the upper secondary school last Saturday listening to the seventy-fifth anniversary concert of the men's Glee Club, and it filled the air like the smell of cooking fat, whatever it is, like a smog, a mist of thin, life-threatening fibers that eat their way in. Is it hate? Is it only my hate?

It's true that I hate my origins. The Glee Club celebrated its anniversary and I recognized every bit of it. I hate their instinct to imitate, their lost memory. I came to consciousness after the war, when a nation of petty bourgeois were on the march with table-ornament flags in hand. They had killed God and the Fight for Right I thought, when I was a young student and heard their patriotic four-part bellowing. They had pulverized history and made it into a cream-and-berry pudding. They had made sexuality reek of carrion, and I was not so stupid that I didn't notice. I thought they had crumbled and dirtied and pawed at everything.

Now the Glee Club was celebrating its anniversary in precisely the same way it had celebrated its arrival in Denmark more than twenty years ago. That time I had stood on the sidelines and seen, really seen for the very first time, that they were timid and ceremonious and had big feet. And sang out of tune. The Danes pretended not to notice, they opened their arms to them and poured their grain aquavit into them and their beer, and they smiled when the Swedes collapsed like rubbish sacks before their very eyes and the swill with which they had nourished their souls ran back out.

That day I saw for the first time how dreary our lives were and how we decorated them with invented feelings and deep notes, out of tune. That day there was no getting away from it. We were traveling as a group. And where could I have gone? I withdrew for a while, but then I sat with them while they had their open sandwiches at long tables, and drank the endless bottles of beer, that popped when they were opened. More of them began to look the worse for wear, but of course no one else wet himself, no one but my Pappa. He had overdone it earlier, on the ferry.

If there is one thing I was brought up to do, it was to shun excesses. The very first time I walked into the Otters' with my rucksack and my teddy bear I was instructed that excess was to be scrupulously avoided. A person who indulged to excess could end up among the weak and incompetent. And then there was no return.

One might end up there owing to illness and accident, of course, but in that case it had to be a traffic accident, since almost all other kinds of accidents were self-inflicted and a consequence of weakness. Of a tendency to indulge to excess. From giving oneself free rein, a lack of will power, stick-to-it-iveness, and *go*. The fact that most people appeared to have to get along without all that spunk only made those of us who belonged to the chosen all the more excellent. That was Fredrik and Jenny's philosophy.

But it sure as hell wasn't Henning's. He was a weak person. He indulged in excesses of all kinds: of sorrow, of hate, of plans, of confidence in himself, of despondency, of self-contempt, of desire and of love. He also indulged to excess in drink.

At the seventy-fifth anniversary celebration of the Glee Club, local councilor Ante Salvehult, who has the deepest most out of tune bass voice in the entire city stepped forward and paid the Club tribute in his mother tongue and Hebrew, in appropriate doses. He had originally meant to become a man of the cloth. I wish I could describe the thick air and my healthy hate. But I can't. The hate I feel is nothing but the dark gray dregs of a love potion. That other time, when I was younger, I also felt deeply for the proprietor of the medical appliance shop when he dissolved slowly in relief and beer after delivering his speech, when the patches of perspiration on the underarms of his wife's spring suit began to dry. These people have given me their world-view of shards of looking glass and their culture of Christmas tree ornaments and table-decoration flags. When they begin to hold speeches there is something in the very depths of me that is moved. Something tugs at my right arm, my chest swells, I see the stars.

I know they aren't real stars — they've just stuck silver foil on bits of cardboard — and I can laugh at the slight tugging at my soul when they insist on singing that Danish song about the gleaming grain. But I cannot alter the feeling.

A few years ago, when Synnöve's definition of the world spanned from the word "bourgeois" at one end to its opposite, "proletarian" at the other, I noticed when the two of us had come home on a visit that she was distressed. Sometimes it would express itself as shame, anxiety, or even grief. It was as if she couldn't really believe in the people she saw around her. Here we found ourselves in a corner of the world where the laws ceased to apply. Here, where so many people appeared to swing between the groundwork of a proletarian existence and the perpetually enamel-blue sky of the bourgeoisie, here rivers could definitely start to run upstream, or Tuesday come after Wednesday. I also had trouble believing in our city. It did not seem to me to be either particularly real or especially compelling. I believed more in Lisbon and Porto, and even in Kiruna where I had never been. Here was not even a city, just gray mist, switching locomotives, people with Co-op bags, mud, black skeleton trees and dog urine.

There is a season, foggy and brown, which seeks this city out. It seems to know that it is its very own season, and the city knows it too, it receives it at whatever time of year it comes. I squelch through the slush with vindictive, longing feet, wondering where I got this desire to torment and torture the city as if it were a being. Is it my mother and do I wish I could make her feel guilty for not being more beautiful, more intelligent, or belonging to a different social class?

Once Lisa was my mother. Now she's dead. Her ovaries have been incinerated. But the city is alive. It looks younger than when I learned to walk in it. Lisa was, despite minor aberrations, a normal mother. She aged and withered until ultimately she vanished forever. I couldn't get hold of her. She was evasive, a timid shadow in a beret and a wool coat, a guilt-ridden smile.

But this city is a shameless hussy of a mother that goes on breeding and multiplying, and it looks younger and more vulgar every time I return.

I've started working for the paper again. Every Tuesday I go down and submit a Sunbeam. We don't call them that any more though, Bertil Sundh and myself. When Bertil gathers his whole staff in the editorial room on the ground floor, I am usually there with the others, listening to him speak. There are twenty-five people on the staff now, but the circulation is still thirteen thousand, the same as it was in the fifties, when there were five of us running the whole show. The only difference is that *The Correspondent* is now a morning paper. Everybody is under pressure, and there are fewer coffee breaks than in the old days.

Bertil calls his Tuesday speech an overview. Although the news editor gives out all the assignments and deals with the everyday business, Bertil wants his people to be in touch with management. And so he gathers us on Tuesdays. Last time, his subject was reality. We have to be closer to it, he said, and closer to the people. I sat there just waiting for the shop floor and the grass roots, but Bertil has a feel for when words start to smell like piss, and they go sour fast at a place like this.

"We've got to get down to earth!" he said. "Out into the community!"

Now there's a word that's had an upswing. I don't really know what he means by it. Is it the very Godhead? In ancient Rome, the first Christians were accused of atheism. Of not having comprehended the divine sense of community.

Who actually used the word community when I was little? I remember the fatherland. Nobody ever sings the praises of the fatherland nowadays, today they talk about the community. In those days if anybody talked about the community it must have been behind the closed doors at Carlsborg, in the smoky meeting room of the town finance department.

I would like to propose to word-aviator Bertil Sundh that we go out to the people, to those down-to-earth places where they are building and living, and ask them what the community is. Whether it's them. Or us. Whether it is the compulsion to which we are born and from which no one can escape. The horizontal and the vertical organizations and the interdisciplinary ones. The cake, the Napoleon gateau with Queen Silvia and her dyslexic King on top. If it is the local councilors and the county council and the MPs and the trade unions and the public authorities and the media, if it could possibly look like a wooden darning mushroom but just as gray as the big mushroom sculpture at Stureplan, the umbrella we are all huddling under. If it is concrete and rustling paper. Rank Xerox and hole punches and non-smoking meeting rooms, coffee in plastic cups, galoshes and Ramlösa, underground pipes, numbers and huge metal drawers full of papers and corpses, that can be pushed in and pulled out. It is, of course, statistics and neat women with headaches and men who smoke and talk and talk and talk and talk. And minutes of meetings.

The community is the ICA supermarket and big villas nobody really owns and the Esso filling station and Tommy's Hamburger Stand and Boutique Veronique and the terrible stench coming out of the manhole in front of the department store. It is bright lights around the hockey rink, assisted accommodation for the elderly, and a sea of unset cement and white lights, a sea where the sharks and the barracudas swim back and forth in gray suits and where the workers flap their polyp arms, unable to come unstuck from the groundwork.

It's not possible to live apart from the community, at most it is possible to float around in it, torn loose with ragged ends. The community is the bunker where people and goods are preserved, the culverts with florescent lamps and Advent candle-holders, the Underground during the period August-to-June, the long crude concrete hangars, the swaying tower of Babel with glimmering lights, the pharmacies and the health insurance offices where there are no dogs and the military shooting ranges where there are shrapnel and dogs, the parks, the demolition properties, the regeneration sites, the wrecking facilities, the rehabilitation clinics. The community belongs to the children, those little lunarnauts, those little Michelin men, who frighten me so. It is the rails, it is the hot gravel and the stained tarmac and the singing wires.

There is no apart. Even at Walden Pond the train whistles were audible, and a civil servant will bury the sick, filthy hermit monks in Vallmsta. The dreamers are there too, the incurables who slog on with their poetry and perpetual motion machines and who ponder over God. All of us are part of it. Atheism isn't a possibility. We will never come unstuck from the groundwork. All we can do is flail and mumble, flail and mumble.

Down to earth! Let's get down to earth! Right. Down under the ground, down into the soil, past the rusty, leaking pipes, down.

Out on the streets is where we must be, Bertil also says. To where the people are. He says the people, enunciating it distinctly. He's already used up the man on the street.

But not out on the streets, Bertil. You're wrong about that. That is the place where the laws and regulations reign, the ones Gabriel says people have adopted because they do not trust one another. In their loneliness and their deep suspicion, they have built up their city of clubs and associations and lodges and societies to unite them and provide them with a sense of belonging. But beyond the streets, behind the buildings, somewhere in there another city has arisen in the meanwhile.

Go in there some time, have a look around and you may catch sight of it. There, the solitary trees are still in bloom, and someone hurries across the graveled courtyard with cup in hand to borrow what she needs. The old houses turn their faces inward, they use their bodies to protect one more worn-down lawn and a bed of bulbs deep down in the earth.

In there the flower of the city may have opened. It is little and barely brighter than a buttercup, perfectly content with nearly nothing, Just being here and having each other. We didn't come just to build a community, you know. We came to live a life with each other.

Now I'm walking its weary streets. Calling myself Ann-Marie Johannesson when I write about the anniversary concert of the men's Glee Club. Because I have to do my fair share of anniversaries and Red Cross meetings if I want to write my series about the city water supply.

The first two articles have already been published. They were about the wells. The first public health issue ever to be tackled here was apparently when the physician in the railway hamlet decreed that the wells must be closed and sealed because they were polluted and sources of contagion. People liked the one about Trash Moat, too. From the outset it was a brook that ran through the community, a stream of fresh water. But it gradually became an open ditch, a moat of thick, flowing, filthy sludge running between the buildings.

The last two articles are going to be about the waste water works against which Ante Salvehult has been so outspoken in the public debate for many years, and the construction of which he has successfully prevented. But now the national government has stepped in, as people say. The old plant has been condemned. The new one will cost one helluva lot more than it would have a while back. People are saying that Salvehult has thrown over five million kronor of the local government's money down the tubes. I'm going to enjoy writing about it. Bertil can hardly refuse to publish it, he was enthusiastic enough about my proposal for the series. He sees it as a contribution to his down-to-earth project. Down into the soil! Under ground.

All right, you old word-aviator you. I'll take you down into the ground. With your mouth full of a tangle of roots. But when I write those words they will remain in the pile of papers on my desk. It's growing in spite of the fact that I have so much to do. Yes, I'm a busy person. We have our tea early nowadays. Never mind, says the Whitepainter who's an early bird anyway, a ruffled, molting, hoarse and sociable early bird.

The pile of papers is growing. Growing in spite of itself, page by page. I have made myself a body of words apart from this aching, miserable one. The stories may be no more than apologies and pleadings. Or else they are as diabolical as those old slides of Fredrik's that Jenny keeps in their plastic trays. If nothing else, I have made myself a body of words.

Gabriel came up to get his books, the ones Elisabeth never read. But I asked if I could keep them. I'm reading some for my water project.

I'm a mover and a shaker. I'm full of energy — meddlesome, and yes— even thoughtful.

Today I've been sweeping up pigeon shit. They've even dirtied the bed. Every time I see it, I think: this is the entry to my life. This high, rickety iron bedstead with its variable brown stains on its box spring. Lisa screamed there. Sweated in the sheets there. There. Between the bars I see my life begin in a tepid little pool.

But it's not true, strictly speaking. My life has several entryways. One is in the leafy treetops, in the acrid, scented wind that billows the curtain like a sail until the box of pins holding it in place falls to the floor and the clatter wakes me.

The curtain is fading and getting dirty. The mattress has been messed on and has strange new stains. Everything changes, even pigeon shit changes with time. Torrents of rain and rainwater running from the roof dilute it, and then it cakes and cracks in the summer heat under the metal roof. It goes crumbly and dry and when I sweep, it rises in puffs of gray-black dust and penetrates my nostrils and settles on my hands and on the front of my blouse. Pigeon shit ages like everything else. In the end, of course, everything goes to dust, even thoughts.

Henning didn't believe in them, not until they were put on paper, anyway. They were just elusive, gray shadows, he called them rats. But I do think it is equally possible to say that a person is his or her thoughts, just as much as a person is his or her flesh and blood and bones. The flesh is still there when the person is dead, if they're lucky, on a bed. It dries up or decomposes and the blood coagulates. Probably it, too, turns to powder or to dust. It's certainly no more real than thoughts, it is not an especially enduring truth about a person.

Paper decomposes more slowly, it goes brittle and it yellows, discolored and mottled like the skin of an old man. When I shake a pile of it to knock off the pigeon shit, the dust rises toward the roof. The handwriting is illegible but a cloud of sunlit whirling dust rises toward the skylight.

I have to get the pigeon droppings off these trunks and chests if I am ever to be able to open them without the dirt falling in among the clothing and papers. Because there might be something among all the rubbish, after all. Not, God forbid, a stack of letters that explains everything. Although actually, Lisa must in fact have written from the sanatorium. But they have eradicated her out of of this house's memory. A couple of flimsy dresses is all tthat is left, a few blouses with a line of dirt around the collar, a carton of brown medicine bottles. "Almenta", it says on the labels. It may have been hers, but of course there have been other people in this house who have been sick, even had lung trouble.

Gabriel coughs a lot, it's probably his asthma. He hasn't really been himself since he was assaulted. His voice is slower and more slurred, he has trouble finding words. The other day he asked when I came home. There was nothing odd about the question, I suppose, if he was trying to figure out how long I had been home. But I don't think he actually remembered I was here at home at all. There was a blank in his memory. Tomorrow he might recall it again, remember that whole long period when I sat at the kitchen table staring down into the courtyard, the time during which Ann-Sophie was sober as a judge and worked seriously with corns and ingrown toenails, the time when she was drinking herself to death, the time when Elisabeth was here, heavy with child and with her fear, and the time that is now, when she sometimes calls and says: not to worry, Mamma. Don't worry about a thing. João Henry has learned to walk.

It frightened me that Gabriel had to ask. Even I couldn't remember right away. There is no one who keeps track of time for us. We lose it.

Lisa's bed is not the entryway to my life, or at least not the only one. I have a fox-burrow of a life, a rabbit hole with a whole system of passages. One of them, perhaps the right one, is when the wind shifts the white curtain and something larger than myself and larger than the house breathes in the trees outside.

A month ago I found Lisa's ashes. Henning had put the urn up in the attic. Apparently he had never got around to burying her. That was how I found out she had survived Birger by nearly seven years. I made a few calls to the parish office in Norrköping again. She never changed her address.

I deposited her in the grave. Jenny came along, and a director from the funeral parlor. But we didn't bother with a minister. Underneath Henning's name it now says Lisa Johannesson on the headstone, but the gold in her letters is much brighter.

What an idea, putting the two of them in the same grave. But what was I supposed to do? What remained of Lisa was in an urn. I opened the lid and examined the ashes. They were black, a little lumpy. That was all and it looked revolting. I was ashamed of having peeked, but I had to be sure the urn wasn't empty.

If you are alone a lot, you eventually have visitors. I do, too. Faces turn up. Not least behind the frosted pane of glass in the door with its pattern of rigid, star-shaped blossoms around the edge, but I don't have to pay any attention to them.

Other faces gradually begin to be visible. I cannot say I see them. But I see something that reminds me of them and with the aid of which they try to make themselves apparent again. They frighten me like the dead do when they return from the outside darkness that seems to press them to the glass and the reflections in lamplight and fire. I remember Jenny telling me about someone who walked out onto Lake Vimmeln on the first dark ice of early winter. He saw the faces of the drowned under the ice. In his horror he started to run and his foot went through. But it was a shallow spot so he didn't drown. He just flailed around for a while among fragments of ice and dark water, and in the end he pulled himself up out of the sucking grasp of the mud by clutching at frozen reeds. They kept breaking, and not until he managed to find the strong necks down at the bottom by the roots was he able to make his way back to the edge, crawling, his mouth full of cold muddy water, but alive. I laughed, of course, as one does at ghost stories, but I have never forgotten those faces. I think they were like the ones I see, those overlaid faces straining to push out and make themselves real, wanting to be moist and soft, to breathe and move. Sometime they shatter with the effort and recede back into the pale wallpaper, with its flowers, cracks and scales, its grease spots and dried up damp, leaving nothing but brown edges. Voices purl underneath the murmuring of the refrigerator and the humming of the radiators; pleading and begging for their lives: rescue me, dig me up out of the piles of refuse.

When I am lying in my narrow bed at 13 Chapel Road I think of myself as a traveler in a region with terrible train connections. Yes, I think about Australia sometimes; of getting stuck in some fly-ridden hole, alone for weeks and months at some hotel. That's from a novel I once read, I recognize it. Someone's waiting for an airplane to appear in the white sky, and the plains are empty and gray and cracked with dryness and waiting. I even looked in the bookcase one day for that book, for a confirmation of my state of mind.

But my novels are gone. Henning sold them. There are only things like *The Nature of the Physical World*, the book where I thought I would find God when I was a child, since he was the nature of things. Strangely, Henning hadn't sold the *Nordic Family Encyclopedia* in spite of the fact that he could have got an awful lot of bottles of booze for a whole finely bound set with those owls on the backs.

Later I realized it was neither a miracle nor a coincidence. It was love and memory. Henning had saved the gold owls. Perhaps he thought they might fly again?

Upon closer examination, they weren't really gold. How could my memory be so wrong? I put on my glasses to search for traces of gold in the reddish indentations in the leather bindings. But not so much as a particle did I find. Then I opened the old book about the nature of the world:

> We have an intricate task before us.
> We are going to build a world — a physical world which will give
> a shadow performance of the drama enacted in the world of
> experience. We are not very expert builders as yet; and you must
> not expect the performance to go off with out hitch or to have the
> richness of detail which a critical audience might require. But the
> method about to be described below seems to give

the bold outlines; doubtless we have yet to learn other secrets of the craft of world building before we can complete the design.

And I thought: yes, precisely. It is not easy, and it cannot be built out nothing.

The faces try to press out, the voices whisper and murmur. Is it Ishnol, is it Wonda? Of scrap and waste they are made.

I cannot make the world out of nothing, but I will demand as little specialized material as possible. Success in the game of world building consists in the greatness of the contrast between specialised properties of the completed structure and the unspeciaised nature of the basal material.†

No, those games have not yet been played for the last time. Of course one may laugh at the props and call them pathetic. Snail shells and branches. Sticks and stones. Shards and bones. You take what you have and make yourself a universe. It's just as Gabriel says: mankind is incapable of creating.

Pull on Robor's skin, in it is where you belong. Stick your fingers into hers: you can reach this far but no farther. See the shimmering images from the inside of her skull, peer out through the gaps in the wall of the cave. You will never have any other view.

Deep down in the house, in the cellar under me, there is a shard from a plate hidden in the crack between two foundation stones, a shard with a blue flower in the glaze.

I suppose I'm not really an action person, you might even call me lazy. Or at least passive, like Jenny says. I can readily fall to musing. When I was younger I mostly fell to dreaming.

Why shouldn't I have? It's amazing, actually, that we are able to imagine anything other than the sludge we are trudging around in, however crude and saccharine our fantasies may be. I drew, too, for hours at a time at the living room table on Henning's graph paper and on cake boxes opened out flat. I even constructed a marshmallow snowball machine, and the fact that it became reality must have given me deep confidence in drawing and in dreams. Unfortunately I wore it thin around the age of thirteen or fourteen by drawing nothing but silhouettes of

† Eddington, A.S. The Nature of the Physical Word, Macmillan 1928, p.230.

women, lovely ladies with waves in their hair, line after line after line in orderly undulations, arched ink mouths, huge eyelids with blue ink shadow, eyelashes like a picket fence, earrings with rubies I colored with spittle and a red pen.

These profiles never became reality. I looked the same as ever. I dreamed with myself in the leading role throughout this time, myself as a life saver, a concert pianist, a competitive diver, a film star, a man-eater, an archaeologist, a dying woman and, of course, a lover. I even dreamed I could drive a car. After some time, I realized that my dreams didn't change things in reality. The air went out of them. They collapsed and plastered themselves onto my reality, mocking it instead of enhancing it.

But it is as if this dreaming had a purpose. I tired of it, and later it began anew.

The fact that something which has never existed, even as an image, can develop and become conceivable seems to me so unanticipated and so peculiar that I find it difficult to accept. I cannot help suspecting that such a strange but almost routine course of events, in which reality and unreality change places, is a miracle.

Jenny was always so worried I would get lost in the wilderness, end up an outsider, perhaps vanish for always. She was so at home in this world, moved it and shook it and seemed to have a strong, convincing presence in all her doings.

Not until now have I realized that she, too, is an *estrangeira*. Maybe she hasn't always been. I think it began in earnest when Fredrik stopped being a blue collar worker. That was a great victory for them both. But they paid a price.

During the last year, Jenny has started talking about her childhood home in a different way from before. She recreates a picture of hard work and simple ways with no ridicule and no contempt. She seems to have found an old, forgotten scale of values inside her, but if she ever applies it to conditions here in the city she sounds like an ultra-stuffy reactionary. She notices that and shuts up.

With those who live under the most shabby, most grievous conditions today she is unable, of course, to feel any sense of community. Their poverty is alien to her, she does not recognize it. She thinks they live a tough but easygoing life. These are the people she blames for having abducted her, with all their demands and their want of norms, from the land in which she was born. They have removed that land from her, abducted it beyond her reach forever. She believes that the world is theirs now and she walks their streets, afraid of being jostled, screamed at and robbed. Deep down, she is uncertain as to whether she talks and thinks correctly, has the right opinions and emotions. In fact I admire her for behaving with such pluck.

I found an old picture of Henning the other day. It was in a box in the attic amongst my Grandfather Abel's forgotten treasures. It was a photograph that was really of the line outside the bottle store; in those days people would talk about lining up for a bottle. Ada's and Lisa's pappa, Wallin, the nonconformist editor-in-chief, published that picture as a deterrent.

Henning was in that old picture, even though it was from the days before he was a regular outside the bottle store. He's part way down the street, standing with a little metal lunchbox under his arm. On his head he has a cap. He is laughing.

Henning on his way to work at Swedish Engineering. He was probably about to start his shift. He went in with his sandwiches in his lunchbox, with his genius, his youth, his enthusiasm. He left a duped and debilitated man.

He never told me he had started at the works. He never mentioned it. No, he never talked about the dankness and the paltriness or the chill in his life. He was undoubtedly ashamed, like most other people, and wanted to forget it.

I bumped into Egon Holmlund. It was last Saturday. I saw him coming out of the Hotel de Winther with his suitcases. He hasn't had an assistant to help him carry things for years, and I understand he performs his act all alone, too. I walked behind him for a little while, gathering enough courage to catch up with him and say hello. He looked younger than I would have imagined, and when I started calculating, I realized he couldn't be much over sixty.

I told him who I was, that I had known Ann-Sophie before her death. When he realized I was the owner of the house she had lived in, his interest was sparked.

"I've got things stored there," he said. "Some idiots tossed everything out of my room."

I said there was nothing left any more. I had cleaned the place out. But he insisted on coming back with me "to make sure there really was nothing left", he said.

We crossed the bridge over the tracks, and I thought: here I am walking with the magician, the sleight-of-hand-man. It's a gray afternoon. Perfectly ordinary. Nothing special about him. A tall man, actually quite handsome. Teeth not very good. He's best when he's not laughing. There's a missing toe but you'd never know it from the way he walks. Or does he have a slight limp?

"I'll give you a lift home," he said. "My car's parked under the department store."

We trudged along and he asked what it had been like for Ann-Sophie at the end.

"She wasn't in pain," I said, "or at least the pain wasn't bad. She just got weaker and weaker."

"Bleeding ulcers?" he asked.

"Mmm hmm."

When we reached the parking garage he wanted to walk down the ramp the cars drive up, which is actually not allowed. You're supposed to go down through the store.

"Yeah, but this way's quicker," he said.

And I followed him down a gray shaft. It looked like a mouth that was open, a throat and a belly at once. It reeked of exhaust and filth, and I could hear car engines from down there, and the noise of the fans. A cold burst of wind that had found its way down to this underworld chased bits of paper over the concrete and churned up the odors.

Suddenly I was irrationally frightened. I thought of dying down here with my mouth to the rigid mass that is not even stone. Of my blood mixing with oil and dirt and of dying in a rainbow-shimmering pool of oily water, in the toxic stench, hearing the roaring fans. Seeking with my fingers along the cracks in the concrete for warmth, for anything, for any kind of life. Dying alone as his steps echoed in the distance.

He turned around.

"What's wrong?" he asked.

"I'm not going down there. I'll wait here."

He laughed, showing those bad teeth of his I didn't like.

"Claustrophobia?" he asked.

With that he descended into the culvert. I didn't wait for him. I turned around and walked home. I didn't dare to take the High Street because I imagined he'd catch up with me in his car. Instead, I went the long way, by Carlsborg and Hovlunda Road, then down Store Street, shabby, much trampled Store Street, the exterior of which has changed so much.

Many of the houses have been torn down. I wonder where the angels went, the ones under the gables of the building Tora Otter lived in. Perhaps the excavator, with its steel beak, started with their faces. I'm sure I can't be the only person who harbors this kind of hate, this childish fury with the past as if it were a disgraceful, duplicitous mother. The people who live here and have the power to demolish buildings and rip up streets live with this rage inside them. They feel contempt for the life they have lived, and need to smash its face when it appears. Then they weep over the rubble, and pity themselves, and rebuild what has been, in crude, distorted images so they don't have to smell it. Because that is also the scent of want and of longing. The scent of lilacs mixes with the smell of rubbish in the back yards, of dung, blood and piss and heavy perfumes, oil soot and stove ash — it rises in the memory of what has been ours and should be safeguarded by time and oblivion. The past has a face and a smell, it has hands and legs and arms and it gropes for us and we lash out blindly because we are not at home in our selves; we hate ourselves and our lives as they were and became and we want to crush them and build them up again with other stones, other skin.

Several times he's been here looking for me. I saw his face against the pane of polished glass, highlighted against the black of his cape. But I didn't open the door. In the end he stopped coming. I suppose he's left town again.

I'm sitting at the kitchen table, looking out of the window. In this silence, which is the present, everything exists. Terrible death and the joy of being alive. The living lambs and the ones in plastic bags, discarded. Elisabeth and João, not too far away. The pleasure I often experience at work. The life blow that must be glossed over or carried, like the house of a snail, on my back. The spring underneath the snow, the seeds sprouting down there. At least in my dreams they extend their pale shoots.

The weather is cloudy and the temperature is hovering around freezing. The light has nearly expired. The streetlamps hang still, their pale glow inert. A little while ago I saw a man on a bicycle who also appeared not to be moving although he was passing by on Chapel Road, stiff and stooped, high on the seat.

I have always been afraid of stillness when it's damp and gray like this. I think everything is going to stiffen up, time is going to come to an end. If it starts to snow it may go on and on until we are suffocated by silence and wet snow. This is the hellish nightmare of the Nordic countries: eternal stillness.

Now lights start to go on in the windows. So there are other people than myself who are alive, cooking, whistling, running the water. I will live a little longer, or possibly much longer. Who knows how?

Hasse will probably come home. He called last night to say he'd been told: Nórdica is going to close down. He'll have to become an auditor, I suppose, or help people do their tax returns. All right then, he may come home and the two of us will take up living here, living and behaving as if this were reality.

It's dusk. Between the two outstretched arms of this house is my garden. The cracked apple tree and the old lilac. The scruffy lawn with the grass whose root ends lie bared to the frost, and the flowerbeds where thin, pale brown residues of soil cover the bulbs of the tiger lilies. They are no longer starved survivors of a disaster, not remnants or remains. They are signs standing in the gloom and the stillness, signs standing for an herb garden.

On the heavy brown door the paint has developed a crazed pattern, and in a few places it has flaked off and the white undercoat shows. It is a French door and each half has three panels. On the middle one there is a carved, flowerlike bud, thick with many coats of paint. It is tempting to touch the buds and the worn handle, it is tempting to go inside.

And yet I often find myself standing outside longing for the coolness that a totally unexpected vista can offer the hot stock of memory and habitual vision.

But we never get what we expect. Nothing is gathered, nothing won. Out of the corner of my eye I may see, and what can I catch when the palms of my hands remain on the ground?

Sometimes I have a longing, a longing for that coolness on the backs of my hands, for the vast companionship that is alive in the midst of solitude, that rustles in the leaves, swishes in the grass and makes the stones whisper.